FATHERLAND

FATHERLAND

by
Karen Schur-Narula

WOOD HORSE PRESS

WOOD HORSE PRESS

9th floor PB Tower, 1000/30 Sukhumvit 71, 10110 Bangkok, Thailand

First published by Wood Horse Press in Thailand in 2016

Cover illustration by Chas Elterman
Concept inspired by Caspar David Friedrich's *Wanderer above the Sea of Fog,*
Kunsthalle Hamburg

Fatherland / Karen Schur-Narula

ISBN: 978-616-92721-0-6

www.woodhorsepublishing,com

Typeset by Apollo Bulanhagui, Perez Numedia, Inc., Philippines

Printed by Aksorn Samphan Press, Thailand

To my mother and my father
lifetimes of love

A FOREWORD

Although more than seven decades have passed since Nazi Germany ended, that era continues, rightfully, to haunt heart and mind. In a last-ditch effort to show intent that the guilty must acknowledge, apologize, and be punished, a 93-year old former SS officer is sentenced to 4 years in prison. "You could have said 'no'," he was told.

That's true. After all, there were citizens of the Third Reich who did. If only everyone then could have said 'no'. But as the temporal distance since those days grows greater, and the number of people who knew them firsthand shrinks, it will become more and more difficult to truly understand the why: why so few said 'no', and why so many others said 'yes' or nothing at all.

For much of my life I have struggled with the fact that my closest relatives once lived in the Third Reich, a regime voted into existence. In 1942 my beloved grandfather was drafted into the Wehrmacht. Like countless other uneasy grandchildren, I would come to wonder what he had seen, heard, or done during the war when he had been stationed in Latvia and the Ukraine. Yet by the time I thought to ask him, he was already long gone, so I will never know. My imagination gives me no peace.

But this is not about Opa, my mother's father. This is about the other side of the family. My father's parents, whom I never met, and my father's sister. The girl who destroyed two families because she chose to say the wrong words. My Tante Lili.

When I knew her, she lived alone in the foothills of the Vosges Mountains in eastern France. We had been visiting my aunt every summer since my third birthday. It was easy for us as we moved around a lot; my father was in the U.S. Foreign Service. My parents had met while he was stationed in Bonn; my mother had been a local hire at the Embassy there. Even though my father's accent was atrocious, when the four of us were together our conversations were in German. My father and his sister didn't seem very close; perhaps it was the thirteen-year age difference. But our summers together in Friedberg were pleasant, filled with birdsong and long walks in the forest. It was Tante Lili who taught me how to play chess, how to cut the eyes from potatoes before boiling them, how to stand motionless in the shadows just a breath away from an unsuspecting deer. She let me look at her books on gardening and answered my questions. In those days my curiosity was of a simple nature.

When I was thirteen, I asked my aunt what she did when we weren't with her. She showed me a stack of papers. These were some of the documents that she translated for the European Court of Human Rights in nearby Strasbourg, where we occasionally went to wander the cobblestoned streets and eat too much *choucroute garnie*. They looked very boring and I quickly lost interest.

Two summers later, while searching for an owl in the attic, I discovered an antique harpsichord. I asked Tante Lili what it was doing there, hidden away under a linen sheet, and she admitted that for many years she had played such an instrument every day; that, indeed, the harpsichord had once been her lifeline. It hit me then that I knew very little about my aunt. I began to bombard her with questions. Each increasingly disturbing answer raised a new question.

Yet even with all her answers, I would come to understand that I hadn't asked nearly enough; the following year, her heart stopped and she died, alone, on New Year's Day, her 57th birthday.

My parents and I went to Friedberg to take care of things. How different it was in winter, white and bereft of birdsong. The house was left to an agency to maintain and we never went back. And yet here I am again, after so many years.

I have come because it is time to write about Tante Lili.

Her story is just one of millions and millions. But, like each and every account of those millions and millions of individual Germans who were part of Adolf Hitler's realm, it belongs to only that one person. It is up to me to tell hers.

I can ask no one else in the family for accounts of that time, to share their memories with me; I am the last of them all. My mother too is dead now, and my father lost, deep in the labyrinth of dementia. Yet I have found unexpected help. Rummaging around in the attic the other day, I took another look at the shrouded harpsichord. Under its fancifully painted lid, wrapped in brown paper with my name written in fading ink upon its porous surface, was a stack of notebooks. An accompanying note from Tante Lili said that she knew I would find them when the time was right. They promise to answer many of the questions I didn't know how to ask all those years ago.

Now, just like during my childhood visits to Friedberg, it is summer again. It is time to write down my aunt's story.

As do so many other life accounts, this one begins with a family.

Despite their having the same parents, the grandparents I never knew, my aunt and my father had different surnames. When the family immigrated to America it made sense to let the nametags fall. Never in his life would my father be addressed as Freiherr Paul von Rittersburg zu Mertz-Tärnekow; my grandfather's son would be known only as Paul Ritter. After all, he was born a U.S. citizen in New York. But Tante Lili had been born in Berlin, and that made all the difference.

PART ONE

Berliner Luft

Lili and the Fatherland

While any day of the week holds within it the possibility of offering up joy or misfortune, it is today, a Friday in 1925, which will mark indelibly the lifepaths of two families who as yet know nothing of each other.

Throughout this winter's day Lili has been silent and watchful of the many preparations. Just when all is in place—the crystal vases with their hothouse roses spilling over, Belgian lace on the tables, the gleam of silverware almost as brilliant as the candles on the Christmas tree just days before—she is led away to the kitchen. She is both peeved and excited, for her temporary banishment signals that the guests will soon be arriving and Papa will have to be there to greet them.

For several years her parents have been in the habit of giving a large dinner party a few days before New Year's Eve. Tonight there will be an unusually mixed crowd; the usual clique of Prussian Junkers as well as some businessmen and scientists and a carefully chosen assortment of prominent playwrights, musicians, and artists. Then, too, several members of the Berlin branch of the DHK, the Deutscher Herrenklub, will be attending, for her father is now a member of this club, founded the previous year with German President Paul von Hindenburg as Honorary President. This evening there will also be a very special guest, one who has been causing quite a stir these past couple years, but whose appeals for a regulation of society will strike a receptive chord in the conservative hearts of the elite.

Lili is waiting for the moment when she will join her parents in the salon for a short while before bedtime. It is Papa whom Lili is most anxious to meet, for he is the center of her universe.

From her very earliest days she has turned to him for confirmation. She has never been afraid of him. It is Papa who tosses her up in the air as if she were but a *Luftballon*, who sings silly songs and pretends to be a tin soldier marching, even though he was in the Navy during the war. When they go to visit Mama's parents on their estate at Alt Eichendorf, deep in the heart of the Mecklenburg Lake District, it is Papa who scoops Lili up onto the saddle of the chestnut Trakehner. Together they pass through hundreds of hectares of fields and forests and all the while she knows she is safe up there with him. And it is Papa who has led her to the instrument that has long been in the family, telling her that on it she will learn a language that needs no words. She believes him, for her trust in him is as wide as the sky.

She hasn't seen him for several days because of his trip to Munich. A few months ago she and her parents attended the Bach Fest there, staying in the Hotel Vier Jahreszeiten. Everyone had been very kind to her, even if Lili couldn't always understand what was being said. Mama explained that this is the way most people in the south speak. It didn't matter though, because most of the time they were just listening to music, no words needed.

In the kitchen, Lotte has already set out Lili's dinner, a small assortment of the dishes that the grown-ups will be eating later. On the floor is the bowl for Sascha, the old borzoi, with whom Lili likes to share part of her meal. With her silver fork and sharp-edged knife, Lili cuts into the *Roulade* rolled two sizes smaller than usual, just for her. Lotte

2

always does nice things for her, like plump her feather pillows into the perfect shape. Lili says that the pillows are plump like Lotte. Lotte laughs, saying it is because she too is made of feathers. Sometimes Lili thwacks her hand deep into the pillows just when Lotte has given the final smooth to the cool linen, but Lotte's scoldings are good-natured, and she always plumps them up again.

A humming sound rises from the double salon whose wide connecting doors are open. The guests are here. Even though it was so very long ago, Lili can still remember last year's party. She knows that the salon will have been transformed through the presence of all those ladies wearing long, silky dresses, the gentlemen in suits with dark tails or jackets festooned with thick gold embroidery. None of the women will be as beautiful as her mother though. Earlier, Lili went into the bedroom as Mama was getting ready and watched her open the small gold case engraved with her initials and filled with a pink orange dust. With a bunch of feathers, Mama fluffed the barest trace of it onto her cheekbones. This evening her hair lies thick like honey in a swirl on the nape of her neck. Her skin looks like cream. Papa has said that there are times when he wants to eat Mama up because she looks so delicious, and Lili giggles because sometimes she too wants to bite into the soft skin of her mother's inner arm.

Mama is dressed in a gown whose pale iridescence makes her look like a fairy princess. Wherever she moves, the scent of her perfume follows her like a shadow, mysterious and a bit sad too. She will look beautiful next to Papa who of course will be the handsomest man in the room. His dark hair will be smooth from pomade and his freshly shaven cheeks smell faintly of Mouchoir de Monsieur, his favorite fragrance, which for some reason makes Lili think of carriage rides in leafy Grunewald. She knows that he will be wearing his elegant new swallow-tailed coat trimmed with satin because this afternoon she saw it laid out, perfectly pressed, on his bed. She can't wait to see him, have him lift her high into the air and then hug her tight.

In the kitchen it is time. Lotte takes Lili by the hand and leads her out into the hallway toward where the buzz of laughter and conversation grows louder. Lili wrinkles her nose as Lotte steers her through the throng of grown-ups and the confusion of scents in the salon—smoke, perfumes, pomade, camphor, roast meats, and *Schnaps* made from the fruits of Alt Eichendorf. She looks out at the faces, their features indistinct, and squeezes Lotte's fingers. She nearly trips on the fringe of a Persian carpet. And then the blur sharpens. Papa and Mama are just ahead. They are not standing next to each other but on either side of a dark-haired man. He is dressed as if he planned to go hiking, not to a party. It would be rude to giggle, she knows, so Lili bites the inside of her bottom lip instead, a remedy she uses for a wide variety of situations. Once safely in front of Papa, she lets go of Lotte's hand. Looks up at Papa, waiting for his arms to enfold her and lift her high into the air.

But he doesn't. He isn't even looking at her. Has she done something wrong? She swallows. Didn't he miss her as much as she missed him?

"Lili," he says. "There is someone who would like to meet you." She stares at him for another moment, searching, then turns to the stranger.

"Why?" she asks, tilting her head back, fixing her gaze on him. "I'm only five."

The man is not nearly as handsome as Papa—nobody is—and those suede pants and poopoo-colored jacket look odd in this room. But she likes the way his eyes soften, even twinkling, as he smiles down at her. The thing under his nose looks like a furry little pet.

"It is because I have heard from your parents that you are already a fine musician, even if you are only five."

Lili narrows her gaze, considering him. She likes the sound of his voice: quiet, smoothly hoarse, reassuring, even if he does roll his r's as do the people in Munich. There are interesting parts to his face, especially the pointy part of his nose. Most of all, she likes the way his dark eyes are looking at her. She nods.

"Yes, that's true."

At this the man bursts into loud laughter, but Lili can tell that he isn't laughing *at* her.

"Why Lili, darling," says Mama, smiling beneath a delicately raised eyebrow. "You must learn to be more modest. What will our guest think?"

Yet the guest is looking at Lili as if he knew that she has told him nothing but the simple truth.

He leans forward, his face closer to hers. She can smell his breath. Surely he has been eating some of the berries that Lotte put next to the silver bowl of whipped cream.

"I'll tell you what," he says, softly, only to her. "Why don't you play something right now? That will both prove your claim and allow me to boast that I have personally heard Germany's youngest talent."

Lili glances at Papa, waiting for the special sign, their signal that means she can perform for their guests. He sees her, gives a nod, and relief courses through her. They still understand each other.

A path clears for her as, back straight, hands at her sides, Lili moves across the salon. She is no longer the baby who needs to hold on to Lotte's hand; she is a performer. Mama follows, the champagne silk of her dress rustling like foam. She opens the lid of the instrument while Lili climbs onto the stool.

There is an ugly sound from behind her.

"Ladies and gentlemen," announces the dark-haired man, stepping into sight not far from Lili. He clears his throat again, vocal chords rasping. "Your attention: it is our privilege to be present this evening at the debut of Lili *Freiin* von Rittersburg zu Mertz-Tärnekow who will perform for us on the harpsichord."

For a moment, Lili wants to protest that she knows what debut means and that this is definitely not the first time she is performing.

Papa and Mama are proud of her playing and this past year she has often been invited to do so before guests at home. She opens her mouth to let him know. But he is looking at her again, ever so kindly, only at her.

She presses her lips together. No, it is true. Tonight she is not playing for the other guests. Of course they will hear her but today Lili is going to play only for him, this man who is very kind and interesting even though he did make such an unpleasant noise with his throat just now, twice even. And because today is the first time he has come to visit, it actually is a kind of debut.

She touches her fingers to the keys so that he will hear how much she loves music. As Papa says, it is a language without words. She feels something special about the music of Johann Sebastian Bach even though she is still only five years old. However, in just a few days, right at one minute past midnight on New Year's Eve, she is going to be six. Her fingers begin to move. They call forth sounds that lead her as far away as the stars, to a place inside her head.

And then she folds her hands, waiting. The applause always comes. She glances over at Papa, who is beaming at her, and gives him the other secret nod, the one that means that she too is pleased. She watches the man raise his clapping hands. Suddenly he begins to move forward, toward her. Mama gives a tiny nudge from behind and Lili slides down from the stool.

The man leans over her, catching her palm in his, warm and moist, and Lili bends at her knees, curtseying, pulling her midnight blue velvet skirt out with her left hand. But now he bends further, his face coming toward hers, the eyes sparkling with light or tears, she can't be sure, and Lili feels the knock of his nose and then the thick brush of bristle against her skin as he presses his lips upon her cheek.

"So, little miss," he says, when he has drawn back up to his full height. "When I hear such playing from such a charming young person as you, it reassures me about the future of both our culture and civilization." His eyes look like coals that are beginning to burn. Lili

6

opens her own eyes wide in surprise at the sudden seriousness of his tone and the way he stresses his words.

"It must be your duty to the fatherland to ensure that such tremendous talent be shared with all of your *Volksgenossen*. Such music embodies the very heart and hardiness of the German people."

He pauses, as if he were going to say more to her, then simply smiles again and looks over her head at Papa.

"*Freiherr*, it is obvious that your daughter has determination. Her generation will be the hope and strength of a new Germany; I will see to that. And your committed support will help see to it that I can."

Lili doesn't understand all the big words he uses, but she feels their intensity and the burning gaze of his eyes. And when the man with the mustache has to turn away from her to address the swell of people gathering about him, Lili senses a light kindling within her and knows that she will do her duty not only for her own, but for all the other Papas in the fatherland.

What is Destiny?

While every generation of the von Rittersburg zu Mertz-Tärnekow family has included at least one person with genuine musical ability, over the next years it becomes apparent that Lili does indeed have a remarkable gift. Great consideration is given to with which teachers she should study, each helping raise her to a higher level.

She works hard to master the discipline of the serious musician. That this leaves her little time for childhood games with classmates at her girls' school, or the neighborhood children, is of no concern. Occasionally, when the windows are open during a fermata, the sound of their laughter and teasing and shouting rises to her ears. There are moments when she imagines herself with them on the wide sidewalk, pushing a doll stroller, intricately woven reed bassinet on giant wheels, or jumping rope. And because she has a few times joined the girls, she knows how fleeting is the satisfaction derived from their play, especially when the boys come along and rile things up. But such thoughts last only as long as the count in the empty measure.

Her parents have no worries about the level of her passion at such a young age. Indeed, they encourage and enable her to follow her love of the harpsichord. Within the confines of their day's society they are liberal. While her mother occasionally attends meetings of the complacent Deutsche Damen Klub in the Hotel Adlon, at other times she wanders about Berlin, alone, exploring the canvases of painters whose works seem to mirror the changes taking place in the city. Lili's mother seems content with the privileged life she shares with her husband in the cosmopolitan Berlin of the day. It is a resilient and vibrant city and they are at home in it. As the youngest son, Lili's father hasn't inherited the family estate but he is well off. He enjoys sufficient social standing to have been chosen as a member of the prestigious DHK. And of course his own musical abilities have given him an understanding of his daughter's needs.

For the rest of the 1920s, the lives of Freiherr Erwin Junker von Rittersburg zu Mertz-Tärnekow and his family go by smoothly, their days affected by neither the state of the German post-war economy nor the financial shock waves that cross the Atlantic. The seasons pass as they have always done. Lili and her parents attend performances at the Opera House, sit at Kranzler and eat cream-infused cakes, stroll through Grunewald on clear-skied Sundays, and sail on the limpid blue of the Wannsee. In winter they warm their gloved hands on roasted chestnuts and cross the filigreed iron bridge to the Pfaueninsel to examine artifacts in the Pergamon. And Lili sits at her harpsichord, practicing.

They travel again to Munich, making time to attend a performance of the Münchener Vereinigung für altklassische Musik where Lili is spellbound, watching Li Stadelmann at the keyboards. After a while she has to close her eyes; there is something about Li Stadelmann's face, and the way she holds her neck, that Lili doesn't like. The woman might be the most well known harpsichordist in Germany now, and Lili is somewhat pleased that they share half a first name, but she, Lili von Rittersburg zu Mertz-Tärnekow, will be the more famous. Her playing will have to be the more important.

♫ ♪ ♫

If Lili most loves any time away from her music, it is those near endless summer days at Mama's family estate at Alt Eichendorf, when the sun seems reluctant to part from above the forests and ripening fields, its quiet reflection lingering long into the night upon the surface of the myriad lakes. At bedtime, the drawn drapes outlined gold with the night sky, Mama reads fairy tales aloud from books whose cloth covers are worn from the touch of generations of mothers' hands.

On some days Lili and Papa walk deep into the forest, and while the woods of the Seeplatte are not as dense and dark and overpowering as those of Hänsel and Gretel's Black Forest to the south, her father makes sure that she does not stray from the pathways. On those long walks Lili learns much that makes her warm with gratitude for having been born German, for the Great War has not left an indelible stain on the nation. She is free to feel innocent pleasure in the centuries' worth of accomplishments of her countrymen.

Papa makes efforts to introduce German literature to her. Johann Wolfgang von Goethe is his favorite but he quotes from Schiller and Herder, Lessing, Novalis, von Kleist. Most of their words Lili forgets nearly as soon as she has heard them, even if their spirit might linger within her. Her father quotes Mann and Zweig and tells her how the words of poets like Heinrich Heine are made even more moving through the Lieder of Mahler and Mendelssohn. The latter names she will remember, for it is music that fuels her being.

After all, one day she will be recognized as the greatest harpsichordist in Germany. It is her destiny; her duty. Even if she, unlike most of the illustrious Germans before her, is a girl. She has no doubts.

♩♪♫

For a time it seems that she will travel to Munich twice a month to begin studies with Li Stadelmann. By this time, Lili is prepared to give full attention to the woman. But for some reason Papa changes his mind about Li Stadelmann. Something about her political leanings. Lili protests that she doesn't care about the angle of her neck anymore but Papa just smiles and shakes his head. Lili isn't too disappointed, especially as he intimates that in the future she might study with the brilliant Madame Landowska in Paris. This is good news. Not only is Wanda Landowska expert in interpreting old music, she was the first to play the harpsichord in a modern orchestra. Lili doesn't care about that part so much as her tastes are already firmly set in the Baroque, but it does reinforce the expertise. Landowska even lived in Berlin, twice, leaving for Paris the year before Lili was born. It is exciting to think that one day her own career will be linked to that of such an illustrious harpsichordist.

Bad Timing

There comes the day that Lili begins to look at her father in a different way. Is it that she is becoming aware of herself as a separate person, her intellect and sense of self awakening? There is a bigger world than the one lit up by Papa. From source, he goes to being but a resource. On its own, perhaps this will afford her a natural progression toward maturity. Yet timing is everything.

Some years earlier, she asked her father when the man with the mysterious eyes would be coming back. He had been there again some months after his first visit but on that evening Lili was in bed with measles. At first Papa tells her the man will be back one day soon, although he is growing busier as more and more people want to be around him. Later Papa tells her that he doubts the man will return for a visit. And then comes the day on which Papa informs her that under no circumstance will that man ever again set foot in their home.

It is bad timing for such an announcement.

On farms across the country, in hamlets and villages and *Gaststätten* and schools, on town and city streets, the name of Adolf Hitler is being whispered louder and louder as the possible answer to Germany's prayers. He might indeed be the long hoped for savior who will take away the shame of Versailles and the November Criminals, give freedom and bread to the millions; who will right the wrongs and turn the fatherland into a land as proud and strong as it deserves to be.

But Lili isn't yet aware of the real import of all of that.

She simply likes knowing that the rising star was in her home, listened to and encouraged her, kissed her cheek. Even if she keeps this knowledge to herself, not wanting to share it with classmates with whom she hasn't concerned herself in years, she knows it is something special. Adolf Hitler has seen something in her. That is why he gave her so much attention that evening and told her of her duty to play. Why, he has spelled out her future! It is more than frustrating to think that he isn't going to be back for a visit so that she can show him how much further she has progressed.

Her father has it upside down.

♫♪♫

So Lili is drawn to those who are open in their enthusiasm for the man of the hour. She looks anew at those boys whom she has so long considered bothersome. Those boys are neat and clean and as well fed as the boys who continue to wear ordinary clothes and whistle as they go about their business in the neighborhood, a district of spacious apartment buildings and villas set among trees. But the boys in the *Hitler Jugend* outfits move with a new confidence in their step. There are even some girls who are wearing outfits that show they are connected to the movement. There aren't many yet, but it signifies that girls, too, can share in the excitement. Lili can feel something new crackling in the air and she hopes to be a part of it. Soon she tells her parents that she wants to join the *Jungmädel* section of the BDM, the *Bund Deutscher Mädel*, now the official girls' branch of the Hitler Jugend.

Papa and Mama say that they will consider the Young Girls League; meanwhile, how are her lessons coming along? Perhaps it is the perfect time to take a trip to Paris so that Lili can meet Madame Landowska as well as see how filled with marvels the city is. Off they go in diversion, exploring the streets and museums, attending concerts and eating lovely food in the City of Light. Although the name of their hotel is short, the Ritz makes Munich's Hotel Vier Jahreszeiten seem like a provincial *Gasthof.* The French capital is imbued with an elegance and beauty that Lili has to admit even Berlin cannot match. It is magical, as if a siren symphony by some unknown composer had transformed itself into a physical being. Her French is still that of a schoolgirl but she decides that if ever she must live anywhere but Berlin, Paris would not be the cruelest place.

One evening before dinner with some Parisian acquaintances, Papa says that the following day they will set out to nearby Saint-Leu-la-Forêt where Madame Landowska makes her home. Through introductions, the harpsichordist has already expressed an interest in meeting Lili, who is nervous but eager. Madame Landowska's large house and garden are said to be teeming with students and musicians, alive from morning till night with study and performance; the place even has a concert hall. Lili can barely imagine what such an environment is like. She has never played with any musicians but her teachers and Papa. It makes her anxious but at the same time she is certain that Madame Landowska will lead her, or at least point her in the right direction, to where she needs to go.

But at some point during the course of the dinner Papa must have second thoughts. By morning he has changed his mind. Lili is still too innocent and impressionable a girl to live away from home in such surroundings, he says. In a few years Lili will be grown up enough for such a free-thinking teacher like Madame Landowska, but not yet. Lili is disappointed—much more disappointed than when he changed his mind about Li Stadelmann— but diversion arrives that same morning in the form of a gift from Papa. Madame Landowska has recently become the first harpsichordist in the world to record the *Goldberg Variations*. Now Lili has her own black-ridged recordings. A gramophone player is quickly located in the hotel and Lili listens for what will be the first of countless times.

Even if she has not yet met Madame Landowska, she senses her presence. There is something so real, so true, so calm and confident of its being; it is as if Lili can feel the red blood flowing through the invisible hands. As if Madame Landowska knows that Bach is listening, nodding his head at her interpretation of his meaning, and she is smiling up at him. Using that spirit is how Lili will learn to play the Variations, in her own way.

So the time passes, and the old Germany too.

A Bit of Knowledge Can Be Dangerous

"Papa, it's wrong."

Her gaze of ocean gray is on him where he stands near the window. She still sees the man who has instilled in her that love of Bach, who taught her the art of sitting in silence to watch a woodland deer; the father who, from earliest memory, has made her aware of the existence of right and wrong. He has been wrong far too long now.

Her tone is firm.

"We shouldn't be leaving our homeland."

His back to the view outside, Papa remains silent. His expression is one Lili does not recognize. If she were a few years younger, she would stamp her shoes in frustration. Instead, she taps her feet with impatience and pulls at a long braid.

"Everyone says it's the best time since the war. He says we'll be the most powerful land in the world. He says he's going to make Germany great again."

"I have told you before, Lili. That man's aims are not best for Germany."

"Well, I think he's wonderful. Everybody says he's just what we need." She pauses. "Everybody but you." Her tone grows sulky. How difficult Papa is being.

"It's not fair that we have to leave just now when it's so exciting." She twists the end of a plait around her finger, tighter and tighter.

"A bit of knowledge can be dangerous, Lili. You would do better to read the works of Goethe and Aristotle instead of listening to those parrots in their neckerchiefs."

Lili scowls. It's mean when he speaks like that. And it's frustrating. The past is history. Papa needs to see that the future is all that counts.

"You shouldn't talk that way about them, Papa. They're the ones helping make Germany a country we can all be proud of." Their fathers are supportive of them. Their fathers even joined the Party *before* the election. If only Papa would at least join the Party.

Her heartbeat quickens at the thought of the two older boys with whom she sometimes walks home. How attractive they are when they talk about their hopes for the future. Their eyes shine as they speak of the Chancellor's plans and promises. They tell her that one of his visions is that the youth of Germany will help lead the nation into prosperity and a return to true German values. Even if she doesn't understand all the terms, she can feel the intensity of their faith in the Chancellor, and trusts it. When they call out "The new age marches with us," Lili burns to sing and march with them; to belong to the youth of the nation.

Papa walks over to her. With gentle touch he takes her hand from the braid.

"My dearest daughter. I have always been proud to be German. But I will not let pride dictate against reason and morality. If it does, then there is nothing of which to be proud."

He looks past the gathering storm of her gaze toward where the heavy curtains of moss green velvet frame a window. Outside, the bare limbs of the trees are claws against the empty white of the afternoon sky. Inside, there is a pulsing stillness.

Lili presses her fingers hard against the oak wood of the harpsichord case. It isn't fair.

"We made plans for me to study with Madame Landowska some day. You know I need to learn the *Goldberg Variations* with her." There is accusation in her voice. Surely this above all things will make him change his mind.

He says nothing. She cannot read the look in his eyes.

With the cry of a wounded bird, she rushes to the window. She pulls open the handle, her breath rapid. The winter falls inward, over her, carrying with it the scent of snow and cinnamon, coffee, smoke, and childhood. Lili stares out, the cold creeping upwards layer upon layer.

"Papa."

Her voice is filled with salt tears that should sting a father's heart.

"How can you do this to us?" Her mouth is dry and bitter-tasting now. "How can you make us leave Berlin?"

At last she turns to face him, her gaze glacial. The words crack the air before she can stop them, leaving only a crevasse of silence.

"Sometimes I wish you weren't my father."

FATHERLAND

PART TWO

New York,
Spring 1933- Summer 1937

How to Adapt to America

The braids slap hard against her chest as Lili stomps her way through the city streets. She hates it here. Too much noise, too many ugly people. She hates passing the drunken, beaten down men of the Depression who mumble and peer at her with empty eyes as they lean against the buildings, sheltering from the wind. She hates the women in shops who call her 'honey' and try to win her over with their toothy, lipstick-smeared smiles. She hates the children who in the beginning tried to drag her into their senseless games and gossip. The twang of American twists her inner ear.

In the apartment she will speak nothing but German, with her parents and with Lotte and her husband Oskar, still housekeeper and driver for the family. Lotte still plumps her featherbed and cooks her favorite foods even though they taste different here. As ever, Oskar doesn't say much but he usually has a warm smile for Lili. She is glad that the couple is with them, but she'd be even gladder if they had all stayed at home where they belong.

Before reaching the perimeter of Yorkville on her way to the only place that means anything to her in this city, she walks alongside a bakery, breathing in the yeasty warmth hovering above the sidewalk. She quickens her pace to get away from it. The bread in America might smell good but doesn't taste like real bread at all; it is empty inside. There is probably something wrong with the flour or the water or the very air here. Across a street the sound of German emerges. In some ways it is even harder to be away from Germany when she walks along the Yorkville streets where there are so many things that remind her of the treasure of home. Like the Fool's Gold she learned about in Social Studies class. It looks right on the outside, but inside it is all wrong.

Familiar-sounding names hang above the establishments on both sides of 86th Street: Cafe Hindenburg, Bremen Haus Markt, Schaller & Weber, the Gloria Palast where Mama took her to see the latest Zarah Leander film in the cinema on the main floor. The people here must have come from all corners of Germany; their voices carry the varying inflections of the regional accents. From having listened to radio programs on Sundays in Berlin, she can recognize some of them. Bayrisch, of course, and Plattdeutsch, and Sächsisch too, that dialect that sounds as if liquid were being swilled about in the mouth.

Now she is in the heart of Yorkville. Netted shopping bags in hand, three women stand gossiping on the pavement. Small boys in short pants run about hiding and seeking in a game of *Blinde Kuh*, their loud laughter eliciting a sharp reprimand from one of the women. Further ahead, a man with a Kaiser Wilhelm mustache seems in earnest discussion with another whose face is shaven clean. A man on the other side of the street shouts out to them. Last week Lili learned that only the previous month there had been fighting in the streets of Yorkville, not for the first time, and it was those defending their faith and trust in the Chancellor, Adolf Hitler, who were the victors.

She enters a shop that sells products imported from home. The smells of pipe tobacco and newsprint envelop her and for a few moments it is as if she were breathing familiar air. But the illusion disappears as she hears the radio program being aired, a baseball game between the Giants and a team named after a bird. The announcer sounds as if he were foaming at the mouth. She picks up a packet of HARIBO Goldbären from the counter. The shop attendant, blond and heavyset, looks over from where he has been staring up at the radio on the shelf and tells her the price in American English.

She continues eastward, biting the heads off the gummy bears before eating the bodies. A young couple passes her on the sidewalk, their raucous laughter infused with the sound of *Berliner Schnauze*, and for a second Lili is back in Kreuzberg, in the noisy neighborhood to which Lotte occasionally took her to visit Lotte's sister Berta. *"Na, Lili, da biste wieda,"* Berta would say in her thick Berliner accent as she stood with a gap-toothed smile in the doorway of her tiny apartment. Yes, there she was again. But the deception here never lasts for more than a few moments. And Lili doesn't spend more time than necessary on the streets of Yorkville. Papa has chosen to avoid living in this area, perhaps because he wants to stay away from Germans. Lili avoids it because she refuses to settle for anything less than Germany itself.

She turns right on York Avenue. There it is. The only place in New York that means anything to her.

School is little more than a source of annoyance. Unlike in Berlin, here both girls and boys are in the classrooms and too many of them are interested mainly in making eyes at each other. The school's bonus point is that the building is closer to home than if she had gone to the private one in which Papa had initially wanted to enroll her. At the last minute, he changed his mind (again) and decided against Manhattan Park Preparatory or MPP as the Americans call it—as if it were so very difficult to pronounce the proper name. Robert becomes Bob, Philip Phil, and Catherine Kit. They like to shorten everything in America. If only Lili could shorten her stay here.

At home she spends most of her time at the harpsichord, working her way through the *Goldberg Variations*, one bar at a time, by herself. So far, she has no proper teacher. But she is fueled by a silent pact with herself: when she has perfected the Variations, somehow, somehow she will get to go home.

As for the rest of the family, when he is not at his office, a business on Madison Avenue that deals with real estate, Papa often spends long hours in his study. Mama and she occupy themselves with baby Paul. Paul is the best thing that has happened since their arrival in America.

When it rains they stay home and play games or puppet theater. Paul is still too young to play, but he will learn by watching. Sometimes Lili slips a princess in blue satin or the grinning Kaspar over her fingers and speaks in silly voices. Paul reaches out to touch a shiny bell on Kaspar's cap and Mama and she giggle, united in their adoration of this precious creature with silver blonde wisps on his perfect head. On sunny days, Mama lures Lili to Central Park with the promise of ice cream. Lili licks at it, tricks her taste buds, remembers the cool sweetness of it in Germany. With begrudging honesty she admits to herself that the ice cream in New York is different but good. Pistachio is her favorite. Then Mama and Paul wait as Lili sets a miniature sailing craft upon the liquid pewter of The Lake. Lili is silent as she watches it float away, borne by the wind or an unseen force below the surface, and wishes it were the salty ocean and she on the vessel, streaming home.

Home no longer feels right with a father who has abandoned the fatherland.

Now she comes to a halt in front of the building on York Avenue. The small sign next to the door reads "German-American Cultural Club". Papa and Mama believe it is a place for Lili to forge friendships and learn how to adapt to America. They have never been here.

She presses the doorbell. The trio of F-sharps will give her access. Three is the perfect number for her only connection with the *Reich*.

The door opens. An arm shoots out, fingers pointing straight as blades.

"*Heil Hitler!*"

Lili glances up at the boy with his sun-kissed hair. He is not looking at her but out into the distance, past this street on this block, past the Statue of Liberty, the Atlantic, and the shores of France, to Germany, to the land of their blood, their homeland. The fatherland.

"Heil Hitler!"

Lili is facing the other way, but she too can see it, reflected in his inner eye: the glory of the Third Reich.

Then she crosses the threshold to join the others like her, youths whose spirit belongs to a man none of them know—and by whom only one of them has ever been kissed—and the door closes firmly behind them.

A Birthday Surprise

Fingers tap lightly against her door.

"Lili?"

"I'm here." She looks up from her writing desk.

The door swings open. Clad in a dark pinstripe suit, Papa passes across the polished parquet and onto the worn carpet, a pale blue Persian that used to lie on the floor in the salon in Berlin. Though he looks tired, perhaps older, he is still handsome.

"I'm sorry I missed dinner with the three of you. It was a long day at the office." Papa leans over to give her a peck on the lips.

"What are you working on?"

"A birthday letter."

Papa takes a nearby chair and places it next to hers.

"A birthday letter. How thoughtful. Is it for one of your friends?"

She grimaces. "I don't have any friends."

"Surely there are some classmates that you like?"

Lili purses her lips, remembering an afternoon during her first few weeks at school.

Most of the students had already left for the day, and now she too was walking down the sepia-colored hallway toward the exit.

"Hey, Lili!"

She had turned. These students weren't in her class. How did they know her name?

"How come you're in this school? Why aren't you in the Lower East Side?"

"Or New Rochelle?"

Lili eyed them curiously. They grouped about her in a semi-circle, three girls and two boys.

She was still learning English. "Excuse me. What do you mean by this question?"

A couple of them exchanged amused glances. The biggest boy answered.

"What we mean by this question," he said, turning to the others and smirking, "is why can't you kikes go to school somewhere else?" The others nodded.

"What is this word—kike?"

They burst out laughing.

"Ha—she doesn't even know what a kike is!"

"A kike who doesn't know she's a kike—that's a real kicker!"

One of the girls spoke. "You're one of those who left Germany because your government is kicking you out of everything, right?"

Lili's cheeks burned. "No, of course not. We—"

"Well, they don't want your type in Germany, and a lot of us here don't want you either." Their expressions were so strange. What in heaven were they talking about?

"Those Nazis have it right," said the shorter boy. "Get the Jews to get out. But why'd ya hafta come here?"

For a moment there was a great whirling blur of black in front of her but suddenly it cleared.

"No, no. You have it wrong." She smiled. "I am not Jewish." She raised an eyebrow. "It is very ignorant of you to think that every German who comes to America is a Jew."

"No kidding? You're not Jewish?"

One of the girls spun around to him.

"See, I told you! You never listen to me, you dumb lummox. With a name like that she's not Jewish."

The big boy shook his head. "So what are you then?"

"Well, if she's German but she's not a kike then she's a Nazi of course," crowed the third girl.

"A Nazi, right!" The boys began to goose step down the hall, lifting their right arms before them in exaggerated salutes.

"Heil Hitler! Heil Hitler!" For a few moments they pursed their lips as if twitching a mustache. From their mouths issued forth a stream of guttural shouts, crescendos, and staccatos that grated the air. The girls were doubled over in laughter.

The boys clicked their heels and stamped about, accelerating their actions like wind-up toys. Now the girls raised their arms. "Heil Hitler," they giggled, making it sound like "Hi Hittel."

Lili had turned away. Stupid Americans.

Papa is talking.

"I'm sorry about that, Lili. I was hoping that by now you would have found someone to play with." Quickly he corrects himself. "I mean with whom to talk and share things."

Her tone is dismissive. "It doesn't matter."

Papa strokes his chin as if he had a beard.

"But what about the German-American Cultural Club that you go to every week? Surely you've made some acquaintances there? Why don't you invite them home some time?"

She shakes her head.

"I have enough to do with my music and studies." And she would never bring anyone from the club to the ten-room apartment off Central Park.

"Then I'm glad that you have a satisfying inner life, Lili." He winks at her. "Of course, don't forget that you have Mama, Paul, and me, too."

She gives a brief nod.

"When you've finished writing your letter, why not come into the salon and join us? We could play a board game. Or charades. Or you and I could perform a gala concert for Mama and Paul."

A grin escapes her. She remembers those times in Berlin when Mama would slip into an evening gown and, fluttering a fan, pretend she was attending a grand concert at the Berliner Philharmonie. If they perform like this tonight, it will be only the third time since coming to New York.

As he sees her smile, Papa's dark blue eyes shine and for a moment it is as if the past year had never been.

But she glances down at the letter and everything shifts back into focus.

"So tell me," he says. "For whom are those birthday wishes?"

"I'm writing to the Chancellor."

Lili can hear Papa's breathing. Then the sound is covered by the wah wah wail of a fire truck racing toward somewhere in Manhattan.

"Ah. Today is his birthday. Your greetings will be late."

She plays with the tip of a braid, drops it.

"Yes, I know. But he will get so many cards on his birthday. This way, mine will stand out."

Papa's eyebrows rise and he nods.

"My compliments. A well-thought out strategy."

There is a momentary rush of satisfaction, the same warmth that she once knew when, after having learnt a particularly difficult passage, Papa praised her.

"Papa, when can we go home?"

He glances at her, then the card. He looks at the painting of the Brandenburger Tor that hangs on the opposite wall. There are views of Berlin on every wall of her room. He sighs.

"I know this has been difficult for you, Lili. It is never easy to uproot oneself, and for a person of your age probably especially hard.

Please try to understand that our move is not a temporary one. At least not until certain changes have taken place in Germany."

She moves forward on her chair.

"That's the point, Papa. Changes are taking place. We should be a part of them. You know, Papa, you're so nice and so smart. I think you could be an important man in the government."

For a brief moment he smiles, thin-lipped.

"Thank you for your confidence in me, Lili, misplaced as it is. You're still young, my girl, and there is much you can't understand. You will simply have to trust me."

The words burn her ears. There was indeed a time when she trusted him in all things. When she was young, Papa told her the sky was actually green, not blue, and for one whole day she had seen it thus, until Papa himself had realized what was happening and apologized for his teasing. Perhaps he will apologize again, soon. Because this is different. What she hears at the German-American Cultural Club is what is really going on in Germany. Papa no longer knows. He is still seeing blue when he should be seeing *brown*. She snatches up her pen, gripping it.

Her father rises from the chair.

"Finish your letter then," he says as he turns from her. "Let the Chancellor know that he has an unquestioning supporter all the way across the Atlantic."

Alone again, Lili pushes the pen across the paper so hard that the nib breaks off. She starts over. Tomorrow she will paste a stamp and drop it into the corner post box. Some time thereafter, the Chancellor himself will slit open the envelope and his hand, the same hand that once held hers, will hold this very paper. He will read these words that she is writing, words that come from the depths of her heart. He will know how even though she is so far away, she is in awe of the enormous, self-sacrificing mission he is undertaking for the German people as he leads them to freedom, greatness, and power. That it is with deep and fervent respect that she honors him. That she will devote her life to honoring her duty to the fatherland and that she believes in the Chancellor with all her being. And that she wishes him a long, long life as leader of the Third German Reich.

As for making music with Papa, that is of no importance today.

In Us Alone Lies the Future

"Attention!" Herr Krüger barks from behind the podium that stands in front of a medium-sized portrait of the Chancellor. Herr Krüger is particular about the *Umlaut* here even though outside Yorkville he is called 'Krooger'. Not much older than many of his audience, he is a baker in Queens; sometimes he seems to still have the sheen of flour upon him.

"Everybody in their seats," Herr Krüger calls out, wrinkling his nose in a deep sniff. He has a slight cold today. Only the three older boys standing at attention behind him do not follow his order. Lili glances at the tallest of them. His posture is the straightest, his chin lifted the highest. He looks a lot like the boy on the Hitler Jugend poster by the door.

The seating in the large room is mainly of wooden stools. Her back trained from years at her instrument, Lili sits easily on one at the front, where Herr Krüger is waiting to begin. All around are the familiar faces of children, teenagers, and young adults who have come from Manhattan as well as from some of the neighboring boroughs for this afternoon's meeting of the German-American Cultural Club. Lili knows the names of only some of them; that is more than enough.

"Today," Herr Krüger declares, glancing down at his notes, "today I will open today's meeting with a famous speech by the Chancellor. All Germans can sleep well at night, knowing that the Chancellor cares so much for the wellbeing of the German Volk. Of course," he says, his expression serious as he looks over the collection of rapt faces, "we all know that the Chancellor himself never sleeps. He's too busy looking out for the future of the German people."

He motions to the standing boys.

"Friedrich, the gramophone player!"

Friedrich, the tallest, the one who looks a lot like the HJ boy in the poster, rushes to the nearby table and with great ceremony places the 78-rpm plate onto the turntable. As he adjusts the needle, the room falls into frozen silence, not even a creak from the dozens of stools.

At first they hear only a crackling, followed by hissing. And then what they have all been waiting for. It is his greatest speech of the past year and the voice draws them in as if he were there with them at this very moment.

"Comrades of the German Volk!" he begins, and this opening statement to the people of Germany sends a warm rush of pride or pleasure or solidarity, or all of that together, through Lili's chest.

"We don't want to lie and we don't want to cheat!" At first it seems that there is a scratch in the gramophone, for a heavy swell of noise bursts through the speaker. But the swells are capped by shouts of "Bravo!" and Lili realizes that the sound issues from the thousands and thousands of hands clapping together in front of the Reichstag in a vast sea of applause.

After nearly every sentence, there are shouts and more clapping. The Chancellor is speaking from the heart, and her own is beating faster. He tells them how the resurrection of the German nation can be made only by reclaiming the strength and health of the German Volk. That this is not an easy task. Since 1920 he himself has been unwavering in his work to build up the movement. From a mere seven men, the number has risen to 12 million members who understand the importance of his vision.

"Everything is rooted in one's own will, in one's own work."

"That's right!" somebody calls from behind Lili.

The 'Bravo!'s are like punctuation marks as the Chancellor continues, now warning against foreign support and assistance.

"In us alone lies the future of the German Volk...in our own diligence, our own resolve, our own stubbornness."

The skies above Berlin must have split open that day through the sheer volume and vibration of joined hands. Lili feels herself swelling with a longing to do as the Chancellor says, and help the people of Germany upwards to greatness. She wants to both follow and lead.

He stresses the importance of the preservation of the German Volk and the earth, the roots from which strength can be drawn. Their forefathers were not presented with a readymade Germany but had to create it.

"We don't live for ideas or for theories, not for the fantastic Party program—no, the German Volk lives and struggles for the preservation of its very existence."

"German Volk, give us four years, then judge and form your opinion of us! Give us four years, and I swear to you: So as I entered this office, so will I also go. But know this: I did not do it for salary nor reward—I did it for you."

Within her she feels the wild cheering that has traveled through time and space. He is speaking to her.

"Even if today we are misjudged and millions want to curse us, the hour will come when they march behind us."

"Bravo!" Lili hears the clapping and the hurrahs all around her but now her spirit is no longer in the room. It has crossed the ocean and joined the millions cheering the Chancellor, trusting his vision of hope and pride and strength for the land of their forefathers.

"I cannot renounce the conviction that this nation will again rise. Cannot distance myself from love for this, my Volk... the hour will indeed come...millions will stand behind us and greet with us the jointly created, painstakingly battled for, bitterly

earned new German nation—of greatness and honor and strength and magnificence and justice. Amen!"

This final word jars her. For a brief moment she squints in confusion, then joins in with the 'Heil!'s and 'Bravo!'s and applause hissing out of the speaker. The recorded sounds are soon lost in the stamping and cheering that shake the room on York Avenue. Lili's eyes too are ablaze. If it is like this here, what must it be like in Germany?

Like a Celestial Herald

"Attention!" Herr Krüger shouts. "Now we are going to learn some important terms. This will help us understand the issues that are the essence of the Reich." He sucks in some nasal congestion as he peers down at his notes. "*Gleichschaltung.* This is a vital tool of alignment for the Reich. With Gleichschaltung, everything is getting coordinated, running on the same track. All organizations must work together for the good of the nation. The citizens of the Reich, the true German people, look with pride on the accomplishments of the Reich, with the Chancellor at its supreme head. With Gleichschaltung, we can and must all contribute to the smooth running of our country. Even when we are," and here he looks up from his papers, straight into the center of their gathering, "so far away from our beloved homeland. But of course our love for the Reich beats strongly in our hearts!"

One of the older boys cries out "Heil Hitler!" and within a split second the room echoes his call. Lili feels another rush of excitement.

"I know you're disappointed about not being able to play an active role in the organizations created especially for young people by Reich Youth Leader Baldur von Schirach who is of course a very busy man." Here Herr Krüger coughs, clears his throat, fidgets a bit and pulls his thick shoulders back. Two of the older boys glance at each other and roll their eyes; Lili is glad that Friedrich is not doing the same. Earlier this year Herr Krüger attended some gatherings in Germany and was even in the same room as Baldur von Schirach, head of the Hitler Jugend, an event he has alluded to many times since then.

"In Germany, Catholic youth groups have been disbanding to join the HJ and BDM in large numbers. This is also an example of Gleichschaltung. I know you're sad not to be able to join those activities that our Volksgenossen are taking part in with such enthusiasm. That's why I'm pleased to announce that at next week's meeting you'll have the chance to meet two members of the HJ and BDM who are coming to New York. They're going to share with you some of their inspiring experiences as part of the Reich's most important resource—you, the youth."

Hearing this, Lili is so excited that she nearly loses her balance and falls off the stool, but catches herself in time.

"As the Chancellor himself has said," Herr Krüger continues, peering down at his notes, "'what can befall a people whose youth gives up everything to serve its great ideals?'

"To show our visitors that we in America are also doing our part, we'll begin collections for the be *Winterhilfswerk*. We can contribute to the needy. It's our duty to our Volksgenossen! As of next meeting, ten cents will be collected from every one of us every week until November when the money will be sent to Berlin." He looks across the room to where the banner with the swastika is fastened to the wall. "We may be far away in body, but our spirit is close as ever to the needs and goals of the fatherland."

"*Sieg Heil!*" they all call out.

Beginning next week, Lili will make sure that no one is looking and slip several dimes into the collection box for the Winter Relief Fund. Even if she cannot go home to help do her part, her savings will.

"Now we will discuss the term *Ariesierung*." Herr Krüger peers at them as if he were taking in the assorted specimens of German

Volksgenossen. He wrinkles his brow and stares at his notes. Lili wonders if he writes them himself.

"Your pamphlets explain the importance of reasserting the cultural values of the German Volk. For too many years our Aryan actors, artists, musicians, writers, professors, lawyers, and doctors have been shoved aside by Jews. But those days are disappearing. These professions are now going back to where they belong. Into the hands of real Germans." He removes a handkerchief and blows into it with a loud blast.

The atmosphere in the room is electric with excitement at what is taking place back in Germany. Two of the boys and one girl will be moving there next month; their parents have decided to return. The economy is doing much better and they will quickly find work and positions. The girl has bragged about how her parents are members of the Party and that when she is old enough she too is going to join. Lili bites the inside of her bottom lip, a habit she hasn't managed to rid herself of these many years.

Herr Krüger blows his nose again. There are a few snickers around the room.

"Now we will sing."

This is the cue for Otto, a boy from the Bronx, to move to the front of the room with his accordion strapped over his wide belly. He presses some buttons. The instrument wheezes then wakes. Otto's lips are clenched but his eyes are open wide, and as the familiar chords from *Die Fahne Hoch* stream out, arms are stretched out toward the Chancellor on the wall behind Herr Krüger.

"The flag high! The ranks tightly closed!" their voices rise in unison.

At the words "shot dead" and "spirit", there is an exquisite harmony that thrills Lili. Her voice soars with the sopranos. It is the same in every verse; when they come to those particular parts of the melody, she wants to jump up and run out and do something important. Otto's accordion captures perfectly the rhythm of marching drums. The blood flows into

31

her feet, charging her, and she just can't keep them still. Somehow, when the simple arrangement, not unlike a folk song or even a nursery rhyme, is combined with the lyrics of sacrifice and anticipation, they metamorphose into a sentiment so uplifting that Lili finds her heart hammering and her vision blurring. Her very favorite verse is when they sing out "Already millions are looking to the swastika, filled with hope. The day of freedom and bread is dawning!"

Lili turns to look at the banner on the back wall, then at the portrait. It is true; countless millions look to the swastika and to Adolf Hitler with hope in their hearts. Hope and faith and proof that he is leading them to a secure future in which every single citizen will sing with joy to be German. And he is putting much more than bread on the table. Yes, Adolf Hitler is a man who makes promises, and then keeps them.

When the last chord of the accordion has faded, Herr Krüger sniffs deep and continues. "Even though we're so far away from home, all of us can take strength from knowing that we're part of a bigger vision. The vision of the Chancellor himself. Even here in America there are many who recognize the wisdom and foresight of the Chancellor and his desire for world peace." He gives a brief smile. "Herr Charles Coughlin is a Catholic priest who broadcasts radio programs to millions of Americans. He looks to the Chancellor for guidance and inspiration. He's also a friend of U.S. senators and other government people, so there are lots of good opportunities for him to spread the message."

Now Herr Krüger no longer looks like a baker with a cold. His cheeks are rosy, his eyes shining, his garments iridescent from flour. Like a celestial herald, he too is spreading the word of the Chancellor who wants peace for the world.

Behind him, one of the older boys looks down at his arm to check his wristwatch. Lili glances at Friedrich who catches her eye. An eyebrow lifts a fraction. Quickly she averts her gaze and concentrates on Herr Krüger.

"Let's not forget how an American congressman, Herr Louis McFadden, made a speech to the government warning about how the Jews have a plan to take over the world. Americans are beginning to recognize the light of reason, and inspiration, that is our own beloved leader." Herr Krüger is beginning to sound hoarse. "I know that last month many of you were at the rally. It was heartwarming to see such a crowd. I'm truly sorry for those of you who couldn't be there to share in the spirit of that event."

Lili feels intense sorrow, and shame, for not having been among the thousands who gathered in Queens that day in support of the National Socialists. Papa had remained unmoved by her pleas to take her there. Neither smiles nor sulking had changed his mind. Perhaps he will relent for the next rally.

Please Don't Disappoint Me

"The answer remains 'no', Lili."

Seated at the head of the table, Papa addresses her above his boiled egg. There is a tiny flush on each of his cheeks but he still looks calm and elegant in his suit of pale beige. "Some members of the German-American Cultural Club may be at the rally today, but it is not necessary that you attend." He slides the top of the egg onto his mother-of-pearl spoon.

Her lips clenched, Lili looks down at her own unshelled egg. The rally at Madison Square Garden will most likely be even bigger than the one in Queens.

"Papa. You didn't let me go to the last one because you were worried there might be trouble. But nothing happened, so why can't I go to this one? Americans are going too, Papa. Not just Germans. As you said, members of the German-American Cultural Club will be there. If they can go, why can't I?" She can feel her voice rising.

Papa touches the linen napkin to his upper lip.

"By now you should be aware of how I feel about what is going on in Germany." His voice is infuriatingly even. "The Germany I love and respect is being transformed. The current regime is altering more than the face of Germany; it is rendering its body unrecognizable. Yet still it seems that people both inside and outside the country are taken in by the rhetoric.

"I shall misquote Goethe, in spirit at least, for surely he meant it differently: 'A person places himself on a level with those he praises.'" Papa pauses. "In this case, not the best place to be."

His dark blue eyes focus on her. "So the answer remains no, Lili. Even if some of your acquaintances may have taken part in the rally last month, you will not be attending this one. We do not support such spectacles."

Lili bites down on the flesh of her inner lip.

Papa shakes his head. "All this heady talk of Volk and *Vaterland* and values only masks the fact that with each passing day more basic rights are being taken from the German people. Last year it was the Enabling Act. Then Gleichschaltung." He glances at his egg. "Now they've set up the so-called *Volksgericht*. But what sort of a People's Court robs its citizens of both the right to a trial by jury and the right to appeal?"

He seems to be waiting for an answer, but Lili will not speak. She could tell him how these measures were taken to safeguard the nation from internal threats by Communists and Socialists and other agitators, but doubts he will listen to her. Even if he does, he won't hear what she is saying.

Papa frowns. "It seems that Gleichschaltung excuses everything." There is silence in the room.

"Lili."

She can feel his gaze traveling over her face, taking in the tight lines of her mouth and the hardness in her eyes.

"I allow you to spend time with those German and American youngsters at the club because we are in America and because I have faith in your good sense." He returns to his egg. "Please don't disappoint me."

L'Heure Bleue

In the following years it is Lili's devotion to the harpsichord that fosters an uneasy peace between father and daughter. Still, the harmony between them is not counterpoint but more like dissonant intervals, most certainly not always resolved. The notes of that time are scant and fragmented, progressions in interrupted cadence.

Lili spends less and less time with Papa. The memories of how they once were conflict with how they are now. There seems to be nothing that will convince him that they are wrong for having turned their backs on Germany; that he is mistaken, gravely, in his opinion of the Chancellor. With every passing day, the pedestal upon which her Papa has so long stood is sinking. He is her father, but when she looks at him she sees beyond the familiar contours into the nothingness of his being.

She works on the Variations.

She goes to school and does her homework.

And once a week she walks to Yorkville so that she can learn more about what they left behind.

In her room are the pamphlets she occasionally brings home with her, guides to help her look at life. To see what is important, and what should be discarded. Everything makes perfect sense, all derives from the wisdom of the Chancellor. To be neat, she keeps these pamphlets in her desk drawers. Or is she simply hiding them from Papa? From Lotte? She does not consider Mama, for Mama is not overly rooted in the here and now.

♫ ♪ ♫

This summer morning in 1934 Lili can sense her presence even before she hears her calling. L'Heure Bleue has followed her mother to America.

Seated on the bed, Lili looks ups from the newspaper spread out before her.

"Yes, Mama?"

Her mother stands just inside the door frame of Lili's room, serene and dreamy in a cream-colored dress, pale blue hat at an angle atop hair swept up in strands ever as thick and gold as the sweetness gathered from the hives at Alt Eichendorf. Rays from the open window bathe her face in luminescence.

"It's such a lovely day. Let's take Paul to the park, shall we? We can eat ice cream in The Boathouse Cafe and then have a look at the building on Sheep Meadow that they are turning into a tavern."

The lure of ice cream is strong. But the half-finished article in the paper—Lili hesitates.

"We could leave in fifteen minutes," Mama says.

"All right. Fifteen minutes."

Her mother nods and smiles. As she turns away, the delicate scent drifts toward Lili.

"Mama?"

She turns back.

"Why do you wear only that particular perfume?"

"It is my signature scent of course," she says, tilting her head slightly as she begins to speak in a voice soft as rain.

"I was already in my twenties and had never before been in love." Her lashes flutter once. "A young naval officer and I were out walking along Schwerin Lake. It was the hour when the sky begins to lose the sun but has not yet found the stars. It was the hour when all the elements unite to express something, something filled with infinity, an unutterable tenderness..." Mama's gaze slides past her, into an unseen blue.

"What happened next?"

"Hmm. The officer and I returned to the lodge where our families were staying."

"That's all?"

A hint of mischief plays at the shadowed corners of her mother's mouth.

"No, my darling. A few weeks later, that same gentleman came to visit us at Alt Eichendorf. He spoke to Großpapa Hugo and then to me. And aside from a beautiful gold band in a velvet box, he presented me with a bottle of perfume."

"Of course," Lili laughs, forgetting all but delight at her parents' history. "It was Papa!"

"It was Papa, and this is the ring." Mama holds up her hand, showing Lili what she has seen every day of her life.

"And the bottle of perfume was L'Heure Bleue."

"Indeed it was. In the meantime, Papa had been visiting his *Onkel* Wilhelm and *Tante* Aletheia in Paris and had gone to the Guerlain shop. He sniffed his way through the perfumes and when he came across this one, knew it was perfect." Lili smiles as Mama blushes. "Papa said it was as enchanting as I. He told me that Jacques Guerlain himself had created this scent in 1912. He wanted to evoke the mystery of that last moment of light before the sun disappears and the sky darkens."

Lili sighs as Mama floats out of the room. How young her parents once were. Falling in love on the shore of a lake in Mecklenburg-Vorpommern. Wondering what their life together would bring. Never imagining they would leave their homeland, country of their forefathers.

She snaps the newspaper open to the right page.

It is written in English, which she can now read as quickly as German. Over and over again she absorbs the sentence stating that with the death of President Hindenburg, Chancellor Adolf Hitler has declared himself Commander-in-Chief of the German Armed Forces and, assuming position as head of the German nation, has taken the title of leader, the *Führer*.

She breathes deeply. A faint scent of L'Heure Bleue still hangs in the air.

Wrong Wrong Wrong

Yet another summer away from home turns into September. There have been no walks in the park. As if the sky were trying to wash away the entire city of New York, the rain is relentless. Lili takes comfort in watching the endless streams outside her windows, for if the sky succeeds perhaps then they can at last return to Berlin.

Time, the Atlantic, and Papa have kept her away from yet another milestone at home. If only she could have been there that day last week, a tiny but present part of the crowds swelling the streets in celebration, breathing in air ripe with relief and hope. And, under the guidance of the Führer, the gift of confidence in tomorrow. Last week, out of more than 42 million people, only four million voted against him. Today's newspaper said that there were also nearly a million ballots that had been defaced, whatever that means.

She sits down at her harpsichord and begins to practice a stupid piece assigned by the new teacher whom Papa has hired for her, Mr. Farqhas a.k.a. the Jackass who doesn't understand her capabilities at all. Within five minutes she has mastered it. She goes over to the gramophone player and puts on the Landowska recording of the Variations, Number 10. This is how she truly advances. As ever, her aim is not to copy Wanda Landowska but to understand her. Once she has understood, then she can take the work and tune it to what she feels, both of J.S.Bach and deep inside herself. This is hard, time-consuming work that she knows she will one day perfect. Perfect in her own way while always heedful of Bach. This knowledge has its usual calming effect on her. It will take time, but she will do what she has set out to do.

♫ ♪ ♫

Eventually the rains stop and the American autumn takes on its colors and cold. Paul entertains them. With Paul there is laughter, as if his presence enabled a neutral territory. While he is in the room it is often possible to put aside the resentment that smolders in Lili. Sometimes she watches Papa with Paul and remembers how it was when she was still so small that he could throw her into the air and catch her. She too must have crowed with delight and brought that same radiance to Papa's face. There was safety in his arms. She remembers how it felt, her hand in his, as they walked through the darkening woods, remembers his helping boost as she learned to climb higher and higher into the beeches and oaks. Now when, occasionally, he reaches out to pat her hand or smooth her hair, she stiffens. She will never forgive him. Not just for bringing them here but for not even trying to understand what the Führer means for Germany.

If Papa thinks that she will forget their homeland and be American just because they are here, he is wrong wrong wrong. Again. That will never happen, especially as each week she renews her ties to the land of their ancestors. She has no interest in becoming friends with any of the others at the German-American Cultural Club. They are interchangeable. But even though it is in the wrong country, all them, united, are able to call forth from within the overflowing force that is faith and love for the Führer. If she believed in God, she would say that the Führer is indeed His answer to Germany's prayers.

Who Is Vogner?

In English class they have been taking turns reading aloud from passages in their new textbook, *The Romance of American Literature.*

"Who can tell me who the Romantics were?" Miss Mackery asks, peering out at the class through metal-rimmed spectacles. Her voice has a feline whine to it.

The boy next to Lili raises a hand.

"I know. They were them wop foot soldiers that killed Julius Caesar." He folds his arms and nods for emphasis. "They wore togas."

Lili stares through his freckles to see if he is blushing.

Miss Mackery frowns. "Thank you, Patrick. Does anyone else have an idea who the Romantics were?"

Lili tenses.

Slouching in his seat, the class troublemaker slides his hand up. Although his lids are half-closed, his eyes flash jet black.

"Sit up, Tony," snaps Miss Mackery.

Slowly he pulls himself up, not looking at all contrite. If this were Berlin, Tony would be getting his knuckles slammed with the edge of a ruler.

"Sorry, Miss Mackery," he claims, grinning out the side of his mouth. "Everybody knows The Romantics. Or should. They're the bee's knees of a ragtime band down in Greenwich."

The class breaks into giggles and snorts.

Fogging up with sternness, Miss Mackery's spectacles stare at Tony as she commands him to go to Principal Larson. At the door he turns and winks at the class. Lili gnaws at her lip. Don't these students have any manners?

Miss Mackery faces them. "Who can tell us who the Romantics were? Anyone?"

All of the students are sitting like dummies except for Patrick who is picking his nose. Even the one who really should know who the Romantics were is just staring at his pencil; he comes from a first-generation German-American family. If this were her school in Berlin, everybody would know the answer. If this were Berlin, the teacher wouldn't even bother to ask such a stupid question. Miss Mackery's whining vibrato lingers in the air and she looks as if she were about to open her mouth again.

Lili's hand shoots up and the words explode even as Miss Mackery nods at her.

"The Romantics were musicians and writers like Goethe and Beethoven and Wagner."

There are a few titters in the classroom. Miss Mackery moves to the blackboard, chalk in hand.

"Thank you, Lili. Very interesting. However, this class is about Americans."

The girl on the other side of Lili raises her hand. Miss Mackery nods.

"Yes, Dorothy?"

"You mean American writers like Nathaniel Hawthorne and Washington Irving and James Fennimore Cooper, don't you, Miss Mackery?" she says, then throws a triumphant sidelong glance at Lili and sticks out her tongue.

From somewhere behind her, Lili hears a voice stage whisper "Dumb kraut," and she knows exactly who is meant.

Chalk squeaking, Miss Mackery writes 'Rip Van Winkle' on the board. "Any questions?"

A girl in the back raises her hand.

"Yes, Betty Lou," Miss Mackery sighs.

"I know Bate-Hoven but who is Vogner? Does he play in a ragtime band?"

Miss Mackery frowns. "That's enough discussion for today. We will continue silent reading now.

Lili closes her eyes. Why in heaven did they have to come to America?

What Will Papa Do When He Sees It?

Lili's membership in the German-American Cultural Club gives her access to some of the popular newspapers from Germany, periodicals her parents would never have at home. Occasionally members are allowed to take one along to keep but by then its condition is generally so worn that it is good enough only for lining a birdcage. Herr Krüger says that someone in America should publish a newspaper like *Der Stürmer* or the *Völkischer Beobachter*. That would show support and make it easier to get up-to-date news. A few local sheets do occasionally fall into Lili's hands. And of course there is the slender pamphlet she studies now while curled up on an armchair in her room.

It is a modest catalogue listing some of the products from the shop at the NSDAP headquarters in Yorkville, Pennsylvania. These, imports and some locally manufactured pieces, combine in an array of items that will be perfect for Christmas. The crudely bound catalogue, given out to those present at the last meeting of the German-American Cultural Club, features nearly a dozen pages offering framed portraits of the Führer, adorned picture frames, swastika-decorated pinwheels, plates, cups, lamp shades, and ever so much more. She chooses the perfect gift for Paul, after which she will post her order and then wait for Christmas Eve.

There is little snow this year. A few days before Christmas, Mama suggests that they visit Union Square where fir-trimmed booths are set up. It is not like the Christmas markets in Berlin, where the air is thick with that particular scent of the season. The smell is not the same. On some of the counters there are jars filled with red-and-white striped candy sticks and canes. There are toffees and chocolates, and miniature cakes with colored icing called 'cupcakes'. Few of them resemble the Christmas sweets in Berlin. There is music as well, but not the choral, string, or organ works that signal the advent of Christmas at home. No, here the music blaring out from the gramophone players is bouncy, like toys made from plastic instead of wood. *Santa Claus is Coming to Town.* Lili pulls her coat tight against her.

And then it is Christmas Eve.

Paul and she are waiting outside the salon. The gift to Paul has arrived and been wrapped in red paper dotted with fir cones outlined in gold. She is sure that she has chosen well, for it is the perfect gift for a perfect little boy who must never forget his heritage. Will Paul shriek with delight? What will Papa do when he sees it?

He and Mama are still behind the closed doors, getting the tree ready, transforming the sturdy fir thick with plump needles and the scent of the forest into a creation of radiance. When the time is right, Paul and Lili will be called in. Then all will gaze at the splendor that comes but once a year and lasts only moments.

Amidst the dark fir will hang hearts cut from *Lebkuchen*, frosted white and sweet, the spice of their ginger and honey blending with that of the forest's needles. There will be sugar-sprinkled cocoa rings on red ribbons, and chocolate birds wrapped in colored paper, bright-eyed, hovering in the hollows. The branches will be hung with *Lametta*, icicles of foil catching every flicker of light. Golden bulbs, and apple red, too, will burnish the glow. Tucked safely along the sturdier parts, clipped on with tiny silver acorn-shaped holders, will be candles, white, their flames glowing tawny. Yet even their brief blaze will last longer than that initial moment, glorious, when Mama and Papa at last call out to the two of them in the hall and the tree will be at the pinnacle of perfection, its branches festooned with slender wires coated with phosphor, all of which will have been set off so that when the doors are flung open, they will stand together to see the Christmas tree streaming with sparkles like the stars that fly in brilliance across the night sky.

Of course in Berlin it was always only Lili who stood outside the door. Even now she remembers how it felt, all alone there in the half-light. That strange mixture of fear tempered with excitement and knowing it would all work out in the end. For the moment the door opened, her exile in the hallway would be over and once again she's safe with Papa and Mama.

This, their second Christmas away from home, passes in the same blur of fir and light and bittersweet longing as the last. The only moments that are clear for Lili are when Paul's gift is unwrapped. It is Mama who removes the paper for him, carefully, so that it can be reused next Christmas. All four of them are grouped in a tiny circle so it is easy for Lili to look at Paul's sweet face. She is momentarily disappointed, for at first he doesn't understand what it is. But an instant later she turns to Papa, and it is clear that he has immediately recognized the doll. She watches how his eyes widen and then shrink as his eyebrows sink inwards, drawing lines. A tiny tremor of something she has never before felt fills her chest; it is delicious, like an appetizer. Then Paul reaches out for his Christmas gift and, as he does with Lili's old dolls, tries to kiss its tiny cheek. But his lips miss when the jutting visor of the black cap of the perfectly detailed miniature SS uniform gets in the way.

Ragged Underwear from a Clothesline

By January 1935, a more suitable teacher has been found for Lili. Germans have been trickling into New York since 1933 and not all of them are Jewish. *Frau* Kuhn arrived on the S.S. Bremen; Third Class, as she told Lili with a faint smugness. Lili sneaks a glance at her teacher now and stifles a giggle. Thin and wiry, Frau Kuhn drifts around the room, hands stirring the space in front of her as if she were directing an entire underwater orchestra rather than a lone harpsichord working through the new section of a Haydn sonata.

"Ta de da tum tum!" she calls out. "You must see the mark! Feel the empty space! Haydn is witty and subtle in his transitions. Play it again!"

Lili plays it again, the rhythm correct, and has to look down quickly when she notices Frau Kuhn closing her eyes and swaying like coral in an ocean current. Then Lili is off into the piece, her flying fingers guided by the black squiggles dancing on the sheets. For some time there is nothing but the notes that ripple and rush in lightly overlapping layers.

When she comes to the end, there is silence. Usually Frau Kuhn immediately has something to say but now there is nothing. Has Lili played the piece so badly? So well? She looks over to where her teacher sits on the petit point seat. In her bony hand is the pamphlet Lili was looking through before the start of the lesson.

Lili pulls herself straighter. Frau Kuhn peers at her with a gaze even darker than when she is displeased with her playing.

"Are you another one of those who have fallen in love with that man?" Her voice is nearly an octave lower than usual.

Lili meets her look.

"They should have kept him in jail," Frau Kuhn growls. The pamphlet slides onto the chair as she gets up and begins to pace, leaving the Führer's stern stare directed toward the chandelier.

"It's because of him that I lost my position at the Potsdamer Musik and Kunsthaus." Her gray-streaked bun bobs with indignation as she slams a fist into her open palm. Lili doesn't move a muscle.

"For so many years I worked as a teacher. I'm a spinster with only my own efforts to fall back on. I had my certificate from the Moscow Conservatory—I had a scholarship there. My credentials were im-pec-ca-ble!" she states with staccato bursts." Frau Kuhn peers at Lili, who can feel the blood draining from her cheeks.

"I was fully qualified to teach anywhere. I could even have stayed in Moscow."

"So why didn't you?" There is a snarl in Lili's voice.

Frau Kuhn stops short just in front of her.

"Because I'm German, you silly girl. That's why! I love my country. I went back to Berlin to be of service—musical service—to the land of my birth." She sniffs; compared to her voice just now, it's a delicate sound. "The fact that I took back with me not only increased knowledge of music but also an awareness of how things could be better in Germany doesn't make me a bad person.

"When I returned from Russia they teased me and called me a Bolshevik." She snorts. "Yes, Miss Lili, I'm a Communist. But I joined in Berlin, not Moscow."

She waves a hand at Lili. "You're too young, and not of the people. You don't know how bad it was both during and after the war. Crime. Food shortages. Housing shortages. Everything shortages! Hundreds of thousands of Germans dead of starvation because of the Blockade. *Ach,*" she breathes, and Lili can hear her vocal chords vibrating, "most of the twenties were horrible. Horrible!"

Suddenly Frau Kuhn grabs the chair with the pamphlet, pulling it over to the harpsichord.

"I'll tell you how bad it was." She pushes the Führer to the floor and seats herself.

And in an endless stream she explains to Lili who, once a German schoolgirl, already knows some of it. Frau Kuhn rages on about hunger and disease, the billions of marks that eventually bought nothing but perhaps a heel of bread. About how even the ragged underwear from a clothesline might be stolen by someone without any at all. About the impossible reparations that needed to be paid for losing the war. The loss of German territories. The loss of dignity of an entire people.

Finally she sucks in some air, lets it go with a sigh. "Sometimes," she says, and her voice is softer than before, "when we had no fuel, not even splintered wood, my mother had to light our tiny cooking fire with million Mark notes. Worthless. In 1919 a loaf of bread cost 1 mark. By 1923 it was 100 billion marks. I watched my father shrivel up into nothing too, and he a man who had always taken such pride in his workmanship. But what could he do when no one had work for a carpenter? My father always told me to defend myself against the capitalists. He said we went to war for the capitalists." Frau Kuhn breaks off. "But your family is very good. Very fair. Even paying my transportation costs every week."

"So what did you do?"

"I joined the Communist Party, of course."

Lili frowns. "Why didn't you join the National Socialists? There are more jobs in Germany now than ever."

"Ach, back in 1924 the *Hitlerbande* didn't have such a strong presence." She shrugs her narrow shoulders. "But I wouldn't have joined in any case. They're small minds and a violent bunch to boot. No, they've had it out for the Communists since the very beginning.

"All those brutal fights they picked. Beating up our boys in empty lots. Bashing them with beer bottles. Shooting them dead. Then saying our boys were the ones who started it. Of course, to be fair, sometimes they did." She sucks at a tooth. "From the moment the Nazis got in, they've been pinning the blame on the Communists." She blinks. "And the Jews."

She raises her voice, turning it harsh and deep. "It was the Bolshies and the *Judenbande* that lost us the war." Her laugh is ragged. "That's their refrain. And when they finally got in, the trade unions were taken over right away by the Labor Front and those SA *Heinis*." She shakes her head. "No, no. There is no worker paradise in the Third Reich."

Lili raises an eyebrow. "You say you love Germany, Frau Kuhn. So why did you leave?"

Before replying, the teacher examines a hangnail on her finger. "I might as well tell you. We are, after all, in America, supposedly the land of the free." For a moment, her eyes light up and Lili isn't sure if it is because of America, or that she is remembering the past.

"I was helping distribute the *Communist Manifesto*. Sometimes we even managed to get papers into that rag, the *Völkischer Beobachter*." She doesn't seem to notice Lili scowling.

"People would find a copy lying around somewhere, and then come across the leaflet, usually tucked between pages 4 and 5." Frau

Kuhn grins and Lili sees that her teeth are gray. "That was good work. But the SA began to sniff around. Several members of my cell were picked up. Worked over, sent to prison." She leans forward. "And I tell you, they didn't have such a pleasant stay there as did Herr Hitler in Landsberg." Her breath smells of peppermint and tobacco. "Then, after April '33, off they went, to that resort in Dachau.

"Two of them are still there. One isn't anywhere anymore." Her lips press together. "They were closing in on us. My superiors advised me to leave Germany right away. Said it was too dangerous for me to become a beefsteak." She glances at Lili who thinks she must have misheard. "You know, it means only pretending to be Nazi. Brown on the outside but red inside. They said my background was too risky, what with my music studies in Moscow. Said I could continue my work in America where there's still much room for growth. So here I am." She folds her skinny arms in their worn woolen sleeves. "Perhaps I won't stay forever in New York. Perhaps I'll go west, someplace like Minneapolis or Seattle. Out there will be something active I can do. Now Germany is lost to me."

Lili stares at Frau Kuhn, the first Communist she has ever met. Yet as angered as she is by the woman's insults of the Führer and the party, she is oddly moved. Frau Kuhn too has had to leave and lose her homeland.

Frau Kuhn pushes the chair.

"Enough talking. Get back to practice."

Lili follows her directive, for now Haydn's spirited notes smoothing over doctrinal discordance.

Papa Speaks Out

Today's meeting at the German-American Cultural Club begins with a feature film entitled *Then and Now*. The screen is a sheet on the wall. A deep, earnest voice accompanies the flickering black-and-white images.

"Where once the people of our nation struggled under the burden of the Treaty of Versailles, having lost the war thanks to the perfidy of Communist treachery and the abominable scourge of the Jews,"–here the camera moves silently down a street where barefoot and filthy children, their gaze empty, wait for soup from a large cauldron on the corner—"today we are in a new age, a return to German strength and rejuvenation." The narrator's voice is at once reassuring and uplifting.

There follow news flashes some of which Lili has seen several times already. But she is happy to see them again for they illustrate, in more ways than mere words can, how far Germany has come in the two years since the Führer stepped in to take charge. The camera moves through rows of villagers, their eyes shining, their mouths opening in silent cheers, their arms waving at near frantic speed as they welcome the troops reclaiming the Saar. Next comes the Führer, posing with cabinet members at the announcement of the reintroduction of military conscription. This scene is followed by a rush of bodies as truckloads of intent police spring into billy club action against those few outlawed anti-government protesters still intent on stirring up trouble.

Around Lili there are indignant murmurs. The nerve of those men—how foolish they must be to think that they know better than the Führer what is good for Germany! The next scene has a broader panorama. There is the Führer, in full regalia, officiating at the opening of another stretch of the great Autobahn. Voiceless, grinning, flag-waving crowds line the sides of the new four-lane highway as his vehicle rolls into the official ribbon, tearing it apart. The narrator exclaims, "Soon the Führer's roads will cover thousands of smoothly asphalted kilometers, enabling drivers to reach the incredible speed of 50 kilometers an hour. Buy your government-issued savings stamps toward the purchase of your own model of the Volkswagen—the people's car!"

Lili smiles at a sudden mental image of Mama driving a Volkswagen. Her mother has never driven any car. But, if they lived in Germany, Lili would ask Papa to get a Volkswagen so that one day in the future *she* could drive it. And then she would drive across the Reich, north to south, east to west, on both the Autobahn and the normal roads, the windows down and her hair blowing in the 50 kilometer-an-hour rush of homeland air.

The next shots are images of factory assembly lines: off they roll, the high-quality cameras, the lamps, armchairs, wooden rocking horses, and dolls, the planes, tanks, and armaments. "Thanks to the Führer, in just two years, the unemployment rate has already been cut by more than half. The building industry is enjoying a boom." There is the Führer again, poring over blueprints with his favorite architect. Cut to a selection of monumental public buildings, impressive sports arenas and ordinary homes for the ordinary citizen. "The Führer will not rest until every German has work and bread. Until every German is free and happy."

A voice rings out in the room. "Sieg Heil!" Lili joins in the salute. How fortunate Germany is, at last to have such a leader. With him, there has been not only renewed confidence for a brighter future, but results, results that everyone can see.

Yet her euphoria fades when she gets home and overhears Papa talking on the telephone.

"It's already too late for a civil war, but mark my words: at some point there will be war.

Who Can Bring Back Even One Hour?

In Central Park the trees are turning green. Some days she goes to The Mall to stand before the bronze bust of Beethoven who from his pedestal looks out over the earth of Central Park with a gaze she can identify only as angry longing. When she is with Mama and Paul—for she is not permitted to go there on her own— they occasionally walk alongside the shallow waters of the Gill through the wilderness of The Ramble until they come to the bust of Schiller. His softer gaze holds an expression of both distress and defiance. It is disconcerting to see two of Germany's greatest men isolated in Central Park. Lili can stare at them for a long time. Today she must content herself with a walk on Terrace Drive.

She stands still and listens very hard, sure she can hear the tiny *pffs* of leaves popping out along the branches above, then moves forward to touch her hands to a trunk and feel the bark as she did with the trees of Grunewald and Alt Eichendorf. When she was younger, she would close her eyes and sense the sap rising through the body, from the roots in the earth up to the farthest limbs. This afternoon she halts in front of an elm and presses her palm against the ridges of gray, furrowed and scaly. She feels nothing.

Sitting down on a bench, she stares into the distance until she sees what she needs to see. Alt Eichendorf. Every season is wonderful there, but summer is—was—is—her favorite. First the automobile trip from Berlin, a picnic lunch along the way. Then their arrival, the warmth of her grandparents' embrace; *Großmama* Maximiliana's so strong for one so slight, *Großpapa* Hugo's so gentle for such a giant, as if he were holding back, fearful that he might crush her with his welcome. Once the adults had finished their coffee and Lili her black currant juice, along with thick pieces of the season's fruit *Torte* topped with a white hill of freshly whipped *Schlagsahne,* she would dash around the table to grab hold of her grandparents' hands, pulling the two of them to their feet. It was time for the inspection tour.

Lili was always eager to see what changes there had been since their last visit. It might be an iron bench under a weeping willow, a thresher or a painted carriage. There was the excitement of meeting the new animals, from chicks to foals. On their tour around the grounds, she loved greeting members of the estate staff, who had been there as long as she could remember. They always clucked over Lili as if she were a precious treasure her grandparents had the privilege of displaying.

The long hours of the season stretched out before them like a buffet filled with the specialties of summer. Mama and Lili had skipping races across the meadows, rolled down gentle grass slopes, coming up for air to find their hair netted with wildflowers. They rowed across their favorite lake, mooring at the island midway. There they tramped about, looking for the jewelry that Mama told her had been lost centuries ago during a time of battles between fairies and goblins, tiny rings and bells of silver that she and Mama unearthed and then strung together, hanging the gossamer strands from the trees so that the wind would catch them up and the afternoon once again tinkle with fairy music. It was years before she realized that Mama had hidden them all there in advance.

Yet the highlight of those days was the walks that Lili and Papa took, opposite the fields, past the towering rows of oak trees, far into the forest of Alt Eichendorf. The centuries-old oaks for which the estate had so long ago been named were giants cloaked in stately splendor. Steadfast and enduring, they were the Teutonic guards to the thousand hectares. As Papa and she set out for the woods, wild and deep, a strange feeling would take root in Lili.

It was a feeling much holier than that which she felt when she went to the Protestant church in nearby Posenwell with Großmama Maximiliana. Lili moved forward through the temple of the forest, reverence in every step. It was as if she were entering a primeval sanctuary, each footfall bringing her closer to a source; the spirit of something ancient was always nearby. At times she wanted to lie down on the earth and embrace it, breathe in the spice of moss and mushroom, feel the wellspring flowing deep beneath the fertile soil against her cheek. Other times she wanted to step aboard a branch and have it lift her high to the top of the tree so that, like the hawk, she could look down upon the forest and know it.

In the woods were myriad trees with magical names like Bergahorn, Sommerlinde, Schwarzpappel. Others were more simply called but just as magnificent in their leafiness. Papa and she walked among the birches, beeches, elms, and poplars whose branches brushed each other in a filigree canopy that dappled the sunlight on the forest floor. There were firs, too, of every shade between green and blue. And whenever they passed a linden tree, Lili would think of Papa walking nearby, for the linden is the tree of love, and how she loved him, her dearest Papa.

He spoke to her of beauty and of truths, reciting poems by Goethe, telling her of his strange tale of a lion, a lily, and a green snake, recounting legends. There were heroes, like Ariovist of whom Caesar spoke, and Karl the Great whom the rest of the world knew only as Charlemagne. There were ancient tragedies captured in verse, of Etzel and the Good Queen Heche. Lili bridled at the treacheries of Hagen and Gunther, mourned with Kriemhilde. As they walked beneath the endless bower, Papa told her how it was said that Friedrich Barbarossa, beloved red-bearded Emperor of the Germans, was not really dead. No, he was merely sleeping these past centuries, in a mountain stronghold of Thuringia, his red beard growing long and blanched with time. It was said that no other emperor would ever take his place and, one day, when ravens no longer winged their way around the mountain, Barbarossa would awaken and restore Germany to its ancient greatness.

The woods were deep, filled with hidden life. Papa told her to hear music in the murmur of the stream and in the weird call of the grouse. It was he who taught her to listen to the wind, even when it was silent. Whatever they saw along the way became inspiration for what he would share. She learned to see the myriad shades of the color green, sylvan tones glowing deep and moist as the moss and foliage in the paintings of Cranach the Elder. Sometimes they caught sight of a deer in a thicket, or a gray rabbit trembling beside the path as if it had lost its way from a canvas by Dürer.

Late one evening, an orange-eyed creature flew across their path, a young mole limp in its talons. Lili started, for Mama had told her that local lore was rich with tales of witches and their owls. Papa's voice was calm when he told her that sense must always vanquish superstition. A short time later they came upon a hedgehog trapped in the ridges of a moldering trunk. Together they rescued it, placing it on the forest floor, watching it scuttle into the underbrush. Papa said that acts of kindness should be undertaken for the benefit of the recipient alone.

"Feeling fulfillment is but a gift, never the goal."

"Did Goethe say that too, Papa?"

He smiled, shaking his head. "No, Lili, those are my words."

With Papa at her side, Lili could walk the world and understand it.

On the bench in Central Park, Lili wakes up. Her neck is stiff.

Back in her room, she needs music, but doesn't want to play. Instead, she places the needle on the gramophone. By the time she is at the window, the fusion of Schubert and Goethe has begun. At times she almost wishes she were a pianist. The piano's lingering tones are perfect for Lieder, especially for drawing out the nuances of longing and loss. Lieder don't work with the harpsichord. It would be like piercing honey with a fork. With the harpsichord, the journey is through the inner recesses of the honeycomb itself.

She looks through the window to the street, at the lone cherry tree, whose branches are already tufted. There is an entire orchard of cherry trees in Alt Eichendorf. Goethe's poem of first loss floats through the air. A breeze must be blowing in from the Hudson for, ever so delicately, the branches tremble and the pale blossoms shiver and shimmer and finally blur under the New York sky.

O, who will bring the lovely days,

Those days of first love,

O, who can bring back even one hour

Of that cherished time?
All alone I tend my wound,
And with renewed lament
Mourn the happiness that is lost.

Just Like Ordinary Germans

She knows that she left the pamphlets scattered on her bedside table last night. Now they are back on her desk, piled up in a neat stack. Lotte must have put them together while she and Mama were in the park with Paul.

He cried today when he saw Lili eating ice cream and stopped only when she began to spoon-feed him; it's official that Paul too loves ice cream. By the time they got home, dribbles of it were all over the front of his smock. Mama took it off, handing it to Lili to carry to the washroom for soaking.

Lotte stepped in then, saying "I'll take that." Being so occupied with Paul, did Mama notice how oddly flat Lotte's tone was? It probably has something to do with the pamphlets. Lotte must have read them.

Some of the pamphlets talk about the issue of the Jews in Germany. For example, in one it explains that Jesus Christ was actually not a Jew at all but a Nordic warrior killed by the Jews. That the Führer is the new messiah sent to save the entire world from the Jews.

Papa has said that the Bergs are lucky to be away from Germany these days, that Lotte and Oskar would be having more and more hardships if they still lived there.

This is ridiculous. The Bergs aren't lawyers or doctors or journalists or any of those Jews who took important jobs away from Germans. People like the Bergs aren't like those ones in Berlin who wear robes and long black coats and head coverings and look as if they were still living in the Middle Ages. People like the Bergs look and smell and act just like ordinary Germans.

They eat the same things the rest of them do. Lotte's *Königsbergerklöpse* are still the best pork and beef dumplings in the world, or at least in America. Oskar doesn't say much to anyone, including Lotte, but he has that wonderful smile. No, people like the Bergs are nothing like those other ones who caused all the problems in Germany.

If Lotte ever wants to talk to her about the pamphlets, Lili will assure her that it's nothing personal. She knows it's not the Bergs' fault, neither about the economy nor Jesus. She would hug them, just as she did when she was small. But now she is probably too old for that.

Dear Adolf Only Has Peaceful Intentions and Lili gets Angry

Exact change in her damp palm, Lili boards the uptown bus on Broadway. Instead of heading straight home after classes today like a good little schoolgirl, she is going all the way to 122nd Street; on a secret mission. Last week there was a newspaper article about a school founded nearly thirty years ago by a German immigrant, a godson of Franz Liszt. Its original name was the Institute of Musical Art, a name Lili prefers, for it sounds so much closer to the spirit of music than its current one, the Juilliard School of Music. But, names aside, it seems to be the right place for her to continue her harpsichord studies now that Frau Kuhn has gone west. Lili got the idea only the other day when yet another new teacher proved unsuitable: rather than looking for the right teacher to come to her, she could go to the teacher. Or teachers. This school sounds like the best music school in New York and, if so, it is obviously where she belongs. However, she has said nothing to either Mama or Papa. It will be a surprise to them that she, all on her own, has found the perfect place for serious instruction. Perhaps then Papa will begin to take her more seriously in other ways too.

There are two empty places available behind a tall man with a tired gray fedora. She slides into the window seat and watches Broadway roll by. A few girls in brimmed hats and clunky shoes are already in their summer dresses; an occasional spring breeze snatches up their hems in splashes of color against the drab storefronts. Children on their way home from school amble along the sidewalk, the straps of their book belts trailing. At a crossing, a man still dressed for winter stands motionless, a painted sign hanging from his neck. "Hungry for work" she reads, just as the bus lurches forward. Further up the avenue, a dog wags its tail as an old woman tugs at the leash. The dog reminds her of Helembertus, the dachshund belonging to their elderly neighbor in Berlin. "A long name for a long dog," the widower would always joke with Lili when they met on the street.

The sound of German is right there on the bus. A new passenger, face flushed and hat askew, has stopped at the row ahead.

"Why, Professor Hoffstadt—you too are here! So far from German shores." The man in the seat in front of Lili turns. The profile under the fedora is a handsome one.

"Ach," he says at last. "Good to see you again, Professor Mengel." He draws closer to the window and the newcomer sits down.

"When was it we last met?"

From this short distance, Lili can hear every clear word of the Hochdeutsch they are speaking.

The other man shifts his shapeless suit into the space available.

"It must have been in '31." "Yes," the other nods. "'31 at the Heine symposium in Hamburg." "I still remember Schaps and how adamant he was that Heine sold out. Two years later, he himself converts. I wonder how long that will see him through." "Yes, my friend, life is full of changes. Dresden is in the past." They fall silent. Is this the same Heine whose poems were set to music by Schumann? "These days I'm teaching the young ladies at Barnard. And you? When did you leave Heidelberg?" "Just after Oschki and Lederer got their papers. It took time to find something here. Pritzker was most helpful." "Now I'm at Columbia." He doesn't sound happy. "I always had such hope. To me, the university always symbolized the best in Germany." "You know what I mean." "Of course, of course, my dear colleague. No offense taken. You are absolutely right about Heidelberg." He pauses. "You *were* right."

He glances back at Lili; she raises her wristwatch as if checking the time. "Columbia, yes. Too bad you weren't already here when Luther addressed the Institute of Arts and Sciences. That could have been an occasion to speak out." "Perhaps. It does still get mentioned from time to time in the halls. Some continue to be outraged. Others gush about having raised a glass with the ambassador at the reception. After all, they say, Hans Luther should know what's what, right?"

What does he mean about Hans Luther? Papa met him several times in Berlin, first when he was Chancellor, later when he was President of Germany, and then again when he worked for the Reichsbank. Now he is the German Ambassador to America. But Papa hasn't mentioned seeing him here. "Luther knows for a fact that dear Adolf only has peaceful intentions." "Yes, he says it himself on the radio, then gives a clear indication of how he's going to go about getting it." They fall silent. This is truly a testimony to the Führer. Although these professors have moved to New York, they too carry the firm conviction that he is a man of peace. It would be wonderful if they could talk to Papa. If she can't convince him, perhaps he would believe these professors.

"My stop."

"I'll get off too, Mengel, and walk with you."

Only a few streets later it is Lili's stop. Her heart beats faster with each daring step that brings her closer to the Juilliard School of Music. At last she arrives at the newly renovated limestone building. So this is where she will further her studies. The entrance hall reminds her of the one in the Empire State Building. In the Admissions Office, a woman whose hair is streaked with gray like the marble out in the lobby looks up from her desk and speaks with a warm tone in her voice, almost as if Lili were a little girl. Lili is quick to tell her she has decided that, given her abilities, this school will be best for her; in this way the woman will recognize that Lili is quite grown up and in control. There is a sweet smile on the woman's face.

"It sounds as if you would be a good candidate for the special program we offer for people your age. If you pass the audition, you'll have a good chance of becoming a student at the Juilliard School of Music."

Lili gnaws on the inside of her mouth. No need to say more. If the woman would simply point her in the right direction, she will go off to do it.

"Do send in your application next year so that we can schedule an audition for you."

Lili's eyes widen. Application? Next year?

The woman winces. "Oh dear, did you not know that the deadline was May 1st?" She reaches out to pat Lili's hand. "You needn't be concerned. You're still very young. In the meantime you can continue to practice, and next year be sure to fill out your application in time. Good luck!" she adds as she returns to the paperwork on her desk.

For some moments Lili continues to stand in front of the desk. Next year! Doesn't the woman realize that a year is a lifetime for a young musician? How good can this school be if they won't recognize commitment standing right in front of them? She bites down again on her lip, this time hard, keeping her teeth in the flesh, and turns. She says neither thank you nor goodbye. She walks out of the Admissions Office, across the lobby, and into the street. The growl of running motors passes through her. At the bus stop she feels a cold sweat on her skin and squeezes her forearms. Is she going to be sick here on the sidewalk? She swallows, fixes her gaze on an ugly building across the street. No. New York will not stop her. She will not let it. She will keep practicing on her own, but not for the Juilliard School of Music. One day they will be sorry they didn't take her when they had the chance. At last she breathes in, a syncopated intake of air that soothes her chest. It's just too bad that now she has nothing with which to surprise Mama and Papa after all.

Such a Bone to Pick

Most of the apartment windows in the city are already open, inviting in whatever solitary breeze might be passing by this early in the evening. Lili leans on the windowsill, looking out toward the park. Mama and Papa are entertaining guests in the salon. Lili was called in to curtsy nicely to each and spent only a few minutes before asking to be excused. Some of the guests live in New York and she has met them before. Others are new arrivals from Germany. She remembers such evenings in Berlin. Often, someone would sit down at the piano and there would be singing. Laughing, too. When she was young, some of the guests would pick her up and swing her about or cuddle her cheeks with their knuckles. One of them even wrote a poem about her, *The Girl with the Earnest Eyes*. The anthology in which it was published is sitting on a bookshelf here even though books by that man are now banned in Germany.

It is another half hour until dinner, when she will go back and join everyone. She leans against the window frame. The air is stirring. Voices from the salon next door drift across the front of the building, some getting caught in the stonework. At times she can hear clearly what is being said. Now, like lather, laughter floats. A voice cuts through.

"After all, how much worse can it get?"

There are some murmurs.

"What's the mood in the streets now?"

Coughing, snatches of sentences.

"Depends on whom you ask, Max."

"It's getting impossible for intelligent people to stomach, that's for sure." Indistinct voices, like bees buzzing.

"Hold on. I've brought along a joke that's making the rounds at the moment: Goebbels thinks that Hitler's getting too big for his britches. So one day he goes to him and suggests that instead of everybody saying Heil Hitler! they should go back to the traditional *Guten Tag*. Hitler shakes his head. 'No, no, my dear Goebbels. As long as I'm in power there will be no Guten Tag.'"

There is a burst of laughter and Lili's ears burn but she leans forward to hear more. Her braids flop forward, out the window.

"Very good," declares a deep voice. "But that's not the mood in all the streets of Germany."

"True. Nowadays, even the smallest streets consider themselves to be avenues."

Lili doesn't understand this, but there is a lot of guffawing.

"Out on the country roads, the farmers are a lot happier these days. Their debts are forgiven and, for the first time in years, a lot of them have real money."

"True, Alfred. But not the Jewish ones! They can't even farm anymore."

"I know a joke about farmers. Who's the biggest farmer of them all?"

"Who, Felix?"

"Adolf Hitler of course."

"I don't understand."

"It's Adolf Hitler. He has 65 million dumb oxen in the biggest pigpen of all." Garbled talking.

"Well, I detest the man but I don't think that joke is very funny."

"You're right, Marta. It's not amusing."

"Well, isn't that because it's true? We're all dumb oxen for having voted him in."

"I didn't vote for him!"

"Speak for yourself. Anyway, you're going back to Germany. I'm staying here. So who's the dumb one?"

"Children, children." Lili recognizes Mama's voice.

"You're right as usual, dear Wilhelmine. We're behaving like squabbling children."

"That's just the problem!" High-pitched, emphatic. "We—that is, the German people as a whole—are like the children who followed the Pied Piper of Hamlin. And Hitler's promises are like the mystical music of the pipe. You know where that led."

"Depending on which version, they either emigrated or drowned. You don't look wet."

"Stop it. To a certain extent you're correct, Luisa."

"You have to admit he's done a lot to pull Germany up out of the mud of the post-war years."

"Ernst! How can you talk like that? You lost your job, your apartment and everything in it. You paid thousands of Reichsmarks just to leave the country. What are you saying?"

Lili chews on the inside of her cheek.

"I feel the man has accomplished a great deal of good." The voice is steady. "It's only unfortunate that he has such a bone to pick with us Jews."

"Oh, that will blow over after he's consolidated everyone. It's just a tool."

"Did you know that back in '33 Gerda tried to join the BDM? Her biggest dream was to wear the skirt and blouse and belong. Wanted to throw herself into the current of excitement that was carrying off most of the girls in her school. Of course they turned her away. Devastated for days, she was. Some of her classmates felt bad. Others didn't care."

"Don't forget to mention the ones who were glad!"

"So now she can join the Girl Scouts of America, right?"

"It's not the same."

"Good."

Some mumbling.

"I'm going to ride it out over here. Direct some plays and build up my repertoire. Broadway here I come! When all the excitement has died down, I'll go home."

"Just make sure it's not to Dachau." This comes from the mouth of Papa. "They still haven't forgiven you for your last play. It's remarkable that you lasted so long. Even Fiedler and Ruben were banned with the others in '33. And you know how mild they are."

"But I was subtle."

Lili grips the window ledge. Unintelligible chatter floats across.

"With due respect to Goethe," says Papa, "I fear that too many Germans are taking moral shelter under his saying that they would rather commit injustice than endure disorder."

"Erwin," someone addresses Papa. "I still don't understand why you didn't stay. As a Junker, what do you have to lose? Your older brother has the estate in any case. As a former naval officer you only stand to gain in this regime."

For some moments there are no sounds at all.

"One could of course view it that way," Papa says, and the words are clear and separate. "Although I must confess that I am sorry to find you doing so."

Again there is silence.

"There's no doubt in my mind, Alfred." Papa's voice is grave. "Like your joke earlier, but in earnest. Germany will not be at rest until Hitler is."

Lili bites down on her lip, tasting blood. There are layers of murmuring from next door.

"...outrageous..."

"...ethics..."

"Really, Ernst!" a woman calls out. "I still have to laugh out loud when I think of that scene. You know, the one in which the SA man is trying to provoke the Jewish clerk. How does it go, Ernst?"

"Oh, it wasn't that funny. I just used something that was making the rounds."

"Funny enough. Tell us. Please."

He speaks in a loud and harsh but somehow stupid-sounding voice.

"'Tell me, Jew, whose fault is it that we lost the war?'" Now his voice changes tone.

"'I was told it was the Jewish generals.'

"So the SA man puts his hands behind his back, nods and says, 'Good, good.' There's a long silence while he seems to be contemplating the sky. Suddenly he looks at the other man, frowns and exclaims, 'But we didn't have any Jewish generals!'"

"Oh, yes, this is the part I love!" a female voice calls out.

"And the Jewish clerk says, still in his smooth voice, 'We didn't, but the other side did.'" More laughter.

Lili recoils. She has heard enough. She slams the window shut with such force that the glass cracks.

Despite the Uneven Application of the 14th Amendment

"It's a good idea to observe how Americans celebrate their national day," Papa said at breakfast, "as we will eventually be citizens of America."

The butter knife fell out of Lili's hand and onto her plate, the clang of metal like a bolt being pushed into place.

Papa seemed not to notice. "Of course our Paul was already born American," he added, reaching out to tousle Paul's hair where he was sitting on Mama's lap, as if at already such a nascent age Paul had performed an amazing feat.

Since then, Lili has said barely a word all day. She is glad that Paul's requests for her attention require few, for even these stick in her throat. In the automobile she avoided having to speak, by leafing through a book of poems.

It was Papa's idea to drive out of the city, have a picnic in the forest, and see the 4th of July fireworks in a town along the Hudson. So here they are, in New Hamburg. If it were only an outing, Lili might actually be enjoying herself. It has been so long since she walked through real woods, and the trees along the Hudson River are quite agreeable even though they lack the intensity and spirit of those in Alt Eichendorf. She has eaten a 'frankfurter' and tried salted popcorn, which stuck in her throat, and in the afternoon they sailed on the cloudy waters. In a short while the fireworks will begin.

But Papa has turned this family outing into a political statement. As if springing the disturbing news on them at breakfast weren't enough, he went on to talk about the American Constitution.

"I have been reading this document. We are fortunate to be in a country where laws seek justice for all. The 14th Amendment is particularly inspiring, although it doesn't seem to be as evenly applied to all citizens as it should be. Despite that, my dear ones, Paul is an American and I would be honored for the three of us to become citizens of this country." He had paused over his coffee and it looked as if he were struggling to keep from coughing, for his face grew flushed. Was he fighting some residue of shame? For then he added, "Even if it means that we have to give up our German citizenship."

That is why Lili has barely gotten out a word all day; she was rendered speechless. Are there no limits to how Papa can betray his country? How can he make such a decision for her? For Mama? Although her voice is back now, she still has to keep quiet. If she doesn't, she will scream fortissimo. Not even the fireworks will mask her frustration and rage.

All She Wants

"If we were still at home, I would be in the League," Lili says as Mama tucks her in. In Yorkville the German-speaking shopkeepers address Lili by the formal "Sie" now instead of the familiar "Du" but it still feels good to have the childhood ritual of Mama's three good night kisses. This evening it has been just the two of them as Paul has been asleep for hours. Papa is at a meeting at the Waldorf Astoria; perhaps he is buying another real estate office.

"I missed being in the Young Girls League but now that I'm 15, I'd be with all the other girls in the BDM. I'd get to do something important for Germany instead of just thinking about it." She frowns at the blue drapes.

"Darling, you are doing something important. And one day you will be an even finer musician than you already are."

Lili kicks her foot against the feather quilt. She has never told anyone about the Juilliard School of Music. She keeps practicing but it seems to be getting her nowhere, certainly not to Germany. How is she going to honor the Führer's directives from so long ago from so far away?

"It's not the same, Mama."

Mama strokes her cheek. Her touch is as light as the trailing silk sleeve of her dressing gown. "I know you miss being home, Lililein. I do too. But we are building a new life for ourselves over here. We have so much for which to be thankful." She pauses. "Papa is working very hard to ensure that our future will be safe."

"I don't like Papa anymore."

The words vibrate in the shadows, a diminished seventh. She feels Mama flinch, but she will not stop. "All he can think about is himself and his business. He doesn't care about Germany anymore. He doesn't care about us either. He wants to turn us into Americans. He doesn't care that I'm dying over here."

Her delicate features drawn, Mama tries to wrap her arms around Lili. For a few moments Lili relaxes against the familiar contours, warm and comforting; life used to be as simple as this. Then she pulls away.

"It's lucky for Papa that we're here, because if we were at home, I'd, I'd tell someone about all the disrespectful things he says about Germany and the Führer."

Lili folds her arms in front of her. For a long moment, Mama searches her face in the lamplight.

"Oh, Lili," she says, softly, and Lili does not know if Mama has found what she is looking for. "Then I am glad that we are here."

♫ ♪ ♫

Lili twists and turns under the eiderdown. Did the Führer ever receive her birthday card? Not that she was expecting a reply. His birthday must have been really something, nearly two million girls singing and marching and showing their support for him while she had to content herself with imagining. It makes her sick with longing and envy. Some of the girls get to meet him on his birthday, present him with flowers. Have their photos taken with him. Mama is right. She could do more than that. She could perform for the Führer; it wouldn't be the first time.

Eyes open in the dark, she sees herself seated at a harpsichord on an elegant stage. She is playing Haydn, no, of course, the *Goldberg Variations.* Suddenly the conductor raps his baton. No, it has to be a Haydn concerto for this performance, otherwise there is no conductor. Perhaps Keyboard Concerto No. 3 in F. The musicians abruptly cease their playing and look up from the pit. From the dark, a voice singles her out. "Lili von Rittersburg zu Mertz-Tärnekow!" Her heart begins to beat allegro. "Rise and receive the acknowledgement of your Führer for your exquisite interpretation of Josef Haydn's masterpiece. Young musicians like you inspire the greatness of the Reich."

Above a sea of hundreds in the audience, Lili floats to where the Führer is seated, waiting for her so that he can pin a shining Medal of Service to the Reich upon her chest. In bed, her chest is swelling with emotion and effort. She tries to see the next moment, but it is difficult. She concentrates. The perspiration is growing on her forehead. At last she is able to raise her eyes to look into those of the Führer. Deep within her is a strange sensation. Photographs cannot capture the fire and intensity of his inner vision, but now she remembers the burning black of his eyes. They are ablaze with sincerity and goodness and a knowing that is vastly beyond her own. They lock onto hers, a single white ember glowing on each pupil, drawing her farther and farther into their depths until she is rendered powerless to do anything but bow before his very being. And that is all she wants.

He Looks Ashamed

Lili settles her flowered skirt on the seat. She is wearing new shoes of red leather and when she crosses her ankles, the angles of her feet are elegant. They must be visible from the front where Friedrich and the other older boys stand. Herr Krüger announces that today they will first watch a film and then he will give his talk, so the boys move down the aisle to find seats. Friedrich approaches then stops in front of her.

"May I?"

She manages to nod.

He lowers himself onto the seat next to hers. For a few moments, Lili stops breathing. When she begins anew, the air is already filled with his scent, a fusion of something sour, something sweet, and something spicy too. It is disturbing but not unpleasant, like the scent of horses after a run. Friedrich doesn't speak. Lili too is silent. She can feel him only centimeters away. If she bends her right elbow, she will brush against his shirt. She forces herself to focus on the white sheet Herr Krüger has released from the ceiling. Someone at the back of the room turns off the lights. For a few seconds the room is black and Lili can feel heat radiating from Friedrich. He is so tall. She turns to look at him in the darkness but then the light bursts onto the screen and she jerks her head. Did he notice? Her muscles contract. Her teeth sink into her lip.

The film begins. Herr Krüger is showing them *Then and Now* again. By now Lili is familiar with all the scenes, yet there is always something new that springs out at her. The camera focuses on the street where the children wait for soup. One child, who seems only a year or so older than Paul, looks directly into the lens and Lili is seared by the expression on his little face, pale and drawn, hollows under his empty eyes. It is as if he knew nothing other than a life of waiting for a bowl of soup. It is as if he knew nothing of hope. Oh, that Paul should never know such an existence!

Again there are the villagers cheering in silence as the troops reclaim the Saar, the truckloads of smiling young people off to their year of community labor, the truckloads of police springing into action.

Friedrich laughs out loud as a protestor is dragged away by his ankles. He leans over to her. "When are those monkeys going to learn?" he says, and Lili can feel his warm breath. "They should put their efforts into helping the Reich, not trying to hurt it."

For a moment she can't form a response because her pulse is racing.

"Yes," she manages at last. "Everyone needs to unite under the Führer. We should all be marching in step."

The light on the screen is bright, and Lili can see Friedrich glance at her with approval.

"Right. Anyone out of step is out of the picture."

Suddenly there is a new and shocking image, a new segment to the film. Men in uniform storm a shop front, pulling down the flag.

There is a collective gasp. Lili senses Friedrich flinch. She too is outraged. But the announcer clarifies this action as the camera moves around the sidewalk.

"Only Germans have the honor and the right to fly the flag of the Reich. This does not extend to Jews who just happen to be living in Germany for now." The camera halts near the storefront, focusing on a middle-aged man whose gaze is on the pavement. He looks ashamed. Yet it is hard to say if he is Jew or German.

Lili can feel Friedrich relaxing.

Now the screen is filled with stark black lines that form an illustration. On the left is a shadowy man who looks sick, holding his chest while he supports himself against a placard on which is written RM5,50. On the right is a healthy-looking family of five. The father holds in his arms an identical placard showing RM 5,50. The narrator's tone is indignant. "For the same five Reichsmarks fifty that it costs the state to feed, house, and clothe one disabled person for a single day, an entire healthy German family could survive."

The scene changes abruptly to an open field that stretches to the horizon. The sky, white as the sheet, is cloudless, and only wrinkles in the fabric mar the otherwise pristine heavens. "Boundless energy fills these lovely Nordic maidens," booms the speaker as the camera pans the field alive with young women in light exercise suits who run and hurtle over poles and ropes held by other young women. Their faces shine. Lili leans forward to examine how they are wearing their hair. There are braids and buns and braided buns. In the background, and the foreground, flags of the Reich unfurl in splendor.

"Baldur von Schirach announces that membership in the Hitler Jugend has swelled from 100,000 in 1933 to nearly three million today!" Lili sees Friedrich rising from his seat and then she too, along with everyone else in the room, is up and calling out "Heil Hitler!" Of course many of them must know that the Hitler Youth actually began back in 1922, even if there were some growing pains along the way.

But the film is still rolling and soon they are seated again, watching a row of young boys outlined against the fair sky. Their expressions are intense as they raise their arms and place trumpets against their mouths. Smooth cheeks swell with the effort of blowing. For a few moments the room fills with tinny blasts of inspiring fanfare pasted onto the soundtrack. Lili glances at the boys' chubby knees, each pair pressed together above tightly stretched socks, and for a long instant imagines how little Paul would look some day, he, too, sounding a glorious hurrah for the Reich.

Planters of Trees

"Who is this? I've never seen her before."

The late afternoon sun filters in through the library's voile curtains where Mama and Lili are on the floor looking through family photographs. Paul has lost interest long ago and contents himself with stacking the new ABC blocks bought yesterday at Schwarz Toy Bazaar.

"That was my Great-Aunt Margarethe."

The sepia photograph shows a slender woman dressed in the high-collared, pinched waist fashion of the 1880s. One hand rests on the back of an armchair while at her feet is a slim-headed hound. The dog reminds Lili of a skinnier version of long dead Sascha. The woman stares out of the photograph with good humor.

"Did I meet her?"

"No, indeed," says Mama, picking up the photograph. "Nor did I. She must have left Prussia shortly after this was taken."

This is something new. An ancestor who left Germany.

"Where did she go?"

"Hmm. Someplace Swiss or Scottish-sounding. Tess--" She tilts her head. "Ah, yes. Tessonia. Niss Tessonia."

"Is she still there?"

"No, she died many years ago. She would have been in her 80s now."

Both of them look over at Paul who is humming as he arranges the blocks. Mama and Lili exchange a smile in silent agreement at how darling he is with his light curls and the cheeks that always have a bloom to them. His tiny hands, dimpled, are adept at placing the blocks in perfect columns. The two of them return to the photograph. With a light touch, Lili runs a finger over the dress in the photograph.

"What strange fashions they had then. Look at her waist. It must have been hard to breathe."

"Every era has its ideals. Sometimes misguided. In fashion as well. Look at us now with our sack dresses." Mama smiles, pulling at the soft wool of the mauve suit she is wearing. "We can hide a lot inside the draping."

"You don't have anything to hide, Mama."

Her mother looks down. "It's true. I wouldn't have made a good model for Rubens."

Lili giggles. As long as she can remember, Mama has been slender, even when she was pregnant with Paul. Lovely as she is, it is true that she wouldn't have been an ideal for those painters who liked solid flesh on their models. Compared to the women pictured in newspapers and magazines from Germany, Mama doesn't have the figure popular there these days either. And Mama always wears lipstick. Mama wouldn't fit in.

"How old was your great-aunt when she died? And where is Niss Tessonia?"

"Let me think." Mama tilts her head. "Großmama Maximiliana always told me that she left in the mid-1880s when she was about 25. She died when I was about seven, so that would have made her 45. I imagine that her life was rather difficult. But she chose it."

"Tell me about it, Mama." Lili leans back onto her palms on the soft carpet.

"I can only tell you what Großmama Maximiliana has told me." Mama shrugs her slim shoulders. "From early on Great-Aunt Margarethe was known for her stubbornness and determination. If she wanted to do something, she would, no matter what. If she didn't, then no amount of threatening or coaxing could ever get her to change her mind." She smiles at Lili. "I can almost imagine that she was a bit like you. Or you like she."

Lili moves her feet so that she is sitting cross-legged. "Tell me more."

"My mother said that Margarethe, who was her oldest aunt, spent much time on horseback, hunting in the woods around the estate. She grew up making her own rules."

"Why did they let her?"

"I suppose it must have been because she had lost her mother at such an early age."

"But then how did Großmama Maximiliana's mother--"

"Margarethe and Großmama's mother had different mothers."

Feeling wise, Lili nods. "So people felt sorry for her and just let her be."

"Yes," says Mama, smoothing the corner of the photograph. "It must have been like that. And I suppose too that her father's second wife was more involved with all the new babies that came. Perhaps Margarethe felt left out."

Lili can't help but glance over at Paul. He is the most brilliant baby brother in the world. In no way does she feel threatened by his presence. Perhaps it is because she has already had so much time alone with Mama and Papa. She nods, feeling wise and fortunate.

"So eventually she left."

"Yes. Quite early on, Margarethe developed an interest in farming. Fruit trees, actually. She loved experimenting with grafts. She began to study scientific journals on how to improve yields."

"In those days that must have been very unusual for a girl."

"I don't think it would have been possible without her father's support. He must have loved her very much to let her follow her dream."

Lili is silent. She would like to have met this great-great aunt in the flesh. A headstrong woman whose father let her follow her dream, wherever it took her.

"So she went to study botany at a university?"

Mama shakes her head. "It wasn't like that."

"Mamaleeleelook!" crows Paul.

They turn to where he has built up two block towers. All the letters are facing in one direction.

"Clever Paul," Mama coos. Lili cups his small cheek.

"So what did she do?"

Mama's voice takes on that special dreamy quality she has when talking about the past. "Großmama Maximiliana's grandfather enjoyed giving parties. Guests came from all over Prussia, and at times from further east as well. On one occasion, a young Russian who had recently arrived was also present. He'd been away studying at the university in Moscow when Cossacks burnt his hometown to the ground. His entire family had been killed."

"That's terrible."

"Indeed. But at the party he met Margarethe."

"And they fell in love," says Lili.

"Yes. And imagine this: at the university he was studying agriculture."

Lili grins. "So they got married and grew apple trees and lived happily ever after, right?

Mama smiles, her teeth the color of cream. "That's almost right. They went off to a new land where they had to work very hard but, so it was said, the trees blossomed into orchards and on the horizon there were no Cossacks." She pauses. "Of course her father didn't want them to go so far away and at first refused permission. But Margarethe had always known how to get her way." Mama hesitates and then, as if coming to some decision, continues. "Sensing the seriousness of her father's refusal, Margarethe chose a drastic course. She locked herself in her room and refused to come out or eat until he changed his mind. It took two days before he did. After the wedding, Margarethe and Jakob packed their bags and special boxes with saplings and went east."

Lili sighs.

"So Margarethe got to ride horses and work in fields and was, from what Großmama Maximiliana told me, for many years the happiest woman in Palestine."

Lili looks over at Paul. The afternoon light is loosing its intensity, dissolving into murkiness.

"Why did they go there?"

"Jakob felt there was no longer a future for him in Russia."

"Then why didn't they just stay in Prussia? Surely they could have planted orchards there."

"It seems that he felt that the German lands too would not long be a safe place for them to make a home for the family they hoped some day to have. I suppose planters of trees look further into the future than most of us."

"But why, Mama?"

"Because Jakob, who was Jewish, was not willing to give more of his family's blood."

Lili frowned.

"But why did Margarethe agree to go so far away?"

Mama gives her an odd look. "She loved him, darling. It was that simple."

"Mamaleeleelook!"

They peer at the three blocks that his tiny hands have arranged with arbitrariness, and, for the first time in her life, Lili meets the bizarre.

In letters of red, the blocks spell T O D. Death.

The Strongest Brotherhood

The snow falls in silent beats. For some measures Lili stands motionless on the path. The flakes alight upon her nose and cheeks in microscopic crystals cold but soft as a baby's breath. There are few people about in Central Park and she is glad. She does not want the sound of American to break the spell. In ten minutes she will meet Friedrich at the bust of Schiller and nothing should spoil the illusion that they are in a forest far from New York.

Yet the silence is infused by the notes that stream through her inner ear, the fifth of the *Brandenburg Concertos*. She has been playing them even more than usual. They are the comfort food of her music. When she is exhausted by her work on the Variations, she relaxes and finds strength again through the Concertos. Now her hands lie still inside the lambskin gloves but within her she is following the flowing notes, the line of music that moves in swirls and makes her feel as if she were melding with the landscape.

She inhales through her nose, slowly, the cold burning the membranes. The soles of her boots, new and overly elegant for the frozen earth, are of leather too thin for her to stand motionless. She walks toward The Ramble. Now there is the molding of white into tightly packed hollows, a trail of guilt that follows her with every step.

She lied to Mama and Papa this morning. Told them that she had a special school project on Saturday afternoon. At the time, she hadn't yet thought of a why. By the time she returns home she will have figured out a better reason than that she has arranged to meet a Yorkville boy in the forbidden part of the park.

It was after the last meeting at the German-American Cultural Club, while she was winding her scarf around her neck, that Friedrich stopped her. His gaze was steady as he asked if she would like to take a walk with him, suggesting Carl Schurz Park adjacent to the East River.

"No," she breathed, then was afraid he might think she meant that she didn't want to walk with him. "That's too far for me. I would prefer Central Park." There was no thought of asking him to pick her up from home.

"Let's meet at the skating rink," Friedrich said. Then his forehead wrinkled. Perhaps he thought she might want to go ice skating and he would have to buy the tickets. "Wait. At the bust of Schiller. I'm sure you know where that is."

She had hesitated. After all, Papa and Mama have forbidden her to go there on her own. But by meeting Friedrich there, she wouldn't really be alone. At least not for very long. And if he arrived before she did, she wouldn't be alone at all.

"Of course I know where the bust of Schiller is. I'll meet you there." Now she heads toward it. Last night she read a few of Schiller's sayings that she hopes she remembers well enough to quote to Friedrich. They will walk together under the snow-draped trees and speak of poetry.

There, that must be him, the tall figure standing near the pedestal, both forms stark against the clearing. Despite the cold, a wave of heat surges through her. They greet each other with outstretched arms.

"Heil Hitler."

What direction will the conversation take? She can feel his eyes roaming over her face.

"Your nose is red," he says.

Lili lifts her gloved hand to touch it.

"It has become very cold these past few days." Her cheeks must be red now too.

"Yes," he agrees, rubbing his arm. His jacket doesn't look very warm at all.

Lili's feet are getting numb again.

"Shall we walk?" Friedrich says, and they set out.

Their crunching footfall creates a cadence on the snowy ground. Lili glances at him. Strands of ash blonde hair are parted to the side, looking pale in the winter light. He is so tall, his shoulders so broad in the thin jacket—as if the muscled bones wanted to burst out. They must be very strong. What would it feel like to touch them?

Friedrich glances at her. Her gaze slides past him toward the linen-white forms lining the side of the pathway. When she looks back, Friedrich turns too and their eyes meet. She says the first thing that comes to mind.

"The bushes look as if they were wearing pyjamas." Ach, he must think her a fool.

But Friedrich laughs, a belly laugh that warms her.

"Frau Holle shakes out the bedclothes and dresses the trees," he says, and Lili knows that he too remembers the fairy tale of the old woman who causes snow to fall on the world by shaking her featherbeds out the window.

"Where did you live?" he asks, and Lili knows that he means in Germany.

"In Berlin. What about you?"

His smile is lopsided. "My parents had a small farm in the Alsace. They had to pack up and leave it behind."

For a few steps they walk in silence until a slurring rasp pierces the cold air. Both of them look up to where a bird hovers, its wings wide and beating slowly. On its belly is a dark stripe.

"That must be a hawk," says Lili.

"It's a very common one here," he says, "the red-tailed hawk."

"We have hawks in Germany too. Like the *Habicht* and the *Sperber*."

Friedrich frowns. Lili can see tiny blond hairs sticking out above his mouth.

"There's a lot I don't know about Germany because we left when I was so young. I know that my parents lost the farm when France got Alsace-Lorraine after the war, because of the Versailles Treaty." He kicks at a lump of snow. "They didn't get much for all the years of work they'd put into it, so they couldn't even go buy someplace else in Germany. So they decided to leave." He glances at Lili. "I wish they hadn't. Germany is the place to be."

Lili nods. "I feel the same way. It was the worst day of my life when I found out we were moving here."

"*Ja*, I don't understand why your parents made you leave just when things began to change for the better." His eyes narrow. "Your family isn't Socialist, is it?"

"Of course not. My father was a naval officer." With any luck, Friedrich won't probe further and she won't have to admit that Papa is practically a traitor.

Friedrich smiles. "I didn't think so. I know you come from a good family. Maybe your father has some special work that he has to do here for the Führer." There is excitement in his tone. "Maybe he's a special agent who's preparing for the day when the Führer takes over America!"

She laughs. "I think he's busy enough with Germany right now."

"True, but we can always hope, *nicht wahr?*"

"That's true. Remember how Herr Krüger told us about that congressman—"

"Louis T. McFadden," he says.

"Yes, he said that America is being cheated by bankers and the government. That hundreds of thousands of people lost their houses when they couldn't meet their payments because of bad things in the economy." She likes the way she has used the word 'economy', even applying it to America.

"Jewish bankers," says Friedrich.

"Perhaps what America needs now is some advice about the economy from the Führer!" They laugh. It feels good to be having such a deep conversation with someone like Friedrich. There is no need to explain anything to him because he already understands.

"Can I tell you what I wish, Lili?"

She looks up at him. Friedrich is probably already 17 but even with the mustache bristles his expression right now is so eager that he looks younger.

"If I could, I would go to Germany and try to be a bodyguard to the Führer." His features harden and in his fierceness he suddenly looks like a grown man intent on playing his part. "I would give my life to protect him. He's the best leader in the world. I want to wear the uniform for him; the SS uniform."

"I hope that one day you will, Friedrich."

He sighs and his features relax into their usual form. "Nowadays my parents are saying that it might've been better if we'd stayed in Germany. At least my father would have a better job there than mopping floors in Yorkville." He looks at her and there is some defiance in his voice. "It's not easy for farmers to find work here, especially when there're barely any jobs available."

Lili nods. What can she say when her own father has so much work to do that he brings it home with him?

"But in Germany," Friedrich continues, "things are getting better every day. The Führer looks to the future because he's making it. He said the youth of Germany is the strongest brotherhood."

"If we were in Germany now, we would march with them," Lili says.

Friedrich's eyes are shining. "The Führer promised that he would boost the economy and create jobs for the people, and that's what he's doing. Even when times are hard, he never accepts defeat." He slams his fist into a palm. "He gives us hope." He pauses. "Sometimes I love him more than my own parents."

A deep thrill passes through Lili. She is out walking in the park with a handsome young man who is just as excited about the Führer as she is. She stops short and takes a breath. Friedrich takes another step and then he too stops. She looks past him to the trees draped in winter, the biting blue above. The sky is infinite. It touches all, beyond the horizon, and thus, even here, connects them to Germany. The music is so loud in her head that for a moment she thinks Friedrich can hear it. *'Thy magic reunites those whom stern custom has parted; all men will become brothers under thy gentle wing.'*

Friedrich follows her gaze. "Is it the hawk again?"

"No," she says, still looking up. "*Ode to Happiness*, Friedrich."

"What do you mean?"

"Schiller's poem. Beethoven set it to music." She turns to him. "You know it." She hums the first phrase and his face brightens.

"Ach ja!" He begins to sing the well-known chorus. His voice is somewhere between tenor and bass.

"Be embraced, millions! This kiss for all the world!" Their gazes meet. As Lili joins in the last phrase, she can see that Friedrich feels the same as she.

"Brothers! Above the starry canopy a loving father must dwell."

As yet there are of course no stars to be seen but they are there, high in the heavens. It is a moment she knows she will never forget, the two of them in the snow near the trees, their voices united in praise of the Führer. And then Friedrich leans forward. Her eyes widen. For one long moment, soft and surprisingly warm in the winter air, his lips touch hers.

Where the Truth Lies

"That man is going to bankrupt Germany."

Lili looks up from the sofa where an unread book lies open on her lap. Papa stands near the fireplace, a glass of brandy in his hand. He is wearing his favorite jacket, a burgundy velvet. It is infuriating to hear him insult the great man who usually wears a khaki jacket. Lili snaps shut the book and looks over to where Mama is working on the petit point tapestry she often pulls out after Paul has been put to bed. Mama's gaze is on the threads.

Lili's voice quivers; there is going to be an argument.

"That's impossible," she says to Papa. "The Führer has created so many jobs. So much is being built."

"Yes, but shortages are increasing."

"Whatever do you mean?" She doesn't wait for his answer. "All those big projects like highways and buildings require a lot of money. They couldn't be built otherwise. The Führer has kept his promise to keep employment growing. That takes money, doesn't it?" Papa still doesn't have his facts straight.

"Your faith in him is certainly reliable." He takes some brandy. "But Herr Hitler appears to be a master at juggling the nation's financial books to suit his purposes. He is both devious and deceitful, Lili. The Autobahn and the Volkswagen are just airy schemes for him to distract everyone. Not to mention," he adds, "that highways are supposedly his invention—what a brazen falsehood." Papa grimaces above his brandy. "Well, for the moment, Herr Hitler is happy enough to play with building blocks. But on the day he is ready to turn to his toy soldiers, everyone will have to turn with him. And then adequate supplies, and food, will be only a memory."

Her chest tightens. "The Führer is doing things right! Everyone says so. He should be giving advice to the government here." She glances at Mama who is still absorbed in her stitches. "America is the one that is bankrupt."

Papa looks at her over his glass. "I wonder what it will take for you to understand that there is more to it than what meets the eye."

This silences her. Could Friedrich be right? Perhaps Papa actually does work for the Führer and the Reich but must pretend that he doesn't. She looks more closely at him. There might be signs that she can read. He does look different than last year, older, more tired. She bites the inside of her lip. It would indeed be tiring to be a secret agent.

"You're right," says Papa, his tone light. "Herr Hitler is a clever man. He has put together a team that is dedicated to him and his objectives, and who will go the extra mile."

Lili nods. "The Führer needs to have good people around him to protect him." People like Papa? Perhaps he speaks badly of him as a disguise. Instead of a trench coat, Papa wears words.

He puts the glass on the mantelpiece and comes over to sit next to her on the sofa.

"Now that is an interesting choice of words, Lili. Protect him from what? There aren't many people who dare say anything against him anymore. Think about it, my girl," he says, taking her hand. "If Hitler has to surround himself with henchmen and so much armed protection, it must be because he is afraid."

"Afraid?" Lili rips her hand from Papa's. "The Führer isn't afraid of anything!" This is not how an undercover agent speaks to a follower of the Führer. It is outrageous how Papa talks about the strongest man in Germany. Perhaps the greatest man Germany has ever had.

"And why," Papa continues, as if nothing has happened, "why do you think he might be afraid?"

"I told you. He's not afraid."

Papa eyes her. "Fair enough. Let's say then that he is not afraid, but concerned."

That sounds better. The Führer must have many concerns.

"He probably worries about being able to keep all his promises on time," she says.

Papa rubs his chin. "Or perhaps he is concerned that people will find their voice and he'll lose his power."

Lili's eyebrows go up. "Why in heaven would he be concerned about that? Almost everyone in Germany voted for him, Papa. He's more powerful than ever." For a few long moments the only sound in the room is an occasional sputter that comes from the fireplace.

"It is my hope that soon enough you will see where the truth lies." Papa sounds old when he says this. It is confusing. Perhaps Papa is indeed a secret agent and is speaking to her in code. But she doesn't have the key.

She frowns and stares at the fire. She is being ridiculous. He wouldn't need to pretend to her. Would he? She glances back at him. He is looking at her in a way that makes her feel half her age.

Mama begins to wrap up her tapestry, carefully pushing the long needle into a pincushion. "It's getting late," she says. "Perhaps we should make our way to bed." She stands up and slides a hand down her dove gray skirt.

"You are right, my dear." Papa's face brightens as he looks over to her. "Sleep is a wonderful restorative." He turns to Lili. "As Goethe said, 'All that is noble is in itself of a quiet nature, and appears to sleep until it is aroused and summoned forth by contrast.'"

By the tone of his voice, Lili knows that he has chosen this quote especially for her. Ach, Papa and his Goethe.

Something the Naked Eye Can't See

Lili tries her best to read *Mein Kampf* but flounders, unable to concentrate. At last she finds a way of absorbing it, in little bites. Like those people who open the Bible to a random page, ready to take in a holy message, she picks out a passage to read, silently, so that the voice of the Führer resounds within her.

One passage her finger points at states: 'A man can change his language without any trouble...but in his new language he will express the old ideas; his inner nature is not changed. This is best shown by the Jew who can speak a thousand languages and nevertheless remains a Jew.' Words like this bring her comfort for she chooses to see them as consoling her in the loss of her homeland. Although each day she must face New York with its loud people and the unpleasant timbre of their tongue, the Führer is telling her that these sounds will not blot out the music of her own language. Living in America will not change who she truly is: a German in America.

But what about the Jews? At first, the law about Jews no longer being considered German citizens is confusing. For different reasons, she doesn't want to discuss this with either Friedrich or Papa. Even if citizenship is but words on a paper, how can Jewish Germans suddenly stop being German? Jews have been in Germany for centuries. Lotte and Oskar have relatives whose families have lived in the same house for four hundred years. She briefly considers talking to Lotte. Does Lotte feel German or Jewish? But their relationship is no longer the same; they keep out of each other's way.

Never mind the pamphlets. What would Lotte say to some of the books that Lili looks through at the German-American Cultural Club?

The books arrive from across the sea, courtesy of special deliveries from the Reich. Some of the covers are frightening. One shows a gruesome creature with long pointed beard and cloven feet, a hideous being towering over a flaxen-haired girl who cringes in fear. There are posters too. One has an evil-looking face with a nose like a giant 6 under bushy eyebrows that meet in a V.

Lili thinks about the Jewish Germans she knows—people like Lotte, Oskar, Berta, friends of Mama and Papa—who don't look like those examples in the illustrations. In fact, the only one who comes closest is the bushy-haired pastor in Posenwell.

After mulling this about for some time, Lili has the idea that, in light of the Führer's words in *Mein Kampf*, there has to be something else inside the Jewish German that makes him or her different. Something the naked eye can't see. Perhaps it is in the blood.

After all, everyone knows how important blood is. Blood is what unites the German Volk. So if blood is thicker than nationality, then the

Führer's words simply mean that citizenship should be reserved for those with true German blood. Not Jewish German blood. Not the Jews.

Flying Along the Shadows

The first movement of the third concerto has been twisting its way through Lili's head all day like an earworm. As much as she appreciates this movement, it is time for it to leave, make way for other music. She knows what to do. She opens the lid of the harpsichord and lets her hands fall onto the keys smoothed down by the generations before hers. She plays the first movement so that not a moment of silence slips between the ceaseless plucking of the quills. The violin, viola, cello, and bass are as clear in her inner ear as if they were in the room. Together they ride a wave pulsing with joyfulness. They call to each other, echo, surging ahead with steadfast beat toward grandeur and glory, elation, until the viola raises an element of doubt. Lili flies along through the shadows, through peril and fear, relentless, the concerto slicing the air in structures that her fingers call into being, commander and commanded at once. Through courage nearly flagging they forge ahead. Through tension and panic, enduring. Onward, their spirit resilient. Within themselves and together, their strength renewed. Climbing, scaling ever higher, at last out of the darkness and into the light, and then, once more, breathing in peace.

Winter Wonder Tour

It is their third Christmas away from home. Paul and Lili wait outside the closed door of the salon while Papa and Mama put the finishing touches on the tree.

Back home, it was not always only her parents who were in the salon, but Großpapa Hugo and Großmama Maximiliana, as well as Tante Frederike and Tante Amalie, Mama's sisters, and their husbands. Neither aunt has been able to have children, so Lili was always the star. The two aunts carried on a good-natured competition about which one might possibly be her favorite, an impossible choice as they have always been so in harmony that there is no dividing them. Both aunts live in Hamburg, their husbands partners in a shipping company. Tante Frederike's Julius is a stout and good-humored man with wire rim glasses. When she was small, Lili liked to watch the reflections on the round lenses. Occasionally he would pass them to her and she would hold them up, peering through the lenses so that the Christmas tree and room blurred into prisms of light and color. Tante Amelie's Eberhardt is less jovial, and when Lili was very young, she wondered if it was because he is so much thinner than Onkel Julius. She was always pleased when she could coax a smile out of him. Yet it was always Onkel Eberhardt who had a bag of special fruit bonbons for her.

Now Lili wonders how they are celebrating Christmas. It must be very quiet with only adults around the tree. Her grandparents must feel old and sad. How they would enjoy seeing Paul. Last year he was practically still a baby, but this year he knows that something exciting is going to happen soon. He keeps chattering away and his eyes are wide open. If only they could all be together in Germany for Christmas.

It is not only the Eve that is so enchanting but those days before, when the streets are covered with snow even as there is a feeling of warmth everywhere.

While different areas of the city have their own *Weihnachtsmärkte*, the largest Christmas market is at Schloßplatz on the Spreeinsel. At other times of the year Mama would take her to the island in the middle of the river to look at paintings in the Nationalgalerie or to climb the steps of the altar in the newly opened Pergamonmuseum. But it was most exciting in the days before Christmas.

Dressed in winter finery, Mama and she walked through the narrow lanes set up in front of the palace, past garlanded booths from which floated the most delicious smells of the year. Roasting sausages, gingerbread, red wine mulled with clove and cinnamon and orange. In some of the booths, wooden puppets, tin soldiers, and golden-haired porcelain dolls stood in neat rows next to elephants, camels, and monkeys. None of these wild creatures were made as well as those in her collection of Steiff animals but they were exciting to look at in passing. Mama and she stopped before various displays, this one for nougat rich and creamy in shades striped from pale taupe to cocoa brown, that one for paper cones of almonds coated in melted sugar, roasted rust red, warming the air with waves of sweetness. When she bit into a *Gebrannte Mandel*, the kernel burning hot and smelling like heaven on earth, the burnt sugar shell would crack and the almond taste explode in her mouth.

And always there would be one evening in which only she and Papa took a walk. Darkness comes early in the Berlin winter. Wrapped in wool, leather, and fur, Papa and she would set out, a different destination every year—their Winter Wonder Tour. It didn't matter to Lili where they ended up, whether in a brightly lit café with red velvet seats and gypsy violins, a wood-paneled Gaststätte, a bookshop with a table displaying a tree made of children's Christmas books, or a Weihnachtsmarkt with a carousel that had camels instead of horses. The journey itself was all she wanted. Just she and Papa, together on the wonderful streets of Berlin at Christmas time.

There were other times when Mama was there. Oskar would drive them to the street where the Kindertheater was and they would walk along the frosted sidewalk, under the strings of lights that hung in shining stars and moons from the roofs of one side of the cobblestone street to the other. The two tales she remembers best are *Peterchens Mondfahrt*—how amazing it was to see a giant ladybug and two children fly upwards across the stage on their way to the moon—and *Hänsel und Gretel.* Lili could never decide who was the more frightening, the cruel father who abandoned his children to starve in the woods or the witch who overfed Hänsel only so that she could later eat him. Both performances were packed with excitement and colors and spectacular costumes. Both ended with joy, and packets of *Pfeffernüße* for the children both onstage and in the audience. Lili shared the hard cookies steeped in anise and cardamom with Mama and Papa. In the night, the scent would trail through her dreams.

Now Lili sighs and turns to Paul.

"*Mäuschen,*" she whispers. "Poor little mouse." He lifts his arms and she gathers him into her own. Sadness washes over her. Will her sweet little brother never get to go to the Kindertheater before Christmas? Papa is even worse than the father in *Hänsel und Gretel.* Here they have more than enough to eat, but still he is abandoning his children far from home.

The Quiet Strength of the Camel

"Won't you play with Papa?" Lili can hear an undertone of concern in her mother's voice. "It would mean so much to him to end the year in harmony with you."

For the past half hour she has been watching the snow as it falls, blanketing the street, just as she is trying to blank out the thought that in a few hours it will be her 16th birthday and she is still in America and nothing will have changed. Like a metronome, she is simply marking time.

The last day of the year began badly at breakfast, another bitter exchange of opinions with Papa.

"At the risk of sounding inadequately poetic," he said, half a buttered roll in his hand, "I think the clouds that are gathering these days are only a faint shadow of the darkness that will eventually black out everything we ever held dear about our homeland." He put the bread down. "Hitler will have his revenge. But more than Germany will suffer for it."

The anger welled up, a familiar sensation that swells like a storm inside her chest.

"I really don't understand you, Papa." Her gaze was steady above her coffee cup. "Those shadows are simply those of the countless people bustling about, busy with jobs that the Führer has created. Also, Papa," and the word did not sound as soft as it once had, "the only revenge that the Führer might want to take is on those people who have insulted him and not contributed what they could have." She had narrowed her eyes. Let him know whom she meant by that.

"Ah," said Papa. "Herr Hitler must be thinking of Goethe's words: 'Be above it! Make the world serve your purpose, but do not serve it.'" He brushed a crumb off the table. "It is intriguing to see how Herr Hitler is so often able to twist things to his advantage. I would never have believed that the German people could be so misguided. The cost will be bitter."

Mama interrupted them then with the information that the lead had been delivered from the printing shop. After dinner they will take turns melting bits of it on a spoon, and then throw the liquid into cold water. The fun has always been in examining the different shapes of the contracted lead, analyzing them to see what might be in store for each of them in the New Year. Last year, Lili's had looked like a perforated creature with a hump. A camel. It was almost insulting; to be called a camel is the same as being called dumb. But time has shown her its quiet strength. Like the desert creature journeying far through the emptiness, she too must carry enough of her own nourishment to sustain her until she returns to the oasis of her homeland.

Now, violin in hand, as if he had known all along that she can do nothing but obey his wishes, Papa is waiting for her in the salon. His dark eyes meet hers in a smile. Paul is nestled under his favorite red blanket, looking like a lumpy tomato. Mama is resplendent in a pale gray tea gown, especially now that her forehead is clear of the worry lines from earlier. Lotte's *Nußkuchen* suffuses the air with the scent of butter and nuts.

"What would you like to play, Papa?" Lili looks over at the new harpsichord that Mama and Papa presented to her on Christmas Eve and her lips tighten. Why have they given her this French creature, as elegant as its painted casing is? She much prefers the plain German heirloom that has now been moved to her room and gives forth a tone of which she knows Bach himself would have approved. Even Wanda Landowska in France prefers such a heavy 16-foot stop model.

Papa rubs his chin. "Perhaps my favorite from Bach's Six Sonatas for Violin and Harpsichord. It ends on a note of hope."

Lili sits down at her instrument and waits for Papa to place the music sheets on his stand. For these sonatas she no longer requires any notes. Mama settles down next to Paul on the armchair.

"The audience is ready and attentive," she laughs, hugging Paul.

How to Make it Happen

"Lotte?"

Lili finds her on the stepladder in front of an open cupboard in the kitchen.

"Mama said to give you this money for tomorrow's groceries." She hands over two five dollar notes. Lotte takes them without touching Lili's fingers. In Lili's pocket is the third bill Mama gave her. If someone notices the difference, Lili will say that she made a mistake. If no one asks, those five dollars will go into the secret compartment at the bottom of her jewelry box. She has made a decision. Beginning today, she will amass as much money as necessary.

She has almost worked her way through the *Goldberg Variations.* It will soon be time to leave New York. America is not, and will never be, the place for Lili von Rittersburg zu Mertz-Tärnekow. If Mama and Papa and Paul will not go home, she will leave without them. And she will find every way possible to raise the money for this.

She will be like that Tante Margarethe and follow her dream. But her dream is not to marry a Jew and grow fruits in Palestine. No, Lili's dream is much more meaningful: she will at last join the German Volk and follow the Führer. There are others who have done this before her. That girl from the German-American Cultural Club who left just last month with her family when her father was offered a job in Hamburg as an electrical engineer. And only yesterday Lili discovered that she will soon be losing the only interesting person she knows here.

Friedrich had been waiting for her at a corner two blocks from the Club. Already from that distance Lili could see that something was different in the way that he stood. As if he were holding his muscles taut to keep from leaping into the air. Close up, his eyes were a brilliant blue. When he told her that he and his family will be returning to Germany at the end of next week, Lili could feel three very separate sensations. Excitement for him, loss, and an almost physical pang of envy. Friedrich's relatives have sent money for tickets because his father has found well-paying work in a chemical factory near Hannover. Instead of mopping floors with chemical solutions as he does here, Friedrich's father will soon be helping to make them. Later, during the meeting at the German-American Cultural Club, Lili could sense that Friedrich was no longer entirely present. It was as if his mind were already far away. The goodbye peck that he gave her when they parted seemed distracted, as if even his lips were no longer quite here. Her own lips pressed tight against each other, Lili watched him walk away, and it seemed as if his every step grew firmer, higher, ready to march for Germany. There will be no more kisses from Friedrich.

Disappointment burns her heart, bittersweet, even as she forces herself to feel gladness for him.

Yet his and that girl's departures make her own more possible. If others can go home, so can she.

Following Friedrich's announcement, the subject of returning to Germany was raised during the meeting. This led Herr Krüger to discuss with particular enthusiasm the most famous example of someone turning his back on America. It was inspiring.

Although, like Lili, Baldur von Schirach was born in Berlin, his early life was different from most other Germans because not only did his father come from a family with an American background, but his mother was American. In fact, he didn't even learn how to speak German until he was five. Of course he was fortunate to have parents who let him grow up in Germany. Despite such a background, he didn't get uprooted from his country to move to America. But what really impresses Lili in its relevance is that, while on a visit to relatives in New York in 1928, Baldur von Schirach was offered a job in his uncle's Wall Street firm and he said, "No, thank you. I am going back to Germany to work with Herr Hitler because I believe in his dream for the rebirth of our nation." Or he said something like that because he did go back to Germany and he did busy himself doing wonderful things. Just look at what he has accomplished so far. The BDM alone is the world's largest organization for girls! If Baldur von Schirach could turn down a privileged life in America, then so can Lili von Rittersburg zu Mertz-Tärnekow. Even if she has to steal to make it happen.

♫ ♪ ♫

"Lotte?"

Lili crosses the yellow tiles to where Lotte stands in front of the kitchen table stuffing an empty shopping net into her purse. At the sound of her voice, Lotte turns toward Lili, her face expressionless. Lili moves to the other side and holds her hand out over the vase of flowers on the table. "It seems that I dropped one of the bills. Mama gave me fifteen dollars, not ten."

Lotte nods and takes the note. Her gray eyes move over Lili's face. For a long time she is silent. Her purse snaps shut.

"You were always a good girl, Lili," she says, her voice without expression, before leaving the kitchen.

Fingers clenched at her sides, Lili continues to stand, staring into the space Lotte has just vacated. It is obvious that Lotte no longer likes her. Not that she cares. She has more important things to consider than whether Lotte is bothered by her pamphlets.

By giving Lotte the five dollars, she has whitewashed herself. For, after a sleepless night, she has come to the conclusion that she doesn't have it in herself to take the money. Not from Mama, and most likely not from anyone else either; it is wrong to steal. After all, irony aside, Papa taught her the difference between right and wrong. She doesn't yet know how she will raise the money to go home but, in the meantime, she will not be judged by Lotte. She bites her lip. Nor by Papa, who is still more than wrong. There is an angry thrumming in her head. She swallows her rage, yet almost before she realizes what she is doing, her foot slams against the kitchen table. The contact of wood and bone shoots pain up her leg while the force of the kick shakes the table. She watches as the pale blue vase, the one that Lotte brought with her from Berlin, totters and falls onto its fluted side, water spilling out over the white blooms, now horizontal, in a rapidly widening pool. Surely the porcelain has broken. Lili reaches for it. It is still whole. She carries it to the sink and refills it, then replaces the flowers before getting a cloth to wipe away the evidence of something for which as yet she has no name.

Part of Germany in America

Early this morning as she was rushing out the door, Mama and Papa kissed her goodbye, wishing her a good day on the school field trip. Yet Lili is not on the way to Fire Island with her 10th grade class. Even if she will not steal, if they will help her get closer to her goal, lies have now become acceptable. There is no field trip today. Instead, she is on a train that is overflowing with German-Americans of all ages, a special train that rolls out of the subterranean blackness of Grand Central into the blinding light of the Manhattan summer.

It was only last year that the Friends of New Germany Picnic Grounds was opened by the German-American Settlement League, but the campsite's name has recently been changed. Today the wagonloads of excited passengers are heading toward Camp Siegfried. That sounds ever so much better. Probably in honor of the Führer's appreciation of him, the wooded lakefront retreat on Long Island was renamed for the hero of the Niebelungenlied. Today is the first time that Lili has been able to join such an outing.

The journey on the Camp Siegfried Special is filled with singing and laughing and good-natured chatting in both German and English. Lili sits near Herr Krüger and some of the others from the German-American Cultural Club. It would be nice if Friedrich were here but these days he must be singing and marching in Hannover. Lili listens but says little. Most of the talk is gossip about people she doesn't know or care to know. She joins in some of the singing. And when those around her raise their right arms, she joins in with a resounding "Heil Hitler!"

At Yaphank station the train comes to a halt and the passengers spill out. Many of the women look just like those on the newsreels shown at the clubhouse, their faces unadorned, unlike Mama's. They tug back into neatness the kerchiefs, white shirts, and dark shorts or skirts of their little ones. Older children pull themselves into shape, tucking in their tops. Many of the men are wearing gray shirts with black ties, black breeches, and boots. Those are the members of the German-American Bund. Perhaps today Lili will get to see Fritz Kuhn, head of the Bund, whose name has often been mentioned at the York Avenue meetings. She doubts that he could be related to her old teacher Frau Kuhn. If Lili had been at the rallies, like the one at Madison Square Garden that had over fifty thousand attendees, she would have seen him. Herr Kuhn is working hard not only to give assistance to the NSDAP in Germany, but to promote its messages here in America. It would be exciting to see him up close. Of course it would be even more exciting to see the Führer again.

The groups form one large contingent as they begin to march past welcoming shopkeepers in Yaphank on their way to Camp Siegfried. Once again voices are raised in song, the bittersweet melody of the *Horst Wessel Lied*, borne high above them on waves of heat. Lili drinks from the canteen Mama gave her to take on the field trip to Fire Island. She walks near some members of the German-American Cultural Club. The girl who never puts in her dime for the Winter Relief Fund is complaining that she lost one on the train and that someone must have stolen it. Lili chews on her lip. She is glad to be here today even if she has little in common with the members aside from commitment. Together they and all the others feel the calling. Dozens of banners sail up out of their midst. The swastika flies in the gathering breeze and Lili lifts her chin higher into the blinding blue of the sky. The blood surges through her. If she cannot yet march in Germany, she will still march, filled with pride, under the flag of the Führer, here on the soil of America.

She stares in wonder as they pass an inn with a restaurant surrounded by flowers, a profusion of red, white, and dark blooms. How clever—a giant swastika of blossoms. Coming up near her are two of the older boys who used to stand next to Friedrich at meetings. One smacks his lips so loudly that Lili hears it above the song and chatter. "I'm getting myself a Linden later," he says as he strides along. "Hauck charges ten cents a beer at the inn, and they're a good size." The other boy grins.

"We can have a Linden chugging contest." "That sounds swell. We might as well drink up before we have to fork it over for the cause." The other laughs, and Lili does not like their tone, but soon enough they are out of earshot.

Arriving at a wide expanse, she wanders about. In one part of the grounds marchers are being organized, linked together by sashes. Further on, rows of children form lines in preparations for the younger ones' sporting events that are being announced over loudspeakers. Here and there, just as they do on 86th Street, men stand around in groups, deep in discussion, their expressions serious. Nobody seems to care that Lili is on her own. She strolls past a low building and notices the street sign just on the corner. Hitler Street. Further on is Himmler Street. All she wants to do is explore this place and breathe in the air which, like the giant flags flying to the left and right of a two-dimensional triumphal arch towering in the distance, is both American and, somehow, gloriously German.

"Lili!"

A girl from the German-American Cultural Club runs up to her, chest heaving.

"What are you doing, wandering around like a lost sheep? We're supposed to be attending a lecture in the Great Hall now. Come on!"

Lili follows, relieved not to be missing the next event. As they enter the main building, she recognizes a scratchy aria from *Das Rheingold*. Immediately she thinks of Papa. Last week she overheard him saying to Mama, "I was willing to overlook some things, take the music over the man. But now he's even spoiled Wagner for me." Without hearing anything else, Lili had of course known who *he* was, and added yet another black mark next to Papa's name.

The hall is filled to bursting. Lili and the girl manage to find free seats at the ends of two different rows. A uniformed man stands at the podium. His voice is soft and he seems a bit shy, as if unaccustomed to public speaking.

"...and while we are disappointed to have with us today neither Herr Kuhn nor Herr Weiler, it is with an enormous sense of pride that we acknowledge the reason for their absence. Those of you who've been with us from the beginning know that an important part of our efforts is financial support for causes. You'll be pleased to hear how much has so far has been raised to help support the Winter Relief Fund. Some of you are among those contributors who signed the Golden Book Herr Kuhn took with him to Berlin." He pauses with a dramatic flair that seems out of character. "In a special message, Herr Kuhn and Herr Weiler have informed us that while at the Olympics, they had the enormous honor to meet with the Führer himself." Cheers swell through the hall as the audience rises, their arms thrust forward. "Sieg Heil, Sieg Heil!" they call out. For some moments the speaker's voice is lost.

"Now I give the podium over to Herr Kappe, who has very important information on the links between international Jewry and Comintern." He smiles. "Herr Kappe has promised to help transform the Friends of New Germany in America into a new branch of the SA!"

Lili is squirming in her seat. Her canteen is empty and it is no longer possible to ignore the pressing need to find a toilet. It is urgent that she leave the meeting immediately. The further she gets from the hall, the more eerily quiet the building becomes. She passes through a corridor from whose walls hang a strange assortment of German and American finery—stars and stripes and swastikas. A painting of the Statue of Liberty and a photograph of the Lorelei. At last she finds the rooms, one marked "Herren" and the other "Damen." It is strange to think that so many people whose ancestors left Germany to come to the land of the Statue of Liberty are now here in Camp Siegfried because of their belief in one man in Germany. Unlike the towering statue in the harbor, he is of flesh and blood, thousands of miles away yet inspiring them all from a pedestal of hope and faith.

She returns to the hall just as the meeting lets out and is swept up with the others toward the fields where they will march under the leadership of the Camp Siegfried officials. For one exhilarating instant it looks as if Lili will be given a banner to stride forth with against her shoulder but then the moment is gone and the flag goes to the young boy beside her. Next are the competitions and feats of strength for both boys and girls. In a relay race Lili's heart hammers as fast as the notes of a Bach fugue but she manages to pass the baton to the next girl without missing a beat. When her team is declared the winner, she screams with the others. A group of older boys is standing on one side, watching, grinning, eyeing the girls' bare legs. Some of the girls begin to flirt but Lili stays back.

Later there is food, platters of *Knackwurst* and rolls, deep bowls of peppercorn-studded Sauerkraut and pickles. More singing follows, in a grand swell of voices that must be audible all the way to Manhattan. Loudspeakers order them to move to a field and there they all stand, tightly packed, a giant rectangle of children and women, some holding babies, and men of all ages. They stand at attention and salute the leader of the Reich. A great welling up of pride and belief in something bigger than herself, bigger than all of them, moves within Lili.

"We belong to you!" the children call out to the Führer.

The sunlight is soft and tinted gold as they head back to the Yaphank station. They are exhausted yet glowing with energy. One of the girls walking near Lili chatters on about all the things she has been learning since her parents started taking her here on weekends. "...they say that Camp Siegfried is really part of Germany in America and it's important we come here often to get ready for when America is part of Germany." Lili tries to imagine Mama and Papa here and sees only a blank. But she knows what Papa would say to such talk.

As the Camp Siegfried Special rolls back toward Manhattan, Lili swallows the bitter truth that, in her family, she is alone in her allegiance to the Führer and the Reich. At dinner, Mama and Papa ask about her day on Fire Island and she tells them it was glorious.

Watching Her Through the Darkness

Mama has taken Paul to Central Park, Lotte and Oskar have gone with the car to collect crates of apples from a farmer upstate along the Hudson. Lili and Papa are having a rare day together. So far it has been quite calm.

With a brusque rustling of sheets, Papa thrusts the newspaper onto the armrest of his chair.

"What are they thinking?"

He sounds aggravated.

"Dressing up like Nazis and parading around the streets of Manhattan."

Now she truly must keep silent. If Papa finds out that she was one of those cheering on 86th Street yesterday when the German–American Bund marched by with a band and the flags of two nations hoisted upon uniformed shoulders, he will lecture her yet again. But it was so exciting, different from the seclusion of Camp Siegfried. Yesterday's display took place in the city in the middle of everyday life, just as it does in Germany.

"It's ridiculous," he continues. "Nearly all those people live in America and are American citizens. Why do they persist in trying to convince people that what Hitler is doing is so good?" He looks at Lili with what seems curiosity. "Tell me what you think."

Her chest contracts. Papa often used this phrase when she was young, encouraging her to find her way. Yet during these past three years it is as if he has not wanted to hear the results.

"It's simple, Papa," she says, striving to control her voice. "He has a vision and people want to be a part of it. A vision of greatness that you refuse to see."

Rather than look annoyed by her accusation, Papa crosses a leg, as if settling down for a long fireside chat.

"You too have been drawn into the Hitler fervor," he remarks, his tone gentle. "I don't quite understand how you persist in it for so long, being so far away from Germany. Tell me, Lili."

Again, it is almost as if she needed to catch her breath. Here is the beloved father of her childhood who, with infinite patience, picked her up when she fell, who soothed her tears and told her all would be well; the parent to whom she turned when she yearned to understand the world around her. As she looks into his eyes of somber blue, one memory in particular comes to mind.

Mama and Papa were giving a dinner party. Lotte had carried her out to say good night to the guests but it was Papa who lifted her into his arms to take her back to her room. He had a special way of folding her into the featherbed so that she felt encased in softness. "Good night, my little one," he whispered. When he bent to kiss her she could smell the scent of Mouchoir de Monsieur. She raised her arms to encircle his neck. "Stay with me, Papa." He took off his shoes and lay down with her. She snuggled against his shoulder and they spoke about the funny way Sascha had barked that day, about the moonlight streaming in through the open window and how far it had traveled to arrive in her very room. "The stars are even farther away than the moon, isn't it, Papa?" "Yes, little mouse. The sky is as vast as eternity." "Eternity?" "Forever." She pushed at his cheek with her pointer finger. "Papa," she said, "what was there before there was forever?" He took her finger and kissed it lightly. "Nothing, Mäuschen." She took back her finger and rubbed the side of her head with her fist. "But nothing is something, Papa. What was there before nothing?" "Ah, Lilichen," he chuckled. "One day you will be a white-haired philosopher and everyone will come to you with their questions." "And I will tell them to wait while I ask my Papa for the answers," she said, laughing at the moonlight. Papa's smile was silent. "By then you will no longer need to ask me about anything, dearest one, for you will be wise and grown up." Again she poked him. "I will ask you, Papa, because you know everything."

Now Papa made a chuckling sound, but it sounded sad. "Don't worry," she told him. "Even when I am an old woman with white hair and wrinkles and a mustache like the flower shop lady, I will still ask you, Papa." She stroked his cheek with her palm, comforting him. "Ach," he said, giving a little sigh, "by then, like the grumpy old trolls in the fairy tales, I will be gone." The words cut into the night. "There, there," said Papa, smoothing her hair. "I am here. I will be here for a very long time yet." Still she wept, and the weeping felt different from any other in her four years of life. Then Papa told her she must grow up first, and that would take a very long time. "Forever, Papa?" she sobbed. "Almost, my little mouse." He kissed her brow. "Sleep now. All is well." And so she slept, knowing Papa was at her side, watching her through the darkness.

He is watching her now, waiting for an answer.

Agreeing With Someone Else

"My thoughts, Papa?" She glances down at her hands. "My thoughts are like those of millions of Germans who know that the Führer is leading our nation from the fears of the past into hope for the future."

Papa nods. "Yes, this has already been said too many times. And at some point, ready or not, the future becomes the present. But what do you think of the German-American Bund? Why are Americans, citizens of a land of freedom and democracy, marching about the streets in praise of Hitler?" He gives a lopsided smile. "Perhaps it is precisely because it is such a land."

"I think the aims of the German-American Bund are to promote friendship and business between the two countries, Papa. Also, many of the measures that the Führer has been taking to strengthen the economy in Germany would work over here. Perhaps the Bund wants to encourage America to do the same."

"Measures such as?"

This is easy. "For example, the youth labor groups, Papa. Young people should be out there giving themselves to their country, not just taking from it. The Führer understands how important that is, and that's why he set up so many programs to get the youth involved and helping out—raising money to help the truly needy, working on farms, building dams, ditches, streets. Anything that is useful. Everyone needs to work together to create a true nation. All it takes is one year of service to your country." She breaks off. "I wish I could be useful like that. For me it wouldn't be an obligation; it would be an honor." Papa is silent.

"So," Lili continues, her tone belligerent, "if the German-American Bund is marching in the streets of New York, it's to help America learn how to help itself."

"You do have a surprising flair for rhetoric," says Papa, smiling for the first time. "Your argument even has some convincing points. Helping one's country is an admirable responsibility and one should indeed be pleased to do so. A year of youth service might be a good idea, depending on how it is structured." He sighs. "The Germans have been waiting for a long time for someone who will tell them what to do, and how to do it."

Lili is unsure of how to take this. But before she can say anything, Papa continues.

"Since taking office, Herr Hitler has been busy molding a new national consciousness. The youth are, as you conveyed, especially zealous in adopting his outlook. But it's worrisome that they are being taught to overlook so much else." His thumb and forefinger rub his chin.

"Yes, I know," she says. "There's a quote from Baldur von Schirach: 'Adolf Hitler, we believe in you; without you we would be individuals, through you we are a nation. You give us the experience of our youth.'" She sits back and folds her arms.

Papa chuckles. "I will tell you what Goethe said, and this can be applied to today's youth: 'If a man or woman is born ten years sooner or later, their whole aspect and performance shall be different.'"

Lili shrugs. "For me it is different. I'm not in Germany."

"And if we were, Lili, what would you say about those other changes that Herr Hitler has been instigating? Not labor for the sake of the nation, but to break men's backs and minds."

"What do you mean?" She frowns. "Oh, the concentration camps."

"Yes." His voice is soft. "How do you justify sending anyone who disagrees with Hitler to jail or one of those camps? Why doesn't the German-American Bund point out these details when they praise what is going on over there?"

Lili looks down at her hands again. The nails need to be cut so that she can fly unimpeded through her music.

"Do you know," he continues, "that people are being killed because they dared to speak out against some of the wrongs being perpetrated?"

Her eyes widen. "What wrongs? What possible wrong has the Führer done? Any mistakes are made by his underlings, not by him."

An expression of exasperation passes over Papa's face, as if he were a teacher and she a reluctant student in the classroom.

"For one, Lili, the incarceration and execution of good and decent people for nothing but their refusal to see eye to eye with the National Socialists. You should know that there are more world views than theirs." His eyes are growing darker. "Just one example. Ever since the military service was reinstated last year, Jehovah's Witnesses have been having a hard time of it. Among other reasons, it's because their religion doesn't permit them to bear arms. The men are being arrested for not showing up for conscription. The children are being ostracized or expelled from school."

"I've heard about that. It's because they won't salute or sing patriotic songs." Again she shrugs her shoulders. "It's their own fault."

"And what about the fact that many have been sent to concentration camps for their refusal to turn away from their belief system?" Papa persists.

"That too is their choice," she counters. "It's hard to imagine they would make such a choice. They need to change their ways. All they have to do is salute and serve and they're free. They live in Germany and they are Germans. So they need to conform to German ways. Religion isn't as important as nation. If they don't like it, they should leave."

Papa nods. "So you're saying that in Germany citizens are not free unless they do what the authorities want them to."

Lili's chest tightens. Papa has twisted things.

"No! That's not it at all. Almost everybody is free, but it's our duty to do what we can for the government of our country. We must all make sacrifices." She leans forward. "The Führer is doing everything he can to make sure that the Volk is well taken care of and safe. I've told you that before. The Führer is working toward his objectives. The government has to spend a lot of money to help people build up the country and that's what the Führer is doing, Papa. His leadership is giving us back our pride in Germany." Her thoughts are getting jumbled, tumbling out too fast to order.

Papa holds up a hand. "Slow down. What you're saying is that everyone must make sacrifices for the good of the nation, and that Hitler and his party have the power to choose what that good is."

"Yes. *Most* Germans trust the Führer."

"So you are saying that the Communists and Socialists have been rightfully beaten or thrown into Dachau and Sachsenhausen or even killed for not trusting the Nazis to know what is right for them."

Again Papa is twisting things, making them sound bad.

"Not to mention that Jewish Germans don't even get to be a part of this process, as their rights as citizens are gone. Legally taken away from them."

"No," Lili says. "It's just that some people have to be re-educated or kept away, for the good of the nation. In the end it will all be worthwhile." She ignores the Jewish issue as it is too difficult, and thinks of Frau Kuhn. "The Communists and the Socialists will be finished in Germany, and the undesirables will eventually leave. Then we'll have a country of committed citizens that are German through and through." She pauses. For a few moments she has actually forgotten that they are in America. But perhaps her arguments are at last convincing Papa. Perhaps there is something else she can say that will make him see the light. And then they can go home to Germany and to being a perfect family, the way they once were.

"Did you know, Lili, that one of the reasons that the unemployment figures have gone down so much in Germany is that they are no longer including women and the Jewish—or those with Jewish ancestry—in their calculations?"

She hasn't heard this, and frowns. "It's not only about prosperity, Papa. There are other things too. Like the *Kraft durch Freude* program." It is such an inspiring name, true to its nature. The KdF is indeed Strength through Joy. She warms to the subject.

"People who have never ever in their lives gone to a concert or had a holiday somewhere, well, now they can take train and boat excursions all over Germany and attend cultural performances." She stops for a breath. "You know how important music is, Papa. Now everybody can afford to go to a concert, or even the opera and ballet. The Führer is the one who has made this possible, Papa, by making it affordable. Now all Germans can share in the joy of our nation's cultural heritage!"

One of Papa's eyebrows arches. "You sound as if you had memorized those propaganda pieces by Goebbels."

Lili swallows. "You should give me more credit than that." She tastes bitterness on her tongue. "But I suppose it's easier for you to believe that I'm just an ignorant parrot who can't think for herself. Yet even then you want me to agree with *your* thoughts. It just upsets you that I've chosen to agree with someone else." Her eyes feel like two stones. "We should have gone to the Olympics, this summer, Papa. Even your beloved Americans went and came back full of praise for what the Führer has accomplished. Then you would have seen how much has changed since you took us away from Germany." Now her voice too is cold and flat as stone. "Then you would have been ashamed to have left our homeland."

Not once in her life has Papa ever raised his hand to Lili but she is sure that he will slap her for the way she has spoken to him. She waits for him to strike her so another bond linking them will be broken. But Papa sits in silence. She looks at him. She cannot read his expression. He draws a deep sigh and the words come out with his breath.

"Why don't you trust me the way you did when you were younger..."

Trust him? She has more to say.

"Also, I don't need propaganda, Papa. In my heart I know that the Führer is the right government for the Reich. The Führer truly cares about his country. Our country. He went to jail for his beliefs. Every single thing he does is for the good of Germany." She fixes him with her icy gaze, now more cutting than ever. "There is something else you should know." For an instant she pauses, but only for an instant. "More and more I consider you a traitor to Germany." She looks away.

Let him strike her now.

Lili hears the blood pulsing inside her head.

She glances at Papa.

He is looking at her with eyes of fading indigo, his expression puzzling.

Yet when at last he speaks, his voice low and still soft, the words make her want to scream or scratch out at something with her uncut nails.

"You still have much to learn, little mouse. "

You Shall Go Home Again

At last! After nearly four years of autodidactic effort, it has finally happened. Through her commitment and perseverance she has at last accomplished what she set out to do. Today, for the first time in her life, she has played the *Goldberg Variations* through from start to finish, without pause. Frau Kuhn would have appreciated her refusal to be sidetracked. But these days her old teacher is most likely gliding around Minneapolis giving out copies of the *Communist Manifesto* to unsuspecting passersby in snowshoes. Lili giggles as she turns around under her quilt, unable to sleep. Part of her restlessness is due to the uncomfortable cough she has had for the past few days.

She has not forgotten what she promised herself nearly four years ago: the reward for learning the *Goldberg Variations* is to go home.

It remains to be seen how she can accomplish the last hurdle: she still does not have enough money. Getting a job is impossible. What could she work at? How can she make enough money to buy the steamer ticket and travel expenses? And where will she go once she arrives? The apartment in Berlin has been sold. She coughs again, the effort making her chest sore, then bites her lip. How aggravating it is to be at the mercy of Papa.

Like threads pulling her in thirty directions, the *Goldberg Variations* loop through her thoughts, over and over again, the musical weft and warp weaving possibilities throughout the long night.

By morning, there is only one solution.

When she enters the breakfast room, Papa is turning a page of *The New York Times* while Mama has the mail in front of her.

"Good morning, darling." Mama smiles.

Papa greets her. Then, an odd request at this time of day, he asks her to play the harpsichord.

Lili is about to say no when she changes her mind, choosing a sarabande. The minor key infuses the room with melancholy. Yet at a deeper level the notes are pierced with gladness and optimism so that despite its grave opening, the piece ends like a tapestry in harmonic counterpoint. A perfect finish to her night's labors.

Papa's voice is gentle.

"Is there a reason why you chose that particular piece?" Ach, Papa. How attuned they once were. She shrugs.

"I like it."

He says nothing more.

Mama's clapping is delicate. "It is such a joy to listen to you, darling."

"Thank you, Mama."

"Indeed it is," says Papa, looking at her. "Yesterday the *Goldberg Variations* in entirety. Today a simple sarabande, exquisite."

Lili's heart is thumping faster. She must do it now.

"Papa, Mama." She turns to face them, her fingers gripping the wooden edge of the harpsichord as she coughs before continuing.

"I'm sorry if this will trouble you. You're my family. I love you. But I think you both know that I haven't been happy all these years in New York. My body is here, for I was given no choice. But my heart and mind both are still back home. I was a child when we arrived. Now I'm 17." She can no longer focus on their faces; her eyes are tearing up.

"All I can do now is ask you to let me return to Berlin. Please let me go home." A lump in her throats forms and she catches her breath in a sob. "Mama, Papa. Please."

Even through the blur she notices her parents looking at each other, their features twisted. Both of them rise then, moving toward her, and their arms enfold her with all the familiarity of a childhood haven. Lifting with it part of the weight from her tight chest, the relief begins to flow through her in a delicious surge. She bites her lip to keep from smiling. Any moment now, Papa will say the words of release she has been longing to hear; she can feel it in his embrace.

"Darling Lili." His throat sounds choked with sadness. "We understand your longing. You shall go home again, one day. But not yet."

How to Open the Window

Lili stares out through the windowpane. The limbs of the tree are empty and dark. She feels like the tree.

Since Monday, she has neither left her room nor eaten anything save for a stale biscuit discovered on the windowsill. This morning she pushed back again not only the tray with food—her favorite dishes; how could they be so cruel?—but the glass of black currant juice as well. Her cough has grown deeper, her chest more painful. Since last night, her head has been throbbing, her skin hot to the touch. Yet there is a certain pride that comes with the pain. That Tante Margarethe endured only two days of deprivation. Today is Lili's third. She is made of tougher stuff. And so, apparently, is her father. Unrelenting.

Mama and Papa have come to speak with her several times already, both separately and together, pleading for her to understand why they cannot let her go, but to no avail. They can say what they like as she lies on her bed, refusing to respond. Let them beat her if they like. She will remain silent. (Except for her cough, which sounds like the roar of a baby dragon.) Last night they changed tactics and enlisted the help of Paul and Lotte and even Oskar. Poor little Paul. How unfair to subject him to such a task. His distress was pitiful but her resolve unwavering. Before sending him back out, Lili gathered him into her arms and the two of them cried together for a while. It was a new experience. A tear slid into her mouth.

Lotte and Oskar appealed to her love for her parents.

"*Fräulein* Lili," they said, crossing into her room, their faces creased with strain. "How can you continue this, knowing that your parents are suffering with you?" Lotte's voice was taut. "They have always only your very best interest at heart. If they believe that going back to Germany now is not a good idea, then you must trust them. They are much wiser than you."

Lili let her eyes move over them but remained silent.

Oskar had no smile. "Things are not right in Germany. There is much injustice these days, Fräulein Lili. For everyone." He paused. "Honor your mother and father. When all is well again, surely you can go back for a visit. Maybe one day we can all go." These were more words than he had spoken in a long time.

Lili closed her eyes then. How glum Oskar sounded. But he and Lotte didn't want to go back. Lili did. With every fiber of her self she must go back. She heard them standing in front of her for some time more before Lotte said "Na ja, what can we do?" and they left the room, a floorboard creaking.

Now Lili's head feels strangely light as she stares at the lines of the tree, black against the sky of palest gray. It seems to be dancing in the winter air. How strong a wind it is that the branches can twist and twirl so lithely. Is it a fruit tree? Perhaps Margarethe planted it outside when she rode by on her way to Palestine. Lili lifts her hand. It feels as if it were being drawn up by threads. Like a puppet. And now they have snapped! Her fingers fall back onto the bedclothes and she stares at them. What strange creatures. Little tentacles tipped with shells. She tries to blow them away, but her rasping breath is not strong enough. Perhaps what she needs is air. Is there a window in this room? She looks up, her gaze traveling across the white snow above her but finding no opening. A faint light catches her eye and there it is—a window. She has seen it somewhere before, long ago. She slides a leg over the bed, then another. She checks to see if perhaps there is another leg she has left behind but no, the bed is empty. She floats toward the light, the tentacles streaming along at her sides. Ach, the tree. What amazing things are hanging from its branches now— sausages and trumpets and lampshades with swastikas. Why, outside is

Schlaraffenland! It is true then, that centuries' old legend. All she has to do is figure out how to open the window and she can pass right into the land where the houses are made of gingerbread, and milk flows in the streams, and all she has to do to succeed is sleep. She moves closer. A pheasant sits atop a plate on a branch. It is already broiled, with a carving knife stuck deep into its breast. The bird looks friendly. It smiles and juts out its beaked head, beckoning her to come nearer. Lili presses down on the handle and with a last burst of effort pulls open the window into the land of flowing milk just as her head explodes in a thousand stars.

"Lilileinchen."

Floating up through the strange sound of rasping that seems to issue from the burning in her chest, Lili slowly opens her eyes. And sees Mama's face. There are new lines on it. Her eyelids are swollen. Her hand reaches out and strokes Lili's cheek. Lili closes her eyes to the exquisite comfort of it. When she opens them again, it is Papa who is there. Darkness sits beneath his gaze, shades his mouth and chin.

"My darling girl."

With infinite gentleness, he takes her hand. The tentacles are gone. It is her hand, one of the two with which she once played the harpsichord. Connected to the limpness of it is a rubber tube which runs up to a bottle hanging from a metal stand.

"Rest now, my dearest," Papa whispers into the darkening space around her. "You have conquered the pneumonia. Now you must get strong for your voyage across the Atlantic."

Germany is Much More than Berlin

"Berlin is out of the question. I will not have an impressionable young woman without supervision exposed to the fervor of the capital." Papa's tone is as dry as the logs in the fireplace.

Oskar has just finished lighting the fire. Papa and Lili, both already comfortable in their dressing gowns, are sitting in front of the growing flames while Mama must have fallen asleep putting Paul to bed. Lili would like to glower at Papa, but the truth is that she is just so relieved to be going back that it no longer matters where in Germany she goes. Yet she must at least make an effort.

"We still have friends in Berlin, don't we? And Alt Eichendorf is just a few hours away. I could always go visit Großmama Maximiliana and Großpapa Hugo."

Papa laughs. "I can't imagine that you would want to spend that much time out in the country with your grandparents."

"But we always spent our summers there." Her voice sounds peevish.

"Yes, but you were a child. Now you are a young woman and I imagine you could very well find yourself bored by long hours chasing butterflies in the country."

"I still love butterflies." She pretends to frown, thrusting out her bottom lip.

The corners of his eyes crinkle up, giving her for a moment that delicious feeling that all is well with her world because Papa is smiling at her. Yet there are still shadows beneath his eyes.

"That may be. But I don't want you to become one yourself in Berlin."

"Whatever do you mean, Papa?"

Again he smiles. "No matter. Trust me in this at least, Lili."

She stares at the wood. Three big flames wave, one from each of the logs. It is a good sign. She returns her gaze to Papa.

"What do you propose instead?"

He crosses one leg over the other.

"You remember my telling you about my Onkel Wilhelm?"

"I think so. He was an art collector in Paris, right?"

Papa nods. "Correct. His love of art was more powerful than any other allegiances at the time. He left Berlin long before the war, so, by the time it began, he wasn't treated as an enemy—certainly not by his friends in Paris."

"What does he have to do with my going to Germany? He died a long time ago." She taps a toe against the floor, eager to discuss her future and not Onkel Wilhelm's past.

"Patience, Lili. I'm getting there." Papa reaches out for the glass of cognac on the side table. "He married in France, to a German woman many years younger than he. Tante Aletheia. It was she who inspired him to begin painting so late in life. He even became rather successful, certainly with the critics in Paris." Papa swills the brandy around, breathing in the spirit. "Over the years, I have met Tante Aletheia several times and we remain in contact. She is a fine person. It's a pity that you only met her when you were so young. She was no longer living in Paris when we were last there." Papa sets the glass down. "After Onkel Wilhelm's death she moved to the countryside. Soon you'll have the opportunity to meet her again."

Lili sits up. The countryside? Then why not Alt Eichendorf?

"For some years now," Papa continues, "Tante Aletheia has been living in Heidelberg."

Heidelberg! Why, that day on the bus those professors said that it has the best university in Germany. Does Papa plan to send her there?

"It's true that Tante Aletheia has always been somewhat of an eccentric," Papa is saying. "Her father, Egon Beck, was a famous conductor in Hamburg. Her grandfather on her mother's side was a renowned archaeologist in the Ottoman Empire. Not as famous as Schliemann, but highly respected in his circles. It was he who gave his granddaughter her Ancient Greek name. Tante Aletheia herself grew up as something of a free spirit, I suppose, and this is what must have brought her and Onkel Wilhelm together." Papa rubs his chin. Perhaps he is having second thoughts about sending Lili to someone like that? Lili presses her teeth into her bottom lip.

"Yes, she's a rather peculiar old lady." Papa grins. "But true as a blade. For the past couple of years she has been running a boarding house in Heidelberg."

A boarding house--they have a relative who does that? Her amazement must show on her face because Papa laughs.

"As Goethe says, 'People of uncommon abilities generally fall into eccentricities when their sphere of life is not adequate to their abilities."

Lili frowns. What is so uncommon about running a boarding house? Indeed, it seems rather common.

"After Onkel Wilhelm died, Tante Aletheia spent some years in their home in Alsace. The house is right near the Vosges Mountains."

Lili interrupts. "You've been there?"

Papa nods. "Yes, indeed, and so have you."

"I have no memories of it."

"No, you were too young for that. You were just a tiny sprite, toddling about." He smiles, and Lili memorizes the way his lips reveal his teeth only slowly.

"Nearly two kilometers from the house, through the forest, is Friedberg, a small village on the river Bruche. For some years after Onkel Wilhelm's death, Friedberg was enough for Tante Aletheia. She only occasionally traveled to Straßburg, or, as it is called in French, Strasbourg." The French version has no 'sh' sound at the beginning. It sounds strange. "Even more rarely, when galleries or museums wanted to arrange retrospectives of Onkel Wilhelm's work, she went to Paris or came across to Germany."

"So he became a famous artist only after he was dead?"

"Famous enough," says Papa. "He certainly never sought fame. Onkel Wilhelm was a man with great humility as well as a great appetite for life, a combination rare in a man."

Lili thinks of the Führer and his humble origins in Austria. He began his life hoping to be an artist. Yet life did not reach out to meet him in this. How disappointed he must have been. Yet his loss must have fueled him on to search for greater meaning, for himself, and now for the nation he has made his own. Papa's Onkel Wilhelm was a much more ordinary man than the Führer, even if he was eventually successful in his art. He had to die first. The Führer is still alive.

"...and eventually she decided to move back across the Rhine. She chose Heidelberg on the Neckar, which is only a few hours away."

"But why did she open a boarding house, Papa? Is she poor?"

Papa laughs. "I asked her the same question. As I said, she's rather eccentric, this Tante Aletheia. Her answer was that a boarding house would allow her to keep her finger on the pulse of things."

"What things?"

"Ordinary daily life. She feels that the people in a boarding house will let her see which way the wind is blowing, so to speak. It's good to know that in Germany these days."

Lili sighs. Here it comes. Another lecture on how bad things are in Germany, when Lili knows that they are better than ever.

"So you see, Lili, on your trip to Germany you will be staying in one of the country's most beautiful towns, with a *Schloß* dating back to the 15th century." Papa coughs and subtly swallows to clear his throat. "In fact, her house isn't far from the base of the hill where the castle sits."

Lili chews on her bottom lip. She should resign herself to it—she is not going to Berlin. But this Heidelberg alternative does sound intriguing, even if she has to put up with a crazy old great-aunt. Besides, she has won. She is going home. And Germany is much more than Berlin, even if that city is the most wonderful place on earth. So let it be Heidelberg.

"So I'm to stay with...*Großtante* Aletheia."

Papa picks up his glass.

"Of course you'll have to do something constructive there, Lili. That should go without saying. Tante Aletheia will help you in every way she can. Certainly you must continue your harpsichord studies. Another possibility would be for you to attend classes in a high school there."

"A high school? But I'm graduating in June!"

"It's not the same. High schools in Germany are more advanced than those here. In any case, it will only be for a few months."

Her chest tightens, like an echo of when she had pneumonia. A few months—no, that is not enough. As deliriously happy as she is to be going home, even now she knows that it has to be for more than a few months. She bites down. Breathe. Breathe. She will find a way to solve this, just as she found the way to get back home.

"Of course it is indeed a pity that you can't attend the university in Heidelberg," Papa is saying. "It's one of the best, and certainly the oldest in Germany. But I fear that your American high school diploma wouldn't be adequate qualification for entry."

University in Heidelberg. It sounds exciting. Would she study music—or? Papa says it is impossible. But it seems that nothing is impossible. Looking at Papa, she remembers one of his Goethe quotes: "The human mind will not be confined to any limits." She won't remind him of this; it is enough that she knows it.

"It will be interesting to stay in Heidelberg with your Tante Aletheia, Papa. For when is my ticket?"

Papa keeps the glass near his mouth but doesn't drink. He seems to be breathing in the scent of the cognac. At last he puts it down but the glass doesn't land flat on its base and nearly tips over. He rights it. When he speaks, there is a slight catch on the consonants.

"The week after your graduation, Lili."

She leaps up and plants a kiss on Papa's cheek. She cannot remember the last time she has.

Not Every German Girl is a Follower of Hitler

During the day she picks up the magazine. Its pages already worn, the magazine opens easily to the right place. As soon as she sees him flat against the paper there is a fluttering deep within her. Over and over again she takes in the image. Her blood quickens already at the sight of the boots that rise halfway up long legs. Her gaze roams along the taut black of his uniform, slides up his narrow waist to the wide shoulders studded with braids. Slowly she raises her eyes to meet his. As always, he stares straight at her. The wings of an eagle spread silver across his cap. He, nameless, has become her daily secret. But it is in the darkness of night that he gains a dimension. She waits for him there in the untouched wilderness, shivers in her sleep.

♪ ♪ ♫

"There are certain modes of behavior that you will follow while you're visiting Heidelberg, Lili."

Papa and Mama have called her into the salon and seem ready for a serious talk. Lili sits prim and straight upon her hard-backed chair. June is still in the future. Are they going to lecture her every week until then?

"Yes, Mama, yes, Papa."

Paul suddenly falls face down against the sofa, then looks up at them, wailing. "I want to go with Lili. I want to go on the big ship and see Germanmany too."

"Hush, Paulchen," says Mama, reaching over to smooth his hair. "One day you will go back to Germany."

He stops crying. "I already goed to Germany?"

"What a clever fellow you are," says Mama. "Yes, you began your life in Germany, my little clam. You were still tiny then, growing inside me. We came to America before you were born. Now we live here. But you must always remember that, like everyone else in your family, you began your life in Germany."

Papa turns to Lili. "And you must never forget that you are the daughter of a noble house. You are still Freiin Lili von Rittersburg zu Mertz-Tärnekow, a baroness. Your family name may mean nothing in this country, but even now in Germany it commands respect. Make sure you honor it in all that you do." Papa sounds so grave. He gives a little cough. Mama looks over at him, her eyes narrowing.

"Are you quite well, Erwin?"

Papa shakes his head slightly.

"It's nothing, Wilhelmine. Just a little frog in my throat." Lili smiles. It wasn't until she was about six that she realized there was no tiny amphibian that came to visit Papa from time to time.

Mama too smiles, but continues to watch him closely.

Lili studies Mama's face. For a moment, like Paul, she looks as if she were about to cry. Poor Mama. She too misses home but rarely speaks of her feelings. A wave of pity passes through Lili. Soon she will be in their homeland while Mama still has to make the best of being here. How does Mama do it? She is always so calm. She has given up so much to be here with Papa: her family, her friends, all the joys of living in Berlin. Yet she never complains.

Lili sighs, watching Mama tickle Paul to take his mind off the subject. Perhaps her mother simply doesn't feel as deeply as she, Lili, does.

"You return to Germany at a dangerous time in its history," Papa continues, his tone still somber. "We know your enduring enthusiasm for the current regime, but fervently hope that you will observe everything around you with an open mind. Look, listen, and learn. Goethe once said that the best government is that which teaches us to govern ourselves. Ask yourself if what you see can meet those standards."

Lili decides that this is the perfect opportunity to give some Goethe back to Papa.

"Did you know, Papa, that Goethe also said that the destiny of any nation at any given time depends on the opinion of its young people, those under 25?" She tries not to sound smug even though 25 seems quite old.

Papa grins at her. "Goethe was indeed a man whose thoughts were timeless." Then he turns serious again. "Apropos the thoughts of Goethe as to the importance of youth, Mama and I would like your assurance that you will not involve yourself in any of those Nazi organizations that feed on the youth of Germany." They wait for her response.

Lili's stomach contracts. "What do you mean?"

"Exactly what I just said. For example, you are not to involve yourself in an organization like the BDM."

Mama interrupts. "We prefer you not to surround yourself with such people, Lili." She gives a little shudder. "It is all very difficult."

Lili exhales. "But how am I supposed to look, listen, and learn if you won't let me behave like an ordinary German girl?"

"First of all, not every German girl is a follower of Herr Hitler. Second, you are not an ordinary German girl." He pauses. "When in doubt, ask yourself if Goethe would approve—of your own actions as well as the actions of those around you."

Lili taps her toes on the floor. Mama glances down. Lili stops.

"Yes," Papa says. "I know you find my constant harping on Goethe bothersome. But there is much wisdom in his simple sayings. You would do well to reflect upon many of them. To that end," and here he turns to pick up from the side table a package wrapped in pale yellow tissue, "even if it's a bit early for a farewell gift, Mama and I would like to present you with a copy of some of his finest thoughts."

She kisses them both.

"Thank you."

They watch as Lili unties the violet ribbon. It is a small volume entitled *Secrets of Goethe*, published in 1837.

"It's already a hundred years old!" Lili says, running her fingertips over the ivory title page. It is one thing to have grown up enduring Papa's incessant Goethe quotes. Yet to hold Goethe's words in a book printed only five years after his death feels different somehow, more solemn. She closes the deep blue leather cover.

"I will take it with me. When I read it, I'll think of you both. Especially you, Papa."

There is shared laughter then. Just like in Berlin, when they all still understood each other.

A Close Call

His voice vibrates with rage. "From where did you get these? The German-American Cultural Club?"

Papa has called her into his study. Before him on the desk are two stacks of pamphlets. Her collection. How did he get them? It must have been Lotte. Oh, she could shake her. Never has Lili seen Papa looking as angry as he does now. His face is shaded purple like a plum, his eyebrows meet at the middle.

"I—I got them at school." It is the first thing she can think of.

The muscles in Papa's face tighten. "We are not in Germany! What school in America hands out German propaganda by Goebbels? With disgraceful advice on how to spot a Jew?"

"It was for Social Studies." Lili forces her eyes to remain focused on a spot straight ahead. "We were learning about Germany."

"How can that be possible? And how many of you can read German?" Papa inhales long and loud. "It's an outrage if such material has been given to students at your school." He shakes his head. "It's bad enough that you bring home those skewed German newspapers."

She seizes on this. "Do you remember, Papa, when I told you about the music programs of KdF and how you said I sounded as if I were quoting propaganda by Goebbels?"

His tone is frosty. "Yes?"

"I do look over the newspapers. That's also because we were studying about Germany in class and the teacher thinks that it's important to get firsthand information."

Papa peers at her. Now his skin is pasty pale. "And where does she get this so-called information?"

"I'm not sure, Papa." She tries not to bite her bottom lip, even though she can feel it trembling. A wave of nausea is rising.

"I believe," he says with deliberation, "that it is time I paid a visit to your school."

"Yes, of course, Papa." She nods and nods. "But that teacher is no longer there."

"Ach, is that so? Did she leave or was she fired?"

"I don't know, Papa. And now we're studying South America in Social Studies." At least this is true.

Papa leans back in his chair. A good sign. He exhales, and the only sound in the room is his breath. "Now that you have read them, it doesn't matter anymore. Tell me. What have you learned?"

Again he is peering at her as if trying to see what lies beyond her eyes. It is important that she speak carefully. If she says the wrong thing, it is possible that Papa will change his mind, just as he has at so many important crossroads in her life, and not let her go back to Germany.

She raises her chin just a fraction.

"There's so much to think about, Papa." She forms the words with deliberation. "The Führer is doing many good things for Germany. Not everything is perfect, but he has instilled a sense of pride. Given us back belief in our nation." She looks directly at him. "But people shouldn't get too proud, right Papa? When I'm home I'll look around to see if that's happening." There. Is this enough to reassure him?

He is silent for some time. "Not everything is perfect because perfection is impossible to achieve. But a nation and its people must always strive to reach the goal of perfection and not allow themselves to be misdirected. If they do, they must quickly get back on course."

With a sudden movement he pushes the stacks of pamphlets away from him.

"Throw these out, Lili. And never again bring such filth into our home." He seems about to say something more but stops himself. His jaw muscles clench. "By God, Lili, keep away from the Nazis while you are there. They are sucking the goodness out of the German people."

Lili bites her lip. What a strange thing for Papa to say, considering how much good the Führer is doing for the German people. But she will keep quiet. She bites down harder, to keep from smiling. She is still going home!

How Can She Leave Her Family?

"Lili?" Mama calls out from the kitchen where she and Lotte are preparing the meal, roast goose with potatoes and asparagus. Ever since the day of the pamphlets, Lili tries to look right through Lotte just as if she were invisible. Surely it was Lotte who stole the collection to show to Papa; she had no right to do so. Yet the way things now stand, it is best not to have a confrontation. If Lotte were to complain to Papa or Mama it might still affect her trip. Besides, Lotte just isn't the same Lotte anymore. If Lotte doesn't like her just because Lili likes to inform herself about what is going on in Germany, then she certainly doesn't care about Lotte anymore. If they were in Germany, she'd be right not to. After all, it is as simple as Lotte's blood being different from hers.

"Lili, please bring this to Papa. He wasn't feeling so well this afternoon." Lili picks up the small tray with its linen napkin on which sits a thin porcelain cup filled with chamomile tea, sweet tendrils of steam rising. With careful steps she moves down the hall to where Papa spends so much of his time when he is at home. Considering the amount of effort he has put into his real estate business these past years, he must already have sold half the city. But he could have done the same in Berlin.

With so many Jews leaving since 1933, he could probably have made even more money, through both volume and the profit on each transaction. The newspaper says that buyers in Berlin and elsewhere have been picking up wonderful apartments, properties, and companies from Jews who are in a hurry to get out of Germany. But there are thousands more who simply refuse to leave. And there are those who don't have enough money to do so, even if they wanted to. It's going to be especially hard to get them out.

She knocks at the study. No answer. Shifting the tray to one hand, Lili presses down the bronze handle and pushes open the door. Papa is not at his desk but on the chaise longue, lying on his back, partially covered with a light woolen shawl. His hands lie on his chest, the long fingers laced in repose. From this angle he looks younger than usual. His skin is smoother, the lines around his mouth more shallow. In sleep, his brow is less furrowed. In sleep, he looks both familiar and like a stranger. The tea grows cold as she watches him breathe.

Her gaze goes over his fingers, hands that smoothed her hair and soothed her fears for so many years. This is Papa, the same man who kissed her tears, telling her that she could be brave. And when she grew older, her problems bigger and more abstract than a bruised knee, it was this man, her Papa, who would tell her that every new day held in it the promise of light.

If this is what he truly believes then why did they leave Germany? She watches the rising and falling of his chest. His eyelids flutter. Of what does he dream? Surely his dreams are not hers. She wants to reach out and shake his shoulders wildly until he wakes up and tells her that all of them are going home, together. She wants to pick up his hand and kiss it, like when she was younger. But she is no longer so young and he no longer the man he once was.

She blinks, three times. She watches him inhale three more times.

"Papa," she whispers, just as she did on that night so long ago when she realized that one day she would lose him. "Papa." He does not wake. "Papa."

Without looking back, Lili slips out of the room.

♫ ♪ ♫

And now, at last, the day has come.

She stands against the railing of the S.S. Hamburg, looking down onto the pier where two and a half tiny figures wave white handkerchiefs into the wind, as if in final surrender to her wishes. Her chest tightens. For the first time in her life, she is leaving her family.

She has given Paulchen a last squeeze and tickle, has breathed in the sweet scent of his four-year old head. She has wrapped herself inside the slender arms of Mama, felt the love in her long, delicate embrace. And she has stood before Papa, looking into his eyes until he gathered her to him. A horrible lump then formed within her, moving upwards, swelling her throat, making it hard to breathe. As Papa held her close, her muscles seemed to give way and she sagged. Yet the shelter of his arms remained, until she had collected herself and, at last, pulled away.

Now, looking down upon the three of them, the pain sears her heart. Why is it that she is leaving them? The steamer horn sounds and for a wild moment she wants to tear away, down the metal stairs, across the gangplank and into their beloved midst again. How can she leave her family?

Far below in the crowd of those bidding farewell, Lili sees a movement of familiar colors. And as the unknown well-wisher moves an arm back and forth, she remembers, and draws strength from the waving flag with its red, white, and black.

The steamer horn sounds, its great bellowing knell blasting the hot sky.

FATHERLAND

PART THREE

On German Soil

All Things are Possible Now

Gulls careened shrieking above the wake as the ship cut into the pewter waters of the Elbe. For some time the wind still carried with it the tang of the open Atlantic. Gradually the breezes that blew across the deck were infused with the acid bite of the herring and eel catches of the fishing vessels the steamer passed on its way southeast through the flatlands of Holstein. Earthy smells began to waft through the air, sweet and ripe with summer growth. Nearer the city, fresh winds floated by bearing the yeasty aroma of bakeries and breweries, the fragrance of flower shops and tobacco and teas from around the world.

Lili leaned over the railing to watch their arrival in the thousand year-old port city of Hamburg. After five days at sea it was now only a matter of minutes before they would dock. She was giddy with excitement and a faint nausea. The Elbe, much broader and deeper than what she remembered of Berlin's Spree, afforded, from the vantage point of the ocean liner, an enormous panorama of harbor and metropolis. The skyline stretched out, a thick spread of brick and plasterwork structures with verdigris steeples poking up into the cloudless cerulean.

From her childhood visits here, she recognized the spire of Sankt Nikolai, once the world's tallest building. This time she would see little of Hamburg. There would be no sojourn with Tantes Frederike and Amelie, for the aunts and uncles were off holidaying together in the Alps. As soon as Lili disembarked, she would head to the train station. Tonight she would sleep in Alt Eichendorf, in the same carved oak bed she had known all her life.

As the steamer blew its horn for the first time on this side of the Atlantic, three long blasts, Lili's excitement grew. All around her, passengers waved and called out to those waiting on the rapidly nearing dockside. Underneath the shouts and laughter, a thumping sound grew louder and louder. Peering at the throng on the quay, Lili discovered a group of bearded seamen with brass instruments and an accordion pumping out the patriotic refrains of the century-old *Die Wacht am Rhein*, somewhat peculiar here along the Elbe. Next came *Lieb' Vaterland, magst ruhig sein*. Beloved fatherland. Her breath was jagged from a giddy happiness. The smells, the sounds, the sights—all were coming together now to form a setting that was both wondrously familiar and strange.

A loudspeaker urged passengers to collect their belongings before making their way toward the gangplank. It was the last shipboard announcement made in both languages and it was wonderful to think that from now on she would no longer hear English. Despite the slow progress on the deck toward the gangplank, her pulse was quick, her legs trembling. After all these days of keeping to herself on the ship, she was eager to discover what lay before her.

A vendor with a voice as deep as a foghorn called out from behind a white stand, offering "*Knackwurst mit'n Rundstück—heiß un' knackig!*" and Lili was sure that even from the deck she could smell the steam rising from the boiled sausages. Women in summer dresses stood out like bright blooms. Tow-headed boys and darling little girls with braids fidgeted about, impatiently awaiting their homecoming fathers or relatives visiting the Reich. And scattered everywhere were the children and young people clad in the colors of the Hitlerjugend, and earnest men in uniforms, the guardians of the Führer's vision. How proud all of them must be to wear those clothes that marked them as committed to the peace and prosperity of their great nation. The sight thrilled Lili, sending blood rushing through her veins in a surge that seemed as great as that forged by the vessel crossing the swells of the Atlantic. Yes, she was at last come home. In but minutes she would be standing on German land, even if it was only the worn cobblestones of the dockside. Yet already she loved the very stones, for they touched the earth beneath. She watched her compatriots. Nowhere else in the world did the swastika fly so very proudly, held in so many hands. Looking out upon them, it seemed to her that in the blurring field of flags all were waving to her, welcoming her home to the fatherland.

♫ ♪ ♫

It was already late morning as she arranged herself comfortably in the first class compartment. So far there were no other passengers. What a delicious feeling to await the departure of a train that was going somewhere she wanted to go. She could already feel the excitement of those first few moments when the wheels would begin to roll, silently, catching one by surprise, before being followed by the creaks and squeaks that signaled the official start of a journey. Leaning back against the velvet seat, she breathed in the smells of coal and steam and summer that poured in through the open window. She wiggled her toes. But the air was vibrating with unseen events and Lili jumped to her feet to poke her head out the window. The great glass dome of the Hamburger Hauptbahnhof bathed everything in milky daylight.

The station was alive with passengers and those who had bought platform tickets to be able to see the travelers off. Porters pushed through with carts piled high with suitcases of leather or cardboard, straw baskets and bundles. Toting rucksacks, girls with glowing cheeks and BDM neckerchiefs walked arm-in-arm with pleased-looking young men in light brown shirts. Lili could barely tear her gaze from them. There were businessmen too, hurrying along with well-worn briefcases, felt or straw brims shading their faces. Families on their way to farm holidays in the country or seaside bustled about, some smiling with anticipation, others frazzled with exasperation. Some of them must have been KdF travelers. One small group, two couples, two girls, a boy, seemed especially strained, their faces drawn as they stood close together. The children appeared reluctant to be going on their journey. Indeed, all of them in this group looked out of place in the bustle of the station, as if they belonged elsewhere. The boy was scowling. All at once his foot shot out and he kicked the nearest suitcase. His glowering gaze met Lili's before sliding past. Could they be Jews leaving Germany? Where were they going?

From up ahead one, two, three, four, five children ran by laughing; Lili smiled at the blonde heads, each smaller than the one preceding. Behind them was their mother, obviously pregnant again, certainly doing her part in building up the Reich.

At the kiosk further down the platform there were stacks of newspapers laid out neatly upon the racks. Lili was too far away to be able to read their headlines but the mere sight of the Führer's face looking out at her brought a rush of warmth. Soon she too would be able to do her own part for the Reich. In New York Papa had told her to stay away from the Nazis, but surely that would be impossible here. Soon she too would be one of those girls wearing a uniform and waving a flag; there was nothing Papa could do about that. She was in Germany now. All things were possible. At the thought of the contradiction between the impossible and the possible, she burst into giggles and stepped back from the window to regain her composure.

The station clock said 11.27. Five more minutes. Around noon she would make her way to the dining car to savor her first truly German meal in four years. What would they serve? A lovely venison roast and red cabbage with a hint of clove and a solid pat of good German butter? What about afternoon coffee? Would there be a piece of *Haselnußtorte* with Schlagsahne? Her mouth was already watering. Yet no matter what they served, today everything would taste delicious. While she ate, she would gaze out at the landscapes of her homeland and dream of good things to come. At this, she couldn't help but smile again.

Her glance met that of a young man in a group of three approaching the space on the platform opposite her window. Looking straight at her, blue eyes flashing, he returned the smile. She had to hold on to the check rail as she grew weak behind her knees and below her belly. It could not be the man of her dreams, the man in the magazine, and yet he appeared just like him. Taut black uniform, polished boots, dark cap. Her startled gaze swept over the other two and she saw that they were all like that; tall, blond, beautiful, yes, beautiful men moving with leonine assurance through the parting crowds on the platform. Lili looked back at the first SS officer and found his eyes still on her. Then he closed one in a quick, flirtatious wink before moving past, shoulders wide and back straight as a sword, leaving Lili with her insides flipping like a speared fish.

Caught in a Time Warp

Becker was waiting for her at the station in Posenwell. He and the '21 Daimler seemed in good enough shape although the patina had faded on both of them. The chauffeur was grinning from ear to ear and Lili could see that despite his renowned prodigious intake of apples for strength, he had lost a tooth in the years since she'd last seen him.

"Welcome back, *gnädiges* Fräulein." He bowed his gray head just as he would have to Mama.

Lili was so delighted with this figure from her childhood that it wasn't until much later that she realized there had been no Hitler greeting from him, nor from the other staff. By then she had noticed that Alt Eichendorf seemed caught in a time warp, as if the Kaiser still reigned or, at the very least, the Weimar Republic had not yet disappeared.

The countryside along the way to the estate was as she had remembered it, fields and forests snoozing under the summer sun. It was like dreaming while she was awake. As Becker turned onto the gravel driveway, Lili caught sight of her grandparents and almost leapt out of the car. Alt Eichendorf was inseparable from them; it was impossible to even imagine one without the other. Großmama Maximiliana and Großpapa Hugo, backs straight as if they were twenty years younger, were seated on wrought iron chairs upon the raised terrace that lay in front of the main building. They looked like proud relics of the Prussian aristocracy surveying their centuries-old domain. Why, Großpapa had been born the very year Otto von Bismarck became Chancellor of Prussia.

As the Daimler neared the terrrace, she remembered Papa telling her that there had been times when the Junkers felt Bismarck had betrayed his class. There was no doubt that he had unified the German states into the Second Reich, linking a sense of national identity and socialism for the masses. Then Papa had said that Hitler was taking Bismarck Realpolitik to new heights, but the question was whether there would be a Kaiser Wilhelm II. Lili hadn't understood what he meant, and pointed out that the old Kaiser was in Holland and what did he have to do with the Führer? Papa's smile was wry as he said that it had been the Kaiser who had dismissed Bismarck. It was only now that she understood what he had meant. A black mark for Papa.

She ran up the stone steps.

"Here she is at last, our Lili," said Großpapa Hugo. The intervening years had silvered his hair, softening his well-carved features. His embrace was as Lili remembered it, that of a man who had power but used it sparingly.

Time had not been as kind to Großmama Maximiliana. Although her face still showed the delicate beauty that had captivated Lili's grandfather so long ago, her gaze had changed. As if she were seeing a place where no one else could follow. She was frailer, too, fragile as the slender birds that rested at the edge of the nearby lake. Nevertheless, her grip was talon-like as she held on to Lili, peering at her.

"At last you look like a true von Eichendorf." There was satisfaction in her tone. "Except for your eyes. They must be your father's—gray as the sea, blue like the lake. Green like the river." Her laugh was an old woman's, high and raspy. "Do they turn murky like the swamp when you are angry?"

Lili glanced over at Großpapa Hugo, whose expression was mild as he looked down at his wife. His palm rested against her shoulder, the fingers moving back and forth, slowly, with tenderness.

"I don't think so, Großmama," Lili giggled. "Papa says my eyes look like ice floes when I get angry. But his are always clear," she added.

"Yes, it's a good man that Wilhelmine married," Großmama Maximiliana said, her voice trailing off. "Even-tempered and a looker too. A pity that he had to take her so far away." She peered at Lili. "What time did you say they are arriving today?"

Lili looked over at Großpapa Hugo. He was watching Lili now, a silent plea in his eyes.

"Ach, Großmama Maximiliana. Soon everything will be resolved and we will all be here together again." She smiled as she said it and willed her grandmother, and herself too, to believe it.

Later she took a short walk under the chestnut trees with Großpapa Hugo and an Alpaca elbony cane that he used only intermittently. She learned that Großmama Maximiliana was, as her grandfather put it, his voice breaking as he uttered the words, 'slowing down'. Then he had taken her hand in his own gentle giant's and Lili felt a quiver of the quiet strength that had always marked him.

So there were changes after all at Alt Eichendorf.

Still, nature kept to its old habits at the estate, garnishing the gardens with a rainbow of amaranth and freesia, hydrangea and yellow roses, coating the birch trunks with sheets of silver. On thousands of trees the leaves glistened green. The air was perfumed. Lili spent the week revisiting her favorite haunts: the animals in their paddocks, the lake where Mama and she had rowed to the fairy island, and, of course, the woods. Passing the linden trees, she thought of Papa. Each day of her stay she went deep into the forest of oaks and beeches, rowans and ash. There, walking amongst the ancient growths, she again sensed the presence of a primordial essence. It was not the god of any church but something much older.

One day she came upon a clearing and slipped off her shoes. The grass was peppered with tiny petals of white and blue, the ground pliant beneath her bare feet. The touch of the earth was astonishing, as if connecting her beyond the source where tree roots themselves took their nourishment for life. Birds trilled and warbled and cooed from the branches, squirrels scurried and leapt. Otherwise, she was alone. It was one of the strangest sensations she had ever known. There was no fear to be so far away from others but, instead, exhilaration. A thousand strings of Baroque notes wove through her inner ear yet none could match the simple call that rose up through her, as if she herself were the instrument, and the spirit of the ancients the player. Its force was such that she sprang forth, pushing her limbs through the air, skipping and swirling through the rays of light that shimmered in the clearing. She swayed with the new knowledge of sorrow among the shading trees. She leapt and bowed and twirled and danced because her feet were touching the hallowed ground.

First Dinner at the House on Kornmarkt

A week later she stepped from the train in Heidelberg. Tante Aletheia had sent a cablegram to Alt Eichendorf, letting Lili know that she would not be met at the station. Lili called for a porter and followed him to the taxi. The burly man asked neither whence she was coming, nor how long she had been away. Apparently he didn't notice anything different about her; she was just another German girl.

Heidelberg was a fraction of the size of Hamburg and Berlin and its Alstadt had only one main road, the aptly named Hauptstraße, straight and narrow yet wide enough for a tramline as well as automobiles and the blinkered horses drawing delivery wagons over its cobblestones. Finally the taxi rumbled past a solid and imposing church, passed by a large square and turned right. Immediately Lili's gaze was drawn to the sky, for hovering, no, looming in front of her was a giant, golden ray-crowned Madonna. Perspective was a curious thing. As the taxi drew closer, Lili's focus shifted to what lay behind the statue on its pedestal. Poking up from a forested slope, dwarfing the buildings of the square they had turned into, were the broken edges of a wide group of what looked like rose-tinted brick walls. That had to be the Heidelberger Schloß. Moments later, the taxi came to a stop in front of a building on the left side of the square.

With some hesitation Lili rang the doorbell. She looked up to the open windows where lace curtains hid the rooms. There was a slight stirring of fabric on the first story. Was it a faint breeze, or was someone watching?

Then the door opened and immediately she knew that this woman with eyes of intense green was Großtante Aletheia. Slightly taller than Lili, her silvery chignon made her appear even loftier. The scent of unknown flowers hovered as she ignored Lili's hand and instead pulled her into her arms.

"*Grüß Dich, mein Dirn*," she said, kissing Lili on both cheeks, and Lili's eyes widened with surprise at the provincial but sweet address. Then Großtante Aletheia stepped back to examine her, green-eyed gaze flickering over her face. A part of Lili was glad that her great-aunt hadn't come to the station. Großtante Aletheia looked as if she had fallen into a vat of paint; all her clothes were tinted or patterned in varying shades of green. Even her shoes.

"Come in, my child," she said. "You have had a long journey. Let's sit down and have some coffee."

As if on cue, a plump woman who appeared to be in her fifties stepped through the doorway.

"This is Frau Brinkmann," Großtante Aletheia said. "She has been with me for many years and takes good care of all of us here."

Frau Brinkmann grinned, wiping her hands on her apron. "*Wilkommen,* Fräulein." While the driver brought in Lili's trunk, Frau Brinkmann grabbed hold of her suitcase with arms that looked accustomed to heavy work.

The foyer was tiled with faded black and ivory stone. On one side, standing on a stone base and giving Lili a start, a sizeable statue of an almost entirely naked young man looked into the distance; perhaps it was a work Großtante Aletheia had inherited from her grandfather's excavations. Near the stairwell sat a potted orange tree replete with tiny fruits. From the adjacent wall a mottled mirror inside a large gilded frame doubled much of the foyer's scenery. Lili followed her great-aunt into the dining room. Its windowpanes looked as if they had been cut out of thick sheets of amber; the sun shining through bathed the room in honeyed light. Several colorful paintings hung on the walls. Despite her age, Großtante Aletheia moved gracefully from one side of the room to the other, pouring coffee from the silver pot, placing biscuits on a porcelain plate, then bending down to scoop up what Lili at first thought was a white pillow.

"Meet Fragonard. He is my constant companion, as dear to me these days as are few people on earth."

Lili reached out a hand, tentatively, but her great-aunt slid the furry creature onto her lap. Fragonard looked up at her with an expression she found impossible to read—his eyes too were green—then settled himself over the contours of her thighs. Within moments he was vibrating, and Lili couldn't help but stroke the cat purring on her lap.

Großtante Aletheia nodded. "You must tell me how your dear father and mother are. And of course there is the little brother now." She seated herself opposite Lili, spry and engaged. "Tell me everything."

"Certainly, Großtante Aletheia. But first, would you please explain why his name is Fragonard?"

"What does he look like to you?"

"A powder puff?"

Großtante Aletheia pursed her lips. Even though she must have been nearly seventy, they seemed to have a layer of lipstick. When she laughed, the wrinkles on her face moved upwards, smoothing out her cheeks. "An excellent comparison. He is Fragonard because when I got him he looked like a puffy white cloud, and of course Fragonard was such a brilliant painter of clouds. Apropos name, my dear. No need to call me Großtante. Tante will do." She passed the platter to Lili, who took a biscuit with a hazelnut sticking out of it. "Now tell me all about everything and especially about you."

Lili was surprised to realize how at ease she felt with this rather strange woman. Still, there was much she did not tell Tante Aletheia, especially about herself.

♫ ♪ ♫

After they had finished their coffee and chat, Frau Brinkmann took Lili two flights up to the second floor. Its walls a warm hue of gray blue, the room that was to be hers was large, with a good amount of light coming in from the two double windows that looked out upon the square called Kornmarkt. As soon as Frau Brinkmann had gone, Lili crossed the parquet and its worn carpet to stand before the window on the left. From here she had a fine view of Kornmarkt and the Reich flags that hung from many of the surrounding windows. She noticed that the statue of the Madonna and Child, which had now taken on more earthly dimensions, had stone water basins surrounding its lofty pedestal. The opposite side of the square was dominated by a large establishment, probably once a grand hotel that now looked somewhat tired around the edges. Some of the buildings had, next to the flags, boxes of geraniums that spilled out over the balconies, while others contented themselves with store signs between the ground and first floor. Behind those buildings to the left rose the wooded hills that must have led to the castle, which was not visible from this direction.

Lili walked over to the bed that was neither too soft nor too hard. Nearby stood two chairs covered with a worn fabric of petit point, a polished round table, and a further two chairs of glossy cherry wood. Lamps with tasseled shades, rather horrid, were placed on both a narrow writing desk and the nightstand. There were two small side tables that seemed to have come from the Orient for they were lacquered black and painted with chrysanthemums. The closets had been built into the wall itself and their doors were padded by silk the same gray blue as the wall except for the one which had a full-length mirror. There was also a recess that offered empty shelves. A border of white stucco ran all around the room under the ceiling from which hung a small crystal chandelier. On the side farthest from the window a paravent offered modest changing space. Lili peered behind it to discover a small door. Inside was a porcelain sink with taps for both hot and cold water, a toilet and the tiniest bathtub she had ever seen. She went back to the window and turned to survey her new domain. The only thing missing was a harpsichord.

Dinner would be served at 18.30. By the time Lili arrived in the dining room at 18.31 everyone was already seated around the large table, but as she stepped inside, washed and neat in a pale blue skirt and blouse of white cotton, chairs slid against the floor and all the men began to stand up.

"Heil Hitler!" said the first out of his chair. His palm flew up and Lili returned the salute, delighted to have before her someone so obviously enthusiastic.

He was followed by another boarder who, judging by his leaner and younger frame, should have been first on his feet. His thick dark eyebrows reminded Lili of the leading actor Karl Martell. For some moments he seemed frozen as he stared at Lili through eyes brown as a hazelnut. "Heil Hitler," he said, his voice hoarse.

The third rose as if in slow motion, his hand going up as if pulled by a string. Perhaps he was not well; his ash blond hair accentuated the shadows under eyes of watery blue.

It did not seem as if the fourth man could ever move quickly. In New York, Lili had become familiar with the Christmas season advertisements of the Coca Cola Company. This man, portly and rosy-cheeked, looked as if one day in the not too distant future he were destined to become Santa Claus himself.

They waited until Lili sat before reseating themselves, the dark-haired young man still looking at her. Aside from Tante Aletheia, there was only one other woman at the table. Her shoulders seemed to press in against each other and there were lines between her brows and on either side of her mouth, as if she had spent years crying. Although she must have been a good fifteen years older than Lili, her smile seemed that of a shy girl.

"Frau Dierck," said Tante Aletheia.

The meal was delicious yet wasted on Lili, who was so tired that she could barely recognize what she was chewing or follow who was saying what. It was not until shortly after dinner, when Tante Aletheia came to her room to say good night, that Lili learned more about the boarders. The plump one with the bristly hair and quick salute, Herr Poppe, was a civil servant in a government office in Heidelberg. The youngest, Herr Malter, who had kept glancing over at her throughout dinner, had only recently completed his studies at the university and was already working at the Kaiser Wilhelm Institut for Medical Research. Herr Tischborn was a representative of a wine firm and occasionally traveled to France and other regions of Germany. The would-be Santa Claus was Dr. Hempel, once a music professor, now a teacher of violin.

"What about Frau Dierck?" Lili asked, as Tante Aletheia turned to go.

"I will tell you about her some other time," were the last words Lili heard on her first day in Heidelberg.

Never Mind New York Now

In the morning, Lili began her explorations of the town, riding the tram up and down Hauptstraße a few times. There were a good number of *Konditoreis*, their displays tempting, and Lili made a note of the one that had the most enticing cakes. At one point a group of HJ boys marched by, flags hoisted. Through the open window of the tram she could hear their song praising the Führer. At the next stop she got off. That she was now on the same soil as he made her press her lips together to keep from grinning like a lunatic again.

Heidelberg boasted a variety of building styles, from medieval to Baroque and beyond, represented in the structures that lined Hauptstraße and its sidestreets. She liked the way that the designs of window frames changed with each upward story. Wooden signs hung from iron bars that jutted out from the shop fronts of half-timbered houses, and many of the roofs looked as if their russet tiles were about to slide into the street. How she had missed living in a land whose civilization spanned millenia. In New York the emphasis was on modernity, the destruction of all that was dated. Not that New York had much that was old. But never mind New York now. Thoughts of it brought those of Mama and Papa and Paul. She looked up at the flags hanging down from many a window ledge, pure white and brilliant red as poppies, their center seed the swastika, and pushed the thought of New York out of her mind.

She strolled through Marktplatz in front of Heidelberg's largest church, Heiliggeistkirche. It was market day and the air laden with the aromas of freshly cut flowers and smoky sausages. Wagons and booths of metal and wood stood parked in rows, the ruddy-cheeked vendors inside on platforms, calling out how tasty their wares. In the temporary alleys between, housewives with summer kerchiefs or neat natural curls clutched their string shopping bags, comparing quality and prices. Children jumped and skipped while even younger ones sat in their carriages plumped against pillows like fat little kings. Somewhere to one side of the square, an organ grinder was turning the crank on his music box.

Lili ambled along, buying a kilo of strawberries, and, unable to resist eating one right away, had to wipe off from her chin the juice that burst out with the first bite. At one of the many sausage booths, a vendor held out a sample, urging Lili to try the peppery slice that prickled her tongue. Further on there were ladybugs, bright red and spotted with black, and Lili nearly sighed with pleasure as the sweet almond of the marzipan insect settled onto her taste buds. But there was much more than just food to be had. She bypassed the useful kitchenware to choose a tiny wooden horse, its painted saddle exquisite in detail, for Paul, and an emerald green vase into which she could stuff a bouquet wild with flowers of every imaginable color for Tante Aletheia. Purchases in her arms, Lili headed back to the house to drop them off before going out again, this time to cross the teal gray water of the Neckar via the cobblestones of Altebrücke.

Once on the other side, she turned to see the town dwarfed by the red-hued half ruins of the Heidelberger Schloß that lay above it. She climbed the winding steps of the Schlangenweg toward the flat path of the Philosophenweg where Goethe and Hölderlin and other great German thinkers had strolled through erstwhile vineyards on their visits to Heidelberg. Perhaps later that afternoon, if she were not too tired, she would visit the castle. Today she was still a tourist. Tomorrow she was going to join the BDM.

Papa Plays His Part

"Where are you off to?" asked Tante Aletheia the next morning as Lili came down the stairwell, purse in hand. Dressed in a well-cut suit that would have been quietly elegant if it hadn't been in grass green, Tante Aletheia was watering the orange tree in the foyer. "The weather is perfect for a walk on the Philosophenweg."

Lili shook her head. "Another day. I have some errands I must attend to."

Tante Aletheia's left eyebrow rose. "Here two days and errands already? You are obviously a person with purpose."

She smiled, but her eyes were watchful and Lili wondered what exactly Papa and Mama had written in the letter that they had sent along with her. While at sea, Lili had been tempted to steam it open. All she had to do was hold it over the running hot water in the bathroom sink. It would have been easy, but she had held back.

"Ach, just a few small things. I'd like to go to a music shop. I need to find out about where I can find a harpsichord. I've never been without one and I don't want to fall behind in my practicing."

Tante Aletheia tapped her chin for a moment while regarding the orange tree. "Your parents agree. The best person to consult about that is Dr. Hempel as he has excellent contacts in the music world."

"I'll ask him at dinner," Lili said, already excited. "Is there anything you'd like me to bring back?"

"No, but thank you for asking." Tante Aletheia accompanied her to the door.

Lili waved goodbye then turned. She could feel the green eyes upon her all the way across Kornmarkt.

As if she had drunk too much coffee, her heartbeat seemed to accelerate with each step. It took fifteen minutes to find the right building.

"Heil Hitler," she said to the receiving clerk in the entrance hall. When she stated her intent his eyebrows rose a notch but he nodded briefly, gave her a form to fill in, and told her to sit in an adjoining room. Inside were mainly mothers with daughters years younger than she, whispering and giggling with each other. Lili examined her fingernails.

At last her name was called and she headed for the designated room. Rays of sun streamed through the open windows, lighting up the wooden desk and wall of filing cabinets. Like fairy dust, minute particles of paper floated gilt-edged in the air. Behind the desk, his head bent over a stack of documents, sat an official; his brown hair was thinning on a pale scalp. After a few moments he looked up at Lili.

"Heil Hitler."

Lili bent her right arm, lifting the palm into the air with grace and precision, as perfect as if she were a dancer in her debut performance. After all, this was the very first time in her life that she was addressing an official of the NSDAP.

"Lili von Rittersburg zu Mertz-Tärnekow," he said, glancing down again. "Hmm. Papers, please."

Opening her purse, Lili took out the document.

The man's eyes widened.

"What is that?"

"My passport."

"No need to get snippety with me, young lady." His tone was gruff. Grunting, he reached for it and began flipping through the pages.

Lili bit into the inside of her bottom lip. How frustrating it was to have received this American passport only days before her departure from New York. There was another document too, tucked into the safe in New York, that had her name below the printed words: Certificate of Naturalization, Derivative. Papa had begun his citizenship process already on his first trip to New York, just in case, while Mama's and hers had been processed only later, after that horrible 4th of July. Paul had of course always had American citizenship. Did this mean that he could never be German? The possibility of Lili herself being refused admittance into the BDM because she was American filled her with dread.

"M-my family moved to America when I was 13. They made me get this passport." The drumbeat in Lili's chest sprang into double time. "I didn't want it."

The official rose. "Wait here."

Nausea began to rise. She looked around the room. They had to let her join. She had been dreaming of this for years, could not have come all the way here, so close, only to be denied because Papa had insisted she become American. It wasn't fair to rob her of this. There was so much she wanted to do as a German, for the Führer, for Germany. So much she *had* to do.

What was taking the man so long? A potted plant stood on the windowsill. On the desk was a tray with two pencils sharpened to perfect points. A sheaf of papers lay neatly on one side of the stack of documents that seemed to be applications. Nearby, a beer bottle, empty. There was also a breadcrumb that seemed to grow larger the longer she stared at it. She raised her head. A framed picture of the Führer hung on the wall behind the desk. The Führer did not look pleased and Lili too did not feel like smiling.

The door opened. She swallowed. The first official was back with another, a slightly older man who gave off the strong scent of stale tobacco.

"Heil Hitler," he said, almost breezily.

"Heil Hitler." Lili willed her voice to steadiness.

The second official walked over to the desk, waited for the first to pick up the passport and hand it to him.

"So, young Fräulein," he said, speaking over the green booklet. "This is an interesting situation. One we haven't yet met here." His smile wrinkled the skin around his eyes, made him look like a nice man. Lili began to hope.

Yellow-tipped fingers turned the pages of her passport.

"I can read some English. It says here that you were born in Berlin, January 1st, 1920." He looked across at her. "A New Year's baby, eh?" he chuckled. The first official gave a faint snort that faded almost as soon as it had formed.

"Yes." Papa always said that while the rest of the world had been popping champagne corks and lighting fireworks to toast the advent of the 1920s, at home it was Lili's arrival they had celebrated.

"On the form you say you were born to Erwin and Wilhelmine von Rittersburg zu Mertz-Tärnekow." He closed his mouth, pursing his lips and nodding. "An aristocratic family of Prussia."

"My father was a naval officer in the Great War," Lili said with emphasis. Perhaps this would show that Papa had once done something for his country.

Yet the man merely tutted. "The Führer was deeply disappointed by Junker von Lossow in 1923..." Lili's breath caught.

"You said that your father took you to America in 1933." His eyes narrowed. "Shortly after the Führer became chancellor."

"Y-es." She could her blood pulsing louder and faster in her ears.

Both officials were staring at her now. It was going wrong here. They were looking at her as if they could see what was wrong with her family. With Papa. The second official's voice was neutral now.

"Kindly explain how that came about."

For a few moments, Lili had no idea what to say. How could she tell them that Papa had taken them away because he did not believe in the Führer? That he had turned his back on his country. What could she possibly say to convince them that she was not like her father? The eyes of the Führer were on her as she began to speak, faltering at first, then with growing conviction. Even so, in her inner ear her voice sounded alien.

Hours later, after having passed through other departments and undergone an examination (a test of ideological knowledge on which she scored 100%, the display of some marching steps—thank goodness for the German-American Cultural Club and Camp Siegfried—and the singing of a verse from the *Horst Wessel Lied*), Lili and several 10-year old girls from the outskirts of Heidelberg raised three fingers of their right hands.

"I promise in the Hitler Jugend to do my duty at all times in love and faithfulness to help the Führer—so help me God."

Then they sang together and Lili wondered if a heart could actually burst from relief and happiness.

Afterwards, she walked the Heidelberg streets with a new sense of ownership. In her purse was a new sense of identity. It no longer mattered that she had been teased for being one of the oldest girls ever to apply for membership in the BDM. In the end it hadn't even been bad, after all, that she had American citizenship; the officials had been rather pleased that an American wanted to join. It demonstrated that the ideals of the Reich held universal appeal. Besides, they informed her, legally she was still German because her parents had emigrated at different times. They told her it would make a good feature story for the newspapers, proving that blood, German blood to be precise, was thicker than anything. Lili had shaken her head, saying she didn't need to be in the news and, besides, it would be best to keep certain information quiet. The officials had to concede that she definitely had a point there and Lili felt an easing of anxiety. At least the story wouldn't go out into the world, where Papa might one day discover that she had confided that her father was helping the Führer in America.

Lili was stunned by her brazen lie, and, as she walked down side streets and along the Neckar, feelings of shame as well as pride at her ingenuity washed over her in equal measure. So she kept on going until the shame had been walked off.

Herr Poppe Pontificates

"Dr. Hempel has found a harpsichord for you," Tante Aletheia said, pouring wine into Lili's glass.

"Oh, that was quick." Lili looked over to the portly professor. She felt like smiling when she saw him.

As if he didn't want to be caught blushing, Dr. Hempel lowered his head for a moment.

"Our young Fräulein will soon be in possession of a Dolmetsch, " he told those around the dining table. Only Herr Malter's seat was still empty.

"A Dolmetsch!" Lili hadn't expected such a good make.

"I remembered that one of my old students from university days often complained about his grandfather's harpsichord being stored in his room. So I made a few inquiries and *voilà!* You are pleased to have a harpsichord, and he is relieved to have some more room. Everyone is happy."

"If only every situation in life were as easily solved," said Herr Tischborn, holding his glass up to the light to examine the wine, a Riesling he had brought from Trier.

"Indeed," agreed Herr Poppe. "Dr. Hempel has illustrated the point that order is the best way to efficiency." He nodded for emphasis and bit into his bread smeared thick with creamy cheese.

Tante Aletheia had told her that Herr Poppe had become a full-fledged member of the Party in 1934, adding, "He's a real 110-percenter." Lili had never heard the term and would have liked to ask Herr Poppe how this felt but of course that would never do. Instead, she would observe and learn from him. Just like Papa and Mama had told her to do. She smiled into her glass.

"*Ordnung muss sein*," he continued, addressing all of them. Lili thrilled at the familiar words. Großpapa Hugo often used this very phrase about the need for order. The thought that Herr Poppe, a member of the NSDAP, agreed with her Bismarck era grandfather was pleasing, for it underlined that all Germans respected order. It must be in their blood.

She would have liked to hear what else Herr Poppe had to say, but Tante Aletheia was asking Herr Tischborn about the wine.

Just as Herr Tischborn began to explain about the ancient Roman settlement at Trier, Herr Malter stepped into the room, his dark hair ruffled. He excused himself for his tardiness by explaining that he had just come from a re-run of a film at the cinema on Hauptstrasse.

"Have you seen it before?" he said, addressing Lili. "It's got that new actress Christina Söderbaum in it. I think she's going to be a big star."

"Yes," Lili replied with enthusiasm. "I loved her in *Onkel Bräsig* last year. Has she made any new films? I haven't been to the cinema in ages."

"Herr Malter," Herr Poppe spoke, setting down his glass as if he were putting a stamp on an important document. "Perhaps you should introduce the young Fräulein to our cinema in Heidelberg."

Now it was Lili's turn to look at her plate so that no one would notice the blush stealing up into her cheeks. Mama would certainly not have approved of Herr Poppe's suggestion. It was the kind of statement that could make both the object of the suggestion—in this case she, Lili, and the one being suggested to, Herr Malter—feel awkward. But Herr Malter did not look at all uncomfortable with the idea.

Please Don't Tell My Parents

At her first meeting she was introduced to the 39 girls of her BDM squad. She was the 40th because one girl had recently died of diptheria, leaving a space open. The members seemed welcoming enough, even if she could overhear some of them whispering the word 'American', just as she had once been labelled 'kraut'.

Meetings took place at rooms a few minutes' walk from Tante Aletheia's house. The atmosphere there was different from that at the German-American Cultural Club. Already on the very first day Lili could see that not all the girls were there only because of their commitment to the Führer and she felt a certain scorn for them; she had worked so hard and surmounted so many obstacles to be able to belong to the organization while those particular girls seemed to think it but a lark to have joined the BDM.

The squad leader was a sweet-faced girl of 16 who knew how to keep the others in line as they went through all their activities, songs, and exercises.

"You're very lucky," she announced to Lili after her third attendance, this time at the weekly political evening in which NSDAP ideologies were read out loud in turn.

"We can see that your enthusiasm is really strong. So although you've only recently joined, and have missed almost all our preparations for attending this great event, it's been decided that you get to go with us." As if waiting for a drum roll, she paused. "To this year's rally in Nuremberg."

♪♪♪

Later that week Tante Aletheia invited Lili to join her for a walk and now the two of them were strolling along the pathways of the lush terraces and woods around the Heidelberger Schloß. For a moment Lili had thought that Fragonard would be joining them, for Tante Aletheia had scooped him up just as they were leaving the house. But she had simply planted a kiss on his furry forehead.

Tante Aletheia was wearing a dress of silk chiffon that fluttered around her ankles in a shade of sea froth. The billowy sleeves were trimmed at the cuffs with what looked like a band of tiny shells. Lili wondered where Tante Aletheia got her clothes. Certainly there was no tailor in Heidelberg who could come up with such exotic creations. Perhaps they were leftovers from her days in Paris.

"Next month I'll take you to my house in France," she told Lili, who was craning her neck to look at the lacework of leaves overhead. "I suspect that you will appreciate it."

"Papa says that I visited you there when I was very young."

"That's true. You see, our connection already goes back quite far. Perhaps when you are there you will find yourself remembering things from the past."

"I don't know," Lili laughed. "I have so much to think about for the future."

"I'm glad that you now have the harpsichord on which to practice. You are obviously determined as well as talented." She smiled. "And you are also busy exploring Heidelberg," she added, her green eyes looking more deeply into Lili than was comfortable. "Have you decided about joining a high school in September, even if it is only until December? Or do you have other plans for now?"

Lili glanced over at a crumble of bricks covered with vines and purple blooms. The Heidelberger Schloß was nothing like the elegant palaces of Berlin. Closer up, she had been surprised to see the level of decay in the brick walls. Of course the castle was centuries old. Tante Aletheia said its oldest part dated back to eleven hundred something although new parts had been added over the years. No one in all those centuries had ever bothered to repair it in its entirety, always leaving portions at the mercy of the elements, man, and time. Lightning bolts and fires had brought their own brand of destruction. The Thirty Years War, the Nine Years' War, the tearing up of stone, wood, and iron for homes and palaces elsewhere had ravaged it even more. Yet still the Schloß stood, wearing its stains and wounds like medals of endurance. It made Lili think of German warriors. She spoke with a trace of defiance in her voice.

"I'll be making a short trip to Nuremberg in September."

"Ach, is that so?" Tante Aletheia murmured. "And will you be going by yourself?"

It was here. The moment that she had known would have to come. Yet surely Tante Aletheia was different from Papa. After all, she had a member of the NSDAP living in her house.

"No," Lili said, slowing her pace as well as her words. "I'm going with—" She broke off and halted, turning to Tante Aletheia. "Please don't tell my parents. They won't understand." She was pleading, whining; she heard it but could not help it.

Tante Aletheia's left eyebrow rose.

"I-I've joined the BDM. I'm going to the rally." There. It was out. She was putting herself at the mercy of an old woman.

"Mm, yes," Tante Aletheia said, resuming their walk. "I was waiting to see how long it would take you to tell me."

Stunned, Lili did not ask how she knew.

"You should be aware of this, Lili," she said a few minutes later, her tone conversational as they stepped along the pathway toward a ruined wall with only the lintel of an old door still discernible. Beyond was a tangle of foliage, leafy trees and bushes and creeping vines. It was obvious that here too it had been ages since the touch of human hands. Time had made a wilderness of what had once been a well-laid out garden. Lili bit her lip as she waited to hear what was coming.

"I am a believer in the freedom of thought," Tante Aletheia continued. "But this does not naturally follow into freedom of expression. Here one must consider the well-being of those around." She glanced over at Lili, her own expression mild. "Yet oftentimes one must be free to discover for one's self that not all doors need be opened. Some doors should be left closed even when the key is there. A peek through the keyhole, even with the key lying in it, is usually adequate." Suddenly her voice was infused with anger, surprising Lili.

"And never ever should anyone be forced to what lies on the other side of such a door."

Lili turned toward her great-aunt, but just as the ire had been sudden, she was again calm and for a moment Lili wondered if she had imagined the outburst. What in heaven had she meant by that last sentence?

"Look," Tante Aletheia said. "We have arrived." She moved over to one particular tree, a large, somewhat tired looking specimen with a deeply furrowed trunk and long leaves like flattened poppies fluttering chartreuse in the slight breeze.

"It's a gingko biloba," Tante Aletheia explained while Lili took in the stubby branches. "For nearly 150 years it has stood here in silent witness to the comings and going of the castle. Goethe himself plucked a leaf from it as an old man—well, a man near my age—to give to a young woman who shared his love of poetry, both German and from farther east. Marianne von Willemer. He wrote a poem to her about this very tree." Tante Aletheia reached out to run a bent finger over the ridged bark of the old tree and sighed. "I believe its days too are numbered."

"Do you know the poem?"

Tante Aletheia turned to her.

"That I do, for it is the reason I have brought you here." Tante Aletheia lifted her chin, finely-lined yet still well-formed, and as she spoke Goethe's words to Marianne von Willemer, Lili could imagine the years slipping off her great-aunt's shoulders so that she was once again the emerald-eyed young woman whom Onkel Wilhelm had married, so much younger than himself, because she was creative, bold, and filled with the sap of life.

"This leaf from a tree in the East,

Has been given to my garden.

It reveals a certain secret,

Which pleases me and thoughtful people."

When she had finished, Tante Aletheia closed her eyes for a few moments.

Lili frowned. That poem was why she had been brought to the tree?

"So, now we will go home," Tante Aletheia said. "Frau Brinkmann has made a cake with fresh raspberries. We shall have a feast and be pleased and thoughtful. And, for now, I will say nothing to your parents." Her gaze shimmered iridescent in the golden light. It reminded Lili of a snake she had once come upon in the woods, green and glistening, watching her. She had trusted the snake not to harm her.

They began to walk but at the last moment Lili bent to the ground, picking up a souvenir from the gingko biloba tree. Once back at the house, she ran up to her room and placed the already fading leaf between two pages of *Secrets of Goethe* before joining Tante Aletheia in the salon for berry cake with an absolutely shameful amount of whipped cream.

The Vast Multi-Limbed Creature With But One Mind

Banners of enormous length flowed crimson from the battlements, walls, and towers of the medieval trade center glowing gray in contrasting harmony. As Lili and the members of her squad marched toward the heart of the old town, it was as if they were moving through the illustration on the top of a Nuremberg Christmas Chest filled with holiday sweets, or through a Dürer print from one of the storybooks that Mama had read to her. Or perhaps she had traveled through time to another age. Never before had she seen any place as perfect as Nuremberg. It was almost like a fairy tale come true that she was even there, in the city that had once been, and was now again, a center of the German Renaissance.

Camp Siegfried was but a pale sketch compared to the vibrancy of what surrounded her.

Lining the streets and squares through which they passed were houses that looked as if they had been constructed of creamy nougat or gingerbread mortared with layers of marzipan and dark chocolate. Some had roofs that seemed like steps ascending into the cloudless sky— real *Führerwetter* today. Branches of pine had been festooned to walls and window frames while from countless sills the flags of the Reich were draped or hung off poles jutting out from under the windows. The very air was festive, joyous, filled with voices that rang with anticipation. Agile young *Pimpfs* and HJ boys were climbing high onto the iron railings outside second story windows to ensure a good view of the Führer who would pass by later in his open automobile. The boys looked healthy and happy. Lili wished Papa could have been there to see them, further proof that the youth were enthusiastic participants in the Reich. No one was forcing them to love the Führer.

"Over there," a squad member called out. "The SS are keeping everyone behind the barrier. Onwards!"

Lili followed her glance. While the SA men in their uniforms of milk chocolate brown were dispersed throughout the mass of people, the men in licorice black seemed to be concentrated around the edges of both sides of the street, standing about a meter apart from each other. Long bands of leather separated them from the growing throngs of men, women, and children. Despite their imposing posture, there was nothing threatening in this. They carried no weapons save for the ceremonial daggers hanging off their belts. Several people in the crowd were joking with the SS men, and several of these were smiling back. All of them looked so handsome, tall, strong, capable.

"The Führer is on his way!" someone shouted, and Lili felt as if her heart were tripping over itself.

"He's on his way to the Town Hall!"

"We'll push our way to the front," the squad leader ordered, and Lili was thrust forward with the others. Her embarrassment at forcing past those people already lined up quickly evaporated in the heady realization that if they did manage to get to the front of the crowd, there was a chance that she would have a completely uninterrupted view of the Führer.

"*Aua!* Watch it, girls—that's my foot!" a woman complained. Lili was close enough to overhear her neighbor's response: "If it weren't for that inflamed bunion of yours, we'd already be drinking coffee at home."

How could anyone choose coffee over a glimpse of the Führer? Lili craned her neck. So far there were no vehicles approaching. Several of the girls in her squad were getting closer to the edge and she was amazed at their audacity at pushing others aside. Didn't everyone want to fight to be at the front?

From her current position she could see that an automobile was just rounding the far corner, its headlights shooting forth brilliant reflections of sunlight. The squad leader renewed the pushing. There were more grumbles and a couple of shoves back but the throng parted at the force of the BDM girls and Lili felt a surge of pride and power. An SA man grinned at them, his face flushed and damp under his cap. The vehicle drew near and she peered to see if it was *him*. The crowd began to cheer and disappointment coursed through her. So very close as she was, it was still too far away for an unimpeded sight of him.

Then they were at the edge, spreading the front-liners into even tighter formation, or sending them backwards, just as the vehicle passed. All Lili saw was the backs of several uniforms.

She asked the girl next to her if that had been the Führer.

"No, silly. He's still on his way."

Now her heart was thrumming, her throat dry. A few more open automobiles filled with stern-faced party officials passed and Lili joined in the cheering but she was saving the full force of her voice for later. For a small eternity the street was empty. At last a single motorcycle appeared, its engine droning as it rode over the cobblestones. From the handlebar fluttered a flag as yellow as in the days of the Kaiser.

A strange sound thundered from far off, like water falling in a distant cascade, and for a moment Lili was confused. But as the next vehicle rounded the bend, she understood, for all around her the voices were swelling to a volume she had never before heard, and she too was swept up in the endless roaring. Her head was knocked hard by a hand shooting up from behind. But she did not care, as her own arm was rising, reaching out high and straight toward the open street, and she too was screaming, one mouth of a vast multi-limbed creature with but one mind.

"Sieg Heil! Sieg Heil!"

The automobile moved ever so slowly but this was perfect, for the longer it took, the longer she could draw in the wondrous sight of the Führer himself, coming closer and closer.

He stood with his left hand resting upon the windscreen. His right arm was raised, unwavering, in the very same salute as that of the ocean of people who adored him, and Lili thrilled to think that it was them he was saluting, no, blessing, for they, all of them and she too, were his hope for the future, the people to whom he was devoting his life and his dreams and his energy—the German Volk.

The automobile rolled ever closer to where Lili stood pressed in by bodies on three sides, their voices swelling in a crescendo of jubilation near deafening. For an instant she imagined a Caesar in Rome, an emperor with laurels, immobile upon his chariot. And in that moment she realized that it was true here, today, too, with this great leader who had taken it upon himself to unite his people in a new age of world peace.

Her eyes were burning and then brimming over and she squinted, ferocious, so that her vision would not be blurred. For a few moments, the tears streamed down. This was a day of her life that she must always remember. Like Dürer's etchings, she would engrave it upon her heart for ever more.

Now, at last, he was near enough so that she could begin to make out his features, gaze at the expression on the face she had so longed to behold. And perhaps, just perhaps, he would look at her.

Lili was astounded at what she saw, for her childhood memory of him had clouded with time. Despite having studied every possible photograph of the Führer these past years, she now realized that no camera had ever been able to adequately capture that which was his reality. Despite that he was a slim enough man, and that he was standing perfectly still in a moving vehicle, the Führer was larger than life. He wore a simple SA uniform of brown shirt, breeches, and black boots, and had no cap on, yet he was the embodiment of power.

"Heil!" she cried into the air. "Sieg Heil!"

Closer and closer he came, so that she could see clearly the contour of his dark hair against the skin of his face, the shadows of his eyebrows and the mustache that was his signature. There was a deep line etched into his forehead and she knew it must be there from the weight of his burdens. She could barely believe that now it was but meters that separated her from his actual person. Her view was perfect, the spacing of the SS men affording her an unbroken vista. Her breath was rapid, fueled by the rush of her heartbeat. The Führer's gaze was in the same direction as his outstretched arm and now, at last, Lili could look into his eyes.

They were burning. In them she saw a flame of intensity and will that seemed superhuman. Yes, he was beyond human! But in their depths there was something else, something else—what was it? Lili gasped. This great man who devoted himself to the good of his nation had in his gaze strength and purpose and resolve and yet there was sadness too. Or was it fatigue?

The automobile was almost upon them and Lili knew already that the Führer would not avert his gaze from whatever vision he was following to look at her alone. She knew but was not disappointed, no, not in the least. She was exhilarated. She had experienced the Führer in Nuremberg. Today was the best day of her life, so far.

The Voice For Which They Had Been Waiting

"I slept like the dead," one of the girls said the next morning over their breakfast of poppyseed-speckled rolls, butter, and steaming coffee.

The hostel was filled with the excited jabbering of those who had reserved their spots ages in advance. Lili was sleeping in the dead girl's bed. But the vast majority of the youth groups who had come to Nuremberg from all over the country were camping in a sea of tents outside the city.

A heavy-boned girl with stringy hair and an expression of continual amazement stopped her cup midway to her mouth.

"Slept? How could you have slept? I was awake all night."

"So was I," Lili confessed. "My mind was racing."

Another girl fixed Lili with a severe look.

"Yes, I can see that your mind was racing away. Your *Fahrtentuch* is on wrong."

Lili bent her head to look down at the proud symbol of her membership in the BDM, the black neckerchief which she had so recently first tied at her throat. "What's wrong with it? I tucked it under my shirt collar."

"Ach ja, you're new." The girl reached across the half-empty plates and tugged at the scarf. "Look. You've got it on upside down. The shiny side is supposed to be worn up."

Lili's lips tightened as she strained to examine the material under her nose. It was true. One side had slightly more sheen than the other. She was unsure whether she should take the whole thing off now to adjust it, or do so later in the privacy of the room upstairs. She was spared the decision when the squad leader arrived at their table, breathing fire.

"What are you doing sitting around here munching away? We need to get to the Zeppelinfeld." She flung a braid over her shoulder. "The Führer is going to start reviewing the HJ troops. Do you want to be a part of it or are you going to tell people you came all the way to Nuremberg to sit on your fat asses and eat *Schrippen*?"

Lili was out of her seat in an instant, stuffing the upside down black cloth back under the white as she and the others ran out of the hostel.

For the next few hours she reveled in the force and fervor of the tens of thousands attending the Labor Rally on the newly completed grounds of the Zeppelinfeld. The grandeur and the pageantry reminded her of the Führer's imperial passage yesterday, as if all of them had been flung back to some earlier time like Rome or Ancient Greece. Or perhaps even further back, to the legendary days of the Nordic gods themselves. Marching with those on the field—the youths of today, the adults of tomorrow—Lili imagined what it must look like from above, from higher than the rows of spectators or even from where the Führer himself was sitting upon the tribune. She, Lili von Rittersburg zu Mertz-Tärnekow, was just a speck on the enormous field, a single meaningless speck lost within the tens of thousands that marched upon German soil to honor him. As one individual she was nothing. What could she, one individual, do? Yet it was these very thousands of individuals, come together under the Führer's guidance, that were the strength and future of the Reich.

The days at the Nuremberg Rally were a collage as colorful as the ever-changing pieces of glass in a kaleidoscope. From the torchlight processions through the historic streets to an entrancing performance of *Die Meistersinger*, from a thousand dancing girls to displays of gymnastics, one spectacle flowed into another. After a while she could no longer remember the order. But it did not matter; all were visions of beauty and might, bedazzling and enflaming. The dreams and ideas she had nurtured in New York had not prepared her for the magnificent reality of what Germany had become. The faces of those around her were aglow with the splendor of it. And she was a part of it.

Only on the first day did she think about how Papa and Mama had ordered her not to be. But how could she not?

The Nuremberg rally of 1937 was the Rally of Labor. Lili watched as legions of 19-year old men doing their year of service in the *Arbeitsdienst* marched through the stadium, knapsacks on their backs, gleaming spades carried against their shoulders, goose-stepping as they passed in front of the Führer. They performed an expert military salute with their spades, demonstrating that all service to the nation was glorious and needed no weapons. Lili strained to see if she could spot Frau Brinkmann's son Willi among the thousands. But aside from that she had never met him, seen him only in a worn photograph Frau Brinkmann had shown her, it would have been near impossible. Their faces blurred in similitude, an endless stream of strength and endurance let loose by open floodgates, unstoppable. Lili would go home and report to Frau Brinkmann that she had indeed seen Willi, ten thousand times.

In his address, the Führer told the multitude that what they had just witnessed was the greatest demonstration of peace the world had ever seen.

"*Ein Volk, ein Reich, eine Gemeinschaft, eine Kraft.*"

And this one folk, one realm, one community, one power rose to its feet and how could Lili ever describe what it felt like to be among the cheering clapping 200,000 who were united in their faith and steadfast devotion to this simple man?

All too soon, the rally was over, and Lili on the train back to Heidelberg. She and the other seven girls in their compartment were subdued. What could they say that would bring forth again the energy they had absorbed, and radiated, these past days? It was perfectly clear to Lili why for so many of them this rally had not been the first and why they sighed, "Ach, I can't wait until next year." She had marched and sung and shouted and cheered and been among those moving like one giant, perfectly calibrated flag-bearing machine. Her life had taken on an intensity that made the sudden quiet excruciating. She had stood before the greatest men of the Reich. She had heard their voices from atop the tribune, under the shining sun of the gold-plated swastika. The Führer had spoken in words real and true, and his men—Göring, Goebbels, Hess, Ley, Streicher, Rosenberg, Frank, and Baldur von Schirach—all had stood there above her, in flesh and blood. She had heard their call and answered with a resounding yes.

Now, through the window of the compartment on the Heidelberg-bound train, the sky was as black as her neckerchief, no stars visible. Lili stared into the darkness, remembering one scene in particular.

It had been on Friday night and they were all outside, she and the tens of thousands of others sitting in the dark of the stadium, waiting for the Führer to address the political leaders. Then, in one long and astonishing swoop, they were delivered into a vast temple as pillars of light soared up straight from the ground, so high that the rays were lost in the heavens. For some moments it was enough simply to feel the magnitude of this temple of the Reich created by 150 floodlights pointed upwards. But there was more. Slowly coming into sight from the back, bathed in eerie luminescence, a procession moved forth. Scarlet banners hung on poles from whose countless spear tips the reflected light glinted. Mesmerized, all had watched this stately stream that looked like ghostly warriors from an epic past. When at last the men and banners arrived at the front, below the tribune, everyone rose to their feet with a reverence born of hope and faith and pride. Why, the entire Reich must have heard their voices as they joined in singing

Deutschland, Deutschland über Alles and the *Horst Wessel Lied*. The trumpets resounded with fanfare until, abruptly, the heralds stopped. For some moments yet the timbre of brass lingered on the air. Then it was silent, so silent, until at last they heard the voice for which they had been waiting. It was soft, calm, only gradually growing quicker and more urgent and louder and fiercer and soon the sparks of its message flew out through the darkness of the night as the word of the Führer ignited all of those who were there in that temple, and surely most of those who were not.

There Are Not Enough Plum Trees in the World

"You have certainly been working hard these past days," said Dr. Hempel, meeting Lili on the stairwell. Since returning from Nuremberg, she had spent most of her time at the harpsichord, the only way to channel the exhilaration that still swirled through her. "I wish at least one of my students were as committed as you."

Lili nodded. "I have to practice." She moved aside to give him enough room. "Experience has taught me that without a teacher I must be very strict with myself if I want to progress."

Neither the dimness of the stairwell nor the thick lenses of Dr. Hempel's horn rim glasses could hide the sympathetic light in his eyes.

"I don't know about a teacher, but perhaps there is something else to consider." He muttered a few words under his breath. "The last few years have seen a dearth of so many of our finest musicians and singers, gone from nearly one day to the next. To think that music itself should also bow to..." He shook his head then tipped his hat at her. "Let me think about it," he murmured. "Good day." And then he was past Lili.

How very odd.

She forgot about Dr. Hempel as soon as she entered the salon where Tante Aletheia was seated at the coffee table with a stranger. The man seemed to be a few years older than Papa, his forehead creased with vertical lines. Like Papa often did, he was running his thumb over his chin, but on him there was a real beard, streaked with gray. The two of them spoke in hushed tones. Lili gave a delicate cough.

Tante Aletheia looked up. For a moment her green eyes widened and then she smiled. Her companion rose from his chair.

"This is my nephew's daughter," Tante Aletheia announced.

"Ach, the young lady from America," he exclaimed, extending his hand. "I'm pleased to meet you at last."

The hold on her hand was the grip of someone with confidence. For a moment Lili was taken aback. This was the first time since coming to Heidelberg that she had been offered a hand to shake. Obviously this man was of the old school. She almost slid into a childlike curtsey. But those days were gone. There would be no more curtsies from her.

"Lili, this is Dr. Morsch," Tante Aletheia said. "For many years he has been one of Heidelberg's best doctors as well as being an old acquaintance of mine."

Dr. Morsch's smile was wry. "The sand is running through the hour glass on that."

Lili frowned. "Are you unwell, Tante Aletheia?"

Her great-aunt waved her palms in the air as if to brush away the very idea. "No, no, Lili. I'm fine. And I will be even better when we get to Friedberg next week. Dr. Morsch was passing through the neighborhood and stopped by for a glass of my world-renown plum brandy."

Lili glanced at the table where a bottle of Schnaps stood between two tiny glasses.

"Would you like to try some?" Tante Philomena asked. "Perhaps just a taste."

Dr. Morsch interrupted. "Your great-aunt was being modest. Her Schnaps is not only world-renown—it is perhaps the best plum brandy in the universe." He spoke as seriously as if he were delivering a medical diagnosis.

Laughing, Lili went to get a glass from a cabinet and joined them at the table. "Papa and Mama allow me to drink wine and champagne occasionally. Although I've never had Schnaps, I think it would be morally wrong of me to refuse a glass of the universe's best."

Dr. Morsch nodded, filling her glass only half full. "Indeed. Your great-aunt has managed to capture the essence of the humble plum and turn it into an elixir." He picked up his own glass and sniffed. "Perhaps in this very liquid resides the panacea for all woes."

Tante Aletheia rolled her eyes. "For that, there are not enough plum trees in the world."

"So we're going to France next week?" Lili asked once her throat had stopped burning.

"Yes," Tante Aletheia said, glancing at the wall opposite them. "I need to make sure Wilhelm's works are safe."

Dr. Morsch said nothing but poured them all another shot. This time he seemed to forget that Lili should have only half a glass.

Paintings Disappear and Mothers Think of Children

After dinner, Herr Malter approached Lili.

"Do you remember we spoke about the cinema? Tomorrow evening they're playing a film that you might enjoy. I thought we could go together." A muscle twitched in Herr Malter's cheek.

A sudden heat rose to her own. "That sounds like a good idea." It was only once she had gone to bed that she remembered that she would be in Friedberg by then.

But in the morning she had awoken with the now familiar tightening pain in her belly. It would be long hours before the cramping began to ease. The only way to get through it was to spend the day in bed with a hot water bottle.

Tante Aletheia had been concerned. "Should I call Dr. Morsch? Shall I stay here?"

"Thank you, no. I've had this several times already; it's only a matter of waiting. Please don't postpone your trip."

"Hmm," Tante Aletheia replied, looking skeptical. "Your color is the same as the cheese we had last night." At the thought of food, Lili's insides shuddered. If only the bleeding would begin. During the past few years she had learned that once it had, the nausea and cramping would disappear.

"I'll make sure that Frau Brinkmann looks in on you from time to time. A hot broth for lunch will do." She sat down on the bedside. "Sleep is the best, although, during my days, I often resorted to a healthy gulp of brandy as well." When Lili shook her head, Tante Aletheia reached out and slid her palm over Lili's forehead, her touch cool and dry. Comforting.

Lili closed her eyes.

"Sleep now," Tante Aletheia whispered. "You will see the woods at Friedberg another time."

And she would have to wait for another occasion to go out with Herr Malter.

♫ ♪ ♫

Feeling quite well again the next day, Lili wandered about the house, examining the various rooms. She was surprised that Tante Aletheia had taken with her several of the largest canvases, their departure leaving darker spaces on the wallpaper, and wondered if anything would be hung in their place. She liked the house. It was roomy and filled with light, and she was always coming upon some fascinating decorations in it. On a shelf in the salon was a small lamp that looked as if it had belonged to Aladdin, and because she was alone in the room, Lili rubbed its darkened surface. No genie appeared so she went to the foyer. Frau Brinkmann had left an ivory envelope for her on the table there. Later Lili would cut out the portion with the stamps for Frau Brinkmann's young nephew. It was the boy's mother who collected them now because apparently all little Fritz cared about these days was hiking, cycling, sports, and outings with the *Jungvolk*. Frau Brinkmann was quite proud of him.

"He's only a Pimpf but he knows how to take orders, and he's already showing leadership qualities," she had told Lili. "That boy will go far in the HJ."

As for Frau Brinkmann's son, Willi was still doing his labor service. After Nuremberg he had returned to working on Strecke 46, part of a new highway coming up between Fulda and Würzburg. It was several months since Frau Brinkmann had last seen him and it would still take a while because once he was out of the Arbeitsdienst he still had to complete his apprenticeship at a bakery. Apparently Willi was a terrible correspondent.

"A mother's heart," Frau Brinkmann would say as she kneaded dough or mopped or cleaned the windows, "is either over-flowing with love, or breaking."

Now Lili took the envelope with her to a sofa and opened it. Two creamy pages covered with lavender ink slid out and Lili bent to inhale the scent of her mother's touch. Mama thanked her for her recent news. (Lili had written to say that she would be going to Nuremberg but avoided giving the dates.) Mama hoped that Lili had made the most of her visit to such an historic town and she looked forward to having Lili tell her everything about it. Papa and Paul were well, even if Papa occasionally got tired. He was as busy as usual but enjoyed spending time with Paul who too was missing Lili terribly. He was asking for a puppy. Perhaps they would indeed get one as her allergy seemed to have finally disappeared. She was glad to hear that Lili was keeping up with her harpsichord practices. Had she begun classes at a school yet? She would need to keep busy until her return to New York in December. Mama was already counting the days. She enclosed a recent photograph of the three of them, and Lili studied their faces. Papa did look tired. Mama was beautiful as always. Paul looked as bright as she remembered him.

Sighing, Lili folded the letter to put in the desk drawer with the others. Then she got together the papers she had brought with her from New York, putting them into her satchel. It was time for the next step.

Dream No Small Dreams

The heart of the university lay around the area radiating out from Grabengasse and the Alte Aula. Lili ambled about, examining the sturdy buildings in which generations before her had studied and made life-changing discoveries. Robert Schumann had studied law there before turning full-time to music, and Joseph Goebbels with his PhD in literature had walked these same streets. One narrow house had been a student jail. In disuse since the war, the rooms had once imprisoned students for bouts of drunkenness or rowdiness. During their confinements they had nevertheless been allowed to attend classes; apparently nothing should get in the way of learning.

On her earlier walks, the streets around the university had seemed to be slumbering under the summer sun. Now, in September, the air stirred with excitement. The semester was beginning soon and students were afoot. She had seen a few groups setting out with flags and it made her a bit nervous but excited to think that one day she might actually be marching with them.

It was slightly disappointing that the Faculty of Law to which she was now headed lay quite a distance away from Grabengasse. There didn't seem to be the same bustling atmosphere in this greener area. The decision to study law had come to her only last night. Through it she would get the knowledge she needed, with information based on legal facts, to counter all of Papa's arguments.

The stocky receptionist greeted her with a hearty "Heil Hitler." She swept past him toward the Registration Office.

Within a few minutes she was seated before a man whose graying brows squeezed together as he stared down at her pristine BDM card and the high school transcripts from New York. Lips pursed, he listened to her request. If it hadn't been for the happy outcome of the BDM registration, she would have grown anxious. But she was an old hand now. All she had to do now was give the man—whose fingernails could have used the sharp end of a nail file—some time to realize that a grade A meant 1 and B meant 2 and she had several of those. Unfortunately she also had a few 3s. But surely the sciences weren't important for the study of law. Next she would answer his questions about her American passport and tell him how this was merely an irritating technicality, and then she would sign the forms that would turn her into a student of law at Heidelberg University. She had already perfected a new signature, looping the L with a flourish.

The man cleared his throat.

"Very interesting, Fräulein. The study of law is a noble pursuit." He paused. "The university is honored by the request that you, member of a respected family, a young woman with the initiative and motivation to enter the arena of German law, be admitted into the faculty."

Lili's chin rose just a fraction.

"However, I advise you to take this application no further."

Her eyes widened.

"You will only be disappointed."

"Is it the notes in Biology and Chemistry?" she breathed. "I know I can do better now." She swallowed. "If I'm permitted to enroll in the Faculty of Law." Her teeth bit down on the inside of her bottom lip.

The man brushed off her words. "Despite your evident enthusiasm, this is not the time to become a law student."

"With all due respect," she countered, her eyes flashing. "I have already told you that I am committed to advancing the laws that the Führer has judged best. I will take my studies seriously. I came all the way from America to devote myself to the Reich." Frustration was rising and she had to make an effort to stop her heels from clunking against the wooden floor.

The man examined her from under his immobile brows. "If you want to be a successful student at this university, try *Germanistik*. You may still find a seat there. Good day, Fräulein."

Lili found herself in the street with her transcripts before she realized that there had been no Hitler salute.

Her cheeks burning and her heart beating a protest, she crossed Friedrich-Ebert-Anlage. Surely there must be someone in the university administration with whom she could lodge a complaint. How dare that man thwart her plans! Yet by the time she arrived at the Alte Aula, her heels thwacking against the stone with every step, the frustration was spent. Perhaps it was for the best. Law was a complicated subject with a high degree of technical terminology. How much could she absorb by December when she had to return to New York? Perhaps the man had done her a favor. She would investigate the field of Germanistik. After all, she loved the German language. She could still prove Papa wrong in myriad ways.

Was it her determination, the intensity of her drive, or the look in her stormy blue eyes that got her into that examining room in the Germanistik Faculty? Was it her being American or was it simply that the moment was right?

"Dream no small dreams, for they have no power to move the hearts of men," she told the four university examiners sitting in a row, an ancient troll with white hair and three middle-aged men who looked more like grocers than professors but studied her with even greater deliberation than had the man at the Faculty of Law. As yet their expressions were neutral. It was her next quote that seemed to raise the stakes and stir them.

"'How can we know ourselves?' Goethe is said to have asked," she stated with careful elocution, her chin held high. "'Never by reflection, but only through action. Strive to do your duty', he said, 'and you shall know what is in you.'" She could feel her eyes burning.

"For years I have known that my duty is to serve the Führer. My every action will be undertaken with that purpose in mind."

The longings and disappointments of the past years now gave her strength, as did a strange need to have Goethe with her. Her voice was firm, her answers succinct, and not once did she bite her lip. She watched the faces of the examining professors and it seemed that even if some in the university's Faculty of Law were still weighing certain considerations, those in Germanistik had whole-heartedly embraced the evolution in Germany.

It's in the Blood

A few hours later, Lili raced upstairs. Tante Aletheia was sitting on a sofa in her bedroom with Fragonard at her side. Her face brightened as she looked up from her book.

"It's official," Lili called, waving the card before handing it to Tante Aletheia to examine, then sinking into the velvet armchair across from her. How good it was to be able to share the sense of accomplishment with someone from her family. It would have been lovely if Papa and Mama too could have been there to appreciate it. How surprised and proud they would have been to learn what Lili had managed to do, all on her own. Now she could easily forget the fiasco of the Juilliard Music School—how naive she had been then. Today, despite having only an American high school diploma, she had been accepted into Heidelberg University's Faculty of Germanistik. Undoubtedly her lifelong, if superficial, acquaintance with legends and sagas, and Goethe, had stood her in good stead. Surely Papa would have appreciated hearing her quote him.

Tante Aletheia handed back the student card.

"Congratulations," she said, moving her hand gently over Fragonard's fluff. "It is an honor to be a student at the university here. Let us hope your studies follow its true spirit..."

Lili glanced at her but Tante Aletheia was looking elsewhere.

"We must open a bottle of champagne tonight," she suddenly announced. "Becoming a student in Heidelberg deserves to be fêted in any age." She scratched Fragonard's forehead. "There hasn't been much to celebrate these past few years, has there?".

A shiver of pity moved Lili as she watched Tante Aletheia communicate with the cat. Although she had been a widow for so many years, she must still have felt the absence of Onkel Wilhelm.

"Thank you, Tante Aletheia," she said with warmth. "I'm certain that Mama and Papa would approve of my having a full glass, today of all days." She had, after all, proved both of them wrong about not being able to attend university in Germany. "And I'll have a glass for them too."

Tante Aletheia presided over the dinner table with not one but two bottles of Möet Chandon.

All the residents of the house were there, Fragonard curled up on a chair against the wall behind Tante Aletheia, and Frau Brinkmann was invited to raise a toast to Fräulein Lili. Herr Poppe made a small speech on the importance of Germanistik. It was punctuated with pauses, as if Herr Poppe were listening intently to his own words.

"German language, history, and culture are the backbone of the German Volk," he concluded, his bulky bottom half-rising from his seat as he leaned forward in a small bow directed toward Lili. He picked up his glass again. "You have made an excellent choice of studies."

The others echoed the toast. When Herr Malter added that the university was now even more attractive than it had been in the past, Lili understood what he meant and blushed. Herr Tischborn spoke up in his soft voice, congratulating Lili on seeking to expand her knowledge. He reminded her of the comedian Heinz Rühmann in one of his mousy roles.

Turning to Tante Aletheia, Herr Tischborn said, "Frau von Wohlitz, I must say that your choice of vintage is impeccable as usual."

Herr Poppe was swift to point to the bottles. "It is the year, good people, it is the year."

Tante Aletheia's lips pressed against each other in a tight smile.

Lili peered at a label. 1933.

Spurred on by their questions, Lili recounted how she had been interviewed by the rather intimidating panel of male professors—"Yes indeed," interjected Herr Poppe. "You must realize that the Führer prefers to see the women of Germany busy with the all-important work of raising families. Still, you are young enough for now…"—and how she would soon be receiving her NSDStB membership card for the National Socialist Students' Association.

At this, Herr Poppe raised his glass in yet another toast and Lili was again congratulated with a clinking of glasses and a healthy swallow of champagne. Frau Dierck looked sallow and nervous but managed to smile and tell Lili that she was a lucky girl. Tante Aletheia expressed the hope that Lili's studies would not interfere with her music.

"I don't intend to let them," Lili declared. "But if necessary, I'll simply sleep less. After all, the Führer himself barely sleeps." Quickly she added, "Not that I could ever compare myself to him."

"Indeed," Herr Poppe nodded. "But he inspires us."

Tante Aletheia called for Frau Brinkmann to bring in the *Knödel*, for today's dinner was hot. As they ate the raw potato dumplings with meat and sauce, Dr. Hempel and Lili began to talk about music. The professor pointed out that the number of his younger students had been dropping off, due to time commitments to their youth groups.

"Perhaps I should have made my specialty the trumpet or drum," he said, giving a lop-sided smile, and Lili wondered what he meant. She drank some more champagne.

Despite what must have been a joke, Dr. Hempel looked somewhat glum. It couldn't have been easy to make a living as a music teacher. Lili remembered Frau Kuhn, going from house to house, giving harpsichord lessons to students of all levels. While the harpsichord was one thing, the plectra providing a certain equality of sound, Lili certainly would have hated to hear the off-key whining and screeching of violins in the hands of beginners. As she sipped from her glass, she vowed never to be a music teacher.

"Is it too late for you to change?" she asked Dr. Hempel.

He looked a bit startled.

"Yes, Fräulein," he said, sounding resigned. "It seems that I will just have to keep fiddling until my last student marches off into the big beyond."

Lili was not sure what to say in response and in the ensuing pause her attention was pulled to the other end of the table.

Herr Poppe gave a hearty laugh that was shaking his jowls.

"But, Herr Tischborn, of course your Rhineland wines will be safe, at least for the next thousand years."

Lili looked around the table.

Tante Philomena had her face down, petting Fragonard who at some point had settled on her lap in a wispy cloud. Herr Malter was busy cutting a dumpling, a shock of dark hair hanging down over his forehead. He was not particularly good-looking, his head narrow and his teeth crooked, but still there was something attractively mischievous about him. Lili tilted her head, contemplating him. Herr Malter looked up over his plate, directly at her, his mouth forming a slanted smile.

Immediately the blood flowed into her cheeks and she glanced away, her gaze alighting on Frau Dierck. How quiet the woman was. She never had very much to say at all. Her hands lay on her lap but from the movement of her shoulders it looked as if the bony fingers were pulling at each other. It seemed that all Frau Dierck did every day was stay in her room and knit. How boring. Lili raised her glass and drank, glancing back at Herr Malter, but now he was talking about scientific things with Herr Poppe, who was nodding as if he too understood biology and chemistry.

"...it's in the blood..."

Lili couldn't help smiling. Here she was, drinking champagne—perhaps a bit too much—and sitting in Heidelberg, part of a group of adults who understood and felt Germany. So did she. Why, she had been in the presence of the Führer himself. She sat straighter in her seat. Next week she would go to another BDM meeting and begin classes at the university. She was already a part of it. A wave of wellbeing washed over her, prickling her blood, and Lili could scarcely believe her good fortune to be here, in the most wonderful, most heartfelt, dearest land in the world.

She hiccupped, loudly.

The Importance of Girls in Dirndls

The bells of Heiliggeistkirche were pealing as Lili turned into Steingasse on her way to Neckarstaden above the river; she would walk off the residue of last night's champagne, and her frustration. Thoughts of Papa's lack of understanding were worse in Heidelberg than in New York. To be faced daily with idyllic scenes that advertised participation in the pursuits of the Volk and family Gleichschaltung stung. Countless times a day she fretted about how misguided Papa was. And countless times a day the church bells sounded in the background.

She liked hearing them. Heiliggeistkirche in its nearly six centuries of existence had been both Catholic and Protestant. She passed it many times a day but hadn't been inside. There were better ways of honoring life—or a God—than sitting in a stuffy old church, whatever the denomination. After all, as Baldur von Schirach had said to all the youth groups in the land, "Whosoever serves Adolf Hitler, the Führer, serves Germany. And whosoever serves Germany, serves God."

Religious institutes might have been all very well for the older generation, but young people needed to focus on the good of the nation. Personal salvation, in whatever form that might take, was fine, but the greater good was, well, simply greater. Alone, the individual was nothing.

The chiming continued. Those very bells had been pealing for centuries, through the lifetimes of more generations of Germans than she could try to count. And now she was again a part of the continuum. It was as if all of them, German citizens past, present and future, were notes in an undying, harmonious composition that was the Reich.

Lili's step quickened and she even skipped a bit on the footpath, something she hadn't done in ever so long. She felt happier and lighter than she had in years. If she had any heavy thoughts, they were of Mama and Papa and Paul so far away. Had they too been here, they would have seen that the picture that Papa painted of a harsh and unjust Germany was not that of reality. Lili looked at the people promenading along Neckarstaden. In their faces she found yet another confirmation that she was right and Papa wrong.

Her pace slowed as she observed the family of four just ahead. Father and son, looking very pleased with themselves, seemed to take up most of the path in their potato-starched uniforms. Behind them were mother and daughter, braided and dressed in dirndls, picturesque and wholesome. Lili had never worn a dirndl but now she considered that such a traditional outfit might suit her very well. She would go shopping for one later in the week. After all, in many of those newspaper photos it was almost always the women and girls dressed in dirndls who were presenting the Führer with flowers.

And there—a young couple, hand in hand, with crazy grins pasted on their faces. They certainly looked pleased with the world. Or what about that old couple over there? Their pace was slow, both of them moving forward with canes, but they seemed at peace. Where was all the disagreement and social upheaval that Papa kept talking about?

A Different Duty

All around her the students were listening to the lecturer, taking notes. Lili too had begun the morning with her notebook open and pen poised. But it was difficult to write anything down because all her attention was spent on trying to understand what was being said. By the time she thought she might have grasped the meaning, the professor was already a few sentences further.

"If one attempts to envision these Kunstschaffen machen, darf man deshalb nicht willkürlich die early circumstances nach den heutigen Grenzen betrachten und weite Gebiete German culture... "

The metallic taste of blood seeped into her mouth. She had been biting down too hard on the meat beneath her lip. The professor was speaking too fast. How could she understand the meaning if she couldn't even understand the words?

By the time the class was over, Lili's mouth had tiny swellings where her teeth had pressed into the flesh. She put her books away.

"Hallo." A broadly smiling young woman came up to her. "You look new," she said. "I'm in my second semester but I had to change courses so I'm in this class."

Lili smiled back, causing some of the tension in her face to relax. "This is my first semester."

"Well, there aren't that many of us women here, so you do stand out. I'm Hildegard."

Lili nodded. "I'm Lili." She was unsure of what else to say, or if she could even utter a more complex thought. Her mind was still a jumble of terms she had never heard of and sentences that went on for minutes.

"Are you going to the Mensa for lunch? We could walk there and sit together," Hildegard offered. She radiated warmth.

Drawn in, Lili agreed and they set out. It was galvanizing to walk through the university with Hildegard, passing dozens of students along the way. Several cast appreciative eyes at the two of them and Lili was glad she had worn her new sweater, blue gray as her eyes. She began to relax. After all, it was only her first day. Did she expect to be an expert before even hearing the lectures? Surely she would soon become comfortable with the vocabulary and everything would slip into place. She took a deep breath as they passed into the sun-filled freshness of the late morning.

"How is it," Hildegard said as they stepped onto Grabengasse, "that von Eschenbach could be so clear on the virtue of fulfillment of duty, his ethical interpretation so poetically inspired, yet all the same von Strassburg chose to question his meaning?" She shrugged, "Perhaps there were other influences. Besides, it's of no real importance."

Lili glanced down. Apparently her knowledge of German stories and legends would not be adequate, neither in class, nor outside. Still, Hildegard didn't appear to require an immediate answer so Lili too gave a little shrug, and a smile that she hoped was wry enough to signify something meaningful. It seemed to be, for Hildegard began to talk with enthusiasm about a film she had recently seen.

As they left the Mensa after a lunch of *Hackbraten*, red cabbage, and potatoes, a large group of students bearing flags and banners passed them on the street. "Come with us!" they called out. "This is more important than going to classes!" One of them hoisted his flag higher before moving on. "Didn't you hear? Today's classes have been cancelled so that we can march!" and Hildegard and Lili were swept up with the others. It was Lili's first university march, and the suddenness of it made everything—the footfall, the singing, the streets, the faces of those they passed, and the scent of the overheating bodies all around her—pass by in a haze so that at the end it felt as if she had still marched only in a dream.

They came to a stop in the small square in front of Alte Brücke. Someone suggested they take their banners with them and go for a drink before breaking up. But Lili had a new piece to practice and texts to study, not to mention the need to absorb the new awareness of her inadequate abilities, so she told Hildegard to go ahead without her. For a few minutes the group remained, milling about on the uneven incline in front of the drawbridge.

One of the students pretended to scold Lili, saying she took her studies too seriously.

Hildegard nodded her braid-wrapped head.

"He's right, Lili. Whatever interest we might have in our subjects, it's really enough just to go to class. If we want to get ahead in our careers, our NSDStB activities are much more important than our studies."

"But Hildegard," the student interrupted. "I hear your career plans are already set. You're getting married next year, aren't you?"

"That's true. Then I begin the most important career of all for a German woman these days."

He grinned. "But you'll need someone capable of delivering those fat babies every nine months, right?"

Hildegard scowled at him; Lili could see it was in jest. Still, it was disconcerting to think that someone as knowledgeable in German literature as Hildegard appeared to be would give up her studies just so that she could have babies. Lili tried hard to imagine having to give up her music for that. Impossible. A chill passed through her. Thank goodness the Führer had given her a different duty.

The Virgin of the Tavern

"How is the student today?"

Lili looked up from the armchair in the salon where she was reading through a commentary to a poem for her class with Professor Dr. Hetzenrath, a squat man who always looked serious. Unlike her other professors, so far he hadn't said a word about the Führer or the Third Reich. He spoke only on old literature. It was hard work, especially as she had to keep looking up words in the dictionary. How was she going to understand the commentary when she could barely understand the poem? Her next task would be easier, to think of a list of German words that could be substituted for those of foreign derivation. In that class the professor, who took every opportunity to remind the students that he had been a part of the Putsch of '23, had given the example of 'restaurant'. To take it away from its current French origins, such a word should be called *Esshalle*, a place where proper Germans would be proud to dine.

Herr Malter was watching her where he stood in the doorway, his hair scruffy as usual. It was becoming a distinct pleasure to share a few moments, or minutes, with him.

"I have so much work…" she sighed.

First there were the cramming sessions that all first semester students now had to attend in case their schools had not brought them up to university standards. In some ways they really were helpful, but not in the way that she had expected. Today she was tired from the sports activities. It was something that all students absolutely had to do during their first three semesters: 150 crucial points worth of fitness exercises. Gymnastics, running, broadjumps, rounders, somersaults, jump rope, and marching, her favorite. She was getting quite fit, fitter than ever before. She had already been to one NSDStB political evening get-together. How different it was to be among university students rather than the girls who attended the Wednesday evening BDM meetings. The students had been louder and more boisterous than they were in class, and all of them looked older than Lili. For the entire evening she had not said a word, only watched and listened, hoping that no one would address her so that she would not shame herself, and them, through her ignorance.

Herr Malter nodded sagely from the doorway. "That's the punishment for every student—studying!" He chuckled. "But afterwards, the reward is an evening at a Heidelberger *Studentenkneipe*."

Lili smiled but kept quiet.

"What?" Herr Malter peered at her, his expression one of incredulity. "Don't tell me that you haven't been to one yet. When I was a first-semester student, I spent as much time in the tavern as in the classroom." He moved into the salon; the usual floorboard creaked. "Of course it's different for you girls. There aren't too many of you at university these days."

Lili nodded. "I heard that we make up only about 10% of the student body. It used to be 20%."

"Well then," said Herr Malter, "you are really very special indeed."

This made her blush and it was some moments before she could look him in the eye again. In the meantime, she focused on her book even though the words were swimming away.

"Fräulein Lili." Herr Malter slapped his palm against his temple. "I have suddenly been hit by a brilliant idea. Possibly one of the most creative thoughts yet in my illustrious three-month career as a scientist.

Why don't I act as your escort, seeing you safely there and back, on a visit to a famous Studentenkneipe of Heidelberg." He bent forward, fixing his face with a mock expression of gravity. "This is a serious cultural element you are lacking. One especially essential for a student of Germanistik."

Lili giggled. Why not? It would be something new and exciting, and he did have a point. She should examine all the traditions of her homeland. Now that she was a student, she was old enough to do such things, and going to a tavern was undoubtedly an important student tradition.

A few hours later they stood at Karlsplatz, the square just past Kornmarkt, directly below the Heidelberger Schloß. Herr Malter pointed up the street. "That tavern over there, Zum Sepp'l, has been around for over 300 years. The other one is a latecomer. Zum Roten Ochsen opened its doors only in 1703. I would suggest the latter. Their beer has more bite."

In a few steps they were downstairs inside the most amazing locale Lili had ever visited. Neither Coney Island (which she had endured once soon after their arrival in New York) nor the hall at Camp Siegfried could compare in volume. Filled to near bursting, the smoky hall held a few hundred customers, mainly students but also officials in uniform, who were drinking, eating, talking, shouting, laughing, singing, linking arms in good-natured swaying at the tables, and generally making the walls vibrate. The tavern could have been a life form in itself. Like its namesake, Zum Roten Ochsen seemed to be a red ox hoofing the earth, getting ready to burst up and thunder outwards.

"How does anyone hear anyone else?" Lili felt as if she were shouting at Herr Malter.

He understood her instantly.

"It's not so bad when you get used to it."

Truly, within minutes, the roaring had receded into the background. They were seated at one of the tables around which perhaps a dozen other people were already comfortably settled. All the students wore the insignia of the party.

"Hallo, Malter!" someone called over. "Heil Hitler!"

"Heil Hitler," he said, raising his palm. "How are things?"

"Good, good." The man glanced at Lili and slid his chair back to rise to his feet.

"Hallo, I'm Egon, an old friend of Benno's from his university days so long ago." Aha. Herr Malter's name was Benno.

"Meet Fräulein, no, Lili Freiin von Rittersburg zu Mertz-Tärnekow," Herr Malter said, and Egon lifted one eyebrow rakishly as he shot a quick look at his friend.

"An honor," he quipped, then kicked his heels and leaned over to kiss Lili's hand.

Lili couldn't keep back a giggle.

Herr Malter grinned. "The Fräulein is visiting a tavern for the very first time. She's just begun her first semester."

Egon leapt up.

"Then we must have a toast!" He grabbed a fork and then a large boot blown from glass, filled to the calf with beer, and rapped against the thick heel with the tines. "Hear ye, hear ye!" he addressed the others at the table. "We have with us this evening a virgin of the tavern!"

Lili could not believe her ears, but they were burning, for the blood was rushing out from her cheeks into the flanges. Everyone within hearing range pushed back their chairs and got to their somewhat unsteady feet and all of them lifted their glass boots to her.

"Heil Hitler!"

"*Prost*, young lady!"

"What's her name?"

"Freiin Lili," Egon announced. "Freiin Lili von and zu." For a moment Lili was shocked at this, the shortening of her name into something as frivolous as of and at.

"Prost, Freiin Lili von and zu. Welcome to the eternal tavern of the eternal student!" "*Semper apertus est tavernus!*"

Despite the waves of embarrassment washing through her, Lili was pleased that her schoolgirl Latin could still recognize this as a grammatically incorrect rhyme using the motto from the university seal 'Semper apertus'.

She certainly did have a lot to learn. And when someone pushed a small beer into her hand, and Lili found herself holding up the earthern *Krug* and grinning back at the people around her, and taking a taste of beer while everyone at the table clapped and cheered and Herr Malter put his hand on the back of her chair and from one of the walls the Führer was smiling down on all of them, well then, she decided that studying here had more to offer than she had anticipated.

Heated Words around the Campfire

Lili dropped her pile of twigs at the base of a silver birch whose branches still dripped with butter yellow leaves. It was unlikely that anyone would notice her here on the inner edge of the forest. Most of those girls sent out to gather firewood for the evening bonfires had stayed closer to the camp.

Earlier that day, after a train trip to Freiburg and then a long march, she and legions of BDM members had at last reached the Schauinsland in the Black Forest. Although the climb had not been steep, the view from the mountain here was so wide that even the Vosges, the darkness of their firs and pines smoldering through the blaze of autumn's palette, could be seen from the inclines of the valley. Perhaps Tante Aletheia's property in Friedberg was included in the vast view. It seemed that the

Rhine and its plain had torn apart what must once have been one great, unified forest.

Immediately upon arrival, dozens of tents had been pitched and the girls guffawed, imagining how they would slide and roll in their sleep on the sloping ground. Sports and games would take place tomorrow. For today the ordinary members were occupied organizing the cooking and washing up stations, the storing of gear. The *GD-Mädels*, specially trained in health services, had set up the first aid tents, complete with medical supplies, equipment, and log books. They oversaw the setting up of the latrines, where Lili had been busy with a shovel and already had the blisters to prove it. She had watched the girls, impressed by their efficiency, both in content and manner. Perhaps she could apply for such training once she was physically as strong as they.

Now, although her feet burned and her calves ached, she wanted to spend a few minutes by herself in the woods. She slipped in among the trees. After only a few meters, the sound changed, the tree line forming a natural barrier to the world beyond. Ginger and sepia-colored leaves rustled beneath her feet here and there. Elsewhere, the dark earth was soft and silent under the firs. The air was flavored with moss and nature's mulch and mushrooms and herbs. Despite the soreness in her legs, Lili felt she was right to have gone among the trees. The quiet was soothing.

She remembered a different forest far away. Papa, Mama, Paul, and she had driven upstate to view New York's first capital at Kingston. Lili had been sullen throughout the trip, saying she was interested in neither America nor its history. What did she care about a town that had spent only twenty years as a capital? Twenty years. What sort of a history could come from only twenty years? The Third Reich was going to last at least a thousand, further extending Germany's great past. Papa had smoothly ignored all her complaints, and Mama had been soothing, coaxing, promising that some sort of delight would assuredly manifest itself at some point along the way. They had sung folk songs, teaching

Paul, so that for moments at a time, Lili had been able to pretend that they were driving along the Havel or Elbe rather than the Hudson. She no longer remembered the town of Kingston. But the memory of their walk in the forest, just beyond St. Stephen's College with its chapel of gray stones, was still with her; perhaps it was simply because of the name, the same as that of the Catholic church in Posenwell. In the end, there had indeed been a delight when a family of wild turkeys, creatures of the New World, had scuttled gobbling across the path ahead of them.

She remembered that forest now as she moved through the Black Forest. These woods were of the Old World, a fairy tale forest long known for its wolves and witches. Of course she no longer believed in witches, but the legends ran deep. She decided to head back to where she had left the dried branches and twigs. For a moment she shivered under her jacket. Was she moving in the right direction? She halted, stood under the trees, felt the pulsing silence cut only by the explosive trill of a wren. The weathered trunks and branches pressed in on her. The shadows were deepening, turning the forest true black. Had she been paying too much attention to the past and not enough to the present? She bit her lip, hearing the breath pass through her nose. Surely this was the way she had come. There were no witches, nor wolves. The forest was no monster from a fairy tale, neither dangerous nor forbidding. It had never been. Lili shivered but managed to turn it into a little shake. She was a BDM girl. She could prove herself. After a few paces, she stopped again, leaned down and pushed her fingers into the moist earth, wiggling them just a bit. As she walked, she sniffed at them.

She came out of the forest to find Ursula, a girl from her squad in Heidelberg, walking by, twigs sticking out of the rucksack on her broad back.

"My goodness, it's the American Girl," she gushed. "Did you go visit your grandmother in the woods while the rest of us were gathering kindling?"

Lili couldn't help but roll her eyes. "Don't be daft. My share is just behind you."

Ursula clumped over to Lili and tickled her nose with the fuzz atop a stalk.

"I'm only joking." She puffed out her cheeks. As usual, her brown braids looked as if they had not been washed in at least a week.

"I know." Lili scratched her nose. "But I do wish you and the others would stop calling me American Girl."

"It's not meant badly," Ursula said lightly as she helped stuff Lili's twigs into her rucksack. They set out for the campsite.

"Tell me an American joke."

Lili frowned. "A joke? My memory is good, but not for jokes." And certainly not any American jokes. Their sense of humor was so different.

Ursula pouted.

"Then make one up. You're smart, you can do it."

Lili was silent. The rucksack thudded against her back, one twig poking her in the neck.

"Do you know what they call a *Frikadelle* in New York?" She was careful to give it the right name, for while in Berlin the name for a ground beef patty was *Boulette*, around Heidelberg it was called a Frikadelle.

Ursula cocked her head to one side and nearly lost her balance.

"A Frikadollar?"

Lili giggled. "That's really very good. I might even remember that one. But no, the answer is a hamburger."

Ursula looked puzzled.

"So what do they call someone from Hamburg?"

Lili gave an unlady-like sniff. "All Germans are called Kraut in America. At least by ignorant people. Obviously they think that all we eat is Sauerkraut." She looked out toward the hills in the distance.

"There were people in the school I went to who used to call me a Kraut, and worse."

"What did you say to them?"

"Not much. I just told them that they had a piece of food stuck between their teeth."

"What was the point of that?"

"Usually they'd put a hand to their mouth right away. By the time they realized that there was nothing, it was too late. I would simply smile. It's so stupid. New York is full of immigrants. Everybody in America is from somewhere else. But the name callers were mainly from Ireland or Italy or England. The really idiotic ones were those whose grandparents came from Germany."

"What did you tell them?"

Lili smiled, remembering. "That their leaving Germany had raised the intelligence level of both countries."

Ursula nodded then frowned. Lili could tell she was thinking that through. After a while Ursula asked, "Did that annoy them?"

"I hope so."

Again Ursula was silent.

"You study at the university, don't you?"

"Yes." This was the longest conversation Lili had ever had with any of the BDM girls.

"I wish I could go to university."

Lili was surprised.

"So why don't you?"

"Goodness," Ursula blurted out. "That's impossible. I finished school when I was 14. First I helped in a laundry but now I work at the store where my father works. He's hoping to buy the store soon. The owner isn't going to last long." She paused. "My father always agrees with the Führer about everything. So he doesn't think women need much education. Not that he ever did think they do." She ripped at a dirty fingernail. "But he'll be glad I'm so good at numbers when it's time for me to do the books—that is, if he ever lets me near them. Maybe even if he buys the store I'll still only be putting the cans up on the shelves, and mopping." Ursula flicked the nail into the air.

A bird warbled nearby. From afar came another sound.

"Listen," said Lili. "They're singing."

Ursula began to run.

"Hurry! We don't want to be late."

The song about carrying and building, *Wir Tragen und Bauen,* grew louder. Lili and Ursula raised their voices as they hastened to the great woodpile to add their gatherings to what held the promise of a massive bonfire. They assembled with the others clad in black shorts, white kneesocks, white shirts, sensible shoes. Some had added jackets, for it was a crisp fall day.

"Attention!"

On the camp parade grounds the corps of the obedient drew themselves up.

"Announcement!"

Hundreds of faces turned toward where the speaker with the megaphone stood.

"Tonight there will be a campfire discussion. No one will want to miss it."

There were, after all, a few games before dinner. Relays, jumping, gymnastics, ball throwing. How fit most of the girls looked. Surely all this exercise was good for their health. The amber rays of the late afternoon sun coated their skin with a sheen of gold. Lili surveyed the legions. If they were like those in the news films, then they were the shining vessels, the Nordic maidens from whom must soon pour forth the new generation, pure and of German blood.

♫ ♪ ♫

Later they lined up to receive their food.

"Mmm, a hot meal for dinner," Ursula murmured as the chunky liquid was ladled into the enamel bowls they held out. Lili and she each took a heavy piece of black bread and searched for space amongst the clusters of girls munching and chatting. For a while they threaded their way through until a group from another squad let them squeeze into their midst.

"Did you hear? A troop of HJ boys might be passing through the camp tonight."

Some of the girls began to giggle and fidget about. There were a few exaggerated sighs.

"I hope they get to sit with us around the fire."

"Do you remember that really cute boy we met in Nuremberg?"

"Oh, him! He was a darling. I loved the way his shorts were so tight in the back."

"Especially as that's all you ever saw of him, Gertrud."

More laughter.

Gertrud seemed to take it in stride, however, and turned toward the other girl. "In any case, they're right about you, Beate. BDM: Beate Desperate for Men." Gertrud stuck out her tongue.

Beate ignored her but glanced at another girl.

"Hey, Marlies," she called to a slender girl sitting on the fringe of the group. "If they come, maybe you'll finally find a real boyfriend!"

Marlies ran child-like fingers through a strand of flaxen hair. "I don't need a boyfriend."

Beate's nose wrinkled in scorn. "Are you still seeing that Jew?"

Marlies did not answer. Even in the waning light Lili could see her lips tighten.

"How can you go out with a Jew?" Beate burst out. "You're not allowed. You're an Aryan, you dumb cow."

"So what?" Marlies said. "I like Karl and he likes me. That's all that matters."

Beate's cheeks were flushed. Her words flew out like shrapnel, hot, fast, and in all directions. "Haven't you heard of the Nuremberg Laws? Haven't you read your Social Studies book? You have to keep your blood pure. It's not just yours. It belongs to Germany. The Jews aren't German. Your Jew boy might pretend to be, but he's not!" On and on she fired, and Lili was fascinated by her ferocity.

"Jews steal from Germans," Beate growled. "They stole all the best jobs from us, and our money. They even tried to steal our culture."

Marlies's arms were wrapped tight around her knees. The kneecaps looked shiny and pale, as if all the blood were being squeezed out of them.

"You stupid sow." White spittle gathered at the corners of Beate's mouth. "Maybe you're part Jew too, eh? *Saujud.*" Her voice was ugly and loud. Other girls began to look toward their group.

A girl with an upturned nose and slanted brows called over to Marlies.

"It's not just yourself you're dragging down by going with a Jew. You're doing it to all of us."

Several of the girls nodded. Their mouths were twisted so that it looked as if they had wrinkles, like bitter old women.

"*Uns alle!*" another girl called out, the 'a' of the 'all of us' guttural and harsh.

The swelling mass of voices reminded Lili of an opera, but she couldn't think of which one.

"What would the Führer say?" someone cried out.

One girl leapt up from the ground, her braids flying behind her.

"Jew lover!" she shouted, looking at Marlies.

Yet another sprang to her feet, taking up the call, pointing her finger at Marlies.

"Jew lover, Jew lover…" More voices joined in the rising chorus.

Lili rolled the words in her mouth, mild and mellow sounds that burst into brutality only when they were laced with venom.

Marlies sat motionless as Beate rushed at her, kicking her with the sensible shoe on her right foot. She shrieked once before rolling herself into a ball but didn't fight back. Beate, grimacing, kept kicking. Right, right, right. Lili stared. It looked as if it were happening in slow motion, the girl, the shoe, the huddled limbs. Even the queasiness that rose in her came slowly, and all she could do was swallow.

Suddenly a BDM squad leader stomped into the midst of the commotion. She scowled at Beate who stopped her footwork, and then turned to Marlies who was unfolding herself. Marlies was pale, the dazed expression in her eyes something Lili had never seen. The chattering of the other girls had risen. Lili couldn't hear what the squad leader was saying, but the sound was harsh. Beate, her arms folded, smirked as Marlies, head lowered now and hands curled into fists at her sides, left the group with the squad leader.

For a few moments the girls stood and watched. Then they sat down and resumed their dinner. Lili took up her bowl but it was no longer warm and she put it down.

Beate scoffed.

"Marlies better watch out. What she needs is a really good thrashing. Or maybe some cooling off time somewhere. She needs to be re-ed-u-ca-ted." She grinned, then spooned some stew.

Someone began to sing.

"*Erst wenn vom Messer...*"

"That's right," Beate said, making the gesture of slicing something with a knife. "The Aryan race has to be kept pure. Not polluted with stinking Jewish blood."

Then they were made busy again with chores. Dishes washed and stored, the girls gathered in an enormous circle around the now blazing bonfire. The sky was almost dark, great streaks of slate and mauve that swallowed the amber clouds. Stars emerged through the curtain of night. Lili breathed in slowly. No matter what discord there might be, nature was always a source of serenity. Surely Marlies too could take comfort in that, even if she had brought the discord onto herself.

There Can Be Nothing Weak or Soft About Them

The group leaders clapped their hands.

"Girls! It's time to begin the evening's program," barked the senior leader, her starched white blouse and tight bun lending her even greater authority. "We'll start off with some of our favorite songs." Silence reigned as from her pocket she pulled out a triangle and struck a small bar against it.

"Aaah." The multitude of voices tuned to the metal. The leader replaced the triangle and raised her arms. Half hidden behind her accordion, a girl sounded the opening phrase, her fingers skipping lightly along the keys.

"Girls of the Reich, take pride in your duty,

Find joy and happiness and beauty,

Sing loud while stirring the ladle,

Sing low while rocking the cradle,

La ra la la, la ra la la.

Girls of the Reich, the day will come,

When your husbands and sons will march off for honor, Your hearts will be strong and forever young,

For yours is the German Volk of purity and valor.

La ra la la, la la ra la la."

Some of the songs that followed Lili remembered from New York, but they had sounded different there, a longing contained in the confines of their city meeting place. Here the legion of voices rose into the sky. For a moment her heart thrilled yet again, secure in the knowledge that she was truly here in the fatherland. For a moment she saw again that strange look in Marlies' eye, but she blinked and it was gone.

"Now our respected squad leader is going to speak to us on the importance of motherhood in the Third Reich."

"Heil Hitler!"

"Young women of today, young mothers of tomorrow," she began. Despite her youth, the squad leader carried herself with an assurance that seemed to have been decades in the making. What poise she had. Lili bit her lip. If she had not left Germany perhaps by now it would be she addressing the BDM girls. The faces around her were aglow. Marlies was nowhere to be seen.

"All of you are here at this wonderful camp because you've shown you are true daughters of the Reich. Each and every one of you is ready to do whatever she can and must for the Führer, and for the Volk." The squad leader paused, letting her gaze sweep over them.

"There's nothing nobler for a woman than to devote her life to the good of our nation. A nation is its people and you, its young women, are those who will carry the glory of the fatherland in your wombs."

A ripple of excitement passed along the co-centric rows around the flames. The glory in their wombs would come from boys, as yet unknown men, who would press them close and part their legs to give them the gift of life. For most of the girls, this must surely have been an as yet mysterious rite, enough to make them shiver in delicious if somewhat nervous anticipation. Lili was sure that for her it would be years in the future, but for many of the girls around her, it could be quite soon.

"Most of you have already left school. Others still have a year or two to go. Some of you insist on going to university." At this the squad leader rolled her eyes, as if the mere thought of this were nothing if not silly and superfluous. Lili bit her lip and shifted her bottom on the ground. There must have been other girls here who were students. She wondered if they had reconciled themselves to being singled out like this.

"For the rest of you, by now you've learned enough to enable you to be good citizens, wives, and mothers. Remember! The strength of the fatherland is its willingness to follow our Führer. Heil Hitler!"

After the speech, the girls divided into small groups around individual fires. Lili and Ursula were assigned one on the far side. As they walked, they could hear the groups already beginning their lectures. One leader gave her girls instructions on how to make potato pancakes and dumplings in the regional manner. Elsewhere someone spoke on German minorities scattered about Europe and how the pull of blood would surely bring them home some day.

Lili and Ursula found places around the fire. The girl in charge stressed the importance of clean housekeeping and the plumping up of feather beds as a way of pleasing husbands. Lili grinned, imagining what Lotte would have had to say about that. She shivered. Now that the sun was gone, the air was chilly. Tomorrow they were going to have a workshop on qualities of obedience and community responsibility. Lili focused her attention on a recipe for window washing soap, then found herself drifting off, the lines from a poem floating through her mind. Even if she didn't quite understand everything yet, the personality of the German landscape in the poem was enchanting.

The leader asked if there were any questions.

Startled into awareness, Lili voiced the first thought that came to her.

"Yes. I don't remember who wrote this. Can someone tell me? Listen." The words flowed. She was filled with a sense of amazement—not only that she could recite the poem, but that she was actually doing so here in front of these girls who were watching her with their own wide-eyed amazement. Perhaps, without even knowing it, she too had gained enough confidence to aspire to qualities of leadership.

"On the pale shore of the sea
Lonely and with troubled thoughts I sat,
The sun sank lower—"
She came to an abrupt stop.

"That's all I can remember for now. I'd really like to know who wrote it." She paused, tilting her head just like Mama. "It might have been Heine." Lili looked around at them then, at the circle of eyes staring at her. For goodness sake. Her rendition hadn't been that wonderful.

For a few moments more the silence weighed, and then the leader began to sputter.

"What do you think you're doing, quoting Heine's words to us?" Perhaps it was only a shadow from the flickering flames but it looked as if a vein were bulging on her forehead.

Lili frowned. Professor Doktor Hetzenrath had read them that poem in class. So it couldn't have been Heine.

"Don't you know that Heine's works are banned? He was a Jew!"

Lili swallowed. "He wrote *Die Lorelei.*"

"Watch yourself, young miss." The words sounded strange, coming from the leader who was still in braids.

Lili tugged at her own braid. "I'm not even sure if Heine wrote it. Perhaps it was Goethe."

The girls in the circle shifted their positions, as if trying to move away. Lili heard the word '*Amerikanerin*'.

The group leader glowered. "You really are an arrogant girl. Trying to impress us with your intellectualism. Who do you think you are?"

By now, the metronome of Lili's heartbeat must have been at 110. Everyone was staring at her. Even Ursula looked more astounded than usual. Lili knew that if she appeared guilty, she would lose her strength. Like Marlies. She didn't want to be like Marlies.

She turned her gaze to the leader and forced herself not to break it.

"For goodness sake," she said, her tone as even as she could make it. "I just wanted to know who wrote the poem because I don't remember the rest of it." She lifted her chin. "I didn't even know Heine was a Jew." The lie came out smooth.

"Hrmmph." The leader peered at her. "All right. I'll take you at your word. But forget that poem. We don't need any fancy words. There are beautiful songs about the Führer that fill our hearts with joy." As if to make her point, she began to sing in a thin voice, and the others immediately joined in, their voices weaving together, wrapping the air tighter and tighter.

"We, the youth, stride filled with faith, our faces toward the sun, Germany, you must stand illuminated, even if ever we're done."

By the time the gathering was over, Lili's heartbeat had calmed. Two of the girls cast faint smiles at her. The fires were put out and everyone moved toward their tents by the light of lanterns that some girls swung in dangerous arcs before being scolded. Higher up, stars mottled the black sky. Lili was sharing a tent with Ursula and four others. They lay down. Tomorrow morning's tent inspection would come soon enough and they knew the importance of rest for healthy bodies. Still, the others were in the mood to continue chattering.

"I wish the HJ boys had come. Then we wouldn't have had to listen to Lili's stupid poem. We could've been visiting with them."

Lili chewed on her inner lip. She wouldn't make such a mistake again.

"They probably didn't get back from their march in time to make it here."

"I heard they had to go somewhere to do some training with airplanes."

"Oh, my cousin did that during his last HJ training drill. It's a lot of work. Aside from pretend battles, they have to remember all sorts of things about the airplanes and engines."

"I wish I could've remembered my times tables when I was in school. Then the teacher wouldn't always have hit me with the ruler!"

Laughter.

"Ready for a joke?" Without waiting for an answer, the disembodied voice began. "A German, an Englishman and a Jew go into a pigpen to see who can stand it the longest. Guess who comes out last?"

Lili waited for the punch line, but there was no answer. Instead, the girls' breathing began to sound and the tent filled with the faint flavor of stew and apples.

The night air was cold. Lili arranged herself under the blanket but her teeth began a soft percussion against each other and she bit down to still the trembling. She needed to toughen up, on so many levels. Closing her eyes, she thought of the Führer and how strong he was to lead a country. He wanted strong followers too.

"What I want is a youth that is violent, dominating, fearless, and cruel. The young must be all of this. They must endure pain. There can be nothing weak or soft about them."

The Führer had said this.

No, there should be nothing soft about the youth of Germany. And she too was a youth of the Reich. She should make a true start to toughening up. She threw off the comfort of the cover until, ashamed, she could bear the cold no more and returned to the refuge of the blanket.

Kaffeklatsch

Like mad weeping, the rain streamed down the windows, blurring the glass, but inside the house at Kornmarkt the mood was cozy and calm. It was Sunday. Usually at this time Lili would have joined the others in the salon. Now that the weather was turning colder, the fireplace would be lit. Sunday afternoon was a favorite time to enjoy the flickering flames. Herr Poppe could be found with a copy of the *Völkischer Beobachter* in front of him, his terraced chin nodding in agreement with every turning page. When finished, he would give a satisfied sigh and leave the newspaper on a table for another resident to pick up. At some point in the day it would disappear. Herr Tischborn seemed to enjoy the humor in *Kladderadatsch*, a magazine that always had a cartoon on its cover. As he read, his pale forehead would bunch up until suddenly a breathy laugh, thin-bodied as Herr Tischborn himself, wheezed out. Tante Aletheia and Dr. Hempel preferred novels and Herr Malter always had a scientific journal somewhere in reach, although more often than not, he was not there on Sunday afternoon. Lili's reading was for her class with Professor Doktor Hetzenrath. It took a long time to get through the course material, and, as she read, she grew increasingly distrustful of her interpretations. Too often she would go to class thinking that this time she had grasped the meaning, only to find that she had merely skimmed the surface.

As for Frau Dierck, when she did join them, she simply knitted invisible wool and looked into the flames.

For a space of time, the silence in the room would be broken only by the crackling in the fireplace, the rustling of paper, an occasional chuckle or throat-clearing. It was peaceful in the salon on Sundays. It was so peaceable and quiet that Lili couldn't understand why Tante Aletheia chose to welcome such strangers in her home. Perhaps if they had been artists or actors it would have been intriguing or at least interesting. But they were—ordinary. Nice but dull. Only Herr Malter was not that ordinary.

Today Tante Aletheia had come to Lili's room after lunch to invite her to join her later. As usual she was in green. "I have some cakes from your favorite Konditorei, and we'll have a nice pot of coffee too." Lili's mouth began to water at the thought of the hazelnut cake from Schafheutle. It was true that she had already sampled enough from the various Konditoreien to qualify as some sort of Heidelberger pastry expert.

This afternoon Tante Aletheia had made sure that there would be enough pastries even for Lili's seemingly insatiable sweet tooth. Her taste buds stood on alert at the sight of the table laid out with slices of hazelnut and rum butter cream cakes as well as a whole one with unseen layers of marzipan and apricot jam lying in wait under the chocolate glaze. As if these weren't enough, a host of tiny tarts laden with berries and creams and nuts dotted a crystal plate. Off to one side stood a large bowl of Schlagsahne.

"Tante Aletheia! Is it a special day or are you trying to bribe me? If so, I will do anything."

"In any case, my dear, I'm sure you will do it justice." Tante Aletheia's eyes flickered with amusement.

As if setting out on an arduous task, Lili took a deep breath. "I shall do my best." For some time, they ate and chatted companionably. Lili spoke about the activities in the recent BDM *Heimatabend*.

"They certainly keep you busy," Tante Aletheia murmured.

"Yes," Lili agreed. "From the moment we arrive, it's a whirlwind. Arts and crafts, singing, and—" she made a face, "sewing, which I hate. Then of course we continue to learn about the Führer and his top officials." She slid a chocolate-covered almond horn onto her plate. "We sing all the verses of all the important songs and memorize the dates and reasons for all the important party holidays, and of course all the names of all the martyrs of the HJ and party itself. We study the map of the Reich and the details of the Versailles Treaty and—"

Tante Aletheia interrupted.

"Are not those matters you have been, emm, studying already for years?"

"Ye-es, that's true. I do know most of the material. From the German-American Cultural Club."

Tante Aletheia said nothing. Fragonard stared straight ahead.

"So you could probably tell those BDM leaders themselves a thing or two."

"Well, quite honestly, if I could, I would try out for a leadership position. I'm the right age, after all." She nibbled at the chocolate *Mandelhörnchen*, crunchy and chewy at the same time. "We seem to cover the same material quite a lot. I suppose there are girls who find it difficult to remember everything the first time they hear it."

"Perhaps," Tante Aletheia said, her voice mild although her green eyes were flashing across the rim of her cup, "the very point of it is that you hear it over and over. In most schools, rote learning has always been a favored method of teaching—no need to think." Now she seemed to be talking into her coffee. "Which is why Rudolf Steiner is so out of favor…"

Lili didn't know who Herr Steiner was so she said, "I suppose you're right. Even good will isn't always enough to make up for a lack of intelligence."

Tante Aletheia looked up sharply. "In what way do you mean, Lili?"

Lili shrugged her shoulders.

"Some of the girls seem a Pfennig short of a Reichsmark. I mean, they're very committed and full of enthusiasm but," she went on, feeling as she were about to say something disloyal, "in many cases it would be hard to have a conversation outside the meetings." She picked up her cup. "I suppose they don't understand how important my music is to me."

Tante Aletheia took a deep breath and busied herself spooning some cream onto Fragonard's saucer.

"It's different with the students at the Uni." Lili swallowed some coffee, strong and hot, and put the cup down, feeling a great lump rising inside her throat.

"I have the opposite problem there." Suddenly the tears welled up. "I have so much trouble understanding them in class." There. She had admitted out loud that she didn't have the ability, or the intelligence, neither to speak nor to understand the level of German used in university circles. She began to cry, bowing her head. Something wet splashed onto the top of her hand. She hoped it wasn't from her nose.

Tante Aletheia rose and came to her side. She wrapped an arm around Lili.

"My dear child."

For a moment Lili fought, but the concern from her great-aunt was too heartfelt, and she gave in and sobbed onto the green shoulder.

"All those years I wanted to come home but I had to wait and study in English. Now I don't have a good enough grasp of my own language to do what I need." She gulped. "What I want to do." She sobbed again. "I can't talk or understand enough." She buried her face in her hands. "The only language I really understand is music."

"Ach, *Kindchen*," Tante Aletheia said, smoothing Lili's shoulder, her touch soft. For a while she said nothing further.

With a last sniff, Lili raised her head. "I'm different from both the BDM girls and the university girls." Her voice was flat. "I've lived in America too long."

"Darling Lili." Tante Aletheia said, her green gaze clear. "You *are* different from most of them. This is a fact that cannot be changed. First of all, consider your heritage. You come from a family whose name can be traced to the 13th century. I imagine that some of those girls don't even know who their fathers are."

It was rather shocking to hear someone Tante Aletheia's age speaking like that.

She continued, her tone matter-of-fact.

"Many, but not all, of the BDM girls with whom you come into contact here must be the daughters of shopkeepers, craftsmen, clerks. Factory workers. For those girls, education comes in terms of learning a trade, not in academics or the arts."

Lili remembered what Ursula had said about her father. Then, too, even in the German-American Cultural Club she had felt the difference in interests. In four years there had not been one occasion in which she had come across any of the members outside the club. Not once at the ballet, opera or museum. Not once in a restaurant. Aside from Friedrich, not even in Central Park.

"About the Uni students, however," said Tante Aletheia. "Yes. You will have to accept the fact that, at least for now, your German is not at the level adequate for academic purposes. Your entire high school education has been in English. You have not learned to write essays and research papers in your mother tongue. University level German is much higher than what we use in everyday speech."

She must have noted Lili's dismay at having the truth corroborated, for she did not pause.

"You have other strengths, my dear. First of all, as you said, your music. Through it you have a complicated and sophisticated form of communication which nonetheless speaks to the universal." Fragonard jumped up on her lap and Tante Aletheia began automatically to smooth his fur, with rather more vehemence than usual. "You have a strong sense of discipline and commitment which displays a certain maturity. Then too, and not to be underestimated, is your sense of adventure, your willingness to take risks." She smiled at Lili. "Look at how you came here, not knowing what you would find, but willing to take a chance." She stopped petting the cat and opened her hands. "So for now you can't communicate in the manner of academics or would-be academics. It may be difficult, but it is not the end of the world."

It wasn't just difficult, Lili acknowledged, it was humiliating. She didn't possess the proper vocabulary or means to understand one.

Tante Aletheia peered at her. "Lili, you must recognize that your years in New York have given you a view of the world that is larger than what most of the students know. Even those with a high level of academic agility." As she spoke, one eyebrow arched. "You have lived in a place where differences are not denied but adapted. You have walked the streets of New York. Even among the Uni students, I am sure that few of them have traveled far from home."

Lili wiped her cheek with the back of her hand. The lump in her throat was shrinking. Now she felt compelled to argue.

♫♪♫

"That's not true. Almost everyone has been to Nuremberg—even more than once. And it's such an inspiring place."

"Of course." Tante Aletheia gave an odd chuckle. "How could I have forgotten that?"

"And several of them have been on Kraft durch Freude trips with their families. By train around Germany. One even went along the Norwegian fjords on a KdF steamer. She said it was the most beautiful scenery in the entire world."

"Where else has she been?" Tante Aletheia's tone was neutral.

Lili paused. "And there was a leader from another squad in Nuremberg. She and her parents went on a KdF trip to Madeira. She said they had ever so much fun on the ship. That everybody felt equal and filled with good-natured camaraderie. Every day they had meetings about important aspects of the Reich, and when they got to Lisbon they were taken on a tour of the harbor area so that they could truly understand the difference between living conditions for German workers and those of the workers in Portugal. She said that certainly was an eye-opener. It made them appreciate even more what the Führer has done for the workers." Winded, Lili leaned back against the carved designs of the chair.

Tante Aletheia regarded her for a while.

"It must indeed have been a wonderful feeling for the people on that ship. Undoubtedly the KdF has been a boon to the railroad and ship builders and holiday centers as well."

Lili nodded. This was a subject she understood.

"KdF was one of the first programs that the Führer thought of and put into action in 1933." She felt pride at the thought of how far-reaching his unique vision was.

Tante Aletheia picked at the cake on her plate.

"Have you heard of *Dopolavoro?*"

Lili was puzzled by the change in topic.

"Is it a brand of coffee?"

Tante Aletheia burst out laughing. "No, but you're probably thinking it is Italian and you are correct. It means 'after work.' Dopolavoro is a program begun in Italy in 1925 on somewhat the same lines as KdF. It was taken up here with enthusiasm." She sipped at her coffee. "Of course, both the Social Democrats and Communists have long had such programs in place. In fact, I remember when Germany was known for having the most varied youth groups in the world."

"The Führer has always been able to take useful concepts and adapt them to the needs of the people," Lili said, her tone slightly stiff. "Just like Chancellor Bismarck in his time. That is the mark of great leaders."

Tante Aletheia smiled, then clapped her hands as if signaling a change of scene.

"Enough of this serious talk! Have I shown you what Fragonard has taught himself to do?"

Lili smiled too. Tante Aletheia's relationship with her cat was always entertaining, probably because she had never had any children on which to lavish her affection.

"Watch closely." She pushed away her table setting and then, most improperly, laid her head with chignon atop the tablecloth. She closed her eyes.

Lili watched Fragonard. Back on an armchair, he had been posing in sphinx-like stateliness. Now, in one swift and elegant move, he sprang onto the table, landing perfectly alongside the cups and saucers and their creamy rests. He ignored it all to pad with light paws to the head reposing next to the coffee pot. There he sank down. Thinking this was it, Lili chuckled at the sight of the white fur and hair side by side. But then Fragonard reached out a paw, gentle as a wisp of cloud, and stroked Tante Aletheia's forehead.

"Did you teach him to do that?"

Tante Aletheia sat up and scooped Fragonard back onto her lap. His purring was immediate.

"Not at all," she grinned. "He's a funny darling, isn't he?"

Lili agreed. "When we were in Berlin we had two Russian wolfhounds. The first was Sascha. But Mama developed an allergy and we had to give the next one away. He was even taller. His name was Napoleon but I called him Napola." She blinked. Goodness. "Well, if he's not dead, he has most likely been renamed." Imagine, calling one's dog by the name of the most elite party schools in the Reich. It certainly wouldn't do.

There was a knock.

Slowly the door opened and Frau Dierck appeared. The skin under her eyes was stained pale purple. Her hands moved without task. She did not seem to notice Lili until she was fully inside, and then she started.

"Oh, forgive me," she said, dismay in her voice. "I didn't mean to disturb you. I just thought if you had some time, Frau von Wohlitz…"

"Come in, Frau Dierck," said Tante Aletheia, an encouraging smile upon her lips. "Will you join us for a strengthening cup of coffee?"

Frau Dierck wrung her hands.

"I don't know if I should." Her eyebrows were nearly vertical.

"Of course you should. Here, sit down." Gently, Tante Aletheia led her to a chair at the table. "By now you should know that in my home, my door is always open, even when it is shut."

Lili was as silent as Fragonard, watching.

"Now drink this," Tante Aletheia said, handing over a cup, "and we can talk when you feel stronger."

Noticing that Lili had been looking at a painting, Tante Aletheia chose the topic of the canvases that hung on the walls. She would be taking these along on her next trip to Friedberg. Two were quite large and colorful. Every time that Lili entered the room, she enjoyed studying the unframed works. There was always something new to be found, something exciting even, while at the same time the paintings were calming. She didn't quite understand how that could be, but was intrigued. They reminded her of art she had seen at home in Berlin and the New York Metropolitan Museum, works by Cezanne, Kirchner, Matisse—yet different too.

"That one he painted back in 1908, when we were living in Paris. He used to call it a portrait of his little muse…"

It was a languid mosaic of limbs and features that somehow came together in a mesmerizing seascape. Lili focused on the eyes, of a green that seemed very familiar.

"These two used to hang on loan to a museum in Berlin," Tante Aletheia said. "Fortunately I got them back in time."

In time for what, Lili wanted to ask.

"Wilhelm might have been amused to have them hanging at Germany's most well-attended exhibition ever, but I couldn't have stomached that."

Lili had to interrupt.

"But it would be wonderful to have so many people see his work, Tante Aletheia. He must have been a gifted artist." While the one painting was swirling with emotion, the other was dry, a wasteland. It made Lili feel as if her insides were being sucked out.

"Yes," Tante Aletheia agreed. "That he was, even if he came into it so late in his life, after spending so many years concerning himself with other artists' works." She shook her head. "Even at the end it was difficult for Wilhelm to acknowledge that he had extraordinary talent, not just in recognizing greatness in others, but of his own." There was sorrow in her gaze, but Lili could see satisfaction too.

As Tante Altetheia spoke, she glanced over at Frau Dierck, who was drinking her coffee, holding the cup with both hands.

"The exhibition is still on. So far, hundreds of thousands have been to see the works there. They have even had to close it down at times. Too many people, it seems." Now Tante Aletheia had the oddest smile, as if were tinged with—Schadenfreude? "In fact, there have been countless more visitors there than at the other exhibition in the Haus der Deutschen Kunst."

"Why is that?" Lili asked.

"That one features symbols of the 're-energized pure German being' in the 'healthy present.' She emphasized the adjectives. "There are heroic and pastoral scenes, families and farmers. Nude women who are pure. That sort of thing."

Lili was confused. "Those are works of art. Important ones. Why are so many more people going to the other one?"

Tante Aletheia briefly pressed her lips together, as if she were going to laugh out loud.

"Over one thousand works are on display there. Even more than that have been removed from museums around the country and brought to Berlin. Wilhelm's paintings would have been taken too if they had still been on loan. The public is being encouraged to see the works of such artists as Kollwitz and Nolde and Kirchner—not to mention foreign artists like Klee and Kandinsky and Picasso and van Gogh and Pisarro and and and—"

"Great artists," Lili interrupted, nodding.

"—and agree that all those artists should be viewed with disgust. That their work is a sickness." Tante Aletheia gave an abrupt shake of her head. A tendril of hair, slender as a serpent, slipped out of her chignon. "The Degenerate Art exhibition is to show everything that German art is no longer allowed to be. And that I would spare my husband—even if he is already dead."

At this, Frau Dierck began to weep with such woeful abandon that Lili fled the room.

Frau Dierck is Disturbed

For long moments Lili stood on the carpet in the half light of the stairwell, shifting from foot to foot. Frau Dierck sounded wretched. The woman had looked half mad too. Her eyes reminded Lili of those of a cow she'd once seen being led out of a stall in Alt Eichendorf. At the time, she hadn't understood why the creature had seemed so crazed. Later she had felt a passing sadness, but the sausage had tasted too good.

Poor Tante Aletheia, stuck inside with that woman.

She cracked open the door and peered into the room. It sounded as if Frau Dierck were keening out her insides.

"Lili," Tante Aletheia called out from where she sat over the huddled form of Frau Dierck. "Please go bring Dr. Morsch. Frau Brinkmann is out today and the phone line is down."

"Where does he live?" Lili stammered, relieved to be sent off.

Tante Aletheia gave her the number on Unterer Fauler Pelz. "Tell him she's having one of her attacks. Hurry!"

Lili flew down the stairs, stopping only to grab her jacket before rushing out the door. The rain had stopped but the wind still blew, cutting against her cheeks like slivers of glass. She lowered her head as she sped up the square, turning right at the crossing.

What sort of an attack was Frau Dierck having? Kidney stones? Asthma? With asthma, would she have been able to mumble and cry for so long? Whatever condition, it must be painful for her. Otherwise she was always so quiet. As much as she found Frau Dierck disturbing, Lili felt bad at her own dismissive attitude all these weeks. She quickened her pace.

Reaching the wooden gate set inside brick walls over which loomed leafless tree limbs, she pushed open the latch and ran up the short path to the house. Her fists hammered against the thick wood of the entrance until she noticed the doorbell. After a seemingly interminable time, the door was opened by a woman with steely gray hair.

"Dr. Morsch," Lili burst out. "We need him at home. My aunt needs him. It's for Frau Dierck. She's having one of her attacks." She took a breath. "I don't know what kind of attack, but it's urgent." What if he wasn't in?

"Come in," said the woman. "I will inform Dr. Morsch."

Lili stepped out of the wind. Compared to the gloom of the day, the interior of the house radiated light and warmth. Biting her lip, she looked around. A large lamp with an ivory shade stood in the corner of the foyer while other fixtures were sunk into the ceiling, casting down rays like tiny suns. An oriental carpet of pale gold caught the warm tones of the parquet surrounding it. At the center of the foyer stood a table holding an amber vase filled with an array of branches and berries. In the connecting salon, curtains of yellow silk framed a large window that looked out upon a garden, now bare.

"Fräulein Lili." Dr. Morsch was at her side, already holding his black medical bag.

The doctor kept step with her, faltering only once to avoid a puddle. Lili would have liked to know about Frau Dierck's problem but as Dr. Morsch offered no information, she refrained from asking. Perhaps it was a woman's matter and he found it indelicate to discuss. Or it could have been that Frau Dierck was his patient and he was bound not to speak of her condition to others. This was because of the oath Dr. Morsch would have had to make long ago to be able to practice as a doctor, something about never doing harm to anyone. It had always seemed rather odd to her, to make doctors take an oath as, after all, wouldn't they be the last people to willfully hurt others? She leaned against the wind.

"When did the attack begin?" Dr. Morsch was asking.

"Perhaps twenty minutes ago," she said, glancing at him as they hurried along. "We were having coffee upstairs when suddenly she began to cry and rave quite terribly. She must be in great pain." Perhaps now he would mention what the pain was due to. But still he said nothing.

Once at the house, she watched as he threw off his jacket, which just caught the hook on the rack, and went straight up to Tante Aletheia's rooms. He entered without knocking then closed the door behind him.

Lili paced the foyer, her heels hard against the stone. All these weeks and she had not even once asked Frau Dierck how she felt. If Mama had been here, by now she would have arranged a hundred kindnesses for Frau Dierck. Lili didn't even know what was wrong with her. But it wasn't only Lili's fault. She hadn't reminded Tante Aletheia to explain. And, after all, Frau Dierck barely made any attempts to be a part of things. She rarely spoke. Her expression was usually odd too, hunted or haunted. It was as if she had cocooned herself off from the world because of her condition, whatever it was. In truth, Frau Dierck was a rather tiresome creature. Sometimes Lili wanted to shake her.

Lili stomped over to the mirror and scowled at herself. Her eyes were dark, a brooding gray. She turned away as the front door opened, bringing with it a gust of wind that smelled of earth and life. Herr Malter was home. For once his hair looked neat, as if the contrary wind had combed it.

"Freiin Lili," he said. "Have you been waiting for me?"

She shook her head. "No, Herr Malter. Not at all. It's—"

"Ach," he said, shrugging his shoulders. "To think that I've spent all Sunday hard at work in the laboratory, with only the thought of your beautiful Aryan face at the end as a reward." He sighed melodramatically. "And now you tell me you don't care."

After the tension of the past half hour it was a relief to grin.

"Won't you make it up to me? Accompany me to Zum Roten Ochsen and I'll be able to forget your callousness." He took a step back, peering at her with exaggeration. "It's a mystery how someone so sweet and lovely can be so cruel." He shook his head slowly.

"I thank thee, kind sir, for thy charming invitation." She curtsied, coquettish, felt her cheeks burning as she rose. "But I must bid thee drown thy sorrows in solitude, for I rest at home this eve and—" She couldn't continue, for a giggle escaped her.

Herr Malter chuckled too. It was a warm and wonderful thing to stand there together in the foyer, laughing.

"It's a pity today is already Sunday," he said at last. "I'd very much like to show you some more sights in Heidelberg if the weather is fine. Perhaps next week?"

"I'd like that, Herr Malter."

"Call me Benno."

They parted at the stairwell then, and for the next two hours Lili sat at the harpsichord playing Bach. It felt as if she were climbing through the clouds, and by the time she reached the clear skies she had forgotten everything, even the disturbing Frau Dierck.

♫ ♪ ♫

The following evening, Lili retired to her room early. The monthly bleeding was about to begin and her insides felt as if they were being wrung by a particularly vigorous washerwoman. She had managed to finish half a bowl of vegetable soup, then excused herself as Tante Aletheia glanced at her with concern.

Lili was curled up in a ball on her bed when she heard muffled noises coming from the hallway.

Unfolding her limbs, she moved to the door. As she pressed her ear against the wood, a wave of nausea rose in her. There was the sound of something heavy slumping against the floor, then a long drawn-out throaty groan, ugly and deep. It sounded like Frau Dierck. Lili bit down on her lip. Not again!

She heard Tante Aletheia murmuring.

Lili stayed pressed against the door. Perhaps she was mistaken. Her heart doubled its beat. No. There was nothing for it; she had to help Tante Aletheia. She opened the door.

Just as yesterday, Tante Aletheia was bending over Frau Dierck, who lay folded on the floor in an angular heap. Ragged moans rose from her even as she sobbed.

"Lili," said Tante Aletheia, her voice stressed. "Help me get her into her room."

Tante Aletheia pushed her hands under Frau Dierck's arms and began to pull her back. For a moment Lili could only stare. Then she moved to take over on one side. The feel of Frau Dierck's body was startling to her fingers. Fleshy, real. Lili could smell mothballs and perspiration and something indefinable.

"Come now, Frau Dierck. You must be brave," soothed Tante Aletheia as they got her onto her feet. "One step at a time."

Frau Dierck's room was at the end of the hall. By the time they arrived, Lili was exhaling hard. She glanced over at Tante Aletheia. She seemed to have regained her composure but Lili could see that her hands were quivering from the strain. They got Frau Dierck onto the bed; Lili untied her shoes while Tante Aletheia covered her with the quilt.

"She can stay in her clothes," she whispered.

"Shall I get Dr. Morsch?"

Frau Dierck was sobbing, strands of brown hair stuck to her cheeks, caught in the tears. Lili had to look away.

"No, it's all right. Please get the small blue bottle and spoon from the painted cupboard in my room."

Lili was grateful for the momentary reprieve.

Without spilling a drop, Tante Aletheia measured out the dose. "Help her sit up."

It was awkward, getting behind Frau Dierck and pushing her up as if she were a roll of dough, lumpy and warm. The sour smell came her scalp too. Lili fought to hold back her gagging reflex.

"Swallow this, Frau Dierck," Tante Aletheia urged. "It will help you." Frau Dierck opened her mouth but the lips quivered, contorted.

"I'm so sorry," she stammered, beginning to cry. Some of the liquid ran out.

Tante Aletheia glanced at Lili. "Let's try again." This time, she aimed the spoon toward the back of Frau Dierck's throat.

Lili rose, letting the head slide onto the pillow.

Tante Aletheia nodded.

"It's all right now, Lili. Thank you."

Lili hesitated. Half of her was ready to rush from the room. Yet perhaps Tante Aletheia still needed her. Her belly was twisting. She wrung the words out of herself.

"I can stay if you like."

"No, dear. She should fall asleep now."

Lili slipped out, taking a deep breath to flood her lungs with the comforting smell of the hallway. The scent of Frau Brinkmann's wax and polish on the stairwell worked like an astringent. In her bathroom, she washed her hands for a long time in the porcelain sink. The strange odor had disappeared yet she continued to rinse. What was it she was trying to rid herself of? She shuddered. Whatever was wrong with Frau Dierck, it couldn't be only physical.

Too shaken to sleep, and her cramping growing in intensity, Lili picked up a book of 19th century German Romantic landscapes and sat in the armchair, the hot water bottle against her belly. The colored pages of the Rhine and the fields and forests were soothing. She stared at *Wanderer above the Sea of Fog*, taking a deep breath. This time it did not come in jagged but as a smooth flow. As always, it was Germany that comforted her.

With a perfunctory knock at the door, Tante Aletheia entered, carrying a small tray with chamomile tea and a bottle of Schnaps. Fragonard followed at her heels, he too settling into the armchair opposite Lili.

"Thank you, my child. You were of great help again." Tante Aletheia looked tired yet composed. Her chignon had been tidied. "You yourself were not feeling well earlier this evening."

"My days are coming."

"I thought so," Tante Aletheia replied, nodding toward the bottle. "A shot of Schnaps will help."

"What in heaven is wrong with Frau Dierck?"

Tante Aletheia took a long breath, letting it out slowly.

"I'll explain."

How to Lose Twenty Kilos

Feeling quite grown-up, Lili poured them both a generous glass of the plum brandy.

"Frau Dierck," said Tante Aletheia after swallowing some of hers, "is the youngest niece of someone with whom I went to school in Hamburg. After marrying, she broke off with her family; they weren't pleased with her choice. It was a hard life but she and her husband were close. A good thing, for Frau Dierck truly gave up everything of her former life to be with him.

"At first things went well, relatively speaking. Her husband started off as a sales clerk in a department store. Soon two children arrived. At the time, they were living in a small flat in Mannheim. Then the husband lost his job but found part time work as a night watchman. His pride was wounded. He took up drinking and became unruly, then mean. Next he began to withhold household money."

"Oh," Lili said, sipping at her tea. "Is that why she's so distraught? She behaves in such a strange way. Quite dramatic. But what about the children? Where are they?"

"Her story is not yet finished," Tante Aletheia said.

"The husband was squandering money when the children needed food. Frau Dierck appealed to his sense of responsibility but his response was a fist in her face."

Lili sucked in her breath. She had never known anyone, neither man nor woman, who had been assaulted. Tante Aletheia certainly had a disturbing mix of boarders.

"She tried to keep the children out of his way. Eventually he lost that job as well. Their savings flowed out in the form of alcohol. But Frau Dierck's pride kept her from turning to her family; her body was covered with bruises. All she did was plead with him, until he slammed the children against a wall. Then she went to the welfare authority."

Leaning over Fragonard, Tante Aletheia poured herself some tea. Lili said nothing. She thought of Paul, of Mama and Papa. It was unimaginable that something like that would ever happen in her family.

"They took him to the station, gave him a warning, sent him home."

Lili was outraged. "That's all?"

Tante Aletheia nodded. "Still, the experience must have shaken him up enough as for a while he behaved himself. Home life improved, he looked for a new job. But either no one wanted him, or he didn't like the sort of jobs he was being offered. It all started over again. He attacked Frau Dierck with a bottle. When he went after her with the kitchen knife she hit him in the head with a pan and ran to the authorities."

Lili shivered. This was the worst thing she had ever heard. Such coarse violence. No wonder Frau Dierck was so traumatized.

"Thank goodness. What did they do to him this time?"

"Because she had injured him, Frau Dierck was given a warning. Both had their rights of guardianship stripped, and the children were sent to a foster home. Two years on, they're still there. Last year I took Frau Dierck in. As for her husband, he was labeled anti-social, sterilized, and sent to Dachau for training and correction. He is still there." She paused. "Frau Dierck blames herself for all of it."

"But it wasn't her fault!"

Tante Aletheia shrugged. "This is what I tell her. But the heart is stubborn."

"That certainly explains her behavior," Lili mused. "So she's actually not really sick, is she?"

"At the very least heartsick, my dear."

"She must miss her children."

"She takes comfort in knowing that they are on a farm in Bavaria. She might get them back next year."

"Why didn't she send them to her family?"

"She's afraid that, because of the father, they would treat the children badly. Besides, it is the state that decides where the children go." Tante Aletheia reached out to smooth Fragonard. "It is her husband's condition that is causing Frau Dierck so much anxiety. Despite his so-called re-education in Dachau, he's not improving. He was again denied permission to leave."

Lili sighed. "Then it's good that he's being treated there."

Tante Aletheia rubbed her finger at a spot on the armchair.

"The methods may be questionable."

Lili frowned. "You said that he was sterilized. Wouldn't it take off his skin—and what about his eyes?" It was rather difficult to imagine someone being boiled in a large pot.

For a moment it looked as if Tante Aletheia were going to laugh but instead she cleared her throat. "In this case, sterilization means that Frau Dierck's husband will never give her another child."

"Oh." Lili felt her cheeks flushing. She would have liked to ask how this was accomplished but felt shy. Surely there was no boiling involved with that.

"Well, that would seem to be a good thing, wouldn't it?" she said. "He sounds like a very dangerous person."

Tante Aletheia was silent, her hand moving through the white fur on her lap.

"That's a difficult subject, Lili. There are people, not just here but in other countries, who believe that those who don't conform to the given ideals of a particular society should not have certain human freedoms. Those with mental or physical problems are at the top of the list."

"Of course," Lili nodded. "That's why the Führer stresses that Germany's youth be healthy and fit." She glanced at Tante Aletheia who was looking at her with a green and unblinking gaze. "Herr Dierck must be crazy."

"His behavior," Tante Aletheia said thoughtfully, "might certainly be labeled crazed."

"Poor Frau Dierck."

"Yes," Tante Aletheia said. "Now and then she succumbs to her despair, as she did again this evening. I try to keep her away from the others then, for there are times when she says things against the government that she later doesn't recall having said. Occasionally Dr. Morsch needs to tend to her, give her an injection or medication. He has given me valerian for her. Today Frau Dierck learned that since arriving in Dachau her husband has lost twenty kilos. Even though he behaved so terribly, she still cares about him. She fears that all this will affect the children's future wellbeing."

Despite having washed her hands, Lili could still smell that particular odor of Frau Dierck. "Isn't there someplace else he can go aside from a concentration camp? A hospital or a sanitarium? Even so, Dachau must be better than being in prison."

Tante Aletheia grimaced. Lili had never seen such an ugly expression on her.

"I have my doubts."

Suddenly Lili was reminded of the girl at the BDM camp, Marlies, and how someone had suggested she be sent away for re-education. Many of those camps had sprung up around Germany these past few years, places, as she had told Papa, where people were concentrated so they could be encouraged to change their ways, to understand and embrace the ways of National Socialism.

It was sad that there were people who refused to live peacefully in the Reich.

"Well, Herr Dierck should have thought about all that before he began hitting his wife," Lili asserted. "Perhaps even now he's still unrepentant and that's why they're not letting him out."

Tante Aletheia closed her eyes. When she opened them she looked as if she were going to say something else but all that came out was, "So, Lili. We have both had a long evening." Gently she nudged Fragonard off and rose. "Again, thank you for your assistance. I hope that you're feeling better now." In passing, she laid a hand on Lili's shoulder, giving it a faint pressure.

Once Tante Aletheia had gone out, Lili settled into bed. Whether from fatigue or the Schnaps, her muscles had relaxed, the cramps faded. The bleeding had begun. She stretched her calves, pointed her toes, luxuriated in the soft comfort of relief enveloping her. She felt light as the eiderdown. Herr Dierck must have been very heavy to have lost twenty kilos.

Lili Feels an Enormous Power

During dinner a few days later, Herr Poppe cleared his throat with a loud guttural inflection, catching everyone's attention.

"Frau von Wohlitz, I must inform you that for the next four days I will not be at table." It sounded as if he were addressing a grand audience instead of the usual boarders at mealtime. "I will be on an official trip to Munich where I am to attend the opening of the new exhibition there. It promises to be a most detailed and comprehensive examination of the nature of the Jew." He bit into his *Salamibrot*. "I will tell you all about it upon my return."

"Exile, that's the nature of the game," said Herr Tischborn into his wine.

"Indeed," said Herr Poppe, giving a curt nod of approval as he chewed. "Our government has the right approach. Make life difficult enough for them and they'll all leave Germany. Problem solved. Frau von Wohlitz, this sausage is delicious." His tongue licked his lips. Then he patted his mouth and forehead with the napkin.

Lili had to look away. Herr Poppe's attempts at what he must have thought genteel manners were often crude or ridiculous, like when he raised his pinky while drinking coffee. She glanced at Tante Aletheia. One day Lili was going to ask her why she took in a guest with so few social graces as had Herr Poppe. Tante Aletheia herself was always gracious. Even now, she was polite enough to disregard Herr Poppe's poor manners. She was merely looking off into the middle distance, and perhaps it was only Lili who noticed that her green eyes looked like slits.

Lili turned her gaze to the others. Frau Dierck looked washed out and dowdy but now that Lili knew why, she could ignore her. It was difficult to always feel sorry for someone who had so little self-control that she let herself melt into such misery. It made it unpleasant to be around such a person. As for Herr Tischborn, he was easy to read. Whatever Herr Poppe said, Herr Tischborn would be right there, echoing him. The faint creases between his brows lent him an air of being a serious thinker, but Lili could see no evidence of any great reflection on his part. Perhaps one didn't need to be overly clever to sell wine. As for Dr. Hempel—well, the sweet man had no thoughts about anything other than his music and training his students to be good musicians for the Reich. Admirable. Then there was Herr Malter, or rather, Benno. He looked at people through those hazel eyes and Lili was never sure what he might be thinking.

As usual his hair was a mess but, somehow, this was endearing. As if he had such important scientific matters to consider that he couldn't be bothered with fixing his hair. Perhaps that was why he hadn't yet asked her out again: he was too busy with his work. She picked up her glass and sipped her wine. When she glanced back across the table, Benno was looking at her. She hoped he didn't see the little shiver that moved through her.

She turned back to Herr Poppe, who was talking about how much work civil servants had these days, and how the workload was constantly increasing. Lili didn't know what his actual work was, but he spoke as if he enjoyed it. She could tell he was pleased to be a civil servant in the service of the Reich. Even if he didn't seem to come from a very cultured background, it was obvious that he took his work and responsibilities seriously. Perhaps it was Lili herself who needed to make some changes in her manners. Rather than belittle Herr Poppe for his lack of finesse, and for his somewhat porcine features for which he could do even less, she should respect him for his dedication. He was a man of the new Germany. Lili looked into his light blue eyes. Herr Poppe smiled at her, his cheeks rosy under the chandelier.

Once dinner was finished and they were all leaving the table, Benno turned to her.

"Do you feel like taking a stroll?"

"Why not?" She hoped that she sounded more nonchalant than she felt.

Kornmarkt was empty as they stepped out of the house and turned left. They began to walk up Unterer Fauler Pelz, reminding Lili of her mad dash to Dr. Morsch's house.

"What branch of medicine will you be practicing?"

"I'm in research. I wouldn't practice unless someone has an emergency and I needed to step in. Which I hope never happens because as much as I'm fascinated by blood and what it holds, amounts larger than that on a slide are not for me."

Lili glanced over at him and grinned. "You mean you're one of those who faints at the sight of blood?" Benno stopped short and for a moment she thought he was angry.

"I've seen more spilt blood than you can imagine. My older brother was a professional boxer. Came home with bloody noses and cuts all the time when I was growing up." He motioned to the empty street. " Come, let's walk."

"Is he still boxing?"

"Let's just say he met his match in a dark alley in Magdeburg shortly before the Führer was elected. Take a mob of those *Reichsbanner* fanatics and even a prize boxer didn't stand a chance. The Führer sent a wreath for his funeral."

"I'm sorry," she said, suddenly understanding. He had lost his brother. Magdeburg had seen a lot of troublemakers for some time before the Führer was elected and put an end to their disagreements.

"It's been several years," Benno said with a thin-lipped smile. "Life goes on."

How strong Benno must be, to have survived the death of a brother. She did not even want to imagine what that must feel like.

By now they had passed Dr. Morsch's house and others on this quiet residential street, and were nearing the Heidelberg prison. It seemed strange to be able to take an after dinner walk in the middle of town and pass by a prison, but there it was—lights were still on in some of the windows of the red brick building that bordered the university area. Yet this was not a prison for drunken university students. What sorts of people were in jail? Perhaps it was only thieves and murderers, and everyone else got what they needed, and deserved, in the concentration camps.

She looked up at the looming outline of the building. Was that dark shape silhouetted against the light of a window an inmate? Perhaps a robber was looking down at them, wondering when he too would be free to walk the streets.

This was disturbing, not the romantic stroll she had imagined. She bit her lip. She didn't know what to say now. Benno wasn't saying anything either. At Kettengasse they turned right, and as they neared Hauptstraße and the familiar lights and sounds of people laughing and talking along the street grew clearer, she realized that she had been clenching her jaws.

When Benno suggested stopping for a glass of wine, Lili shook her head, saying she needed to go back to the house.

♫ ♪ ♫

Once upstairs, she went immediately to the harpsichord. Her hands moved over the keys, drawing out the sounds hidden within so that her tension began to ebb. She closed her eyes. There really was no haven like that of making music. Perhaps not even that of nature.

After a few minutes, she stopped to sort through her new sheets, then began on the harpsichord part of a work called "La Fougade." For the past few days she had been entertaining herself with some peculiar pieces found in a musty little store not too far from Akadamiestraße.

Peculiar too had been the sight she'd passed on her way there, a good dozen men in those long black coats and black hats, with curls that bobbed on either side of their faces as they hurried by, probably on their way to the synagogue at Plöck where that type of Jew seemed to gather. They looked like a flock of strange black birds. Why did they dress in such clothes? There had been people like that in Berlin and New York too, pale and pasty, as if they rarely breathed in the invigorating tonic of fresh air. How contrary they were to live their whole lives in Germany and America and yet still look and behave so foreign. The people whom she saw going into the synagogue on Große Mantelgasse weren't like that; *they* looked normal. That day, as the group of black-coated men had hurried along, several people stopped to watch and one man made a rather loud and rude comment about the annoying influx of Polish *Juden Gesindel*. Riffraff did seem a somewhat strong term for the men, as the cloth of some of their outfits looked to be of excellent quality even if the style was odd. Still, it would be better if they left. Clearly they didn't belong in Germany.

Once inside the store, Lili had been delighted to find a wealth of music sheets, but was disappointed that a patina of dust lay over everything; many of the books and pages looked as if they had long been nibbled at by mice or feasted upon by silverfish. What a pity. She glanced at the owner, a man with a silver beard and hands that trembled. He did not seem aware of the crumbling state of his wares; perhaps he had lost his glasses long ago. Lili thought of Großpapa Hugo's favorite saying: "Ordnung muss sein." Someone committed to order really needed to come into that store with a broom and duster and the resolution to use them before all the musical treasures were lost.

She had already chosen to rescue two works by Bach, a sonata by Scarlatti, and one by Telemann, when she came upon *Suitte d'un Goût Étranger* by Marin Marais. The title intrigued her, as had the spelling of 'suite', and as she opened the worn cloth cover, Lili knew immediately that she would buy this work too although the score was for an ensemble of six instruments. The names of individual pieces, like "Allemande la Singulière" and "Allemande la Superbe" jumped out at her. Even if the allemande was a type of dance, she would interpret it as a charming homage to Germany by the French composer.

After these past days of practice, her fingers now moved easily over the keys. The short pieces were a pleasure although of course they were missing the other instruments. She had to imagine them. It was rather like a puzzle, but with limitless possibilities as the answers. Perhaps one day she would hear the work performed, or even play it in the proper ensemble. What would it be like to make music with other musicians, perhaps total strangers meeting for the first time across a musical score?

Her fingers danced across the keys. What she was playing now, "Le Labyrinthe," was the longest and one of the most intriguing of them all. She loved the satisfaction of figuring out the bars, then flying away with them. And her playing had been improving. Technique was only the beginning, In New York, as she moved back and forth across the room, Frau Kuhn had often told her, "You must live fully, you must suffer, so that your music can soar." Then she would glare at her, as if wondering what form of suffering Lili might have in that spacious apartment so close to Central Park. Yet Lili had discovered there were many ways to suffer. For example, although she had so longed for Germany, now that she was here she missed Mama and Papa and Paul. And the thought that she would have to leave Germany in December made her suffer even more. Of course there were other forms of suffering, for example that of Frau Dierck, but thank goodness, Lili herself was healthy and fit, especially now that she was exercising so much with the BDM and NSDStB. And marching too.

The piece "Gavotte" came to an end. Before she could begin "La Reveuse" there was a knock at her door.

"Come in," she called out.

The door opened slowly but no one entered. Was it Benno? Perhaps by now he was in a jolly mood.

Lili rose to investigate.

Dr. Hempel stood in the hallway.

"Please excuse the interruption, Fräulein Lili. I'm on my way to retire, but couldn't help noticing that you have been practicing much of the evening."

Masking her disappointment, Lili glanced at her Wempe wristwatch. "I'm sorry if I've disturbed you." No one had ever complained about her evening playing and it was disconcerting to think that it would be Dr. Hempel who would be the first to object.

"No, young Fräulein, not at all." He shook his head. "I merely wanted to inquire if you would care to join an old music teacher at a concert in the Stadthalle tomorrow. The program is entirely Baroque. I believe you will appreciate it."

"But that's lovely!" she said. "Thank you very much, Dr. Hempel. I'd be delighted."

Dr. Hempel, who had been looking a bit anxious, brightened and clapped his hands together.

"Splendid. Then let us set out with enough time to walk at a leisurely pace and find the right seats as well." His eyes twinkled as he turned to go. "The orchestra is of especial interest to young ladies."

What did he mean by that? Was there going to be a special fashion show modeled by young women from *Glaube und Schönheit*, the women's group for those above the age of 18? But wait, Dr. Hempel had said 'orchestra'. Well, she would find out tomorrow. This would be her first concert since arriving, even though the season had opened already in September. Now she picked up the music and was about to put it away when she saw a silverfish, looking somewhat like a plump bass clef, poised on the top sheet.

The silverfish sat very still. Perhaps it was hoping she wouldn't notice it. After all, it wasn't very large. At first Lili was not going to bother with it, just brush it off the page. How much paper could it eat? But perhaps it was a female, and about to give birth to a whole swarm of little silverfish, and then these too would have swarms of silverfish. This one must have been feasting its way through the shop and been swept up with the music sheets she had brought home. She picked up the paper. For a moment the insect ran in a circle, then clung on, as if knowing something was about to happen. She walked over to open the window and let it drop onto the street below, but the knob was stuck and she needed both hands. If she put the sheet down, the bug might disappear into the carpet and she would never find it.

She had to get rid of it. She couldn't squash it on the paper. It would leave a mark, perhaps even blur a note or two. She went to the sink and shook the page; the insect did not budge. She waved the paper over the porcelain but still it stayed fast. She held the sheet up and stared at the silverfish. Why was it called that when its color was a pale golden brown? She knew so little about these beings. Aside from the instinct for survival, did anything go on in its brain? She peered closer. She couldn't even see any eyes.

Snapping the page downwards, so hard that a piercing pain shot through her wrist, she managed at last to dislodge the insect. Now it was in the basin, skimming over the smooth porcelain, avoiding the drain that must have loomed like some dark and giant void. For a few moments Lili watched it scrabbling about, a miniscule figure against the white. For one moment she felt an enormous power. It was rather exhilarating. Then she turned on the Cold tap.

Once she had splashed the silverfish into the drain, she added the Hot and bathed her forearm in the running water. Then she went to bed and by the time she was about to drift into sleep, her wrist had stopped hurting.

Girl Talk

Filled with hungry students, the Mensa was noisy. Lili sat with Hildegard and another girl from Professor Dr. Hetzenrath's class. Today's special was Königsbergerklöpse but they did not taste like any Lili had ever eaten, especially not Lotte's. Lili put down her fork with distaste and watched as the other girl juggled three small Schrippen for a moment, expertly, as if they were balls. Then she offered two to Lili and Hildegard and bit into hers. For some moments the three of them chewed the rolls companionably. Lili had come to enjoy these shared lunches. The very casualness of them underlined the fact that she was a university student.

"Last week I met an American girl who's studying German in that program for foreigners," Hildegard said. "She's engaged to a medical student here. You should meet her, Lili. Her name is Nancy."

Lili's answer was a non-committal "Hmm." She didn't want to meet an American girl any sooner than she had to, especially an American girl who was going to marry a doctor and probably stay on in Germany while Lili herself had to return to New York next month. It simply wasn't fair.

The other girl chewed on her roll for a bit.

"What do you think of Karl-Heinz?"

"The Karl-Heinz from Hetzenrath's class?"

Glad for the change in topic, Lili glanced across the hall to where the student in question, tall, with a chin that slid directly into his throat, was approaching with his tray. If Lili had been here last year, Benno would have still been at university. Perhaps they would occasionally have had lunch together here. "He's rather sweet," she said of Karl-Heinz, then added, "But not my type."

The other girl seemed to relax.

"So what is your type?"

"Ach, I don't know." She put an index finger under her chin, resting her head. She considered the only man she knew. "I think, perhaps, someone older. Someone who has suffered and is already out there in the world, making things happen."

Hildegard gave her a sly look.

"Are we talking about someone around here, or someone like, perhaps, the Führer?"

"Really!" Lili scolded. "You're very naughty."

"Heil Hitler, girls," said Karl-Heinz, arriving at their table. "What theories are you expounding?"

All three of them burst into laughter, and crumbs flew across the table.

No Words to Express It

A few hours later, Lili and Dr. Hempel made their way toward Stadthalle for the concert. Except that his gait was the sideways sway of an overweight man, Dr. Hempel almost looked dashing in his dark gray overcoat, subtly patterned bow tie peeping out from between the lapels. His beard was freshly trimmed and he had obviously splashed on an eau de cologne. Lili wore the new Loden coat she had bought only the previous week, with a matching dark green felt hat, traditional but feminine, a tiny spotted feather stuck in its band of velvet. They crossed Marktplatz where, aside from a squashed bit of cauliflower underfoot, there were no signs of that morning's market. As they reached the square in front of Alte Brücke, Dr. Hempel pointed to the bridge.

"Did you know that for two centuries, until the bridge was blown up in the Palatinate War of Succession, a monkey sat over there?"

"A real monkey?"

Dr. Hempel winked. "A statue, symbol to the people of Heidelberg that neither those who lived in town, nor those who lived outside it, were better than the other. The monkey was there to remind them of this as they crossed the bridge." He chuckled. "People need reminding of such matters from time to time."

Lili agreed. "It's a lovely town." She frowned. "I shall be very sorry to leave."

His bushy brows rose. "But that day is still far in the future."

"No. Unfortunately it's getting closer and closer." She looked across the river at the darkening hills above Philosophenweg. "I don't like to think about it. I'm to return to New York in December."

"Already! Oh dear," said Dr. Hempel, looking rather distressed. "I thought you were here for the academic year."

"No. Although my parents are pleased that I was able to join the university, they still expect me home for Christmas." She imagined that she looked as glum as she now sounded.

"Hmm. That is understandable of course," Dr. Hempel said, and grew silent. Only their steps sounded against the pavement of the Neckarstaden.

Once in front of the deep rose stone facade of Stadthalle, he explained that the building had been constructed quite recently, in 1903.

"It was built with the desire to preserve the spirit of the German Renaissance. On the south side there are portraits of such shining lights as Bach, Beethoven, Liszt, Mozart, and Wagner."

Lili felt compelled to object. "Liszt wasn't German."

Dr. Hempel countered. "Nor was Mozart."

"I suppose," she admitted. "But Mozart was German in the greater sense."

"Ah yes," Dr. Hempel said.

They passed the main entrance that faced the river, and continued on to the entrance on the west side. Once inside the large hall, they left their overcoats and hats at the cloakroom. This was the first time that Lili was wearing her new dirndl. At home, examining herself in the foyer mirror, she had noted that her eyes reflected the shade of the finely woven wool, a blue so pale as to be gray. The dirndl's piping was black and its apron, ending just a few centimeters above the skirt's ankle-length hem, black with vertical stripes of delicate gray. The crème de la crème was the blouse. Its slightly puffed sleeves ended in lace just below her elbows while the daringness of its décolleté was saved by another trimming of ivory lace. There was a definite hint of the swell beneath, and with her hair set high in a crown of interlacing braids, a fair amount of bare skin; she felt rather risqué.

Professor Hempel led her to a set of doors, and they stuck their heads into the great hall that at this time was still empty of spectators. How grand it looked, even with the endless rows of wooden seats. It was the ceiling with its gilded ornamentation and the huge molded eagles that made it so splendid.

"As it is still quite early," the professor said, "I would like to meet with a colleague of mine who has been working with some of the musicians in the orchestra. Would you like to accompany me backstage?"

They passed along the hall to a passage on the right and found themselves in the foyer of yet another side entrance. Dr. Hempel opened a door. The heavy wood swung shut behind them and they entered a corridor lined with closed doors. A sound began to pulsate, hitting Lili in her belly: a thrumming, clawing, growling sensation that grew with each step they took nearer its source. The sound seemed to be coming from the one door that stood slightly ajar at the end of the corridor. A relentless vibration of some great bow across strings, deep, intricately layered, intensifying with each stroke, yet at the same time striving upwards with incredible lightness. In Lili too the sensations were moving higher and higher, from her belly into her chest. She stopped walking. She could not bear to expend energy on anything but listening.

Dr. Hempel too halted, then nodded slowly.

"The music of a virtuoso, no less."

For a few moments he shut his eyes, as if he were savoring it or remembering something.

"Why don't you stay here and enjoy this private concert while I go and find my associate?" he said. Lili nodded.

She was alone in the hallway, all her senses taut. The bow drew the strings into rhythms and realms that made her heart beat wilder. The cadenza left her breathless, ripping her along through terrifying undertones that suddenly swept into sweetness, sorrow, longing. She was transfixed.

Now silence resonated. She could feel it in every nerve. Still, she waited. And was rewarded by the plucking of a solitary string. Notes began to weave in and out of long, tremulous phrases, then joined to float on the air in a piece she knew well. Yet she couldn't quite identify the instrument—not a cello, nor a bass—that could descend to such depths, then rise with such bittersweet hope. Now it was teasing, coaxing. Surely she had heard it before.

She moved one step closer to the door, paused when the music, too, found a double rest. At the next measure the mysterious instrument took up again, warm, full, quick, and she followed it to the doorframe.

There was enough of an opening to see into the dressing room. Lili looked, and sucked in her breath. The lone bulb in the room glowed with a soft light, illuminating the blond-haired man who sat, bare-chested, his eyes closed, a white shirt hanging behind him on the chair. He appeared to be in his mid-twenties, with skin that looked as if he had been anointed with honey and milk. Filaments of gold shimmered on his chest above the lean muscles that played there and in his neck and along his broad shoulders and well-formed arms. He was holding, no, embracing a large auburn instrument that looked like a cello but had no support peg. The base rested between the long boots he wore.

Lili looked upon his face framed by high cheekbones. Dark shadows fringed lids under brows that arched like wings, as if his thoughts were taking flight. Although pressed together, his lips were wellshaped. He seemed to be listening intensely to the music he was making. He was the most wondrous man she had ever seen. Cautious, she pushed the door wider open, just enough to watch without craning her neck. Her hands hung at her sides now, fingers tingling.

There was nothing she could do but stand here, fascinated by the half-naked man and the music, creator and creation at once. He seemed to understand the essence of each note. Where they were leading. She had never felt such playing.

All at once he lifted the bow, opened his eyes and found hers. She had never been looked at like that. She saw blue, of course, and so much more. A string deep within her quavered, the ripples reverberating all the way up to her cheeks. But these did not burn. Instead, she felt the blood draining away.

"Do you love music?" he asked, as if they had already been in conversation. In his voice, Lili could still hear the sound of his instrument.

She nodded, as yet unable to speak.

"Then you are welcome to come in." He motioned to a chair. She slipped into the room, her skirt brushing the edge of the wall. She sat down but did not lean back against the jacket that was draped over the back of the chair.

He raised the bow.

"Marin Marais," he said.

She nodded, as if she had been expecting it. Would the piece be from *Suitte d'un Goût Étranger*?

He began to play, this time conjuring a chameleon of sounds, an organ, a bagpipe, both at the same time, along with a host of violins and other strings. All issued forth from this one instrument. She did not recognize the piece.

The man bent his head, looking down, his cheeks and lips only centimeters from where his fingers, long but not at all feminine, stopped the strings, sometimes lightly, then with quivering intensity. He glanced up at Lili and smiled.

It was as if the room had suddenly been suffused with light so brilliant that she nearly forgot everything else she had ever known.

Once more he closed his eyes. He nodded, softly, smoothly, in secret time with his fingers and the bow and suddenly Lili gasped, for it was as if he were communicating, holding and caressing with infinite gentleness a living creature, a beloved. It was as if she were watching, hearing something so intimate that her cheeks began to burn, and she knew that she wanted to be the one sharing the secret. Yet even at this thought and her sudden trembling, she could not tear herself away from the sight.

Now he looked at her with even gaze and, slowly, lifted the bow and laid it down. The tremors lingered.

"Do you play an instrument?"

"Ye-es," her voice, near breathless, flattened the vowel. "The harpsichord." She swallowed, her throat dry.

"Do you play it well?"

"Very," she said, this time with firmness.

Again he smiled, and again Lili was drawn to the warmth in his eyes.

"Then surely you have played with a viola da gamba."

"Ach, of course, it's a viola da gamba," she exclaimed, glad to distract herself with a factual discussion. "I thought it was some kind of cello I'd never seen."

"Well, you're partially correct. The viola da gamba is an ancestor of the cello." He pointed to the base. "But as you can see, unlike the cello, it doesn't have a leg to stand on." Lili studied the glossy wood curving upwards from the floor.

"Why doesn't one simply put a leg on it?"

"A valid question," he said, holding the instrument at an angle. "But purists—and I am most certainly one of them—believe that the quality of sound is affected by the way it's held, tucked in by the legs."

Lili understood. "*Gamba*—like the French *jambes*, right?"

"Yes, you're correct." His lips parted. His teeth were very white. "So now I know three things about you. You play the harpsichord very well and you speak French." At this Lili permitted herself a smile. She couldn't help it.

"What about the third thing?" she asked.

"You look charming in blue gray."

Now he wasn't smiling.

Instead, he inclined his head slightly.

"If I had known I would already have an audience, I'd have put on my shirt." At this Lili had to blush even more, for she had never been alone in a room with a strange man not wearing a shirt, and certainly never carried on a conversation with one.

"Oh, think nothing of it," she said, brushing off an imaginary thread from her skirt. "Musicians are artists, and artists must be allowed every freedom."

At this, he laughed. The sound filled her with longing for more.

"Well said, Fräulein." His expression changed so that he suddenly looked older, with lines near his eyes. "A sentiment voiced only in certain circles."

Unsure of what to reply, Lili said nothing. Voices sounded from outside.

Lili sprang from her chair, suddenly remembering. "I must go find Dr. Hempel. We still have to find our seats."

In one towering movement the bare-chested man rose, his hand easy upon the instrument. He was even taller than she had expected. "Then I wish you an enjoyable concert, Fräulein."

"Thank you. Oh," she suddenly realized, looking up at him. "You're performing in it."

He nodded. "I am."

"Toi toi toi to you then," Lili said.

"Thank you." He paused, his eyes going over her face so that she felt as if he were studying her, just as she had studied him when his eyes were closed. "Perhaps one day we will meet again, on the stage. After all, many pieces have been composed for the harpsichord and the gamba."

Lili shook her head. "I've never performed anywhere."

A muscle rippled across his jaw. "You're still young," he said.

"Not that young," she shot back. "I'm almost 18."

"Ah," he nodded. "Now I know four things."

"That's not fair," she said. "I know nothing about you."

He moved to place the viola da gamba upright against the chair and Lili sensed a fragrance in the air—a mixture of lemon and wood and something wild. She didn't want to leave the room.

"I wouldn't exactly say that, Fräulein," he said, drawing out the 'that'.

"You're right," she answered, somewhat primly. "I do know that you're an excellent musician."

"Thank you," he said, bowing his head briefly.

"I also know that you don't always wear a shirt when you practice." Her eyes flickered with daring.

His flashed with amusement.

"Let me think," she continued, looking around the room to avoid immediate eye contact, for it was causing her to feel breathless again. "Perhaps I know even more about you than four things. For one, it's highly unlikely that you come from this region of Germany. Your accent shows that you have spent a fair number of years in Pomerania."

"Just like you," he replied, grinning. "Perhaps we were neighbors."

"Perhaps," she said lightly. "I also believe that you are over 20 and under 30."

"That doesn't qualify," he objected. "Surely you know that most of us are in that age range. If that's your fourth, then you only know three."

"Most of whom?" she asked.

It was his turn to raise an eyebrow. At the same time, his glance went across to the jacket hanging over the chair, and Lili turned.

The jacket was black, but it was not the typical one worn by performing musicians. On the right collar, embroidered in silver, were two runes; it was the typical jacket of an officer of the SS

"Yes. I'm with the SS Orchestra," he said, his tone indulgent. "We're quite good. It is often our great honor to perform for the Führer himself."

Her eyes grew wide. She was alone with an SS officer. No wonder she was growing weak in the knees. She had to get out before she passed out.

"Are you all right?" His eyes had darkened cobalt toward their center. He seemed to waver for a moment, as if he were going to reach out and touch her, keep her upright. His finely muscled hands brought to her mind those nights in New York when she had dreamt of tall, blonde, broad-chested SS officers with blue eyes.

"Ye-es," she croaked, her chin down. She couldn't look back at him; she knew her gaze would go straight to his bare chest. Or, perhaps even worse, she wouldn't be able to stop looking into those eyes.

"I have to go," she managed.

He stood aside then.

"*Auf wiedersehen*, Fräulein." His voice carried a strange mixture of tones, leaving her longing for more even as she left him.

As she fled down the hall, she could sense him looking after her, sense it on the skin of her neck, just below where her hair was gathered up at the back. Fortunately the corridor door was open. She rushed through it and stood to the side for some moments, her heart galloping, hoping he had gone back into the dressing room. At last she peered round the doorway and was relieved to see no one but Dr. Hempel moving up the hall.

They returned to the now teeming lobby where the sound of laughter and conversations ricocheted against the walls. Lili calmed herself by distraction, observing their surroundings. The waiting audience stood around in groups, in pairs, alone. While not as elegant as the dress worn in Berlin, their clothing and its cut was as varied as their money purses. Of silk, satin, cotton and wool, fabrics threadbare and with the sheen of velvet, the variety of styles and stitching provided a cross-section of Heidelberg citizens. One couple looked about cooly, as if they'd enjoyed attending premieres for the last half century. Another seemed to be at a concert for the first time; the man pulling at his badly tied tie while the wife gaped at the ceiling and fanned herself noisily with the program. Although there were boys strutting about with an air of authority in their HJ uniforms, and girls looking serious in their own neatly pressed garb of the BDM, Lili was glad she had on the dirndl this evening. Several women were wearing lovely models, but hers truly was stunning. Now her blood again thrummed at the thought of the bare-chested SS man with the viola da gamba who had said she looked charming in blue gray. There were a lot of SS officers scattered throughout the lobby but of course he wasn't one of them. He was backstage.

Lili turned to Dr. Hempel as they waited for the doors to open. "Is this a KdF concert?" That would undoubtedly explain the disparity in dress.

"Yes," he said. "Nearly all performances have tickets available for KdF attendees."

"And are there usually so many SS officers attending, or is it because of the orchestra?" She had never seen so many good-looking men in one place.

Dr. Hempel smiled mischievously. "It is indeed a very special orchestra, isn't it? But then, many of the SS officers are from cultured families. One could say that their love for music is in their blood. Even Reinhard Heydrich is himself a gifted cellist and violinist, as well as being the son of a composer whose inspiration is Wagner." His glance darted to the side, as if he were checking that no one could overhear. "Might I say that the father has not absorbed all of Wagner's strengths?"

Lili gave a playful smile to show that she had understood his insinuation. It was exciting to move in the adult world. Especially with Dr. Hempel and the connection of music, she felt as if she belonged.

As they stood in the lobby, Lili grew aware that several men were glancing at her. At first she worried that perhaps a strap was showing, or that she had a smudge on her face. Then she overheard one SS officer murmur to another, "What an Aryan beauty." With sudden and overwhelming clarity she realized what their looks meant. It was exhilarating. It made her lift her chin so that her bare neck would be even longer above her décolleté.

"This promises to be an excellent performance," Dr. Hempel said as the doors opened and they joined the crowd in making their way to their seats. "This SS Orchestra is among the finest in the Reich."

Lili looked around the great hall. She remembered the special feeling that would wrap itself around her with comforting familiarity when they attended concerts in Berlin. There had been happy anticipation in the atmosphere created by the high ceilings, the chandeliers, red velvet drapes, marble pillars, the ornate golden moldings on the balconies—the feeling of being part of a rich cultural life that had existed for centuries. It had been different from those cold halls at Carnegie Hall where Papa and Mama had taken her to concerts and ballets. Despite the excellent performances, the audiences in New York seemed as if they were still trying something on for size.

The hall of the Heidelberg Stadthalle was not as magnificent as the greatest concert halls of Berlin but still she felt at home here. The air was bathed in gold. Everything was perfect as it was, the stately Reich flags adding to the grandeur.

She caught sight of Hildegard, far off toward the rear, sitting next to a young man Lili did not recognize, probably the fiancé. They were leaning toward each other, talking and smiling.

The lights dimmed. As the heavy curtain began to move, the clapping began. Yet within moments the hall was filled with the sound of wood against wood as seats were emptied and the audience got to their feet, facing the towering portrait. "Heil Hitler!"

Onstage, the black uniformed members of the orchestra stood at attention before their chairs, instruments in hand. A shiver shot through Lili and her shoulders quivered even during the playing and singing of the national anthem and *Horst Wessel Lied*. When an official came to the stage to give an introduction, praising the orchestra, Lili searched for one particular officer. Her gaze passed over each in turn, over shoulders wide and waists narrow, across the faces of men most of whom were fair-haired. All of them were looking directly ahead, past the audience. She searched each and every one of them but the man with the viola da gamba was not among them. Had he lied to her?

Then the concert began. For some time Lili was aware of nothing but creation of the exquisite. Truly, these men were masters. As the last movement of the first piece, Telemann's Trumpet Concerto in D major, came to an end, it must have been apparent to everyone in the hall that these officers, the most elite of the Reich, were also men of heart-breaking sensitivity. Lili sighed. They had touched purity, and shared it with all present.

The applause at the end of the final movement was thunderous, with several interspersed shouts of "Bravo!" A HJ boy appeared before them from the side, face impassive, his bearing dignified as he carried a chair out to the front of the stage. Once the audience had settled back into decorous silence, a tall figure appeared from the right. A surge of liquid heat moved through Lili. It was the man with the viola da gamba.

His stride was that of a great cat, controlled and confident. Once seated on the stage, he made some adjustments and then slipped his arms around the instrument. Lili knew how sleekly muscled these were under the uniform. She could see his gaze travel out into the darkness of the hall as he picked up the bow. For just a moment he looked up, as if toward some distant sun, and then he alone began to play.

Lili shuddered. The sounds filling the hall were coming straight into her. Her chest and shoulders were melting with the warmth of the tones already so familiar to some strange part of her. She wanted to close her eyes to savor them but would not take her gaze off the man. As impassioned as if he were still in the dressing room, he conjured up sensations harsh and maddening, wistful and joyous. She wanted to weep. The pain was a thing of beauty. At some point the orchestra joined in and Lili swallowed, her throat raw.

At this moment there was nowhere else on earth that she would rather have been, not with her family, not even at the rally in Nuremberg.

Her teeth bit hard into her lower lip but it was nothing. She was a musician, she had been playing and listening to music nearly all her life, yet never had she been so moved as when this man touched the strings. She, a musician, had no words to express it, only the knowledge that this man knew. She wanted to know too.

She felt as if she were coming apart.

She shifted in her seat, for she wanted to run, to fly to the stage and be near him even as his playing pained her, burrowing deep within her, a heaviness that grounded her in the earth far below her feet. Yes, the sorrow was exquisite.

And she felt as never before the loss of having to leave Germany. To leave this. She would leave just as she was being born. Into what, she knew not, but the man on the stage had opened something and she wanted to pass through.

The music continued. Her mouth was dry. The notes began to find their way upwards, luring her along. She went willingly. They grew lighter, metamorphosing the sadness of longing into something greater. What was it that Papa had always told her? "Even when everything seems dark, you must look for the light...for in every new day there is always hope." Another wave of warmth shot through her, bathing her in the realization that she had never before understood the true meaning of the words until this moment when the man making the music was calling forth the light.

For some time she simply felt it shining within her.

Then a million other emotions flooded through, borne on the great swells and currents resonating from the strings and bow in the hands of the man too far in front of her. Her belly quivered. He lowered his head, and strands of his golden hair shimmered against the auburn wood and jet black of his uniform. How beautiful he was as he called forth the passion of Bach. Her cheeks burned with her longing to be the one he held, to learn from him, to play music with him. She wanted to touch the sleeve of his jacket, the honey milk skin underneath. He was a Prussian SS officer of the Reich, he was a musician, but, crazy compelling realization, he was also a man. And in some strange way tonight she had become something new. Within her was an as yet untapped power; she could already feel it.

"A wonderful concert," sighed Dr. Hempel too short a time later as he helped her into the sleeves of her coat. "An inspiration to us all." As if still in wonder, he shook his head. "The gamba was superb."

Lili could barely nod, let alone speak. The music still resonated within her. She had looked through the program and found the name. Leopold Arnim von Witzleben. He had told her auf wiedersehen. Would she ever see him again?

A Fascinating Age in which to Be a Scientist in Germany

Lili filled her lungs deep with air scented by the season, chilled and invigorating. The walk up to the castle had not been strenuous but enjoyable enough in the company of Benno.

"Let me give you a tour of the Schloß," he had suggested in the foyer earlier that afternoon. "No matter how often one visits it, one can always find something new." Now they were standing on the wide stone terrace that overlooked the Neckar and hills surrounding Heidelberg, behind the enormous banners that had been hung from the wall below so that they could be seen from the town in all their red, white, and black splendor.

"I was here with the students who positioned the Reich flags," Lili told him. "Not those big ones, but the smaller ones like over there." She felt the timbre of pride in her voice.

"Good work," Benno nodded. He turned his back on the landscape and faced the castle.

His profile was different from the commanding one of Leopold Arnim von Witzleben. She looked past him toward Philosophenweg. Disappointment still pulled at her. After the exhilaration of the days following the concert, when she had spent hours reliving their meeting, and envisioning the next one in a wide and wild variety of possibilities, reality had taken over, raw reality that told her she would most likely never again see the man. After all, he was an SS officer, a musician who performed all over the Reich, and she a young woman who would soon leave Germany. There was no point in letting her imagination get out of hand; why add salt? Now she examined the man who stood before her, for a moment visualizing him as a courtier in the Middle Ages. Or perhaps a royal physician, an alchemist. No. Benno was today's man of learning; a scientist of the Third Reich.

"Let's go inside," he suggested, and they headed toward the inner courtyard. "So now, Freiin Lili," he said, for he still liked to tease her with the title. "Tell me what you know about the Heidelberger Schloß."

Lili pursed her mouth. "Mmm…construction began around 1300. The reason that it is such a hodgepodge of styles is that different rulers kept adding to it."

"Correct," said Benno. "Your grade is a 2."

"Why not a 1?"

"Because you didn't mention the fact that parts of the castle needed to be rebuilt because of having been destroyed during wars with France, by lightning and then again when the stones were removed by the citizens of Heidelberg themselves for building their houses."

"I knew that!" Lili protested. "I didn't think I had to spell it all out." She smiled. "It's truly no wonder why you're a scientist. Such a stickler for detail, you are." Now that she had decided she was no longer a girl but a woman, it was much easier to tease back.

"Truly," he grinned. "I do love facts. They're so undeniable." For a few moments, the only sound was the muted crunching of their soles against the gravel. Lili glanced at Benno.

"Do you truly believe that?"

"What—that facts are undeniable?"

She nodded.

"It would seem an obvious truth. A fact in itself." His tone was smug.

"But couldn't a fact be different, depending on from what perspective one is looking at it?"

"What do you mean by that, little Freiin? That a fact is not absolute?"

As usual when faced with an argument, her heartbeat quickened.

"Well, for example, look at this castle." Her gaze swept over the massive red sandstone they were about to pass into, home of the Prince Electors of the Palatinate for over four centuries. "It's a fact that parts of it were destroyed by the French and that was bad. But—" and here she faltered, for the thought was strange and new and even disturbing. "Most likely the French thought the fact was good. They must have thought that by destroying something, they were creating something else." She stopped walking. "If that's the case, then the fact is two opposites at the same time, and then how can it be undeniable? In fact, how can it even be a fact?"

Benno looked at her, his expression somewhat severe.

"You are troubling your pretty head with too much philosophical thinking, my lady." Like a courtier, he put a gloved hand under her elbow, guiding her into motion. "First comes the tour, then, if there is time, we'll talk about opinions."

They continued on into the castle courtyard, in this season nearly empty. During the summer months it was a favorite site for open-air concerts.

"As a scientist I agree with you on part of one of your points," Benno continued nonetheless. "Sometimes one must destroy something completely in order to create something else that is better. The ancient Aryans in the East knew this. The Führer does too."

During the following hour, they circled the great vat as Benno told her his version of the story of tiny Perkeo, the castle jester, guardian of the wine, and they laughed at his comical statue. They toured the newest addition to the castle, the King's Hall, completed just four years ago. Since then, it had been the site of official dinner banquets, cultural performances, and a host of festivities.

Their walk ended in a *Gasthaus*, warm and welcoming. Lili stirred her tea. The scent of mint rose, blotting out for some moments the cloying aroma of centuries' worth of tobacco smoke trapped in the thick walls.

"Oh, what a view!" Lili looked out the window and over to the hills on the opposite bank of the Neckar. "It makes me think of a painting by Caspar David Friedrich. There's something about the colors of the sky at this time of day."

Benno smiled, his mouth closed. "You must be a Romantic."

"Perhaps," Lili flirted, giving it a double meaning. "I haven't really thought about it yet. What about you?"

"No question about it." His dark eyes looked straight into hers. "I'm a pragmatist."

"I see. That's probably sensible, but is it always easy?"

"So far it has been. Although you make it more difficult." He leaned back against the worn leather chair. Before Lili could think of any riposte to the strange comment, he continued. "I go for what makes the most sense. For example, I was fortunate to be a student at the Wilhelmsgymnasium in Berlin. There I became interested in the work of one of those students who came before me, Otto Meyerhof. Even though he won a Nobel Prize in '22, I doubt you've heard of him. You are after all, a Romantic, not a scientific." He grinned and swallowed some tea.

"Eventually Meyerhof became director of the Kaiser Wilhelm Institute for Medicine here. And because my own interest has grown in the direction of physiology, anthropology, and mental behaviors, I decided to come to Heidelberg and study as near to Meyerhof as possible, which is why I'm here."

"Which," said Lili, "was very pragmatic of you."

Benno laughed. Lili had never before noticed that when he did, the tips of his canines stuck out a tiny bit more than the rest of his teeth.

"No, Lili. It was that regardless of his being Jewish and now living on borrowed time—so far he's avoided being thrown out with the more than 40 University professors who lost their jobs in '33—I knew that I should be doing my research in Heidelberg. That was the pragmatic part."

Lili considered. Here was a striking example of what she had learned so long ago at the German-American Cultural Club: that the National Socialists would help give back to Aryans those jobs that the Jews had stolen from them.

"Forty professors," she said. "That's a lot. Who replaced them?"

Benno seemed amused by the question. "Why, Aryan professors of course."

"Yes, of course," she said quickly. "I knew that." Yet she wondered where one would find all at once so many professors who had the necessary qualifications.

Benno held her gaze across the table.

"Don't fret, Lili. There's a wonderful purpose to everything. It's all part of human evolution." He blinked. "Don't lose a moment's thought for those professors either. Most of them have found jobs in other places, countries that either don't care or aren't aware of our findings." He put down his cup. "Our standards are purer."

"One day on a bus in New York I sat behind a professor from Heidelberg," Lili remembered. "Perhaps he was one of the forty."

"About a quarter of the science professors were expelled. Not all of them were Jews. But science must be pragmatic. We're forging ahead in our research, in ways unimaginable only a few years ago." He sounded excited.

"It's a fascinating age to be a scientist in Germany. 19th century researchers and theorists like Haeckel and Schallmeyer paved the way for our understanding of heredity. Today we're standing at the threshold of an era of Social Darwinism. Never before has the government been so committed to facilitating research into such a wide scope of relevant investigation. Like-minded institutions in America are eager to fund our research."

In America? "What *is* your particular field, Benno?"

"Ah, don't get me started! I can speak for hours on that. But it will have to wait," he said, rising from his seat. "It's time I got you back to the house or your great-aunt may begin to wonder if I've spirited you away." His canines glowed an eerie white as they passed through the smoky room. "I'll tell you about germ plasms another time."

Never before would Lili have imagined that such words would intrigue her.

Her Day Must Be on its Way

There was no other word for it. Throughout dinner that evening, Dr. Hempel twinkled. Lili kept looking over at him, hoping he might say something that would explain the aura surrounding him, but the talk at the table was of the celestial body that had been spotted speeding through the sky the previous week by a well-known comet hunter in Heidelberg. For the last few days of October his observation had made international news.

"It wasn't a comet this time," explained Benno. "Too star-like. Most likely an asteroid."

"Apparently you're as comfortable with the telescope as the microscope," Lili said, relishing the comparison and hoping it would encourage him to speak about his work.

Yet Benno did not use the opportunity to explain about germ plasms. Instead, he asked for another serving of Frau Brinkmann's *Rote Grütze*, her creamy pudding with stewed red berries.

It was Dr. Hempel who spoke, just as Frau Brinkmann came out of the kitchen bearing a bottle of Taittinger *Sekt* that she set on the table in front of him.

"I would like to propose a toast," he announced, breaking into a radiant smile. Frau Brinkmann handed out the glasses. "Let us celebrate what will undoubtedly be the premiere of another shining star—the upcoming performance of Fräulein Lili at our very own Stadthalle." Then he folded his arms over his broad belly and sat back, his gaze, like the wine, sparkling at Lili.

The words seemed to push through a syrupy slow echo in her ears. By the time she had digested their meaning, Lili realized her mouth was open. So this was why he had looked so pleased. Dr. Hempel had arranged this without her knowledge and she had no idea what to say to him now. How? How dare you? I will be eternally grateful to you, Dr. Hempel?

Yet it was Herr Tischborn who spoke first.

"This is wonderful news indeed. Congratulations, Fräulein Lili. I will certainly attend the performance. When is it to be?"

At this, everyone turned toward Dr. Hempel.

Now he looked a bit sheepish.

"In December. That allows for adequate practice time."

A flood of emotions ripped through Lili, bubbling, floating, yet sinking too.

"When?" was all she could manage.

Dr. Hempel cleared his throat.

"Ahem, I have been working on this for some time and was yesterday given the go-ahead. There is no need for an audition. My word is enough."

Tante Altheia was shaking her head, all the while looking pleased.

Dr. Hempel continued. "In order to avoid disappointment, Fräulein Lili, I wanted to wait until everything was confirmed before telling you." He smiled, and it was impossible for her to be anything other than thrilled. Except that he had said December.

"When in December?"

"Ach," said Dr. Hempel and began to stroke his beard. His eyes lost some of their luster. "The twenty-second."

The tension moved from her head, passed through her chest and belly and then settled in numbing mass upon her legs. Dr. Hempel had arranged for her to perform at Heidelberg's premier concert house, her long dreamed-for German debut, on the twenty-second of December. Her ship to New York would set sail on the seventeenth.

♫ ♪ ♫

It was market day, Marktplatz abuzz, vendors calling out, tantalizing smells caught in the heavy air, but Lili ignored it all to walk straight over to the yellow box. With gloved hands she opened her purse and took out the slightly crushed envelope. Then she peeled off the gloves so that she could touch the paper with her fingers one last time. The cold bit into them right away. Please please please: let her have written the right words to make Mama and Papa allow her to stay for the concert even though it meant missing Christmas. If she could stay, she would play the harpsichord as she had never before played it. She would make them all proud. If they let her stay, she would play for Germany. Perhaps, that day, she would even play for the Führer. She smoothed the envelope. The man with the viola da gamba had said that she was young but that surely one day she would perform. Perhaps even with him… She dared dream again. Her day must be on its way. How could Papa and Mama deny her such an opportunity? She lifted the envelope to her lips and kissed the address, then slipped it into the slot. She lingered in front of the yellow box. The cold seared her nose and lungs. If Papa and Mama said no, it would sear her heart.

Playing Meaningful Roles

The promise of snow hung in the air. Wrapped in her Loden coat, hat, and a woolen shawl, Lili was on her way to the University. Near Museumplatz the air was delicious with the aroma of roasted nuts. For some paces she walked abreast of a young mother and child. The girl, a bit older than Paul, called out,"Look, Mami. Gebrannte Mandeln! Please, will you buy me some?"

"Not from him."

The small face sagged with disappointment.

Lili reached the building. Once inside, she flew up the stairs. The hallway was already empty; classes had begun. Today, for the very first time, she was late, having lingered over breakfast with Tante Aletheia.

"Heil Hitler," she said as she entered the classroom. "Please excuse me."

Professor Hetzenrath turned briefly from the podium. His palm made a little upwards wave while he continued speaking to the class. Lili slid into the seat next to Hildegard, who frowned, but Lili could see that she wasn't paying attention to the lecture. Instead, she was drawing lines in the margin of her notebook.

Dr. Hetzenrath seemed to be talking about the role of the Catholic Church and Pope Gregory VII. Like Dr. Hempel, the professor had a beard, but was nowhere near as jolly.

"The plenitude of papal authority was not universally claimed until this ambitious pope's reign during the fourth quarter of the 11th century, when it was made binding in canon law." This much Lili thought she understood. "Throughout the concordance of several councils during the ensuing centuries, by the first half of the 15th, any writings issued by the Pope were law. Any deviations from the basic doctrines of the Church were deemed heretical. As such, they were punishable by penance, incarceration or even death." He removed his glasses. From his pocket he extracted a voluminous handkerchief and began to polish the lenses.

"History repeats itself," he said, as if the s's were breath that would help clean the glasses.

A student in the front row called out.

"What are you insinuating, Herr Professor?"

Dr. Hetzenrath settled his spectacles back over his potato nose.

"This is a lecture. Silence."

The student leaned back in his seat, folding his arms. Dr. Hetzenrath continued and there were no further interruptions.

On the way out of the classroom, Lili and Hildegard fell into step.

"That Hetzenrath," Hildegard complained. Her voice was loud, and Lili thought it a good thing that the professor was across the room. "He's such a bore. It's all I can do to keep from falling asleep. On and on he drones, about things that have already changed. Who cares about whether or not this edict said that or that edict said this? It's all over now. In Germany, the Catholic church no longer carries much weight." She stopped to tie her shoelace. Her brown braids swung in the air as she looked up at Lili. "After all, the Pope has given his blessings for a German ethnic community."

"What are you referring to?"

"That papal bull. Don't you remember?" Hildegard stood up. Both her cheeks had vivid blotches. "My uncle is in some government office and he said that we don't have to consider the Catholics anymore. The Pope hates Jews just as much as anyone."

Just ahead of them in the hallway a classmate lost her balance for a moment, her books cascading to the floor. She knelt to gather them up. A tall, tawny-haired student bent down to help.

Hildegard turned toward Lili, her body blocking the view. "Ach, that Mr. Handsome. He's always the gentleman." Her eyes flashed. "Guess what! We've decided to get married in April. Only four more months." Suddenly her cheeks drained of color. "Oh my goodness!"

Lili felt a spurt of fear. Now what? She bit down on the inside of her lip.

"We could do it on the 20th."

"Do what?"

"We can get married on his birthday and by Christmas I could give the Führer the best gift of all. It just has to be a boy. At least the first one…"

Lili couldn't help but roll her eyes. Hildegard seemed to have lost all interest in her studies. And as pleased as she was for Hildegard, such talk couldn't be interesting to anyone but Hildegard and her fiancé.

The only time she had found babies intriguing was when Mama had Paul. And now that baby was already four years old. How Paul must have grown during these past months. Did he still remember her well? If she were allowed to stay longer, would his memory of her fade?

"You're not listening!" Hildegard was frowning at her. "Are you still chewing through Professor Hetzenrath's lecture instead of what I've been telling you?"

"My apologies. I was thinking about my little brother."

Hildegard was immediately sympathetic. "You must miss him. I miss my own family enormously. I've got three younger brothers and a sister whom I see about once a month. My uncle occasionally takes me along when he drives to Frankfurt for work."

"Then you're lucky," Lili said. "I have to make do with letters."

♫ ♪ ♫

Later, when she arrived at Kornmarkt, Lili found that Frau Brinkmann had left a letter for her on the table in the foyer. Although it couldn't possibly be a reply to her own, she grabbed it and ran up the stairs.

Dearest Lili, she read as she folded herself into the armchair under the window. *The days are growing colder. It was summer when you left, and now the autumn is passing here without you. Winter is on our doorstep but you are still far away. I miss you dreadfully, my darling daughter.*

Paul asks about you every day yet seems to have grown resigned to your absence for now—especially as we have told him the end is in sight; Papa is certain that you will come home with clear vision. Soon we can begin counting the days instead of only the weeks. You will be our very best Christmas gift.

The words, penned in Mama's delicate script, infuriated her.

It was as if claws were gripping her chest and throat, but not at all in the same way as had the sound of the viola da gamba. She knew exactly what Papa meant by clear vision. He was not talking merely about her coming home, but about giving up her faith in the Führer. That she would never do. The whole world now recognized the strength and accomplishments of the Führer and the Reich. Were all of them wrong, and only Papa right? She kicked her foot, hitting nothing but air, and threw the letter to the ground. The shame of it rekindled. Papa should have been here. If her whole family were here, they could all have been playing meaningful roles in the new Germany.

By not being here, Papa had robbed her of a chance to move in important circles. Surely he would have been included in important functions. The Führer had been in their apartment in Berlin. She could never forget that. Papa could have taken up his position again as a naval officer. The German fleet was growing by the hour. Perhaps he could get back his membership in the club. If Papa were here, she would have a true place in society, not just that of a struggling university student. But he had turned his back on Germany, and the Führer, leaving Lili with nothing but her own resources.

Well, she had some now. She was going to play the harpsichord so brilliantly that the Führer himself would hear of it and remember her. Perhaps he would even kiss her cheek again. No, that image didn't fit. Perhaps he would shake her hand. Yes, that would be enough. She swallowed. Papa and Mama simply had to say yes. She leaned over and picked up the letter again.

With all our love, always and forever. Hah. Let them prove it. She dared them.

There Must Have Been a Reason

In the meantime, she practiced. Never before had she practiced so much and so hard. Dr. Hempel had explained that the concert was one featuring young talent from across the Reich, and that the performers were permitted to choose from such composers as Bach, Beethoven, Buxtehude, Händel, Humperdinck, Mozart, Pachelbel, Telemann, and Wagner, among others. It would be the performer's choice whether they were solos or pieces that included the orchestra. Her choice had to be submitted within the week after getting Dr. Hempel's news. In early December there would be a meeting with the organizers to make sure that everything was being done correctly.

Lili had spent an entire day deciding what she would play. Should she go with some of the *Goldberg Variations?* It seemed fitting. After all, it was because she had perfected them that she had permitted herself to wrangle her return to Germany. But no, it would be impossible to play all of them at such a concert. She needed something complete in itself. Something that would showcase who she was as a musician. As an artist. She needed the freedom to choose. She smiled at the thought, remembering what she had said about artistic freedom to the bare-chested man with the viola da gamba. Leopold Arnim von Witzleben… In the end, she had chosen Bach. She would play the Harpsichord Concerto in D minor. It would allow her to show off her skills while letting the orchestra shine. A brave thought, she felt, considering that she had never performed with any instrument other than Papa's violin. What would it be like? As she practiced, she knew the silent spaces would soon be filled with tremendous sound. It charged her not with fear, but exhilaration. She trembled with anticipation and joy at the thought of creating music in time with an orchestra.

But another metronome was ticking. Each day brought her closer to the concert on the twenty-second, just as each day drew closer to the morning of the seventeenth, the day she was to set sail on the S.S. Hamburg for the five day voyage. And each day brought nearer the reply from Papa and Mama.

♫ ♪ ♫

Lili turned onto Haupstraße, slowing her pace so that she could distract herself with some windowshopping. Classes were over for today. The last one had finished an hour early as several of the student leaders informed Professor Dr. Hetzenrath that they had an important leadership meeting to attend. Lili had been disappointed. So far, although she certainly didn't understand everything he said, it was her only class in which the professor seemed to stick to the subject. Other classes, although relevant, had a tendency to slide into discussion of what was important for the Reich. She had to admit that she would have preferred to save those talks for outside the classroom. Her comprehension skills still needed improvement and she wanted to learn more about the roots of Germany. After all, she also went to NSDStB and BDM meetings and heard more of the same there.

The fragrance of Gebrannte Mandeln was floating over from the stand near Museumplatz so she stopped and bought a packet of burnt almonds, their auburn sugar coating still warm inside the paper wrap. She remained in front of the stand, crunching on the nuts, breathing in the aroma that so reminded her of childhood. The vendor, a middle-aged man wrapped in a coat that had seen better days, gave her a slow smile that seemed to lighten the shadows beneath his eyes. She returned it with warmth and raised her hand to slip another almond into her mouth.

"*Du da.*" You there. It was the familiar 'you'. No one had ever addressed her like that, and certainly never in such a harsh tone.

Lili turned around slowly.

Two SS officers stood in front of the stall, hands at their backs, booted legs slightly apart. Yet their severe gaze was not on her but the almond seller.

"Watch out at whom you smile."

Lili looked at the men in their smart black uniforms and then at the vendor. In the space of two moments his bearing had crumpled and he looked years older.

"Has this man been harassing you?" one of the officers asked, altering his tone.

"Why no," she said. "Not at all. Actually, he has sweetened my day with these delicious almonds." She held out the bag. "May I offer you some?"

The seller of almonds seemed frozen, only his eyes moving as he watched them.

The two officers suddenly smiled, looking ever so nice, so much more normal, and one of them made a little bow to Lili.

"Tempting, Fräulein," he said.

"Indeed, most tempting," the other agreed, and Lili suspected they were speaking of more than the almonds.

She kept the bag in the air.

Ever so gently, the first officer pushed it back toward her.

"Please. Keep your almonds, sugar-coated though they might be." His expression was friendly.

"We wouldn't want to deprive such a lovely young Fräulein of even one hot almond on such a cold day as today."

"No, indeed not." Another little bow.

Then both turned to the seller of almonds and the voice lost its sugar coating.

"Two bags. Make sure they're hot."

The man hurried to fill the bags and Lili could see that his hands were trembling. A few almonds fell to the pavement.

The officers laughed.

"Don't try and sell those later. We know your type." The man said nothing but continued to scoop nuts into the conical bags. At last he had finished, and folded the paper down on top. For just a moment he hesitated, then held the bags out.

The officer took them, handing one to his colleague. Then they turned to Lili, saluting with a snappy "Heil Hitler", and set off.

Lili was about to call after them that they had forgotten to pay, when the man motioned to her, shaking his head vehemently.

She paused to watch the backs of the officers as they continued up the street.

"Thank you, Fräulein."

Lili waited for him to say something more.

He said nothing.

"You were kind to give them the nuts," she said.

The man shrugged. "As long as I give them their bag, I have a chance to keep my business."

"I don't understand."

"I used to be a high school math teacher. Now I sell burnt almonds."

"Ach," Lili said. She didn't know what else to say, so shook her head and walked away, heels tapping against the cold stone. She winced. There must have been something wrong with the man for the SS officers to treat him that way. In truth, he hadn't looked all that reliable with those shadows under his eyes and his nervous manner. He said he used to be a teacher. Perhaps he had done something wrong in school. Perhaps it was bad, but not so bad that he had to go to jail or a camp. Whatever the man had done, there must have been a good reason for the officers to behave the way they had toward him. After all, otherwise they had seemed very nice.

How Horribly Unfair

The lecture hall was packed with students and several SS officers as well. The guest speaker told them fascinating things about the Vice-Chancellor of the University in Munich. Not only was *Rektor* Wüst an SS officer but he was also an eminent Orientalist. He had demonstrated that the Führer and the ancient wisdom of the East were linked. Lili took copious notes. Then, rather than go home before the BDM meeting, she went to Schafheutle and drank a small pot of coffee and ate a slice of Nußtorte and then another of *Käsekuchen* while she read through the notes. It was exciting to realize that the Reich had roots that went so deep, all the way to the other side of the world.

…in a long chain originating with the ancient Vedas, National Socialism is the last step in the evolution of Indo-Aryan religious history. The suffering the Führer saw and himself experienced during his early days in Vienna made him realize that he could either 'suffocate in theories or accept the superficiality

of reality.' Wüst said that this expresses the Buddhist middle way between extremes, and demonstrates the link between the Führer and the Buddha, who was the founder of the Indo-Germanic faith...

It was yet another sign that the Führer was indeed he who had been prophesied years ago as the leader who would come to unite the German people. What a wondrous destiny. Aside from its roots in the great cultures of the ancient Teutonic and Nordic peoples, the Reich was directly linked to Buddhism. How many different facets there were to the jewel that was Germany. She smiled at the poetic image as she motioned to the waitress.

There was so much she still had to discover here. How could she possibly go back to America already? It truly wasn't fair. Papa and Mama had no idea how important it was for her to be in Germany. At this thought, the anxiety returned. There had been no letter in this morning's post. December seventeenth was drawing closer. She had increased her practice time and already knew her performance would be brilliant. *If* she were here to perform. Oh, they simply had to say yes. They just had to.

The Schlagsahne and cheese rose slightly from her belly, making her feel a bit sick. She swallowed. She must be calm. Papa and Mama would say yes. Except for those times when Papa changed his mind, in the end they always said yes. As she stepped out onto Hauptstraße she drew in a deep breath, cold and crisp, and set out for the BDM meeting.

♫ ♪ ♫

Inside the hall, dozens of girls were busy setting up the room for the evening's activities. There were more than usual and Lili did not recognize a good many of the faces. It seemed that tonight there was going to be dancing; furniture was being pulled to the sides. Lili hung up her coat and went to help some girls carrying a table. They moved to make room for her.

"…and the squad leaders get to visit the SS…"

"I love traveling by train," said a girl from Lili's squad. "You get to see so much of the countryside."

"That's the least of it," said the other girl, rolling her eyes. "First they go to Munich and visit the important sites, like the Hofbräuhaus where the first speeches were made. And to the street where the martyrs fell. Then they go to the Eternal Jew Exhibition. Next day they go to Dachau and visit the SS there. And," she said, beaming, "before they come back, they march to support the *Volksdeutsche* at the borderlands."

"Ja, they deserve all the support they can get, poor things," said one of the others as they plunked the table down alongside a wall. "I'm certainly pressing my thumbs that I'll be one of the lucky ones who get picked to go to the Sudetenland in April. There's going to be a big meeting just across the border. We want to show those kids over there how great it'll be if they join HJ and BDM. After all, they're Germans."

"It's so unfair. Why do the Volksdeutsche have to live under the Czechs when they could be real Germans again?"

"Well, they're going to love our dances," the first girl said cheerfully. "Let's go practice."

"Don't be silly. We have other things to do right now. Besides, you don't even know yet if you'll be one of those chosen to go."

Lili walked away, passing another table where half a dozen girls were sitting, heads bent, sewing. She moved by quickly. Despite Mama's occasional efforts to convince her, needlework had never appealed to her. She would have preferred to wear a dress with a rip in it rather than have to mend it herself. Although she would be the first to say that her mother's embroidery was beautiful, Lili could not abide the detailed work and patience required. A work that progressed in millimeters—no thank you.

"Lili!"

She looked toward the voice and discovered Ursula hurrying over to her. She hadn't seen her since the campout and noticed immediately that her hair had been cut chin length but looked as greasy as ever.

"Heil Hitler!"

"Our squad is also at this meeting." Ursula beamed. "I was hoping I'd get to see you." They set out toward the side of the hall where the others were congregating.

"So much has happened since we last met," Ursula said.

"Tell me."

"For one, my father now owns the grocery shop."

"Why, that's wonderful, Ursula."

"Ja," she grinned. "He was able to buy it for much less than its original value, so he got a good deal. All the wares were included too."

"What a stroke of luck."

Ursula nodded. "The owner left from practically one day to the next."

Lili nodded. Ursula's father was going up in the world.

"And what about you—are you still stacking cans?"

Ursula's expression was sheepish as she nodded. Then she brightened. "For now. But this is the most exciting thing. I—"

There was no more time for talk as the meeting was called to order and a welcome speech given by one of the squad leaders. The girl behind Lili whispered that her neighbor should get to the back row because she wasn't wearing a uniform. Then they all sang several songs, beginning with the anthem followed by the *Horst Wessel Lied*. Lili paid attention to every word as she glanced around the hall.

So much had happened to Germany since those same words had been penned by Reich Minister Dr. Goebbels. The early days of the struggle had been marked by strife with those who didn't see the Führer's wisdom. But now there would never again be war as long as the Führer had his way. And the song would endure, for it showed clearly the sacrifice and hope that went into making the Third Reich.

"Heil Hitler!" everyone shouted.

It was announced that a squad leader would speak on the importance of keeping Aryan blood pure.

A no-nonsense girl who must have been about 20, but could have passed for 40, stepped up to the podium.

"1937 is coming to an end," she said, her tone shrill. "For many of you, it will be your last year in the BDM. Many of you will choose to go on to spend four years in Glaube and Schönheit where the key words really are Faith and Beauty. There you'll learn more about housekeeping, beauty care, health, and, not least in importance, a good and proper world view of National Socialism." She cast a severe look over all of them. "Of course not all of you will choose to join Faith and Beauty when you turn 18. And a lot of you will be getting married. So for all of you who are ready to set out on that path, it will be useful to have a list that you must absolutely keep in mind when you make your choice of husband."

At this she thrust out her right hand, index finger pointing upwards. She reminded Lili of one of the hefty servants caricatured in the drawings of Wilhelm Busch.

"One!" The word exploded.

"Be mindful that you are German."

Lili smiled. She was indeed always mindful of this because there was nothing else she would rather be.

Two fingers were shoved into the air.

"Two! If you're genetically sound, you must not remain single." Lili cocked her head. What did genetically sound mean?

"Three! Keep your body pure!" That was easy to do. She didn't smoke, nor did she think she drank too much.

"Four! Keep pure your spirit and soul!" She certainly intended to. Music was good for both.

"Five! Choose as husband only a German of your type or Nordic blood!' She wasn't ready to choose any husband at this point.

Now both hands shot into the air.

"Six! When choosing your husband, investigate his heritage!" Shouldn't that be number five?

"Seven! Health is the prerequisite for external beauty!" Yes, of course it was important to be healthy—for beauty and everything else in life.

"Eight! Marry only for love!" That was obvious. She wasn't going to be one of those women who were married off simply to put the family estates together.

"Nine! Look not for a playmate but a partner for life!" A playmate? Was she talking about marriage or kindergarten?

"Ten! Hope for as many children as possible!" Lili giggled. Hope wasn't all that was involved in having children... She looked around. Some of the girls were crying. Was it because the advice had stirred them or because they realized that their time in the BDM was coming to an end? Those years must have been the happiest in their lives so far. From what she had heard of Faith and Beauty, it was not as much fun as either the Young Girls League or the BDM. There would be no more campouts, marching, nor evenings of games. In Faith and Beauty they would have more gymnastics and lessons in housekeeping skills. There would be occasional fashion shows to demonstrate how wholesome and beautiful the young women of the Reich could be. Even if Mama and Papa said she could stay on, Lili too would be one of them bidding farewell to the BDM.

How horribly unfair it was, considering that she had only recently got to say hello.

As the speech ended, Ursula nudged her. "Will you be my partner in the dance?"

"Isn't it a row dance?"

"Then we can stand together."

The girls fell into four rows of 16, each row facing outwards to form a large square. Lili had danced like this a few times over the past months and knew enough to keep in step. A gramophone was crackling quite loud but the girls who were not dancing joined with gusto in singing the folk music. The traditional melodies were comforting and cheerful. How natural it felt to be a part of it, harmonizing in steps that had been danced for centuries. The girls pranced around the hall like a giant set of bellows, the rows moving in and out and, after a while, Lili felt quite winded.

"That's enough for me." She sat down at a table. Another girl leapt up to take her place in the dance. Ursula came over.

"Are you still at university?" she shouted.

Lili nodded.

Ursula motioned that they go across the room to where some dried apple slices had been laid out. "I wanted to tell you," she began, stuffing one into her mouth. "When I found out that my father was planning to keep me doing the cleaning and stacking, I decided to do something daring."

Lili looked at her with anticipation.

"Do you remember I told you I'm really good with numbers?"

"You did say you were hoping to do the books at the store some day."

Ursula flapped her hand in the air.

"Yes, but that's not going to be. My father is too close-minded. I heard about a firm that works a lot with numbers. They have special machines that count things, and they need people to work with those numbers." Pride suffused her face. "I went there for an interview. They talked to me and tested me for a while—and then they said they'd hire me as an apprentice!"

"That's perfect, Ursula," Lili smiled. "But what about your father? Is he angry?"

"Ach, him," Ursula scoffed. "We don't talk to each other anymore. When I start at Dehomag I won't be making much, but I'll give most of it to my mother for household money and then he can't complain too loud." They grinned at each other and returned to the others.

When the meeting was over, Lili went around the room to thank the squad leaders and say goodbye to several of the girls. There was no need to tell them that she might be returning to America next month. Let them think that she was going into Faith and Beauty. All around the room there were salutes, handshakes, and even tears. Lili's eyes stayed dry. On the way home, the first snow melted against her lashes.

Sankt Niklaus Can Be Annoying Too

Crawling about on her hands and knees, Lili peered under the bed, searching for her brown lace-ups. They had to be there. She had looked everywhere in the room and could have sworn that she'd left them near the door the night before. Had Fragonard dragged them off? That didn't seem likely. Fragonard did not usually interest himself with such mundane items. So where were they? They were her warmest shoes, lined with wool, perfect for the temperature these days. But they were not under the bed either. Lili stood up in her stockinged feet, smoothing down the pleats of her chocolate brown skirt. She glanced at the bedroom door from where came a slight rustling sound, and opened it to find Fragonard investigating the wrapping of what at first glance seemed to be a large brown lump. Then she recognized her shoes, filled to the rims with an assortment of tangerines, colored foil, and cellophane. Of course! Today was Sankt Niklaus Tag. Just like on every other sixth of December in her memory, during the night her shoes had been taken out of her room by Sankt Niklaus—or someone—and stuffed with goodies. The cellophane package at which Fragonard was now staring with green-eyed concentration contained a chocolate statue of the favorite saint of good German children. The bad ones were always threatened with switches or pieces of coal, but Lili had never had that experience. Her shoes had always been overflowing with chocolates, hazelnuts, almonds, tangerines, gingerbread, and apples to nibble on throughout the following days.

"Here. Play with this." She removed the silver string from the wrapper, dangling it in front of Fragonard. As soon as he swatted it, she let go and picked up the chocolate statue and her shoes. A tangerine fell to the floor, narrowly missing the cat. He looked up at her, his eyes turning to slits. "Sorry." Fragonard leaned against her ankles and then sauntered up the hallway as if more interesting matters awaited him elsewhere. Lili took the shoes back into her room and emptied them onto the table. Mmm. Marzipan fruits. Tiny apples and pears, perfect in form, fashioned from almond paste. She bit into a miniature banana. Then too there were foil-wrapped chocolates she had never had in Berlin or New York. Indeed, it seemed that Sankt Niklaus worked in a regional manner. She grinned. In this case, it was obviously Tante Aletheia who had come in silence last night to remove the shoes. It was a surprise, for Lili had assumed that at seventeen there would be no more visits from Sankt Niklaus. Yet before slipping her feet into the shoes, she made sure they were truly empty. There. Tucked up inside the toe of one was something hard.

As long as she could remember, Sankt Niklaus had left amongst the edibles a small ornament. Over the years, she, and now Paul too, had looked forward to hanging the new one amidst those of previous years already adorning the tree on Christmas Eve. One year it was a silver acorn; another year a crystal bird, its beak of beaten gold. Yet another year it had been a shooting star fashioned of straw. This time there was a small golden Statue of Liberty that she was to hang upon the Christmas tree, in New York.

The marzipan lost its taste.

We Are Going to Take It All the Way

Lili had never been a nail biter. Instead, the inside of her bottom lip had little lumps on it where her teeth had been pressing into the soft flesh. Every now and then, a ferric warmth seeped against her taste buds. Still no letter from Papa and Mama. It wasn't possible to imagine that next week she would no longer be in Germany. Nor did it seem real that she would be on the ship to New York. It was a horrible twilight world. Only the letter would bring clarity.

Going with Benno this evening to the newly released Zarah Leander film at the cinema on Hauptstraße would be a welcome distraction. He had invited her that morning, and now they were seated next to each other in the dark theater. It was strangely disturbing to sit so close. Only centimeters separated them. When he moved, the smell of wool and smoke and something chemical rose from his sleeve. It reminded her of sitting with Friedrich at the German-American Cultural Club. When Benno turned toward her to whisper a comment in the dark, his breath was warm. Would he try to kiss her? Couples often did that while the film was playing. But they weren't a couple. As the newsreel finished and the film began, she imagined what it might be like to be Benno's girlfriend, holding his pale hands, bony hands that sliced cells and mixed solutions. She imagined running her hands through his unruly hair and nearly giggled; surely her fingers would get stuck. And what would it be like to have him hold her close against him? She couldn't imagine.

"It's starting," Benno breathed in her ear. She focused on the screen. *La Habanera* swept her up with its music and scenery and story. Astree (Zarah Leander) was trapped in a loveless marriage in Puerto Rico with a wealthy ex-bullfighter. Life seemed hopeless until Dr. Sven Nagel, her old flame from home—Sweden—appeared on the island to fight a mystery disease. Now the drama began as longings were re-awakened. Lili sympathized with Astree pining for Nordic winters. Suddenly she shivered. More than just his looks, there was something intense about the scientist Dr. Nagel (Karl Martell) that reminded her of Benno. She tilted her head toward him, inhaling the scent of his jacket. What if she were Astree and he Dr. Nagel, re-united in a love that had survived years of separation and heartache? She glanced at Benno. He turned to her. His yeasty breath tickled her ear.

"They're using the wrong beakers in that experiment," he whispered.

The film finished, and she could feel the faint pressure of Benno's hand against her jacket as they made their way out of the cinema. She still felt under the spell of the film.

"Shall we stop for a glass at that *Weinstube* over there?" he suggested. Lili accepted immediately. She wasn't ready to go home, where she would continue to fret about the concert and the letter.

The Weinstube, not nearly as large as the student drinking halls, was full, and for a few moments it was as if Astree and Dr. Nagel were entering a tavern in Puerto Rico. The background noise was comforting, punctuated by laughter or a sudden exclamation, usually followed by more laughter. Tobacco and wine scented the air and Lili sighed with satisfaction, setting off a coughing fit. Benno waited for her to finish, a look of concern on his face. Was he worried about the Puerto Rico Fever? No, that was in the film.

A waiter brought their glasses, half-balloons with green stems. The wine tickled her tongue with tiny bubbles and left a fruity taste. She sighed again, this time careful not to do it as deeply.

"Did you enjoy the film?" Benno asked.

"Very much," she said. "I'm glad it had a happy ending."

He nodded. "It's best to return to one's roots."

Lili agreed with him. "Just like I have."

He leaned forward, his gaze moving over her face as if she were a specimen under a microscope.

"Indeed you have. Anyone looking at you knows that you are a true Aryan woman. A beautiful one."

She felt herself blushing and remembered the SS officer in the foyer of the Stadthalle who had labeled her an Aryan beauty.

"Don't be embarrassed," Benno told her. "Your beauty is completely natural. Golden hair, pale eyes, a noble profile, almost perfectly proportionate by Aryan standards." His smile showed the tips of his canines. "Freiin Lili."

Wishing he wouldn't address her that way anymore, she said the first thing that came into her mind. "Your eyes make me think of autumn, brown like hazelnuts."

Benno shrugged. "If I'm autumn, you're spring. The most important season in the year. The Reich is the season of Aryan rebirth. And it's easy to see that you're a woman committed to upholding the ideals of the Reich. But of course, your forebears have always been of service to realm and ruler. Your heritage is in your blood."

Lili's lips parted. This was a good opportunity to ask him about his work with blood and germ plasms.

Benno cut her off.

"It's true, as a woman you're more slender than the ideal, but it can't be due to something as laughable as dieting. From what I've seen, your only weakness in life seems to be an excessive fondness for cakes." He chuckled. "Undoubtedly as you grow older you'll fit the form for fecundity. For now, your litheness is an asset for gymnastics and other sports."

She shifted in her seat. Was this how Dr. Nagel would have spoken to Astree? "Are you quite finished?" she asked, sounding somewhat peeved.

"Not yet."

Lili cast a quick glance over at the table nearest them. Was anyone listening? This assessment was discomfiting enough without that. But the group of middle-aged couples did not seem to be paying attention to them.

Benno raised his glass. "When I look at you, I know that we're following the right path."

"What does that mean?"

"My work at the Institute. We're doing research into isolating germ plasms."

She sat up. "What do I have to do with disease?"

Benno laughed into his wine. "Nothing at all, I would think. Did you have chicken pox as a child?"

"I do have a memory of endless days spent itching and not being permitted to scratch."

"And you came through without a blemish. Another successful example of Aryan mind over matter. Resistance through innate strength."

Lili smiled, remembering how Mama had anointed her with chamomile lotion every few hours to soothe her frustrated skin.

"Is that what germ plasms are about—immunizations?"

Benno's hair flopped over his forehead as he shook his head. "In one way you're correct," he said. "Strong germ plasms are indeed an immunity. But for something much greater than any one individual." The waiter was back at their table, standing so close that Lili could smell the leather of his apron. He asked if they wanted more wine. Benno nodded, adding that fresh pretzels would also be a good idea.

"Germ plasms are that which carry the traits of bloodlines. As such, they carry both the good and the bad, or useless."

"Oh!" She suddenly thought of Frau Dierck's husband who seemed to have plenty of bad ones. "So can you find the bad traits? Can you remove them?"

Benno sat back against the wooden chair with its cutout heart and raised both arms. "Slowly, slowly! Your intelligence is shining but we're still working on isolating germ plasms. It's difficult, important and costly work. That's why the Institute accepts funds from the Rockefeller Foundation."

"Rockefeller?" In New York she had often passed by the Art Deco buildings going up in a complex between 5th and 7th Avenues. "Why are the Americans involved in this?" Such important work should belong to the Germans alone.

"Because they've seen that we're serious here. The Führer has always believed in the need for a society built only of the strongest. With his encouragement, we're able to forge ahead in research as never before. Courage, endurance, and obedience are some of the superior attributes of the Aryan." His dark eyes fixed on hers. Combined with thick eyebrows in a narrow face, this made him look very stern.

"You ask if we can isolate the bad traits and then remove them. While other institutes are tackling this, our own work isn't concerned with this aspect, but on isolating and preserving the positive attributes." A prism of salt fell onto the table as he bit into his pretzel.

"But what about the Americans?" Lili persisted.

"It would take me hours to explain everything," Benno said. "I'll make it shorter and simpler.

"Advances in medicine are not what's going to save human kind." His voice took on intensity. "If something isn't done, the German race will deteriorate. Pandering to the weak through medical treatments will only encourage the survival of degenerate human stock. Yet it's the inferior breeds that seem to reproduce most prolifically. One way of dealing with these is to send them off to the Front. But for this, there needs to be war, and of course the Führer is against war.

"But there's another way to approach the problem. Germ plasms. They are the essence of heredity. Through the proper use of germ plasm hygiene, science can orchestrate the selection of only the fittest specimens of human stock. This is for the benefit of both the German race, and humanity itself." Benno paused, gave a little smile. "If I can be so bold as to put it into your musical terms, then I would say that the theme of racial hygiene is not the solo, but the symphony."

For a few moments Lili stared at him.

"That's exactly like what the Führer tells us," she said, excited. "We as individuals are only parts of the whole. Our value is in what we can do for the greater good of the Volk. I read that he thinks Sparta was a good example of how to make a society strong, removing the weakest members so that the hardiest could thrive.

"Very apt," Benno said. "People around the world have been following that practice for centuries. For example, in ancient Rome, and today too in Eskimoland and islands in the South Pacific. Deformed infants are killed at birth." He broke off. "Don't look so stricken, Lili. People there know that raising unsound children will only harm the community as a whole. Or take China. Girls are often killed or left to die, to ensure the economic viability of a household, especially in times of famine. The methods of elimination vary. In some places they're buried. In others, left outside so that the elements can take care of them. Simple, efficient. Considerate, too. In this way, nobody has to feel personal responsibility for their deaths."

What he was saying somehow made sense, even if it made her somewhat uncomfortable. But then, who liked to talk about death?

Lili drank some wine, pushing away the disturbing image of Paul as a deformed Eskimo child lying frozen in the snow.

Voices suddenly swelled and they looked over to where a new group had come into the Weinstube. At least half a dozen men in black uniforms were moving to the table that had just been vacated by the middle-age couples. As they began to seat themselves, Lili couldn't keep herself from glancing at them, one after the other, to see if one of them was Leo Arnim von Witzleben. Her glances crossed with several of them, but quickly she looked away. He wasn't among them. She turned her attention back to Benno and focused on his face.

"In today's world," he was saying, "it's America that has been active longest in racial cleansing. They began sterilizing the mentally defective in 1899. They're also successful in, emm, castration, and implementing marriage restrictions as well as segregating inferiors. In all of this there is good support from big businesses and top American universities."

"So why are they giving money to German researchers?" she asked. It was getting somewhat tiring to try and get the answer from him.

"What do you get when you cross Mendel's pea with Darwin's ape?"

Lili frowned. Now what was he talking about?

"You heard correctly." Benno grinned. "It's a joke. You don't know? The answer is eugenics. It all goes back to Darwin and Galton, and the survival of the fittest. Next step on the thought process was that the children of intelligent people would have to be intelligent. Or talented."

Lili nodded. This she grasped. "Like Bach and Mozart and even Strauss. Musical ability often passes from father to son. Or daughter," she added, and glanced over to the SS table. Perhaps one of them had performed at Stadthalle. Perhaps they knew Leo Arnim von Witzleben. Was he too in Heidelberg?

"That's correct. These breakthroughs happened around the same time that Mendel made his discoveries. So the two lines of thought met and found favor with many, especially in America."

"Why especially America?" she asked, forcing her attention back to Benno.

"You have a good mind," he said. "It must be passed on to future generations."

What was he going on about?

"Immigrants," he continued, "were no longer coming mainly from northern Europe, and many Americans worried that too much inferior blood was being mixed with that of the Nordic blood. Racial purity was being threatened."

"You mean by the slaves from Africa?"

"To a degree," Benno agreed, "but for the most part the Africans and their descendants have been kept away from white people through strict laws. For the others, different action was taken. For example, an Intelligence Quotient test was devised that led to the rejection of immigration for certain ethnic groups. America should thank the far-sighted Charles Davenport for establishing a Eugenics Record Office. In the future it will be the modernizing of data processing that will allow us to monitor and adjust the characteristics of our populations." He rubbed an earlobe.

"The main way of neutralizing the inferior is, at least to begin with, eugenics. Getting rid of the bad bloodlines. Like the posters and schoolbooks explain, these pose both economic and social burdens on society. This erodes the strength of a nation. Eradicating these will eventually leave only the good ones. The ones our team is working on isolating."

Lili glanced at the other table. The officers were toasting something.

"The Americans are excited about the inroads we're making," Benno went on, sounding proud. "Actually, they began funding German scientific institutions already years before the Führer came to power. He himself has studied American laws of eugenics and mentions it in *Mein Kampf*. So there's a lot of friendly cooperation between eugenicists in America and our leaders here. It wouldn't be immodest to say that in Germany, science and government are collaborating to improve human heredity. The Americans know that we'll find the solutions." He shrugged. "If they want to add to our research funds, well, 'never look a gift horse in the mouth', I say."

He laughed just as a great burst of laughter came from the nearby table. For a moment it looked as if Benno were part of it, but of course he wasn't. Aside from that he was sitting here at this table, Benno was a bony, dark-haired scientist, not a strapping blonde SS officer.

"You see," he continued, his eyes now smoldering fuscous, "the Americans may have done the groundwork in eugenics, but we Germans are going to take it all the way!"

"It must be so exciting for you to be involved in all this, Benno."

"It is indeed," he agreed. "I feel honored. Our work deals with matter so tiny that the human eye can't see it without the help of the most powerful microscopes in existence—but its scope extends beyond the horizon."

Lili bit her lip. It was awe inspiring to think that even the tiniest bit of German germ plasm was meaningful for the sanctity of the Reich. When, and how, could she contribute hers?

"Think of it," Benno continued. "Through our research it's likely that in the future it will be possible to ascertain whether someone—or his children—will develop a disease. Then it can either be nipped in the bud, or the entire bloodline purged. Conversely, our work with germ plasms may make it possible for parents to choose from a set of approved attributes that they'd like their offspring to possess. In this way, future generations can be assured of purity and strength."

Lili studied his earnest expression. For a moment she saw again the dark eyes and intensity of Dr. Nagel and his scientific search for the solution that would save the island.

"I'm glad that the Reich has people as dedicated as you," she said. Yet the words were barely out when she was suddenly beset by the image of Leo Arnim von Witzleben, bare-chested and touched by gold.

"And I'm glad that you've come to take your rightful place among your people," Benno said, reaching out to cover her hand with his own, bony and moist. "Your bloodline belongs here."

As she moved her hand away to pick up her wine glass, she couldn't help but glance over at the nearby table.

What the Führer Needs

The first rehearsal was to take place in the Stadthalle, where the SS concert had been. Dr. Hempel saw her off from Kornmarkt.

"They expect you by 13.00," he reminded her.

"It will be fine," she told him, closing the door firmly behind her. Yet, as she set out, her insides felt as if they had looped around themselves. Each step wound them tighter. It didn't help either that the heavy neo-classic columns in front of the Stadhalle made the raw red sandstone building even more imposing. This was the prime performance hall of Heidelberg. She was to play Bach here, play him as brilliantly as humanly possible.

At the entrance, she hesitated, observing the feeling of pleasure mixed with anxiety, delicious in a dangerous way. She relaxed her fingers, then turned to face the Philosophenweg across the Neckar, bleak now in its winter aspect. Goethe came to mind.

What would Papa say if he could see her now, about to rehearse for a public performance? Surely he would have an appropriate Goethe quote. Even though it had been weeks since last she'd looked into it, she had *Secrets of Goethe* right here, in her satchel. In honor of today she would find a suitable quote. She flipped through the pages. *A really great talent finds its happiness in execution.* That was a bit immodest. Perhaps this one: *Every person above the ordinary has a certain mission that they are called to fulfill.* Yes, Papa would like that, but most likely not in the context of doing her duty for the Reich. Her fingers slid over the pages. *Plunge boldly into the thick of life and seize it where you will; it is always interesting.*

Yes, that sounded more like it. She slipped the book back into the satchel. Today she was a bold step closer to turning her dream into reality: one day she would again perform for the Führer. That would be both in the thick of life and interesting. Holding on to that thought, she entered the building.

It was five minutes before the hour so she went directly to the concert hall; the musicians were in their places. A crane-like man stood at the fore, baton hanging from his fingers like a dead eel. Pressing her thumbs against her curled fingers, Lili took a deep breath and climbed the steps leading up to the right side of the stage.

"Heil Hitler," she said, casting a quick glance over the faces of those seated on wooden chairs. All of them were older than she. One of them stared at her as she passed, another gave a quick glance then averted his eyes. The rest continued to study their scores on the metal stands in front of them. The conductor peered at her, his silver-haired head tilted back slightly when he spoke.

"You must be Dr. Hempel's protogée, the young miss from America."

Lili winced.

"I did live in America for a few years but now I'm back in Germany."

"Good, good," he said. "Then in the future we won't have a problem with punctuality." He grinned at the musicians. "You know, in music so much has to do with perfect timing."

Was he joking, or insinuating that she was late?

"I was told to be here at 13.00."

"And so you are." Now his smile was cold. "But you should be at your instrument, not standing in the spotlight like a prima donna." He tapped the baton. "*Avanti.*"

The blood rushing into her cheeks, Lili hurried over to the harpsichord placed near the front of the stage. No one could hear her heart thumping. She opened the case and ran her hands across the keys, rubbed her fingers against each other. Despite having been covered, the keyboard seemed dusty. Was it out of tune too? She played a few scales. It would do.

"And are we ready now?" The question was directed at her.

Once more her cheeks flamed. Why had she been told to arrive at that time? She could have come earlier and been ready to play at 13.00. She raised her eyes.

"Yes."

As she began to play, the knots inside her unravelled. After all, what really mattered was the music. She was rehearsing for her first public concert. At first, the sensation of not seeing all of the other musicians on stage was disconcerting. Papa always stood next to her when they played a duet. Yet, within a short time, the ensemble and she joined. It was astonishing. All of them, together, rose and took flight, a formation guided by the conductor, whose top half seemed to have a metronome built in, while his long legs swayed to the underlying themes of the music. He was fascinating to glance over at.

In so many ways, the musicians became simply an extension of his movements and motivations. In the concertino passages he pressed them to yield to the obbligato of the harpsichord, in the ripieno passages she stayed bass, weaving her way across the layers of their harmonics. The key was of course that every one of them knew the music. Further and further they went into the first movement. Her senses were tingling. It was much more delicious than Schlagsahne. How had she never had this experience before? This particular piece was a perfect blend, showing off her ability to fit in and support the others as well to soar by herself. It was exhilarating. What would it be like on that day, that day which was surely coming, when she would play for the Führer?

And then it happened. It was at the end of the first movement, near the end of the cadenza which up to that point had been flawless. Her finger slipped, landing on both F# and F instead of only F#. It shocked her and she lost the beat, so that the harpsichord sounded as if the wires were snapping. It was inexcusable, she knew, yet the conductor's outburst was so shocking to Lili that she could feel the blood drain from her face. Her hands froze. The others had stopped playing and the hall was filled only with harsh tones.

Who did she think she was, the conductor shouted. Perhaps in America such shoddy playing was tolerated, but not in the Reich. Timing was essential, he bellowed. And there was such a thing as proper notes too. Or did she not have the sensitivity to notice them? Perhaps it was then that he noticed her face, for suddenly his tone softened.

"Just imagine, Fräulein, if you were to make such a mistake at the performance—and the Führer were in the audience."

Lili could only nod. The hall was shrinking, the luminescence on stage fading. Only the conductor's hair seemed to hold the light. A humming sound was growing in her ears. She held on to the edge of the harpsichord as a wave of black spots pushed through her. Her head began to fall forward.

"*Schnell!* Someone get a glass of water!" The silver head was next to her. "Fräulein." His voice was full of concern. "Are you all right?"

She felt the conductor take her wrists and rub them. She could hear the rasp of skin against skin, like paper folding allegro in the key of G. The wave faded. The muscles of her cheeks relaxed.

She took a jagged breath.

"Yes, thank you." She blinked. "I'm sorry. It won't happen again."

A hand thrust forth a glass and the conductor watched as she drank. "There," he said at last, a catch in his voice. "You will be fine." He turned and went back to his stand.

Lili wasn't sure if he meant for the moment or in general. Neither would be thanks to him.

"Enough excitement," he announced, tapping his baton. "We will move on and return to the allegro later."

They resumed playing and Lili felt an undertow of disappointment during the rest of the rehearsal. There were no more mistakes though. When it was over, she closed the case and rose from her seat. Other musicians would rehearse other pieces now but she would not stay to listen. She placed the score back in her satchel. Fingers fumbled as she strapped the leather and she bit her lip to keep it from trembling. Mama would have paled at the rudeness of her exit, for Lili walked by the conductor without looking at him or anybody else. It was only when she reached the top of the stairs that she turned and saluted, for the Führer.

She seemed to have held her breath until she was outside, for she gasped in the piercing air. The tiny park nearby was barren, its trees naked, defenseless in the cold. She crossed the street. The wind from the river bit at her so that her eyes burned, but she welcomed the stinging. If it hadn't been so cold she would have torn off her coat and let it blow through her. No one—neither her parents nor her teachers nor even her music instructors—had ever used such a tone on her. Its harshness resonated even now. So she had made a mistake. But had it been the mistake itself or was it her American aspect, or both, that had caused the outburst? Why had the conductor so demeaned her in front of everyone?

She forced herself to relive the moments. The others had not seemed unduly shaken. Had they ever experienced something like that? Or, perhaps, horrible thought, could this be a normal part of performing? She shuddered. Perhaps she was not cut out for this after all. Perhaps her years in America, where teachers were less disciplined and disciplined less, had weakened her so that she was too quick to take offence. She stopped and stared at the river. The current pulled at the water, relentless. How would she ever play for the Führer if she couldn't perform in public? It wasn't as if he were ever again going to come home for dinner and hear her there. That viola da gamba player, that Leo Arnim von Witzleben, had assured her that some day she would perform. But what did he know of her? Her eyes blurred in the bitter cold. She had no resources other than herself, her music. Moving to America had taken everything else away. No one really understood. No one would ever understand.

She covered her nose and mouth with her gloved hands, breathing through the leather and faint traces of metal until both her face and her fingers felt warmer. She stared at the river. Passing out of the lock up ahead, making its way south, was a barge heavily laden with coal from the mines in the Ruhr. Lili watched its slow progress. Men had gone deep into the earth to bring forth the lumps that would produce light and power for the Reich. What was it like to be a miner picking away in the dark? She had seen Wagner's *Das Rheingold*. But those had been dwarves mining for golden treasure, not smelly black fossil fuel. Or what about a bargeman, loading and unloading coal day after day, in all sorts of weather? Did one need to think, or did these tasks become mindless performances after a while? It was unlikely that it mattered one whit if you dropped a lump of coal now and then by accident. The same couldn't be said of a note.

As the barge neared, she could see two men in work clothes standing outside on the back deck. From this distance they looked like beardless dwarves sharing a laugh in the raw air above the river. Streams of gray blew off their fingers; they were smoking. Lili frowned, peering at the great heap of coal. If embers jumped off their cigarettes and lit upon the load, a fire could start. An entire barge worth of fuel would be lost. Germany needed all the coal it could get. How could those men endanger the Reich just for the sake of a smoke?

She would shout down to them. She opened her mouth then closed it. The wind would sweep away her words. The men would never understand her from this distance. How could she warn them of the danger? Why didn't they realize it themselves?

It was then that understanding came, and a weight as heavy as the burden of the barge slid from her shoulders even while she saw the men wipe their hands and disappear into the cabin. It was as the Führer had said, in so many different ways: the wishes of the individual were not as important as the welfare of the Reich. That was the reality, the only one that mattered. Lili closed her eyes for a moment. What were her feelings compared to the perfection of the piece? She had made a mistake. In a performance it would have been not hers alone, but a shoddiness shared by the entire ensemble and the conductor himself. He had been correct to shout at her; she needed correcting. The Führer needed his German youth to be strong, to be able to endure pain. He needed young men and women who were tough. These were not just words. Today she had failed him. She had let personal feelings make her weak. She bit her lip so that there was blood.

News from New York

"Give to the Winter Relief Fund! Help the needy!"

Taking turns ringing a bell that looked as if it had come from around a cow's neck, three boys in HJ uniforms stood at the snowy corner of Heugasse. Lili, on her way home from shopping for gifts to send to Großmama Maximiliana and Großpapa Hugo, stopped in front of the collection box and emptied her coinpurse.

"Thank you," the boys called out in voices that hadn't yet broken.

A matron walked by, cloche hat tight against her ears. She cast a sideways look at the boys and her nostrils flared, almost as if with distaste. Lili stared after her.

"Lili!"

His hair at right angles, Benno bounded over from across the street. The HJ boys giggled.

"Come on, let's walk together."

"You seem different today," Lili said.

He grinned, canines sharp against his lips. "I'm glad you noticed. I finally feel like the future is opening for me." He stopped. "Look around." They had reached Marktplatz and Benno put his hands to her shoulder, spinning her around so that she was shocked and then giggling.

"This is Germany," he said. "Our land! Look at it and really see it."

During the past few days, the square had been transformed into the Christmas Market. She glanced toward where the tiny forest house booths festooned with spruce and fir stood in rows, like a happy village from simpler days. Everyone, especially the children, had rosy cheeks, and good cheer seemed to have infused the whole square. It did look rather like a wholesome painting by one of those artists whose style the Führer seemed to prefer. Was that what she was supposed to notice?

She smiled at Benno.

"Come," he said again, and they moved on, stopping at a booth filled with Lebkuchen in myriad shapes. Lili watched as he studied the offerings. At last he told the old woman behind the counter which one he wanted. Lili bit her lip. Was it for her? The woman cut the ribbon from which the gingerbread was hanging and took out a piece of brown paper with which to wrap it.

"Not necessary, my good woman," said Benno, and Lili could only stare with wide eyes at his behavior. For a moment he dangled the gingerbread heart as if it were a rat he was holding by the tail. "Here, Lili. It's for you." He began to whistle a tune.

Lili looked back and forth between him and the heart that said *Ein Mädel wie Du* in red icing. A girl like she?

"Come on, young Fräulein," the vendor called out. "What are you waiting for? Can't you see when a young man is wearing his heart on his tongue?"

How embarrassing! The vendor rolled her eyes as Lili bent her face to the heart and breathed in the spiciness of the gingerbread.

"Thank you, Benno. It smells delicious."

A flicker of something passed over his face but then he chuckled. "Come on then, little Fräulein, let's continue our stroll." They passed through the lanes redolent with the scent of clove and cinnamon and roasting meat. "Do you recall my mentioning the name Beger?" he asked suddenly.

"Beger? Isn't he your anthropologist colleague?"

"So you did listen." Benno beamed. "He and I have been in contact more and more. He's an expert in ethnogeny, the study of race. Our work overlaps in many areas. Because of him I've come to the notice of Schäfer himself, and he's one of the most important experts in the field." Benno was talking so fast that a bead of spittle flew through the air. "I've been offered an opportunity that only very few men can aspire to. I can't tell you about it yet, but it's of immense importance to Germany and the future of our Volk."

"That's marvelous, Benno!" Lili said. No wonder he was behaving so strangely. He was excited about his work. She sniffed at the *Lebkuchenherz*.

"Don't mention anything at dinner. I don't want that pompous Poppe to know until it's all set."

"I'll keep it to myself, Benno, especially as you haven't really told me anything at all." She knitted her eyebrows to look cross and that set the two of them off into fits of laughter that lasted all the way across Kornmarkt.

At home, Lili stopped to visit Tante Aletheia in her rooms.

"My dear girl," she said, motioning for Lili to sit down. "It seems like so long since the two of us have had a good chat."

It was true. What with her practicing and the student marches as far afield as Kirchheim, she had not spent much time with her lately. "I've missed you," Lili said. "It seems that there aren't enough hours in the day to do everything one would like to accomplish."

"If you feel like that now, what do you think you'll do when you reach my age and time hurries even faster?"

"But you've already done so much," Lili said, her voice earnest. "What else do you want to do?"

Tante Aletheia's smile was thin. "When I was a young girl, I believed that old people had done and learned so much during their lives that there were those who knew or understood everything; like the proverbial sage on the mountain top. As I grew older, I realized that learning must never stop. Nor should one's efforts to best use that learning." She stroked Fragonard's fur backwards and Lili could hear him purring. "There are those who choose to stop learning, or perhaps get stuck, but that is another matter."

Lili nodded. "I understand what you mean. I used to think I'd be grown up when I turned thirteen." She grinned. "Now I know it takes longer."

"Indeed it does, my girl. So," she said, reaching to pour Lili a cup of tea, "do tell me about how your performance is coming along."

They chatted for a good half hour. Lili refrained from mentioning the incident at the initial rehearsal. After all, she had arrived in good time for the next session and it had gone flawlessly, and she had even exchanged a few words with some of the other musicians. There was no need to touch upon that incident. They spoke of how much fun it was to make music with others, how painting was a solitary art, and what Lili would wear for the performance. Then Frau Brinkmann came to the door.

"Fräulein Lili. I thought I would find you here." She held out a letter. "This just came."

"Oh!" Lili was up on her feet and hurrying across the room. It had to be from Mama and Papa.

Frau Brinkmann was twinkling. "Goodness gracious, did you win the *Reichslotterie?*"

"No, no," Lili breathed, taking the envelope. "It will be even better than that. Thank you." She turned to Tante Aletheia. "*Tchüß* till later."

Once upstairs she closed the door and leaned against it, holding the envelope in front of her. At last. *Fräulein Lili von Rittersburg zu Mertz -Tärnekow,* it read. She smiled. Not Freiin. At Kornmarkt in Heidelberg, Germany. Yes, that was where she was and where she wanted to stay. As soon as she opened the letter she would know. Mama and Papa simply had to say yes. She went to the desk, picked up the sharp blade, then hesitated. At this precise moment the future was open. She could be staying, she could be going. Each was possible. If she never pulled out the letter, both would be there. But no, if the boat sailed without her when she was supposed to be on it... But what if she sailed away when the letter said she could stay here?

She sliced open the paper spine. It was a German style envelope, the letter folded in four to fit. She picked up a corner and pulled it apart like a handkerchief. The paper was light blue, the ink darker.

Dearest Lili. As I write these words, flakes thick and pale are falling, layers and layers of flakes that frost the earth with the icy freshness of the sky. Inside it is warm and cheery, for Oskar has built us a lovely fire. Only the glass separates me from that winter world outside. How like a fairy tale it is. Everything is perfect in the clean white snow that lies on the other side of the clear glass. Yet I feel no need to step into that landscape, for I am content to simply watch its unfolding beauty from my window. It is there; the knowing alone is enough.

This, my dearest daughter, is a sentiment that I hope you will take to heart when you learn that we have given your request much thought. Papa and I have spent many sleepless nights wondering how best to honor your hopes and desires. Music, we have long known, is an intrinsic part of your being. That you would want to share it with the world is an admirable attribute of your character. Yet we cannot help but feel unease in imagining where this might well take you at this time in your young life, and the life of our troubled homeland. Thus, Papa and I have decided it is in your best interests that you forego this event and return to New York and your loving family—

With a cry akin to a shriek, Lili threw the letter onto the table.

It wasn't possible. They were denying her wishes. Her needs. Her entire world was crashing down and they didn't understand at all. She sank into the seat, put her palms to her face so that she wouldn't have to look at that horrible piece of paper. How could those few lines of ink wreak so much damage to a life? Perhaps she had understood it wrong. She picked up the letter, read the damning sentence once more. Dropped the paper again and wrapped her fingers into the hair above her forehead, pulling, pulling so hard it felt like the roots might be tearing away.

She pushed the chair back and ran into the bathroom. Leaning over the sink, she gagged and retched yet nothing but ugly sounds came out. She cupped water, splashing it on her face. In the mirror her eyes were dark, dull, like the bottom of the deepest sea where the light never reaches. She had never seen such an expression on her face; it was not hers, no, she looked like someone else; a stranger.

When it was time for dinner, her hair combed and braided and wrapped across her aching head, Lili went down the stairwell. Her steps sounded against the wood, one by one, like doors shutting.

"Ach, Fräulein Lili," said Frau Dierck, who stood just ahead of her, as if waiting for someone or something. "You startled me. I was thinking about my children."

Lili bit down on her lip. Not another scene from Frau Dierck!

But Frau Dierck's smile was sweet. "Next year we'll be together again, my children and I." Then her features sagged. "But maybe they won't remember me." Her hands moved together as if she were washing them although there was no water. "Maybe I won't remember them."

As if to a small child, Lili tutted. "Come, Frau Dierck," she said. "Let's go down. The others must be waiting."

Everyone was indeed already seated, Frau Brinkmann serving soup.

Benno shot Lili a grin as she sat down. She tried to smile but was sure it came out as a grimace. Across the table, Herr Poppe looked about to burst, as if he had something that he wanted to share. Tante Aletheia was looking at Lili with narrowed eyes. Lili chose to let her own gaze wander over to Herr Tischborn, who seemed preoccupied with the farmland landscape on the wall. Tante Aletheia had hung it there just yesterday. If Lili could disappear into the canvas, then all her troubles would be gone. Next to Herr Tischborn, Dr. Hempel was pouring Frau Dierck a glass of wine. Frau Brinkmann finished ladling the soup and turned toward the kitchen with the empty tureen. Lili let her shoulders fall. This room, these people. In only a few months she had grown so accustomed to them, even with their quirks and strange behaviors. It wasn't that she was fond of all of them, but they had become part of her life. How old she felt, already.

Herr Poppe cleared his throat, his chins vibrating.

"I would like to announce something," he declared with as much solemnity as if he were giving a speech to hundreds. "I have just been informed that with the coming of the new year, I will be receiving a promotion for my years of dedication." The tip of his nose rose slightly as he smiled. "1938 will be an excellent year for the German Volk."

Lili glanced over at Benno. Was he going to make his announcement now and most likely trump Herr Poppe who, although a conscientious civil servant, was not a brilliant scientist? But no, Benno merely sat listening to Herr Poppe. He did catch her eye though, and Lili saw his own flashing, probably with amusement.

Frau Dierck slapped her hands on the table, drawing a momentary look of concern from Tante Aletheia. As if suddenly remembering herself, Frau Dierck picked up her spoon and returned to the soup.

"That is excellent news, Herr Poppe," said Herr Tischborn. "You are a man of loyalty."

"Indeed," interrupted Herr Poppe. "It seems that I'll be busy with another function, in my capacity as Party member." He chuckled. "Helping sort things out in the neighborhood as a *Blockleiter*."

Lili noticed that Tante Aletheia had gone a bit pale.

His own cheeks flushed, Herr Tischborn coughed into his hand. "Let us hope that 1938 is indeed a year of good tidings."

"Yes," said Lili, pulling up her chin. "I'm sure it will be." Her voice was so forceful that everyone turned to her.

Dr. Hempel's eyes grew bright. "Ah, Fräulein Lili. It sounds as if you too have something to share with us this evening."

Tante Aletheia sounded mischievous and her color had returned. "Could it have something to do with a certain letter you received earlier today?"

Lili could feel every cell in her face quivering, as if the muscles were not hers to command. She opened her mouth, afraid of what must come out.

"Ye-es," she said. "Yes. I've heard from my parents." She paused, looking one last time around the table: at pompous Herr Poppe who was still chewing and swallowing; at mild and timid Herr Tischborn; at Frau Dierck who faced such disturbing problems at a distance; at happy Dr. Hempel, always in good humor; at brainy Benno who was full of surprises and often made her feel strange; and finally at dear, peculiar Tante Aletheia and her faithful Fragonard on his chair next to the buffet.

"Yes," Lili said, and this time her voice was firm as the floor beneath her feet.

"I can stay."

Past and Future Become One

Ever since she had made the decision to go against Mama and Papa and stay here, everything felt like a dream. Beginning with the lie at dinner, every day was filled with a fog, fuzzy and desensitizing. It was as if she, Lili, were not fully there. As if she were split into two: herself and her self. Which one was Lili?

"Will you come with me on an outing to the *Thingstätte?*" Benno asked a few days later. Some of the winter festivities at the amphitheater up on the Heiligenberg outside town were said to be spectacular.

Although it would mean several hours away from the harpsichord, Lili agreed to join him and a few of his associates on an automobile trip there. For most of the ride across the river and up into the snow-laden hills, she was silent. The men spoke of microscopes and cells. Every time the vehicle turned a corner, Lili strained her leg, trying to keep her upper body from pressing into Benno's lean frame. At least not too much.

Up and up they went, into a world of white, the trees like legions of monks robed in frost. As the vehicle pushed its way past the ruins of the Stephanskloster, Benno broke away from the conversation to explain to her that the 11th century monastery had been abandoned around 1500.

"This particular Thingstätte was built in 1935," he said, " and some of its power must surely derive from its proximity to the summit of the Heiligenberg. Celts built a settlement up there."

"Did you know that the Romans had a temple to Mercury up there too? That's why it's called Heiligenberg," came from the front.

The driver took his hand off the steering wheel for a moment to object, and the car lurched a bit.

"No, that's not why. In the 9th century there was an earlier monastery up there, the Michaelskloster."

"Doesn't matter," said Benno. "Point is that this hill has been a magnet for spirituality and sanctuary for centuries. You can really feel the ancient roots of the German lands up at the Thingstätte."

"Here we are," said the driver, turning into a parking area between slumbering trees.

They trudged along for a short time before coming upon men in uniform standing guard. Then they were at the side of the amphitheater, tiers of stone blocks pulling the landscape apart in bands of gray, perfectly symmetrical.

"Come on," Benno urged. "Let's climb up."

They took the center path, past rows of people bundled in winter wear, past braziers sending out crackling waves of heat. After several tiers, Lili turned to look. It was magnificent. There, directly below them, was the stage, also stone, with a ramp curving behind it to form a perfect circle. Beyond that, the frosted forest and the blurred shadows of Heidelberg. Off in the distance all was blenched to the horizon. How pure it was, this place of snow and tree and stone. A shiver went through her. Surely she was right to have chosen to ignore the summons that would take her away from all this.

They did not go to the very top, settling midway, spreading out on the tier the blankets they had brought. Down below, the festivities began, and for the next hour and more, Lili was mesmerized. Music, song, speeches, and a short play extolling the honor and pride of the German Volk—all enhanced by sophisticated electrical equipment that allowed the sound to envelop most likely the entire Heiligenberg. Perhaps the vibrations were causing snow to fall off some of the nearest branches, and birds to tremble with confusion. Would ancient spirits awaken and smile upon them?

The sky was darkening. As they waited for the next portion of the festivities, Benno opened the thermos he had brought along, and they drank *Glühwein* that was still warm.

"Can you feel it, Lili?"

She knew he didn't mean the wine, which was swirling its way into her gloved fingertips.

"Oh, yes. This is a wondrous place. Thank you so much for inviting me." Her eyes lingered over his features. Not attractive, but appealing.

He reached out a hand and rubbed it up and down her coat sleeve as if to warm her.

"One day, all in the Reich will understand what this Thingstätte and the other dozens like it mean to the German spirit." He looked down at the tiers. Not all of them were full, but the enthusiasm of those who were here electrified the air. "I was here the day that Goebbels inaugurated it. The place was packed; it was summer. I still remember at least the gist of what he said."

"Tell me."

Benno grinned, the skin around his eyes crinkling from the cold and dryness. "Something about how the style and German life view has been actualized in monumental fashion in this monumental construction. That these sites are in truth the political landscape of our time. That the day will come when the German Volk turn to these Stätte to acknowledge their immortal new life." He frowned. "Something like that."

"Oh, I understand. I do," Lili cried out, holding her hand to her coat somewhere in the area of her heart. "I understand it here."

"Yes, you would."

For some moments they sat in silence. Below, torches were being lit.

"One day, " Benno pronounced, his voice slow and deep like a prophet's, "the Reich will move beyond its present borders. New settlements will arise, new Germanic roots planted in the soil to the east."

Lili's eyes widened, the cold stinging them, and her fingers curled into themselves.

"Our blood will be the nutrient that gives rise to a new and strong crop," he said, gazing out into the darkness beyond the burnished glow of the amphitheater.

Lili shivered again. Was he talking about a battle coming, or something else, something empowering and eternal? She was afraid to ask. She pressed her gloved palms against the solidity of the stone seat.

And then the sky was lit up with a thousand stars. She had been to the Nuremberg rally last year, seen the lights rising into the heavens like space pillars. Here on the Heiligenberg, the spectacle was not nearly as grand, and yet it moved her in a way that went deeper than the glorious events at Nuremberg. There she had been caught up in the present and future, had felt the goodness and power radiating from the Führer. Up here on the Heiligenberg, she was pulled by the earth, felt the ancient source of her land; past and future became one.

Tante Aletheia Minces No Words

Until the last moment, there was the possibility that the Führer would attend. There was always that chance, for the Führer was everywhere. One could never rule out that he might suddenly alight from an aeroplane in some nearby field and appear at the Stadthalle. Preparations were made, just in case. But he did not, and the performance went on without him, just as the S.S. Hamburg was pulling into New York harbor without Lili on board.

On the evening of the concert, Lili put out of her mind the fact that she had lied. She refused to think of Mama and Papa. They should have been here to see her first performance; as they were not, she would waste no bitterness. Such emotions would be of no help in a performance that she intended to be brilliant regardless of whether or not the Führer were there.

Tante Aletheia was in the audience of course. Indeed, everyone from the house at Kornmarkt was there except for Herr Poppe, who had gone to attend a Party seminar. As she waited backstage with the other performers, Lili glanced about, as if Leo Arnim von Witzleben might somehow be nearby and see that his prophesy had come true. But he was not.

And then it was Lili's turn to walk out on the stage. The lights in the audience hall were dimmed, yet she could sense the mass of bodies. Everyone had warned her that butterflies in the stomach were normal even for the most seasoned of performers. Lili could feel their wings of lead beating; they did not remain in her belly but seemed to sink into her feet so that it took hours to cross the stage. When at last she arrived at the harpsichord, she turned on her heels, black skirt swishing against her ankles, and saluted, her arm stretching out in syrupy slowness as if reaching across the entire hall. The Führer was not in the audience. But as the muscles in her raised hand tightened, she gained strength from the thought of him. He was not here but it was for him that she would play. Yes, this was her first public performance, and it was dedicated to him.

Once she had seated herself and the hall was silent, Lili touched her fingertips to the keys. She looked out into the darkness of the audience before settling her gaze on Maestro Ohlig; their eyes met and the music began.

Lili played as if she had been born for the sole purpose of sharing with the world her understanding and love of the harpsichord.

And then it was done.

She looked up. She did not understand why Maestro Ohlig had come over to where she sat at the instrument. He was smiling, the crane-like conductor was grinning, his hand held out to her. She peered at him. It sounded as if rain were beginning to fall. She put her hand in his, and, as he pulled at her and she rose, still in a cloud of wonder, the drops grew louder. With one hand, the Maestro waved toward the musicians behind them while with the other he squeezed her fingers gently and bowed, so that she followed his movement even now, and then both of them saluted the hall and the applause surrounded them like a storm.

♫♪♫

The doorbell rang just as Tante Aletheia had cut off the top of her egg. She and Lili were alone in the breakfast room, laughing and recounting the events of the previous evening as seen from both the audience and on stage. Lili heard the door open, Frau Brinkmann thanking someone. Sensing the impending disclosure, Lili put down the piece of buttered roll she had been about to bite into, and waited. There was a solid thud as the door closed against the winter. Frau Brinkmann's felt house shoes scuffed closer and closer across the stone tiles.

"Frau von Wohlitz," she said, coming into the room. "There is a cablegram for you."

Tante Aletheia sighed as she took the paper. Watching her read it, Lili felt like vomiting up her breakfast, but did not flinch when Tante Aletheia turned to her with a gaze of piercing green.

"Ja, Mädel," she said, shaking her head ever so slowly, not taking her eyes off Lili. "I almost suspected as much. How could you do it to your parents?" But before Lili could even begin to answer, Tante Aletheia rose from her chair, startling Fragonard. Now Lili flinched, for she had never seen her great-aunt with such an aura of menace. Yet the older woman merely passed her on the way to a drawer, as if Lili were air, returning with paper and a pencil.

"There is no time to attempt to reach them by telephone," she said, her tone clipped. "I will send a cablegram to assure them that you have not disappeared from the face of the earth." Once more she shook her head, but said nothing further, as if there were no words possible to describe how despicable was Lili's behavior.

She sat in silence as Tante Aletheia wrote out the cablegram. Her nose itched but she was afraid to scratch it. Instead, she dug a fingernail into her palm. Even when the itch went away, she continued to press. Her throat was dry, her heartbeat rapid; her teeth pressed deep into her flesh. She wanted to know what was in the cablegram but was afraid to ask.

"Frau Brinkmann," Tante Aleltheia called out, folding the paper into a square. "Be so kind as to take this reply to the Post Office. It is urgent."

"Ach, of course." The fleshy cheeks quivered with concern. "I do hope it isn't bad news, Frau von Wohlitz."

Tante Aletheia's eyes narrowed as she glanced over at Lili.

"It is indeed not good, Frau Brinkmann. Now we can only hope that it doesn't get worse."

Lili stared at her plate until it seemed to dissolve.

As the hours passed, there was a flurry of exchanges between Heidelberg and New York.

Tante Aletheia's eyes flashed emerald. Every now and then a glaring glance struck Lili, making her feel wretched, like a creature weakened. For hours she sat, unable to move.

Ever since she had made the decision to go against Mama and Papa and stay here, everything had felt like a dream. Beginning with the lie at dinner and ending this morning with disclosure, every day had been filled with a fog, fuzzy and desensitizing. It was as if she, Lili, had not been fully there. As if she had been split into two: herself and her self. Which one was Lili? The one who had sacrificed her family by lying and hurting her parents, or the one who had somehow found the strength to make her own path? Could the two ever be reconciled?

As if silence were her chosen measure of condemnation, Tante Aletheia did not speak to her, nor did she read aloud any of the cablegrams. But, after arrival of the third, her tension seemed to soften. It was already evening, dark outside and inside gloomy, when suddenly she rose and poured them each a glass of Schnaps. She swallowed hers right away, poured herself another. Then, at last, leaning back in the armchair, she addressed Lili.

"You have behaved in a deplorable manner." Her tone was icy. The cold wrapped itself around Lili's heart; did Tante Aletheia hate her now?

"You wanted to participate in the concert so much that you chose to disregard—and disobey—your parents' instructions. You chose to do so in a way that raises questions about your character, questions that your parents must surely face anxiety in answering. What you have done to your parents is a selfish unkindness whose weight you will bear your entire life." Here she paused. Lili felt the sting of the rebuke.

Yet even now Tante Aletheia was not finished. "Your parents are far away. It is difficult for them to understand the intensity of your motivation. However, I have the advantage of seeing you each day, and I believe that your intention was not to hurt them, but to take life into your own hands."

At this, Lili felt tears welling up.

"You have acted irresponsibly and selfishly," Tante Aletheia continued. "Did you ever stop to consider how your parents—and your younger brother—would feel, what they might imagine, when they waited for you at the dock and you did not appear? Did you have any thoughts at all? What did you expect would follow the inevitable disclosure?"

She glanced down at Fragonard, who was leaning sideways against her.

It felt as if all the blood in Lili's body were rushing into her chest. When she spoke, her voice was choked, for she had not used it in hours.

"I suppose I didn't think that far. I just wanted everything to continue the way it has been. I wanted to play at the concert and stay here." The breath she drew in hurt. But probably not as much as it must have hurt Mama and Papa and Paul when she had not come out of the ship.

"Ach, Lili," said Tante Aletheia with what looked like a shake of disgust. "Don't whine. It is unbecoming in a child, and even more so in a young woman who has turned her back on the past." She lifted her glass, sniffing the Schnaps. "Your parents have asked me to advise you that as you will not be celebrating Christmas with them, it is your duty to spend the holiday with your grandparents. You are to leave for Alt Eichendorf in the morning."

Lili nodded. That was a suitable proposition. Yet—what about afterwards?

As if reading her mind, Tante Aletheia continued.

"Despite the worry, shock, and disappointment that you have caused your parents, they are not ordering you to get on the first available ship. While you are in Prussia, your parents will consider your future, and inform you of their decision when you return here after the holidays.

"It's late," she said, rising. Fragonard landed on nimble paws. "Let's go to the kitchen and see what we can find to eat. Then I suggest you get some sleep. You will need your wits about you tomorrow. Indeed, Lili, it is advisable that they be nearby every day in the future." And then, for the very first time since the first cablegram, Tante Aletheia's gaze softened and Lili felt the fingers of ice around her heart crack.

Later she lay in bed, pulling the quilt around her like a cocoon. As she nestled deeper into the warmth of the eiderdown, her breathing, scented with licorice from her toothpaste, grew slower and more even as she drifted into drowsiness. Eventually Mama and Papa too would forgive her, and somehow she would find a way to make it up to them and little Paul. Tomorrow she was going to Alt Eichendorf. Christmas in Prussia. Her lips curled upwards in the dark. Her conscience might bite her, but its mark was already beginning to fade.

Assorted Sorrows of Sickness

"Good bye, dearest Tante Aletheia!"

Lili is enveloped in the slender, strong embrace that smells of wildflowers. She hugs back hard.

"Bring me a piece of Prussian earth. We will plant it in the garden in Friedberg."

This makes Lili laugh. "I'll bring back some Prussian snow."

"Good idea," says Tante Aletheia. "I shall water the plants with it."

Lili hugs her again, tighter and tighter, but she seems to shrink in her embrace. Harder and harder Lili presses, till there is nothing.

She woke up, the feather quilt bunched up inside her arms, and for some time lay still. From outside came the sound of horseshoes and wooden wheels against the cobblestones, drawing nearer, then fading away. She slipped out of bed to get ready for her journey.

The taxi arrived. As in her dream, Lili wanted to slip into Tante Aletheia's arms, but Tante Aletheia kissed her cheek and then stood back to watch her get into the automobile.

"You might want to look through your Goethe while you're gone," she advised.

For the briefest of moments Lili felt aggravation. "I have him right here," was all she said, patting the brown leather bag at her feet.

Then she was on her way, past Marktplatz and its still slumbering Christmas booths where later in the day the old woman would hang up more Lebkuchen hearts. What would Benno think of her hasty departure? The taxi flew past the empty expanse of the Universitätsplatz where surely this afternoon there would be musicians with violins and a recorder, and someone singing carols for Christmas Eve.

By the time the train crossed the Neckar, Lili had decided that for the remainder of the journey she was not going to think about how Mama and Papa must have felt when she did not get off the boat, and what punishment they might be planning for her at this very moment. Nor was she going to dwell on anything else that was unpleasant. Like that of an eastern philosopher, her focus was going to be on the here and now.

In Frankfurt there were fifteen minutes between connections. From a kiosk she picked up a copy of the *Völkischer Beobachter*. Settling into the next train, she placed her bag on the top rack, slipped out of her coat, and sat down. She hadn't read a newspaper in days. One editorial praised the military agreement signed with Japan. The Japanese were to be considered the Aryans of Asia. Were there Japanese with light hair and blue eyes? Another section had a glowing report on the current exhibition in the newly completed House of German Art. It would be exciting to be able to go and see it. The Führer had said that even if he were to accomplish nothing more in his life than this great gallery, he would have done more for German art than anyone else in the 20th century.

The reporter noted that over three million citizens had already visited the first exhibition of degenerate art—free on order of the Führer—and in February it would begin its travels around the Reich for those unable to visit Munich and see the mad and sick examples of Modernist art. At least there would be no shame for Tante Aletheia; most of Onkel Wilhelm's works were now in Friedberg. The reporter emphasized that art lovers around the world were in agreement with the

Führer's condemnation of the insane ugliness of these Modernist works. That could only mean that the Führer was right in this as well. He was as polished as a diamond, knowledgeable in so many facets. The article flowed neatly into the next topic by way of Jewish artists, Marxism, and a worldwide conspiracy. Herr Poppe had told them about his visit to the exhibition of The Eternal Jew. About five thousand people a day were visiting it. Like the Degenerate Art Exhibition, The Eternal Jew would eventually take to the road. In this way, all Germans could better inform themselves about exactly why Jews should merit disgust and disregard.

A whistle blew. The doors slammed shut. Lili put down the paper and watched the Frankfurter Hauptbahnhof slide by as if it and not the train itself were the one moving. The door to the compartment opened and a woman in a fur-trimmed overcoat of orange pushed her bulk inside. For a moment, a painting by Onkel Wilhelm flashed across Lili's imagination. The woman looked larger—and more garish—than life.

"Heil Hitler," she said, shoving her bag under the seat. She pulled off her coat, a process rather like peeling an orange, that sent a disturbing mix of scents into the already warming air of the compartment. She folded it inside out before laying it on an empty place nearby. Then, huffing and puffing, she dropped onto the velvet seat.

"Excuse me, Fräulein. I was in such a rush to make the train I didn't get a chance to get a paper. Can I read yours when you're finished?"

"Certainly." Lili handed over her copy and looked out the window. They were already passing out of the city and into the open countryside where the snow lay white and pure upon the sleeping fields. In the distance, surrounded by a village whose roofs seemed covered with nightcaps of soft cotton, a church steeple poked upwards in the pallid sky. It was yet another featherbed landscape, and Lili nestled warm and cosy against her coat that lay crumpled behind her. In just a few hours it would be Christmas Eve. The first without her family at her side. Paul would stand alone before the tree. Mama might cry, and Papa look sad. Lili shook her head. No such thoughts allowed.

There was a rustle and the woman peered over the rim of the paper.

"Are you on your way home for the holiday?"

"To my grandparents in the countryside."

"The woman nodded. "I'm off to my son and his family in Wittenberg."

"You must be looking forward to that."

"Yes, indeed. My son's an official, you know. There'll be a big dinner at Party headquarters. The whole family'll be there. He sent me the ticket. That's why I'm traveling First Class." She brushed some lint off her coffee-colored skirt. "Helmut's been with the Party since '29, you know. Before that I didn't travel First Class, I can tell you that."

"That's nice for you," Lili said. "I mean it's nice that you can do so now."

"Oh yes. It makes it easier to avoid the Jews these days too. Then of course they keep to themselves more and more, as they should." She leaned forward, as if there were someone in the compartment who shouldn't overhear. "Of course I'm 100% behind the Führer. I would follow him to the ends of the earth. That man's a godsend." She drew a deep breath. "But I still have feelings for Jesus, you know. I was raised that way so I can't quite help it. It was the Jews that murdered him. Jesus that is. Even though Pastor Niemuller's in jail these days he himself used to say that it's the Jews themselves who brought this all onto themselves. It's those race aliens that brought the Christ of God to the cross."

Lili frowned. "Why is he in jail?"

The woman made a tutting sound. "It's strange how people can get off the track. They arrested him when he protested the arrests of some Protestants, you know. Why that should be though, I don't rightly know. It was Martin Luther himself who spoke against the Jews. Imagine, just last year they brought out a little booklet by him that says we should arrest the Jews, use them as we need, then send 'em away, and more." Folding her plump arms, she sat back against the velvet. "And that was written already hundreds of years ago."

"Well," Lili said, tapping her foot against the floor. "I heard that there was some sort of agreement to have more Jews go to Palestine or Madagascar or somewhere. If they did that, then everyone would be happy, and we could get on with other more important matters." She felt rather sophisticated discussing political matters with the woman, even if their paths would never have crossed anywhere but on a train.

The woman shook her head. "It doesn't look like they're welcome in Palestine. The British don't want them there either." She wrinkled her nose. "Nobody wants them. And why should they? The ones coming in from the East are dirty and strange, and the ones who've been living here are sneaks and cheats."

The door to the compartment opened and a bespectacled man with a cap stepped inside.

"Heil Hitler, my ladies," he said. As he examined and punched their tickets, he spoke of the weather, which was expected to remain clear for Christmas Day. When he withdrew, the woman picked up the paper again but in minutes was fast asleep, snoring lightly.

At Wittenberg, after much fumbling with bag and coat, she descended, wishing Lili a happy holiday. New passengers boarded, a businessman, a wheezing grandfather, and an HJ boy some years younger than Lili, but, aside from the initial greetings, there was no conversation. Lili ate her *Leberwurstbrot* and an apple and for the rest of the journey stared out the window at winter, white upon white.

In Berlin she changed trains with only a few minutes to spare, and cast longing looks at what she could see of the Reich's capital.

Tante Aletheia had notified them at Alt Eichendorf; Becker was there at the Posenwell station. His lined face wore an anxious expression.

"Freiin Lili," he said, taking her bag. "Welcome back. They're waiting for you. But I must inform you that your grandmother has been taken ill."

Her heart skipped a beat.

"It was a heavy cold that developed into influenza. Dr. Hindemann is doing his best to keep it from turning into pneumonia."

"Ach, poor Großmama Maximiliana. Poor Großpapa Hugo," she said as she sank back into the leather seat.

She was silent as the Daimler pulled away from the station, traveling over the Posenwell cobblestones toward the darkening countryside.

"Why isn't Dr. Burckhardt taking care of her? He always looks after everyone in the family."

Becker didn't respond and Lili repeated the question. He cleared his throat.

"His wife has been arrested. He's gone to Berlin to see what he can do about it."

"Arrested!"

"She's been in jail for the last week, Freiin."

"But whatever for? She's such a nice old lady. What could she possibly have done to get arrested?"

"Somebody reported her for complaining about the ban on Jewish doctors in government hospitals."

"But Dr. Burckhardt isn't Jewish!" she protested. "Or is he?"

"No, he isn't, and neither is she. But she was overheard saying that it's not right to deny patients help just because of some, emm, stupid law."

Lili's eyebrow went up in the dark. "Oh my. She said that?"

They passed under a canopy of bare-limbed oaks. Caught in the momentary glare of the headlights they looked like outstretched arms. Snow swished against both sides of the automobile as if they were traveling by sled.

"Yes, Freiin, that's what she said," Becker said, his voice gravelly. "And somebody didn't like it. Now she's in jail and Dr. Burckhardt beside himself with worry."

"Hmm," Lili said to the back of Becker's head. "It's hard, her being so old. I suppose after this she'll know to keep such thoughts to herself."

For the rest of the trip, Becker was silent.

♫ ♪ ♫

Waking up in the familiar folds of her featherbed, Lili stretched with contentment until she remembered Großmama Maximiliana. She bounded out, washing and dressing quickly. If anyone had asked her, she would have admitted being glad that Christmas Eve had passed. Despite Großpapa Hugo's efforts to make her feel at home the previous evening, she had known that his mind was mainly on her grandmother.

With just Großpapa Hugo and Lili before the tree in the salon, it had been a rather sorrowful Christmas. Both aunts and their husbands were in Norway for the holidays, where Onkel Eberhardt had family. Großpapa Hugo and Lili had exchanged gifts, the pipe and silver tobacco box she'd bought at Dürninger in Heidelberg and forgotten to post, and perfume and a Cordoba leather writing set for her. How touching it was that he had arranged this at such short notice. He also presented her with a velvet box. Inside was a strand of black pearls. "Großmama Maximiliana always meant for you to have these one day. I think she would approve of you having them already now," he said, rather loudly, patting her hand. Großpapa's hearing had deteriorated considerably since the summer, requiring him to hold a horn to his ear, making conversations both brief and tiring. There was no music, no singing of Christmas carols. Despite her determination to avoid thinking of them, Lili had wondered how it was across the ocean: were Mama and Papa and Paul celebrating? Did they miss her, or was it now more peaceful without her?

Just when it seemed that the two of them would sink under with glumness, Großpapa Hugo had uncorked a bottle of Pommery and the loud efforts of their toasts, passing from good will to good-natured teasing, somewhat lifted their spirits. A Christmas dinner of roast goose followed, and with their bellies comforted by an assortment of festive foods perfected as usual by Frau Soeding, the evening had ended on a slightly uplifted note.

Now Lili hurried down the hallway to meet Großmama Maximiliana.

"Großmama?" Her footsteps were silent as she entered the room. Her grandmother's eyes were closed, the lashes gray shadows against the creamy parchment of her skin. Further down, two rosy splotches marked her sunken cheekbones. The Swiss cotton and lace of her nightgown encircled her neck. Lili reached out to touch the fragile hand resting on the linen coverlet. The flesh was dry and hot with fever.

"Lili?" The voice was a wheezy murmur. "Is that you?"

"Yes, dearest Großmama. I'm here."

The nearly translucent eyelids slid open slowly, the cracked lips parting in the shadow of a smile.

Lili stroked the pale brow. Mama would look like this when she got old.

"Sleep now. I'll stay with you. When you awaken, you will feel better." Or so Lili hoped. Großmama was so sick that it could go either way now.

For some hours, Lili sat in the straight-backed chair next to her grandmother's bed, suddenly homesick for those seemingly endless days of childhood innocence when she had been loved and sheltered by her healthy and doting family in a world still small enough to know nothing but perfection.

♫♪♫

From across the snowy fields came the muted clang of the ten o'clock church bells. Lili listened until they faded, then returned to the blue leather bound book on her lap. Today she had been sitting with Großmama Maximiliana since after breakfast. The past few days had been difficult, but at last her grandmother had rounded the corner. The fever had broken last night, her sleep restful, her breathing even. Lili was still looking at the Goethe quotes when she heard Dr. Hindemann arriving downstairs for the first of his daily visits. Lili had not entirely warmed to him and his clipped mannerisms that she would have considered fine for anything other than patient administration. But she could see that he was doing his best for Großmama Maximiliana in Dr. Burckhardt's absence, and the results were a relief. She set the book on the seat and went to the entrance hall to greet him.

"Heil Hitler, Fräulein Lili." His right arm straightened. Usually he headed up the stairway immediately but today he lingered.

"Quite a bit of excitement at the square this morning," he said, rubbing his palms. "Put Posenwell on the map, I should say."

"Why, what's happened?"

"Seems like the church can't control its own flock. Or at least its roosters." He grinned at his joke.

Lili waited for him to continue.

"Pastor Schmidt has been inciting his congregation to question the Party. He even had the audacity to protest Niemueller's arrest."

Lili nodded knowingly. "I was just discussing him with someone the other day."

"Some of the Protestant pastors have made quite an about-face." He shook his head. "You've got smart theologians like Ludwig Müller who have always seen eye to eye with the Führer on religious matters, and then you have powder kegs like Niemueller and Bonhoeffer."

She had no idea who Bonhoeffer was.

"One of the radical reformers who's with those idiots at the Confessional Church. He's just asking for trouble."

It was too confusing to follow. "So what happened in Posenwell with the pastor?"

"They've taken him in for questioning of course." He paused, as before a punchline. "They picked up his counterpart over at Sankt Stefan as well."

Lili gaped.

The doctor laughed. "Yes, two for the price of one, I'd say. It looks like Father Matthias hasn't been listening to his church's directives. You recall the concordat with the Führer back in '33?" He peered at Lili. "No, I don't suppose you would, you're still too young. In any case, the priest was heard saying that the Führer would never replace the trinity of Father, Son and Holy Ghost. He went so far as to say that even though Jews crucified Christ, they shouldn't be singled out by secular laws, especially if they've converted, and that people should protest."

Lili almost smiled. It was strange how she had met the woman on the train who had spoken of Jesus and the Jews, and now this. Life was evidently full of coincidences.

Dr. Hindemann snorted. "A fine picture: the two opposing pillars of Posenwell sharing the same paddy wagon. I wonder what their conversation en route was." He leaned over to pick up his medical bag from the polished parquet. Rising, his manner changed back to the man of medicine.

"And how is your grandmother today? She was in fine form last night."

"Yes," said Lili, breaking into a smile. "It's a miracle."

"Nonsense," asserted the doctor. "It's just good German medical know-how." Clicking his heels as he saluted, he went upstairs to where Großmama Maximiliana had been propped up against the feather pillows for the last hour reading favorite passages from her Bible, which was upside down.

Birthday Celebration

On the first morning of the year 1938, Lili wrapped herself in an old astrakhan coat of Mama's she'd found in a closet, pulled on a cap of blue wool and a fur muff, and went out into the winter. It was her birthday; she was eighteen.

During the night more snow had fallen and now lay soft and silent, pristine on the path leading toward the woods. How often Papa and she had walked this way. Far above the white mantle of the forest a goshawk or perhaps a kite screamed, but otherwise only her boots sounded through the fresh snow.

There were the memories of other birthdays. Mama and Papa had always made her feel special. In the morning, they would creep into her room, singing, louder and louder in near harmony, and Lili would open her eyes to a large, brightly colored sign—the color would change each year—covered with birthday wishes. At breakfast there was a special flower arrangement that was hers to take to her room later. In the afternoon, gifts were opened around the lace-bedecked table set with fine porcelain and cake and hot cocoa. The gifts themselves were a delight, often surprising, always thoughtful. Today was the first time in her life that she had not awoken to Mama and Papa. She would not share a moment of her day with them. All things considered, it was only fitting.

She was a woman now and must follow her own path. She pushed on through the snow, myriad prisms sparkling in the strengthening sun.

When she reached the opening in the forest, she halted. The sound of puffing faded as her breath slowed. Her gaze slid over the frosted landscape. Slowly, as if following the call of some ancient rite, she began to turn in a circle. Her fur muff dropped and her arms rose outwards as around she went, faster and faster, wearing away the snow with her feet, her spinning focus blurring the bare branches and the pale sky and the bleached blanket of winter that spread out upon the slumbering earth. Her cap flew off. Free, she tilted her head back and as her hair loosened, her laughter rose, higher and higher until she could barely breathe with the joy of it. Life. Life! Trusting the snow, she stopped, and let herself fall.

It was exhilarating to lie there looking up into the whirling and limitless heavens. Surely there could be no one heaven. If life and the world were already so wondrous, how could what came after death be so limiting? There must be so many heavens, many universes; the infinite was all. And what was more than all? Nothing. Nothingness. She giggled. So nothing, non-existence, must be even more limitless. What freedom came with that wondrous thought. Yet this must be not only in death: in life as well. The freedom of choice, of making the right decisions for the right reasons. She blinked.

The cold began to cut into the astrakhan and under her bare head. Her muff-less fingers were already burning. Indeed, the palm of her left hand was throbbing. She braced herself on the snow to sit up. The blood shifted in her head. Only one movement and how different the world looked. And how silly she must appear, sitting bundled up in the snow with her legs stretched out, like a small child. She looked around; she was alone. After all, who else would want to take to the woods so early on the first day of the New Year? She glanced down and started.

For some moments she couldn't understand from where it came, that crimson staining the snow. Twisted twigs, black as wire, poked up nearby through the frosted covering. She stared at them, reached out to touch one. The tip was jagged and sharp, frozen. Her hand throbbed and she turned her palm inwards to find blood smeared across a rip in the fleshy part. Long and bloody as it was, it didn't look serious enough to impede her playing. Using her right hand, she picked up some snow with which to rub the wound. Stupid idea. Best to go back to the house and wash it. She clambered onto her feet, looking upon where her blood had marked the snow.

In a sudden movement she went down on her knees. Pushing with her right hand, she used the twigs, snow, and her lifeblood to form the symbol. There it was: the swastika. She grinned at her handiwork.

She rose again, breathed in deeply. The cold and the cut had cleared her head. The fog of hesitation of the previous weeks had evaporated completely. Again she looked around at the stark beauty of winter, knowing the silent life beneath that would explode and flourish green and glorious in the coming months. No matter what the season, there was always the enduring reality of the German lands. Clarity. Her place was here. Why, her very blood had spilled on the snow; in spring it would melt and seep into the soil.

Today was the first day of the New Year. Today she was eighteen.

Two Unexpected Developments

After the disquieting mixture of memories and worries at Alt Eichendorf, Heidelberg was a relief. Lili could barely wait for the taxi to pull to a stop on Kornmarkt before ripping open the door.

She had brought along a tiny but perfectly proportioned fir tree, earth still clinging to its roots, even though the exchange with Tante Aletheia had been but a dream. For Fragonard there was a straw mouse with a bell, suitable for batting about. When she had unpacked her suitcase in Alt Eichendorf, she had discovered a gift from Tante Aletheia: original sheet music by Ferdinand Muckelbacher, the 18th century Swabian harpsichordist. She couldn't wait to start playing it.

Now she unlocked the door and stepped inside the house that she had left under such a cloud less than two weeks ago. Warmth and the comfort of familiar smells rolled over her, enfolding her, and she sighed with relief. Everything was as it had been. The gray-striped umbrella was in its customary place in the antique milk bucket next to the door, the potted fern was wilting at the edges, and the Oriental carpet lay at a 45-degree angle at the base of the stairs. The statue of the near-naked man was still surveying his realm. It was odd. Despite neither Mama, Papa, nor Paul being nearby, she felt at home.

No one was in but Tante Aletheia and Frau Brinkmann. The latter welcomed her warmly but, unsure of the former's disposition toward her, Lili had initially been subdued. Yet, as Tante Aletheia and she sat in the kitchen and Lili, ravenous from her trip, ate last night's re-heated *Eintopf*, the atmosphere grew relaxed. They spoke of the journey, her grandparents, Frau Dierck's worst incident (on Christmas Eve), and the comings and goings of Herr Poppe. The only topic they didn't touch on was Mama and Papa and what was going to happen to Lili. But they couldn't avoid that subject forever. At the thought of the chastising letters that surely lay in wait for her nearby, a little of the Eintopf threatened to rise.

Tante Aletheia expressed delight at the fir tree and went to look for a suitable container. "While it is still small, I'll put it on top of the treasure cabinet."

This pleased Lili. The treasure cabinet on the far side of the room was filled with artifacts like hammered gold jewelry, a comb, glass vials, tiny pots. All were slated for eventual bequeathing to the museum in Straßburg rather than that in Heidelberg, as most of the items had been dug up from the grounds in Friedberg.

"The woods there were home to a Celtic tribe," Tante Aletheia said. "I wouldn't be surprised to learn that druids held ceremonies right there on a hill near the house. The museum has a collection of Celtic items from the area and these will augment it nicely one day.

"Now we should talk about what your parents have decided."

Lili swallowed. Suddenly it was as if she had never been away and it were still the day of the cablegrams. She pressed the wound on her palm. It had healed but was still somewhat sore when pressed. It reminded her of the decisions she had made that day in the snow, and that she must be strong.

Yet the news from New York shocked her. Papa and Mama wrote that she could stay till summer. At that time, she was to spend two days in Hamburg before the aunts would see her safely aboard and out of the harbor.

"That's all?" Were there no punishments, no admonitions? There was no letter for Lili either.

Tante Aletheia pursed her lips.

"That's all they wish me to say to you."

Lili bit her lip. This was not what she had expected.

♫♪♫

The rest of the day was spent at the harpsichord, tackling the Muckelbacher until she had memorized the piece, then moving on to Händel with guilty relief. Despite its complexities, Muckelbacher was too sweet. Händel was much more to her taste, and savoring this next piece would blot out concerns about Papa and Mama, returning to America, and her future in general.

In the late afternoon, she went downstairs just as Herr Poppe came into the house. His fleshy cheeks were florid but he seemed more agitated than cold. After a brief inquiry about her holiday, he launched into a lengthy monologue; his much-anticipated promotion was not going as smoothly as originally expected. Just that morning he had received a memorandum reminding him that all single applicants for promotion in the civil service were to make a written deposition setting out why they were not married, and when they intended to do so.

At one point he sucked in the breath through his nose, creating a goose-like honk in E flat. He was completely flummoxed by the worry that if he did not marry within the ascribed time, his file would be reviewed—and who knew what could happen after that. After all these years of exemplary service. Not to mention his newest role as Blockleiter, ensuring that the community was safe from those acting contrary to the guidelines of the NSDAP. Lili had never seen him looking so wild-eyed and shaken, nor heard him speak in this manner.

Even his hair was bristling with anxiety, damp at the roots. He stared at her, and, for a long and horrible moment, she thought he was about to ask her to marry him.

Then, like jelly quivering back into form, he pulled himself together, his voice too growing firmer with each word.

"I shall renew my efforts. I'll do whatever is required." He gave an emphatic nod. "Heil Hitler."

"Sieg heil," Lili said.

Herr Poppe had barely taken off for his room when the front door opened again and Benno appeared with a blast of winter air.

"Heil Hitler," she called out.

"Heil Hitler," he said, moving toward her. "When did you return?" He looked pleased. "Wait here," he said and bounded up the stairs three at a time. Moments later he was back with a heavy package wrapped in flowered paper.

"Belated wishes for a very happy birthday. Now you're not a little girl anymore."

She thought of the Lebkuchenherz and could feel her cheeks warming. "Another present. Shall I open it now?"

Benno grinned, the tips of his incisors sliding into view.

It was a thick book, *Heidelberg through the Ages.*

"It's lovely. Thank you. I shall read this and next time you test me in history, I'll get a 1."

"Then you'd better get reading. First exam is already scheduled."

She glanced over the pages. There were many photographs of her favorite spots in Heidelberg.

"I said it will take place over dinner at Zum Weissen Schwanen."

"Oh," she exclaimed. "Were you talking? I didn't hear you."

"You're rather sassy for an eighteen year old."

"Forgive me. I'm still a freshly baked eighteen."

Benno laughed. "I think I could forgive you anything."

If only Mama and Papa would feel the same way. But the thought didn't go any further because, almost roughly, Benno pulled her to him, pressing his mouth hot and moist upon hers. The kiss lasted only an instant yet Lili stopped breathing. All she could feel was her lips, and his. When he let her go, her eyes were wide open. The book fell and smacked hard against the floor.

Benno looked appalled.

"Forgive me," he muttered, and rushed to the entrance.

Lili was still standing in the center of the foyer as the door closed, leaving only a wave of frigid air. Some moments later, her heart hammering from her own flight up the stairs, she crossed her room to the window and looked out upon Kornmarkt. Benno was nowhere to be seen but her mouth still felt the pressure of his. She hesitated before running her tongue over her lips. They tasted no different than usual. She stood frowning at the window until she was aware that anyone looking up from the square would see her, a young woman who had just been kissed. Abruptly, she turned away

Some Insights into Kladderadatsch

Dr. Hempel had suggested that Lili build up a repertoire; after her success last month, it was probable that she would be performing again soon. She had been to the music store to choose several new pieces, both solo and chamber arrangements, and earlier today had begun work on CPE Bach's Trio in G minor. Although his compositions didn't have the brilliant complexity of so many of his father's, there was something about the son's that drew her. And working at them allowed her to stop thinking about everything else, including that strange kiss.

Yet today held an emptiness, for although it was Wednesday, she had not gone to the BDM meeting. Unless she became a leader, she would never attend another. Next week she would join Faith and

Beauty but of course that wouldn't be the same. It was good that a university student march had been planned for tomorrow. It would be a tough one, for snowfall had been heavy these past hours and by morning the streets would be thick with drifts that needed pushing and tramping through. Yet it would be wonderful to be out there again, following the banners, feeling the power. Perhaps this time she would get to carry a flag.

Dinner was still half an hour away when Lili went downstairs into the salon where Herr Poppe and Herr Tischborn were ensconced in armchairs, reading periodicals. Lili settled down with *Heidelberg through the Ages*. Surely Benno wasn't serious about testing her knowledge. She glanced at the other two. Herr Poppe was going through the pages of the *Völkischer Beobachter* with a great frown of concentration. Herr Tischborn had as usual opted for *Kladderadatsch*. She looked through the leaded panes to the falling snow and for some minutes there was a companionable silence in the room, broken only by the slide of paper as pages were turned.

"It says here that the Party is making great inroads in Austria," Herr Poppe said. "One day all the German lands will indeed be reunited. One Volk, one nation, one Führer."

"The Sudetenland is waiting for that," Herr Tischborn added.

Lili peered at the cover of his magazine. It had a drawing of Father Time standing back as a young boy, clearly a Pimpf, entered a Pater Noster elevator headed up. The message reminded Lili of the Führer's speech in Nuremberg:

"As you stand before me today, so year by year in centuries to come will the young generation stand before future Führers. And again and again they will profess their faith in the Germany which we have fought to create today."

It had made her shiver then, and did even now, when she thought about how she was of the generation helping create the new Germany.

Although what was she doing that could be considered fighting? She shifted in her seat.

"What sort of a magazine is *Kladderadatsch*, Herr Tischborn?"

"An amusing journal, good for a chuckle. Much of it pokes fun at the Communists and the British," he said, passing it to her.

She flipped through the pages. She wasn't sure that she understood the jokes. There were too many references to current events. Frowning, she nodded and handed the magazine back.

"The cartoons are political," said Herr Poppe jovially. "It's not a woman's job to understand politics. Just now I was reading—let me find the page in the paper—ah, here it is, that women ought to be removed from every sphere of public life." He gave her a good-natured nod.

Lili considered this for a few moments. "That would make life rather difficult for everyone."

"Of course it isn't meant in a negative sense, by any means," Herr Poppe said. "It simply emphasizes the point that the Führer believes that the most important and honorable role for women remains that of rearing a family. The future generation. And that is done in the home." He gave an emphatic nod.

"Mmm," said Lili. Perhaps Herr Poppe was thinking about the directive he had been given about getting married. She glanced at his lips. They always seemed wet. As earnest and committed as he was, she certainly wouldn't want to be a Frau Poppe. But the Führer's message was clear. One day she, Lili, would do her part in raising a new generation for Germany. For now she could still march next to the flag and collect clothes for Winter Help Relief and do whatever else to help the nation. Especiallly her duty to play the harpsichord. After all, it wasn't for nothing that 'The state does not exist to serve the individual, the individual exists to serve the state' was such an integral part of the Führer's inspiration to German youth.

"*Kladderadatsch* is one of the oldest magazines," Herr Poppe went on. "Although it was a Jew who started it, these days it's a solid bit of

Aryan work. No more Jews to be found in *Kladderadatsch*. These days they've got their own papers for lying and whining to each other about how bad they've got it here." He shrugged his shoulders. "So let them leave. Ah, I think I hear Frau Brinkmann coming."

The door opened, and Frau Brinkmann appeared, her face flushed from cooking. As they made their way out of the room, Lili noticed that Herr Tischborn, normally so neat, hadn't put the magazine away. *Kladderadatsch* lay abandoned, spread-eagled on the table where it had been since Herr Poppe had told them of its Jewish origins.

Dinner at Zum Weissen Schwanen

Lili wasn't sure who had been avoiding whom these past few days, Benno for kissing her, or she for not being sure if she'd liked that kiss. After all, she only had Friedrich's kiss with which to compare it. There had been a moment alone after dinner at home the other evening when it seemed that Benno was going to say something to her. But Herr Tischborn came into the dining room and the moment passed. By the time they met to go for dinner at Zum Weissen Schwanen, it seemed that both Benno and she had chosen to not mention it.

They crossed Kornmarkt. As they stepped onto an icy patch, Lili began to slip and Benno's hand shot out to grab her. She flinched, but thanked him.

"Are you finally going to tell me your news over dinner?" she asked. "Or can't you talk about it yet?"

This evening she had her own news. Earlier today, Dr. Hempel had handed her an official paper, black eagle hovering on the letterhead: an audition for a concert in the famous Nibelungensaal of the Rosengarten in Mannheim. Perhaps the Führer would attend this one. And if the same SS musicians were involved, perhaps the viola da gamba player would be there too.

"I'll tell you right now," he said. "I've been invited to join the *Ahnenerbe*, under Himmler himself. Well, not directly, but it is rather his pet project."

"Compliments! What will you do with them?"

Benno explained how an expedition scheduled for earlier that year had been delayed and that this had worked in his favor for, in the meantime, because of his work with germ plasms, his name had drawn attention from such luminaries as Ernst Schäfer and Hans F.K. Günther. Now a new scientific research project was in the works, an undertaking that would be of great import to the future of the Reich.

He stopped talking to pull open the door to the 14th century Gasthaus. Inside it was warm, with the comforting scents of good food and tobacco.

"Who are those people?" Lili asked.

Benno looked around at the tables.

"No, I mean Schäfer and Günther."

Benno laughed, baring his incisors. "Schäfer is an incredible zoologist. But I'm surprised that you don't know who Günther is. He's written on the history of the Nordic race and how they conquered the East. That explains why the aristocrats of Japan and China have such white skin. And why the caste system exists in India."

The waiter brought them their beers. Lili still preferred wine, but there was something earthy and wholesome about beer. As if one were drinking a bit of the homeland, distilled.

"I went to a lecture on Buddhism and the East in the Große Saal," she said.

Benno nodded. "According to Günther, Buddha was the son of Nordic settlers in Indian lands."

"When I was at the lecture," Lili said, "Rektor Wüst explained about Aryan gods that created, preserved and destroyed. It made me think about our talk at the Schloß, and how the Führer says that things must be destroyed to be created. From what you just said, it could actually be that our Nordic ancestors taught that to their subjects in India."

His gaze began to roam over her face and Lili looked down into her beer.

"I can imagine you as a brave young woman who travelled to the East to build a powerful new empire ruled by Nordic bloodlines. The pale-skinned Brahmans of today's India would be in your debt."

She arched an eyebrow. "I doubt that any of my ancestors went as far as India to create bloodlines. I imagine that they preferred staying by the lakes in Prussia."

"In any case," Benno said, "we know that your descendants will all have musical notes flowing in their blood." He paused. "I'm not a musician of course, but after hearing you practice these past few months, even I can recognize your amazing talent. You bring to music a sense of confidence that's surely an inherited trait."

It was not the first time he was telling her this. "That's true, I mean, about it being inherited. At least partly. My father is a very confident player, even if he doesn't perform."

"That just goes to show that an aptitude for music is in your blood. Your children too will be fine musicians."

His eyes met hers and lingered. Lili was suddenly reminded of Herr Poppe. He had peered at her in just as strange a way that day when he told her about needing to get married. Marriage meant children too. It meant kissing and more. Did Benno want to kiss her again? She glanced away and gave a high-pitched laugh.

"Ye-es, music has always been an important part of my family." Perhaps it would be a good idea if she were to go home now and practice some. She bit her lip. But it wouldn't be fair to Benno if she left just because she was feeling awkward. She needed to show strength. Be objective and confident.

Benno picked up his glass; his thumb made her think of a test tube, while the other long fingers had knuckles knobby and bleached.

"Aryans have always had a special gift for musicianship," he said. "Ancient sites in Scandanavia have turned up many examples of early instruments."

"I wonder how music first began," she blurted out, and then warmed to the thought. "When did people begin to notice a difference between pounding hides and making rhythms, or speaking and singing? The understanding of music must be what separated primitive man from early man." She nodded. "I think music is essential to human well-being. Sports and art and such, they're all important, but none of them give such lifelong richness. Truly, music must be the gateway to understanding the infinite."

Quite pleased with these unexpected turns of phrase, Lili picked up her glass.

Benno was staring at her again, his eyes glittering dark as a wolf's. She swallowed.

"Did I say something wrong?"

"No, no. It's just that you are so--"

She could see him breathing, his narrow chest moving against his shirt.

She bit her lip.

"If I were a poet," he said, "I would have the right words."

Right words? What did he want to say? Was he going to propose to her?

"But I'm a scientist. So I'll just say what I've told you before—that you're an excellent example of all that is best in an Aryan woman. One day, your bloodlines will be an asset to the Reich." He paused. "Just as the Ahnenerbe expedition I am to be part of will unite past and future, East and West."

Relief flooded her even as she blushed at her mistake. She remembered what he had told her that day up on the tiers of the Thingstätte, that one day the Reich would move beyond its present border, with new settlements arising, new Germanic roots planted in the soil of the East.

"Congratulations, Benno," she said. "The Ahnenerbe is lucky to have a scientist like you."

He reached out and gently, very gently, ran a knobby finger above her lip. Lili's eyes widened. His finger slid off and he held it up, showing her the white foam stuck to it. Her giggle was nervous and he laughed, as if it were a schoolboy prank. Then he called over the waiter and they ordered their dinners, spending the rest of the evening speaking about forgettable matters.

Lili is Astonished

The wind from the Neckar lashed at them like whips, searing their cheeks.

"Brr. What's the holdup? Let's get moving!"

Those with flags hoisted them now, the air current immediately claiming the cloth. The banners flapped and snapped, their red as brilliant as fresh blood against the blenching sky of the winter day.

They were on the march this morning, instead of going to classes. Lili was grateful that she was somewhere in the middle of the group of about three dozen, more sheltered from the wind. To relieve the guilt of her relative comfort she resolved to sing and shout the louder. The student leader gave the command to set forth and off they went, their route taking them through the heart of Heidelberg, from the river to Bismarckplatz. Lili had covered it countless times already. Sometimes they went in the opposite direction. The singing began, with an old favorite from the male students' days in the Jungvolk.

"The world belongs to those who lead, those who follow the sun.

And we are the marchers; none can stop us.

The old world totters, the crumbling walls fall down.

We are the young stormers.

We are victory.

Leap up, march, march!

Raise the banner atop the tower!"

How earnest and deep the men sounded. How sweet they must have looked as young boys. Just like those countless groups of darling young Pimpfs that so often moved in formation through Heidelberg and elsewhere, trumpets blaring, drums pounding, not-yet-broken voices raised in jubilation. All of them, HJ boys and BDM girls, marching till their feet were blistered, their ankles chafed, arches flattened. All of them, the youth of the land, marching and singing, committed with heart and soul to honoring and obeying their Führer, for whom they would gladly spend every drop of their blood.

Two hours later, Lili and several others stepped into Zur Goldenen Gans, their earlobes close to frozen. Lili had never been to this Gasthaus, which seemed to be very popular with SS officers. The marchers rubbed their hands together. No one who had ever marched could say that it wasn't hard work, burning up energy, especially when so much energy was already being used in trying to stay warm. When the waitress came by again, Lili ordered a veal sausage with fried potatoes but today there was only pork.

In the heated air, toes and fingers began to regain their feeling, unpleasant only for those with blisters. Although it was rather late for lunch, it seemed as if everyone were avoiding going back into the icy outdoors.

Lili glanced at the students around the table. She didn't know most of their names.

"Heard this one yet?" one asked. "The Führer goes to a village and enters the Gasthaus. The innkeeper gets excited and sends for the mayor and all the top men of the village to sit with the Führer. He orders his usual, a glass of mineral water. So of course everyone else orders mineral water, except for one fellow at the end of the table who hasn't been paying 100% attention to what's going on. He orders a beer. The other villagers look shocked and worried. The Führer notices, and calls out to the man: 'It seems that you and I are the only honest men in this village!'"

"That's no joke—the Führer has always has been earnest and honest. He leads a very simple personal life."

"He doesn't even take an official salary," said the only other girl among the students.

"Of course not. He stopped years ago. But what did you mean by 'his personal life'? He doesn't have a personal life! Everything he does is for the Reich."

Like the others, Lili nodded. No matter how many times she heard or said this, it was always reaffirming.

"I remember him addressing a crowd in the pouring rain," someone said. "There was no umbrella, but he wouldn't let his own discomfort stop him from talking to the people. He got completely drenched."

"He never stops going. If he's not working on national plans, assessing budgets and discussing new projects, he's out meeting with people and giving speeches. I don't understand how he keeps up his pace."

"Right you are. But you're not a good example in any case. You have a hard enough time carrying the flag, puffing like some dilapidated engine. If we ever have to go war to protect the Reich, I wouldn't want to be in your battalion."

"I can do as much as any man. Except the Führer."

"Obviously."

"No one can compare to the Führer. Himmler has named him the greatest man of all time."

"Heil Hitler," someone called out, and all raised their glasses. A few SS men looked their way, then lifted their glasses to join in the toast.

"*Zum Wohl des Führers!*"

Lili glanced at the SS men nearby. Of course Leo Arnim von Witzleben was not among them. He wouldn't be sitting around, drinking afternoon Schnaps. He would be rehearsing or performing somewhere, or doing something important. She realized that she was staring at a blonde, broad-shouldered SS man who was looking back at her with apparent interest. Quickly she averted her gaze.

"The Führer is pure reason in human form."

"Well spoken from a former student of philosophy."

"And were I a divinity student--" At this there were great guffaws from around the table. "Then verily would I say that the Führer, gentle and kind, loves every German in the Reich."

There were some chuckles and a mantle of comfort seemed to slip over their shoulders.

"It's a pity that the Führer never went to university."

At this the girl looked scandalized. "What are you saying? The Führer is highly educated!"

"I meant only that there are so many fields in which his knowledge could have been awarded with degrees."

"He may not have been to university, but he should be awarded doctorates in every single subject."

"He's certainly a graduate from the school of life, too. Summa cum laude, I'd say."

"I've never heard anyone speak so knowledgeably, and with such conviction, about anything, from architecture to science," said the girl. "Including our esteemed professors. The Führer can make mincemeat of all of them." She paused. "When I was in Berlin last December, my parents took me to a social event at a hotel. The Führer was there too."

Suddenly everyone at the table fell silent. All of them had been to Nuremberg for the rallies, some of them since the very first, but here was someone who had been in a closed room with the Führer, breathed the same air, perhaps even shared a toast. Everyone's attention was on her.

At that moment Lili wanted to call out that she too had been with the Führer—not in an impersonal hotel but in her own home. He had spoken with and even kissed her. He had proclaimed her duty.

But everyone was listening to the other girl and Lili kept silent. What was the use? It was the past.

She felt within her the familiar pain. Yet as she stayed silent, the ache seemed to change its form; transforming those unspoken words and feelings of disappointment, moving outwards from heart to limbs. No longer in discomfort, but with a strange, lightening sense of strength. She could be as tough as she needed to be.

"Was Elsa Wallenbach there too?"

"Where've you been, man? Turns out she's half Jewish."

"Too bad. She was quite a piece."

"Ironic that she used to be in all those Blubo plays."

Blut und Boden, blood and soil. Lili thrilled at the thought. It wasn't just about plays and books. For a moment she wanted to tell everyone at the table about Benno and the other scientists and their research that was so important for the future of Germany's lands and the purity of its people. But she knew how to keep silent, so all she said was "Is there a Jewish version of Blubo?"

"Of course," said the girl, rolling her eyes. "It's called Sano—Sand and Nothing, for when they dream of Palestine."

There was some loud laughter.

"Ah, Blubo. Human procreation and soil fertility on the same pedestal."

"Pretty steamy stuff."

Lili glanced back over at a nearby table. A couple of the SS men seemed to be enjoying the students' conversation. She wondered if any of them had seen her performance at the Stadthalle.

"What about you?" someone said to the girl. "Aren't you getting ready soon for your big day?"

Lili winced. Were all the female students getting married? Hildegard from her class, and now this one too?

She nodded. "We're just waiting for my fiancé to finish his Reich Labor Service year next month. He's been working near Magdeburg where a big housing development is going up."

Benno had told her how his brother had been killed in that city. First people had fought against the NSDAP and now the NSDAP was putting up houses for them. That was the Führer's sense of justice.

"Ja, they need more housing over there. That hydrogenation plant is causing a population boom."

"Must be the lignite deposits in that area. Say, what's with this bread? It just doesn't taste right."

"You've probably eaten too much of it."

"No, it tastes different. Not like it's supposed to. The consistency's different."

"So, good people," one of the students said, pushing back his chair. "I, for one, have to move out."

There was a general agreement that it was time to face the weather. Perhaps the afternoon sun would be kinder than that of the morning. The waitress began her trip around the table with her black leather purse, collecting money. In the background, the buzz of conversations was punctuated by sporadic laughter but it was no longer as loud as before, for the SS men too were making their way out into the deep chill of the afternoon.

As she left, Lili could feel the gaze of some of the officers on her. Their dark uniforms were symbols of security and strength, and something that made her cheeks burn.

"Lili!"

She turned. Around the corner from the main room stood an SS officer. He was calling out her name again. He seemed to know her. For a few moments, she could not make the connection. Then the features swam into focus as he came over, smiling.

"You look surprised," he said.

"I am," she said. "How is this even possible?"

Benno laughed. "I forgot to tell you the other day that in order to join the Ahnenerbe, I had to join the SS."

Talk of Marriage

Lili stepped up to the house just as Dr. Morsch appeared to be leaving, worn black bag in hand.

"Fräulein Lili," he said, his smile as warm as a father's. Lili smiled back and then raised her hand in the *Hitlergruß*.

Dr. Morsch blinked, glanced about, drew closer his bag and overcoat.

"Frau Dierck is resting now. I'll stop by tomorrow again." He passed by her, disappearing into the darkness.

Lili frowned as she wiped her feet on the winter mat. Dr. Morsch seemed such an honorable man. Perhaps he was just too tired to have returned her Hitlergruß. His bag had been in his right hand. She went to hang up her coat. Tante Aletheia came into the foyer, a sweater of leaf green draped across her shoulders.

"There you are, my dear," she said, giving Lili a kiss. "But what a cold cheek you have. Come into the kitchen. There's still some stew left from lunch. That will warm you up." Soon enough, Lili was lapping up beef and vegetables nearly as quickly as Fragonard, who was crouched in front of his own bowl nearby.

"Tell me about your day," said Tante Aletheia.

Lili finished her mouthful. Today wasn't an Eintopf day but she would have gladly eaten Frau Brinkmann's stew any day of the week. That would raise a lot of savings for the good of Germany. But Lili suspected that even the meatless stews in Tante Aletheia's house were so richly flavored with herbs, green beans, and wine that there wasn't much of a savings in any case—aside from energy, of course, for it took only one burner to cook on. Now she frowned again.

"Today's meeting was centered on caring for babies. We had to change diapers on a doll. We learned some lullabies." Lili sipped her wine. The bottle was one of the many in the cellar, hearty reds that Tante Aletheia had brought over from France. "In truth, it wasn't very interesting. It's one thing when you have a real baby, like when Paul was little, but when you have to do all those things for a doll--"

Tante Aletheia laughed out loud. "I can just imagine. And how many of you were there?"

"Our group has 23 members and we can take up to seven more." She lifted her glass again. "I hope next week's meeting is more interesting."

"You don't actually have to go to them, do you?"

Lili shook her head. "No, not to Faith and Beauty, that's optional. Of course, since '36 all girls have to enter the BDM when they turn 10. I wish I could have stayed in the BDM. I wish I could have come back earlier from America. Or never gone."

Tante Aletheia's shapely fingers stroked through the white fur on her lap as Fragonard licked his paws and cleaned his whiskers.

"My dear, I always think it is a good idea to look for the best in situations, especially if they cannot be changed. For example, if you had stayed in Berlin, it's unlikely that we would have spent much time with each other, and then I would have been sorry to have missed getting to know such an independent-spirited young lady. A young woman who is not adverse to taking risks."

Lili smiled, not as ruefully as she might have, at the obvious reference to her having disregarded Mama's and Papa's wishes. What a risk she had taken with their love. Sometimes she even shocked herself at how she was able to put aside her guilt at having disobeyed them. To freeze it. No doubt her punishment was coming but, in the meantime, it might indeed be best to take Tante Aletheia's advice to heart and make the best of being here.

"That's true, Tante Aletheia. I'm glad that I have this opportunity to be here with you." She looked at her great-aunt, brilliant in summer greens despite the winter white outside. "You are like nobody I have ever met."

One silver-gray eyebrow rose. "Shall I take that as a compliment or as a veiled critique?" A smile played upon her painted lips.

"Oh, as a compliment." Lili pushed back her chair and went around the table to embrace her.

"Thank you, Lili," she said, squeezing back.

For a few moments they stayed like that.

"Ach." Tante Aletheia pulled back. "I almost forgot. There's also some Rote Grütze for you. The berries are from a jar of course, bottled in Friedberg last summer, but the pudding was made fresh. Frau Brinkmann put them in the pantry, on the ledge near the window."

Lili went over to the cupboard door and opened it, reaching inside. The outside air slipped over her fingers like gloves of ice. Quickly she took out the bowls and shut the door.

"Would you like some too?" she remembered to ask, just in the nick of time, but Tante Aletheia shook her head.

Lili spooned the bright mixture of stewed cherries, strawberries, raspberries, and red currants over the pudding.

"How is Frau Dierck?"

"A small *crise de nerfs*. I thought it best to have Dr. Morsch administer a sedative before she did herself some real harm." Her tone was dry.

For a moment Lili stopped eating. "Was she throwing herself around?"

"No. Not that. But she didn't realize what she was saying."

"Like what?"

"She is increasingly agitated about the situation."

"Frau Dierck is always worried."

"Yes, of course. But she was rambling on in a way that could add to her problems."

Lili savored the fusing flavors. "Oh, I see."

Tante Aletheia was silent.

"You don't want to have happen to her like what happened to Frau Burckhardt in Posenwell," Lili said, outlining the situation with Großmama Maximiliana's doctor's wife. Perhaps in the meantime she had been released. Perhaps not.

Tante Aletheia listened, her jaw tightening.

"To crown matters," she said, "tonight we were joined at dinner by Herr Poppe's fiancée."

"No!" Lili dropped her spoon. "He's actually getting married. Goodness, he worked fast."

"They've set the date for April 20th." Tante Aletheia pursed her lips.

"The Führer's birthday. That's when Hildegard wants to get married."

"No doubt many happy couples will tie the knot on that auspicious day." An expression unlike any Lili had ever seen on her flickered across Tante Aletheia's face and was gone in an instant. It was like disdain, distaste, and dismay all rolled into one. Someone else might have wondered what she was thinking. But Lili felt only a stab of sorrow for her. Poor Tante Aletheia. It must be difficult for a widow to see other people just starting out on their life together. Even if it was with someone as unromantic, pompous, and porcine as Herr Poppe.

Another Annoying Letter

How calm she felt when she learned that the audition had gone well and she was to play in Mannheim. There was a feeling of not quite smugness, but a definite sense of satisfaction, both for the recognition of her expertise and of tipping the balance of guilt. Surely

Mama and Papa would see the importance of such a performance, even if they didn't care about the honor.

There had still been no letter from Papa. Lili had written several times, reiterating her reasons for staying on, asking—no, in truth, pleading—with him to understand how important it was for her to be there. But every time the postman came, there was nothing from Papa. In a way, that made it easier for her to harden her heart.

Mama had written, enclosing a photograph of Paul holding a band that could have been a leash, with whatever was on the other end out of the frame. The tone in her letter had been kind, loving, as close to forgiving as possible under such circumstances. Lili felt Mama's longing both for her and for the past. For her parents in Alt Eichendorf. This made Lili even angrier at Papa. Großmama Maximiliana was over the influenza but her mind was certainly not getting any better.

Would Mama get to see her mother before it was too late?

Today, along with the notification of the concert, there had been another letter from Mama that Lili was going to read over a soothing drink. She went into the kitchen for a cup of peppermint tea. Frau Brinkmann was busy polishing the silverware but noticed the envelope in Lili's hand.

"Your mother must miss you. I miss my Willi." She smiled, and Lili saw that Frau Brinkmann was missing an upper tooth. "Now he's stationed outside Munich."

Lili waited for the water to boil.

"He says they keep them busy from morning till night." Frau Brinkmann scrubbed at a dark stain on the silver teapot.

"It must be hard work being a soldier."

"Protecting the Reich is important. The Führer himself has become Supreme Commander of the *Wehrmacht*."

Lili poured the water over the dried mint. "He is?" Unlike in America, here she no longer read the papers as often as possible. Now that she was home again, it didn't seem necessary.

"The newspapers say he took over from von Blomberg earlier this month." Frau Brinkmann pursed her mouth, a raisin in a sea of pudding.

"He does everything for the Reich," Lili said, picking up her cup. "I'd better go see what my mother has to say."

"Yes, indeed. A mother's heart beats strongest for her children."

Once in her room, Lii settled into the armchair next to the window.

My darling Lili,

February is nearly half gone and with the promise of spring on the horizon, I can at last begin to hope that your adventure will soon be fin— Lili picked up the cup, drank some tea, scalding her tongue, and skipped to the next paragraph.

Life goes on for us here. Paul is very pleased with our new acquisition, a German shepherd puppy. Although Bella (Paul insisted on naming her) will never replace Sascha or Napola in our hearts, she is a happy addition to our family and I am sure that you will find her a delightful companion. I already dream of the four of us taking walks in the woods with Bella at our side.

We have made arrangements to rent a lovely villa along the banks of the Hudson during the summer months. It is some miles from where we once walked near St. Stephen's College, but the vegetation is the same. Glorious. The villa is situated on one of the hills looking down upon the wide reaches of the river and to the greenery beyond. Of course it is too far north to afford a view of those ruins on the small island mid-river. Do you remember how each time as we passed by, we tried to imagine it was an old castle on the banks of the Rhine? Lili bit her lip. How Mama must miss Germany.

We hear of developments in Germany that make us increasingly uneasy. Yet our solace is that we know you are secure under the watchful eye of Tante Aletheia. And of course you have your wonderful music to bring you comfort and inspiration in troubling times. You have said nothing further about your studies at the university there. Lili shifted in her seat. One very good reason for this was that outside university hours she didn't want to have to even think about them, let alone address them. Her studies were not going well. *Papa and I speak about what your possibilities here are. Barnard could be a suitable college at which to continue your education, if that is what you would like. Vassar is simply too far away.* She shook her head. She didn't want to have to think about any of this at all.

Papa is of course as busy as always. He has now taken on a new assistant at the office, a relief because of his occasional bouts of weakness. Although the doctor cannot find anything wrong, there are days when Papa knows he must stay at home to rest. I am sure that your return will be the best energy tonic of all for him.

Folding the letter, Lili rose and went over to the desk to slip it in with the other missives from Mama. Her head ached as if she had been beating it against a wall.

What Makes Life Meaningful?

"Is Herr Malter back?"

"No, Fräulein Lili."

As the sound of Frau Brinkmann's step faded on the stairs, Lili felt disappointment. Benno hadn't been at dinner. She hadn't seen him in what felt like ages. Even if he didn't look as attractive as so many of the other officers, for there was no disguising those boy-like shoulders, he did look good, much better than before. He kept his uniform neatly pressed, too. Tante Aletheia's eyes had narrowed to green slits the first time she'd seen him enter the house dressed in it. But surely she could see the honor of having an SS officer in her home—even if dark uniforms went against her more colorful bent. Lili blew out a loud sigh.

She walked from one side of her room and back, threw herself into an armchair, then crossed the room again. From outside came the sound of people talking and laughing as they crossed Kornmarkt. They sounded as if they were having fun this Friday evening. She wasn't necessarily looking for fun, but today she was filled with discontent. Why, she didn't even want to sit at the harpsichord. Was she sick?

Earlier on in the day, some students had invited her to join them this evening at Zum Seppl' but Lili had declined, hoping to go out for a glass of wine with Benno instead. Now she had neither. She moved to the window. It was too dark to see anything other than lights behind the curtains in the other apartments around Kornmarkt. A dinner party seemed to be going on in the top floor apartment of the building on the left side of the square. Candlelight shimmered through lace curtains, illuminating the outlines of people.

She slipped off her shoes and lay down on the satin bed cover. What an unpleasant mood to be in. Mama's letter had added to her frustrations. Go to Barnard College in New York, hah. How much longer were Papa and Mama going to try to rule her life? And what was that about Papa needing her as a tonic? As if she didn't feel guilty enough already. *Schwamm drüber!* What a good expression that was. Wipe out everything with a sponge. She kicked a stockinged foot into the air. Papa was obviously still too angry, too busy, and too tired to write. Schwamm drüber. For a while she stared at the stucco near the ceiling. She didn't feel like practicing or sleeping. What should she do? What could she do? In fact, what had she been doing these past months?

Filled with a sense of purpose, she listed the ways in which she had been a contributing member of the Reich, and then felt discomfiting frustration well up again:

1. Attended as many BDM meetings as possible.
2. Went on a campout.
3. Was at the rally in Nuremberg!!!
4. Attended some Faith and Beauty meetings.
5. Sang and marched through the streets of Heidelberg countless times.
6. Collected money and warm clothes for the Winter Relief Fund.
7. Ate a lot of Eintopf meals.
8. Performed in a concert.
9. Might perform for the Führer soon???

This last thought was followed by a rush of anticipation. But as soon as it dissipated, the frustration was back. She tossed about on the bed for some time. What else could she do to prove herself worthy of being a citizen of the Reich? What else to prove that she was dedicated and ready to give her life to her Führer and homeland? She turned onto her side and stared at the lampshade. In her ear she could hear blood pulsing like a basso ostinato. Jumbled images formed behind fluttering eyelids. The Thingstätte. Her blood on the snow—Blut und Boden. Herr Poppe's mystery fiancée. The wide-eyed doll at Faith and Beauty. Benno's germ plasms sliding like raindrops. Papa and she with harpsichord and violin in Berlin; a melody, haunting. And then all faded, replaced by faint popping sounds that gained in intensity as an endless vista of trees, resplendent in the leafy renaissance of spring, spread before her, blotting out everything else, and her breathing grew even.

♫ ♪ ♫

The next morning, Lili set out to walk on the opposite bank of the Neckar, following the path on the right that led through the trees. How still the winter woods were. How glorious the German forest. Trumpets sounded in her inner ear, heralding the aria "Ein Schütz bin ich, in des Regenten Sold" from a romantic opera by Lortzing. Its spirit of celebrating love and the wild lifted her steps through the snow. If she needed to, she had the energy to walk across Germany.

She ate lunch, a Gulasch of game and berries, in Die Hirschgasse, a 15th century inn that looked out across the river toward the castle. It was exciting to have the self-confidence to be able to go alone into a restaurant and order whatever she wanted and just sit by the window, eating and thinking about whatever she liked. There was a lot she had to think about today. She'd had a brilliant idea that needed considering, as it would decide her future.

Later, back in her room, she finished her practice, still not quite sure about what course of action to take. As she closed the lid of the harpsichord, she sighed, pushing the air out between her teeth, making a hissing sound. That felt good, so she did it again. For a few moments she sat in front of the harpsichord, hissing and looking toward the window where the afternoon light was waning, the sky above Kornmarkt smoky amber streaked with lilac.

Suddenly she leapt up and strode over to the gramophone, wanting to hear the other arias from Lortzing's *Hans Sachs*. Once the arm was in place on the zinc disc, she slipped off her shoes and tucked her black-stockinged feet under her.

At first there was the familiar crackling sound but this was all at once broken by horns, as if calling from the distance. Next came strings and a penetrating reed. Then silence. When at last the voice began, it went straight to her heart.

The three verses filled the room. At first the singer told her that neither wealth nor high praise make life beautiful and meaningful, that only the heart creates both gladness and torment. Once the singer understood this, he realized that pure happiness came from the precious fatherland. The highest bliss was to be found in his love for the German fatherland. Lili sighed long and loud, the breath coming from the very depths of her being.

The decision had been made for her.

A Bit Like Goethe and his Lily

"Benno!"

She had immediately recognized the elongated figure in the dark uniform making his way further ahead of her on Augustinergasse.

"Are you already free today?"

Lili nodded, delighted by the opportunity to talk with him, setting her pace to match his, her book satchel against her shoulder.

"We were let out early again because of this afternoon's National Socialist Lecturers' Association meeting. A lot of the professors are attending. Last week it was the big student meeting all of us went to. Then there was another march on Tuesday morning. We're missing a lot of classes. Some of the professors have been grumbling." She didn't add that she was glad to miss the classes. "But the *Völkischer Beobachter* said that the very best thoughts are those that are implanted by marching." Or had it said 'while' marching? "It said that in those thoughts resounds the secret German spirit of centuries."

Benno nodded and Lili felt a wave of pity for him. Now that he was no longer a student but a scientist, did he ever get to march anymore? Perhaps as an SS officer he would get to.

"It's very cold today."

For a few moments, Benno did not respond. Lili gnawed at her lip.

Not breaking pace, he turned toward her. "How do you feel about marching over to your favorite Konditorei for some hot chocolate?"

"Oh yes," she said, brightening.

Once there, Benno ordered her a portion of whipped cream.

As soon as the bowl was again pristine porcelain, she sat back.

"There's no doubt that you're a scientist. You observe me so well."

For a moment his incisors flashed. "You know what I think about you." His lips pressed together, as if he were thinking things he couldn't tell her.

She swallowed. She had something to say to him, and at the thought that this serendipitous meeting might be the moment to come out with it, her pulse quickened.

"Benno?"

"Yes?" His uniformed sleeve slid across the table but his hand stopped just short of her own.

Along with the hum of conversations, the red velvet surroundings blurred into the background. What she needed to offer had seemed clearer as she had lain in bed, walked in the woods, sighed to *Hans Sachs*. Yesterday it had seemed as clear to her as the day her blood stained the snow at Alt Eichendorf.

"All those things you say about me," she began, her voice quivering for several beats, as if she were beginning her first aria alone on a stage. "About how I have certain qualities that are, that are..." she trailed off.

Benno helped her along. "You mean the list of your admirable Aryan attributes?"

Lili nodded.

"You mean how much I value your character as well as your characteristics. How Germany values them," he continued, not taking his eyes off hers.

Now her eyelids slid down and she could feel the featherweight of lashes against sensitive skin, her cheeks heating.

"Mmm. That's what I mean." She pulled herself up in her chair.

"You told me about how important it is for the Reich to strengthen the bloodlines of our people, Benno. You told me about the work of the Ahnenerbe, about Sievers and Wüst and your associates at the institute." She was speaking quickly but clearly now, each word distinct and weighted and earnest. She had put much thought into this the past couple days.

"You know I love nature and the history of our land, Benno, you know how much I care about the Führer and his visions for the Reich." She paused. "You know how much I care about our homeland." She gave her lip a quick bite.

"So. I know that you're going on some sort of an expedition with the Ahnenerbe. And I think I know where you're going and what you're going to do." Again she paused. "So, you go off and do it. And when you've done it, when you've set it up, I want to be part of it. I want to go there too and do my part, to strengthen the bloodlines and serve the fatherland. I want to be with you, to help create the colonies to the east."

She did not blink as she looked at him. Benno was certainly not the most handsome of men. He was not even blonde and blue-eyed. But he was an SS officer, intelligent and committed. She would be proud to honor the Führer and help the Reich by having children with Benno. If he agreed to her suggestion, and his superiors found her to be suitable—of which she had no doubt—she would marry him. She would stay in the Reich, even if in its farthest reaches, and never go back to America. And what would Papa have to say about that? That would surely elicit a letter from him.

Benno did not seem able to take his eyes off her. Lili had never noticed how many shades of brown they held. She could feel herself trembling. At last he spoke.

"Dearest Lili, are you saying what I think you are?" His hand reached out, the pale bony fingers covering hers. His skin was moist. "Shh, say nothing. I know you are." His long thumb moved over the flesh between her wrist and knuckles. He had told her not to speak, but now he seemed to be searching for his own words.

As the silence continued, and his touch was upon her, she bit her lip harder. Had she been wrong and misread everything about Benno? The walks, the evenings out, the gingerbread heart? His poetry-like praise of her. Blood flooded her cheeks and her eyes began to burn.

Benno let go of her hand and drew his fingers across her brow. They felt like slivers of ice melting against her flushed skin.

"I am honored beyond words," he said.

She blinked and gave a light sniff. Honored?

"It would be my heartfelt wish to tell you yes, let us go east together one day. Let us join our blood and help build up the Reich so that it lasts even longer than a thousand years."

He leaned back, distancing himself from her. Her throat was dry with unshed tears.

"Yet there are two things I must tell you. First, as you know, I am indeed going on an expedition with the Ahnenerbe. But it isn't to scout out lands for settlement. I'll tell you, Lili, but you must promise not to speak of this to anyone for now."

She nodded and he moved close again, yet still she felt the distance between them.

"It's true, the team will be traveling east, but much farther east than you can imagine. We're going to undertake research that will prove, without a doubt, that our ancient Aryan ancestors once conquered the highest mountains in the world." He whispered the word. "Tibet." His gaze moved over her, lingering at her neck. His voice sounded raw, as if he could barely say the rest. "It's the chance of a lifetime. Still, part of me wants to forego the expedition and just stay here. How can I turn away from what you just offered me?"

She forced steel into her voice. "No, Benno. You must go. Your scientific expertise is needed. You cannot deny yourself—or your country." She felt as if she might choke on her words, as honest as they were. This was turning out all wrong. It even sounded like a melodrama.

He breathed a long sigh, as if of relief.

"You're right of course, Lili. Sensible and right, and beautiful, which is what makes it so very hard."

"How long will you be gone?" Her voice sounded twisted and pale, thin like a distant oboe.

His tongue moved over his lips. "A year or so. Travel to the Himalayas is difficult."

She was silent; her breath felt like tiny jagged blades.

Benno frowned, his lips pressing against each other so tightly that they went white and almost disappeared.

"Ach," he said at last, sounding angry.

"I'll just say it." For a moment he glared at his cup, then picked it up and emptied it in one long gulp. "You, dear Lili, are sweet and lovely and pure. Blue-eyed and blonde, of age-old nobility. You honor the fatherland and the Führer and are ready to give your lifeblood for your country. On top of that, you're talented." He glanced down at his hands, now balled into fists. "In short, Lili Freiin von Rittersburg zu Mertz-Tärnekow, you're a highly desirable Aryan woman. So, when your blood joins with another's, it must be the right match."

He unclenched his fists. "I'm a scientist. I understand germ plasms." He gave a small bitter chuckle, his narrow shoulders rising. "I wish I could say to you to wait for my return. For me. But I can't. I'll never be the right one for you."

Lili stared across at him.

"I beg you," he said, his dark eyes boring into hers. "Don't look at me like that. It's hard enough as it is." The shadow of a smile flitted across his features. "Like Goethe and his lily. I'll take the memory of your beautiful face with me wherever I go; to the top of the world, and beyond."

For a few more moments, Lili continued to sit opposite him. He must have meant the person, not the flower. Goethe's lily was Lili Schönemann, his first love. Is that how Benno saw her, as only his first? Because he wasn't the right one for her? Oh, how painful his words. She could take no more and, springing to her feet, knocking over her empty cup with her coat sleeve, fled past the blur of startled and indignant expressions and out from the Konditorei. Several times as she hurried along Hauptstraße toward the sanctuary at Kornmarkt she turned, thinking Benno might be behind her, about to reach out and touch her arm to stop her. But although the pavement was filled with people, he was not among them.

Respite in Various Forms

The Mannheim performance would feature the *Brandenburg Concertos*; Lili took respite in practice. It was not unusual for her to spend hours at a time at the harpsichord; no one need notice her humiliation and confusion as she worked her way through the various movements. Perhaps she could work them both out in the process.

While her hands were thus engaged, busy and disciplined, her hair was loose and her feelings too raged unkempt. What in heaven had she been thinking of, to offer herself like that to Benno? Mama would have been horrified—mortified—to hear Lili say that she would go east to make babies with him. Benno himself had declined the joining of their blood. Lili shook her head as her fingers swept across the keys. He'd been rather a gentleman in response to her pathetic babbling. It was shameful. She stopped playing and pressed her hands onto her thighs as a wave of nausea passed through her. She had been rejected. But it was in such a contrary way. Apparently she was too good for him. She made a sound, halfway between a snort and a laugh. Benno had made it seem that she was from a superior pool of germ plasms. Had he found a kind way of pushing her away, or was it truly that he found himself unworthy? And why—because of his dark hair and eyes? Why, the Führer himself had dark eyes and hair. She touched the keys, lightly, and began to play again, gaining intensity. How committed Benno was to upholding scientific principles, even sacrificing his own desires. Like the Führer, he was committed to ensuring the best future for the German Volk. Benno deserved her respect and good will, and her good wishes. She would work out her feelings. And, in truth, deep down, there was relief. His thumbs looked so much like test tubes. She took a long breath of resolution and immersed herself in Bach.

♫ ♪ ♫

An auburn squirrel scampered across the snow, leaving barely a trace of its passing. From where she sat in the depths of an old armchair, chin resting on her hand, Lili watched it disappear into an apparition of white. Ever since her arrival at the Friedberg house, she had been feasting her eyes on the sylvan scene outside the windows. If it was this magnificent now, when the birches, elms, and oaks sparkled under the webworks of iridescent icicles lodged in their bare branches, when the soaring firs that surrounded the property were garbed in frosted ermine, what would it be like in early summer when the world exploded into new life?

Only yesterday Tante Aletheia had decided, seemingly on the spur of the moment, to make a trip to her domain.

"A few days of Alsatian forest air will do you good before the concert," she said. "After all, by now you could play the *Brandenburg Concertos* in your sleep. You probably do."

So here they were, on the other side of the Rhine. Not so long ago this province had been German, for over the centuries Alsace had found itself pulled back and forth between Germany and France, both lands vying for this fertile and creative region in a tug-a-war that had surely left its people feeling torn.

On the journey in the hired automobile, they had passed through the town of Molsheim and entered the Vallée de la Bruche. The Bruche was nothing like the Neckar. Tante Aletheia described it as "narrow, lazy, and thoroughly happy", a slight river that eased through the valley. In spring, a feeder stream cascaded down from a source deep in the hills, crossing the property with decorum before moving on to join the Bruche in Friedberg itself. For now, the flow of this tiny streamlet that divided the snow-covered property was downright sluggish, as if it might still decide to freeze over.

"There you are." As in Heidelberg, the stone floors of the salon were covered with carpets and Tante Aletheia's steps were silent. His tail in the air, Fragonard trotted behind her. "I've just asked Marie for coffee."

If Frau Brinkmann was a solid example of an efficient town housekeeper, Marie would have won in the category of country maid. Every other sentence was interrupted by a giggling that would have been annoying it if hadn't been so genuine. The oldest daughter of a farming family of twelve further up the valley toward Schirmeck, Marie had been looking after the house these past two years.

"Look." Tante Aletheia pointed toward a window. "Deer have come for salt."

Two does, both stepping slowly as if carrying extra weight, moved toward a boulder at the far end of the large frozen pond. How restful the natural beauty of these forest creatures. Papa and she had spent hours watching them in Alt Eichendorf. A Goethe quote came to mind, and she could hear Papa's voice. "In nature we never see anything isolated, but everything in connection with something else…"

"In late summer and autumn they come to eat the apples in the orchard," Tante Aletheia said. "In winter we put out hay. The salt is out year-round."

On the journey from Heidelberg, she had told Lili about how her husband Wilhelm would spend hours painting his canvases in the cottage studio on the other side of the stream, near the salt lick. About how sometimes on late summer evenings, she had walked down the gravel path to cross one of the two stone bridges, carrying a basket filled with delicacies made to tempt. Then Wilhelm had laid down his brushes, and they spread a blanket on the grass, eating, drinking, and watching the fireflies come out until either he went back to the cottage, painting by gaslight, or they packed up and returned to the house where the moon shone in upon their bedroom.

It sounded very romantic.

Now the deer looked up, then froze into the landscape before suddenly turning, becoming a blur of black hoof and tawny legs that disappeared into the snowy curtain of bushes and trees behind the pond.

Over coffee, which Marie placed on the table while peering with unabashed interest at Lili's heirloom pearls, Tante Aletheia and Lili spoke of oaks and stags and how the ancient people were guided by the stars. She told Tante Aletheia how Benno too dealt with an entire universe, only that it was so small that it could fit on a microscope slide.

At this, Tante Aletheia took Lili upstairs to a room that was empty but for an enormous dark canvas scattered with pale dots.

"This is Wilhelm's last work," she said. "He believed that everything in the universe is atoms, and that in death we are atoms still. Always moving, rearranging. Two days after finishing this painting, he died. When I look at it, I can still feel him. Just as I do when I look at the trees, the sky, the water." Tante Aletheia's eyes glistened green as she smiled at Lili.

They went back downstairs to their coffee and an apple tarte that Marie had just baked. Lili thought of telling Tante Aletheia about how she had offered herself to Benno, but now it no longer seemed so tragic, only bittersweet. She could choose to view it as an inspirational incident in her life. She took a deep breath of satisfaction and then chewed on the pastry.

The conversation was relaxed, cosy, and Lili was content that she had agreed for these days to leave behind Heidelberg. Tomorrow they would walk into the surrounding woods, up to the Grotte du Loup where wolves once sheltered but where, according to Tante Aletheia, there was now only silence. She would show Lili where druids must have spoken to the trees and where in summer a hidden meadow was filled with wildflowers. Tomorrow, Tante Aletheia told her, she could slide across its gentle slope on a wooden sled, skimming the soft surface in a ride that would leave a gentle wake upon the snow.

"I hope you take comfort here, Lili," Tante Aletheia said.

Lili looked out at the forest landscape that, save for the seasons, had likely changed but little in the preceding centuries, whether part of France or Germany.

"I do, dear Tante Aletheia. Thank you. Friedberg is a special place."

Tante Aletheia looked pleased. "It has long been my haven. Whatever is happening in the outside world—it stops here at the gate, lopsided as it is." She closed her eyes then, momentarily resembling Fragonard. "I am glad that you can already feel the peace here."

A Fortuitous Meeting

And then, after the requisite number of rehearsals, the concert at the Rosengarten in Mannheim was upon her. She had invited everyone at the house; only yesterday Benno said he would not miss this concert, not for the world. But soon he would be leaving her world, and each of them would become nothing but memories for the other.

While Tante Aletheia and the others were to make their own way, Lili and the orchestra members from Heidelberg travelled together by special bus.

As at the last concert, all the musicians were older than Lili and most were men. But in the weeks leading up to the performance, even though she had exchanged few words, she had come to feel at ease amongst them. After all, she was an accomplished musician and had every right to be where she was, even if not a permanent member of the orchestra.

They passed the time before the performance in a large room backstage. Several of the men smoked. The middle-aged cellist, one of the three other women musicians, walked over to Lili. Her hair was drawn back into a tight bun, her speech clipped.

"I have been a member of the *Reichsmusikkammer* from Day One," she said without preamble.

Lili nodded. "I just recently." Dr. Hempel had helped her join the State Chamber of Music, without which she wouldn't have been permitted to perform. Only Aryans were issued the identity card. Hers was in her handbag. She was rather pleased with the photo which made her eyebrows look more arched than usual.

"The last harpsichordist was a blue-eyed sneak who didn't seem to understand that true Germans don't want Jews playing our music, just like we don't want to play music composed by Jews. It was discovered that his card was forged." Her tone was dry. "There are still a few conductors who don't seem to care who plays what, but fortunately our new maestro is a man with good morals." She fixed Lili with a severe look.

"You should be honored to perform under his baton."

This conductor was even more demanding than Maestro Ohlig had been.

"As a guest performer I do feel quite fortunate," Lili said.

The woman nodded. "We shall all play Bach brilliantly tonight. German music for German musicians. For a German audience."

"Do you know what dignitaries will be in the audience?" Perhaps the woman had heard something. Perhaps the Führer would be there.

"*Jawohl*," she said with emphasis. "There will be prominent Mannheimer city dignitaries with their wives, and of course *Gauleiter* Wagner who has himself requested the performance."

Lili bit into her lip; obviously the Führer would not be among them. He would have been at the head of the list.

"Will there be any SS officers?"

The woman allowed herself a chuckle.

"There are always SS officers."

"I saw a chamber music performance by an SS orchestra in Heidelberg last year," Lili said.

"Yes. Those are a special group, making time from their other duties, performing in various parts of the Reich. The *Leibstandarte's* Music Corps has several dance bands of course, but the group you must be referring to plays only Baroque."

Lili was about to ask if she knew when the group would return to the region, but an attendant entered, telling them it was time.

Opening its doors in the same year as the Stadthalle in Heidelberg, the Nibelungensaal of the Rosengarten had once been Germany's largest concert hall. Today it was still an imposing space. Even though the hall was not completely filled, the audience was larger than the one in Heidelberg had been. Lili had no idea where Tante Aletheia, Benno, and the others might be sitting. For a moment she allowed herself to imagine that Papa and Mama too were there. It made her stand straighter. But by the time she reached her seat, the daydream was over. Only people who cared about Bach *and* the Third Reich were here.

Then it began, fingers flying as the music flowed. It was as if she and the others had been born knowing every nuance of the work. The countless hours of practice had disappeared, leaving only the seemingly effortless fluidity.

Afterwards, she learned that there was to be a reception, courtesy of the Gauleiter of Baden, Robert Wagner. It sounded exciting, very grown-up and sophisticated. Lili went out to find Tante Aletheia. Her passage through the departing audience was slowed by people addressing her, commenting on the performance and praising her playing. It was disconcerting. How was she to react to strangers suddenly behaving as if they knew her? After the first few, to whom she stammered some words about Bach and rehearsals, she simply smiled, nodded, and thanked them before moving on. Her gaze roamed over the crowd and at last she caught sight of Tante Aletheia's jacket of green velvet. She and Dr. Hempel were nearing the cloakroom.

"Lili, darling, it was wonderful," Tante Aletheia murmured, embracing her as Dr. Hempel beamed. "Benno apologizes that he has had to rush away, but he has work that must be finished by morning. He told me to tell you that he is positive that your name will soon be known throughout the Reich."

"Indeed," Dr. Hempel said, "most impressive." He winked. "That was the Li."

Lili smiled, understanding his reference to Li Stadelmann. Yet Dr. Hempel continued. "She will be eclipsed by you. I know it here," he asserted, laying his hand on his chest.

Lili looked down, could feel the blood rushing to her head. She had indeed played very well.

"Will you both come to the reception with me?"

Tante Aletheia smiled. "Thank you, but after such intensity of mind and heart, I am ready to retire."

"Have a glass of Sekt and you'll feel bubbly again," Lili coaxed.

"I doubt that," said Tante Aletheia.

Lili turned to Dr. Hempel but he took her hand, bowing, so that she could see a bald spot beneath the carefully combed-over white.

"*Merci, mademoiselle*," he said, his eyes twinkling. "I will accompany Madame. But I too thank you for the invitation. Let us raise our glasses together another day."

For a moment, Lili was set to pout. Then she smiled.

"All right. Thank you for being here." She paused. "And for much more as well," she called back as she took off.

The reception was being held in one of the many function rooms of the Rosengarten. As she neared the salon, she could hear the humming of conversation punctuated by high-pitched laughter. The clinking of glasses. She slowed her step. Perhaps she should go home with Tante Aletheia now, slip off her shoes and nestle into an armchair. Did she really want to go into that room? It was filled with noisy adults. Were they talking only about the *Brandenburg Concertos*? But she was an adult now too. She bit her lip, looked over at the looming entrance. The double doors burst open and a waiter hurried out with an empty silver tray. Before it shut, Lili saw tendrils of smoke rising, people clustered about in groups. On the far wall, staring at her from inside a golden frame, was a portrait of the Führer. She pushed open the door.

A waiter offered her a glass of Sekt and she took it, then stood to the side, waiting to be addressed as she had been earlier. This time she was going to be witty and charming with her responses to the compliments. She was Lili von Rittersburg zu Mertz-Tärnekow, German patriot and harpsichordist.

Yet nobody seemed to recognize her. Taking some tentative sips of the sparkling wine, she tried to look at ease while studying the room, waiting. It seemed that everyone here knew everyone else. Laughter was flowing as freely as the wine. Many of the women had lips as scarlet as the drapes that hung in great bunches from the high ceiling, and some of the dresses looked as if they had come straight from a salon in Berlin or even Paris, not Mannheim. But it was the women's expressions, and voices, that intrigued Lili. Shrill yet drawling, supercilious or dripping with exaggeration—her ear was piqued. They sounded different from the voices in the Heidelberger streets, different from what she remembered of the well-modulated tones of the women guests at the dinner parties at home in Berlin. The men, outfitted in *Smokings* or uniforms, spoke in tones of bass and tenor, but odd grating laughter or loud interjections pierced the harmony of even these lower registers. Lili drank her wine, beginning to feel that she was both invisible and rooted to the spot.

On the far side of the salon she could see some of the musicians grouped together, drinking and stuffing food into their mouths. Now that the music had stopped, nobody else was paying them any attention. Pushing herself forward, Lili began to head toward them. There was no one else she recognized. It wasn't that she really wanted to chat with the cellist with the tight bun, but at least she would be moving through the crowd with purpose. She passed next to a group of four or five women, inhaling their cloyingly sweet perfumes on the way. No L'Heure Bleue here. A couple shot her sideways glances but otherwise ignored her. It was the same when she moved by a group of men. They looked at her—slightly warmer than the women had—but said nothing. She was beginning to think that there was something wrong with her, and raised a hand to her hair to smooth it. A woman in a nearby cluster of people called out to her.

"Nice necklace." She waved her ivory cigarette holder in the direction of the black pearls.

Lili paused, glancing at the woman's own adornment which appeared to be a cascading collar of roses in aqua silk. She would have liked to thank her, but the woman had already turned back and was chatting with a man in a dark uniform, stroking his sleeve.

An unpleasant feeling began to rise and Lili took a gulp of wine to keep it down as she continued making her way through the crowd. A waiter stopped her to offer a change of glasses, and she was glad to take the colder one.

A persistent clinking of metal against glass grew louder as the cacophony in the room began to die down. Lili stayed in place but turned toward where Gauleiter Wagner was planted in the middle of the salon. Lili studied his face as he launched into a speech about the greatness of German composers and the land that nurtured them. Although the two men didn't really look alike, there was something about him that reminded her of Papa. She couldn't pinpoint what it was. The intensity of expression? Vertical troughs were etched between brushstroke brows although he seemed composed and at ease. A joke about musicians elicited chuckles throughout the salon. There was something compelling about him. He burned with a quiet energy, as if nothing would keep him from doing what had to be done. That was no doubt why he had been chosen to be Gauleiter of Baden. Men like Gauleiter Wagner were the backbone of Germany. His eyes were shining as he spoke of the Führer. No, Lili decided right then. Papa and Gauleiter Wagner weren't at all alike.

As soon as the speech ended, the waiters were back with more Sekt. The buzzing and guffaws began anew. Lili knew she had to move. Perhaps she should leave now, even before reaching the musicians. After all, why would they be glad to see her or care to include her in their conversations? She had performed with them; other than that, what did they have in common? She really didn't care to talk anyway. Yes, perhaps it was best to leave now. She knew no one and no one cared to know her. She was just a woman alone here, without family or social standing. She swallowed the rest of her Sekt in one gulp.

"Mademoiselle?"

Was Dr. Hempel here after all and playing a trick on her? But his voice was not as smooth nor as seductive as this one, and this accent was perfect. She turned.

He was smiling down at her. His gaze was as intense as she remembered, but she had forgotten the dark brows, the angled planes of his jaw. This time he was in uniform, the cloth black and broad against his shoulders. Just as it had the first time she'd seen him, something deep inside her quivered.

"Mademoiselle," he repeated. "You see, I remember that you speak French and that you play the harpsichord...passably well." His cobalt eyes held glints of light.

She blinked. All her anxieties evaporated.

"I suppose that, coming from you, 'passably well' will do me passably well," she said in as gruff a tone as possible. Then she had to laugh, and he did too, all the while looking down at her.

And she couldn't take her gaze away. He was even more compelling than in her memory.

"How did you enjoy performing for this lot?"

"I love the *Brandenburg Concertos*," she said.

"This wasn't the first time you were on the stage, was it?" He gave a sly smile. His teeth were almost perfectly aligned.

"No, that was in December, at the Stadthalle in Heidelberg." This brought back the memory of seeing him for the first time. Again something fluttered deep inside her.

"So," he said, satisfaction in his voice. "Since last we met you have indeed stepped out of your chamber and become a performer." In one fluid motion he took the empty glass from her hand and stopped a passing waiter to whisk two more off the tray. "By the way, your playing is brilliant, but you know that already," he said, lifting his glass to her.

She looked down at the carpet. Her heart was suddenly hammering. "Thank you," she whispered, raising her chin.

FATHERLAND

He said nothing, just searched her face, and it seemed to Lili that a question lingered in his eyes. Yet she did not know what he was asking. All at once she wanted to reach out and touch him, feel that he was really there. All she had to do was put out her hand and trace her fingers over the fabric of his sleeve to sense him underneath. If she had been like the woman with the silk rose neckline, she could have. She would have. But she was Lili, and she only looked.

"There you are, von Witzleben," a voice boomed out just behind her. "Why is it that you, a lowly officer of the SS, are the one who's deep in conversation with the most beautiful and talented woman in this room?" The man guffawed. "Must be the perks of knowing music!"

Lili turned toward the broad-shouldered middle-aged man whose paunch seemed to want to burst out of his cummerbund. His grin was just as wide. Standing before Lili, he clicked his heels and bowed over her hand.

"Fritz von Bieberstein, *enchanté*."

At this, she had to giggle.

"Aha!" he cried when the viola da gamba player introduced her. "I suspected as much, Freiin. Prussian nobility has its finest flowering in the female form." He paused, peering at her. "Why, I do believe I recall knowing a relative surely of yours, in the DHK, hmm, years ago now... yes, Erwin von Rittersburg zu Mertz-Tärnekow."

Lili stopped breathing.

Fritz von Bieberstein pushed on. "Perhaps he's your uncle? Too old to be your brother, I'd say!"

Slowly, as if exhaling, she released the words.

"He's my father."

"Your father." He cocked his head, squeezed his chin between thumb and fist. "I haven't seen him in, well, years. He must have retired early to the family estate. Or wait--"

Lili took a gulp of Sekt but it left her mouth dry. Here it was. Now the man must have remembered how Papa had abandoned the

DHK, Berlin, the Führer, the fatherland. Well, she wasn't her father. She pulled her spine straighter. Took a breath.

"Parents," said Leo Arnim von Witzleben and laughed out loud. "And Prussian parents are the toughest of them all, don't we know it. What about Bodo? I hear he's taken after you and joined Göring's *Luftwaffe*. Heard he's been flying a Junker 87."

Fritz von Bieberstein beamed. "Yes, indeed, my boy's sitting in the front of a Stuka that got to see some action in Spain."

"Franco's counting on the German gunners," said Leo Arnim von Witzleben, glancing at Lili, who was clutching the stem of her glass.

And then other guests joined the small group. The performance became a topic of conversation as several men flirted with her and even a couple of the women who had earlier looked through her now smiled and were charming, and Lili wondered if she had imagined it all. Her heart was still thumping from the exchange with Fritz von Bieberstein. Still, she understood that the others were talking to her now only because she was no longer standing by herself there in the salon. Only he, Leo Arnim von Witzleben, had spoken to her when she was alone.

Now he was listening to an older man commend Himmler as being clear-headed and rational, but that, nevertheless, the *Reichsführer's* eccentric interpretations of ancient history could be questioned. The viola da gamba player's expression showed only engaged interest. Lili wondered if he was taking silent offence at this possible critique of the SS leader.

"There's so much that our scientists and an-thro-po-lo-gists are just now discovering about our German roots," she found herself saying, slurring, even as her pulse raced within her throat. "From what I have been told—by someone in the know—we can look forward to being most impressed at how deep and far they go." She chuckled at the inadvertent rhyming, then quickly raised her glass and drank from it.

The others were looking at her with interest and one portly man remarked that Lili was herself an impressive young lady, a fine example of German womanhood. He sounded like Benno. She frowned, annoyed at having brought the focus to herself, and bit her lip.

And then, for the first time, she felt his hand on her sleeve, a current passing through the fabric to her skin.

"Excuse us, *meine Herrschaften,*" he said to the group. "The Freiin and I have some matters of music to discuss."

Gently, oh so gently, Lili could feel him guiding her through the circle, and she did not resist, for her knees were weak. They moved together toward the left side of the salon. In passing, he murmured something to a waiter.

"Are you well?" were his first words as they stood near the wall covered with striped satin. His eyebrows arched like the wings of a hunting hawk.

Lili parted her lips to reply, but what came out was a hiccup. Her eyes flew wide open, yet she was afraid to look at him. She glanced down at his boots, wondering if her pathetic being was reflected in the shiny black leather.

"Look at me," he said, softly.

Slowly she raised her eyes to meet his.

"It's all right," he said. "I can imagine what has happened. You haven't eaten all day, you were a bundle of nerves before the concert, and when you came into this circus here, you drank too much Sekt, too fast. This will pass. Take a deep breath." His voice was calm, soothing, and Lili could only look up into his dark blue eyes and breathe. In, out, in, out, trusting, all the while knowing his look intent upon her. She hiccuped again. The scent he gave off was like a light rain in a forest meadow. The waiter returned, bearing a glass of water. Lili drank.

"Now," he said, when her breath was even, "perhaps we should be formal and exchange names." He smiled at her surprise. "When last we met, we didn't take the opportunity. So. Freiherr Leopold Arnim von Witzleben." He bowed deeply, in the style she knew from her childhood. "But call me Leo. And you are--"

She did not curtsy but held up her chin, which was quivering just a bit, and looked him in the eye.

"Freiin Lili von Rittersburg zu Mertz-Tärnekow. You may call me Lili."

"So, Lili. I recall that in Heidelberg you laid claim to being an excellent musician." He paused. "It does seem that you're an honest woman."

A tiny thrill shot through her. He saw her as a woman, not a girl. And of course she was an excellent musician.

"Yes, I am." She swallowed. "And I'm eighteen now."

He cocked an eyebrow. "Time passes quickly. You're quite ancient now."

She frowned up at him.

He threw back his head and laughed.

"So tell me, Lili, woman of mystery. Who are you?"

Who was she? No one had ever asked her such a question. She had no idea how she was supposed to answer. He already knew her name and thus her background. But the latter he'd already known the first time they'd met. They were both from Prussian Junker families. She hesitated, searching his eyes.

He seemed to be studying her, looking for something. Did he want to know more about Papa? She bit her lip.

"Perhaps," he said into the silence, "we can talk another time. It's been a long evening. But tell me, Lili, do you live in Mannheim or Heidelberg?"

"In Heidelberg, of course."

"Hmm. Do you have transportation there tonight?"

She nodded. The musicians' hired omnibus would be leaving at 23.45. She looked at her watch.

"Oh!" She started. "I have to go right now or I'll miss the bus."

He accompanied her outside to where the vehicle was already waiting, its rumbling engine battering the chill night air. She stepped up to it.

"Will you always disappear so abruptly?" he asked, his voice so low it could have been a growl.

His question laid bare the fact that she didn't know when or where she would see him again.

When the door closed and the omnibus pulled away, she could feel the distance between them growing, and she looked back but it was too dark to see if Leo was still there.

Bittersweet

What a dreary afternoon it was, the wind sneaking its way into the cracks of the window frame with a high-pitched whistle, relentless. Lili wadded a handkerchief tight into one corner of a window to muffle the whining, and peered through the rain-streaked glass. The clouds above Kornmarkt seemed engaged in a battle of grays even darker than the water-soaked cobblestones of the square. She switched on another light.

Earlier in the day she had spent time at the harpsichord: Bach, Telemann, Händel. Marais too. Of course the accompaniment was missing from that piece, although in this case it was the harpsichord that was the accompaniment to the viola da gamba. As she played, she permitted herself to relive the time with Leo. His hands. His mouth. His voice. His shoulders. His eyes. Where was he? When would their paths cross again?

The notes wove themselves around a mystical undertone, bubbling in her blood and belly like sparkling wine, luring her into a simmering sense of expectancy. It was physically disturbing, yet strangely soothing. Playing Marais was a link to him, thrilling her with the unknown. For some time she imagined scenarios of when they might—would—next meet. She a famous harpsichordist, and he bringing her a bouquet of roses backstage. No, not backstage—right on stage. Or she and he would be performing together for the Führer and they would both receive a standing ovation. Or they would be sitting together, themselves watching a performance of an orchestra, and their fingers would accidentally meet and then—and then? Her heart beat so fast that she lost the rhythm and stopped playing. No, they must meet sooner... She rose, shutting the lid with a clunk. For some time she watched the cloudswept sky, barely hearing the rain slamming against the windowpanes until the wind whistling through the cracks recalled her. The handkerchief was useless.

She chose a gramophone record. The voice blotted out the storm as she listened to "Nicht Reichtum Macht das Leben Schön", the aria from *Hans Sachs* that had so moved her last time. This time it left her feeling chastised, embarrassed at how she had been ready to lap up the praise at the concert. Truly, she must put more effort into playing for the Reich, and not her own personal *Reichtum* or wealth. She winced at the silly joke.

Then she was listening to the words of "Einst Spielt ich mit Zepter, Krone und Stern" from *Zar und Zimmerman*. All at once hot tears welled up, burning her nose, so that she shoved the back of her hands against her eyes, pressing them to stem the threatening flow. She would not allow herself to fall prey to sentimentality. Childhood play, sitting on a father's knee, being a child—no, let someone else weep over that. She had already gone past that. Was she supposed to feel sentimental over a father who did not even bother to write to his child? Yes, she knew that Papa was disappointed by her disobedience. Yet surely enough time had passed since then. Why did he refuse to answer her letters? Did he no longer love her? Every time she let herself think about it the answer could only be the same: it was because of her continuing faith in the Führer.

It was Papa who had encouraged her love for Germany and its history, just as he himself had loved them. Why had he changed so very much? Oh, these thoughts had become tedious, a painful and bad refrain.

The Consequences of Twelve Toes

The rain had washed out the air so that for now the sky was azure, the clouds bleached. After a morning of unsatisfying classes, one too simple and the other too difficult to follow, Lili was roaming Hauptstraße. A few days ago she had spilled a glass of oxblood red wine on the kitchen tablecloth and, despite a treatment of salt, the stain had not come out. A replacement was in order. Yet none of the three household shops she'd been in had an acceptable quality of cloth. There seemed to be only some cheap and artificial-looking material that wouldn't do.

Passing by a Konditorei, Lili peered in at the pastries. Customers must have had a great appetite today, for several of the usual platters of cakes and tarts in the display window were already gone, or, perhaps, hadn't been put out at all. As she glanced back and forth between a lonely *Berliner* and a Mandelhörnchen, Lili noticed the reflection of a passerby and turned.

"Hildegard!"

Hildegard stopped; the look on her face was shocking.

"Are you sick? You haven't been in class for some time," Lili said.

"Sick?" Hildegard grimaced. "I am most certainly not sick. Just livid."

"Let's go inside for coffee and cake," Lili suggested.

While they waited for their orders, Lili talked about the morning. At eleven o'clock there had been a student meeting, so that all classes for that period had fallen away. That meant Professor Doktor Hetzenrath's too.

"No great loss," Hildegard shrugged.

Lili grinned. "I know you think he's boring, but he sticks to the subject matter more than any other professor." She didn't add that this made it the most difficult class of all for her.

"That's what I mean."

The waitress arrived with the coffee and two bare pieces of *Apfelkuchen.*

The coffee was hot, but it didn't taste as good as that at Tante Aletheia's.

After a few bites of the apple cake, Lili looked across at Hildegard. "Are you better now?"

Hildegard put down her fork. "Unfortunately not. I'm angry and upset. Last week Gustav and I went to register for a marriage loan—he wants to open his own practice and isn't keen on taking a loan from either of our families. We thought that we might as well take advantage of the newlywed program. Of course I won't be working, so we'd have to pay it back at only 1%."

"And every baby will reduce the loan by 25%, right?" Lili grinned, remembering her facts from Faith and Beauty.

For a few moments, Hildegard was silent.

"Of course we had to fill out several forms," she continued. "That's normal. Then, yesterday, I got a letter from the State Health Office." She pressed her lips together; they were quivering.

"They said that I have to have an operation."

Lili put down her cup. "Why? You said that you're not sick."

Hildegard shook her head. "Of course I'm not. I'm perfectly healthy—certainly healthier than that horrid clerk with the crotchety cough. I'm healthy as an ox. But my school health records state that I have six toes on each foot." She shrugged. "Everybody on my father's side of the family does. We laugh about it. But, according to the authorities, because of that, I have to have the operation."

Lili frowned. "Well, it's certainly not pleasant, and I don't see what the point is, but it shouldn't be too bad to have the extra toes removed. After all, you don't need them." She chewed on her lip.

Hildegard's eyebrows shot up, and for one moment there was mirth on her face.

"I wish it were only that," she said, her eyes glistening. "It's not my toes they want to remove, Lili. It's my insides."

"What do you mean, your insides?"

"They say I shouldn't have babies. But then they say that if I can't have babies, I'm not permitted to get married!" She made a fist and hit the table. "It goes against everything!"

Lili glanced around to see if any of the mainly elderly women in hats had noticed Hildegard's outburst. So far no one was looking at their table.

"I'm so confused, Lili. And angry. So I have twelve toes instead of ten. Does that make me any less of a person? Does that make me less committed to the Führer and the Reich?" Her voice was rising and Lili cast further glances at the tables around them.

Perhaps noticing Lili's expression, Hildegard lowered her voice. "I'm supposed to have the operation next month." She folded her arms. "I simply won't be there. I'll show them."

"What does Gustav say about it?"

Hildegard's expression softened. "He's as upset as I am. He doesn't care about my feet. We've already booked the hall for the wedding. Now we might have to postpone it."

"But what will happen if you don't show up for the operation?"

"There are still some weeks. A lot can happen in that time." Hildegard jabbed her fork at the cake still on her plate. "I'm not some mentally defective idiot who shouldn't have been born, let alone have children. I'm a university student from a good family. If my extra toes are such a blight on the Reich, I'll cut them off myself. I don't care. But that operation—absolutely not."

They parted outside, turning in opposite directions. Despite being somewhat dazed by what she'd heard, Lili considered Hildegard's situation. It didn't quite make sense. Why would the State Health Officer order her to be sterilized just because of the extra toes? What an extreme measure! It wasn't as if Hildegard were a drunken violent maniac like Herr Dierck. There had to be something more involved to the story. Perhaps the medical records had shown something that Hildegard herself was unaware of, or there was something she wasn't admitting to Lili or even to herself. Yes, that had to be it. Besides, Hildegard wasn't as smart as she had at first seemed to be. She was rarely interested in actually learning something in her classes. Perhaps she had got into university on the strength of her uncle's connections. But then, wouldn't Hildegard's uncle help her to avoid the operation? On which side of the family was her uncle? Perhaps he too had six toes on each foot. But if he did, would he still be allowed to have the position he had?

Lili bit her lip again. Perhaps she should ask Benno. He could probably shed some light on the situation. It might have something to do with germ plasms. So tiny, but so important.

To Life

Frau Dierck had had an intense spell. Tante Aletheia and Lili stood by as Dr. Morsch put away the empty syringe.

"I was afraid she might start up again in the evening," Tante Aletheia said.

Nodding, Dr. Morsch bent over the huddled figure whose sobs had grown faint. He drew the quilt over her shoulders. "The injection will help her sleep through the night without further incident."

"I know," said Tante Aletheia, her voice low. "Your help is always invaluable."

Frau Dierck was snoring lightly as they left the room.

"Do you have time for a glass of wine?" Tante Aletheia asked.

Dr. Morsch hesitated. "I should get home to my daughter." He looked at his watch. "There's still a while before dinner. A glass in your company would be much appreciated."

Tante Aletheia turned to Lili. "Would you be a dear and bring us three?"

The other two were already seated in the salon and laughing about something as Lili came in with the glasses. They looked relaxed, different from the drawn faces of just a few minutes earlier.

"Ah, good," said Tante Aletheia. "Wine is a solace for the soul and music for the mind."

"Is that from Goethe?" asked Lili.

"Why, I would imagine it is one of your great-aunt's own adages," said Dr. Morsch, winking at Lili.

"Indeed," admitted Tante Aletheia. "Goethe would say it with much greater finesse, and less alliteration. And now, will you be so kind as to pour us some solace?"

"With pleasure," Dr. Morsch said, filling the glasses half way. They raised them in a toast.

"*Santé*," he said with Gallic flair.

"*L'chaim*," said Tante Aletheia. She glanced over at Lili. "To life."

Lili had heard this expression in New York. It was what Jews said. How strange that Tante Aletheia would use it, but then, as Papa had said, she was eccentric. Lili shrugged and drank.

♫ ♪ ♫

The door slipped from her hand and she jerked as the wind slammed it shut. For some moments, the reverberation silenced everything else. As she hung up her coat, she noticed Frau Brinkmann dusting in the hallway off the kitchen. They exchanged some observations on the weather but, these days, Frau Brinkmann had only one thing on her mind.

"My Willi was with them when they rolled into Vienna!" she said for possibly the tenth time. "My own flesh and blood, part of history making." She clicked her tongue. "Who would have thought it? There he was, marching through the streets of Vienna, liberating the Viennese,

shouting 'Sieg Heil!' Ach, Fräulein Lili, I can see it my little mind's eye."
She beamed at Lili over the dust cloth.

"Everyone's talking about it," Lili agreed. "One of the students was there, and told us about it today at the Mensa. He said that when our troops arrived, people were lined up along the roadsides, cheering. He could have seen your Willi pass right in front of him!"

Frau Brinkmann's eyes grew large and she nodded her head slowly, as if imagining the scene. "Yes, my Willi was with them."

Lili went upstairs. It was exciting to think that the Führer had brought over four million people back into the German fold. But a student had pointed out that this created a new problem. Apparently, all the Jews that had left Germany over the past five years were back. Of course they weren't the exact same people but, because of the *Anschluß*, the numbers were up again. Now that Austria was a part of the Reich, everyone over there seemed peeved with all those Austrian Jews. According to the talk in the Mensa, the Viennese had begun to be creative in making life unpleasant for them, hoping to encourage them to leave, just as so many German Jews had. This reminded Lili of the day in the Hamburger Bahnhof and that tense-looking group she had seen at the station. Yes, they must definitely have been Jews departing Germany. And now, with the Anschluß, that happy melding of German Volk, there would be so many more Jews who needed to leave.

A Germ Plasm Named Lili and Frau Brinkmann's Discovery

Spring was nesting in. The sky seemed wider, the light softer. The air smelled different too. Perhaps it was this gentling change in season that had caused Benno to invite Lili out for dinner, like old times. Now, seated across from him, she smiled into her wine glass. She had been pleased by the invitation. It seemed to underline the gratifying fact that they were both adults who could share a meal as friends, without thought of kisses or shared futures. She doubted that he had had second thoughts about going against bloodlines and germ plasms. This reminded her that she wanted to ask him about Hildegard, whom she hadn't seen since their coffee and cake.

Benno had selected one of her favorite places, the Goldener Hecht on the square near Alte Brücke. The inn liked to point out that Goethe had visited Heidelberg eight times and had almost stayed at the Goldener Hecht. *Heidelberg through the Ages* stated that the great man had always stayed with friends when visiting. It would have been interesting to discover why he had *almost* stayed at the Goldener Hecht. Was it because he had had an argument that was then resolved, or was it something else—a romantic tryst that had backfired? Something with his great love Lili S. or Marianne W. of the gingko biloba tree? It was unlikely that she would ever know, but it no longer mattered. She sighed with contentment. She was on her second helping of kidneys in a tangy sauce. Benno was wolfing down his *Hirschbraten*. It almost seemed like old times.

Benno cleared his throat.

"It's official," he said. "We leave next month." His incisors jumped into view. "Just think, Lili. Soon I'll be on the roof of the world, finding proof of our forefathers' foresight."

"I'm truly very glad for you. Am I the first person you've told?"

His brown eyes were shining.

"I plan to write my family tonight."

So she was the first to know. This pleased her. Perhaps, somewhere up there on a majestic mountain where their Nordic ancestors the Aryans had once built settlements and forged kingdoms, Benno would indeed think of her and even name a germ plasm after Lili, the girl in Heidelberg.

♫♪♫

Tante Aletheia and Lili were drinking coffee when Frau Brinkmann came into the kitchen. She was holding a neatly folded copy of the *Völkischer Beobachter*.

"Will you look at this," she gushed, spreading it out on the table.

Tante Aletheia and Lili exchanged glances. Frau Brinkmann was red in the face.

"I was cleaning Herr Poppe's room out just now, what with him away for the next couple days, and look at what I found."

Just yesterday Herr Poppe and his fiancée—along with twenty-three other couples—had been married in a mass ceremony at the Town Hall. The newlyweds were now on a short honeymoon in the Allgäu.

The three of them crowded round the open newspaper. It wasn't today's date. Frau Brinkmann, stumbling over some of the words, read the advertisement out loud.

"34-year old pure Aryan civil servant with blond hair, no blemishes, Party member since 1934, residing in Heidelberg, desires marriage with healthy and fertile pure Aryan maiden no older than 28. Candidate must be modest, frugal, and hardworking. Should not wear make-up or high heels. Interested applicants for this position should send photograph to #213/HP."

Frau Brinkmann looked up.

"The new Frau Poppe certainly looked like a no-nonsense type the day she came to dinner. Pulled a face at my Knödel," she tutted. "Said it was wasteful to have so much bacon in them."

"I wonder what she's going to say to your hot dinners," Lili said. "And your Eintopf. She'll find her position even more difficult when she sees how much of it Herr Poppe can eat."

Tante Aletheia put on a serious face, but it was obvious that she was straining.

"I must say that I wonder in what position she now finds herself," she said primly.

At this, the three of them looked at each other in surprise, then burst into howls of laughter. Lili was blushing madly at the hideous thought of Herr Poppe's bare rump in the air.

One of Our Few Remaining

It was bliss to walk through the streets between classes. The air was scented with the promise of new life. Lili would have liked to go up along Philosophenweg or even further on the Heiligenberg, back to the mystical Thingstätte. It was a day meant for being outside, whether marching or lolling about under the trees. She forced herself to ignore the infantile desire to skip across Alte Brücke or twirl in the breeze like a horse chestnut seed.

If she bothered to come, Hildegard would be pleased to attend this next class, for the professor was the one who relished any subject to do with the Third Reich, fanatic about Germans using German words. The other day he had said that with its Latin roots the term *Konzentrationslager* should be thrown out. *Sammellager*, or collection camp, would be more fitting.

Yet Hildegard hadn't turned up in any classes. By now the situation with that unpleasant operation must have been settled, and she and Gustav off on their honeymoon. Surely she wouldn't have had to go through with it. It could have been a clerical error. Yes, that's what it must have been. Perhaps she was already well on her way to giving the Führer a son; Hildegard seemed to be made for being the mother of many. Even though Lili had not got around to asking Benno about the science of all this, she was certain that just because Hildegard had twelve toes, it didn't mean that her children would have them. Didn't Gustav's germ plasm count for something?

Once in the building and up the stairs, Lili passed by a group of students.

"Are you marching with us tomorrow?"

"Of course!" She knew that the plan was that they be trucked out to Kirchheim and then march back into Heidelberg. It would take a while, but with this weather that would be only a pleasure. "How many trucks will we need? I imagine the whole university will want to go on this one."

The man next to her smirked.

"Not everyone, you snappy hazelnut. Not her."

With his chin he motioned toward a young woman just coming out of the toilets at the end of the hall. The severity of her pulled back honey blonde hair only served to accentuate the shadowed hollows beneath her eyes. Lili immediately recognized her from months earlier. She was the student whose books had fallen in such a heap in the hallway.

"What about her?" Lili asked.

"She's one of our few remaining Jews." His tone was curt. "I don't know why they didn't kick them all out with the professors back in '33."

"Maybe she's like Hannah Arendt," someone suggested. "Has a sweetheart in the Philosophy Faculty."

The other sneered. "Not very likely. Look at her. Who'd want to break the law for something like that?"

Despite the legal issue, Lili frowned. Couldn't the man see how beautiful she was? All she needed was more food and rest to take away the shadows.

"Jaspers didn't get much out of messing about with that Jewess Arendt," the other shrugged. "He's out of a job since last year."

"But not because of Arendt," someone else called out. "She left long ago. No, Jaspers is out because of his wife—she's a Jew too."

"He must really be a Jew lover."

"Come on. We'd better get to class if we want to hear old Paetzold talk on yesterday's latest ruling to help drive out the Jews."

Before passing through the doorway, Lili turned. The girl was standing outside a classroom further up the hall. She seemed to be waiting for everyone else to go in first. Alone at last, she raised her shoulders, as if taking a deep breath. Then she stepped forward and disappeared.

But Why Would It?

"Why long for the Rhine when there is the Neckar?" Dr. Hempel asked as he and Lili strolled along Neckarstaden on a Sunday afternoon. They had been taking coffee in the salon when the professor, fidgety throughout, had suddenly leapt up, suggesting that on such a fine day they should promenade alongside the river. Tante Aletheia had declined, citing a headache, so it was left to Lili and Dr. Hempel to enjoy the balmy air.

It seemed ages since Lili had spent time alone with him and she relished his company, comfortable and comforting. As they passed the Stadthalle, Lili stole a sideways look at him. He had lost his one remaining student due to increased involvement in Pimpf pursuits. For some time, Dr. Hempel's hair had grown dangerously ragged around the edges, and his collar frayed—classic symptoms of insufficient funds. But today his white hair was neatly clipped, and he had on a nicely starched new shirt. He had found work again, or the work had found him, for only last week not only had he been given a position in administration, he had been put in charge of a group of HJ musicians. It was sad that there were no strings in the young orchestra, but at least Dr. Hempel had a regular income once more. Still, it seemed that much of the sparkle had gone from his eyes. How he must miss the violin.

As they strolled, they came to speak of Goethe. Lili knew that Dr. Hempel too was a great admirer of Goethe yet, unlike Papa, he generally resisted quoting him.

"It's only natural that Goethe would have been drawn to Heidelberg," he said now. "The town is a crown jewel of Germany."

They came to a stop, staring out across the Neckar to the freshly garlanded green of the Philosophenweg and the soft hills that led to the Heiligenberg. Lili shivered. She had seen this view in all the seasons now. From the other side of the river she had looked upon the ruins of the towering Schloß, in winter frosted white, these days glowing pink under the strengthening sun. She had walked the streets below the castle in every weather, had come to know every twist and turn of the cobblestones. Had followed the uplifting strains of a waltz into an alley to find an old man turning a carillon. Had sniffed her way into courtyards where unharnessed horses stood quiet, feeding upon hay. Had bought licorice snails to toss to the children who ran laughing with hoops through a tiny square. She had opened her window to send Bach out into Kornmarkt, and linked arms with students who felt as she did, striding forth into the moment. Now, with a thickness gathering in her throat, she swallowed. It was true. Like the poets and philosophers of bygone days, she too had come to love Heidelberg.

"There is much for which we should thank Goethe," Dr. Hempel was saying. "His poetry, his drama, his studies of science and color. His sensible counter to the excesses of the Enlightenment, and more. But it is his understanding of music that moves me on the occasion of this rather glorious day in your company, dear Fräulein Lili, to quote him. Even if it does seem one of his harshest sayings. It is likely that you are familiar with this particular one, but I shall utter it nonetheless."

He spoke slowly, enunciating each word, unlike Papa, who slid the quotes out, fluid like spring water.

"The person who does not love music does not deserve to be called human; the one who loves music is only half a human. But the one who makes music," and here he paused, " he is a whole."

His eyes were twinkling a bit.

"At this point in my acquaintance with the young lads of the HJ Youth Orchestra, I am somewhat unsure of the veracity of this particular belief of Herr Goethe. I have never heard such dissonance in my life."

Lili laughed out loud.

"Poor boys. What are they supposed to be playing?"

"We are attempting Mozart. But the deplorable state of musical education these days makes it unlikely that we will progress further than *Ah vous dirai-je, Maman.*"

Her eyebrows went up.

"I know, I know," he said. "To add to my misery there have been whispers that the orchestra might make it to Bayreuth as a little foretaste of greater things to come—if the boys can be whipped into shape in time."

"But that would be so exciting," Lili exclaimed. "The Führer will be there, and then of course there's the Festival itself. What an honor it would be to attend."

"I'm getting old, Fräulein Lili. I don't have that much energy left over for such things." Dr. Hempel sighed, and Lili felt a pang of sympathy. There just weren't enough hours in the day for everything one needed, let alone wanted, to do. Had there ever been an age or civilization as busy as this one? Yet surely Dr. Hempel would be able to train the boys in time if he set about doing it the right way.

"Let them listen to Wagner," she said with assurance. "His music will teach them. If they honor their country—and of course they do—then Wagner's spirit will awaken their consciousness and they'll know what they have to do to practice harder." She thought of how Papa no longer cared for Wagner.

"It's that simple?" Dr. Hempel was looking at her with what could only be amusement.

Lili blushed.

"I mean, I've found it very useful on a personal level, Dr. Hempel." She cleared her throat. "For example, when I listen to *Tannhauser,* or even Lortzing's arias, I'm overwhelmed by emotion. It is this emotion that inspires me to do my best."

She could hear Dr. Hempel drawing in his breath. "Na ja. It has long been clear that you are a musician, and that you love your land at a fundamental level." His gaze returned to the waters running fresh and free below them. "Let us hope that this will never change."

"But why would it?" she laughed. Dr. Hempel was such a funny old dear.

Contemplative Days at Friedberg

A lacework of green stirred in the breeze high above where Lili lay on the grass, blades tender and new. What would it be like to stay here forever, under the canopy of trees in Friedberg?

They had arrived yesterday. Marie was delighted, rushing about to take care of the things she had neglected since Tante Aletheia's last visit. She had insisted on coming in this morning after church to finish washing the windows. Tante Philomena explained that in the 1921 renovation several walls had been partly knocked down to install large windows. With such a view it was understandable, even though the extra sizes had increased the taxes. It gave the house a curious look, trapped between a 19th century *maison de maître* and a modern Bauhaus construction. Indeed, it was unusual to have any house at all set alone so deep within the forest.

A touch as soft as moth wings brushed against Lili's bare toes.

"Fragonard."

The cat moved from her feet and upwards along her side to nestle against her, purring. Lili looked him in the eyes, which he promptly closed. For a few moments she shut her own, a golden darkness, then stared upwards at the profusion of fresh leaves brushing each other in ever-changing patterns against the constant sky.

Her life was changing too. Benno was gone, off to join the expedition. Their parting in the foyer in Heidelberg had been brief, but she understood when his hand held on to hers longer than proper. Even though his heart had touched hers—or was it that her heart had touched his—he was an honorable man dedicated to science. Science and the Reich. That was how Benno would spend his life.

She watched a stork on high, its markings growing clearer as it neared its nest on the roof of the house.

Benno could take pride in knowing that his research would further the findings of the Ahnenerbe as well as knowledge in germ plasms. It was ironic that the man of science didn't have as pure a blood as she, the artist.

It was fascinating to think that blood harbored so many secrets. She recalled the school textbooks with the charts illustrating the importance of bloodlines. Last week there had been an article in the newspapers about a woman who had tried to kill herself because she had once slept with a Jew and now feared that she could never have an Aryan child. Well, that wouldn't have been the case with Benno and her. They were both Aryan. He wouldn't have been in the SS if he weren't. But he was a dark-eyed scientist from Zwickau and she an aristocratic, golden-haired Prussian musician. Perhaps that was enough of a difference in the long run.

She flexed her feet. Benno had explained about Hildegard's toes. It wasn't just that she had two too many. The danger was if such a useless trait continued, eventually thousands of people would have six toes per foot and, given enough time, the entire population of Germany would be twelve-toed. So even something small like an extra toe could have terrible consequences. Imagine if it were something more threatening! This was why one had to concentrate on the best, and cull the worst. This was why Benno's work was so very important. Perhaps Hildegard wasn't aware of these scientific facts. Perhaps if she learned of them, she would feel better. In case she did have to go through with that operation. But Lili still hadn't seen her.

Now Lili puffed out her cheeks, blowing the air in streams. It was going to be different without Benno around the house. He had been the closest to her in age. But she should concentrate on other thoughts, things she had to do. Like practice the *Goldberg Variations*, which she hadn't touched in weeks. Just because she had played them perfectly in New York didn't mean that she shouldn't keep working on them. She had let herself get somewhat sidetracked recently, working on pieces that featured a viola da gamba.

♫ ♪ ♫

Perhaps she had dozed off, for it seemed only moments later that Tante Aletheia appeared.

"Hello, my dear." She arranged herself on the grass, the folds of her chartreuse skirt spreading out like a giant gingko biloba leaf.

"I've brought us something light and refreshing from the winery at Dorlisheim. Almost as clear as water." She handed her a glass from which tiny bubbles leapt upwards in a fine mist.

"Thank you," Lili said, sitting up. "I'm sorry that I've been such a sadsack again." She took a sip of wine. It was indeed almost as light as water.

Tante Aletheia smiled, shaking her head. "I understand. It's always hard to say good bye to a good acquaintance."

Lili looked at a giant spruce, its needles shimmering metallic blue. "I doubt I'll ever see him again anyway. Even if he does survive such a journey."

"I am confident that they will take proper precautions, Lili. One doesn't go off on expedition to the Himalayas without considerable preparation." Her tone was dry. "And, as you know, the Ahnenerbe has the very highest official backing."

Leaning over, Lili rearranged Fragonard's limbs, which were loose and limp in deep sleep. "The *Völkischer Beobachter* says that the Tibet expedition is going to reveal stupendous facts about our ancestors.

I already knew that a long time ago." Her fingers pulled lightly at the grass, twisting a few blades. "It's too bad that Benno wasn't able to leave with the others on the ship from Genoa. He still had some important work on germ plasms to finish up. But he's meeting the team in Calcutta."

"Then I'm sure all will be well." Tante Aletheia looked up at the sky, cerulean and clear above the firs. "Sometimes one must simply trust the universe."

"Well, I don't know about the universe yet, but I do trust the Führer. And I think you're right—they wouldn't be going if he or SS-Reichsführer Himmler thought it too dangerous." This thought brightened Lili's spirits. She picked up her glass again. The wine was lovely and refreshing.

"Tante Aletheia," she said then, slowly. "Do you trust the Führer?"

Finding a solid resting place on the grass for her glass, Tante Aletheia looked across at Lili, her eyes green and unblinking.

"Why do you ask?" Her tone was light.

"Ach," Lili said. "I've been living with you for months, and I can't recall anything you've ever said about him."

Tante Aletheia nodded. "That's most likely true. I rarely speak of him."

"But that's not because you don't like him, right?"

Fixing her green gaze on Lili, Tante Aletheia spoke with severity.

"Surely you are now adult enough, Lili, to know that people and life can be more complicated than a simple question of like or dislike. Generally it is people who make life more complicated, but that is not the topic here, I understand," she said, smoothing out a bunched gathering of her skirt.

"Of course you're right, Tante Aletheia," Lili replied, afraid that she might have offended her. "It's, it's like with Herr Poppe. I know he's a good man, but he can also be rather pompous at times. I'm not saying that the Führer is pompous," she added quickly. "What I mean is that there are so many facets to a person, and some we might not appreciate, or understand as much as others. So what you must mean, Tante Aletheia, is that there might be some things that you don't always see as making sense, but you know that it's for the best." She paused. "Rather like what you just said about the universe." She gave a small smile.

"It appears that you have answered the question very well yourself, so there is nothing more that I need to say." With that, Tante Aletheia rose, brushing off her skirt with intense strokes.

"Hmm," she said. "Grass marks. A sure sign that spring is here to stay. Well, no matter. Chartreuse and grass green go well together." She reached a hand out to Lili. "Come. Let's take a walk, shall we?"

They started off across the lawns, recently trimmed by three men from the village. Moments later there was a streak of white and then Fragonard was trotting next to them. The air was as transparent and clean as the water bubbling in the stream, and when they closed the lopsided gate and set out on a woodland path, birdsong heralded their passage. For a few minutes they walked together in companionable silence, breathing, observing, listening.

Reaching a fork in the path, they stopped.

"I think today is the perfect day to return to the Hill of the Celts," Tante Aletheia said, and they went to the right. Fragonard decided otherwise and trotted back the way they had come.

"Imagine, just a couple months ago you went down the hill on a sled, and look at it now."

The slope was covered with a green velvet sheen out of which peeped at least a hundred thousand heads of wildflowers white and butter yellow. Among them, scatterings of cornflower blue blossoms thrust upwards. It was pristine perfection. Lili had the urge to run to the top and somersault down. Her whole body was straining to leap.

"Go on," said Tante Aletheia. "I know you want to roll down the hill."

Needing no more encouragement, Lili was off, throwing her shoes aside and skimming over the growth, even so smashing dozens of blooms with each bounding step up to the top of the incline. Then she was on the earth, her arms stretched out, the silky swipe of the grass connecting with hands, fingers, the backs of her knees, grazing feather-fine across her soles. Now her hair was streaming behind her, with each turn caught momentarily in the delicate web of flowers and weeds as she wheeled sideways down the slope. Her eyes were open to see the sky and earth moving toward each other, again and again, azure and glistening green. On and on she rolled, through the fragrance of late spring, her laughter in her ears.

"It's been so long since I did that," she sighed, once she had caught her breath.

Tante Aletheia bent over her.

"I have to tell you a secret," she said. "I've done it myself every year for decades. I still do."

"Really?" Lili smiled. The image of Tante Aletheia tumbling down with her white hair fanning out was something to savor. "Are you the only one or is there a secret society of hill rollers?"

"As far as I know, I am the only one around here who practices this ancient rite of passage." Tante Aletheia grinned. "Of course, now there is you as well."

"I will do this every time I am here," Lili proclaimed. Then realized that it was already May. Soon she would be leaving.

♫ ♪ ♫

Tante Aletheia seemed to notice her sudden mood change, for she reached out again for Lili's hand.

"Don't be despondent. You will be back. I feel it and my feelings are, sometimes unfortunately, usually correct. Now, I promised to tell you more about the Celts."

Heading further into the woods, they walked the pathway that skirted the slope.

"This area was settled by Celts when the tribes moved in from further east. Did you know that your father's grandmother came from an area in the south of Germany where there are Celtic burial mounds? Several were found filled with jewelry and artifacts like what you've seen in my showcase."

"But Papa's grandmother was buried in Prussia."

"Of course. I'm talking about thousands of years ago."

Lili rolled her eyes. "Oh. That was silly."

Tante Aletheia chuckled. "In the passage of time, we are all only tiny specks, thank goodness. What are a thousand years here or there?"

Lili brushed off some dandelion fuzz stuck to her sleeve. "If you put it that way... But a thousand year Reich will be important."

From nearby in the lower branches of a tree came a rustling, followed by a tawny blur of feathers shooting forward and then up in soaring flight.

"Oh my," said Tante Aletheia. "That must have been a golden eagle. I haven't seen one in years!"

"Papa and I used to see a lot of eagles and falcons at Alt Eichendorf. Have you ever been there?"

They set out again, their footsteps soft on the springy earth.

"Yes, but only once. Wilhelm had already said his good byes to Prussia before we met, opting to live in Paris. We stopped in Alt Eichendorf on the way back from his brother's funeral."

"Mama told me about another relative of ours who left Prussia. She wasn't Jewish but she went to Palestine."

"Yes, I know to whom you are referring," said Tante Aletheia. "She was certainly a woman before her time. Independent and spirited, I should think."

Lili nodded.

"Tante Aletheia, why don't all the Jews just go to Palestine? Why do they stay here when things have changed so much for them?"

They walked. From somewhere within the canopy, a lark sang its bittersweet notes.

"Germany is their country, just as it is ours, Lili. Not all Jewish Germans want to leave their homeland."

"But nobody wants the Jews here. Can't they see that? Even the laws are making it harder and harder for them." The image of the pale, beautiful girl outside the classroom suddenly came to mind.

"I think you are wrong about that, Lili. Not everyone finds fault with Jewish Germans. Indeed, it is not even possible to know who is Jewish and who not. Do Jewish people have a sign on them that announces, "I am Jewish"? No, of course not. Aside from those who wear their traditional religious garb, most look like the rest of us. We cannot have a civil war, pitting Germans against Germans." She shook her head.

Lili's heart began to hurry. "I don't mean to be rude, Tante Aletheia, but I believe I'm not wrong. I hear and see things when I'm out and about. The Jews are neither wanted nor acceptable as Germans. Why else would the laws be as they are?" She paused, took a few breaths but could not stop, her voice growing more and more heated in the quiet shelter of the woods.

"You are the one who is wrong," she went on. "Or rather, your generation. You might think that because they fought in the war, that makes the Jews Germans. But scientists know that this isn't so. Blood is more than red liquid. Scientists know that blood, and germ plasms, decide a lot about who is what. And Jews are different, even if you are friends with them. They're not Aryans. You can see it with so many of them, even without their traditional clothes. You know that, Tante Aletheia." She glanced at her. Her profile reminded Lili of a tragic Wagnerian heroine.

"So the sooner they leave, the sooner Germany will again be a land of pure Aryans, like it used to be when our ancestors were living. Did you know that the Celts also used the swastika?"

A bitter taste was rising up in Lili as she heard her own voice, knowing how unpleasant she must sound to Tante Aletheia who loved her and who really wasn't to blame for anything. Yet despite Lili's outburst, for the longest time Tante Aletheia said nothing at all. All that broke the silence was their footfall and the brushing of their clothes and limbs against the leaves and branches that jutted out into the path. Even the birds were quiet.

Suddenly, Tante Aletheia turned to Lili. Her eyes were near black in the shadow of the pines but her expression surprisingly mild.

"You have much to contemplate, Lili. These are complicated times, even if you might think the solutions are simple." She raised a hand as Lili opened her mouth to protest.

"Always remember that laws are made by people." She paused. "It is good that you are a musician, for I believe that you will find truth in music."

Then, as if clearing the vibrations, she clapped her hands together once. "Let us not debate this any further. The day is too lovely for that. Let's put this aside for now."

Frustrated yet relieved, Lili nodded. Tante Aletheia was such a good person, even if she didn't see the full picture. She deserved not to be further upset. Right then and there Lili decided, when possible, to ignore Tante Aletheia's weaker points. After all, like Großmama Maximiliana's and Großpapa Hugo's, her days were drawing to a close. Then the new order would reign supreme, and today's youth rise, embracing and embodying the spirit of the times and all that went with it.

Lady of the Woods

Back at the house, Marie had done a good job of cleaning the windows with a vinegar solution. Lili glanced through the spotless glass upon the lawns and gardens as she played a sonata on the slightly out of tune piano in the salon. But the air was still pungent with acidity and when Tante Aletheia invited her to the garden, she willingly shut the piano lid.

The residue of discomfort she felt about the exchange earlier evaporated with Tante Aletheia's good spirits.

"Before she left, Marie put a lovely bottle of Riesling into the stream to cool. Shall we sit under the trees and have some now?"

Lili brightened. "I'll go get it."

Barefoot, she crossed the slate terrace with its marble and clay flowerpots overflowing with ivy and the multi-colored blooms of spring, and went down the stone stairs to the lawn. On the top step was a red bowl where Tante Aletheia had placed extra milk for Fragonard. The scent of the late afternoon air was sweet. Lili bent down to pluck some wild strawberries growing near the raspberry bushes. They tasted of orchard and woodland. At this time of day, the light was golden, rinsing the palette of greens in dreamy hues. It was no wonder that Tante Aletheia loved green—the shades were endless. Out on the grass, Lili stopped and turned slowly. Save for the very tips of the gargantuan evergreens swaying gently in the breeze, nothing but she seemed to be moving. When she had completed her ritual of a few slow circles, she stopped, and the wind died as well. The sudden stillness of the surroundings was loud in her head.

How tiny she was, compared to these deep-rooted giants all around. Her eyes welled with tears. Light and color blurred. The rippling waters of the stream broke the spell.

At the edge of the brook she skirted along the bank, looking for the bottle. Most likely troubled by her shadow, a trout flashed below to hide under stones. Ah, there it was. Marie had placed the bottle in a tiny cove. Lili knelt, bending over to retrieve it, gasping as the icy water covered her arms nearly to the elbows.

Tante Aletheia was waiting for her near the grove of silver birches whose slender trunks glowed like antique gold. There were plates of tidbits on the table.

"Never in my life have I drunk as much wine as in these past months," Lili stated, holding up her glass to catch the sun.

"Wine, like life, is to be appreciated," said Tante Aletheia. "Santé."

"To wine...to life," Lili said, remembering the toast with Dr. Morsch.

Tante Aletheia gave her a curious look but said nothing. Fragonard ambled over and jumped onto her lap and she fed him a small piece of sausage from a plate of cheese and charcuterie.

"Tante Aletheia."

She looked up. "Yes, Lili?"

"Thank you for bringing me here again."

Despite her years, Tante Aletheia was beautiful. She blinked, then looked at Lili with emerald eyes. "You are always welcome." She paused. "I know you will be a comfort to me in my old age."

Lili was taken aback, but noticed the mischievous sparkle in her expression.

They chatted of Tante Aletheia's early years with Onkel Wilhelm, about the many people they had known and entertained in Paris.

"Of course, he was older than I and needed peace sooner that I might have. Not that I was too sorry to leave Paris behind for the serenity of Friedberg even if, at least to begin with, it was rather a shock. Just nature and all these trees."

"It's hard to decide which ones I like best," Lili said, slipping Fragonard another sliver. "The oak is of course incomparable, especially for us. Germans, I mean. How many poems mention the oak? Then there are the elm, the horse chestnut, and beech. I find their shade and leafwork comforting. There's something strange about the birch though—sometimes it even makes me nervous. Still, in the end I'm torn between it and the fir as favorites. Those two seem to call out to me the most." Lili grinned, feeling sheepish. "Or I call out to them and they answer me." She raised her chin. "I've always felt that way. Since Alt Eichendorf."

Tante Aletheia was smiling at her.

"In the Celtic calendar," she said, "each month bears the name of a tree. According to it, because of your birthdate, you are a birch. And because you were born on the first day of January, you fall under the lesser influence of a secondary tree—the fir." She sat back against the wrought iron chair. "So it is not surprising, at least not according to Celtic beliefs, that you feel drawn to these two trees in particular."

This was fascinating.

"But what does that mean: 'I am a birch?'"

Tante Aletheia sipped some wine before answering. "I am by no means an expert on Celtic lore. Over the years I picked up a little knowledge, when the grounds yielded so many Celtic treasures. I wanted to learn more about the people who lived here long ago. It is said that the birch is known as the Lady of the Woods.

Lili shivered.

"What else?"

"Grace and beauty. Renewal. Rebirth. The birch was—or is—a determined tree, hardier than even the mighty oak. The birch will grow in soil where the oak cannot flourish."

"What about the fir?"

Tante Aletheia's eyes had a definite glint in them.

"It is said that those who are influenced by the fir can be egotistic and stubborn, yet they also have dignity and care deeply for those close to them."

Lili pursed her lips. "Hmm. Are any more good things said about the birch?"

Tante Aletheia chuckled.

"You'd like to make a choice between the two?"

Lili bit into a pickle.

"I'm leaning toward the birch."

"Birch people are said to have clarity of purpose combined with a visionary nature. However, at times, a lack of reality can cloud judgement."

"Clear and cloudy at the same time." A paradox. Like creation and destruction—like Benno's germ plasms and the Führer's insights. She nodded.

"So be it. I have decided. I shall embrace my birchness."

Tante Aletheia laughed.

"It's amusing, isn't it? And you are indeed as slender as a birch."

Fragonard jumped off her lap and stretched as Tante Aletheia scratched him behind an ear.

"Our friend is telling us it is time to go inside."

"Yes," Lili shivered. The temperature had dropped.

As they put the tableware onto a tray, Tante Aletheia said, "I just remembered another aspect of the birch. A little poem"

Lili looked across at the birches, whose limbs were now trace lines of true silver and lilac, their pointillist leaves dappled with darkness.

Tante Aletheia's voice drifted out onto the evening. What a good memory she had, at least for poems about trees.

"The silvery birch was noble
Yet armed herself quite late.
Still 'twas no mark of yellow stripe
But of her strength innate."

Lili grinned as she carried the crockery toward the house. In New York she had been called a kraut. Now she was apparently a birch, with a sprig of fir thrown in for good measure.

Someone Standing in the Shadow

Although the classroom windows were open, the air barely stirred. For the past hour, students had been shifting in their seats and fanning themselves with moist hands.

Professor Dr. Hetzenrath paused the lecture to mop at his flushed face above the tight collar. His glasses slid over his nose and he removed them, wiping his eyelids before putting the wire frames back on. From where she was sitting as far in the front as possible, Lili could see that, for once, his eyes appeared to be twinkling.

"Some of you will be more than pleased to learn that I have decided to end the class right here."

There were indeed several cheers upon this, which he ignored. "It is my opinion that nothing will be served if both professor and students are too hot to begin to reflect upon one of the greatest figures of medieval literature—Parzifal." There were a few murmurs.

Professor Dr. Hetzenrath stared down the noisemakers.

"All of us are aware that the quest has been set to music by a 19th century composer dear to the hearts of many in our homeland." He cleared his throat. "However, next week we will examine the original text, as written by Wolfram von Eschenbach. We will also consider its roots in French Arthurian romances, and the connection with Celtic legends. Be warned," he added, looking them over, and Lili could see that the twinkle had disappeared, "our discussion will not move beyond the 13th century."

Soon after, in the hallway, there was some grumbling about the old man and how he should be replaced by a professor who knew how to respect today's world as well as that of long gone yesterdays.

"Are you coming, Lili? We're marching along the Philosophenweg."

"Good idea!"

A short while later the group gathered in the courtyard. Lili sat on a stone post watching the latecomers. Lili recognized one of them as the student who had helped pick up the Jewish girl's book last semester. He was tall and powerfully built, but there was something sweet about him. Now he seemed to be walking over to her. But he passed by her, and she could not help but watch as he crossed the courtyard, eventually reaching someone who was standing in the shadow of a recess. Even from this angle, Lili was able to recognize who it was. Today the girl seemed to have a firm grip on her books, but still looked pale.

Suddenly the Night Changes

"Tra la la la!"

Last year Carl Orff had written a cantata based on the verses of *Carmina Burana*. Lili had heard pieces of it performed on the radio but had not yet seen a production. Still, the rented hall where the *Studentenfest* was being held had been decorated to look like how she imagined the bacchnalian setting of *Carmina Burana*: pillars wrapped with grape vines, with drink in copious quantities. It was good that Tante Aletheia had insisted she eat a *Butterbrot* before leaving the house.

It was thrilling to be a part of this great Fest. Arms linked with others', swaying from side to side, Lili had spent part of the last couple hours at a long planked table, singing out with gusto the songs that raised everyone's spirits ever higher, fervent melodies of love and brotherhood and the fatherland.

Dressed in a cardinal red dirndl that did not make her look at all demure, Lili kicked up her heels dancing the polka. The horns and brass thumped, the accordion rippled as round and round she flew on the wooden floor, her partners a wide assortment of fellow classmates and total strangers. Some of them were masked, or wearing costumes—Roman togas, here and there crowned by a wreath of grape leaves, while others wore garments that echoed the style of the Middle Ages. There were also men in uniform. These were probably students who had recently left university to join the growing numbers of the military and SS forces. Many of these, too, requested Lili as a partner in dance, and the exhilaration of whirling around with them, one blending into the next, was heady.

Yet now the rhythm of the blasting horns was beginning to grate. As this last partner, a black-hatted pirate, began to lead her back to the table, Lili shook her head.

"Thank you, Herr Klaus Störtebeker," she said, recalling the 14th century Hamburg river pirate her aunts had told her about. "It's time for me to leave."

"But you're my booty!" cried the pirate.

"You'll have to find another wench." She giggled, pointing over toward two young women standing by a pillar. They looked like shop girls out for a night of fun. "How about one of them?"

"Grrr!" he growled. "I'll have them both!" and off he went, brandishing his wooden sword.

On the way out, Lili eschewed all offers of being escorted home. At last she was out in the cooler night air. The quiet breeze soothed her head, clearing it somewhat, and she began to walk along the cobblestones.

Some distance ahead, arms slung over each other's shoulders, a group of students tried to march, staggering and dancing like buffoons, bellowing along the darkened streets. Lili grinned. Student life in Heidelberg. The men's pace was hampered by their zigzagging, so it was not long before Lili caught up with them. A fellow with an enormous stag-headed cane stopped short, leaned upon the stick and then vomited into a box of geraniums outside a building. Lili grimaced at the sound.

"Ahah!" called one of the men. "A new type of fertilizer has just been invented."

"Pray tell," said another. "What bloom shall spring from such fertile soil?"

A masked man weaving from side to side held up an arm.

"Judging by the depths from which its creator spews forth, surely a soulful one." At this, his knees gave way and he crumpled into a drunken heap.

Despite the disgusting noises emerging from over the flower box, Lili had to giggle.

One of the others must have noticed the sound, for he turned toward her. His voice was slurred.

"But here it is already, the flower! It's a red one, and in full bloom too." He stared at Lili as if she were the most amazing thing he had ever seen.

A man with a set of cow horns on his head nodded, his head bobbing so that the pointed tips lolled in the air.

"I can see it too! Blonde with red petals." He called to the student at the geranium box. "You've got a winning recipe there, brother. Hey! Make some more of these for us."

He stepped closer to her and Lili could see spittle on his lips shining in the moonlight. He reached out a hand, following it with a lurching movement.

"I want to smell the sweet petals. Come here, little flower."

Beneath the great horns, bleary eyes turned sharp and suddenly the night changed. These were no longer just tipsy students. A rush of some strange substance surged through Lili, heating and chilling her at the same time. Her heart seemed to have sprung into her throat. Her breath was shallow, dizzying, and she turned on the ball of her foot to move away but the movement was too late and the horned man caught her skirt.

"Ach, don't be like that, *Blümchen*. Give me a kiss." Handful by handful he reeled her in.

"Let go of me at once," she hissed, for her vocal chords seemed cut.

The horned man roared with laughter but kept a firm hold, his gaze roaming over her face and body. He licked his lips.

"I remember you. You're quite a dancer but you look like you need a good kiss, and I'm just sober enough to give you one."

Under normal circumstances he was probably not an unpleasant man. But now he looked primitive and raw and Lili had the terrible knowledge that she was not strong enough to fight him off.

He came at her, pulling her against him. She felt his solid body pushing against hers and it was hard and unwanted and still it pressed and then his wet mouth was upon hers. Lili clenched her lips. She could feel a slick heat bearing down on them, pushing at them with increasing urgency, prying them apart with slippery force. And then the tongue was in, her jaws aching as the intruder thrust deeper into her mouth, leaving the bitter taste of beer pooled on the sides. There was a wild humming noise, like that of a trapped insect, and it was coming from within her, vibrating upwards. But she could not free her mouth to let it out.

"That's enough now!"

The voice slashed through the night.

For another moment she was still molded against the man, and then suddenly she was loose. Her hand flew to her mouth, the fingers swiping the slime across her lips with roughness. The night air hit her mouth, cool against the wet. A wave of disgust and lingering fear passed through her but she did not run.

"You are an asshole," the voice said again, using the polite form of 'you.'

An officer in the black uniform of the SS stood on the pavement nearby. He made a tutting noise and stepped forward into the light of the streetlamp.

"Have the brains of you university boys become so weak these days that you can't even recognize a lady when you meet one? You're lucky that I know you're all just drunk from too much partying, or I'd have you hauled off." His booted foot nudged the student slumped on the ground.

"Get him home." He motioned to the one still retching over the geraniums. "Him too. As for you," he turned to the horned student who was now ashen, "you'd better sober up at once and apologize to this young lady. Kisses taste better when they're given, not stolen."

His head cast down, the student addressed Lili.

"Indeed, Fräulein, I'm sorry. It was the drink." His voice was soft, shaking.

Lili peered at him for some moments. Now, with his horns sliding halfway off his disheveled head, he looked ridiculous, pathetic even.

"The officer is right. Your brains are addled." She paused. "You might be a very nice person when you're not drunk. But I'll never know, and I don't care to." She smoothed back her hair and turned toward the officer.

"Thank you. Thank you very much."

She began to walk away, her knees trembling with each step. It wasn't far to Kornmarkt.

"Fräulein!" The officer called out to her.

She halted. In her haste, she had forgotten to say "Heil Hitler."

He walked over to her.

"Would you like me to escort you home?"

For a moment she hesitated, then shook her head. "It's kind of you." She looked up at him. "Thank you again. But I don't live far away and I'm all right now." Glancing over at where the students were sorting themselves out, now greatly subdued, she added, "I doubt they'll bother me again."

He followed her glance and gave a small chuckle.

"No, I suspect you're right. They do look properly chastised. Well then, Fräulein. Get home safely. Heil Hitler!"

"Heil Hitler!"

She set out, her heels sounding on the stone in as even a beat as she could make.

The house seemed asleep when she arrived home. A pot of chamomile tea and biscuits had been left on Lili's nightstand. She brushed her teeth with ferocity, rinsed, gargled, and rinsed several more times before pouring a cup of cool tea. The evening had begun so well and had been so much fun, nearly until the end. She shuddered and went back to the sink to spit.

After she had washed herself and put on a clean nightgown, she couldn't sleep. There had been a few moments with the drunken student when she felt powerless. It was a horrible feeling. What if the officer hadn't come by? She exhaled. Thank goodness for the SS. She stared into the darkness. Gradually the moonlight filled the room. What if it had been Leo? He had already saved her once before, in Mannheim, when that Fritz von Bieberstein had asked too many questions about Papa. What if Leo had come by and seen that demeaning scene? It was good that it had been a different officer. What a disgusting kiss. She ran into the bathroom and spit into the sink again, rinsed her mouth.

Back in bed, she tossed about. In her life, she had already known three kisses: from Friedrich, Benno, and now a nameless drunken student. Each had been different, and unexpected.

Some Differences

L ili was ravenous but a hot dinner was delayed because Frau Brinkmann had forgotten to cook the potatoes. The potatoes were forgotten because at the moment all she could think of was how impressive her Willi looked in his Storm Trooper's uniform. On a two-day leave from Vienna, Willi had stopped by to sit in the kitchen and chat with his mother for several hours. He'd brought along a basketful of Viennese goodies that he—and anyone else who happened into the kitchen—was helping his mother eat. Lili had enjoyed a lovely veal sausage that Frau Brinkmann fried up with butter.

But that had been earlier in the day. For the past half hour, Bach had been competing with the rumbling and grumbling of her stomach until Lili had closed the harpsichord lid and gone back to the kitchen.

Willi was still seated at the table.

Frau Brinkmann beamed at him as she cut a chunk off a large loaf of dark bread. *Schwarzbrot* still tasted nutty and chewy as it should. But these days, some of the other bread had changed its consistency and flavor. Frau Brinkmann's brother, a baker, had told her that the flour was being ground finer to increase volume, and rye and wheat were being augmented by potato flour and maize.

"Maize!" Frau Brinkmann said. "That's pig food. I don't understand why. It's not as if we were at war, heaven forbid."

"There wasn't much blood shed," Willi said after his mother's outburst. "Almost everybody was happy to have us there." The air snapped as he took a bite of another *Wiener Würstchen* that Frau Brinkmann had boiled up for him. All he seemed to do was eat and talk. Lili looked at his sausage and then the pot with the potatoes. They'd be done soon, to be served with a stew that was simmering nearby, driving her crazy with its aroma.

"I guess the Jews aren't very happy though," Willi said. "They had to clean the streets of Vienna."

Frau Brinkmann clucked at him.

"It's a bit much, don't you think, Willi?"

He suddenly looked guilty.

"The sausage?"

"No, you little dwarf. The thing with the Jews and the tooth brushes."

"Ach, that." When he shrugged his shoulders Lili could see that he'd gained weight since the last time she'd seen him, before the

Anschluß. "They could have given them brooms, I guess," he nodded. "That would have covered a lot more area a lot faster." He made a loud sucking noise, as if to dislodge a piece of sausage from between his teeth. "And why they had some of the women scrubbing the cobblestones with their, their undergarments—that didn't make much sense either."

Frau Brinkmann shook her head and made tutting noises.

Lili looked down at her nails. The Jews in Vienna had scrubbed the streets with toothbrushes and underwear. Like Willi said, brooms would have been faster—if the point was for them to actually clean the streets. Obviously sanitation wasn't the only issue. It must have been to make them so uncomfortable that they would get out of Ostmark, the old Austria, faster than they were getting out of Germany. These new, more intense measures taken in Vienna must have been the creative approach, making the point that the Reich had little use for those whom they called parasites.

How unpleasant it would be to have to do something like that. How humiliating. Her blood would have boiled with rage. If it had been she, Lili, she would have refused to do it. That was it. Real Germans would not stoop to do something so stupid and degrading as to clean the street with an underwear or toothbrush. It made you realize the difference between them. There was a popular slogan that said, "Treat your comrade as you would like him to treat you." It was becoming quite clear that only the Volksdeutsche were comrades.

She held on to this thought when she went in for their meal later. Benno was gone; his seat had been taken over by Frau Poppe. It was strange how a simple matter of exchanging one person for another could make such a difference.

Frau Poppe was already at the table when Lili slid into her seat.

"Aren't you hungry?" she asked, her close-set blue eyes alert as Lili filled her plate. "Young women need to eat properly to be strong and fit members of the Reich. Only then will you be ready for the next step.

In *Mein Kampf*, the Führer says that a German girl has nationality, and only with marriage does she achieve citizenship."

With this, she spiked a large potato piece dripping with sauce from the meat. "If you ask me, you university girls aren't doing your duty to the Reich."

"With all due respect, Frau Poppe," Lili said, quickly swallowing the last of her cabbage. "I need to finish my studies before I can think of marriage. Besides, I'm a member of the National Socialist Student Association as well as of Faith and Beauty. We do a lot of marching and physical training and I hold myself to be quite fit." Certainly she looked fitter than Frau Poppe, whose hefty frame might be strong but certainly not lithe.

Frau Poppe frowned, so that her eyes appeared even closer together. "That may be, but Dr. Goebbels says that the finest and most elevated position for women is that of wife and mother."

At this, Herr Poppe gave his wife a smile so silly that he looked like the American cartoon character Porky Pig, with hair.

Tante Aletheia turned to Frau Poppe.

"It would seem that unlike you, Frau Poppe, young Fräulein Lili has not yet found the right man."

"Ja, ja," admitted Frau Poppe. "You have a point, Frau von Wohlitz. Some things can't be hurried. When the time is right—then the woman finds the man for whom she's right."

"I think Fräulein Lili is missing Herr Malter these days," said Herr Poppe, winking above his wine glass.

Lili's nose twitched. Table talk had indeed been less annoying when Benno was here.

"The Führer has the highest regard for music, and considers it a cultural imperative for the German Volk," Dr. Hempel said. "Let us not forget that Fräulein Lili has the musician's soul—sensitive and aesthetic." He looked around the table. "There are many ways to contribute to the goals and glories of the Reich."

Sniffing, Frau Poppe said, "You're correct, Dr. Hempel. There's more than enough for good German women to do without their having to go to university."

When Lili looked up from her napkin she caught a glimpse of Tante Aletheia sucking in her cheeks.

A hot wave rose up through her. Who did Frau Poppe think she was, making such pointed insinuations like that? As if Lili weren't involving herself enough.

"I know that women have been called hen-birds and that we are here to look beautiful and hatch eggs," she said, recalling words by Dr. Goebbels that always caused some of the students to laugh and pretend to flap wings. Now it didn't seem that amusing.

"Some people say that male birds are there to protect us and they're the ones that fly out, roaming the skies. But where, Frau Poppe, is it written that hen-birds cannot sing? Or point out to their chicks the beauty of flying?" She stared at Frau Poppe's ugly dress. The woman had no sense of style.

"And actually," she said, almost as an afterthought, avoiding looking at Tante Aletheia or Dr. Hempel as she spoke, "I will soon be performing for the Führer himself." There, that should shut Frau Poppe up.

Frau Poppe did seem momentarily nonplussed.

"But," she continued, her voice gradually resuming its abrasive tone, "it's interesting what you just expressed. It reminds me of what the Führer said some years ago. That the concept of female emancipation is merely an invention of the Jewish intellect, and its substance bears the stamp of the same mind."

There was a sudden intake of breath from one corner of the table. Lili stared at Frau Poppe who was now sipping her water with a delicacy quite unlike what she knew of her. The woman was impossible.

"Why is it so quiet?" Frau Dierck blurted out. "I remember how it used to be around this table when Herr Poppe told us stories." Frau Dierck giggled. "Talking about birds, there's an old saying about birds from when I was a girl." She jerked her head, looking a bit like a duck, and began to recite in a singsong manner.

"*Mädchen die pfeifen und Hühner die krähen, muss man zu Zeiten die Hälse umdrehen.*"

Frau Dierck looked about expectantly. It had been a long time since she'd spoken up around the table.

Lili recognized the line, from an old book with illustrations by Wilhelm Busch. She had always been amused by the image of girls whistling and hens going cock-a-doodle and both of them occasionally having their necks wrung. Yet it had never entered her mind to consider that she too was a girl who sometimes whistled. And it looked as if Frau Poppe sometimes crowed.

Lili grinned. Herr Tischborn was pale while Herr Poppe's face was red and jovial.

"Na, na, Waltraud," he said, reaching out and patting his wife's hand where it lay on the table like a dead fish. "The rooster is happy to have his little dovey in the barnyard." He threw his head back and crowed. "*Kikiriki!*"

At this Lili and Tante Aletheia exchanged glances. Lili could feel it rising up in her until her shoulders began to shake with the impending explosion. Within moments, everyone else at the table, even Herr Tischborn, had joined in the loud guffaws. Only Frau Poppe did not look overly content with the outcome of today's discussion at the dinner table.

Perhaps This Time

"Lili."

Tante Aletheia was peering at her, one silver eyebrow slightly raised. "When is this special concert you mentioned last night going to take place?"

If Tante Aletheia had come into her room just one hour earlier, and if Lili hadn't felt a sudden craving for an *Apfelkrapfen* and gone round the corner to the bakery to satisfy it, she knew she would have died with embarrassment and shame. But, in the meantime, the postman had been there and upon her return Lili had found, along with a letter from Mama, another one of those official envelopes, its black eagle's wings spread out like an embrace. It was as if fate had suddenly stepped in, and Lili could barely believe that she had been saved from having to lie yet again.

Now she could feel her eyes brilliant with excitement, relief, and anticipation. She had danced around her room and in the mirror they had sparkled so much she couldn't even see what color they were.

"I'm to play at a concert in Berchtesgaden!" she half shrieked.

Tante Aletheia looked stunned, and lowered herself into an armchair.

"Oh my."

"Isn't it wonderful? Berchtesgaden! The Führer will have to be there."

"And when is this to take place?"

"Next month. So it will work it out beautifully. I can perform, and then go to New York." It was so amazing and perfect that even the thought of returning to America was not, at least not just yet, spoiling her mood. She was excited to be able to tell Papa and Mama and Paul about it afterwards.

If fate was handing her this concert, perhaps it was not too much to hope that not only would the Führer be there, but there would also be a chance to see Leo again. Perhaps he would be performing too. Perhaps this time she would get to spend more time with him.

"Yes, it sounds as if this time, the timing works better." Tante Aletheia shot Lili a mischievous glance.

Lili clapped her hands together then jumped up. She felt like bounding about the room again. She felt like dancing her way across Alte Brücke.

"Have you thought about what music you might perform?"

Lili grinned with glee.

"No question about it: the *Goldberg Variations*!"

Somewhere on the Other Side of the Hill

She could barely breathe; no, her breath was so deep that she thought she might burst with the sheer joy of it all.

On the way toward the mountains, the train had passed through countryside increasingly captivating. Yet nothing had prepared her for the view from her room; never before in her life had she been so close to such giants of the earth. And the Führer himself was just nearby, on the Obersalzberg.

Lili would have been delighted to stay in Berchtesgaden. On the drive from the station, what she had seen of the town—medieval houses built in southern style, the pale and shimmering pink palace of the Wittelsbachs, the flash of a stone lion poised atop a pillar rising from the fountain in a square—had charmed her. But the Wittelsbach Hotel was full. Arrangements had been made for her some kilometers away, in a Gasthof high above the village of Oberau, where apparently quite a few of Göring's pilots were also being put up while their barracks were still getting the finishing touches. She hadn't seen any of them upon her arrival, and since then hadn't left her room, unable to tear herself away from the wooden balcony that wrapped around two sides.

The Gasthof was perched on the edge of a height overlooking the *Aus*, those meadows of summer green, and the valleys that looked up toward the Alps. The Königssee, royal lake of emerald water said to be the deepest in the land, lay hidden somewhere to the southwest. It was impossible to focus long on only one view; everything was utterly bewitching. Her gaze roamed across the mountains, some still topped with snow, that spread out before her like a vast white-capped sea of stones fading into the far away horizon.

Her heart was going to burst.

The air she drew in was so sweet and pure it felt as if she were bathing her lungs in elixir. Her fingers tightened on the wood railing and she squeezed shut her eyes for some moments, the sun warming their lids like feathers of light. How could she have spent her whole life never having known such almost painful beauty? The forests of her childhood had been rooted in the lowlands. Here they swept upwards, sylvan garlands linking the ancient ones, the Watzmann, the Hochkalter, the Windechartenkopf. She turned slightly toward where earlier on the driver had pointed out the Obersalzberg, just a few hills over on the other side of the thick forest to the left. That was where the Berghof was, with the Führer in residence. And now she, too, was in the heartland of the Reich. Light streamed through a passing veil of clouds, splitting up into beams that shone down in angles as if the meadows and valleys and mountains were being crowned by celestial rays. The fatherland! Lili could feel a great energy pulsing through the air, coming from the Obersalzberg.

She had arrived four full days earlier than necessary for the concert so that she would have time to explore the region on her own. Another wave of excitement passed through her. It was one thing to travel alone to visit Großmama Maximiliana and Großpapa Hugo. Even cross the Atlantic. But those trips had had definite destinations and schedules. She had never simply toured on her own. It was a delicious feeling. Why, she could do anything she wanted. And anything could happen!

The sudden memory of the horned student and his beer saliva flickered but she would not let it linger. No, she was walking distance from the Obersalzberg. It had to be the safest place in all the Reich.

Her very first outing was going to be into the forest.

But before that she had to unpack. The room was spacious, a large cupboard covered with carvings in one corner, a weathered chest of drawers, two wooden chairs and a small table. A lovely *Himmelbett,* its four un-curtained posts painted over with swirling vines and flowers, faced the three large windows on the long side of the room. How she would luxuriate in it tonight. She climbed up on the feather bed to see the view from it. Perhaps later the moon would hang over the mountains, bathing their pale caps with its milky light. She lay back. How soft the pillow felt. A faint aroma, soothing like memories of holidays and roast goose, rose from it. Every cell in her body tingled with wellbeing. Were her germ plasms singing and dancing in bliss? She giggled, nestling deeper into the feathers.

A symphony played in the distance, drums rolling like thunder across the valleys. She did not recognize the work as it faded in and out of her hearing, Glockenspiel and cymbals, horns and the delicate plucking of a thousand strings.

She woke up, surprised to discover that she had been asleep.

The air flowing into the room smelled different; there had been rain. Now the vista through the window was of a world even fresher, if that were possible.

Leaving the unpacking for later, Lili slipped into her sturdy shoes, then hurried to the bathroom where she splashed water, icy and shocking, onto her face. Almost out the door, she remembered a sweater. Down the stairs then. Men's voices booming from somewhere nearby, but she didn't stop; out, out into the splendor of the alpine day.

She gulped the air. Wildflowers wayward and capricious rose in clusters along the upward path to the road that she already knew split in two directions, one back down to the village and the other right up to the edge of the forest. Even if today she would not hike all the way toward the Obersalzberg--and indeed, she didn't know how close she would be able to go, for she had seen the photos with the metal fences—she would be closer to the Führer than at any time since the Rally in Nuremberg. And the bonus would be the woods.

Rust red cows stood feeding in the Au on the other side of the valley. Occasional clangs from the bells around their great necks drifted across the meadows, tones deep and soothing. She passed by a weathered farmhouse that seemed to be hugging the edge of the hill. Further up, an old grandfather in *Bundhosen* and gray wool kneesocks sat on a wooden chair under a tree, his smoking pipe protruding from out of a mass of white whiskers. He watched her approach, his blue eyes twinkling, and gave her a nod as she drew near. As the road turned, Oberau with its onion dome church came back into sight down in the valley. The talkative driver had explained that the church's interior was painted Maria blue. Another day she would walk there to see its color. Now she stepped off the road.

Within moments, the dense woods had swallowed all sound other than their own. Vestiges of rain still sheltering in the branches fell from time to time, and as Lili moved she could hear the thick drops in the rests between her footfall on the muddy, stone-scattered upward slope. A bird shrilled once, then fell silent. The smell of moist earth was strong. Somewhere on the other side of this hill the Führer was breathing the same air.

She came upon a stack of logs, cut neat and short for firewood, making a little hill of their own to the side of the path. The trail led up and down and up again. How very different it was from the flat forest at Alt Eichendorf. Tante Aletheia had told her that this area had been inhabited since ancient times. The Baiovarii tribe had come to these mountains when nearby Salzburg, the fortress of salt, was still a Roman settlement. Now Salzburg was part of the Reich but salt was still being mined in the area. How happy the Führer must be to have his homeland returned to the German fold. How close to Germany itself he had been born, up there in Braunau am Inn; he had missed it by the river's width. What if he had come into the world on this side... She should visit Salzburg, see the house where Mozart had lived. Quite a few genius minds came from this region. Benno had mentioned the scientist Doppler and his discovery about something to do with sound. Then there was of course Herbert von Karajan. Lili stopped. Could it have been the salt itself that fostered creativity and made minds sparkle? She rolled her eyes at such a droll thought and set out again.

A few steps further she realized that she was ravenous. Why, she hadn't had a bite to eat since the morning. She'd missed lunch, and if she didn't turn around right now, she might miss dinner as well. Tonight, just in case, she would sprinkle extra salt on her food.

Like a Different Planet

Nearly all the tables were occupied in the long *Speisesaal*. Lili stood at the entrance, looking over the diners. Could it be that Leo was among them? Most of the men were in uniforms, black and brown and feldgrau, but there were also *Lederhosen* and leather suspenders over stark white shirts with embroidered collars. There were women in dirndls with colorful aprons, in summer frocks, and one or two in black. HJ and BDM uniforms were scattered around the room. The youngest children looked simply like little heads at table level. No sign of Leo.

"Heil Hitler," a waitress called out as she swept by, her arms laden with foaming beers. "There's a table for you by the far window, gnädiges Fräulein." The buxom woman halted then, the drinks sloshing dangerously close to the rim. "It's you in 106, isn't it?"

"Heil Hitler," Lili replied. "Yes, that's my room."

"Ach, then it's good," the waitress said, nodding. "We kept the table for you as we thought you might like to sit alone. But there've been those eyeing it, so you'd better get over there soon."

"I'll do that," Lili said, smiling.

The path cut straight through the center of the room. At first she focused on her table at the far end. But curiosity was too strong, and she glanced at the diners in passing. Many of the men were quite frank in regarding her. Again it was thrilling to sense that their gaze lingered. She had changed from her forest walk clothes into a linen dress whose pale blue mirrored her eyes. Her hair was still a crown of braids, but she had stuck a white wildflower into one of the plaits.

Before she could reach for the wooden chair at her table, a Luftwaffe officer jumped up from a nearby seat to pull it out.

"Allow me," he said.

The three officers at his table made sounds of encouragement.

"Thank you," Lili murmured as the seat was pushed in for her. How polite these officers were. Was it part of their training or were they innately considerate?

"With pleasure," he replied, making a Hitler salute. Laughter in their throats, the others called him cunning.

Lili turned toward them with a brief smile, and then focused on the menu in front of her. She wasn't going to flirt or even get into a conversation with anyone this evening. Not even such good-looking Luftwaffe officers. There was too much to think about.

A different waitress came to take Lili's drink order, a glass of black currant juice. Tonight's set menu offered a salad with bits of bacon, stuffed cabbage roll with boiled potatoes, and dessert of *Apfelstrudel* with vanilla sauce.

Her table was at a window that looked out toward the northwest, a view of the nearest hills, their pastures and woods glowing for just a few more minutes before beginning their inevitable slow fade into pale purples and grays. How long the evenings lasted in summer! What would it be like to sleep outside somewhere in a clearing in the woods and watch the curved cinema house of the sky? There had been an impressive view where they'd camped on the BDM outing, but this part of the country was incomparable. No wonder the Führer had chosen to build his home here. Tomorrow she would set out for the Obersalzberg. She sighed with contentment, sipped her juice. Mama would likely have scolded her gently but she wasn't here, so Lili pulled out her book, a university text she hadn't finished, and most likely never would.

She'd read only a few sentences when she stopped and looked out the open window. The author had written that the supremacy of German blood had been recognized already thousands of years ago. "Tacitus himself held the same opinion as those who believe that the German Volk, that are not sullied by intermarriage with other peoples, are the original, pure and only like themselves peoples." A slight breeze touched upon her arms, and she shivered. Why, this was what the Führer had been saying all along. Just like the ancients. But the Führer had the courage of his convictions, set into practice through the Nuremberg Laws. People of different races should not mix, for, in doing so, purity would be lost. German women must stay true to their blood. The nation depended on them. And perhaps the Jews wanted to keep their blood to themselves too.

"It must be a very interesting book, gnädiges Fräulein," said one of the officers from the neighbor table. "You keep putting it down."

Lili laughed. "I can't stop looking at the view."

"We too are enjoying the natural splendors of the view in front of us," another one said slyly, and was given a sound punch in the arm by his neighbor.

"What is it about officers," Lili challenged, "that makes you so charming?" She pursed her lips as if in thought. "Every single SS officer I've met has been a gentleman, and now I discover that the Luftwaffe too is filled with amiable examples."

One of the men cocked an eyebrow.

"So you meet a lot of officers, do you?"

The blood shot to her cheeks. "No, no. Not many. But all of you are very pleasant. Considerate." She smiled. "You can be a bit naughty at times, I see, but the Reich is fortunate to have you. You make us feel so safe."

"Ach, she's the cunning one!" said one officer, bursting into laughter.

"Well, we trained like dogs to get to where we are," said the one who had pulled out her chair.

"No," said another. "We trained harder than dogs."

"So you feel safe with us."

Lili nodded. "Very much so."

"I don't know if I'm relieved or disappointed about that," said an officer.

"Fräulein, can I serve the next course now?" interrupted the waitress, thrusting her chest out a bit more than necessary.

"Certainly," Lili said, her tone somewhat prim.

As soon as the plate was set down, the officers wished her *Guten Appetit* and turned their attention back to their own food. Lili pierced the large cabbage roll, sending a momentary tendril of steam upwards. It was different from the way Lotte made the dish, tasty in a southern way, with a light touch of caraway. Lili ignored the open book, instead watching the Au and hills fade to lavender. The Apfelstrudel was a disappointment.

But it was sublime to be here, in the heartland of the Reich, surrounded by her people. She breathed in deeply, relishing the mixture of scents that defined the air. New York would be like a different planet.

A Small-Minded Idiot

In the morning, birdsong was again her only companion as Lili hiked along the forest path toward the Obersalzberg. Like the hundreds of visitors who were said to make the trip up from Berchtesgaden daily when the Führer was in residence, she was headed as near to the Berghof as possible. Like them, she would stand at the fence and wait for the Führer to walk down and greet the pilgrims. How considerate he was in this, knowing that people had travelled from all over the Reich just to be in his presence for a few moments. If she'd been part of a visiting BDM group, she might even have had an audience with him. But she was on her own now, coming from a different direction, over the hills.

As it promised to be a sunnier day, she wore a dirndl, sky blue with an apron of butter yellow. Most of the pockets of mud from yesterday's rain had already dried up, but here and there the dark earth squelched beneath her leather shoes and a few times mud spattered against her calves. The forest was all around her. Conservation of nature and the protection of flora and fauna were important points stressed in all the youth group meetings. Now a song about the forest came to mind and she sang out loud, '*in Deutschlands Wälder...*'

All around her, like the keys of the scale, the array of greens worked infinite in variety. The incessant light and shadow play caused new tones to appear. She halted, lifting her face to look at the verdant filigree glowing lime and fern through the forest canopy. If there were any eternity to be spent, it would be easiest in the woods. How rich the earth was, nurturing such trees. The German forest had moved Goethe and Schiller and other poets to pen their praises. She really must read more of them. It would be good for her soul. Indeed, the forest must be the soul of all the German people. Yet it could not be only in the trees, both ancient and fresh; surely it was to be found as well in the very soil, rich and black, and in the tiniest acorn. These too were the essence of the forest. She hummed as she moved forth, sensing the strength of the earth through the leather soles of her shoes.

The path was dry now but still soft. Perhaps she would come upon a deer, like all those times at Alt Eichendorf. Oh, what was she going to do in New York? And would she see Leo again before leaving? It seemed impossible to think that she wouldn't. Being with him had been—like an unfinished composition.

Aside from her footfall on the forest floor, the woods reverberated with their own rhythms. For some time it remained this way. Then, in an off-key crescendo, new notes entered the air. Perhaps it was woodcutters talking, but no, the sounds were too complex; it was many voices, different timbres. Lili hesitated and then kept on. Through the trees came a procession of people, perhaps more than a dozen. There were uniforms and feathered felt hats and a couple of dresses, and, oh! Was it? Yes--the Führer. The Führer himself! Surely she hadn't trespassed? There had been no fence. If she continued on the path, Lili would come face to face with him. She moved to the side and stood still, although, like that of a startled deer, her heartbeat bounded and her breathing was shallow.

She saw that she had been spotted, but it seemed that no one found a girl in a dirndl on a forest path cause for concern. The first SS *Leibstandart*, his face as chiseled as one of the mountains in the Sea of Stones, glanced at her, his lips twitching in a brief smile. The next simply looked. Lili's gaze flew to the Führer. He was even closer than at the rally in Nuremberg. Would he recognize her as the girl who had played the harpsichord for him in 1925? Nonsense.

She watched him approach; time seemed to decelerate, like the slow motion reels at the cinema. She remembered how he had looked at the rally, an emperor surrounded by adoring subjects. Yet the man whom she now saw coming up the path was not the same larger-than-life being as that day. No, here was the stranger she remembered from that evening in Berlin. A simple man of real flesh. She saw the pointed tip of his nose and where the edges were slightly reddened from the mountain air. She saw his forehead, the skin pale. Even closer, she saw a strand of his hair damp against the others and knew this was real, here, now.

Her eyes were burning, her throat swollen. And then he was there, about to pass her on the forest path. She could have reached out, touching him, but instead stood still, each hand squeezing bloodless a thumb. He turned toward her and his mustache rose in a smile. For a moment his pace slowed and it seemed that he was going to say something to her but *Feldmarschall* Göring spoke and he turned away. Then he was past, leaving Lili both light-headed and heavy-hearted. Yes, the Führer had smiled at her. He had seen a young woman in the forest and smiled. There was a certain humiliation in her anonymity. She wanted more than that. She pressed her lips together, taking little notice of the others moving by, only waiting till they were gone so that she could take a deep breath.

As soon as the entourage had passed, Lili set out, veering off the path and into the woods, bushes slashing against her bare legs like tiny whips. Should she, could she have reminded him of who she was? Just who would she have said she was? Not Papa's daughter. Not the child of the man who had long ago stopped his support for Herr Hitler and his plans for the future. And even if she had said that she was the girl who had played the harpsichord for him, the Führer would have thought of Papa—if he even remembered him. Perhaps the Führer did not even recall her playing for him. It all came back to the same thing. Until she became famous for her music, she was nothing. Not to him, not to Germany.

She sank the edges of her teeth into her flesh.

She continued downward through the woods until the taste of blood brought her back and she slowed her pace. At a tree stump, she sat on its weathered surface and closed her eyes, covering them with her heated palms. The dark heightened the sounds: the breeze whispering against the leaves, a cuckoo calling out. Three more days, and she would play for him again. After that, anything could happen. Her breathing slowed and her legs stung where nettles had grazed them. Served her right. She was an idiot. More than that, she was a small-minded idiot. She had met the Führer in the forest and he had turned to her and smiled. She had made the Führer smile! She was one of the most fortunate citizens of the Reich.

Who Are You?

The same officers were there again at breakfast, ready to pull out a chair, pour coffee, even with an offer to butter her roll. Lili bantered with them and the towering manager of the Gasthof. In a booming voice he suggested that Lili join the officers who were heading down to Berchtesgaden.

"You don't have to stay with them, girl, just take a ride into the big city." He raised an eyebrow at the men. "You'll have me to answer to if anyone gets any other bright ideas."

Laughing, Lili agreed, although Berchtesgaden certainly did not fit her definition of a big city.

"Thank you, but I feel quite safe with these gentlemen."

"Ach, you still do," complained one of the officers in mock disappointment. "What are we doing wrong? No frisson of excitement when you see us? Even one of us?"

Lili shook her head.

"No. Perfectly calm and secure," she said, holding back a giggle, as they climbed into the vehicle. "I consider you my big brothers."

As the motor's roar was loud, Lili did not say much during the ride through the countryside, but stole looks above their blue gray collars at the smooth skin of their necks and cheeks, at their varied profiles.

At last they rumbled over the cobblestones into Berchtesgaden, and the buildings changed from sturdy wooden farmhouses to *Bürgerhäuser* with scenery-painted facades and icing sugar window frames. Lili asked to be dropped off at the large square in front of the Schloß.

"Shall we arrange a time to pick you up again?" the men inquired. They seemed disappointed when she declined.

"I'm on holiday," she explained. "I live by the sun, not the clock."

"Well then, remember that the sun still shines at dinner time—and there's only one serving!"

Lili set out. The light was strong on the rosy walls of the Schloß. From outside, the local palace of the Wittelsbach dynasty was not overly grand; it seemed in good taste. Soon she would see the inside, for it was there that the concert was to be held. The innkeeper in Oberau, a fountainhead of local knowledge, had said that ever since the Crown Prince had moved out in 1933, it was a tradition of the government to offer a residency in the Schloß to well-known artists. In this way, the artists could spend all their time creating works for the Reich. Lili looked up at one of the windows. Perhaps one day such a residency would be given to a well-known musician...

The main street was busy with morning shoppers. Uniforms of every shade were everywhere. After all, this was Berchtesgaden. The Führer could probably look down upon it from the Berghof. Perhaps he was sitting outside having a cup of tea right now, surveying this very square with eagle eyes. Lili eyed the people on the street, the men and women and children going about their daily business, walking and strolling and playing. Did they realize how fortunate they were that they could look up at any time and know that their Führer was there, perched high above them like a protector? This reminded her of the painting of him dressed as a knight, a *Ritter* in full armor. It made sense. The Führer was indeed the greatest knight of the realm. Of course he was that too when he was up in Berlin, or anywhere in the

Reich. But here, somehow, it felt different. Here, in the mountainous heartland of Germany, the Führer could be true to his spirit. Like Barbarossa.

Across the street, a store window displayed some mannequins. Lili gaped at the array of designs. Yes, this was most definitely the place to buy a dirndl.

Half an hour later, carrying paper shopping bags, she emerged wearing one of her three new dirndls, the leaf green one with polka dots tiny and white, and a rose-striped apron. The outfit made her feel fresh, in both senses of the word. Now it was time for coffee and cake. Thank goodness a Konditorei was just up ahead.

Here, too, the variety on display was greater than what was being offered in Heidelberg these days. She stood in front of the glass cases, unable to make up her mind.

"Na, Fräulein," a server addressed her, "If you stand here much longer, I'm going to have to put on some Schlagsahne and serve you up as a specialty of the house." The woman pursed her lips.

Lili pointed to a Nußtorte and walked to a table near the window.

Along with the cake, creamy and nutty and perfect, she drained a cup of coffee, a real Mokka. It made her blood move faster. Three more days until the concert. So far, she hadn't practiced; one couldn't count yesterday's half hour teasing the piano at the inn. Instead, she had spent hours tramping about in the woods and now here she was, indulging herself with dirndls and pastries like a dilettante. This afternoon she really should go to where she'd been promised a harpsichord would be available, and spend some hours practicing. For goodness sake, she was to perform for the Führer! And yet, and yet. These were but superficial thoughts that pushed themselves to the forefront. Deep down she knew, she knew with the pulsing of her blood, that she was ready to play for him at a moment's notice.

She sipped some more coffee, put the cup down with a clatter of porcelain. The two older women at the table next to hers glanced across at the disturbance. Lili ignored them and examined her nails. The tips curved white like tiny crescent moons but they didn't need to be cut yet; a thorough filing tomorrow would suffice. She looked up. Through the window she could see three SS officers crossing the street. Their bodies seemed to move in mysterious unison, radiating confidence and control with each step. She drew in her breath. It was true. The Luftwaffe officers were sweet and funny and charming, but nothing more. They were like big puppies, like boys who still liked to play with toys—in their case, giant airplanes. Of course it was interesting work, but what was it they really did for the Reich aside from soar through the clouds above it? No, they were nothing like the SS men. Nobody was like the SS men.

After a silent debate over whether she should have another piece of cake, Lili left the Konditorei, strolling along Marktstraße and Maximilianstraße and in between. The summer breeze felt as light as whipped cream upon her arms and neck, her bare legs. Life could be so simple; a bellyful of cake and the knowledge that soon she would be doing what the Führer had so long ago said was her duty to her country. What joy! It would have been perfect to skip along the pavement; but she was eighteen, not eight. Still, as she walked, she swung the shopping bags a little.

"Lili."

The voice was low, but she recognized the timbre and something inside her leapt in the same key.

"Ach," she said, turning, catching her breath. "It's you."

"Yes," said Leo. "It is I."

She had never seen him in the day. Whereas before, against the lamplight and in the darkness of the night outside the Rosengarten, he had seemed outlined, now, in the mountain brilliance of the morning, his edges were blurred. She could not sense where his boundaries lay, only felt his presence, broad-shouldered, towering, radiating something, she knew not what.

"Heidelberg, Mannheim, and now Berchtesgaden," he said. "May I ask what brings you here?"

This was the first time she was seeing him in daylight and she looked at how the sun was caught in the hair that grew long above his forehead. At the golden contours of his jaws. At the eyes which were looking straight into hers, as if he were looking straight into her.

"A concert," she managed, her throat tight, so that the sound came out a whisper. "I'm performing at a concert in the palace."

Leo glanced across at the building and Lili's gaze went to his lips, then back up. He was looking at her again. A shiver of warmth began in her belly, slid through her.

"Ah, yes," he said, and Lili saw his left eyebrow rise slightly. "That concert." He paused. "*Komplimente*, mademoiselle."

Lili felt the blood rising to her face. So he knew she was performing before the Führer.

With a sudden glide forward, he took the paper bags with the tissue-packed dirndls from her hands, grazing her fingers as he did. The touch left them feeling barer.

"Now that fate has brought us both to Berchtesgaden, let's walk together," he said, and Lili could only nod as if stricken dumb.

For some steps their pace was off beat, for Leo's legs were longer. Lili doubled her timing but that was too fast. She would overtake him in moments, despite her off-balance gait. Glancing down at her, Leo adjusted his step and then, suddenly, like the time signature change from a syncopated 5/8 to 4/4, their pace was matched. She could see the shadow of a smile on Leo's lips, but he said nothing.

Should she make conversation? What could she say to him? Indeed, all the thoughts that swept through her now only succeeded in emptying her mind. Only her senses were left. She saw the faint curve of his high forehead in profile, the straight line of his nose, breathed in a scent of lemon and wood, heard the leather tread of his boots against the stone, felt his presence nearby in the thrumming of her blood. Tasted the dryness of her mouth. No, she could not speak.

They passed through the square with the fountain topped by the upright lion. Two establishments had their wooden tables and chairs and sun umbrellas of red canvas out to profit from the weather, and several customers glanced up over their ice creams and beers as the two of them moved by. For a moment, Lili saw what a perfect picture they must make, she in her new dirndl and Leo in his uniform, and she imprinted it upon herself so that in future she could look back on this sunny day in Berchtesgaden, across the valley from the Berghof. Now she glanced up at Leo. How well he carried himself. Although only a few years older than she, he looked as if he understood the world. How important was music to him—and how had he come to his particular instrument? How often did he play for the Führer? Actually, there were more and more questions that she wanted to ask. Like what did he like to do when he wasn't being an SS officer or playing the viola da gamba. What sort of a childhood had he had in Prussia, and did he have a big family. Where did he live? She parted her lips, but realized she did not know how to begin. Nothing would sound right.

It was Leo who spoke.

"What will you play?"

Now she would have to say something.

"Play?"

Were they to play a game together?

"Oh, at the concert, you mean." She felt her cheeks burn at her mistake. But at least she had found her voice again, and it grew stronger as she told Leo about the *Goldberg Variations* and how it had long been her dream to perform this work for the Führer.

"I was 11 when I first heard Madame Landowska's recording of them," she said as they turned at the corner pharmacy into a quiet lane off the square. Shadows from the press of old buildings cooled the air and they stopped briefly aside a small wall fountain to dip their hands in water. "It was the first time ever that they'd been recorded. My father brought the gramophone records for me in Paris." She could recall Papa's look of anticipation as he had presented to her the shallow box with its lilac bow. "I still remember—the windows in the hotel room were open, the voile curtains stirring in the breeze. When a gramophone had been found, my father laid the record upon it, set down the needle..." She squeezed her left forearm to still the quiver that went through her even now. "I still remember what it felt like..." She paused. "The questioning chords, the searching notes, all of life before me...it bit into me...and it has never let go."

She looked up again to where Leo was watching her with an intensity that was as if he himself were listening to the music. Inside, where he could not see, she shivered.

"After a few moments, I went to the windows and pulled open the curtains. All Paris should rise with the power of Bach! What strength I felt that day. I was only eleven, but all sorts of thoughts were swirling through me. It was then that I decided that even though I couldn't study with Madame Landowska after all, I would learn the Variations." She fell quiet.

"Why 'after all'?"

"My parents had changed their minds about my studying with her. Later, they said I could go when I was sixteen, but then they changed their minds again."

"So you didn't go back to Paris?"

She bit her lip. Now she would have to explain about the move to America. What would Leo think of her if he knew about Papa?

"No..." She didn't know where to begin.

For some steps they continued in silence.

"So you learned the Variations with another teacher," Leo said.

Relief flooded into her as she glanced up at him, nodding.

"Probably best that you didn't study with Landowska, after all. They'd say you absorbed a Jewish interpretation." The muscles in one corner of his mouth tightened, pulling his lips to the side for just a moment. "So," he continued, "with whom did you end up studying Bach's masterwork?"

"A series of teachers, actually, until the advent of Frau Kuhn," Lili said. "She was the best of them." She didn't have to tell Leo about Frau Kuhn's political views. "But mainly I studied them on my own." Lili's tone was matter-of-fact as she shrugged her shoulders. All those thousands of hours of practice had disappeared into the past, were gone forever. "I worked my way through them, one by one." She gave a tiny chuckle. "I wore out two more sets of gramophone records after the one my father gave me."

Leo's eyebrow shot up as he stopped and turned to her. They had reached a small sun-dappled square.

"Mädchen," he said, looking down at her. Even from here she could feel the heat of him on her skin. "Who are you?"

Again that question, the same as when they had parted in Mannheim. This time the reply flew off her tongue before she could even consider it.

"Who are *you*?"

Their eyes met and the square disappeared, the cobblestones beneath her feet were gone. All she saw was blue, deeper than the deepest lake of Prussia, more profound than the ocean, than the night sky. She was losing herself in those eyes. They dazzled her, turned her insides into a mystery and the world into a new place filled with new life.

And then, so strange a thought that she blinked, she needed to know if Leo knew what she had seen. Yet how could words ever say what she had read in his eyes?

From somewhere across the square, a dog barked. Perhaps it had been barking for some time already.

Leo pressed his long fingers to his nape, moved his head slowly so that the smooth cords beneath his neck stood in relief, like sculpted marble.

"I have an idea," he said, his voice low. "Come with me." With only a sideways glance at her, he set out, leading them toward the upper left side of the square. A miniature schnauzer the color of salt and pepper ran across their path, leash trailing.

The abruptness startled Lili. Where was Leo taking her? His strides were so purposeful; powerful like a lion's. Keeping up with him made her breathless. Again she had a flash of what they must look like—the handsome SS officer and the barelegged girl hurrying to stay at his side. Most likely Mama would be horrified at her rushing off with a strange man even if he was a musician as well as an officer, and Prussian to boot. Surely that counted as some kind of introduction. And, after all, she'd already met him--twice. As for Papa... one day in New York he had read aloud from the newspaper about a young woman who had been found strangled in Central Park. He had looked up from the article then, straight at Lili, warning her never to go off with a stranger. Still, even if he understood that Leo was no stranger, Papa wouldn't approve of his uniform.

She glanced over at Leo, at the way his lips sealed themselves against each other. At the way he carried himself, one broad shoulder slightly ahead of the other, as if cutting the air, leading the way for the rest of him. None of her daydreams or memories of him had managed to capture his likeness. She had put the features together in a way that didn't begin to add up to what she was seeing today. Yet she had carried the tone of him with her all these weeks. Again she stole a look at him. He moved like a leader, sure of his territory. A tremor passed through her. Why didn't he tell her where they were headed? It wasn't that she was frightened to follow him. But where was he leading her?

They turned from the square into a street whose half-timbered buildings had surely not changed much since the Middle Ages. Leo glanced over, as if to reassure himself that she was still there, and even though she was moving, Lili felt another thrill course through her, liquid as quicksilver. Near the end of the street he stopped before the entrance to a *Hof*. The two great wood-planked doors with their weathered iron fastenings stood ajar. Wisteria clung leafy and thick to the archway and surrounding walls, botryoid blooms trailing down purple.

Leo turned to her.

"Let's find out," he said.

"Find out what?" she asked, but he was already moving ahead.

She could hear her breath as she entered the shaded passage into the Hof. She raised her chin and followed. The mystery was exhilarating.

In the passage, where several rows of barrels rose in neat stacks, the air was heavy with the flavors of oak and fermented fruit. Inside the Hof, more wisteria hung from the walls, and clay pots filled with leafy plants and flowering shrubs gave the cobblestone courtyard a garden-like atmosphere. Leo opened the entrance to the large, half-timbered house. He was waiting for her at the wrought iron stairwell, one black-booted leg thrust onto a step.

"It's upstairs," he said, and Lili didn't bother to ask him what, although she was trembling.

Colored light flooded the stairwell, glowing through the lead windows in scenes depicting life from earlier centuries. The house must have belonged to a well-established bourgeois family of Berchtesgaden. Intricately grained, the wooden bannister shone golden with the touch of generations of hands. It was strange how she was noticing such unimportant details. Everything seemed heightened, and yet, at the same time, dreamlike. At the landing of the first floor, Leo paused for a moment, turning to look down at her. Lili's heart was thumping so loud that perhaps it could be heard, there in the sudden silence of the stairwell. Then he continued to climb. On the third floor, he grasped the brass door handle.

"We're here," he told her. "Come inside."

With no idea why they had come to this place, Lili entered.

For several moments, all she could do was look out the open windows through the clear sky toward where the Berghof lay hidden within the green folds of the Obersalzberg. It was as perfect as a painting, capturing the enduring epitome of their homeland's beauty. How fortunate were the descendants of that prescient Burger who had built this house. She turned toward Leo, ready to acknowledge such sentiments. He was watching her, his grin spreading.

"So you think I brought you here for the view, hmm?" She didn't respond, and couldn't tell if she was turning red or pale or both.

He gave an odd laugh and glanced across the room. She followed the direction, past the old-fashioned furniture, solid and dark, past the tasseled lampshades and the collection of Bavarian pipes on the wall next to a closed door. What lay behind? She glanced back at Leo. He wasn't focusing on the door. She looked back, and this time noticed the familiar shape that stood near a far window. How had she missed that? A short distance away rested a large, stringed creature.

"There," he said. "That's why we're here." He motioned toward the windows. "That's only the backdrop."

She made her way over to the harpsichord.

"Is this yours? Is this your house?"

Leo laid his hand on the neck of the viola da gamba, fingers long and light upon the strings, and for a moment Lili remembered how it had looked when he'd played; how she had envied the instrument.

"This one is mine. The harpsichord belongs to family friends. They're all in Berlin right now, but I have full use of their house."

"So this is where you're staying," she mused, "all alone." She turned away quickly, leaning over to examine the harpsichord.

"Ach, it's a Hass! Has it been in the family long?"

"I have no idea," he said. "The family history includes several mayors, although I don't think harpsichordists were a part of the line. I recall seeing it some years ago but it seemed to be gathering dust back then. These days it's the young nephew who likes to tinker around on it, pretending he's the next Buxtehude." He grinned. "Old Dietrich's reincarnation he's not."

Lili chuckled, both relieved and disappointed by the casual conversation after the previous minutes of heart-thrilling mystery.

"Last time I was here, I promised I'd bring my gamba along to play some duets with him. But, as I said, the whole family went up north the day after I arrived, so I've been spared." He moved closer to Lili, bringing the scent of lemon and wood. "And now you're here."

And again her blood was thrumming.

"Yes," she said. "I am here."

Through the open windows came the sweetness of the summer air, the light floating. It settled on Leo's brow as he bent toward her. It shimmered in the short distance between them. Her whole world was suffused in radiance.

"Here," Leo said, keeping his eyes on her as he reached behind where she stood. "I must have been thinking of you when I brought along these pieces," he said, presenting the sheet music to her.

Her fingers trembled as she took them, but although she sensed he was watching her, she could not focus on the squiggles of black ink. It was a terrifying, exhilarating thought. If she were to move forward, she could lean her head against his uniform, press her cheek against the material covering his chest, breathe in his flavor, taste it.

He was waiting for her.

She swallowed.

"Is it," he said, "that you play only German composers?" She shook her head; her vision began to clear.

"Mainly, of course, but not only." She forced her attention to the top of the sheet. With a rush of excitement, she saw "Allemande la Singulière" from *Suitte d'un Goût Étranger* swim into focus.

"Marais," she said, recognizing it from the folio she had bought in Heidelberg. "You were playing Marais when I first met you."

Again she saw the transformation in the commanding lines of Leo's face when he smiled, sliding from chiseled presence to warmth and light.

"So this is why you brought me here—to have me meet an old French man," she said, infusing her voice with flippancy and arching an eyebrow.

His gaze narrowed. "Why do I get the sense that you've been expanding your horizons in more directions than one?"

She lifted her chin.

Leo's gaze continued to move over her face.

Her knees were trembling; the quivering threatening to spread. It was the most curious sensation: as if she were cold, but she wasn't, not at all.

"All right then," he said. "Let's see."

Moving past, he pulled out the seat for the harpsichord and gave a brief bow.

"Mademoiselle."

She draped her skirt over the stool. She clamped down on her lip to keep it from vibrating.

"Merci."

Moving over to the viola da gamba, Leo slipped off his jacket and hung it on the chair.

Lili ran her fingers up and down the scale a few times; the sound of the instrument was good and she could find no major fault in the tuning. She waited as he positioned himself, adjusting the angle of the gamba. With a start of sudden understanding, she noticed its carved scroll—a lion's head, mane full. Leo. At last he drew the bow across the strings. As when its call had first come to her that evening in the dark hall of the Stadthalle in Heidelberg, the stroke went deep through her belly, growling.

She watched as he adjusted the tuning, tightening one or two pegs. She could already see him drawing into the sound, his features intent, his eyes darkening and nearly hooded. He withdrew the bow. The loss of the wide, vibrating graze of strands against string brought a sudden absence of energy to the large room. Laying the bow across his thighs, Leo unbuttoned and rolled up one sleeve, then the other. His forearms were long and muscular, gilded with smooth hairs that caught the light like gold dust.

"There are the others," Leo told her. "But let's see what we can do with this allemande."

"Yes," she said. "It's singular."

He shot her a grin and, like a quaver note, the thrum was back inside her. They began.

The opening was almost festive. He led them, an upwards striving toward the wholesomeness of the major key. It was like taking a pleasant holiday walk together along a gently undulating sun-dappled country lane, no stones or shadows along the way. Just the dreamy drift of slivered white clouds and the brush of some birds' wings in the air above as they headed toward a grove of trees suddenly seen in the near distance. It was over too soon.

Keeping the bow in his hand, Leo raised his eyebrows. Lili nodded, pulled out the next sheet. "Allemande La Superbe." Another dance with roots in the fatherland. She glanced over at Leo, who gave her what must have been a sly smile.

She scanned the bars then met his eye again. With a barely perceptible nod, he took them back into the music.

Ah, the richness. Together they stood before a threshold, hovering at the doorsill. Then, almost as if on tiptoe, they entered. Moved through the chamber, explored the fineries of where they found themselves; paused, waiting for each other. Asking. Imagining. Asking. Tiptoeing.

Lili took her hands from the keys, laid them in her lap. Her heart beat faster than the count of the allemande.

Leo raised his fingers to his nape; she could see him pressing into his neck. He almost looked as if he were frowning.

"More Marais, or Bach now?" he asked.

Lili bit the inside of her lip, swallowed.

"I think Marais," she said, so that there would be more of those velvet sweeps of the bow vibrating through her.

"Let's play something wilder," he said, rifling through the sheets on the stand. "Le Tourbillon."

Barely three beats into the bar, the gamba was already raging, the harpsichord the anchor against the swelling swirling crescendoes and turns that were tugging at her, daring her to let go and be swept away. She glanced over at Leo. His upper body had become a part of the churning, his strong fingers fueling the force, hair down upon his forehead, his nostrils slightly flared, his expression fierce. It thrilled her.

The sound disappeared.

Lili blinked, caught her breath. Leo didn't move. Then set down the bow. How wide his shoulders were. He was across the room from her but she could sense the tension of the muscles that held the viola da gamba close to him.

"Now you choose one."

She tore her gaze from him and shuffled the sheets; the room roared with the sound of paper against paper. Her fingertips had never been so sensitive. Each sheet held within it the promise of new sensations, strange voyages into something both inside and outside herself. And so this next one. How fitting.

"La Reveuse," she said.

Leo gripped his chin with one hand, studying her. She sat perfectly still and let him look. Meanwhile, she would examine him. How was it that she had not yet noticed the way his cheekbones pulled his face taut? Or that his brows were several shades darker than his hair?

"And are you a dreamer?" he asked her.

"What do you think?" she asked.

But Leo merely smiled that twisted smile of his and took up the bow.

Already the first slow strokes pulled her toward him. She watched as he leaned closer to the gamba, his lids lowering, and nearly missed her entry, a ripple surrounding the deep slide of the bow. Together they moved upwards. Then it was just Leo again, his fingers moving sure yet soft over the strings, as if in a half-waking dream. Such sorrow, such resignation and then, daring, growing, such hope, over and over again. She watched the mirror of his features. Heard the sharp intakes of his breath, the long sighs, as if he and the wooden body within his embrace were one.

She felt him in the notes, in the chords that coursed and looped, knotting them together without words.

And once, when she had finished her measures, she looked over at him and he was watching her. In his eyes she saw that he knew.

There were no mountains, no valley, no room. Just he, and she.

And the music. For the first time in her life, she could truly understand how much lay within it; music was not only creation. It was wordless discovery.

Strange New Notes

"Duty calls," Leo said, opening the door for Lili to get out of the automobile, gray with a roof that folded back. There was just enough time for her to make it to dinner at the inn and him to get back to town for his officer duties. The evening sky was still infused with a pellucid light. They had spoken little on the ride; Lili sensed that for Leo, too, the music still sounded within. From time to time she had looked over at him, noted the easy way he held the steering wheel, as if he were as comfortable with a ton of metal as with the scented wood of the viola da gamba. Those hands. She wanted to reach over and press her pointer finger against the one vein that rose, pulsing, in the valley near his thumb. Just that one touch. That would be enough; for now. But she had kept her palms on her lap. Once, just as they were rounding a curve that passed through a small forest, he had turned to her. A shadow flickered, cloaking half his face, but she had sensed the way he was looking at her.

Now he stood before her and the black broadness of his shoulders was as high as the mountain crest behind him.

"I'll be here at ten," he said. Glancing down at her sandaled feet, he added, "It would be best if tomorrow you wear walking shoes."

They parted then, their looks lingering like the last note.

Through the entrance hall window she watched as Leo drove past the trees and disappeared, the motor's rallentando fading. She turned toward the dining room but, after some faltering steps, knew it would be impossible to be amidst all the people there. Instead, she climbed the stairs to her room two at a time so that she could sit out on the balcony and watch the mountains and the sky and anticipate tomorrow. She wasn't hungry anyway. Her sleep that night was dreamless.

♫ ♪ ♫

In the morning she was ravenous and for breakfast ate three rolls. Today there were no Luftwaffe officers in the dining room; perhaps they were airborne, looping loops like little boys blowing smoke rings. At ten to ten, wearing a green dirndl with a pale blue apron, her feet in dark brown walking shoes, she went outside to wait. How clear the air was, clean and full of promise. The birds had been awake for hours. An Italian named Resphigi had composed an entire suite inspired by their music. A motor sounded. It rounded the bend, Leo at the wheel. She could tell when he saw her by the way his face changed.

"Mädchen," he said, moments later, grinning. "You look perfect for our outing."

"Perfect?" she asked.

"Look at you." He pointed to her clothes and shoes. "Forest green, sky blue, earth brown. You're the essence of our homeland. Golden sun, too," he added, sliding his fingers over her hair, making her shiver inside. He had touched her again. "Leni Riefenstahl is missing a great photo opportunity. But we're not going to let her know." He put the car into gear. "Today it's just you and I."

There was nothing to say to that, nothing at all, just bliss. Lili settled back against the leather seat, the wind in her face delicious, as they set out for Schönau am Königssee. Once there, Leo bought tickets for the tourist boat. Families and couples passed along the pier in orderly fashion. Two boys horsing about nearly caused a third to fall into the water. Those nearby scolded them, and one man cuffed the first two boys. Then, like an afterthought, he gave the third a smack. It looked like a scene from a Ludwig Thoma story. Despite her sympathy for the boy, Lili had to hold back a giggle.

Gliding across the emerald waters, the vessel paused under an overhanging cliffside while the captain blew a trumpet for the tourists. Echoes sounded across the lake. Next was a folk tune that used the reverberations as part of the refrain, eliciting expressions of awe and enthusiastic clapping for the captain's musical abilities. Leo and Lili exchanged amused glances.

At Sankt Bartholomä they watched most of the visitors disembark and head toward the garden restaurant near the double-onion-domed 12th century church. The Führer had been there recently. As the boat pulled away from the pier, bound further south, the air flowed cool through the open windows. Hillsides steep and raw-rocked slid by. Side by side they sat, Lili closest to the water, her dark skirt grazing Leo's thigh. She leaned her head more to the right so that he wouldn't see her as she stared down at the fabrics touching.

At Salet, they left the boat that would now turn around, for the Königssee ended here; they were to catch a later one for the return trip. Leo had brought along two walking sticks, but the ground was even as they followed the path toward the smaller Obersee.

They walked without speaking. The sticks smacked against slabs of stone, a thumping like mortar and pestle. The sky was blue as in a painting by Cranach, the air honeyed with summer. Woodland tufted the craggy sides of the valley in uneven clumps, the highest points of the firs rising against the bare rock of the encircling mountain chain. A hawk rode the wind. From some Au in the distance where the grazing was lush came the placid chime of cowbells. Wildflowers in mauve and white dotted the grass on either side of the meandering path, and, by a low thicket near a boulder, as if in unvoiced unison, they stopped to lay down the walking sticks, side by side, for they didn't need them in this terrain.

Lili slowed her step so that she could see his profile. Leo fit this landscape with its rugged mountains rising; commanding space, at home in the heights. Yet it was easy to imagine him in the flatlands of Prussia too, striding across the marshes or meadows, the fields of wheat, silhouetted against the setting sun. There was something about his presence that made him seem at ease anywhere. She'd already seen him with Sekt amongst the high officials. He caught her examining him.

"Have you joined the Party?"

"No," she admitted. "I've been meaning to, ever since I turned eighteen. I really should do it when I get back." She bit her lip. Did he think her uncommitted?

They walked on.

"It will help your career," he said as they entered a small grove.

A group of middle-aged hikers appeared round the bend. Catching sight of Leo's uniform, they moved to let the two of them pass.

"A beautiful day," boomed one of the hikers, a large man with knees puffing out like yeast dough over his high gray socks.

Leo turned. "You can say that again."

"A beautiful day," said the hiker, his grin wide as the waist on his Lederhosen.

Lili giggled.

"And at whom might you be snickering?" Leo asked once they were out of earshot. "Him? Or me? Say the wrong answer and I'll get you..."

She narrowed her eyes. She took a step sideways. His hair gleamed gold, his eyes glinted; a lion ready for the chase.

"You!"

And they were off.

For a few paces, Lili stayed on the path. Then she shot out to one side, onto the thick grass that blanketed the ground between patches of rocks. Darting this way and that like a deer, she kept ahead of Leo but could feel his tread behind her, vibrating the earth. Crazy laughter bubbled up, making her weak in the chest and knees.

"I'm getting closer," he roared, and she thought she could feel heat near her neck.

Like a wild horse now, she gathered her energy and ran. She heard her own ragged breath, hysterical giggles rippling through her, weighing her down, but then, with a tremendous surge of power she was suddenly calm, floating, fleet-footed, cutting through the air. She headed to the right, skirting round another gathering of trees.

"You run like you play!" she heard him call from further behind.

She grinned into the wind.

And then she was at the lake, and couldn't help but stop short before the reflections in the turquoise transparency, the mountains mirrored therein. She turned away to face him and her blood went wild as Leo reached her.

"You," he breathed.

She knew he was going to gather her to him and already her body began to go limp.

He reached out a hand and touched her, let his fingers slide down over her cheek.

Surely everyone in the valley could feel her heartbeat; the earth was trembling with it.

One finger trailed warm across her mouth. The faint scent of wood and earth rose from it, and her lips parted.

She could hear, ever so clearly, the trills of a bird's song, the hum of a bee's wings, the whisper of the leaves. She could hear the sounds, but all she felt was warmth as his hands encircled her face, and all she could see was fathomless blue until she thought she would drown in it, and closed her eyes. She nearly gasped at the way her other senses came alive.

This would not be the hasty touch of a schoolboy in New York, nor of a scientist nor drunken student. Leo's would be the kiss of a man who understood how to coax beauty and poignancy from the virgin wood of a viola da gamba. Any moment now, she would feel his lips against hers, gentle yet compelling, his breath sweet. She would open to him. Leo. This was real. She sensed him moving closer. Already the heat of him was flowing into her.

His mouth was soft and warm against her forehead.

Her eyes flew open.

"You," he said, looking down at her.

She blinked.

His hands still encircled her face.

Suddenly they slid over her shoulders, bringing her closer to him. Her arms moved up to find hold, her head against his chest, her cheek against the solidity of his heartbeat. Strange new notes sounded within her, an ancient tuning. A passing breeze rippled the surface of the lake. Lili could feel Leo's breath slow and heated upon her hair and met it with a silent sigh that could have gone on forever.

All She Could See

At some point they realized that they were ravenous. A small Gaststätte near the ferry dock served them fish fresh from the lake, and they sat at a wooden table under the trees, lingering over their green-stemmed wine glasses.

It was hard to remember what only yesterday she had wanted to ask him. All those questions, and their answers, were now so unimportant. All that mattered was being with him.

They spoke of the butterfly that fluttered nearby, wondering about the bittersweet brevity of its life as they watched it wind its airy way into the woods. They smiled at the discovery that each of them found Pomerania an excellent place for a holiday, but otherwise rather dull. Holding them tip to heel, they compared the size of their hands. Leo decided that Lili's looked like a tendril against his paw. Lili protested that his were not exactly paws, but the leonine hands of an artist. To prove his point, Leo encased hers within his. "I could crush it, you know," he told her. "We SS officers are trained well."

"I trust you will not," she said.

Leo told her that he had begun with the violin before discovering the gamba, that as a boy he had imagined running away to the gypsies to learn more. Stories about their devilish ways had never impressed him. Anyone who could play violin like so many of those gypsies did understood both hell and heaven.

Lili told him about the bridges at Friedberg and how she sometimes imagined an evil troll sitting under one of them.

Leo laughed. "It's refreshing to hear that turning eighteen hasn't robbed you of fantasy."

"Of course not," she shot back. "Imagination is one of the most important attributes of a musician, don't you agree?" Before he could answer, she continued. "Just think of it. All those works composed by old men and performed by people decades younger. How can we know what feelings went through them as they created their music? What thoughts of life inspired them?" She was swelling with energy at this line of reasoning; she had never put it into words but it seemed she had felt it forever.

"They had hopes and dreams and ideas that they put into sound. They lived in different times than we do, under different conditions." She was looking at Leo but seeing further. It was exciting. "There may be little we can truly know about how they lived but still we, the inheritors, have to try our best to feel the music so that we can interpret the language of their lives." She stopped short, felt herself blushing.

"And that's why imagination is so important to a musician," she finished, as primly as possible.

Leo's right eyebrow had ridden up. "You do make a convincing case for fairy tales." He grinned across at her sudden frown. "I agree with what you've said. Imagination is without doubt an essential aspect of the musician, but I don't think it should be reserved just for artists." He paused. "Everyone should be taught to foster imagination. And empathy." He picked up his glass. "Nevertheless, an overriding sense of order does compel me to point out one slight fact distortion in your presentation just now." He winked at her over the wine. "Not all composers were wizened old men when they wrote their music. Some had barely begun to live. Think Mozart."

His eyes shone with mirth, as if he were enjoying her search for a riposte.

"Ach," she said at last, pulling at a strand coming out of her braid. "You know what I mean. But tell me," she continued, turning toward him, feeling a rush of adrenalin. "How should a musician feel when playing something that was written in a foreign land by someone he has never met? In a different age? Should he—or she—strive to feel what the composer felt when he created it, or can the feelings be completely new, and unique to him? Does the music speak alone, or is it melted inseparably into the culture and life of its originator? And, does it really matter?" She picked up her glass to steady the palpitations, gave a mock toast and a grin which she hoped was mischievous, not flustered.

Leo bowed his head for an instant then looked across at her, his Prussian blue gaze unwavering.

"I like you," he said. "Very much."

He picked up his glass. "It's a thought similar to what happens when we look at a painting, especially one of the modern ones. Are we seeing what the artist saw or was inspired by, or something else? Each of us carries his own perception of the world within." He paused, looking toward the lake. "Perhaps that's one of the motivating reasons for Degenerate Art." He drank.

"But surely there can be overlaps of meaning..." She couldn't finish the sentence. What did he mean by bringing up that show of art rejected by the Reich?

How lonely life would be if each being felt only what was within him or her alone. Was it only fantasizing that had led her to feel that she and Leo were sharing the same understanding of the music, of life—of each other—yesterday? No, no, it couldn't have been. Surely her imagination wasn't that good.

Perhaps he heard something in her voice. Perhaps he just wanted to reach out to her at that moment. He leaned toward her, sliding his fingers over her hand and its delicate fantail of bones until it disappeared under the warmth of his touch. She stared at the hand, at the way the shadows from the branches crisscrossed it in constantly changing patterns as the breeze passed through the highest reaches of the trees, sunlight flickering in its wake, and saw how the hand met the wrist and became Leo's arm, baked gold by summer. She followed the skin to where it suddenly disappeared under the rolled up white of his sleeve. That skin was connected to hers; she could feel it pulsing, warming, sheltering her very bones.

"We'll make music together again, Lili. In the meantime, don't worry." Those eyes could see into her! He had understood. She couldn't stop looking at him. How was it possible that this certain combination of features could come together to create such a face? He was without compare. Where did it come from, that light in his eyes, that glint that made her know that he was truly seeing her? She wanted to see what he was seeing. But her gaze held his and all she could see was Leo.

On the ferry back, they watched the same green waters and cliff sides, heard the rush of the wake, breathed in its aqueous fragrance. They had left the gnarled walking sticks behind, still lying hidden to the side of the boulder. Perhaps, one day, if no one else found use of them, the wood would return to the soil, nurturing new growth. Leo turned toward her. She was trembling. At times, she could barely breathe. The next moment, she found herself breathing deeper than ever before. Everything was new, and yet, at the very same time, everything seemed as if it had always been.

That Goldberg

The day of the concert dawned pristine. Snug in the featherbed, luxuriating in its softness, Lili gazed out through the windows whose curtains had been left open the previous night. Already the sky was vast, cerulean, blotted out only on the left by towering firs that covered the hillside. For a few minutes the lure of memory kept her abed.

Yesterday, after some hours dutifully practicing the *Goldberg Variations*, she had met Leo for lunch at a charming Gasthof set in a garden-like courtyard, and then they had gone back to the house opposite the Berghof—to make music. Now her heart raced under the feathers, recalling what they had spoken of without uttering a word.

Only their fingers had called forth emotion and idea and something that surely must have to do with the spirit. It was to be admitted that Goethe was right: "The world is so empty if one thinks only of mountains, rivers and cities; but to know someone who thinks and feels with us, and who, though distant, is close to us in spirit, this makes the earth for us an inhabited garden."

Hours later, when Leo had driven her back to Oberau, several groups of Luftwaffe pilots were milling about and, upon seeing the two of them enter the salon, welcomed them. Leo knew some of them. There had been casual conversation and even a few good-natured comments from the ones she had already met, about Lili's apparently preferring SS officers to those of the air. As this was indeed true, she merely smiled, lips closed, a response that had given rise to some more ribbing until something unspoken but merely sensed had made the men stop. Further discourse had been respectful and perhaps even a bit reserved on the part of the officers. How it had come about, she didn't know, but Lili had been relieved, preferring it so.

Later, she had gone to her room, to stand on the balcony looking out at the valley toward the lilac gray horizon with its endless sea of mountains. Closer in, the sky was still alive with colors soft and dreamy. How it must feel to fly across it, not as an airman but as a bird—no, as herself. She would climb barefoot atop the railing, open wide her arms and soar upwards, feel the sweep of the air against her arms and legs, untangling the weave of her hair so that it too would stream in the wind. When she was high enough, she would level off so that she could see the world, more beloved than ever, below. She had stood on the balcony, her fingers pressed against the curve of the wooden railing, as if only they knew to keep her from throwing caution and her shoes away.

She had not tried to fly last night. Now she bounded from the bed to look out the window at the landscape beyond the trees.

There they were. Germany's massive magnificent marvelous mountains; the same as always, and yet today they looked even more majestic. How wonderful was her homeland, how clear the air. Everything was so much more defined. What a glorious day! Papa and Mama and Paul would love it here. Back and forth she ran, from the window to the closet, to the balcony, to the window to take a photograph, back to the balcony for a better one, to the bathroom to brush her hair and prepare for the day. Leo was coming to get her. They would walk along the river together before the concert. She shuddered. Her heart really was going to burst.

Today was at last the day she had so longed for. In just a few hours she would show the Führer who Lili von Rittersburg zu Mertz-Tärnekow truly was. By the end of the evening, the Führer would know that name, and never forget it.

And Leo would be there too. On duty as an officer, but in the audience, watching her, listening to her. Yes, he would hear, and know.

Only a few more hours. And after the concert, he would be at the reception. They could walk together around the large salon, talking to guests just as they had in Mannheim. Except that this time she would be toasted as the soloist of the evening. Perhaps later Leo and she could walk in the palace gardens, under the moon. Perhaps there would be a kiss, a real one, on the lips. Her heart was beating accelerando again.

♫ ♪ ♫

"Are you nervous?" he asked later as they sat on a bench next to the Salzach. This water was different from the flow of the Neckar. Chalky teal, it was wilder, closer to its source in the mountains.

"About what?" she countered, feeling almost giddy.

He gave his twisted smile.

"So, is there anything at all that makes you nervous?" he asked, moving closer to her, his voice low. "Aside from the interpretation of music and art?"

She raised her face. How near he was. She could see the faint line of an old fencing scar on his cheek, just above his chin. The muscles on his neck were taut.

She felt her cheeks heating, and turned to pick up the score that lay next to her on the bench. Instead of saying that it didn't seem real that she would soon have to leave for New York, and didn't know when she would return to Germany, she said, "I have been practicing for this moment nearly all my life." She corrected herself. "I mean, for this evening,"

Leo laughed.

"Don't worry, Lili. You'll be brilliant. Our Führer will be overwhelmed by your Variations." He lifted his hand to her cheek, let his fingers trail along its burning contour. "I know I will be."

Without further thought, Lili took hold of his hand, put it to her lips and kissed his knuckles. Shock at her audacity coursed through her and she looked up at Leo in near panic. But he was already lifting her hands to his own mouth.

"Here," he murmured, kissing each of her fingers. "Here and here. Not that you need any magic spells to make your beautiful fingers fly."

Ah, the delicious warmth that flooded her then. How she would play for Leo. She would feel each and every one of his kisses, and he was wrong. There was magic in them. Magic and delight and anticipation.

♫ ♪ ♫

Dressed in a long black skirt and puffy-sleeved blouse that would show off her arms, her hair in a crown of golden braids studded with tiny wild roses of red, Lili sat at the harpsichord, going over a few passages in the still empty hall. All was well. She was ready. The hall itself was resplendent with the accoutrements of the Wittelsbachers' sense of decor. Aspects of it seemed more baronial than princely, especially the stag heads jutting out from one wall. White roses filled giant vases painted with pastoral scenes. Of course there were also the giant symbols of this age, blood red flags of the Third Reich draped and stately from the ornate ceiling. Beneath them stood row after row of wooden chairs. Lili looked up as a door opened and several officials swept in. As if in choreographed movement, they parted, heading in different directions throughout the hall.

"Heil Hitler," said the one who came straight over to her. It looked as if he had fallen into a pit, or rolled on the shore of the North Sea; everything about him was pale as sand, even his brows and eyelashes. "So you are the charming young lady who will be performing this evening,"

"Heil Hitler," she replied, raising her hand from the keyboard. "I'm looking forward to it."

"Of course. " Then, in a tone of reverence, as if he were giving her a gift, he said, "The Führer has expressed his pleasure at the intended program. "

"I'm honored to be able to perform for him."

"Yes," said the official. "After the performance, you will be presented to him in the great salon." He paused, cast an eye over her, head to toe, as if summing her up. "I'm sure there is no need to tell you how to comport yourself, Freiin." He turned to go. "Heil Hitler!" For a few moments Lili watched him cross the room. How pompous he was.

She returned to the keys. It was somewhat annoying that all those men were in the hall; better to have had a few more minutes alone. How she had longed for this opportunity that was hers by right. No— by virtual decree of the Führer himself so many years ago. Tonight she would at last be able to begin the path that was her destiny: to make music for the fatherland. How far she had come, to be able to do so. Years of hard work, passion, commitment, even deceit. Tonight it would be worth all of that. The Führer would recognize who she was.

And Leo. He too would be there, watching, listening, understanding her need to make music. When Leo looked at her, he seemed to be seeing something she herself had not yet fully discovered. A frisson of anticipation shook her. She would be with him after the concert. Feel his gaze, his touch. Learn more. She could barely wait.

But how strong she was. Like steel in her resolve. There were moments when she was tempted to take the same course as she had in December and not get on the ship, for now there were even more reasons for her to stay here. She could miss the sailing. Yet, if she did that again, it would be turning her back on her family forever.

She breathed in deeply; the scent of roses was slight but sweet. Golden light streamed in through the tall windowpanes. What a moment to savor. Where did one moment end and the next begin? Moments linked together, forming a chain of time that led back to that dinner party at home in Berlin. If even one moment had been different, would the chain have taken a different direction? Under other circumstances, Papa and Mama would be amongst the guests this evening, Mama in one of her gossamer gowns, Papa in an elegant suit. Or uniform. Or, Lili would have a bob, blowing the trumpet in a school band in New York, sending out excruciating blasts, off-key. Or she could be a pastry taster in Heidelberg, round as a Berliner, jolly as jam. A pig farmer in Dieksanderkoog, standing knee-deep in mud and smelling the tang of the North Sea just over the dike. A gypsy fortuneteller with smoky black eyes and the mournful strain of the violin in her blood. She paused. What was it that had led her to be who she was—a member of the greatest nation in the world?

A short, portly older man whose comportment indicated he must have been with the old palace staff stepped into view.

"Freiin," he said, his voice as courteous as his words. "Might I suggest you retire to the room that has been prepared for you. You will find some refreshments have been laid out there for your convenience. We will inform you when it is time for your entrance."

Just before leaving, Lili laid her hand on the harpsichord. Whatever else, it was thanks to this instrument that she had been brought to this moment.

♫ ♪ ♫

The hall was full. Although the summer evening still glowed through the glass panes, candles had been lit and their flickering bathed the great room in a shimmering light. She crossed the stone floor to the sound of applause. She bit down on the inside of her bottom lip to keep herself from peering over toward the seat where the Führer was.

"Nevertheless," the official at the podium said, as the clapping died down and his well-modulated voice filled every corner of the hall, "it was decided to continue with the concert as planned. Our beloved Führer would have it no other way."

"So, without further ado, I present to you the harpsichordist Lili von Rittersburg zu Mertz-Tärnekow. Despite her young age, she has come to the attention of those who are alert to the talents of musicians gifted in celebrating the timelessness of our well-known German composers. These authorities are convinced that this lovely young lady has that," he paused, giving a little laugh, "magic touch."

He cleared his throat. "This evening we are fortunate to have the opportunity to hear a Bach masterpiece performed by this brilliant new star of Germany's shining womanhood." He turned toward Lili and then back to the guests. "If only our beloved Führer were with us. But we all know how he is. For him, the needs of the nation always take precedence!"

He motioned to Lili to take her seat, but she couldn't move.

Her gaze was frozen on what had suddenly swum into focus: the empty chair in the center of the front row.

A numbing wave of disappointment flooded over her, making her shoulders sag and her fingers go limp.

How long it was before she could push her muscles into movement and make the steps needed to reach the harpsichord, she couldn't tell. But at last she sank onto the stool. Like lumps of clay, her hands brushed against the silk folds of her skirt, pushing it about on the seat. Spent, the useless appendages collapsed onto her lap. She stared at them. Had no idea what had happened to so change this evening. The Führer wasn't here. It seemed impossible. She looked up then, out at the blurred aspect of that gorgon creature, the audience. It was waiting for her. There was only so long that she could prepare herself without the audience growing impatient. All those people in front of her hadn't come to see her stare at them or her numbed hands. Her fingers felt lifeless, all the feeling drained out of them in the wake of her disappointment.

She would never play for the Führer. She would return to New York a failure to the fatherland, a stillborn. Already she could hear the restlessness of the audience. They were being robbed of both the Führer's presence and Bach. Yet her fingers were immobile.

Leo. He had kissed each and every one of those fingers. He had looked into her eyes and told her that her fingers would fly. He knew what she could do.

Sinking her teeth into her lip, she straightened her spine. Clenched her fists. Spread her fingers, felt the blood stirring within. Raised her hands to the keyboard. There were no notes in front of her, for she didn't need them.

♫ ♪ ♫

Lili slipped the latch and leaned against the door. Now at last her fingers could tremble, just as her legs were quivering as if shot through with an electric current. She wouldn't be able to stay here long though. They were waiting for her outside. Putting her hands to her face, she closed her eyes. She had done it; alone on a stage she had played the *Goldberg Variations* to an audience.

The outside door opened, bringing in the hollow tapping of high heels against the stone floor.

"So Goldberg wasn't a Jew?"

"You goose," another voice shrieked, cackling with laughter. "Of course he wasn't. There wouldn't have been a performance if he was."

"Ach, I know that." The voice was querulous. "But the music is so complicated. Almost devious, like a Jew. It was too long, too. Are you sure Bach wrote it? Maybe it was that Goldberg after all."

"Ach, believe what you want. By the way, your lipstick's swell. Where'd you get it? Did you see what Frau Schmittberger's wearing?" Again there was that shriek of laughter. "Now that her husband's been transferred and left her here, she's sharing more and more of herself."

"Finished? Let's go get some more Sekt. Thank God that concert's over." Swishing of fabric, footsteps, door, and then silence.

That was all that could be said? 'It was too long... Thank God that concert's over.' What ignorant women. Her playing had been sound. And Bach wasn't devious—he was a genius! How could anyone listen to the *Goldberg Variations* and not be amazed?

She had performed the entire *Goldberg Variations* without notes, without any mistakes except for one sharp deep in the 16th Variation. All in all, it had been a superb interpretation of Bach's brilliant masterwork. And she had done this without the Führer being there.

Yes, the Führer hadn't been there, but even that disappointment couldn't change the fact that she had performed in Berchtesgaden.

Her name would be known. One day, somehow, she would play for the Führer. The future belonged to the youth of Germany, swift as a greyhound, tough as leather, hard as steel, and anything was possible. It was impossible to say this too often.

"Is everything all right, Fräulein?" asked another voice, and Lili remembered that the *Toilettendame* was also there.

"Yes, yes," she called out. "Everything's fine."

Heil Hitler, You Lovebirds

Birdsong woke her. Sunlight streamed through the open windows, warming her bare arms. Pointing her toes, Lili stretched her legs into the air and kicked off the quilt. Today was the last day. Tomorrow morning she would take the train back to Heidelberg and only a week later another one to Hamburg. There wasn't a moment to waste. She scrambled out of bed. Leo was picking her up in less than an hour.

By the time she got downstairs, he was already there, outside, standing with his back to the window, looking toward the mountains. Lili paused at the window. It was crazy delicious to think that the man out there, tall with Prussian bearing and an air of knowing the world, that such a man—masterful musician, SS officer, wanderer, good-natured prankster, knee-jellyingly handsome, with a touch so gentle—was waiting for her.

"A fine example of German manhood, isn't he?" said a voice nearby. She turned.

An older SS officer, tall, wide, and with a wealth of ornamentation upon his shoulders and chest, stood near the newspaper rack, holding an open copy of *Der Stürmer*. His expression was benign.

"Ach, you've caught me out," she admitted with a grin. "He really is wonderful."

The officer smiled. "Our young men are the best in the land. Carefully chosen from among thousands of aspiring candidates. So many hope to become SS officers, but our standards are rigorous." He used the paper to motion toward the window. "That fellow is a particularly fine specimen indeed. I've known him since he was a boy. If he has any fault, it's that he's too sensitive. No room for that in the new Reich." He eyed her. "Is he your young man?"

Lili pressed her lips together to keep from bursting out with a great grin.

"I'm not sure."

"Hmm. I understand. You need to ascertain if you're his girl before answering such a question. That's wise."

Lili didn't reply. She glanced outside to where Leo was beginning to pace. She should go out to him now.

"Ah," the officer suddenly said. "You must be the young lady who gave the concert in the Schloß last night."

Lili nodded. "I am she." How that sounded—a mixture of pride and amazement.

"Well, then, it looks like a match made in heaven," he chuckled. "Just make sure you both keep your feet on the ground. Von Witzleben needs to have all his wits about him."

What a strange man. Lili raised her hand.

"Heil Hitler. I must go," she added.

"Heil Hitler," said the officer. "Run along now. He looks as if he's wondering where you are."

With a parting smile, Lili hurried out. Her steps sounded on the gravel and Leo turned, stepped forward to meet her.

"You look like you have a secret," he said.

"I did hear something good about you just now," she said, quickly, to still the sudden shock of fear that he had found out about New York and Papa. "An officer who seems to have known you since you were a boy. I met him inside—" her cheeks burned, because of what he had said about Leo and her— "and he told me that you're actually quite a nice fellow."

"Hah, yes, that must be SS-*Oberstgruppenführer* von Preigenlitz. Our families have known each other forever. He's a good sort."

"He seemed very pleasant."

"Quite. He gets along with most people. Last night he told me he's being transferred to Prague. A promotion, it seems."

"There's so much going on, all over the Reich. There's so much enthusiasm with all this reunification. It's very exciting," she said.

Leo turned toward the automobile.

"Speaking of exciting, I have a special day planned. Come on, your carriage awaits you."

They headed east. The wind, summer soft, flowed over them in the open vehicle as they passed along tree-lined roads set in valleys of a green so lush that it seemed a new quality of light should be named.

"My father told me that Goethe spent years working on light and colors," Lili announced, and then bit her lip. Would he ask about Papa now?

"He did," Leo said, his hands easy on the steering wheel. "In fact, some of it brought him in direct opposition to Newton."

Lili wrinkled her brow. History was not a strong point. "Didn't they live at different times?"

Leo shot her a sideways grin. "True, but I was speaking more in principle."

She didn't feel humiliated or embarrassed. "Explain."

"Despite, or perhaps because of Goethe's deep understanding of human nature," Leo said while changing gear, "he felt that it's impossible to express the inner nature of a person or thing. He said that all we can do is gather the effects of this being's existence—these outward manifestations will form a picture of the character."

That sounded like how music was. "What does that have to do with Newton?" She had learned a bit about Newton in school. Aside from gravity, Newton had discovered that, under certain conditions, light focused through a prism creates a rainbow. She had seen this a thousand times in the chandeliers at home.

Leo turned the automobile to the right. "Goethe didn't get the same results in his experiment with a prism. But instead of looking at the differing conditions, he simply wrote Newton off. Very strange behavior for Johann Wolfgang, who was otherwise generally open-minded and rational."

What would Papa say to that? She had never heard anyone speak of Goethe in such a familiar, almost flippant manner. And yet there was no disrespect in Leo's tone. It was more as if he felt so comfortable with Goethe that he wasn't in awe of him.

"So," Leo continued, his voice clear above the motor, "it seems that Goethe's pride tripped him up. He might have had some truly great insights about science making mankind more perceptive to the world around us. But he did have an excellent point about theory vs. experience."

The image of Benno flashed before her. "But isn't that what science today is doing?" Lili said. So often, Benno had pointed out to her to really look at something. He was a scientist. It was odd how Benno had spoken of Goethe's poetry while Leo, an artist, chose to address Goethe's science.

Leo glanced over at her. "Sometimes it seems as if today's science is trying to force us through a prism. But I'm not sure if everything will come out rainbows."

"Well, one thing I love about Goethe is his descriptions of colors and how they change, especially blue and yellow. Like the sky and sunlight," she said.

"So, where are we going?" she asked, even though it made no difference. The concert was over, she was free. She would be perfectly happy to spend all day driving nowhere with Leo.

"You'll find out soon," he said.

She settled back against the leather upholstery.

Indeed, it wasn't too much longer and they turned onto another road. "Salzburg", read the signpost. Within minutes, they were pulling into an enormous square pale as chalk. Leo parked the automobile at the far end. Elegant horsedrawn carriages stood along the perimeter, their drivers liveried. Many of the buildings surrounding Kapitelplatz were festooned with flags brilliant in red, white and black, resonating an aura of importance and power, making Lili thrill. She straightened her back. Now she would walk the lovely old streets of Salzburg with Leo resplendent in his uniform.

Their first stop was the birth house of Mozart, an airy, parquet-floored apartment where the young Wolfgang Amadeus had first experimented with sound. Lili tried to imagine him there, younger than Paul and already playing a violin. What a life of chaotic creativity he had led. Later they ambled along the cobblestone streets, ducking into a shop for a handful of creamy *Mozartkugeln* wrapped in silver and blue foil. On one of the squares, a great market was set up, with a string quartet playing to one side, and Leo and she passed among the pots filled with flowers whose aroma nearly overpowered the flavors of foods drifting over from nearby stalls. They stood at a stand and ate sausages and rolls, grinning at each other over mouthfuls. A fleck of mustard stained her blouse but she only laughed. Velvet-curtained shops studded with violins and flutes beckoned, and they entered through creaking doors to choose musical scores for their own instruments. Lili bought a small marble bust of Mozart for Paul. Who knew where his life would lead? Without doubt, music would be an essential part of it. Perhaps he would take up the violin from Papa. And where was music leading her own life? Someplace wonderful.

Coming upon yet another chocolate shop, she picked up gifts for Tante Aletheia and the others at Kornmarkt. For Mama and Papa she would find the right thing in Heidelberg. Leo took the packages from her. Across the street, a shop was being boarded up while a policeman stood by. They stopped to watch as an eager HJ boy, his mouth twisting with effort, dipped a brush into a bucket of black paint. "JUDE", he wrote on the planks of wood. It reminded her of how Paul had put the blocks together to form a word when he was only a baby. But of course this boy knew better what he was doing.

They turned the corner in silence and came upon a horse and carriage.

"Let's take it," said Leo, holding her hand and helping her up.

As the horse moved into a trot, its shining rump jounced from side to side, tail swishing like a feather boa. Salzburg slid by in a blur. Leo's arm lay next to hers. She could feel the two limbs pressing into each other over every bump. She drew a deep breath. Was this what was meant by bliss? It was odd how everything else in the world lost its urgency when she was with Leo.

"That's the museum," he pointed out. "There's an intriguing 360 degree painting of Salzburg and the outlying countryside. Would you like to go inside and see it?"

Lili shook her head. Leo gave his twisted smile, took her hand between both of his, as if holding a small creature, and ran his thumb along her wrist for a few moments. Then he stretched both arms out on the backrest. Lili stared out into the pastiche of pastels that was Salzburg under the late afternoon sun.

At last they descended, halting before a large *Gartenhof* with music floating forth from a billowy pavilion. Dozens of guests were seated at the rows of tables, while others danced in the space in front of the orchestra. Most of the men here were in uniforms, the women in dirndls with colorful bodices and aprons. Strings of lights hung from the trees like slumbering fireflies waiting for the night.

"Next time, we'll take in an operetta," said Leo when they were settled at a table smack in the midst of the others. It almost seemed that the waiter wanted to show them off.

"I've never been to one," Lili admitted. "Only operas."

"We'll have to change that then. There's nothing quite as delightfully light as a good operetta. And nothing as horrendously heavy as a bad one," he added.

The waiter brought their glasses of cool Grüner Veltliner. The wine was as refreshing as fruity water, yet there was an underlying bitterness in her mouth.

Next time, he had said. When would that be? He knew that she was returning to Heidelberg tomorrow. But she hadn't told him about next week. She kicked at the gravel under the table, sending up a faint cloud of dust on one side. No, she wouldn't think of that tonight.

"Mademoiselle," Leo was saying. "Would you care to dance?" The orchestra was already playing the opening bars of Strauss's *Rosen aus dem Süden*.

"*Avec plaisir*," she said, as coquettishly as she could, so that her tone would mask the almost painful anticipation.

Threading their way through the maze of tables, she followed him to the dance floor. Two hands met, the others found their places at waist and shoulder.

"Heil Hitler, you lovebirds," interrupted a young man with a camera up near his freckled face. "I'll take a photograph of you and have it back here tomorrow. I'll never win in Lotto, but speedy service is my motto." His expression was so beseeching that, laughing, they agreed. Leo pulled her closer and Lili leaned her head against his shoulder. The bulb flashed.

'And then they were gliding off into the swell of the dancers, sweeping and turning and sailing to the strains of Strauss, more dizzying than champagne.

No past, no future. Only this moment.

And the bright burning within her.

They danced into the shelter of an arbor of roses, and, when there was nowhere left to turn, Leo drew her to him.

Oh, the Shame of It

"In the morning I will take you to the train station," he said, much later, when they parted at the Gasthof in Oberau.

She could barely speak. Words were intruders in the swollen silence that linked them. If only they could make music together now, right this instant. How they would play this time—the harmonic dissonance of their polytonality would render the previous times but the sound of a white plain. Now there would be landscapes of brightest tone color and passacaglias of soaring heights and valleys most profound, of iridescent waters with free form unfathomable. Oh, if only they could play together again before she left.

Instead, he kissed her again.

♫ ♪ ♫

And then, a sleepless, agonizing night later, she was on the train. Leaning over the half open window, white handkerchief between her fingers, waving, watching Leo in his SS uniform grow smaller and smaller until he was just a speck of black and then gone.

For some time she stood at the window, letting the gathering wind flow over her. The air was still near enough that it was the same that Leo was breathing. But the wagons moved on, into the valley that ran along the Salzach, and with a violent jerk she pulled up the pane. Immediately the rumbling of iron wheels over the track was muted. She was alone in the compartment.

Leo had placed her suitcase on the overhead rack. She reached up to touch its handle, then sank down onto the green velvet seat. The train passed through a grove of trees, shading the pane so that her face was reflected upon the glass. Was it the lighting or did her features really look as drawn as that?

From the traveling bag at her feet she took out a sheet of music, stared at the notes, laid it aside. Put it back into the bag. Looked out the window. Unbuckled her shoes. Slipped them off. Slipped them back on. Buckled them. Looked out the window at a farmhouse. At a cow. Two horses.

Just yesterday Leo and she had sat in a horse drawn carriage. Already it seemed so very long ago. At the same time, it was only a moment ago that he had kissed her under the night sky, the scent of roses in the air. She could still smell them. Taste him. How was this possible? What was time?

Which brought her straight to the gaping abyss of all the thoughts that she had been avoiding.

What a mess she had made of things. During all these days, never once had she told Leo that she was returning to New York next week. Although she had at last confessed that she had spent some years living there, she had allowed him to infer that this would remain in the past. And she had allowed him to infer that Papa had gone to America to do important work for the Reich. When she said that, his eyes had narrowed a bit but he had said nothing.

If Leo did not pass through Heidelberg in the next few days, neither would she see him again, nor would she have the option of telling him the truth.

For some utterly mad reason, she now felt impelled to do so.

She bit the flesh inside her lip. The patch was already raw from her gnawing on it most of the morning. Leo had asked for her address, to call on her when next he would be in Heidelberg, and she had given it. But because he was always on the move, she had no way of contacting him. What would he think if he arrived and she was gone, gone so far away that it might as well be that she did not exist for him?

Which brought her to that other awareness that she could barely bring herself to acknowledge.

A knock, and the door opened.

"Heil Hitler," said the conductor.

Lili swallowed.

"Heil Hitler."

"All the way to Heidelberg today, young Fräulein," said the conductor, punching her ticket. "There'll be a dining car from Munich on."

"Thank you. I'm not hungry."

When he was gone, she turned back to the window. They had come down to lower lands, passing through fields and meadows; the great mountains had faded. Further and further away the train was taking her. Away from Leo, from happy days in Berchtesgaden. From the Führer. And there it was, that terrible awareness.

It had been a disappointment that he hadn't been at the concert. But it had not been as crushing as she had first imagined, because someone else had been there to hear and watch her. Knowing Leo near, all she could think of was him. When they had played music together, all she wanted was him.

Her eyes burned, her nose was stuffy. A welling pain built in her chest and she was still reaching for the handkerchief as the sobs burst forth. Oh, the shame of it.

She had forgotten the Führer.

For some time she wept, the wheels beneath her rumbling and turning and syncopated, a rhythm without respite. What a weakling she was. What a weakling. What a weakling. On and on the train went.

She sucked back the liquid in her nose, pressed the damp cloth to the swollen skin beneath her eyes. A chill passed through her. No wonder the Führer hadn't been there. She didn't merit it. She had been thinking only of herself. Her name, her fame, and Leo.

A wave of nausea swelled. She shut her eyes, tasting bitterness.

♫ ♪ ♫

"Darling Lili, it's so lovely to have you back," said Tante Aletheia, enveloping her in a green-sleeved embrace in the foyer of the house on Kornmarkt. Fragonard was there too, winding about and pressing himself against Lili's ankles. She bent to pick him up, rubbed her cheek against the fur of his jaw.

"He too has missed you." Her gaze green and direct, Tante Aletheia eyed Lili. "Freshen up, and then we can talk over peppermint tea and your favorite cake. I have so many questions."

Once upstairs, Lili opened the door only slowly, so that she could take in the room where she had spent so many months planning and looking toward a mythical future. The familiar smells of music sheets, pamphlets and books, of clothes and knickknacks, of everything she had been living with for nearly a year, flooded over her. Together, they were the scent of hope and meaning, for the fatherland, for the Reich and her role in it. If only she could have bottled it to take along.

FATHERLAND

PART FOUR

Season of Discontent

It Is All So Painful

It is easy to lose track of time, here, along the wooded banks of the Hudson. The soft scents of summer drift through the elms and beeches, casting a spell of contentment and ease so that it is enough simply to lie on the ground and doze. Birdsong is drawn out and dreamy, bugs buzz as if in afterthought. Wildflowers and grasses bask in the sun, their earthy perfumes enmeshed in its lingering rays. Occasionally Lili opens her eyes to watch a wisp of white high above, but even the clouds are too charmed by the air to do anything other than continue their stately floating, and soon she is asleep again.

Yet her dreams are not of here. Even as her body curves against the warmth of the woodland shore, it is another land that calls to her. A land of meadows brushed with velvet blades of grass, a land of countless lakes, cold and clear, of hills patterned by thousand year-old vines, of forests dark and deep, of red gables and cobblestones, of earth that trembles with the step of a million marchers. And, sensing the silent soil beneath her is not of that land, Lili shudders and awakes.

Her watch reads nearly five o'clock. It is time to make her way to the cottage. Later they will pick up Papa, who arrives on the 18:12 from

Grand Central. That complex is one of the few in New York that Lili admires, because of its colonnades, like that of the Brandenburger Tor. If she cheats a little, she can imagine that Mama, Paul and she are in Alt Eichendorf and Papa is coming from Berlin for the weekend. But she does not want to do this because then she will have to think about all that has been left behind. Again.

When Papa is there, dining is more formal than during the week, when it is only the three of them. Then they eat quite early, often putting their food into a basket and finding a spot along the sun-dappled river for a picnic. Just the other day they sat on an old wooden pier; that pleased Paul enormously. His tiny fishing rod hung over the side, but Lili was glad no fish was hooked. Other times, they dine on the terrace between the turrets. It is odd that the owners call the place a cottage, as it seems modeled on a Tuscan country estate complete with a fountain spouting up from the middle of the courtyard. It must be an American figure of speech. Papa enjoys taking meals on the Italian marble terrace overlooking the Hudson, but tonight they will be eating in the dining room. Lotte has already laid out the settings, and the crystal and silver sparkle as meticulously here as they do in the city.

Lili walks along the gravel path that skirts the river, rewinding her braid as she goes. Tiny wildflowers drop out of her hair. She catches one in her palm and blows on it, sending it out onto the breeze. The petals hover before her and then the flower swirls away toward the trees. For a moment she envies the fragile white its freedom to go where it will. Life is repeating itself; it seems that she is fated to long for what she cannot have.

Yet it has been meaningful, these past weeks, to be together once more as a family. She is glad for all the moments. Nestling up against Mama, inhaling her special scent; having conversations with Paul—ones in which he is able to articulate five-year old thoughts; and walking with Papa to look at the wild geese on a nearby pond. During the week, Mama, Paul, and she giggle and play hide-and-seek in the garden, tramp about the forest while singing songs that Lili remembers from when she herself was five. They pedal their bicycles and roll in the grass and occasionally drive to the nearest village to eat ice cream at the soda fountain. On weekends, Papa comes home, his briefcase filled with silly trinkets: a mother-of-pearl fan for Mama, for Paul a wide-eyed wind-up monkey clapping tiny brass cymbals in his paws, a necklace of South Sea shells for Lili.

There is a dreaminess to it all. After the first day of questions about her studies, Tante Aletheia, Heidelberg, and her music, neither Mama nor Papa has asked her what she did or saw during the past year. It as if life had taken up from where they left off before her departure. Papa and she play duets on the piano and the four of them laugh over cards and board games, or speak of deer and rhododendron and hot air balloons. All of this has in a way been wonderful, but it as if the world at large no longer existed. It as if life—her real life—had suddenly stopped. And she does not have a key to wind it up again.

♫ ♪ ♫

They are to take a horse and buggy excursion in the early afternoon, over the gentle roads that skirt the valley's potato fields and apple orchards, along the shaded paths that cut through the profusion of forest. Later they will have a picnic. Everyone but Lili is busy. Mama is scrubbing Paul's hands, black under the nails from the construction of a mud castle. He can't stop talking about the *Suppenkaspar* who refused to eat his soup and died of starvation.

"He was a silly boy. I always eat my soup."

Lili smiles. Paul is so pure and sweet in his earnestness. What a darling. She is glad that Heinrich Hoffman's stories are still part of the family tradition. Her favorite tale was always that of Pauline and the matches. Little Pauline never listened to anyone. They warned her not to play with matches, but she did anyway. One day, when no one was at home, she took them out, played with them, and burned to a crisp.

Lili wanders through the house. Passing in front of the study, she sees Papa at the desk, a pile of papers before him. Although it is the height of summer, his face has the pallor of winter. His forehead is lined with concentration. Papa seems to work most of the time, even when he is here with them. Just like in the city.

Mama said that the house owners are traveling in Europe, buying paintings for their apartment in Manhattan. She says that Papa and she are thinking about building their own summer cottage, somewhere in a forest near the river or a lake. It would be a simpler place than this, but peaceful. It would remind them of Alt Eichendorf where they spent so many happy days.

Lili's insides knot up at the thought of yet another break with their homeland. Building a country house in America means that Mama and Papa must plan to stay away forever.

She turns the corner and comes upon Lotte carrying the picnic basket. For a moment they stand in front of each other. When Lili was little, she and Lotte would often make such an encounter in a hallway into a game, each one blocking the other's passage until both burst into giggles and Lotte would swing Lili up in the air as she shrieked with laughter. Now Lotte moves to one side.

"It's a beautiful day for a picnic," she says.

Lili looks into Lotte's eyes. "Paul is looking forward to it."

"I'm sure he is." Lotte continues to stand alongside the wall.

Her tone suddenly annoys Lili. What is this attitude that Lotte has these days? If she were still in Germany, Lotte would be lucky to even have a job. If she were in Ostmark, she would be cleaning the street with a toothbrush. But Lotte is here. Because of Papa. And Lotte's luck is Lili's misfortune.

"Did you boil the eggs properly?" Lili asks. Her voice carries an undeniable timbre of haughtiness.

At this, Lotte's eyes widen, then her face tightens. "Yes, Fräulein Lili. The eggs have been boiled just the way I've always boiled them."

"That's good then," Lili calls over her shoulder as she continues down the hall, her legs strangely weighted.

She can sense Lotte's gaze on her but wills herself not to turn around.

During the afternoon, she plays chase with Paul in a meadow, lets Mama braid her hair, and tries to pay attention when Papa tells them about his latest real estate venture, blocks of houses in the middle of nowhere.

"But the trains pass by, and sooner or later there will be a stop. Then there will be a community that lives in the country and works in Manhattan." He smiles with satisfaction. Papa has been right about all the other ventures; undoubtedly this one too. Of course he is always right about everything. Except one thing; the biggest in their lives. Lili bites her lip and looks out toward the Catskills. Once again, Germany lies far behind her.

It is just after dinner, before dessert, when Mama leaves the table to take a sleepy Paul up to bed, that Papa clears his throat.

"Lili."

She looks up from her whipped cream and strawberry cake, freshly baked by Lotte this afternoon.

"Yes, Papa?"

"I would like to address a matter which gives me some concern. Perhaps you will be able to set my mind at rest."

Is he asking her for advice? She puts down her fork.

"When we gave you permission to spend a few months in Germany," he begins, and Lili winces at the implication that the other months were without their permission, "it was our understanding that you would revisit aspects of German culture that you have missed these past few years. Schlagsahne included." For a brief moment he smiles. "You would strengthen your language skills and enjoy the natural beauty of the fatherland. You would get to know your great-aunt Aletheia and, unexpectedly, even have the opportunity to study at a famous university." He pauses, and Lili senses that the crux of the matter is coming now.

"We knew that we were letting you return to German at a most disturbing time. Aside from concerns about your personal safety, which we would have no matter where you might be, we were especially aware of the social changes that have beset the country these past several years." His eyes find hers.

"Yet we have always relied on your upbringing and good sense to prevail. We have always felt that you have within you the ability to choose correctly between right and wrong."

Lili's muscles tighten and she glances over at the golden clock on the wall.

"Therefore, when I sit at my desk and overhear you speaking with insolence to someone who has been a faithful part of our family for longer than you have even been alive, it makes me wonder what else you took with you from your stay in Germany."

Lili feels the blood surge into her head.

For long moments, the only sound is the ticking of the clock.

At last Papa makes a sound something like a tired sigh.

"Your silence says enough. So. Arrangements have been made for you to begin your studies at Barnard College." He looks at her but doesn't pause. "It is a college affiliated with Columbia University. The American system allows students to explore several areas of study before committing to any particular field. I believe this is the way of the future. One must broaden one's outlook and knowledge to better understand life's interdependencies and consequences. Your application has been accepted, and you will enter the college in September."

Her head feels as if it were on fire.

"I never applied!"

His eyes dart to the side for a moment. "That is true, Lili. The application was indeed completed without your knowledge. However, you were not here at the time."

Again the insinuation of her disobedience. Well, she isn't going to insinuate anything.

"Why didn't you write and ask me, Papa? In fact, why didn't you write to me at all?"

Papa's shoulders move inwards a fraction.

"There wasn't enough time for an exchange of correspondence or we would have missed the deadline." He clears his throat softly. "In filling out the application for you, I took the liberty of using paragraphs from one of your letters to Mama. You spoke of wanting to play an active role in your country, and of how you aspire to do great things, whether large or small. Apparently your enthusiasm was convincing enough for the Admissions Board, even if your grades were not overly impressive."

Her mouth is open.

"But I was talking about Germany--"

He cuts her off. "Lili." His voice is calm but firm, as if he were willing her to stay composed. "It is my belief that you require a full regiment of activities to broaden your base. For some time I considered enrolling you in the Juilliard School of Music, but then decided against this. You are already a talented musician. More attention needs to be paid to strengthening your humanistic education. At eighteen, you have shown that you are not yet the best judge of what path to take. That is why I had to act in haste."

Lili's throat is dry. Her limbs feel bolted to the chair.

"Like it or not, your future lies here, Lili," Papa says, leaning forward on his seat. "In America. It is the land of opportunity, and for those who have ambition and intelligence, there is no limit to the successes possible. I was right to bring our family here.

"The Germany we once knew has disappeared. America is a nation that grows greater each day, and it owes this greatness not to might and repression, but to the spirit of freedom. Here, as in no other land on earth, you are truly free to make your own life choices."

Lili speaks, acidity in her words.

"If there is indeed such true freedom here in America, then why are you always making the choices for me?"

Papa remains silent.

"You're a hypocrite," she says. "You talk about freedom, about free will, yet you tell me what to do. You say that you still love the fatherland, yet you want nothing to do with it. A hypocrite. You've taken Paul's freedom away too, making him an American."

His face takes on a pained expression.

"I was there, Papa. I wrote to you and told you that your accusations about the Führer are false. He's not ruining the country. To the contrary!" She is so tired of having to repeat this to him. "I saw them, Papa. I was there in Nuremberg too, with thousands and thousands of others who are proud to be German, who love him and want to help him build up the Reich." So she has admitted to going to the rally. And she is proud of it now. "I have friends who are doing important things for the Reich because they see that the Führer wants what's best for everyone. It's about much much more than the Führer alone." She stops short. Papa is watching her with an odd expression. He makes her feel like such a child again. Yet she is no longer a child, even if he has had the effrontery to enroll her in college. She brushes that impertinence aside to deal with later.

"You still don't understand what I'm talking about," she continues. "You're here in your own world and have no idea what's really going on over there." It is like being in a nightmare, the same words, over and over again.

"You," says Papa, "are like a thirsty young mare trotting earnestly forward toward the water. Unfortunately, your blinders do not allow you to see the poison being poured in further upstream."

Lili blinks back her fury, but there is venom in her voice.

"And *you* seem to spend all your time here listening to Jewish lies. From the ones who left. They're the only ones who say bad things about Germany." She is breathing fast. "That's just because the Jews in Germany are finally getting what they deserve for having done such awful things to the country to begin with. Even American Jews don't like the German ones, and don't want them coming here. I heard that on the radio yesterday."

Papa makes a gruff sound. "It's apparent that I have been inadequate in clarifying things to you over the years."

"Since we left, you've never had anything good to say about Germany."

"Ah my dear, you are so very mistaken. I still love the fatherland, even when, year after year, that man continues to turn it into something it should never be. His relentless harassment of Jewish Germans is only one particularly ugly and disturbing facet. He wants people to be afraid that Jews everywhere are plotting to take over the world. That *The Protocols of the Elders of Zion* is real, even though years ago that inflammatory text was proven to be a fraud, a conspiracy theory hoax."

"That man. Why can't you ever call him by his name? And why can't you understand that almost everyone is happy to have the Führer?"

Papa looks past her. "To begin with, even Hitler had the sense to know he wasn't the messiah. But as he watched the masses, he realized that he could easily transform himself into what they, the desperate and deluded, wanted. And that they would follow him wherever he chose to take them." Now he looks straight at her. "His henchmen will do his dirty work. Already we have the terrible outcome. Germany has lost many of its best and brightest to this casting aside of the Jewish. And, in the process, it has lost its right to be called a civilized nation."

Lili rolls her eyes.

"You should remember that not everyone is happy to have *the Führer,*" he says, stressing the name. For a moment his mouth tightens, as if he had tasted something bitter.

"Austria is not the first nation to be invaded by the Nazis, Lili," he says. "No. It is Germany itself."

Now she gapes. Papa's thinking is even more warped than she remembered. It is all so painful.

♫♪♫

"Lili," Mama calls from where she sits on the terrace, her delicate fingers pulling off the tough fibers of a heap of fresh beans. Paul is curled up asleep on a nearby canvas chair. "Have you seen Lotte?"

"Not since this morning before Paul and I went on our walk." Lili sits, hoping Mama will not ask her to go in search of Lotte. It is more and more uncomfortable to be around her. It is the way Lotte looks at her, as if Lili had done something wrong. But there is nothing for which she should feel ashamed. Those words about the eggs the other day, why, she was just showing Lotte that she is growing up and taking on her rightful role as daughter of the house.

Mama stares out at the rolling landscape on the other side of the Hudson. Is Mama too remembering the hills of Germany?

"I worry about Lotte," Mama says, her voice soft, as if Lotte could overhear. "No matter how much she urges her sister, Berta simply refuses to leave. Lotte is afraid for her."

Lili shrugs. "Nothing will happen to her, Mama. She's just a simple *Hausfrau.*"

"A Jewish one, Lili."

"Even so. What could she do or say that would upset anyone?"

Mama picks up a bean from one bowl, pulls the pale thread off, drops it into the other bowl. "Lotte is very close to her, Lili. She wants to know that Berta and her family are safe."

"I'm sure that if they obey the laws, they will be." Lili too picks up a bean, snaps the top off, and strips it of its seam. She throws the cleaned bean into the bowl, examines the rejected spine, snapping it open and shut like a tiny whip, and then tosses it back into the other bowl.

Mama's brows meet. "There seem to be so many laws in Germany nowadays. How is one to remember them all?"

"They get posted, Mama," Lili explains. "You can read them on walls and buildings. And in the newspapers too. It's everywhere. Everyone knows what the Jews are not allowed to do anymore."

Mama's fingers stop moving and for a few moments she stares at the vegetable in her hand. Lili too pauses, but when neither speaks, they resume their labor. The beans plop into the bowl, one by one, an efficient system. There is something comforting about working together like this in such a simple task. No need to think, just do. Separate the good from the useless. It is fulfilling in its own way.

♫ ♪ ♫

From where Lili is nestled between two boughs, the view is soothing. Best of all, nobody can see her. She takes an apple out of her skirt pocket, pats the cloth to make sure the letter is still inside, and bites into the fruit. Sweet and sour at the same time. It is a relief to sit here, high up in the branches. These past days have been strained, what with the news from Germany that made Lotte cry and turned Oskar more silent than usual.

A few days ago The Great Synagogue in Nuremberg was demolished. Not that Lotte's sister or anyone from her family was there, and in any case, none of them are the religious type of Jew, but Lotte was very upset about what she called the disrespect shown to Jews in Germany. When she finally managed to tell Papa and Mama what had happened, she kept glancing over to where Lili sat on a sofa, as if, in some mysterious way, Lili herself had something to do with it. It was rather annoying.

"What has it come to in Germany that a synagogue is destroyed and the government says nothing? That the government itself commands it." She said this as if she were not expecting anyone to answer. "What would happen if a Jew burnt down a church?" Then she laughed in a rough and rather disturbing way.

Lili could have told Lotte about Father Charles Coughlin and his new group, the American Christian Front, in which Catholics and Protestants are uniting against Jews. Would it comfort Lotte to know that Germany isn't the only place that doesn't think highly of Jews?

Lili takes another bite. In its own way, the Hudson Valley is quite beautiful. Just last month there was a big international conference in France convened by President Roosevelt. Over thirty countries attended, to discuss what to do about the hundreds of thousands of Jews who have decided to leave the Reich and are looking for visas and entry permits to all sorts of countries. After all, no one in Germany cares where they go, just as long as they get out. But who wants them?

A black bug scuttling along the tree bark stops to unfurl its tiny cape-like wings, revealing an undercoat of brilliant red, then soars, landing on Lili's knee. It is so light that she cannot feel its passage until it arrives at the more sensitive skin of her thigh. She watches it for a few moments, then leans forward, making sure to maintain her balance so high above the ground. Lightly, lightly she blows against the creature until once more it opens its wings and flies away.

For eight days the delegates debated about which countries would be willing to take in so many Jewish emigrants. In the end, despite feeling sorry for the people looking for new homes, no country was willing to increase its annual quota of immigrants. No governments want to increase the number of Jews in their countries. Except for Costa Rica and the Dominican Republic, who said they will take more as long as some Jewish American committee pays them millions and millions of dollars for doing so.

The big question is what can be done, now that it is clear that nobody really wants the Reich's rejects. True, most of the Jews brought it onto themselves with their greedy ways—still, it is not actually their fault that they are not Aryans. Apropos that. Lili throws the apple core into the air and reaches into her pocket.

The postmark and date are blurred and the envelope looks as if it had been carried overland across mountains and through deserts by a hundred sweaty hands. Tante Aletheia has forwarded it to her. A letter from Benno.

There has been no letter from Leo.

There are a dozen possibilities as to why this might be so, but only one satisfactory one. That Leo hasn't yet had the time to go look for her in Heidelberg.

Benno writes that he thinks of her from time to time—which can't be too often as since leaving Germany he has been endlessly busy. First of all, he had to hurry to catch up with the other members of the expedition, who were already in Calcutta. From there it was a train ride far to the north, to Gangtok, in a land called Sikkim. Then, on the auspicious day of the summer solstice, they set out for the highlands with an entourage of dozens of porters and colorfully decorated mules and horses. He writes that despite the hardships of the journey—heavy rains from something called monsoons, bringing mudslides, more mud, and leeches—he is exhilarated. He and SS Officer Dr. Beger are ready to begin their studies of the people inhabiting the Himalayas. While Beger will examine them from an anthropological perspective, Benno has brought along his microscope and slides and instruments for blood taking. It is there in the Himalayas that solid evidence of millenia-old Aryan supremacy will be documented. And he, Benno, will be at the forefront of it. He closes in haste, explaining that a report is being sent to Berlin and that her letter will have the honor of accompanying it in the postbag.

Lili runs her finger over the stains on the paper. Because of this letter, in a small way she too is a part of what is happening over there, so many thousands of kilometers away in the east. She remembers Rektor Wüst's lecture about Aryan ancestors becoming aristocracy in the Himalayas. She looks out over the valley where high in the distance the brushstrokes of clouds could be mistaken for a chain of snow-capped mountains. How small the world and the struggles of humanity must appear from such summits.

For some moments, this thought brings relief. But soon enough the seething frustration is back. Even if she gets a letter from Leo, what then? No kisses can be sent through the paper, no more duets can be played. The mystery of being that their music was unlocking is unrealized. She rocks back and forth on her perch, whispering the nursery rhyme into the breeze. *Ach Du lieber Augustin...alles ist weg, alles ist weg.* Everything and everybody that meant something to her in Germany is gone.

And now Papa and Mama expect her to enter Barnard and start a new life in America. This is her punishment for disobedience; the one she knew was coming.

If only she could stay up in the tree.

Poor Paul

"Did you meet anyone interesting today?" Mama asks as Lili slips off her jacket. "Surely you had time for some socializing outside of classes." There is a note of pleading, irritating, in her voice. Now Mama is trying to get her to become friendly with her classmates at Barnard. Papa has forbidden Lili to return to the German-American Cultural Club. Life has become a nightmare of repetition, this time without even the haven of York Avenue.

However, as it goes, she hasn't spent much time in college yet, for after the summer holidays both Paul and she were down with influenza. She missed the first two weeks of classes. If she does anything at all, aside from losing herself in the harpsichord, it won't be socializing, but catching up. If she falls too far behind, it will be almost like classes in Heidelberg. At least English is not as sophisticated a language as German.

She tucks a wisp of hair back behind her ear and looks at Paul, who is concentrating his efforts on placing neat forkfuls of cake and whipped cream into his mouth. How sweet he is, her little brother. So innocent. She gets up to hug and kiss him as he munches. Mama pours him some more cherry juice, and coffee for Lili and herself.

"I might have, Mama," she says, "but if I did, I didn't notice."

"I know it is hard, Lili." Mama sighs. "But you are so talented and diligent. I am sure that among the students of Barnard you will come to find a friend here who appreciates you." All this is worse than a nightmare of repetition. She doesn't care about having friends.

Papa comes home and Mama tells him that Lili might soon begin to feel at home in America. That surely such a lovely young lady will eventually find fulfillment here. Lili's cheeks burn with the absurdity of her statements.

Papa listens, his gaze soft.

"Your Mama is always thinking about you. You are fortunate to have such a loving mother."

"I know, Papa." She glances to where Mama is smoothing Paul's hair. Mama is always thinking about her children and Papa. Her world is so small.

"That reminds me," Papa says, rising. "Let me see if I can find it." Mama and Lili exchange glances. While he is out of the room, Paul tells them about his day at kindergarten. He can already reach the bell because he is the tallest boy in his class.

"Here it is," says Papa as he returns with an open book. He thumbs through the pages. "Ah, now listen well, you immigrants.

"'What, then, is the American?'" he reads. "'A mixture...which you will find in no other country...an American, who, leaving behind him all his ancient prejudices and manners, receives new ones from the new mode of life he has embraced, the new government he obeys, and the new rank he holds...here they are incorporated into one of the finest systems of populations which has ever appeared... Here individuals of all nations are melted into a new race of men, whose labors and posterity will one day cause great changes in the world.'"

Papa looks pleased. "This was written by a former Frenchman in 1782. Imagine what he would see in America today: a great melting pot of people."

Paul looks as if he were going to cry.

"But what is it, darling?" Mama asks.

"Please, Papa," Paul says, his voice quavering. "I don't want to be melted in a pot. Can you tell them I'm already a real American boy?"

Lili turns away. Poor Paul. She bites her tongue. Let the Americans believe what they like. In the end, the world will see that it will not be as Papa's American Frenchman claims. It will be the German Reich that causes great changes in the world.

Out in the Open

Another New York autumn is upon them. Lili sits at the harpsichord, her fingers moving through the first movement of C.P.E. Bach's Sonata in B minor. Papa and she used to play this together. Of late there is something different about him. Often when he looks at Lili it makes her feel as if he were examining a stranger. It is disconcerting.

She will play it alone. Now she hears every note. Feels every missing one. Remembers Berchtesgaden and Leo and how it felt to be filled with both hope and happiness. For a few moments her blood stirs. Her life is like the leaves outside. Once green and filled with the sap of new life, she too is drying out. And when the autumn rains beat against the windows and trees, the dead leaves will turn gray and wash away, just like all the dreams she once had.

♫ ♪ ♫

Today the air in Central Park is cool and earthy. Around the sea lion pool there is the added tang of salt. Papa, Mama, Paul, and Lili head out of the zoo and west, toward The Tavern on the Green for afternoon coffee and cake. Paul wants to take a nearby horse and carriage, but Lili can see that Papa and Mama would prefer to walk.

"If you get tired, I'll carry you *Huckepack*," Lili assures him, knowing how much he enjoys riding on her back. "Although I'm not sure how much longer I can carry you. After all, you're the tallest boy in your class."

This makes Paul stand up even straighter, his still babyish haircut glowing golden in the autumn sun. As he sets out, gamely striding along the pathway, his chest pushed forward, he reminds Lili of the rows and rows of little boys marching with pride for the Führer. Paul too would be proud to become a Pimpf one day. She turns away.

The park is filled with a jumble of people, with baby carriages, dogs and kites, with vendors selling refreshments.

"Breathe in the air," Papa urges the three of them, taking a breath that is deep and dramatic. "Aside from being full of oxygen, this is the air of freedom. Look around. Every person here is free to walk in the park and enjoy the same rights as everyone else."

Knowing full well that he has said this for her benefit, to make yet another point, Lili nonetheless obeys him, glancing at some of the people nearby. Americans, yet all so different from each other. Blond, brown, red, black hair, both frizzy and straight. The clothing, too, signifies varying origins, as well as economic backgrounds. America is indeed a hodgepodge of humanity.

"Get your hotdogs," a vendor calls out. "Kosher hotdogs here!" They turn toward the sound and watch the young man expertly spearing sausages into buns, adding mustard and sauerkraut before handing them with an occasional professional smile to the small crowd of customers gathered around his cart.

"I like hotdogs but I want cake more," says Paul, and skips on ahead while Mama starts off behind him.

Papa and Lili watch the vendor.

"That is a perfect example of America's liberty for all," Papa says. "Come, Lili, let us walk at a slower pace." They walk in silence for some steps.

"It is a sad but true fact," he continues, "that here too not everyone accepts the Jews. Even in America there are clubs and hotels that bar them from membership. They might do it subtly, but they still keep them out. Just as in Germany, there are even universities that have quotas for Jews. American discrimination against Jews restricts their presence in education, jobs, and even housing. Here too there is resentment and prejudice."

Lili does not respond.

"Yet there is a great difference, Lili. A publication such as the *Christian Century* can make the erroneous claim that America is a Christian nation, and thus permitted to be indifferent to Jews, saying they deserve God's punishment for their treatment of Jesus. And because this is America, they are free to print such rubbish." He glances at Lili. "I must catch my breath. Let us stop for a moment."

They pause under a magnificent tree whose great branches are ablaze with leaves of amber and tangerine.

"But," Papa says after some moments, "another publication is free to point out the mistaken and morally reprehensible views of that magazine—without fear of government reprisal. And that man back there is free to sell his kosher hotdogs in the middle of Central Park and anyone who wants one is free to buy it. He is free to marry anyone. Not everybody likes him or wants to be his neighbor, but no one will ever take away his citizenship. There will never be Nuremberg Laws here, Lili."

For a moment, he stares at her with an odd expression, as if he had never really seen her before. Then he says, "That is one of the many differences between America and today's Germany."

Lili kicks lightly at a clump of gravel.

"There don't have to be Nuremberg Laws in America, Papa. From what you just told me, Americans are perfectly able to keep Jews out of wherever they don't want them, but in a backhanded, dishonest way. In Germany I heard people say that a lot of Jews are glad about the Nuremberg Laws because everything is neatly stated, out in the open, with no room for doubt or error. Ordnung, Papa. Everybody in Germany likes order."

Papa grimaces. "It is undoubtedly true that there are some Jewish Germans who prefer to live apart from gentiles. Probably from other Jews as well. There are always fanatics, Lili, in every religion. But do you really believe that people want to be told that they cannot sit on a park bench?" He looks ahead to where Paul is running along the gravel. "Do you think they appreciate being told that their children cannot play in the same parks as other children?" Eyes cobalt blue, he peers at her, and again she has the sense of him seeing a stranger. "That men in black uniforms have the right to deny human freedom?"

"Hah!" she says, glaring back at him. "If America is such a perfect example of freedom and equality, then why are there so many places, especially in the south, that have separate facilities for black and white people? Why are black people kept apart? It's just like for the Jews in Germany." She snorts.

Papa takes a deep breath. "You are correct, Lili. There is still much room for improvement in America. But because it is a democracy, change can—"

Lili interrupts him. "That 14th Amendment you praised so much is just—"

A wail pierces the air. Mama calls out.

"Erwin! Paul is hurt!"

Papa and Lili break into a run and Lili reaches them first. Paul is still on the gravel, his left arm looking odd with an extra angle.

"Aua aua aua," he cries.

Papa arives, looking ashen, and while onlookers gather, he and Mama manage to scoop Paul up.

"Go find a carriage!" Papa calls to Lili.

She turns on her heel and runs to where a short while ago they passed the waiting carriage. It is still there. Lili hesitates, unsure whether she should ride in it or run back.

"Didn't you get a carriage?" Papa fumes when she returns on foot.

"Yes, it's coming."

His face is plum now, Mama's pale. Paul looks gray as he lies in Papa's arms while Mama gently keeps the little arm in position. Lili stands alone, clutching her elbows. Finally they are all in the carriage, the horse trotting toward the doctor's office on Park Avenue. Paul whimpers.

"Paulchen," Lili exclaims. "If we had known you wanted to ride in a carriage so very much, we would have taken one right away. You didn't have to go and break your arm for it." She forces a smile and a giggle in his direction.

Paul stares at her, his blue eyes liquid with more tears, and his bottom lip quivers. "My arm is broken?"

"Lili!" Papa is almost shouting. "What are you doing?"

"I'm trying to make him laugh," she says.

"Ach, child," says Mama, "I don't think he feels like laughing right now. Can't you see that?"

At the doctor's office Lili sinks down into an armchair in the waiting room. It seems as if she waits for hours; no one comes out to tell her anything. Through the thick door she can hear Paul shrieking, and she squeezes her fingers into fists, chomps upon her inner lip. Poor little Paul. The silence is sudden. She looks out the window at the tree in front of the building. She hears Papa's voice and sits up, expecting the door to open. But it is silent again and the door stays shut. Do they think she doesn't care? Perhaps they believe her still too young to be truly concerned about Paul. Have they forgotten her? Perhaps they believe her too old now, an outsider. There is a touch upon her shoulder.

"Come," says Mama. "We can go now."

"How is he?" Lili asks.

Mama gives a weak smile. Lili sees lines around her mouth.

"He will be fine. The break is not as complicated as they had initially feared. But setting it was very painful for him."

Now Papa comes into the waiting room, Paul in his arms. Her brother's eyes are closed, the shadow of his lashes darkening his cheeks, and, for a moment, Lili is afraid. She doesn't want to lose him, ever.

"They gave him some medicine to make him sleep." Papa sounds tired and strained, but at least his color is nearly normal. "So that they could finish putting the bones back into place."

The ride home is hushed, all three watchful as Paul breathes and occasionally wrinkles his brow. Then they are at the apartment but everything feels different. Squeezing her elbows, Lili stands in the doorway of Paul's room while Papa and Mama kneel at his bedside, watching over him.

After a while, Lili whispers good night and they answer her but she knows that their attention is on Paul. She understands, but when she goes into her room there is a new sense of aloneness.

Lili Decides to Be Someone Different and Mama Wonders about Mankind

By Saturday afternoon Paul is well accustomed to his encased arm, admiring the drawings with which some of his kindergarten classmates have decorated the cast. A fire has been lit in the salon. Mama is at work on a new tapestry that looks as if it came from the Middle Ages. How it is humanly possible to have so much patience with such fine and detailed work is a constant source of mystery to Lili. But if anyone can do it, it is Mama. She seems to have infinite patience. Papa puts his newspaper down.

"Lili, it has been a very long time since we played together." He looks at the harpsichord then back at her. There is deep sadness in his gaze. "I have missed it. We used to understand each other so well through music."

The regret in his eyes moves her even as his words call Leo to mind.

"Yes, Papa. Let's play some Bach right now." She rises, leaving her still unopened book on the seat.

Papa gives a strange little smile and they go to their instruments. His violin is quite out of tune. Lili wonders if he has played at all this past year while she was gone.

Finally, they are ready. As a first piece, they have chosen an old favorite from Six Sonatas for Violin and Harpsichord, the Sonata in B minor. As ever, the phrases pull at her, and, as the piece progresses, Lili is filled with an indefinable sadness.

The first movement finishes. Papa's bow lingers on the strings.

Paul begins to hiccup, giggling at the same time. Mama apologizes for the interruption and says they will go off to the kitchen for a spoonful of sugar. In the meantime, would Lili please go to the bedroom and get her another spool of gray thread, most likely from the top drawer on the right.

Lili leaves Papa standing next to the harpsichord, violin in hand, lamplight softening the shadows on his face.

In the bedroom, Lili goes to the cupboard, rummages around in the drawer. It is filled with her parents' handkerchiefs, some delicately embroidered by Mama, others discretely lined or plain. No spools of thread to be found here. Just to be sure, Lili opens another drawer. This one has papers in little stacks. She picks up a heavy cream-colored envelope with a German postmark, March 1937, to Papa from Tante Aletheia. A light blue envelope marked with her own handwriting lies underneath, one of the letters she sent to Papa. Beneath that is a plain white envelope. She picks it up. It is unsealed. She opens the flap and pulls out the photograph.

It is as if her heart's blood suddenly surges upwards through her chest and into her head.

The photograph is clamped between her fingers.

She stares at it.

Leo looks up at her, and he is more beautiful than she can bear.

For some moments she cannot understand this photograph and why it is in this drawer.

Slowly the figures come into focus. She recognizes the dirndl. She remembers how it felt to lean her head against Leo's chest. The flash of the bulb.

This is the photograph taken on their last night in Berchtesgaden.

How did it get here?

Still staring at it, she sits on the bed.

Its presence here means that somebody sent it. The only somebody that could be would be Leo, who must have gone back the next day to get it from the photographer. Which means that Leo wrote to her. But no letter came to her.

She jumps up, searches the drawer for the right envelope. It is not here. Only that white, empty envelope.

Sinking her teeth into her lip, she stands in front of the cupboard. There are several possible scenarios. Leo went to Heidelberg. He didn't find her, but he met Tante Aletheia and discovered the truth. He gave her the photograph as a parting gift, asking her to send it to Lili. But if Tante Aletheia had sent it to her, then she would have received it in a letter. And no letter from Tante Aletheia had this photograph in it.

Which means that Leo must have got her address from Tante Aletheia, and sent her the photograph himself.

So why didn't she get it?

The answer is obvious; inside her erupts a new rage born of betrayal.

Papa never gave it to her.

A sudden tremor shakes her. Where is her letter? She storms out of the room and down the hallway back to the salon, yet when she speaks, her voice is deadly quiet, glacial.

"Where is the letter?" she asks Papa, who is plucking a string with a light touch. Mama and Paul have not yet returned.

Part of her registers that Papa has the decency not to deny it.

"Ah," Papa says, glancing down at her hand that holds the photograph.

"The letters."

Letters? Leo has written to her more than once? This knocks the breath out of her.

"How many letters?" she asks, her throat swollen with distress. "How many letters are there?"

"Three," says Papa, and slowly sits down in a nearby armchair.

Her jaw tightens.

"Which one of my letters had the photograph in it?"

It is crucial that she know. If it was in the first or second, then the next would be wondering why she hadn't written back. If it was in the last, then the photograph was a farewell.

Papa jerks his head. "I don't recall, and it makes no difference. My daughter and an SS man." He looks aside. "Your behavior is more disappointing than I can express."

Lili stares at Papa. "That's exactly how I feel about you." She sits down opposite him. "Where are my letters, Papa?" Her voice rises. "Where are my letters?"

He looks at her then, his color ashen, his voice uneven.

"When the first one came, I picked up the envelope to take to you at the summer house. But then I noticed the emblem, an eagle and swastika. Lightning bolts. My daughter gets mail from the SS?" He shakes his head. "That was a Monday. I put it aside for some days. It could be related to her music, I told myself. It could be about her music. But that Friday, two more envelopes arrived, all of them with the same sender. Then I sensed that they weren't music related. I opened them. Found the photograph. Threw the letters into the trash. I didn't tell Mama either. I wanted to forget about them, and I tried; but I cannot." He looks exhausted from his confession.

Nausea churns through her. "Did you read them?"

Papa shakes his head again.

"No. I didn't read them. They weren't mine to read."

Lili bursts out with a laugh, harsh as a witch's cackle.

"They weren't yours to throw away either! Or to keep the photograph from me!" Her face contorts. "Why did you keep it if it's so distasteful to you?"

Papa swallows, his Adam's apple sliding against his throat.

"You may think me unjust, Lili. But how do you answer to consorting like that—with an SS man?" His eyes look old. "Who have you become?"

For some time she is silent, ignoring the fact that he hasn't answered her own question. The blood is racing through her head. She will not sully Leo by telling Papa anything at all about who Leo is, nor even about his music.

"I thought I was already discovering that, Papa." Her tone is calm, cadential. "But from now on, I am going to be someone different."

♫ ♪ ♫

Just how she is going to put her plan into action takes some days.

On the surface, she goes through all the motions necessary for ensuring that none of them, neither Lotte, Oskar, Paul, Mama, nor Papa, will know what is going on inside her. She has become an expert at hiding her emotions. But all the while, she is preparing.

"How were your classes today?" asks Mama, looking up from her embroidery. The gray thread was eventually found in her old sewing bag, and the tapestry is growing in shades of bleakness. Once she begins adding burgundy it will surely revitalize. From another room comes the sound of Paul demonstrating his ability to blow a toy harmonica as loudly with one hand as with two.

Lili takes a calming breath before she speaks.

"In history class we learned that we'll be going on a field trip to East Hampton the day after tomorrow, to visit the site where one of the first witch trials in America took place."

Mama raises her eyebrows.

Lili continues.

"The area is also rich in American history about the early settlements, the Indians, and slaves too. And the hurricane," she adds for good measure. "We're going to look at what the hurricane did last month."

"Is that safe?" Mama asks. "There was so much destruction. And loss of lives."

"Oh yes," Lili reassures her. "We won't be going anywhere that's dangerous. But it will be a very long day."

"It does seem a rather far way to go for a field trip." Mama lays down her embroidery. "We visited a business associate of Papa there shortly before you returned. We even went swimming in the ocean." Her voice begins to trail away. "It is important to see where historical events have happened. They can give us inspiration, or make us hope that history does not repeat itself." Lili nods, her stomach knotting.

Yet Mama is not finished. Her voice is dreamy.

"I remember walking through Versailles, knowing that it was there, in the Hall of Mirrors, that the deaths of so many good men of so many nations were simply signed away. After all those years of fighting, the world was suddenly at peace again." Her gaze is clouded, as if she really were seeing the great halls of the palace. "As I passed through the royal rooms, I wondered why it is that mankind must continuously be at war with itself. Why so many are born only to die at the hands of their brothers..."

The nausea is rising. Lili gazes at this person who gave birth to her.

"Mama," she says, holding on to the back of the chair and swallowing. "I'm so glad that you're my mother." Then she moves over to Mama, whose delicate features are elongated by a look of surprise, and bends to kiss her, inhaling the scent of mother, holding it in as long as she can.

"Why darling, you look pale!" Mama holds her hands out to her. Lili stares at the graceful fingers whose touch, all her life, has only been soothing.

"Mama!" The call comes from the other room where the toy harmonica has fallen silent. "Mama!"

"I'll be right back, darling," Mama says to Lili, smiling as she rises.

Lili nods. "It's all right, Mama. I'll come with you." They find Paul holding the harmonica to Bella's muzzle. Lili kisses her brother's forehead and presses her cheek against the softness of his.

"I'm so glad that your arm will be fine, Paulchen. You are my little treasure. Always remember that."

His tiny teeth whiten his smile.

"And you are my big treasure," he says to Lili.

Then she has to hurry out of the room because she knows she is truly going to be sick.

By dinner she is able to sit at the table with the three of them. Mama smiles occasionally, and Paul giggles as Papa tells them about his day, but Lili isn't listening to his words. When she was young, his voice, gentle, low and even, meant safety; it was the loving sound of reason and reassurance.

Today it is but the sound of the past.

PART FIVE

In the Fold

Missions

Lili stepped off the gangplank. She was back.

The pain of the darkest hours of the Atlantic passage dissipated with the swish of red, white, and black against the brilliant blue of the sky above Hamburg. There was only one thing to do before abandoning herself to the relief of arrival. The cablegram was short: ARRIVED STOP WILL WRITE STOP LOVE COMMA LILI. Then she climbed onto a train. With only one bag, she traveled light and needed assistance from no one. Where she was going to sleep that night was still debatable. Before embarking on the ocean liner, she had posted a letter to Papa and Mama, telling them not to worry, that she was on her way to Germany. Her tone had been apologetic but not remorseful. They should accept her as an adult. And for an adult, the words of Goethe were to be taken to heart: "Every human being must think in his own way."

It was likely that upon reading the letter they had telegraphed Tante Aletheia, expecting Lili to go to Heidelberg. In this they were correct. Rather than Berlin, it was indeed Heidelberg to which she was going home. Whether or not Tante Aletheia would take her in—that was to be seen. Yet even if the door were slammed in her face, something Lili could hardly imagine, she knew that she would be able to manage on her own. This time she had money, enough to last quite a while, for before leaving she had sold the necklace of black pearls. If still in her right mind, surely Großmama would have understood, if not approved. Then, too, when Lili wasn't performing, marching, studying, or doing whatever else it was that she was going to do from now on, she would earn money by giving music lessons.

By the time the train pulled into Hauptbahnhof, it was dark. She peered out the taxi window. Here and there, the street lamps highlighted the facades of buildings and glass storefronts that had been so familiar but now seemed dreamlike. Was she really and truly here again? Exhaustion was taking hold. By the time she got to the entrance of the house at Kornmarkt, she felt as if she were floating. She rang the bell. Her heart was beating faster, and despite the contingency plan there was a genuine worry. What if, out of respect for Papa and Mama, Tante Aletheia really did refuse to take her back?

The door opened.

"There you are." The voice was the same. "Come in out of the cold."

And then Lili was inside and there was Tante Aletheia, wrapped in a striped jade shawl and holding Lili at arm's length, looking into her tired eyes with her own piercing green ones.

"Young woman, you have again done a great deal of mischief." Lili could feel herself swaying with the effort of standing upright but she bit her lip. Tante Aletheia's fingers pressed into her upper arms as if trying to measure Lili's pulse right there, and all the time she kept looking at her. At last she let her hands drop.

"You should get some rest. We will talk tomorrow." Her voice was calm and reassuring and all at once Lili was ready to collapse. But before that, she needed to say something.

"We can talk tomorrow, Tante Aletheia, but I can already tell you this: I am not going back."

The green eyes glittered. "I know that, dear," she said. "Indeed, I was wondering when you would return."

♫ ♪ ♫

There was a telegram for her from Mama. HOW COULD YOU LEAVE WITHOUT EVEN SAYING GOODBYE QUESTION MARK.

It was a bittersweet but rather silly cablegram. If she had said goodbye, she wouldn't have been able to go.

While in some ways it was a distorted repetition of December, this time there were major differences. For one, this time she didn't feel the same guilt as before. Even if Mama didn't understand all the reasons why she had left, Papa certainly would, although she doubted that he would tell Mama about the letters. Because then Mama would blame him, and that would hurt her too much. So Lili too would keep that reason secret, and write a different letter to each of them.

To Mama she would talk about needing to come home. She knew that Mama longed to be here too, so certainly she would understand that. With Mama she could be more apologetic for, truly, she was sorry that she had hurt her and left with a lie, without a good bye. But with Lili living here now, there was always the chance that they would eventually make the trip to Germany to visit her. She would hint at that too. To Papa she would say that she could not bear to stay where she was treated like an incapable child. She was an adult now. In case Mama read her letter, she wouldn't directly remind him of Leo's letters, but he would understand what she meant. She would tell him that she wanted to be in the country where people appreciated her for what she believed in and what she could do. In any case, both Mama and Papa could find solace in Paul. As for Paul, from now on she would send him cheerful postcards from Heidelberg and wherever else she went in Germany. She would make sure that he still had a link with the fatherland.

And she would do her best to look ahead, not back.

Over mid-morning coffee it was decided that Lili would stay in her old room, fortunately still available, but that she was expected to be more communicative with her parents from now on. After all, if she wanted to be treated like an adult, she must behave like one. Lili could finally take a deep breath that didn't hurt. And she could finally ask the question whose answer she already knew.

"Tante Aletheia," she said, pouring them each a second cup of coffee. "Did Leopold Arnim von Witzleben come here?"

The eyes glinted. "You mean the well-spoken SS officer who was shocked to learn that you had gone off to America?"

Lili looked down into her cup and bit her lip.

"Didn't he write to you?" Tante Aletheia asked. "He took your address. Said he was going to be traveling a lot in the coming months."

"I suppose I should tell you the whole story," Lili said, and began. If Tante Aletheia thought less of Papa after this, it would not be Lili's fault.

♫ ♪ ♫

In the afternoon, she went to re-register at the university.

This time it was easier. However, there was a nasty surprise—in truth, not that much of a surprise—when she was informed that unless her work improved this semester, she would be out.

To console herself, Lili stopped at Schafheutle for cake. There were fewer varieties than before the summer, and they didn't taste as good as before either. But the Schlagsahne was delicious, and she slathered it on. She would do her best with her studies, but that was all she could do. If by the end of the semester she was no better, then, well then, she always had her music. And not being at university would free her to put all her efforts into that. Just because she couldn't keep up with classes didn't mean that she was stupid.

Feeling slightly sick from the sweets, she left the Konditorei and headed home. The autumn air was crisp. At the corner of Floringasse, a Party official held out a lottery box, his cape spread out over its sides like a tent. All the proceeds were slated to help welfare organizations. Perhaps some good luck would cheer her. She bought a ticket. The drawing was immediate; Lili's was a no-win but she shrugged. It was for a good cause. She walked down the narrow lane and turned into Ingrimstraße. From up ahead at the next corner came a large troop of the Hitler Jugend. A drum was beating, a bugle sounded, and, in voices soprano to bass, they began to sing *Es Zittern die Morschen Knochen.*

Lili moved to the side as they began to pass, and when their arms moved upwards, she too saluted. Unlike in the song, her bones weren't trembling and they weren't rotten. Like the youth of the song, she was committed to doing her part to help keep building Germany up. That was why she was here again, this time to stay.

Nearby, a woman turned away, muttering.

Lili frowned. Like millions throughout the Third Reich, these HJ members were singing out about how their elders might rebuke them, but even if the whole world decided to fight against them, they would still be the victors. A swell of anger rose in Lili. The youth should and would stand firmly behind the Führer.

She moved in front of the woman.

"What were you complaining about just now?" Lili's tone was icy.

The woman, middle-aged, wearing glasses and clutching a cloth shopping bag, looked up, and her mouth sagged.

"Nothing, Fräulein, nothing. I said nothing at all."

Lili peered at her while the sound of the marchers' shoes against stone grew fainter.

"You didn't return their salute either."

The woman paled.

"I, I didn't see it."

Lili grimaced. It was a heady feeling to be able to tell this adult that she was not behaving as she should.

"You're lying. You're lucky that it was I who noticed," she said, with a satisfying surge of pomposity. "Someone else might do more than simply point it out to you."

The woman was nodding, shuffling backwards in little steps as if trying to disappear offstage.

"Thank you, Fräulein, thank you."

Lili nodded once and walked away; she didn't look back. The sense of satisfaction was deep. Today she had at last done something immediately useful for the Reich. In future, that woman would certainly think twice about her behavior and lack of respect for the Führer.

♫♪♫

It was the first time since her return that all were at the table for dinner, even Frau Dierck. Lili had been sorry to learn that the court had not yet returned her children. At the same time, her husband was no longer in Dachau, but had been transferred to some other concentration camp where he was still being re-educated. What a difficult case. Frau Dierck looked even more agitated than before. Perhaps she was just worried that he would be released soon and, blaming her, beat her again.

Since Lili's return, Herr Tischborn had been more talkative than usual. Yesterday he had asked a few questions on what life in America was like, both for long-time citizens and recent immigrants. She told him about the way that immigrants transformed into Americans and how these in turn were often quite vehemently against the arrival of new immigrants, even when they were from the same country of origin. After listening intently, Herr Tischborn asked no further questions.

Dr. Hempel seemed as delighted to see Lili as she was to see him. He promised to let it be known that a teacher was available to students wishing to learn the harpsichord. However, he was not overly optimistic. Instead, he expressed excitement about future performances for her.

The Poppes had just come back from Berlin where Herr Poppe had civil service business to attend to while Frau Poppe met with other leaders of the BDM for an intensive leadership training session.

"Waltraud is taking on more and more responsibilities," Herr Poppe said. He had grown stouter over the past few months, of course no thanks to his wife's cooking.

Frau Poppe nodded as if acknowledging that this was only as it should be. She turned to Lili and spoke; the grating quality in her voice was unchanged.

"So you decided to return to the Reich."

As annoying as Frau Poppe was, the woman was truly committed. She devoted nearly all her time and effort to helping girls and young women, shaping them into citizens who were capable and ready to carry forward the ideas and ideals of the nation. Just as she had with Herr Poppe, Lili decided that she should persevere in learning to put aside personal feelings, and consider the admirable spirit of service exemplified in Frau Poppe. She was a *Ringführerin* with already 600 girls under her.

"Indeed," Lili said. "I've come home."

Frau Poppe pursed her lips.

"I thought you were an American citizen.

"Mm, I—" Lili paused, flustered. Her American passport was sitting upstairs in the desk drawer. Her old German passport had already expired. "Actually, it turns out that I have two citizenships."

Tante Aletheia interrupted, picking up her glass.

"Everyone at this table is German in heart and mind. I suggest we raise our glasses in a toast to the spirit of those poets who praised some of the aspects of the German character. Let us drink to kindness and truth." Frau Poppe called out a toast to the Führer.

Tante Aletheia blinked, and her glass swayed in the air. The others repeated Frau Poppe's words, and Herr Tischborn seemed alarmed as Herr Poppe's glass clanged into his, although nothing broke. Dr. Hempel knocked his glass against Lili's, his eyes twinkling, and she was reminded of the previous year and her first toast around this table. Then she had been but a girl. Now she had returned a woman determined to do her very best for the Third Reich. In tasks small or large. She would show Papa that nothing would stop her now.

She called out, echoing Frau Poppe's toast to the Führer, and her voice rang out over them all. She knew what she was going to do, first thing, tomorrow. So that no one could ever again doubt her, she was going to the proper department. There she would file the papers necessary to reissue her document of German citizenship. And if in doing so she had to turn in the American passport lying upstairs, so be it.

♪♪♪

When was she going to see Leo again? Like an unending chaconne with all sorts of related thoughts circling round and round, this overriding question had consumed her from the moment she'd opened her eyes today. She tried to drive it out by playing, but that made it even worse.

From how Papa had described the envelopes, there had been a return address. But she had never seen them. Nor had Leo left an address with Tante Aletheia. Lili had nowhere to which she could send a message to let him know that she was here. Where might he be? On a grand tour, making music across the Reich? Or he could be in Berlin, visiting relatives, or in some other city attending to whatever duties SS officers had; perhaps he was with the Führer. He could even be here, rehearsing in the Stadthalle, shirtless as she had first seen him. A wave of longing tore through her as she remembered his broad shoulders, golden in the light of the dressing room. Remembered how he had caught her near the lake. How he had pulled her to him, kissing her beneath the roses. How they had touched each other through their music.

She grabbed her coat and headed out to walk off her longings. Yet as frustrating as all this was, she no longer felt as she had during the past months in New York. She was here now, and she wasn't leaving. Sooner or later, preferably sooner, Leo's and her paths were bound to cross. She had to think like that, otherwise she would grow distracted, mad.

In the meantime, she would continue her mission to be more active. She would practice and perform, she would march across Germany until her feet shredded, she would try to stay in university, collect donations, and do her part to guard respect for the Führer.

Her lace-up boots sounded along the pavement, one heel louder than the other. Ah, her first mission, trivial as it was. She needed to go to the cobbler. The small square in front of the Alte Brücke was empty. She passed the Goldener Hecht where she and Benno had eaten dinner together. Since then, she had learned that there was no deep mystery behind Goethe's almost sleeping there. The truth was as simple as a clerk having turned him away.

Untere Straße seemed to have more people on it than usual. She followed the flow toward Heumarkt. The closer she got, the slower the pace became. At first she couldn't see why people were looking at the man and the woman who stood flanked by a few men in uniform. The man, eyes cast down, blond hair parted neatly on the right with one wayward strand sticking up near the back, appeared to be in his early thirties, the woman a few years younger. Her brown eyes were staring straight ahead, as if she were blind to the passersby milling about. The two stood about a meter apart, each with a large cardboard hanging down over their chests. The black paintwork was from two different hands, as if they had each written their own words.

"I am a race defiler," read the man's, letters trailing down like tears of ink. In thick broad brushstrokes, the woman's shouted out: "I'm worse than a slut. I slept with a Jew!"

Lili could feel her cheeks suddenly aflame. It was obvious that this had nothing to do with sleeping. She couldn't help but stare at them. Both were dressed in nice clothes, fashionable suits of good quality. She stared, and under her burning gaze their clothes seemed to fall away. With one movement, fluid and helpless, the two came together, their pale limbs wrapping, entwining each other. Their words were warm and breathy. The two heads, dark and light, closed in, blending, blotting out the faces in a kiss that seemed to have no end.

Someone stepped on Lili's foot.

"Oh, excuse me, Fräulein," said a middle-aged man with a scrub brush mustache. "Too many gawkers." He grimaced and moved on.

Lili blinked, and the two people were still standing there, stiff in their suits and cardboard signs. Some of the passersby glanced at them, then averted their eyes and kept going. Others slowed down or even stopped, and some of those milling about smirked or nodded approval. Others were murmuring, too low for Lili to understand. Still others cast down their eyes, as did the man with the sign. The shame of it. Three years already since the Nuremberg Laws were decreed, and still there were people who didn't respect them. Some of the bystanders shook their heads and moved on.

Lili too had seen enough now, yet she stared at the woman for some moments more. Brown curls framed a face that would have been pert if her eyes hadn't been like two dark stones. She had risked such horrible humiliation just to sleep with that man. Was it that she didn't care about the laws, or that she cared too much for him? For a moment, Lili remembered Marlies from the BDM campout. Perhaps one day Marlies would have to stand like that woman, shamed by society.

Lili turned away and continued on her errand, past Heumarkt and up to Hauptstraße. She really should get to the cobbler for her uneven heels. As the expression went, that woman had made her bed and now had to lie in it. Or, in this case, she had lain in the bed and now she had been made.

What Could it Mean to be Just a Number?

Fragonard lay on Tante Aletheia's lap as if it were his personal pillow. Even from where she sat across from them, Lili could hear him purring. He opened one eye.

"I do miss the new dog," she told Tante Aletheia. "Bella's nearly as big as my brother but ever so gentle. She adores Paul."

Tante Aletheia shifted, and Fragonard's other orb opened, then both eyes narrowed until his silky pillow was once again still.

"It's true," she said. "Size doesn't really have much to do with whether an animal or, for that matter, a human being, is gentle or not." She stroked Fragonard, who already seemed to be dozing peacefully. "Some of the gentlest men I have known were real giants. Nearly two meters high."

Perhaps one day Paul would be a tall man. Most likely Onkel Wilhelm had been one of those giants. Lili glanced over at where his paintings used to hang before Tante Aletheia had carted them off to Friedberg. During Lili's absence the remaining empty spots had been filled by mirrors in gilded frames, making the room look larger and deeper. Next week Tante Aletheia and she would visit Friedberg and Lili would look at the paintings again. Try to understand why art could be so dangerous.

"So, will you go with me to the concert, Tante Aletheia? Dr. Hempel said it should be rather good. He's been busy with the visiting orchestra all week already."

Tante Aletheia's fingers raked through the snowdrifts of Fragonard's fur.

"If Mama were here," said Lili, "she would want to go. She has always loved Wagner."

"Your Mama has a true artist's soul. Perhaps I will go with you. Let's see closer to the day."

Lili rose, smoothing her charcoal gray skirt.

"I'm sorry that you won't join me now. It's such lovely weather for a Sunday walk on Philosophenweg. The leaves are all the colors of melting metals."

"I do enjoy your descriptions." Tante Aletheia smiled. "I'm sorry too, my dear. But I'm concerned about Frau Dierck. I don't think it is wise to leave her alone today."

Lili hesitated. "Shall I stay with you then?"

"I'm sure it won't necessary. You go on your walk. And take this with you for on the way," she said, handing Lili a flat packet.

Lili's brown lace-ups were still at the cobbler's. Today she moved silently in rubber-soled shoes from New York as she crossed the Altebrücke. Over the summer, nearly every time she had looked at the Hudson she could think only of how the river was moving toward the Atlantic and how she longed to move with it. Now there was pleasure simply in looking at the river. She was where she wanted to be.

From this side the castle appeared smaller but the view of the town was deeply satisfying. She walked the twisting way of the Schlangenweg. It was indeed a serpent's path up to the Philosophenweg, and toward the end she was a bit short of breath. A red squirrel scampered across the path ahead, still close enough for Lili to see its cheeks bulging with nuts harvested from the cornucopia all around. In the Hudson Valley there had been large gray squirrels with bushy tails, dipping comically like sylvan dolphins as they moved across the pathways, but Lili preferred these smaller red ones. In Berlin Lotte had always made sure there was something with which she could feed them and the ducks or deer in the parks, like sunflower seeds or dried bread in a paper bag. Today Lili had nothing but Tante Aletheia's gift of chocolate. She startled now as a loud chattering burst forth from inside a nearby bush.

It was warm enough to open her jacket. The sky was clear, the autumn sun friendly. For some time she walked without thought, just listening and looking. But her pocket began to claim her attention and at the next bench she sat down, tore open the foil and broke off a row of flat squares. The chocolate melted onto her taste buds. Sighing with contentment, she sat back against the wooden slats, pointing and flexing her toes.

"American girl?" A brief pause. "Lili!"

Lili jerked her head. There on the path, moving quickly toward her, was Ursula whom she hadn't seen in months. Another young woman strode alongside. Behind them was a scowling boy.

"Heil Hitler," said Lili, getting onto feet that felt a bit tight in her shoes now. "I wasn't sure if you were still in Heidelberg."

Ursula and the woman returned the greeting. Their fingers were stained with earth.

"Of course!" Ursula smiled. Her hair still sported the extremely greasy look. "I'm very much here." She turned to the woman. "This is Erma. She works in the Reich Statistical Office with me."

Erma peered at Lili. "*Freut mich,*" she said, but didn't sound all that pleased.

Lili glanced at their hands. "What have you been doing up here?"

"Picking mushrooms," said Ursula, pointing to the rucksack on Erma's back. "Would you like to see how many types we found?"

Lili shook her head. "Don't bother. My great-aunt's going to teach me about mushrooms next week, but for now I have no idea about what and what not to pick."

At this Erma smirked and Ursula laughed. "You'd better pay good attention to her lessons then. You don't want to cook the wrong ones and poison everybody."

"I had a cousin who died from just that," said Erma.

Lili looked over at the boy, who still had a sullen look on his round face.

"That's Hans-Peter, the youngest in the family," said Ursula. "He's in a bad mood because he's too young to march with my other brothers. Instead, he's with us." Grinning, she reached over and pulled at a tuft of his dark hair, which looked just as dirty as her own. "Come on, sulky. Only another year and you'll be with the Pimpfs. And then I'll go boo hoo because I'll miss you so much."

Hans-Peter glowered at her. "You're a silly cow."

Ursula tutted. "And you're just a little half-baked calf."

Lili addressed him. "I have a little brother too. He's only five, so he still has a long way before he can become a Pimpf. You're very lucky that you'll be one already next year." She expected him to ignore her but Hans-Peter turned and cast a radiant smile.

"I already know which squad I'm going to be in," he said, and Lili could hear the pride in his voice. "And when I get into the HJ, I'm going to learn about airplanes so that I can go into the Luftwaffe."

Ursula grinned at them. "Hans-Peter has everything figured out."

He stuck his chest out. "I'm a boy. And boys become leaders. The Führer said so."

"Yes, yes, you little pre-Pimpf." Ursula laughed. "You'll do just fine. All of us will be very proud of you."

Hans-Peter kicked his heels together on the gravel pathway and threw out his arm, the seriousness of his expression suddenly aging him by a decade. "Heil Hitler!"

Lili asked if he would like some chocolate.

"Oh, yes, please!" said Hans-Peter, once again looking like a nine-year old.

"Do you still like your new job, Ursula?"

Her face lit up. "I love it. It's so much more interesting than anything I could ever have done at the grocery store, even the bookkeeping. I get to work with enormous numbers every day." Erma didn't look quite as eager.

"What sort of numbers?" Lili said.

"Let me explain," said Ursula, her tone enthusiastic. "Dehomag, the firm we're with, supplies tabulating machines. Just like they trained me, and Erma too, they've been training everybody to get ready for the next census. The last one was in '33."

Lili interrupted. "Isn't a census just a matter of counting heads, and making sure not to count any of them twice?"

Both Erma and Ursula shook their own. "It's much more than that. All sorts of interesting information is gathered during a census, and after, too. The Dehomag machines make it possible to know not only how many people live in a house, but what languages they speak, where they were born, their jobs, religions, and so on. There are even ways of tabulating what diseases people might have had." Ursula could barely contain her excitement. "The machines are fabulous!"

"They do sound fascinating," Lili had to admit. "So you work with them in the Reich Statistical Office?"

"At the moment. The next census is next year."

"1939," Lili said. This time she would be a part of it, one tiny number.

"This one will cover the entire Greater Reich, not just Prussia like in '33. It's going to be the most thorough census ever taken."

"I still don't understand what the machines do."

"It's simple," said Erma. "They tabulate the holes on the cards. Then the statisticians can read the information." She shrugged her shoulders as if this were self-evident.

"What holes?"

Ursula took over. "It's actually a system developed by a German who emigrated to America in 1890. There it's called International Business Machines, but here we go by the name Dehomag."

Erma interrupted. "How do you know all this, Ursula?"

"I was paying attention, dearest Erma." She winked at Lili. "Back to the holes."

"Yes, the mysterious holes."

"Not so mysterious when you know what they mean. Because that's all they are: little holes that are arranged on the cards to give the information." Seeing Lili's expression, she added, "Like when the train conductor punches the ticket in different places, and later other conductors look at it and know if the passenger is tall or fat or has a big nose. Or what station he got on." She giggled. "You know, it's a way of identifying passengers so that nobody else can use the same ticket."

"Oh, I think I understand. It sounds rather like the pianola." Ursula, Erma, and even Hans-Peter with the chocolate mustache stared at Lili.

"The way the music plays because the cylinder only sounds the notes where there are holes on the paper."

"If you say so," said Ursula, grinning.

"Can we go now?" Hans-Peter pushed at his sister.

"I wish we could walk together," Ursula said, turning back to Lili, "but I promised my mother to be home to peel the potatoes." She looked at her wristwatch. "We have to hurry now."

Alone again, Lili continued along the hillsides. How fortunate Ursula was to be able to go home and have a Sunday meal with her family, even with a narrow-minded father like hers. At least in that house the conversation around the table wouldn't be marred by unspoken disagreement about the Führer. Hans-Peter and his sister seemed to have a good relationship. When would Paul come to Germany? Would Papa and Mama bring him, or would he too have to sneak away? How she would love to take him around Heidelberg. But perhaps by the time he was old enough to come on his own, he would be too indoctrinated in American ways to feel true love for the fatherland. After all, he already referred to himself as an American boy.

She bit her lip. How disappointing it was, and only because of Papa. He had robbed his family of their home. He had had the audacity to steal her letters. He had ruined everything for all of them.

He Was Making All of Them Guilty

Later that day, Lili sat at the harpsichord, her fingers flying. When would she and Leo again play together? Would she ever perform for the Führer? Where was Leo? She stayed at the keyboard all afternoon. But if she had any hopes of staying in the university, tomorrow she would have to get back to her books.

At dinner both Frau Dierck and Dr. Hempel were absent, the latter dining out with colleagues. Frau Poppe spoke over the clinking of her utensils.

"...and the Winters who run the tobacco shop around the corner are divorcing. Turns out she's a Jew."

Neither Herr Poppe, who was chewing a mouthful of bread, nor Herr Tischborn, busy wiping at a spot on his shirt, responded, but Frau Poppe didn't require any acknowledgements.

"All those blonde curls," she said, tutting. "I always knew there was something wrong with that simpering mouth." She paused to spear another piece of potato. "Winter made a mistake, but he's taking the proper steps now. At least there are no children."

This reminded Lili of the couple with the cardboard signs. Yesterday she'd overheard a vendor at Marktplatz telling a customer that the man had been sentenced to eight months in jail. He hadn't said anything about the woman. Was the humiliation itself considered adequate punishment?

Dessert was stewed plums. At first Lili refused any, then ate two helpings. Herr Tischborn said he had a lot of paperwork to do, and he retired as soon as Lili had finished her last mouthful of dessert. As the Poppes climbed the stairwell, she could hear a little giggle, but it was hard to tell from which Poppe it came.

A dinner tray was prepared for Frau Dierck, and Lili and Tante Aletheia went upstairs. There was no response to the knock and when the door was opened, Lili nearly dropped the tray. All the drawers had been emptied, their contents scattered throughout the room. Sitting on the floor amid the mess was Frau Dierck, head bowed, hair disheveled.

Tante Aletheia whispered to Lili. "Call Dr. Morsch and ask him to come immediately." But when she telephoned, there was no reply. She ran back to Frau Dierck's room.

"I'll go get him," she whispered.

The late October air bit at her cheeks as she hurried along the pavement. At this time on Sunday evening no one was about. Only one light was burning upstairs at Dr. Morsch's house, and it took a while before the door opened. The housekeeper must be having her Sunday off. The doctor seemed disconcerted to see her.

"My daughter is not well today," he said as they hurried along the street. "She takes everything to heart, and it pains her. It is a difficult time in which to grow up."

Lili glanced over at him. "How old is she?"

"Around your age. An age that she should enjoy. Instead, she is in her room, crying." He stopped speaking then and Lili too said nothing more for the rest of the way.

Before entering Frau Dierck's room, Dr. Morsch glanced up and down the hallway.

"Thank you, ladies," he said. "I will now examine her."

Tante Aletheia suggested that she and Lili sit in the salon with a plum brandy. "My own nerves are rather on edge today. We'll keep a fortifying glass for Dr. Morsch too." They settled into armchairs.

Fragonard appeared from under a table and sprang onto Tante Aletheia's lap.

"You're very worried about Frau Dierck, aren't you?" Lili asked her.

"If it were only that," she murmured.

"What else is it then? Are you worried about my being here?"

At this, Tante Aletheia burst out with a harsh sound that was part sneer, part snort, most unlike her. "Ach, Lili. When are you going to understand?"

Lili frowned. "What do you mean, Tante Aletheia? What don't I understand?"

Tante Aletheia closed her green eyes. "I'm very tired, Lili. We will talk another day."

This was disturbing and unexpected behavior. She could certainly use a glass of Schnaps. Lili crossed her arms, staring at the gilded mirrors on the walls. Substitutes for banned art. She frowned. Surely it wasn't illegal that Tante Aletheia had taken them away. In fact, it was the right thing to do: get them out of Germany. She could still enjoy looking at them if she really had to, just not here. Lili glanced at Tante Aletheia. She seemed to be dozing. After all, she was an old lady and deserved to rest. Some other day she would likely tell Lili what she had meant. Lili got up and walked around the room, Fragonard's gaze following her. Perhaps she should check up on Dr. Morsch. He might need something.

Upstairs, she paused. Best not to knock in case she disturbed Frau Dierck.

The woman was no longer seated on the floor but on a chair, with Dr. Morsch standing behind her, kneading her shoulders. Seeing Lili, Dr. Morsch gave a tired smile. What a good doctor he was. A kind man. It seemed that he was also a thoughtful father.

"She's responding well," he told her. "Relax some more, Frau Dierck," he said into the fluff of unkempt hair. Lili could imagine how her head smelled. "Perhaps it will not even be necessary to administer an injection."

Lili crossed over to them. Frau Dierck looked up, bleary-eyed. "Good evening." Her voice was weak. "How ashamed I am to be so much trouble."

"Don't think about it," Lili said. "Tante Aletheia will be glad to know that you're feeling better. Dr. Morsch, do you need anything?"

He shook his head, another weary smile above his beard. "Not for the moment."

In the salon, Tante Aletheia had woken from her nap.

"Dr. Morsch is giving Frau Dierck some form of treatment on her shoulders."

"A massage. Sometimes that seems to calm her, at least for a while."

"More work than giving an injection," Lili said. "Dr. Morsch is very conscientious."

"I remember going to Baden-Baden with my mother when I was a child," said Tante Aletheia. "While she went off to the baths for her daily massage treatments, my brother and I played with hoops and then sat on the terrace and stuffed ourselves with pastries."

"Those must have been lovely days."

Tante Aletheia agreed. "It was a different Germany." Now she looked into Lili's eyes, holding her gaze. "Lili, you must not tell the Poppes or Herr Tischborn that Dr. Morsch was here today."

"But they know that he often comes when Frau Dierck has her nerve attacks."

"Yes. But that was before. Now we cannot let them know."

Lili leaned forward. "Is something going to happen to Frau Dierck?"

Tante Aletheia closed her eyes for a moment. "I hope not, Lili. But it's not that. You weren't here when the new law came out during the summer. Jewish doctors are only allowed to treat Jewish patients now. Since then, Dr. Morsch has been risking punishment by coming here. His housekeeper has left his employ."

Lili bit into her lip. How had she missed the fact that he was a Jew?

"Tante Aletheia! How can you break the law like that?" Her tone was indignant. "And to think that I'm the one who fetched him!" Before she could respond, the door opened and Dr. Morsch entered.

"She's asleep," he told them. "I don't think there will be any further incidents this night," he said, coming over to sit down near Tante Aletheia. "But I am concerned about you, dear lady." He reached out and took her hand between his own. "The pressure on you is great and I worry about your own nerves. I don't want you to become my patient as well."

Lili was about to say that as far as nerves went, he had some nerve breaking the Reich law. She could have told him that all she needed to do was inform the police that a Jewish doctor was treating an Aryan, and Dr. Morsch would likely be out of a job. Or perhaps he would just have to stand in a square wearing a sign that said his hands had been on Frau Dierck. Would he be sent to jail for that? What would happen to his stupid daughter crying in her room? Lili made a sound of disgust.

Dr. Morsch turned to her. "You are a great comfort to your aunt, Fräulein Lili. Your support is probably worth more than any medication I could prescribe for her." His smile was so very kind. Yet even though he was helping Frau Dierck, didn't he understand that by coming here he was making all of them guilty? Tante Aletheia should find an Aryan doctor for her.

Tante Aletheia was peering at Lili. Her eyes seemed to be sending some sort of a message.

"Mm, I do my best," Lili said at last, but her voice sounded thin and strained and somehow false to her ears.

A Nation of Spineless Hooligans

As shaky as her status at the university seemed, Lili was glad to be back. The halls were full of posters from the NSDStB and other NS bodies, some advising of marches around Heidelberg. She had missed this year's rally at Nuremberg. However, the initial disappointment was erased by the knowledge that from now on she would be able to be there every year. And of course there was so much satisfaction to be had in marching through Heidelberg.

Today's classes in Germanistik included literature (the professor claimed that both Goethe and Schiller would have found themselves comfortable in today's Reich), language (more exercises in substituting solid German words for Latin- and Greek-rooted ones), and a lecture on the music of Carl Orff and the two Richards—Strauss and Wagner. It was mentioned that *The Ring of the Nibelungen* was a clear example of the seriousness of the racial problem. Finally, it was interesting to learn that while German citizens' attendance of concert and opera performances had been rising steadily over the past few years (due to KdF), the President of the Reich Chamber of Music was said to have disclosed that private musical instruction had declined.

This last bit of information was exciting, as it could mean that with fewer teachers she would find pupils easily. On the other hand, Dr. Hempel had mentioned that it was precisely because the pupils were too busy with HJ and BDM activities that his own instruction had fallen off over the years. Perhaps she would not even need to teach, if she could find work as a professional performer. After all, Li Stademann could support herself in this way—why not Lili von Rittersburg zu Mertz-Tärnekow? Li Stademann had been around for years already. Wasn't it time for the new generation to show what it could do?

Classes were over for the day; Lili set out toward the meeting point for today's march. Across the courtyard, she caught sight of a figure standing in the shadow against a wall, and for a moment she thought it was Hildegard. But as she turned, Lili recognized the Jewish girl from last semester.

The students were gathering on the opposite side of the Neckar for the fun of crossing the bridge. A crisp but pleasant breeze was rising, just right for making the banners snap and crack as they waited. When no more students could be seen hurrying toward them, the leader shouted a command and they readied themselves. Their heads held high, they looked out toward the castle and the brilliant blue beyond. Out they moved, voices raised in a spirited song that thrilled Lili. She would never tire of the exhilaration that came from belonging here.

The autumn breezes unfurled the flags so that they rippled and streamed like the Neckar below, the river whose waters flowed on, joining other currents into the heartland of Germany. This new Germany would never again have its citizens lying sleepless at night, listening to their children crying in hunger.

If only Papa would understand.

They marched through the gateway and back into town, their voices swelling with enthusiasm. They marched past the citizens of Heidelberg. Countless of them saluted (perhaps that woman she had reprimanded the other day was among them) or smiled and nodded at the marchers. Further ahead, others seemed intent on their late afternoon errands, hurrying to get back to their workplaces or home to their families, seemingly unaware of anything but the tasks at hand. One young man in overalls jumped into the students' midst and for several happy meters was carried along with them before he was booted out on the other side. This was a university group, after all.

Further up Pfaffengasse, a middle-aged man, neatly dressed and wearing a loden hat with a duck feather in its band, stood on the pavement, staring at them with an odd expression. He called out something but Lili could not hear the words over the singing. Some of the others must have heard them, for their step slowed down.

The student leader, a university boxing champion tall and resplendent with his Party insignia, came to a halt in front of the man. Now that the drumbeat had stopped, she could hear when the leader said, almost just as she had to the woman the other day, "Are you sure that's what you wanted to say?"

The man in the hat shook his head.

"You students are fools." His voice was gruff. "Don't you see where Germany is headed?" Lili could feel the stunned intake of breath all around her.

With a rapid movement the leader slapped him.

The man flinched yet nothing but the muscles in his face moved.

Everyone was staring.

"So this is what they teach you at university these days."

Another student moved closer.

"Watch it, old man, or you'll get more of the same from *all* of us."

"You're nothing but a bunch of hooligans." His tone was flat with disgust. He flapped his right hand. Did he mean to include them all in this, or was he parodying the Hitler salute? His lips curled downwards. "That's what the fatherland has turned into. A nation of spineless hooligans."

A fist flew out, this time shoving the man in the hat backwards. He stumbled, and as he went down he called out something Lili had never heard. The shock of it shot flames through her blood.

"Fuck the Führer! Fuck all of you!"

At this the leader lunged, and no one held him back. Someone else hit out with a black shoe. Lili watched, in a heatwave of rage against the man on the ground, as another student took a flag and began to jab at him with the staff. A student pulled at him to stop.

"You might damage the flag," he shouted.

It was all happening so fast. The man was no longer wearing his hat as his body jerked and danced while the students kicked and hit and slammed him into the cobblestones. Someone pushed Lili forward.

"Go on, girl—spit on the bastard," and she was propelled toward him and then she was trying to gather saliva and fling it at him in a great, vicious hiss but her mouth was dry. Instead, her heart hammering wild, her eyes pulled wide open by furor, she shrieked in a primitive outpouring that gave sound to the outrage of so disrespecting the Führer.

How long she raged at him she did not know, but suddenly someone was taking her by the arm.

"Come on." The tone was matter-of-fact. "He's had enough for now. We're going for a drink." She allowed herself to be led, and turned back only once. The last thing she saw before rounding the corner was the felt hat, its feather still stuck in the band but its spine broken.

Fog and Darkness Descending

Tante Aletheia had been kindness itself, holding Lili's head as she vomited into the toilet bowl, asking no questions; it was obvious that Lili had drunk more than ever before. She helped her into her nightdress and tucked her in, fluffing the pillow to keep Lili's unhappy head elevated. She even put a wooden bucket next to the bed; mercifully, it remained empty. In the morning, she urged Lili to drink two cups of camomile tea. Later, despite still feeling rather wretched, and with little hope of being able to concentrate, Lili forced herself to be present at her afternoon lecture. On the way home, she headed to the river.

The day was growing overcast, a filmy mist dissolving the hills above Philosophenweg. Most of the benches in front of her on Neckarstaden were empty. The events of yesterday were still too blurred to sort out: a horrid man who had insulted the Führer and lost his hat, far too much beer at some Gasthaus she'd never been to. Never in her life had she behaved as she had yesterday. How outraged she had been; it almost frightened her. But the man had needed severe reprimanding. Unlike for the woman from the other day, admonishing words had not been enough. Yet it was Papa's face that kept invading her mind, his eyes staring at her as if in reproach. She grimaced. Who was he to rebuke her? He had stolen her letters, hidden the photograph. Was that honorable behavior? And he had said the same thing about the Führer as had the man in the hat, even if in politer terms. What a father. Some saliva sat behind her teeth and this time she had enough. She gathered it and spat toward the river that led to the sea.

Glancing to her left, she saw a man far up ahead along Neckarstaden. For a moment it was as if somehow both Papa and Leo were on their way to her here and her insides seemed to lurch. But of course it was neither of them. Had the alcohol clouded her brain so much? As the figure drew nearer, she saw that it was the student whom she had seen with the Jewish girl. Hildegard had said he was nice. Perhaps too nice. How would he look with a cardboard sign hanging from his neck? He would look better in a uniform; his shoulders were broad.

For a while she stared into the grayness hovering above the river. The she looked for the man. The student was further along now, but no longer walking. He had stopped at the bench past hers, where a woman sat with a small dog. He was leaning down to pet the dog and Lili could see that he was talking to it. She watched the woman, the dog, and him, and suddenly it was clear that he was not speaking to the dog but to the woman. When she focused on her, Lili could see that it was not just any woman, but the Jewish student.

She turned away then, looking across at the Philosophenweg upon which the late October afternoon fog and darkness were descending.

The Poppes at Table

It was strange to be at the table with only Herr Tischborn and the Poppes. Earlier on, Tante Aletheia had spoken of an upset stomach and gone upstairs. As for Dr. Hempel, these days he was often out for dinner with colleagues from his new administrative position. Most unusual of all, Frau Dierck was off to visit her aunt. It was to be hoped that the trip would help pick up her spirits.

Of course the Poppes could speak of little but what was happening at the Polish border.

"Those Poles!" Frau Poppe snapped, the Salamibrot in her hand hovering. "They're good for nothing, not even taking--"

"You're right, Waltraud," her husband interrupted. "All we get from them is trouble with a capital T. It's all we've ever got from them. And what have they got from us?" He waved his knife. "I'll tell you what: Posen and West Prussia! Now you tell me, Herr Tischborn," he said, suddenly turning toward Herr Tischborn who had been quietly eating his pickle, "don't you agree that as Poland was happy enough to take from us our own German soil, they should open their arms and take back their own Jews—all seventeen thousand of them?"

Herr Tischborn put down his cutlery and reached for his glass while clearing his throat. He took a healthy swallow. "Certainly, Herr Poppe. It is quite unacceptable that so many people should be stranded out there, caught between the two countries. Even if the Polish government has now revoked their passports, their citizenship is still Polish. So, if they're not wanted here, then let them return to Poland. It will certainly be warmer than out there in the middle of no man's land."

Frau Poppe laughed. "Ach, those Polish Jews must be used to the German cold shoulder by now. I heard that they're living in pigsties. If you ask me, they should just stay there. The Poles know what they're about."

"Quite so." Herr Poppe beamed at his wife. "That's one good thing we can say about the Poles. They don't like their Jews either."

"What's to like, Otto?" Frau Poppe giggled like a schoolgirl. Her swollen chin bobbed under her braided head like a yeasty *Hefekranz*.

Lili watched the banter of the Poppes. Neither of them seemed to have any redeeming physical attractiveness, yet neither seemed to notice it in the other. It had to be true love. "You are very quiet this evening, Fräulein Lili," said Herr Tischborn, giving her a lopsided smile. "You must be thinking about your studies."

She started. "I do have a lot," she admitted. Actually, this was no longer really the case. Between her lack of effort and the increased marching, she was studying less than ever. Her language skills were as faulty as before. She would be out if she didn't improve by the end of the semester, but at least she didn't seem to be the only one not concentrating. There seemed to be more marching than before summer. It had been her impression that German universities were extremely demanding and academic. Perhaps she was in the wrong faculty. Surely the sciences required exacting and intense work, like Benno's.

"Perhaps Fräulein Lili is thinking of the mysterious Herr Malter," said Frau Poppe, her tone sly.

Lili blinked. "I did hear from him some time ago, Frau Poppe," she said sweetly. "He told me about some of his important work with the Ahnenerbe in the Himalayas."

For a moment Frau Poppe looked sour, perhaps envious that Lili should be in contact with someone on such an important mission for the Reich.

"Ach," Frau Poppe said, collecting herself. "Who knows when they'll come back from such an expedition. It must be very dangerous up there in the icy mountains among savages."

Herr Poppe cleared his throat.

"Fräulein Lili, would you happen to know what films are playing at the cinema this week?" He looked over at his wife. "I thought we might go and see one later in the week. Dinner out and a film, what do you say to *that*?"

For once, Lili felt grateful to Herr Poppe. He had changed the subject, and, for at least one evening next week, the Poppes would not be there for dinner.

Willi, the SS, and a New Date

For the past few days, Frau Brinkmann's normally delicious food had tasted somewhat like the institutional offerings at the university Mensa. Her raw potato dumplings were undercooked, the meatloaf dry as cardboard. Hungry in the late afternoon, Lili wandered into the kitchen to look for something edible. Frau Brinkmann was seated at the table with someone whose back and shoulders were wide as the kitchen door. It was the coal man, late with his delivery this week, but still taking time out to enjoy his usual glass of beer at the house on Kornmarkt.

"Willi's so disappointed," Frau Brinkmann was saying to him as she cut the peel off a potato. "He was hoping that he'd be accepted for training by the SS, you know, because he was in the HJ-*Streifendienst* for some time, after all. But imagine this: they say my boy doesn't qualify as a candidate. He doesn't meet the physical requirements. And him with such a sturdy build." She shook her head and sighed, deep and long.

It sounded as if it were Willi who was to blame for his mother's culinary confusion.

Frau Brinkmann stopped peeling and, without putting down the knife, wiped the corner of her eye with the back of her hand.

"Ach, from now on it's going to be so painful for him every year on the ninth of November when the men are inducted." She sighed again. "Willi was always hoping that his day would come too. That after years of training and service he would finally get to be an SS man." She started back on the potato. "And to think it's just because of the big bones on my mother's side of the family..." She threw the potato into the pot, forgetting to cut out its eyes.

The coal man shook his head. "Na na, Frau Brinkmann, don't take it so tragically. Your Willi is a young man and one day all this will be just a memory of his youth." He set the glass down with a thump. "Won't he be doing a baker's apprenticeship with your brother? You need big strong arms for that. At least he's guaranteed to always have bread."

"Yes, well, I suppose you're right. It's just that it would have been so nice to have a real SS man in the family. My Dieter, God rest his soul, would have been proud. I think." Now she noticed Lili. "Fräulein Lili, you did give me a start. Are you hungry again? Here, try a slice of my plum cake."

Lili shook her head. She had already nibbled at a piece earlier and found that Frau Brinkmann must have put in three times as much salt as usual. With luck, the coal man's words of encouragement would have a positive effect on her cooking before they all starved.

"I'm just on my way out again," Lili hastened to explain, "and I won't be home for dinner tonight. Dr. Hempel has invited me to a small concert at the Stadthalle."

♫♪♫

Fifteen minutes later, Lili was in the hall where she was to meet Dr. Hempel. For some moments she stood in the middle of the room, remembering. If she were to walk down the hallway to the last room on the right, would she find Leo again? His hands on the body of the gamba, his jawline against the shadows of the wood. The thought of him being there made the back of her knees weak. A sudden longing for him, for his music and his touch, rushed into her belly and she moaned. When oh when was she going to see him again? Her hands flew to her face and she closed her eyes.

At last muted sounds began to float into her awareness. Scattered phrases from Mozart, disjointed, without beginning or end. She moved away from the center of the room and leaned against a wall. From the dressing rooms in the hallway, one violin was delicately picking its way through a measure from a sonata in E minor that she remembered Papa playing, while a horn slid down into the lowest tones from a Horn Concerto. She didn't recognize the notes from another violin, but a clarinet was definitely going over the adagio from the Clarinet Concert in A major. The result was strange, something much more than the polyphonic texture. She tilted her head. If she blocked out the familiarity of the fragments, hearing them without preconception, the whole was an entirely new composition. Exciting and disturbing, it was Mozart, but Mozart in a novel form. As if Mozart himself had taken apart his work and reconstructed it to make his listeners examine each line more closely. Because the lines came together in both harmony and dissonance to form something new that was full of meaning, if one could truly listen for it. Suddenly she knew what the sounds reminded her of: the paintings that Tante Aletheia had hidden away.

A door burst open then, spilling several people into the room, and Lili hurried off to find Dr. Hempel.

"I'm delighted that you could come," he told her, wiping his forehead with a wilted handkerchief. "We have had little chance to speak at the house. When I agreed to help out with these concerts, I had no idea how much time I would have to devote to my duties."

"I'm sure that this one will be splendid. And I'm really looking forward to Wagner next month."

Dr. Hempel's white beard and mustache parted as he smiled. "I think so. These musicians are excellent."

She couldn't help herself. "As good as that SS orchestra?"

"Now, that orchestra is indeed something special." His eyes twinkled. "It seems that you haven't forgotten those young men."

She could feel her cheeks warming. Dr. Hempel had no idea.

He cleared his throat. "I have good news for you," he said, as they began to walk toward the concert hall. "Exciting news. You will be invited to perform again. This time, not in Mannheim or Berchtesgaden but..."

She took a deep and tremulous breath. In January she would perform in the city of her childhood. Berlin. Capital of the Third Reich.

Troubling Travel Plans

"Would you like me to pick Frau Dierck up from the station today?" Lili asked while pouring coffee.

Fragonard stared at her.

"That would be kind, my dear," said Tante Aletheia. "I'm afraid that she will be in a daze."

"Most likely. But at least she was lucky to have been permitted to see her children while she was there. You said that she sounded happier on the telephone last week than she has in months."

"I would like to think that perhaps now she will eventually get them back."

Lili shuddered. "To think it's all because of her husband."

Tante Aletheia took a long breath.

"Yesterday I had a letter from my classmate, Lili. They received news that Frau Dierck's husband has died."

"Died?"

"Yes, my dear. They say it was pneumonia."

"Poor Frau Dierck." Lili winced. "What she's been fearing has come true. But it's probably best for all of them." At least Frau Dierck's worries would be over. Perhaps now she could pull herself together and be normal. "Was he in the hospital long?"

"I don't know if a place like Buchenwald has one."

"Surely it does," Lili said, frowning. "Prisoners get sick and need medical attention too."

Tante Aletheia dipped her finger into the cream and let Fragonard lick it off. For some moments they sat in silence, watching him.

"Dr. Morsch thinks it is time for his daughter and him to leave Heidelberg," Tante Aletheia said. "Life here is getting more and more complicated."

Lili nodded.

"Where does he want to go?"

"Britain, America, South America—he really doesn't know. And these days it's so hard with visas." Tante Aletheia sniffed. "However, it's highly unlikely that he will go anywhere."

"But why not? If he can get in, he should go."

"Because of his daughter. She refuses to leave, and if she stays, he stays."

Lili scowled.

"Why doesn't she want to go? Dr. Morsch's practice must have shrunk considerably over the past few months. Things have changed." She shrugged. "His daughter should see the sense of their leaving."

For a long moment, Tante Aletheia's green eyes stared into hers. "Dr. Morsch's daughter wants to stay because this is her home. Her mother is buried here."

"But they're Jews. Germany isn't their real homeland."

"Lili."

Fragonard seemed as frozen as Lili by the tone in Tante Aletheia's voice, sharper than Lili had ever heard. The green eyes were glittering black.

"The time is at hand that you learn to see clearly," she said.

Lili gaped.

"Hallo?" Dr. Hempel's voice called from the doorway and Lili was filled with a rush of relief at his opportune arrival.

Tante Aletheia's voice regained its usual timbre as she invited the professor to take a cup of coffee with them.

"Has Fräulein Lili told you her news?"

"She has indeed, Dr. Hempel," said Tante Aletheia, sounding as if nothing had ruffled her surface just now. "Our Lili will blossom. The sooner the better."

Lili wrinkled her brow as she looked at Tante Aletheia. Was the old woman going senile? Dr. Hempel turned to Lili.

"I have a sweet little extra to put on your plate." he said, "and I don't mean cake." He paused. "Also performing at the festival will be Li Stadelmann."

Lili dropped her fork, startling Fragonard.

"Li Stadelmann and I will be at the same concert? Oh my." Her chest seemed to have wings beating inside it. She rose from the table.

"Please excuse me. I must get to my harpsichord."

For several hours, Lili lost herself in the Bachs and Haydn. There were no thoughts of Tante Aletheia, Papa, or Leo. Today nothing would come between her and the notes. Not even Li Stadelmann.

♫♪♫

It was already dark when Lili arrived at the station and bought a platform ticket to wait for Frau Dierck. Most likely she would need help with her bag. The train from Halle pulled in, steam hissing, metal wheels shrieking softly against the rails. Lili waited, searching among the disembarking passengers. But the voices and thump of heels faded, and finally there was no one left on the platform but Lili. Even the conductors seemed to have disappeared. She hurried alongside the train, calling out for Frau Dierck and peering through the windows. Perhaps she had fallen asleep. But the train was empty and the platform eerily silent. Terminus.

Inside, Lili inquired at the counter. There were no more trains from Halle scheduled for the day.

"Frau Dierck must have decided to stay on longer," said Tante Aletheia when Lili returned alone. "Perhaps she is trying to get the children back. Or there are complications with her husband's affairs.

Lili searched Tante Aletheia's eyes. There were as green as ever, her voice even. There was nothing in her demeanor to suggest that she was still peeved with Lili. Nevertheless, Lili excused herself and went back up to her room where the harpsichord was waiting for her.

Into the Movement

Dr. Hempel had suggested Lili attend a rehearsal of an upcoming Beethoven concert. A person could never have enough of good music. Yet, upon waking, Lili had decided not to go. She had her own upcoming concert with which to concern herself. As of Monday, all of Professor Hetzenrath's classes had been cancelled; she was free to practice the entire day. But when the morning's post brought the letter from Papa, she changed her mind. It was just what she needed now; an hour or two of music that she could listen to on any level she chose. That could help block out what was in the letter.

To capture in color her current willfulness, she put on a red dirndl with a long-sleeved blouse and an apron of black. Her stockings too were black. Buttoning her jacket, she set off, the letter folded and pushed into the darkest recess of her purse.

On her way past a newsstand, she glanced at the papers on display. "Once again it was a Jew!" shouted the headlines. Something must have happened. She would look at the newspapers later.

At Stadthalle, she entered through a side door and made her way to the hall. The orchestra was already in full sound. She slid into a seat far to the back and for some time barely paid attention to the music. How she had come to despise her own father. Alone his letter was reason enough, traitorous, polluting her purse. She swallowed. Three Gs and and ominous E-flat burst into the hall like shots of warning. Hah, one of his favorite symphonies. How often had her father said that he wished he could hear the whole symphony in one, without having to change the records on the gramophone player. How could she ever again look him in the eye without seeing the betrayal written there?

The orchestra fell silent, the conductor spoke. She was too far in the back to hear what he was saying, and didn't care anyway. A few clarinets sounded, stretching a B-flat. The conductor said something. An oboe wove for a measure. The conductor said something. Lili was tempted to take out the letter but it was too dark to read it here.

The conductor raised his arms. Lili took a deep breath. She would listen to the coming piece without examining the structure of the composition, would let herself be swept away in a primeval manner to wherever the sound imagery alone chose to take her.

The pianist touched the keys.

She was in a vessel on a river. Like waves, the notes lapped at the sides, beseeching and asserting at once. Leaves swirled idly on the surface of the water. The vessel slid along, soft in its passage past banks hidden under stalks of green, thrilling her as it bobbed alarmingly through a valley of white waters sparkling under the sun. A rocky outcrop loomed, drawing ever nearer. But the river, deep, with currents pure and true, carried them through safely. The trumpets sounded their arrival. How sweetly the verdant countryside stretched out. The piano scattered fragrant flowers.

The curves of the unknown river were glorious, each gliding turn opening up a fresh vista of green. Just around the next bend were dancers, simple country folk in traditional finery. Sturdy peasant bodies dipped and swayed and circled in perfect rhythm, their ribbons of red and yellow fluttering in the breeze. For a while, the happy melody drifted alongside the vessel, and then it faded as the river carried her further.

Now they were passing through farmers' fields, where hard work and love for the soil made the crops stand tall. The air was alive with the scent of earth and growth and the warmth of the sun. Here too the nameless river was strong, forceful and determined as its current moved the vessel past tiny islands midstream. On and on she went, borne on the sun-speckled quicksilver.

Now the current slowed. The craft was floating, seemed to hover, and then, with a sense of utter delight, Lili was lifting up as her vessel rose on notes light as air. Higher and higher she went, looking down upon a landscape of forest rising into the hills. Below, in the secret sylvan world, a stag moved out of a thicket, majestic in his stately pace across a clearing. Further and further she floated above the woods that reached toward the horizon. Nearby clouds were lined with copper and gold, so close that, perhaps, if she leaned out, she could touch the colors themselves.

Suddenly the mountaintop was there, snow shining sun-brilliant and unblemished upon its crest. Far below, the world was silent. Here there was only the sound of their passing through air.

And then they were floating back down, once more closer to the ground, riding above a settlement with buildings of brick and stone rooted firm for centuries. Townspeople moved through the cobblestone streets, their step filled with purpose and rhythm. The vessel drifted past them, over the ramparts of the town's castle, past the turrets, just above a path that led into a grove of trees on the castle grounds. She craned her head but could not see where the pathway emerged. The vessel sank. As it alit, she stepped out onto the earth and began to follow the path, at first with hesitation, but, as she walked downwards through the woods, her pace grew ever quicker.

At last she burst through the trees to find herself back at the river, and it was not just any river. Now she knew. It was the Rhine.

As she stood on its solid bank, looking out upon the artery that flowed through the heartland of Germany, voices began to surround her, one after another. They rose clear and decent and earnest from all who embodied the ancient soul of these ancient lands, and the sweet harmony and words of their ode to joy filled her with an almost unbearable gladness.

"Fried und Freude gleiten freundlich
Wie der Wellen Wechselspiel.
Was sich drängte rauh und feindlich,
Ordnet sich zu Hochgefühl."

Yes, oh yes, it was true; peace and joy did flow serenely like the alternating play of the waves, the gentle waters of the Rhine that passed before her here with the grace and dignity of the ages. All harsh and hostile elements were transformed into radiance through music. It was exquisite. A chorus of spirits resounded...when love and power united, humans were lifted up by the divine... She understood the fatherland and its people, peace-loving philosophies, morality, the future that would come through the Führer. Peace. She could never make peace with Papa. She would make her own peace. Here. Where the people had faith in the Führer, the man whose heart beat only with love for fatherland and Volk.

She started. Silence. The conductor was talking again. Gathering her jacket and purse, she slipped out of the hall.

For some time she walked along the Neckar, that wild and meandering waterway which rose in the Black Forest and joined the Rhine, beloved river of the Romantics, at Mannheim. For some time it felt as if she had truly journeyed through and above her homeland. The sensations lingered, tingling her blood. But, like the bubbles in Sekt or mineral water, eventually they dissipated, leaving her flat. She would go to a Konditorei, eat cake and read Papa's letter again.

On the way she stopped and joined others poring over the front page of the *Völkischer Beobachter*. Yesterday, in Paris, the Third Secretary at the German embassy had been shot by a Jew.

The article said that it was clear that the German Volk would draw its conclusions from this. That it was an impossible situation. There were, within German borders, still hundreds of thousands of Jews ruling over stores, going to entertainment venues, and, as 'foreign' landlords, putting German money into their own pockets. And all the while their racial comrades were preparing for war against Germany, and shooting down German officials, like Gustloff in Davos in 1936 and now Ernst vom Rath. The shots in the German Embassy in Paris would not only mean the beginning of a new German position in the Jewish Question, but hopefully be seen as a signal to those foreigners who had not yet realized that the only obstruction in the way of understanding among peoples was the international Jew.

The voices around her were a cacophony of distress, outrage, and fear. She pulled her jacket tighter and walked on. Were Lotte and Oskar considered international Jews? She had barely thought about them since leaving New York. New York made her think of Papa and the letter weighing down her purse. She entered a Konditorei.

The waitress teased her about the second slice of cake, but made no comment now as she set the next piece and more cream down in front of Lili. She was eating but not tasting.

The letter lay on her lap, under the table, away from any curious gaze. She had read it twice already, and now leaned over to read it again.

My dearest daughter. Soon it will be one month since you left us without a word of farewell. Lili's jaw tightened. He knew why she had left. *Since then, words have failed me as well. I, who have always felt at ease with oratory, did not know what to say to a daughter who has chosen to sneak out of her home to squander her life with the dreams of a madman.*

The first time she had read this, at breakfast, she had nearly choked on her coffee. Now she felt only a lump of ice in her throat.

Nor is this an ordinary madman. No, my daughter has made the decision to believe in the ideals of an evil being. It was Papa who was evil— forsaking his homeland and forcing his family into exile. Stealing from his daughter.

It is clear that you have never understood the dangerous waters into which Adolf Hitler has steered our beloved fatherland. You, like so many millions of our countrymen, have been swayed by the rhetoric and promises shouted out into the ether. For every imaginary kilometer of his glorious Autobahn, you have been led astray a distance much greater than you can fathom. You, like so many millions, have been tricked by the greatest magician of all time. Had Papa lost his mind? Waters, ether, Autobahn, magician? She stabbed her fork into the cake and dragged the piece through the whipped cream.

By misusing the honest faith and hope of the German people, he has made German honor disappear.

He continues to use every inhabitant for his own purposes, purposes which are spelled out in that insane piece of writing he has called Mein Kampf. *I believe you have read it. Do you not yet recognize what that loathsome creature plans? What, dear daughter, will it take for you to see?* Forgetting to chew, she swallowed the forkful. A flash of shame prickled her conscience. Papa thought that she had read *Mein Kampf* but she had read only random paragraphs. Yet how dare he call the Führer a loathsome creature?

Need I tell you of the heartache your decision has brought into our home? Were Germany still the land we once knew, your mother and I would support your choice, as last year we supported your need to revisit the land of your birth. Yet you have chosen to applaud and thereby encourage the aspirations of a man who is duping and poisoning an entire nation. He is opening the spigots of a sewer. I cannot repeat often enough the fact that Adolf Hitler is leading the Germans into an abyss of immorality where only human vileness will be rewarded. Are you quite sure, dearest daughter, that you want to be a part of this cold and brutal new order? Were the teachings of your mother and father not adequate to provide you with the code of human decency? I fear that you will find my words unpalatable. At least that much he had right: not even the cakes could sweeten the acidic bitterness with which his words filled her.

Nevertheless, it is my duty as your father, as a father who loves his daughter still, to point out the grievous error of your ways. That you will one day understand, and flee that godforsaken land, remains my most fervent hope.

Ever your Papa.

Lili shoved the letter back into its envelope. That godforsaken land. What a hypocrite—Papa hadn't stepped inside a church since their summers in Alt Eichendorf. And to speak of duping and immorality— what about her missing letters? She would never forgive him for that. Never. If she'd read the letters she would know where Leo was and by now they would have met up again. No apologies from Papa about that either. And where did he even get his special insights into Germany? No doubt from poison pen sheets written by disgruntled Jews. He was probably commiserating with some of them on the other side of the Atlantic right now. Probably feeling sorry for that maniac in Paris.

A radio had been turned on in the Konditorei and the announcer said that it wasn't certain if the embassy official was going to survive. If he didn't, the shooter would be in even more hot water. Lili stuffed the envelope into her purse. What had that Herschel Grynszpan been thinking? Even if his parents were among those caught in the no man's land between Poland and the Reich, what good did it do to shoot an innocent Prussian in the German embassy in Paris? And Papa was talking about immorality.

At last she set out from the Konditorei, walking along Hauptstraße toward home. The mood on the street seemed different than earlier. Here and there, people were standing about in clusters, and snatches of conversations showed that they were giving their opinions on whether or not the diplomat would survive. And if not, then what? How different were French hospitals from German ones? What new troubles would the Jews give decent Germans? What can of worms would be opened? It seemed that the whole town was caught up with the fate of that innocent man, shot down in cold blood. From under their hats, faces were creased with frowns and worry lines. A harried-looking woman kept glancing about her as she pulled at her two children who were tripping over their feet to keep up with her. Perhaps she was afraid of another shooting. A Jew in a black coat and hat hurried by, probably toward Plöck, and a man near Lili shouted out a curse at him. The Jew didn't look back, merely moved faster up the street.

The atmosphere was so odd, like the erratic pulsing of sound waves. She had never felt anything like it. She stopped walking, causing the woman behind her to nearly crash into her. Lili excused herself and moved to stand by the side of a building, listening and watching. It was as if something unseen were building up, like—like contrapuntal strands in a fugue. As if she were still alone, one silent note, while the world was moving by, bodies and voices led by a phantom maestro, their echoes superimposing upon themselves in a tightening blur. For a long long moment she was motionless, as if hesitating. Then, with a shiver that went to her marrow, she pulled her jacket tighter and stepped forth into the movement.

Broken

And then it was already the fifteenth anniversary of the Beer Hall Putsch. Dark red banners hung in strategic spots throughout Heidelberg, the names of the fallen heroes of 1923 emblazoned in gold. This year too marked the twentieth passing of that infamous day when the armistice and the Kaiser's abdication had been declared by those liberals, the November Criminals. But these were new times. Germans could look up to the achievements of their Führer. Throughout the Reich, millions of feet were marching, marching in unison to celebrate the Führer and his Volk.

For most of the day Lili had joined students and the youths from the HJ and BDM, stepping forth, from one end of town to the other, parading their enthusiasm as widely as possible in an endless and toe-numbing fanfare of color and pageantry. Later there had been a glass or two of wine in a Gaststätte. The only blight on the festivities was the continued anxiety about the life-threatening condition of the Third Secretary. On the way home she had seen no black-coated Jews on the streets, not even one. They must have been indoors, thinking about what all the newspapers were saying. That there was a vital need to at last take serious action against them. It didn't matter whether they were dressed in black or had disguised themselves over the centuries to look like Germans. Perhaps even Dr. Morsch's stubborn daughter would at last realize that Germany wasn't her home.

Now, sighing with contentment after the long hours of marching, Lili snuggled deeper into the softness of the quilt. A blister on her heel rubbed against the linen, causing a momentary burning sensation. She closed her eyes on the day, drifting off into darkness.

Snow falls. She is in Central Park. Children are skipping and laughing. The very air seems light-hearted. She catches a snowflake on her tongue, walks on, humming. Perhaps Mama and Paul are sailing a boat on the lake, if it has not yet frozen. The lake is somewhere through the trees. She steps off the path onto snow soft as whipped cream. Now she is alone. The trees in their shrouds press ever closer. The ice on their bark begins to crack, falling off like shards of crystal to reveal the slumbering blackness beneath. Layers splinter and crash. She stumbles through the frozen razors, trying to leave the forest that is closing in on her but the sounds of breaking glass are getting louder and louder and

Lili awakens to hear voices and crashing.

She slides out from under the featherbed, moving barefoot to the window. She presses her forehead against the cold pane, sees nothing but the empty square. Yet somewhere there must be a fire because again and again comes the sound of shattering glass. Now there is more shouting. It grows in intensity until there, from around the far left corner, a group of men in SA uniforms bursts into sight. For some moments they stop in front of the Kornmarkt Madonna. Their voices are rough with bellowing and belly laughs. They set out again. One of them, thick-bodied and slower than the others, has an alpine walking stick.

He looks up toward her side of the square and suddenly he is looking directly at her. She pulls open the window and the November night air hits her skin.

"What's happened?" she calls down.

The SA man halts.

"We're on our way to Plankengasse."

"But didn't the explosions come from the other side of town?"

"What explosions?" Even from up here she can see that he looks puzzled. "*Nee*, that was the shop. Now we're going to their apartment."

"What happened at the shop?"

He wipes his temple. "We took care of it good. Rosenblums won't be selling any more kitchenware, that's for sure." He waves the hiking stick back and forth. "Good solid Bavarian wood, this is. One solid thwack is all it takes." He begins to move. "Well, the night is young. We'll show them what they're in for."

"Wait--" Lili beckons him. "What are you talking about?"

The SA man pauses. "Then you haven't heard yet."

"Heard what?"

"Ernst vom Rath is dead."

A shudder passes through her. "That's terrible."

"Murdered by that Jew," the man says, spitting out the words. "Now it's payback time for the rest of them."

That poor man, dead now for no other reason than that he was a German. How tragic for his family. She nods to the SA man and he hurries off to rejoin the others. She returns to her bed, still warm with her imprint. But she cannot find sleep. What a tragedy for the entire Reich. As it is, more and more governments are closing their doors to German Jews looking to emigrate. Now what country on earth will want to take in troublemakers who are murderers of innocent citizens? Outside, the night air is not yet still. Shouts, crashes and even screams vibrate the windows but Lili does not get up again to look out. If she hadn't spoken with the SA man, she would be terrified by the sounds.

♫ ♪ ♫

It is already late in the morning when Lili runs downstairs. If she doesn't hurry, she'll be late for class. No one is about, not even Tante Aletheia, whose coat is not on its hook in the hall. Frau Dierck still hasn't returned. Did everyone sleep through the noise last night? It seems that Frau Brinkmann has already been busy this morning. The wood is shiny on either side of the carpeted stairs, the stairwell suffused with the smell of wax. Murky light filters in through the frosted panes of the front door. A gray day.

Outside, there is a faint smell of ashes, and strange things are lying about. Books with ripped spines, their pages stained yellow. Shards of what might have been colorful flower vases. A rubber plant lies sideways, some of its fibrous leaves mashed into the ground. It is shocking how disorderly it is.

Something heavier than smoke is in the air.

She hurries along the backstreets. Rounding a corner, she comes upon a group of men, some in SA uniforms, others in neat suits or the garb of their trades. There are a few women as well, one with a thickly blanketed baby carriage. All of them stand and watch. Despite her need for speed, Lili too stops to see what is going on. Two of the workers are shouting through the glassless windows of a street level apartment house.

"Come out, you Saujud!" one of them calls.

"Why wait? Let's go inside," says another and, joined by an SA man, they charge into the building.

Even from the street Lili can hear them beating on a door until there is another crash, wood splintering. Through the empty window frames she sees the men flailing about, throwing plates and glasses, ripping paintings from the walls, then stamping about as if they were trampling grapes. A cupboard is tipped and thunders to the floor. She turns to those standing near her. They seem mesmerized by what is going on, although their expressions are varied.

"Has anyone called the police?" Lili asks, directing the question to any one of them.

A man with a briefcase turns to her. "I've heard that they're not getting involved today."

"That's not true," says the woman behind Lili, her eyes flashing. "They'll come if there's any looting. Germans are not thieves."

"And the fire brigade will come to protect any Aryan-owned buildings from catching fire." The speaker's tone is neutral.

Then the other men are back out on the street again, their hands empty, for they are not thieves, their faces twisted with a mixture of what looks like snarling rage and excitement.

"Who's next on the list?"

Her heart beating in a strange rhythm, Lili turns away and directs her path back toward the university. Here and there, swept up in piles neat but dangerous, are shards and splinters of glass. Occasionally something snaps under her feet, probably leftover slivers. It is all very dreamlike. This must be what the SA man meant last night. They are damaging property owned by Jews. Punishment for the murder of vom Rath.

She passes a shopkeeper who has his head down, as if examining the broom fibers while he sweeps the sidewalk outside a store that no longer has glass in front. Ever since she has been in Heidelberg, Lili has always seen the shop mannequin standing in a frothy but tasteful array of nightgowns. Now it is lying on its back, one arm raised, its head sideways. The glass eyes stare out at the street in a numbing gaze of blue. Several people mill about, observing the shopkeeper as he sweeps, but no one says anything. One woman pulls her child against her.

Lili hurries on; without doubt she will be late for class. They are supposed to hear a lecture about Bismarck. Unless he is back, it won't be by Professor Dr. Hetzenrath. She rather regrets his refusal to link any of the topics to contemporary issues. Today would be a good time to start.

The courtyard is a buzzing mass as students stand in clusters, gesticulating and discussing. Some are louder than others.

"It's the final straw."

"Let's break the Jewish camel's back."

"They just don't get it—we want them out of the country."

"Those deluded fools, thinking they're German just because we've let them live here so long."

"They should all be sent to Poland."

And on and on.

Lili wanders through the crowds toward the stairwell, comes across a sign that announces all classes have been cancelled. She pauses, debating what to do with the rest of the day.

"Hey you, beautiful girl." A wide-shouldered giant who, she notices with a pang, looks a bit like Leo, is calling out, and for a few moments she doesn't realize he means her.

"Yes, you," he says, his voice sonorous. "Come with us. We're setting out on a march—a march to remember!"

"Join us," calls another student, and Lili is swept away by all of them in the group, men and women, as they move out of the courtyard and into the streets of Heidelberg. Today there is more shouting than singing. Here and there, bits of glass crunch underfoot and Lili is glad she is wearing her thick-soled boots.

Someone says he has a list of names and addresses.

The first place is nearby, just off Hauptstraße. Two students pound on the door of the apartment with their fists, a roar like the drums in *Carmina Burana*. After what seems like an interminable wait it opens, and a tiny woman with a cloud of silver hair looks out at them.

"Can I help you?" she asks politely, as if it were every day that a group of university students is waiting, fuming, orchestrating upon her doorstep.

"Yes, you can," says the student who looks a bit like Leo, his eyes glinting, his tone polite. "You can clear out of Germany."

The woman's features pale but she does not flinch.

"Now why would I do that? I've been in this house longer than you've even been alive, you fresh badger." She smiles, revealing teeth of buttermilk yellow, but the corners of her mouth are quivering.

"You dare call me a *Frechdachs*?" The student throws his head back and laughs so hard that Lili can see the mucosal wave of his vocal chords. But when his head snaps forward, his expression has changed.

"I'll show you what a Frechdachs does in a Jew's house."

The woman frowns.

"You're mistaken. I'm not a Jew."

"Oh no?" someone sneers. "And that candelabra over there is for roasting nine sausages at a time, right?"

"It was my grandmother's," the woman explains. She shrugs her shoulders. "I'm a Catholic. Last Easter I went to Rome and was blessed by the Pope."

"Yes, you're her blessed granddaughter."

He strides across the room. The floorboards creak.

"So we'll give you a little show of what we think of your Jewish candlesticks." He turns to the others. "Hey, *Kumpels*! Let's invent a new game. We'll call it 'How many times does it take before the menorah breaks against the wall?' You start."

He thrusts the heirloom into the woman's hands. She seems paralyzed.

"Come on, throw it at the wall," another student urges, his tone playful.

With a sound of disgust, he takes it from her and hurls it. Plaster cracks and the menorah falls to the floor, slightly bent but still whole. Another student bounds over to scoop it up. The room fills with laughter, as if the years had fallen away and they were once again but a group of grade schoolers at recess, taking turns to toss a ball. With each thwack, the wall dents or cracks, and sometimes the menorah ricochets against an object, shooting it onto the floor, shattering it. The woman is pressed against a wall, her hands covering the hollow of her throat.

When it is Lili's turn to throw, she looks down at the tangled silver arms warm to the touch. Her hesitation breaks the rhythm.

"Throw it!" they command.

The student who looks a bit like Leo calls out. "Think of Ernst vom Rath!" And she throws it so hard that this time when it falls, a piece of silver breaks off and skitters across the floor.

After that it is easy.

Armed with their list, they roam through the neighborhoods. In some homes, everyone seems to be in, from grandparents to infants, and Lili's gaze slides over faces that show shock, bafflement, outrage, and finally fear by the intrusion, and at each place a new form of nuisance is devised for them.

Some of the men look like those time-frozen ones, with thick black coats and wispy curls hanging down both sides of their faces, the women wearing wigs. In those homes, the students sweep across the table or cabinet where the menorah stands, knocking it to the floor. There is no more time for games. Hebrew tomes are torn along the spine. When that happens, someone has to hold back the men who want to lunge out and protect their holy books, whose eyes seem crazed.

"They really went berserk this morning when the synagogue was burning," says a student. During the night, the synagogue on Große Mantelgasse was set afire. Much of the religious paraphernalia was taken away to the police station, but there are still objects left inside. Later in the day, when the heat of the fire is less intense, they will go to see what else can be found.

In one home on Unterestraße, a young man bursts out of the hallway and throws himself atop a student, knocking his glasses off. Lili stands to the side as the thin figure, probably the oldest son in the family, is pummeled by a few of the students. It doesn't seem quite fair that he should be so outnumbered when he is obviously so inept at throwing punches. A middle-aged woman, her wig askew, is shrieking at them and the mood here feels wild. For a few moments Lili stares at the scene, loud and tempestuous like some dramatic opera she is seeing for the first time. Wondering, just for a moment, what she is doing here. But then reason prevails. This wouldn't be happening unless this is what the Führer wants, and he knows why. He always has his good reasons.

If this were wrong, he wouldn't allow it.

At the apartment downstairs, one of the students pulls at a boy's blond sidelocks as if checking to see that they are real. The boy begins to sob. His delicate features twist into a grimace, and a wave of something that looks like shame passes across them. Another student makes it his task to pull the caps off the younger boys and toss the cloth out the window. They look like black birds failing to take flight.

Ripping open cabinets and cupboards, Lili helps hurl wine glasses onto the floor, stomps on decorative items so that they crack and splinter and crumble to the original powder of porcelain. Windowpanes burst and shatter under the swing of a walking stick or umbrella handle, their shards flying outwards onto the street, oblivious of passersby. It is like cymbals of crystal, crashing together in a mysterious symphony, otherworldly. And nearly everywhere in the background is the chorus that scolds and shouts, sometimes in silence, that pleads for reason. Woven deep within it all is an almost overwhelming undertone, somber and rather depressing to Lili's ear. Those making this sound aren't even doing it in German but in Yiddish or Polish or some other strange language, making the atmosphere all the more distant from the feel of a true German home.

In other apartments, the residents look like real Germans but the students know that these looks are deceptive. In these homes, it is the family portraits that are torn, the Biedermayer furniture gouged with blades, service medals from the war smashed with an iron. They have no right to such accoutrements of a good German household. Yet it is these people who act most scandalized, and protest the loudest.

At some places, the inhabitants aren't at home but the students exact their revenge for vom Rath's death with just as much dedication. Like for those SA men and workers that Lili saw this morning, it is a simple matter of breaking in. Force will open most doors. Of course their shoulders are beginning to ache from all the thrusting against wood and so, every now and then, they stop at a *Wirtshaus* to rest and re-tank. Nobody has time to eat, just gulp down some beer and get back to work. Revenge for the death of the diplomat. Get the message to the Jews, loud and clear. There is really nothing to think about but that they need to be urged out. Purged from Germany. It's as simple as that. Get rid of the Jews and the Reich will once more be pure.

In one large apartment overlooking the river, two elderly women and their ancient mother, staring into space, are sitting at the coffee table when the overpowered maid lets them in. The daughters look up in surprise.

"Did you invite them?" one asks the other.

"No," she replies, shaking her head. "I thought you did." Both women gape at the visitors.

"There are so many of them," says the first. "Do you think there is enough cake?"

Lili and the others look at each other with raised eyebrows. Someone sniggers. A burly student bows.

"My ladies, do not disturb yourselves. We are not here to pay a social call. In fact, you might as well drink up your coffee now because you won't be brewing any for a long time."

At this, the mother looks up over her collar of lace.

"What does he mean, Elfriede? I must have my coffee every day." She holds her cup in vein-laced hands.

The daughters look alarmed.

"Why are you here?" they ask.

The student purses his lips. "Let's say that we have come to renovate your kitchen." The women look at each other in perplexity.

"Did you call someone in?" asks one.

"Certainly not," says the other, shaking her head. "I don't know what he's talking about but I do wish Mitzi hadn't let them in. I don't like them." She frowns.

"Where is Mitzi?"

"I'm here," a thin voice calls from around the corner.

"Ah, Mitzi," says the student who looks a bit like Leo, his voice like syrup. "Would you be so kind as to show us the way to the kitchen?"

The slight figure creeps into the room. It is obvious that she is more than reluctant to do so, but too frightened not to.

Another student turns to the three women at the table.

"Please. Do finish your coffee." He clicks his heels and salutes. Some of the students chuckle.

With that, they move into the other end of the apartment. Mitzi, her cheeks bloodless, stands to the side while drawers and cupboards are opened and crockery and glasses crescendo against the floor in broken notes. A bottle smashes, flavoring the air with the fruity acid of apple vinegar. The wooden coffee grinder, its sides painted with scenes of sailing ships and palm trees, is splintered by a meat pounder. Just as Lili lifts a gray and blue flour pot from a shelf, she notices that one of the daughters is standing at the doorway, her gaze wide and unblinking as a crab's.

"But what are you doing here?" the woman gasps.

No one stops to answer her.

Lili drops the pot, its burst shards blasting flour onto her feet as well as the floor. Particles of white dust rise like vapor.

The woman shrieks.

"What is the meaning of this? Why are you destroying our kitchen?" She fixes Lili, closest to her, with a look of bewilderment.

Lili opens her mouth but cannot find the right words.

The woman lunges forward, grabs Lili by the forearm. Lili shakes her arm to rid herself of the fingers but their grip is tight as a pincer.

The bug eyes seem half-crazed.

"You—you look nice. Tell them to stop this at once," she rasps. A drop of saliva flies out from her lips and into the air. "What have we done to you?" The pitch of her voice rises in a jarring key.

Lili pushes her.

She lets go and staggers, then finds her footing and remains rooted to the spot, staring at Lili through those awful eyes.

Lili runs out of the kitchen.

Some students are back in the salon where the mother and other daughter seem frozen in their seats.

For a moment, Lili stands in the middle of the room casting about for what to do next. The others have already begun shoving books out of cabinets. Someone is pulling framed etchings of castles off the green wallpaper. Lili is drawn to a carved wooden box on a credenza. Inside are scrolls of paper, rolled up and each tied with a faded ribbon of blue or red. They could be love letters or messages from relatives far away or even secret messages. The paper is worn with age. She is not sure what to do with them. All around her, the students are busy with their work of getting the message across.

Jews out of Germany. That is what the Führer has been aiming for, and he knows best. Everyone should do his or her best for the Reich, even if it means personal hardship. It is not the individual who matters but the entire nation. Lili steels herself. It is an unpleasant task but must be done. She reaches into the box and draws out one of the hollow tubes.

"We're about finished here," one of the students calls out.

No time to read it first.

Lili tears the scroll and drops the two halves onto the carpet. The ribbon dangles from her hand. There is a strangled wail from the table and Lili glances over to see the old mother making indistinct sounds and pointing a trembling finger at her. Like a ghost, pale, with shadowed gaze, the daughter begins to rise, but one of the students fixes her with a stern look and she stays seated, clasping her mother's hands, closing her eyes.

Lili's movements are deliberate as she pulls out another of the fragile scrolls and rips it into pieces, the aged paper tearing easily. The old woman is sobbing, gulping, a silver thread of tears trailing down her parchment cheek. Crossing the carpet, Lili scatters the bits of paper soft as petals. They are crushed underfoot as the students leave the apartment.

If Papa could see her now.

The November air on the street is welcome after the heat inside. Lili's throat is dry and craves another beer. They march along toward their next destination, a house on Theaterstraße. The cold air is invigorating. Someone begins bellowing out a song and everyone immediately joins in, their voices hoarse. The banner that they have been leaving outside the buildings has been hoisted high again, its trinity yet bold against the sky. At one street corner they pause to watch a band of Pimpfs giggling and shrieking as they throw garbage into the broken window of a health food shop. A stout man who looks like a schoolmaster appears from around the corner. He stops abruptly, then barks at them. At the sound of his voice, the boys jerk to attention.

"You rascals! Halt your actions immediately or I'll use my cane on you." He raises it, shaking the stick at them. "The Führer would be appalled to see this sort of thing. He expects more of his young folk than such scoundrel behavior!" His eyebrows, thick as paste, meet just above his nose.

The boys begin to slink away, some muttering and looking annoyed, but Lili hears two of them say "Sorry, Herr *Schulleiter*." Still frowning, the principal nods, and continues on his way up the street.

Some of the university students look at each other and shrug their shoulders. The man must be a fool. Or he has just stepped out of his door for the very first time since Wednesday.

A young man runs up, pauses to gasp for breath.

"They're taking more stuff from the synagogue."

They set out, hurrying across Hauptstraße and through Heumarkt, back down toward the river toward the synagogue that, as Lili knows from *Heidelberg through the Ages*, is a mishmash of architectural styles, from Romanesque to Renaissance. The closer they get, the stronger the smell. Now she stops and stares. Smoke is still rising from the charred synagogue. The roof is gone. A few passersby have gotten down from their bicycles and are standing on the damp cobblestones, watching. Here and there, children too are silent, looking at the ashen facade.

A man explains to someone how the SA set the fire around three in the morning, using wood shavings and cans of gasoline. About an hour later, the fire brigade arrived. Like the man with the briefcase this morning said, their job was to make sure that the neighboring buildings didn't catch fire. Aside from the Jewish prayer hall in the community building next door, of course. Later in the morning, the NSDAP-*Kreisleiter* came to check on the situation, and, around seven o'clock, the fire brigade and the SA men left. The synagogue has been smoldering ever since. Fortunately there is no wind today.

For some time even the students seem taken aback by the sight of the once solid building smeared with stains of smoke, a patina deep with darkness. High up, a few windows are still intact, mirroring glints of insouciant light and clouds.

It is time to get busy.

There is still enough left inside to make a statement that reinforces the message to the Jews. Get out of Germany! Lili looks over to the entrance where for a moment it looks as if a game of tug-of-war were taking place. An older man holds on to one end of a length of cloth while a student pulls the other side. Both are grunting with effort but their expressions are vastly different. In the end, the Jew collapses onto the stones and the victor walks off, trailing the cloth on the ground.

Various objects are being piled atop a wooden cart while a few Jews run around with contorted features and inarticulate shouting. Lili helps carry a strange-looking table. At one point she has to slap at the hands of someone who is trying to remove a particular book from the cart. If Papa could see her now. Lili hasn't entered the synagogue, but even the air outside is steamy, infused with smoke. It is all very dreamlike, wild, a fantastic fugue that is growing more and more frantic in sound and intensity.

The cart rumbles over the cobblestones as they move up toward Heumarkt and then through Unterestraße. Turning the corner, they find an amazing sight, as if history had suddenly burst into life. Like a scene from the Middle Ages, a bonfire is being set ablaze in the square. People gathered around watch as loads are dumped from carts, and books and scrolls and cloth and an untold number of Jewish possessions are thrown into the fire. The flames rise into the November sky, the smoke following.

For a while the students stand and watch. But several of them are coughing, still bothered by the smoke from the synagogue.

"Let's go get something to drink," one suggests. "My throat's parched again." Soon thereafter they set out anew, fortified, to find that the atmosphere is even stranger, highly charged, as if the fire had set off electric sparks. Many of the people out on the streets are behaving in ways that Lili has never seen.

One group walks along dressed only in pajamas and bathrobes. Very odd. Two of the men are on crutches while some of the others are holding on to their sides or supporting each other. Their expressions are dazed, bewildered, as if they had taken too much medicine. Across the street, a bearded man with red paint on his bald head is staggering along, his eyes to the ground. Up ahead on a side street, a kerchiefed woman hurriedly pushes a baby carriage filled with three crying children. She knocks on a door that opens immediately. An older woman sticks her blonde head out, peers up and down the street, and then quickly pulls the carriage inside, closing the door. The other woman races back in the direction whence she came.

On a nearby street some Pimpfs are throwing pebbles at a fish store. As she nears them, Lili can hear the 'ping ping ping' against the glass. One boy pries up a loose cobblestone. When he throws it, the storefront shatters. An especially large shard comes down right atop a plump flounder, slicing it in two, body and tail. Two matrons with empty shopping nets stand nearby, watching, shaking their heads.

"The police should do something. This is vandalism."

The other tuts. "And he always has such good prices."

One of the students overhears. "No, my good ladies," he addresses them. "This is not vandalism. It's retribution."

Then they are off again, bashing and smashing whatever they pick up in the apartments they visit. By now everything is a blur of beer and brawn, a mind-numbing exercise of lifting and throwing that is making Lili's muscles ache.

"By the way," one of the students says later, his voice slurred over his beer at another Wirtshaus.

Outside it is dark. They are exhausted, at last having run out of places.

"Where did you get that list of names?" he continues. "Has Himmler put out some sort of directory of Jews?"

"Insider information, my friend," says the student who looks a bit like Leo. His tone is smug. "Got it from an occasional acquaintance, if you know what I mean." He grins above his glass. "She works at some firm that's involved with the census. They know everything."

Lili looks up from her beer. Could he be referring to Ursula? To Erma? They work in just such a place. But Lili doesn't want to ask if it is one of them. Rather, Lili would like to contribute some insider information too. Her mind is racing, searching for an idea. She looks at her hands. How filthy they are. If Papa could see her now. She giggles. She'll show him. She doesn't have to listen to his anti-German rot anymore. She'll show him the difference between right and wrong. She must know something. Or someone. Ah, and there it is. Someone. Someone who needs some help with doing the right thing. Someone who needs some motivation. Someone who should get out of Germany. Someone called Dr. Morsch. He and his daughter are Jews and la la-la la lah she knows where they live.

She swallows some more beer. Pros and cons. Dr. Morsch drinks plum brandy with Tante Aletheia. He has a beard on his chin and a kind smile. He helps Frau Dierck. But Frau Dierck isn't even here. Besides, he's not supposed to treat Aryans anymore. She should protect Tante Aletheia because she's too nice for her own good. Teach Dr. Morsch a lesson too. Teach him that he shouldn't give in to his daughter. Teach his daughter that she should get the hell out of Germany. Damn him for doing what his daughter wants. Damn his daughter. Damn him. Lili laughs out loud at her language.

"I know an address," she offers up.

Her voice quivers from the attention focused on her. Or from the way her heart is racing now.

"Ah," says the student who looks a bit like Leo. "It's always the quiet ones who come through in the end. The deep ones." He shoots her a grin, and despite her exhaustion and a lingering dissonance, and because he looks a bit like Leo, she smiles.

They drain their glasses and make their way up Hauptstraße past several open storefronts, some of whose display shelves lie empty. Did they have special sales, everything at half-price, or were there looters after all? Lili stumbles over a piece of wood, giggling. The closed shutters of another shop are in the process of being hacked down by three SA men. Scrawled on the wall of a building nearby, in big red letters nearly black under the streetlight, is DEATH TO INTERNATIONAL JEWRY.

A dark car pulls up near the curb where Lili is standing, unloads three figures in dark overcoats and hats. Gestapo for sure. With brisk movements one of them opens the door of the building and they enter in single file. They look like they mean serious business. Lili glances over at the students and smirks. None of *them* need to consider the Gestapo or police or worry about anything at all because everything they are doing is for the good of the nation.

In the distance a siren wails. Smoke hangs in the air. Lili and the others move up Kettengasse and turn left. The gate to the house is shut but quickly torn open. By now all of them have a disheveled, glazed look. Lili wants to look in a mirror, check if she too looks like that.

Someone raps on the door. The lights are off but that means nothing. Yet the possibility that no one is home loosens some muscles in Lili that, until now, she hasn't realized were tight. They wait a few moments before two students try to smash the door with their bruised shoulders. Tough as Krupp steel. Of oak, the door is far too heavy. Someone takes a crowbar acquired along the way and begins to splinter the wood along the hinges. When it is loose enough, the men push and the door comes down nicely.

Lili remembers where the light switch is.

The salon looks restful; the velvet armchairs inviting. Perhaps she should curl up in one and take a nap. A vase of white flowers brings lightness. The drapes are a deep yellow. During the day, the room glows.

"We've got our work cut out for us here," someone says. "This place needs real attention. Almost looks German." At this there are a few snorts.

Someone takes out a pocketknife and begins to slice long gashes into the silk drapes, a methodical whirring sound. Another moves around the room, picking up porcelain figures, surely Meissner, then dropping them as if they were but dirty socks. Lili flinches with each smash. Someone else is busy carving messages into an antique writing desk. From where she is emptying an inkwell onto the carpet in sloppy spirals, Lili glances over at the words.

GET OUT, JEWS!

That's perfect. Dr. Morsch will have to force his daughter to leave.

"Are you positive no one's here?" someone asks of two students who have just come from upstairs.

"No, completely empty. Too bad. Maybe they've already left the country, hahah!" A mirror in a gilded frame hangs above a credenza. Lili walks over and stares into it. Her skin and eyes are a strange color, as if her heart were pumping beer, not blood.

The student with the knife comes over and continues his writing across the polished walnut surface of the credenza. He pushes aside several silver-framed photographs. One of them topples over the edge and, as it falls to the floor, Lili glimpses a face. With a sudden catch of breath, she moves over and picks it up. The doe-like eyes looking into hers are filled with love; the portrait of a beautiful girl. She lifts the other frames lying there, one at a time. All of them are of the same person, some of her alone, some of them from years ago, with a woman who looks very much like her. Even before she sees the photograph of the girl together with Dr. Morsch, the truth hits Lili in the chest. The Jewish student is his daughter. It almost seems stupid not to have realized it earlier.

Where are they tonight? Have they gone out or are Dr. Morsch and his daughter hiding in a closet upstairs? Should she go and search? And then what?

"Let's go," someone says. "We've done good work here for now." The student with the knife slips it back into his pocket. His messages are gouged deep into the wood. The salon looks as if a herd of oxen had passed through, hoofing and horning everything in sight. Lili hasn't seen the rest of the house.

Someone is roaring with laughter from where he is pissing on a pile of medical books, their pages open.

"This is the real thing, my friends," he says. "Much better than that Blubo and KdF crap. This is what it's all about." He gives a parting shot.

"Good aim," says someone else, grinning. "Preparation for the tabula rasa of the Reich."

Lili is momentarily dazed. Blubo and KdF crap?

"Well said," someone shouts out. "Let's go celebrate the New Order."

"Hey, don't forget. This is about vindication too."

"Oh, right you are."

"We should definitely raise a toast to the dear departed diplomat. He's going to be a big help in solving the Jewish problem."

The November sky above Heidelberg is hazy, the stars hidden behind a mottled film of clouds and smoke. Like on a cinema screen, the movements of the people, streetcars, and automobiles still out and about have a disjointed rhythm to them; the sounds emanating form a music strange and new, more neo-pagan than anything Carl Orff could have written. But the sound inside the tavern is familiar. So many students with so much to say. Lili drinks half her beer, then gets up. She needs to go home. Her feet and arms are aching, burning, and her head is throbbing.

"What—you're leaving already?" they ask as she begins to slip into her coat. She can't find the sleeve. Someone helps her.

"Come on," somebody else urges. "Rest up for a while and then we'll go see what's happening at the other synagogue. Maybe someone has some matches left, eh?" At this there are a few belly laughs from around the table, but they sound more tired than hours earlier.

Lili shakes her head. "I really need to get home. My great-aunt is probably wondering where I am."

"Well then," says the student who looks a bit like Leo, "be a good girl and go home to the old lady. You've done a lot today. You can be proud."

There is a general nodding of heads and a few smiles shoot in her direction. Lili's lips are lopsided. All of them here have been through a lot today. A new age is dawning. Everyone at the table looks exhausted, but the fuel of retribution and beer will see them through.

Back at the house, Fragonard is lying on Tante Aletheia's bed. His tail moves back and forth, slowly. Although her coat is back on its hook downstairs, Tante Aletheia herself isn't anywhere to be found. Lili hasn't seen her since the day before yesterday. How odd. But then today has been the oddest day. Perhaps it is best that Tante Aletheia not see her in this condition.

Despite her whirling head, Lili brushes her teeth, drinks water, and even washes. The cloth is coated with gray. She climbs into bed, ready for sleep, but it refuses to come.

She stares at the dark ceiling. The Jewish student with the boyfriend is Dr. Morsch's daughter. Dr. Morsch won't leave Germany because his daughter doesn't want to. He won't make her. It's not fair. It's ironic. They are Jews and they won't leave, and she is Aryan and Papa made her leave. It's not fair. She kicks at the quilt. Papa has no idea what is important. But she does. And she is glad that she took the students to Dr. Morsch's house. Glad that they ripped it up and gouged it out. Glad glad glad. She turns onto her side, closes her eyes. Over and over, the events and sights of the day replay themselves as if they were newsreels without commentaries. The pulsing silence in her aching head is now near deafening.

Perhaps some cold air will be useful. She slips out from under the quilt and makes her way over to the window. She breathes deeply the somewhat acrid flavor of the night. Despite the late hour, despite all that has gone on this Friday, all the lights are on in an apartment across the square. A party? Lili puts her elbows on the ledge and rests her cheeks on her palms, watching.

Several people are moving about inside. Suddenly the night cracks and for a long moment the moonlight lights up a hundred shooting stars as glass shards fly through space. Lili straightens, her hands on the ledge. Now she can hear the sounds from within the apartment. It is not a party.

Curt shouts, a scream of anger or frustration. With the windowpanes gone, the figures inside come into focus. People in pale clothes, men in uniforms. A massive shape looms in the opening, blocking out the view inside. Another scream, muffled. Then the dark mass moves forth, hurtles to the ground, smashing with a discordance in E-flat minor that rips apart the air of this November night.

A piano is lying on the lamp-lit cobblestones, its wooden casing split open like pieces of chocolate, broken, dark and bitter. Yet Lili's gaze is drawn upwards again when she sees what else now sails forth from the window. Armchairs seem to have sprouted wings, for they fly out gracefully before hitting the ground, the impact dulled by their stuffing. Next comes a bed frame with headboard attached and right after that a mattress descends. Their landings are drowned out by the sound of harsh voices and screaming, screams now at a pitch and tone she has never heard before, and shrieking mixed with a wail that makes her bile rise and then a white object sails out from the upper story window.

Bedclothes flutter from the object as it moves in a bizarre tarantella through the night before landing across the upright headboard with a thud and a crack that can be nothing but a finale.

Lili's fingers fumble as she closes the windows, in a hurry to blot out the dissonance. She moves across the room, to bed. To bed. Waves of nausea well and swill their way through her, borne on the hammering of her heart, but nothing comes out. She curls into a ball and her limbs begin to burn as if pierced by a thousand shards.

♫ ♪ ♫

Her first thought upon waking is that the sun is shining. How soothing the light is, soft, shimmering, bathing the morning in quiet. In her mouth she can still taste the residue of the night but the water she drank has helped, for at least her head is no longer spinning. Surely today all will be resolved. It has to be.

Washed and dressed, Lili goes to the kitchen, but again no one is there. The Poppes and Herr Tischborn must be off to work already, but where is Dr. Hempel? Where is Tante Aletheia? If Lili hadn't seen her coat last night, she would truly begin to worry. Frau Dierck's coat hasn't made its reappearance yet either, but that is nothing much to be concerned about. Lili notices a single red glove lying on the floor and picks it up. How soft the leather is. She puts it on the table next to a basket of fresh rolls. It seems that at least Frau Brinkmann has been in. Lili smears some butter on a half and eats it while getting together her books. Unlikely that classes will be cancelled two days in a row. Fragonard comes into the kitchen and looks up at her.

"Here, have some of this." Lili pours milk into a saucer but Fragonard flattens his ears at the offering and disappears around the corner.

Still chewing, she slips into suede shoes and pulls on her dark gray coat, winding a scarf of white wool around her neck. It doesn't seem to be overly cold. Once outside the house, she glances around. The furniture that only hours before lay scattered on the street is no longer there. Yet there are signs that it was no dream. Whoever cleaned the street this morning was not thorough enough. Near the edge of the pavement, looking like a squashed black beetle, a typewriter is spread in a mangled heap. Piano keys lie sprinkled over the cobblestones like salt and pepper. She turns away, unwilling to investigate the spot where darkness stains the stones.

The sun is shining, but as she crosses Kornmarkt it is clear that there is still tension in the air. Will today be another day like yesterday? How much destruction will it take to get the message across to the Jews? She shudders. How awful for everyone if this sort of thing has to continue for some time.

Marktplatz is filled with people, like on market day. But today is not market day. A crowd has formed around something on the far end of the square. It cannot be another bonfire, for no smoke is rising. She weaves her way closer, passing people of all ages and sorts; men in woolen hats and jackets, in overalls; housewives in baggy coats, their reddened fingers clutching net bags; children barely out of diapers; gangly boys and girls. And of course the SS and SA men in their uniforms.

Lili moves into the throng, so close between two SA men that she can smell the breakfast sausage and beer on their breath. The air is humming with gruff voices, with murmurs and whispers, tones both scolding and shrill, inharmonious. Underneath it all, she can hear the sound of silence too. What is everybody looking at? Of course there are not nearly as many people here on Marktplatz but, just as she did that day when she learned how to force her way through the crowds to get to the front of the lines and see the Führer in Nuremberg, Lili now pushes through with her book bag toward the innermost row.

In the open space before her, a man is on all fours. His bare fingers are splayed against the ground, the knees of his dark suit bent against the cold stone of the church square. A line of blood traces the curving fringe of his beard. His head is bowed, so that Lili can see the hair that fluffs out at his nape. She sees something else, too; a dull red collar attached to a long twine that is swallowed up by the crowd.

"Crawl on, Jew!" a voice calls out.

From somewhere else in the mass of spectators, a man shouts: "If you were Herschel Grynszpan we'd show you more than a thing or two!"

A HJ boy runs over to the man on the stones, holds up a paper, and then sticks it onto his backside. There are some roars of laughter.

Someone calls out, "It says 'The harder you kick me, the faster I'll fly out of Germany!'

There are strangled sounds behind Lili.

Another HJ boy, his mouth toothy with a wide grin, skips out and thrusts his boot against the man, causing him to jerk forward and lose his balance. He falls onto his forearms. Someone pulls the leash.

"Up, Jew dog!"

This morning's roll threatens to rise in Lili's throat.

A woman marches out to the man and stands in front of him, arms akimbo.

"Why don't you just drop dead and save us all the trouble?" She spits on his head, then walks around and kicks him in the thigh. Someone guffaws. The man flinches but stays on all fours, his head still down. Turning to the crowd, the woman shrugs before walking back to her place in the circle. Now, as if they were gathered to watch an outdoor folk theater, there is some clapping.

Lili's heart beats faster and faster but the rest of her is firmly rooted, even when the person behind seems to push against her briefly.

Next comes a young man with a kindly face. He strides over and bends down, as if to comfort the man on the stones, then takes a fistful of hair and pulls the head up by it. There are some sharp intakes of breath as people see the eye swollen half-shut, the bloodied nose, the hanging lip.

Just as the sickening realization of who that man out there is hits her, there is a moan from behind Lili, and a thin voice whimpers "Papa".

Immediately, just above Lili's ear, a masculine voice drowns out the next strangled cry of "Papa" with a jovial cry of "*Papperlapapp*" and a hearty laugh, hysterical around the edges.

"Papperlapapp," he says again. Oh yes, it's all papperlapapp, fiddlesticks and nonsense. All this is nothing but good-natured horsing about.

The blood is rushing icy cold through Lili. She feels the straining of Dr. Morsch's daughter behind her, as if her body were being forcibly pulled back to keep it from moving forward. But Lili does not turn around, because she cannot take her eyes off Dr. Morsch. In his eyes she can see disbelief and humiliation and fear and bravery and disappointment. It is a look that is horrifying.

Why is he here? Why are they doing this to him? Someone jerks the leash. Dr. Morsch's head and shoulders jerk too. Some of the people around Lili are laughing and pointing, as if it were a Kaspartheater and he the *Hampelmann* in the middle. There are other voices too, an indistinct murmuring. Dr. Morsch's horrible gaze goes over the crowd. Is he looking for his daughter, does he hope to find her here—or not? Can he see her struggling to get to him? Does he see Lili? Her knees are starting to tremble. Dr. Morsch is in the middle of Marktplatz, attached to a leash.

"What's happening now?" someone further back in the crowd calls out.

Someone else shouts, "This one might not make it to the Promised Land."

The woman next to Lili murmurs, "I know him. He was a good doctor. Such a pity he's a Jew."

"Why is this happening to him?" Lili stammers.

"His house got a good going over last night. The SA went there this morning to finish the job. One thing led to another." She clicks her tongue. "One can almost feel sorry for him."

Lili's insides rise in an awful whooshing. Her teeth clamp down hard upon the flesh of her inner lip. Behind her there is muffled shrieking.

Dr. Morsch is here because of her.

It was *she* who told them where to go. *She* who showed them where he lived. Her legs are shaking. In front of her Dr. Morsch is on his hands and knees, and his face is his and not his.

The blood drains from her head and slams into her chest.

The leash is jerked tighter and his eyes close, then open wide. He cranes his neck to the right as with one hand he pulls at the collar. His face is changing color. His mouth opens and his chest heaves, as if trying to gasp air into himself.

The man next to Lili lifts a child.

"Look," he commands.

And Lili looks. Sees a father she has betrayed, a father she has abandoned.

Behind Lili, as if muted by a pressing palm, Dr. Morsch's daughter is making noises like how an ensnared animal must sound, primal howls, helpless.

Dr. Morsch's skin is darkening. Does he still see his daughter, or is she becoming just a memory?

All around are voices, yet, underneath the cacophony, Lili hears the silence roaring, louder and louder.

As in the transforming final frenzied movement of a fugue, Lili drops her book bag and moves forth. Something, she knows not what, powers her every step as she crosses the empty cobblestones toward Dr. Morsch whose eyes are bulging. As she hurries to him, she strips off her gloves. The voices begin to die away, from the front first, like diminuendos rippling backwards. She drops to one knee on the stones, thrusts two fingers under the collar to give him some air, and then abandons that. His features are still dark. She tugs at the leash to give him some slack.

"Let go!" she shrieks at where the leash disappears into the crowd. The fury of her scream sounds ugly in her ears.

"If the Führer were here he'd tell you to let go!" she cries.

For a few moments there is an eerie silence and the leash loosens enough for her to slip her fingers under the collar and unfasten the buckle holding it. The dull red strap falls to the ground. Dr. Morsch turns, gasping, looks up into her eyes. Does he recognize her? Can he see her?

Lili lifts her face to the crowd.

"He's still alive!" she shouts. She stands up. She is Lili von Rittersburg zu Mertz-Tärnekow, musician, kissed by the Führer a lifetime ago. She will be heard.

"I'm going to tell the Führer about this!" she promises them.

Now that Dr. Morsch is free, she can give vent to her outrage. The blood is thundering through her as never before, but she has to tell them, she has to tell them even though it is her fault that Dr. Morsch is even here. Because he is here. Like in a performance, everyone is staring at her, their faces a blur, as if it were but one big face before her.

"This isn't how we are supposed to behave," she calls out to them. "Germans are peace-loving people." Her throat is going raw from the fortissimo of her spontaneous oratory. "The Führer has said that he wants peace. He would be appalled to see what has just been done to this man—and he a doctor who helps people. The Führer—"

Something flies through the air, just by her head.

"Shut your trap, you stupid cow!"

The words stun. Her mouth is open; the air cold on her teeth.

Arms grab her from behind—she didn't see them coming—and in the sudden onslaught of voices there is a slap across the side of her head.

There are faces, strangers' faces with mouths twisted into expressions she has never seen, directed at her, and so very close. The sounds coming out of them are brutish, atonal. All at once there is a new sensation and she must be breaking in half at the waist, crumpling forward while the pain blows through her belly and into her back. Now she is on the stones again, this time with both knees. Her breath is heavy, heaving. Something is pulling at her scarf. Colors swirl all around her, distorting what she sees. Like the paintings of Wilhelm von Wohlitz. Is she in a painting? No, impossible. All is real but she can't find the focus.

Yes, she is here; whistles and shouts and thumping hard against her sides, her neck, her arms. Her hands—she must protect her fingers. They curl into fists and she works at tucking them under, pulls her arms against her chest. Fist against her jawbone then, burning. Other hands, pushing; she is flat on the stones. Her coat. Brown shoes near her face, hard into her shoulder. A pressing against her ankles; her legs lifted into the air. The sky is a churning sea of faces but far in the back she can see the brooding shape of the castle against the sky. Now her fingers are out, straining to hold on to her coat which is bunching up in the back and cold air rising up her legs and moving toward her heart and against the stones some bone is going bump, bump, bump, bump. Such a rhythm inside her head. The theme weaves around the beat, up and down, over and over, looping through chromatic translations and harmonies. Bump, bump, bump. She knows it, yes, it is the 21st Variation, the distance between the parts preventing them from crossing, then the change in key...No, wait. Slower, heavier, it is the 15th, it is. There is the clearness of the canon...from the darkness will come the light...but... why is it getting so dark?

Because of Her

For some days she had done nothing but hide in bed, her mouth dry from shock. Every position spread pain so she had chosen the one that let her close herself off from the world, curling into a ball. At first the medication they gave against the injuries and inflammation allowed her sleep, a black slumber broken only by hideous thoughts even in her deepest dreams. Then she would awaken with a cry that would have Tante Aletheia at her side.

She would strain to open her jaws but manage only a whisper.

"Where is Dr. Morsch?"

"Sleep, darling girl," Tante Aletheia said then, her fingers soothing against Lili's brow, pulling back the hairs that stuck to her fevered forehead. So Lili slept, but now her dreams were accompanied by the relentless movement of a Fugue in B Minor, tinny and frantic to her inner ear. Under the bedclothes her bruised fingers searched for missing keys, filling her with agitation.

In those moments when the shock wasn't coursing through her, she relived the savagery on the square. That they had beaten her was only right. She deserved it, every last kick and punch and fist in her face.

It had begun with the breaking of glass that night. The SA men had instigated the violence but it was the others, she and so many others, who had taken the humiliation and harming of the Jews to full heights. It had been mass insanity, a giant dose of drug-like wildness. The Führer could not have known. If only the Führer had been informed in time. He would have called them to reason. What they had done was no way to treat people. The Führer would put a stop to the ugliness and violence. He would put his erring Volk back on the path of humanity. Would he forgive them? Could he?

"Where is Dr. Morsch?" she asked again.

"Hush, my dear," Tante Aletheia said. "Sleep and heal."

Lili closed her eyes to see Dr. Morsch kneeling on the cold stones, dog leash around his neck, face turning dark, eyes looking into hers with such sorrow that she awoke gasping for air. What horror she had wrought.

"Where is Dr. Morsch?" she asked, after Tante Aletheia had made her sip some chamomile tea.

This time, Tante Aletheia did not tell her to sleep.

"My dear girl," she said. "You were very brave. You tried so hard to help him." The room was quiet. She swallowed, and Lili could hear the liquid pressing sound of the pharyngeal phase. Tante Aletheia put her hand on Lili's palm.

"I am so very sorry," she said.

"Dr. Morsch has died."

Lili closed her eyes. He was dead. He was dead because of her. She was the one who had led the students to his house. Because of her, Dr. Morsch was dead. She had as good as killed him herself.

Over and over she tried in her head to go back and not take the students to his house, not take them past the door. She tried to take them to another place, take them nowhere; but it didn't change anything. Dr. Morsch was dead. Because of her.

She tried to tell herself that someone else could have taken the students there but it didn't change anything because she was the one who had led them there and now he was dead. Because of her.

Unworthy of the comfort of tears, she did not weep.

Dr. Morsch had died because of her.

The vomiting began. She was sickened by the concern in the voices around her: did she have serious head injuries after all? It had been a long time since she had eaten. What could she be bringing up in such relentless spasms?

Unable to utter any words, to say what she had done, she knew exactly what she was choking up from within her. The smell was appalling. No matter how much the room was aired and perfume sprayed on her pillowcase, no matter how many times her head was lifted and her mouth rinsed with Vademecum-steeped water, Lili could smell it. It was the stench of wrong, of evil, and the shame kept it with her.

Perhaps she could vomit herself out of existence.

But Dr. Morsch would still be dead.

And then, at some point, a thick needle pushed into her skin and the nausea began to recede, leaving Lili on an unknown shore with only herself.

Now her eyes stayed open, staring at the window. When there was light, the pupils contracted, when the pane turned dusky they dilated. She had to find the right words. A vast and silent emptiness loomed. There were no notes in her head, no devastating melody that might help her find the right words to confess what she had done. She was on her own.

Time had no measurement, there was only now, burning.

The door opened.

"Lili?" said Tante Aletheia. "There is someone who has been waiting to meet you. I think you will want to hear what she has to say."

Tante Aletheia entered the room, followed by a tall man and a slender woman with honey-colored hair.

Lili bit into her flesh. Blood seeped into her mouth. While Tante Aletheia propped her up, she forced herself to look at Dr. Morsch's daughter.

Now let Dr. Morsch's daughter look into her eyes so that she would know the guilt that was Lili's.

Delicate, dressed in black, her skin the creamy smoothness of porcelain, his daughter looked more fragile than ever. She came to the bedside. As ever a towering protector, the student too approached.

Lili pressed her teeth deeper. Now. Now the horror would be upon them.

Dr. Morsch's daughter bent over her.

"May I call you Lili?" Her voice was soft, mellifluous. "I am Bettina. I feel as if we must be sisters."

Lili watched Bettina take her hand, raise it to her lips and kiss it. She stared at her, bewildered, her heartbeat galloping with dread.

"I cannot thank you enough," Bettina said, her voice catching. "Of all those there that day, of all those many many people, there was only one who tried to stop the madness." She turned toward the student whose shoulders shuddered as he restrained a sigh. "I know, Volker," she said. "You were too busy trying to keep me from joining Papa out there. I know that Papa would thank you with all his heart." She turned back to Lili, her eyes wet with a startling shade of blue.

"In all that crowd, you were the only one decent and brave enough to help my father. The only one who was willing to stand up for what was right." Bettina took a breath and swallowed. Her voice was frail. "You didn't join the others in what is so terribly wrong these days." She paused. Lili could only stare at her.

"Thank you," Bettina said, her voice stronger again. "From the depths of my being I will always be grateful, Lili. You tried to save my father. Whatever else may come, I will always have that solace." She knelt down next to the bed and put her forehead against Lili's shoulder.

There were no words; she could find not one word to say to Bettina.

Inside her head there was only discordant achromatic dissonance, ugly echoing of all the vile and evil things she had done, to Dr. Morsch, to Bettina, to countless strangers. And Bettina had kissed her hand and told Lili she would always find solace in what she had done.

Lili turned aside as the deep spasms of retching began anew.

"Best you take your leave now, my dears," said Tante Aletheia to Bettina and Volker. "I will see to her."

And Tante Aletheia held the basin while wild images skittered and crashed through Lili as she thought of Bettina and her father and Papa and what he would say when he learned of what she and others in Germany had done.

Afterwards, empty, bent inwards, she slept again. Then woke and slept again. The days went by. Her dreams changed, chasing her when she ran from them, pouncing upon her with talons of truth as she hid along the outermost edges. There were figures, too, furious, accusing her of showing sympathy for those who had done nothing but suck out the lifeblood of the German people.

"I would tear their tongues out of their throats," said an aged Martin Luther, his tone as savage as his words, his earth brown robes dragging along the hallowed ground of his church. There was Beate, face shining in the flames of a campfire as she shrieked at Lili. "Remember how you pledged yourself to the Flag, Führer and Fatherland!" Twisting from side to side in her fevers, Lili stumbled on, through heavy fog. "You must believe in Germany," a voice, disembodied and stentorian, intoned through the depths, "or you are the enemy."

And what did Goethe have to say? Suddenly she wanted to hold in her hands the book Papa and Mama had given her. She began to pull herself up but a whirlpool of dizziness sucked her in and she had to lie back, her skin growing clammy cold with perspiration.

Yet regardless of what others had said or done, it was she who had led the way to the death of Dr. Morsch.

Lili Begins to Think

Then, one afternoon in December, she sat up in bed, her head strangely calm, like the sea after a tempest. She would never know which of the many festering thoughts had hit the nerve that spurred her to begin anew. But she knew that forevermore she would taste of bitter gall.

When Tante Aletheia next came into the room, Lili asked how she had reached home that day in November.

The emerald green eyes peered into hers.

"So, Lili, the time has come."

"Tell me that, please, and what has been happening since then."

Tante Aletheia sat down. Her tone calm, she explained what she had learned from Bettina and Volker. In the ensuing pandemonium that had broken out after Lili's actions on Marktplatz, the two had pushed their way through to Dr. Morsch. Neither Bettina nor Volker had known who Lili was. Dr. Morsch had gasped out to them to get Lili to Tante Aletheia's, a selfless thought for her safety. SS men were already there, barking commands, moving the people, but doing little to halt the blows to Lili. She had been dragged over the cobblestones and, in the confusion, Volker was able to get to her and scoop her up while Bettina touched her father one last time before he was taken away.

"Was he still alive then?"

"Yes. He was still alive then."

Lili bit into her lip.

Tante Aletheia explained how just a day earlier she had gone back and forth, urging Dr. Morsch and his daughter to shelter in the house on Kornmarkt. How they had stayed upstairs there, safe that night, until in the morning Dr. Morsch said he must go out to see if any of his patients had been hurt. Tante Aletheia said that he must have gone home to get medical supplies, and had been there just when the SA men had come to the house. In the meantime, Volker had come by Kornmarkt and he and Bettina had gone off together, ending up at Marktplatz. Since that day, Bettina had been staying in Frau Dierck's room.

Lili shuddered. The blood red glove lying alone on the kitchen floor must have been Bettina's.

"Have you heard from my parents?"

"Yes, they telegraphed, asking if we are safe." Tante Aletheia paused. "I replied, and hope it was not wrong that I did not inform them of what happened to you. There will come a time when you can tell them yourself."

"Where did they take Dr. Morsch?"

"Are you indeed ready to hear everything, Lili? It is painful and terrible."

And Tante Aletheia told her how Dr. Morsch and thousands of other Jewish men across the land had been taken into custody, for their own protection, it was said—in police stations, jails, barracks, schools, even in trucks. The women and children who had been arrested during those first days had since been released, but the men transported to three of the Reich's concentration camps. Of course none of the camps had been designed for such numbers. So the old and the sick and the handicapped had been sent home.

"Apparently," said Tante Aletheia, "the initial correct, even apologetic manner of *some* of the arresting officers, SS or Gestapo, differed wildly from the treatment the men received once in the camps."

"How do you know all this?"

Tante Aletheia glanced to the side. "I learned this from someone who was released. But you must tell no one about any of this." Now the green eyes fixed Lili with a piercing stare. "No one."

By mid-November the temperature had dropped dramatically, she said, was already freezing, but the men were made to stand outside at attention for up to twenty hours. And all that time, nothing to drink, nothing to eat. Some fell, and began to die right there on the gravel. Others were told to run between two rows of camp guards armed with clubs and whips. Some more began to die even as the guards laughed. For several days, Jewish men continued to arrive. The political prisoners, many of whom had been there since 1933, were vastly outnumbered by the Jewish men who stared at each other, shock mirrored in their eyes; they were there simply because of their ancestors?

On the first night, SS guards, men with the face of death pinned to their collars, had entered an overcrowded barrack to pull outside three of the prisoners. Their agony cut through the night, screams and cries that none of the newly arrived men had ever before heard. By morning, one of them had chosen to listen no longer and lay in a pool of blood, the artery on his leg severed with a shard of glass snapped off from a broken window. Still, there were too many in the camp, and not enough water. Each day the loudspeakers cracked the late November air, a cold voice announcing the names of those who were now free to leave. The names of the dead were included in these lists. The man who had been released said that Dr. Morsch's name had been among them.

He said that the message could have been neither louder nor clearer: it was more than advisable for the Jews to quit Germany.

"What has the Führer said about what happened?" Lili asked. "Surely by now he has made some announcements condemning it."

"He?" Tante Aletheia grimaced. "He has said nothing."

Nothing! What did that mean? He must be in shock. Yes, that would be it. The Führer was in shock at the way his people had erupted, destroying valuable property, and lives.

Tante Aletheia continued. In the intervening weeks, even though the Führer had said nothing, Goebbels and Göring had not been silent. Goebbels had issued an initial statement in which he said that the justifiable indignation of the German people at the cowardly murder of Ernst vom Rath had manifested itself in a wide degree. Completely spontaneous reprisals had been carried out against Jewish buildings and places of business. But now the whole population was strictly enjoined to abstain from all further action of whatsoever nature against the Jews. The final reply to the outrage in Paris would be given to the Jews by legal means—by decree.

Göring had announced the first new decrees: one ordering a billion Reichsmark fine to be paid by German Jewry as punishment for the crime of vom Rath's murder. One instructing that Jewish owners of any property damaged during the days of revenge bear the costs of repairing such damage—there would be no insurance payments. One eliminating the Jews from the German economy by January 1, 1939.

She lay back against the pillows. Such measures would certainly squeeze the Jews out of the Reich. Any means of financial support for them would be suffocated. Goebbels and Göring were talking. Why wasn't the Führer?

And there was more, Tante Aletheia said. Jews would no longer be allowed in Aryan theaters or cinemas, exhibition or concert halls.

Lili stared at the wall. It was absurd. How would the authorities even be able to tell who was or wasn't Jewish unless they were wearing those dark old-fashioned clothes. It was baffling. New boundaries were being laid out, not only for the Jews, but for the citizens of the Reich too.

"The Führer has said nothing?" She was begging now. How could he be silent for so long? For her own selfish and vital reasons, to know his censorious judgment on what she had done, she needed to hear that he had condemned those who had participated in the events of those ghastly days in November.

"Nothing."

Lili looked at the window. Outside, snow was covering the roofs of Heidelberg with a layer of unblemished white. She could imagine the streets, snow filling the spaces, soft and hushed, covering the traces. Cold and silent.

With a violent motion, she threw back the covers and climbed out of bed. She could hide no longer.

Tante Aletheia looked startled, then gave a sad smile.

Lili was unsteady on her feet, but sheer force of will would take over now.

"You need to eat something," said Tante Aletheia. "Frau Brinkmann has a nourishing bouillon waiting for you."

Later, after finishing the cup and sensing some energy, Lili wanted to go outside, breathe in the searing cold. Then she would write to her parents. She managed to wash and dress herself and got halfway down the stairs before realizing that a walk was not going to work, not today. The perspiration chilled her forehead and a wave of dizziness passed through her. If Herr Tischborn hadn't been coming up the stairs just then, she might have fallen. But he must have seen her pallor, for he offered her his arm, escorting her back upstairs.

"I heard about what you did, Fräulein Lili," he told her, his voice low, as they made the climb with slow steps. He seemed even more withdrawn than usual. "I would like you to know that you have my respect." He did not cross the threshold of her room but stood waiting as she sank into the armchair near the window, her heart thumping with the effort of the trip. Then, nodding briefly, he left.

Once her chest had quieted, Lili considered his words. She had his respect. But he only knew what she had done that day in Marktplatz, not how it had come to happen. How she had as good as put Dr. Morsch there herself. A snowflake blew against the windowpane and she watched it melt on the glass. An idea was dawning, possibly the most radical thought she had ever experienced.

First she counted the people. Certainly Tante Aletheia—it was now clear to her. Volker too of course. She couldn't count Bettina. She bit her lip. And now Herr Tischborn. There had to be others she knew as well. Dr. Hempel? Her mind raced, recalling conversations and words that could be interpreted in different ways. Pauses or hesitations. And what about Professor Dr. Hetzenrath with his lectures that limited themselves strictly to the epoch under study? Was that because he did not care to address the present? She didn't know if she could fully count poor Frau Dierck with her ravings. Oh, it was becoming clearer by the moment.

Papa was not the only one.

There were a thousand signs, everywhere, if only one knew how to look. Even here there were people who did not approve of what was happening in Germany! Did not approve of where the Führer was leading his Volk. Who felt he was leading them in the wrong direction.

If people she knew personally felt like that, how many others might be out there? How could she recognize them on the street? And then, bizarre idea—what if some of them were wearing uniforms? Like Benno. No, not Benno. He was committed to the Führer, even if in a different way than the Poppes. Leo?

She tried to recall words exchanged with Leo, whose SS insignia had banished him from her mind until now. Yet what was it he had said, that very first time, in the dressing room at the Stadthalle? She had made a grandiose statement, saying that musicians were artists, and artists must be allowed every freedom. And he, what had he replied? She closed her eyes, trying to see and hear it again. He had laughed, yes. And said...yes, he had said that it was a sentiment voiced only in certain circles. Yes! At the time she hadn't understood what he meant, but now... And there were other insinuations, so subtle that she had missed them at the time. Perhaps it was necessary to consider everyone's words. They could have more than one meaning. Or there could be meanings lying beneath the words. Unspoken and hidden meanings.

This brought with it a tremor of apprehension. Her thoughts were disloyal, no—traitorous. She who for so long had marched and sung with the youth of the nation, believing with all her heart that the Führer was the conscience, the savior, the hope of Germany, *she* was now questioning *his* integrity.

For anyone who condoned, or was silent about, such destruction, violence, and murder—yes, murder—could not be just.

With a sudden panic, Lili looked around the comfortable nooks and furniture of the room as if someone hidden might be reading her thoughts. It was new and disturbing. Had she, from one moment to the next, become an outsider? It was a stroke of good fortune that Volker and Bettina had gotten her away when they did. Her cheeks burned with the terrible irony of this thought. She had condemned him to death but Dr. Morsch had saved her. Did he know what she had done to him? Had the truth come to him before the end? Oh, if only he had died not knowing! And what would have happened to her, where might she be at this very moment if the SS had arrested her for helping him in Marktplatz?

This was something she hadn't yet considered. The women and children arrested had been sent home, but then they hadn't done anything other than be Jewish whereas she had gone out and taken action. Surely that was different. A cold wave passed through her and she bit her thumb, trying to keep from trembling. Yet when she saw in her mind again the image of Dr. Morsch out there on his hands and knees, when she heard the jeering voices—and the silence—of the people watching him, she knew that whatever else she had done before, at least there she had done the right thing.

And in this she knew that Papa would agree.

For the first time in years, she felt some tension and anger dissolve just as a sense of excitement was building. It was a strange sensation. She needed to tell Papa and Mama what had happened, both to and within her.

Supporting herself on the armrests, Lili rose and began to move toward the desk. Halfway there, she halted. She couldn't, she shouldn't tell them that she had led the students to Dr. Morsch's house. The thought of Bettina finding out was frightening. Bettina should never feel that no one but Volker had cared. If she found out Lili's true role, trying to save Dr. Morsch in the square would never outweigh her having put him there in the first place.

And, did she have to burden Papa and Mama with her hideous crime, just to have confessed it? No. Let the weight of what she had done be hers alone to bear.

She pulled out the stationery. For the next hours she wrote, explaining to them everything she could think of, making no excuses, sparing no details except what she had done to Dr. Morsch. It was harsh writing, would be harsher reading. Her fingers cramped but for once she did not care about the possible effects on her playing. She had to get it all out, in every tiny detail, even down to the desolation of the old woman, the anguish Lili had read in the faded blue of her eyes, there in the apartment where Lili had torn up the be-ribboned scrolls.

She wrote of her continuing love of another Germany, but that she had lost her faith in its leadership when not one condemnatory word had been spoken in the face of such a happening as had taken place. She told them that her regret was deep for all she had done in the past, not listening to Papa's warnings, lying to them both, making them worry about her for years. Hurting Lotte and Oskar too. She said that from now on, her path would be different. She told them that Goethe was more than a comfort, he was a window to make sense of the world, and she thanked them for the unwavering love they had shown her all her life. And that she hoped that someday they could forgive her. She closed the many pages with a simple "Loving you always, your daughter, Lili".

After sealing the envelope and addressing it, she realized that she could not mail the letter. What if it were opened by the Post Office? She would be considered a traitor. She would be arrested, perhaps worse. No, the letter would have to stay here for now, tucked away in the drawer until such a time as would be safe to send it. She would have to find another way of letting Mama and Papa know.

Despite that she hadn't yet sent the letter, despite the unchanging fact that Dr. Morsch was dead and his daughter fatherless, Lili's sleep that night was calm, dreamless.

The Importance of the 1% and More Bad News

For the first time in weeks, she joined the others at breakfast. Since the onset of what, with viciously cold irony—for it sounded like a night of beauty and rainbow light through prisms—had been termed

Kristallnacht, Bettina had been staying upstairs, where she took her breakfast too.

Frau Poppe tapped at the shell of her soft-boiled egg with her spoon, cracking the top.

"At our headquarters," she said, her tone boastful, "we learn about the new regulations sooner than most." Pulling the shattered egg shell off in one movement, she dropped the white cap on her plate and dipped her spoon into the yolk. "Now it's no longer a crime for Jewesses to have abortions. Really, they are to be encouraged."

Lili would have liked to smear the egg in her face. But then she caught herself and flushed. Who was *she* to judge?

Frau Poppe was herself expecting. Lili looked around the table at the others. Tante Aletheia's eyes were flashing a dangerous green. The muscles on his cheeks twitching, Dr. Hempel was clearly at a loss for what to say. Herr Tischborn seemed to be examining the texture of his breakfast roll with the utmost interest. Herr Poppe munched on his bread while pouring himself another cup of coffee. He didn't seem to have noticed the change in atmosphere around the table.

"Frau Poppe," said Tante Aletheia, her tone neutral. "Did you ever consider that such morbid considerations could be detrimental to the health of your child?"

Frau Poppe was silent for the rest of the meal.

Some minutes later, Lili stepped outside the house, on edge. It was one thing to have new and traitorous thoughts while sitting in her room, quite another to carry them with her as she moved through the town. Tante Aletheia had asked if she would like her company this morning but Lili wanted to be alone. She needed to walk about, observing. But now she seemed mainly to be noticing the guilt and fear coursing through her. The streets, their edges smeared with muddy snow, seemed to have changed during these last few weeks. The stone, brick, and plaster walls of the buildings no longer leaned toward her in a protective way, but as if they were trying to hear what she was thinking.

Would anyone recognize her as the woman who had stepped in to help the Jew? And if someone did, what would he or she do about it? Lili stopped short, debating whether it might be best to return to the house after all. Perhaps she wasn't yet ready for this. But curiosity and shame conquered the hesitation. As she walked, she snuck looks at the passersby, both in and out of uniform. Their faces seemed the same as usual, with varying expressions that she could no longer take at, well, face value. She would be cautious and avoid Marktplatz today. That way nobody who had been there that day could catch the association. She decided to go to a Konditorei for a cup of coffee and to go through the newspapers. It had been a long time since she had read any. Later today she would sit down at the harpsichord. For a brief moment she allowed herself to think of Leo. What would he think of her if he knew what she had done?

The closest Konditorei was boarded up. Had the owners gone away? Or had they been taken away? Further up the street was Schafheutle, still open. The familiar scent of smoke and yeast and bad coffee enveloped her. She picked up several old papers and skimmed the pages as she waited for her coffee. The *Völkischer Beobachter* claimed that no fewer than nineteen synagogues had been set on fire during the early hours of the tenth of November. There were articles that stated that there had been no plundering or looting during the uproar. Another claimed that not one Jew had been harmed at the time. It did admit that a few windows had been broken. Lies!

In a copy of *Der Angriff* she read a letter from someone who was actually protesting the recent events. The writer complained that the murder of vom Rath had given Germany an opportunity to gain world sympathy. Did he or she mean that other countries might take in the German Jews after all? Lili read on. The writer expressed dismay at the disgust that the excesses had engendered in nations well disposed to the Reich. These had no doubt damaged the friendly ties that the Munich Conference had done so much to foster. The newspaper's response was intriguing. The writer was pooh-poohed as belonging to the negligible one percent of the German population that did not agree with the way things were.

Lili's eyes flew over the following sentences. *Der Angriff* found the assertion of foreign nations being well disposed to the Reich outrageous. That by now everyone should know that it was surrounded by enemies who only wished harm on the Reich. Yet all Lili could think about was the other sentence.

The one that said that one percent of the German population did not agree with the way things were. And how she, despite what she had done to Dr. Morsch, now found herself in that one percent.

What did it matter if Jews weren't Aryans?—whatever 'Aryan' even meant.

They were human beings.

It was that simple.

Setting aside the papers and the barely touched coffee, Lili left the Konditorei, heading toward the Post Office. It could no longer wait; she had to tell Papa that she was no longer the girl he thought her to be. Or perhaps she was at last the girl he thought her. Trembling with anticipation, she hurried up Hauptstraße, passing the fur and winter coats store where the sign Pelzer Pelze had been replaced by Pelzhaus Schmidt.

At the Post Office, Lili gave the number to the washed out looking man behind the counter. He peered at her some moments before telling her to go sit on a bench and wait until the connection was made. For some time she stole glances at the people going in and out. An SA man carried a packet that had to go out that day; important mail for Berlin. The clerk scurried to process it. A few people made calls in the booths, but they seemed to be for connections within Germany because their waiting time wasn't long. Lili went back to the counter.

"Excuse me. How much longer will it take for my call?"

The clerk gave her a withering look.

"Patience, young lady. America is a long way from here. Sit down. You will be called when the connection is there."

Made uneasy by his tone, Lili returned to the bench. A magazine lay nearby. She picked it up but its cover, showing a HJ boy sneezing, with dozens of caricatured black robed Jews riding the blast of snot, almost made her drop it. Reasoning came at lightning speed. If she cast the magazine aside, someone might notice. She still remembered her visceral reaction to the woman on the street who had not raised her arm in salute when the parade of HJ boys went by. So she flipped through the pages, stopping at the bold script set in a box. "German Volk," it said, "you have now seen how the Jews—enemies of morality—have harmed you. What kindness did not accomplish must now be undertaken with harshness."

"Fräulein," the clerk shouted. She dropped the magazine and ran to the booth.

"Mama? Papa?" she called into the ether.

At first the response was only silence, but then there was a hiss as if all the foam in the ocean were converging upon the cable.

"Hallo, hallo," she called, and again there was silence and finally a faint voice that seemed to be speaking from much farther away than America.

"Lili?"

Then the hissing returned, and no matter how much she called out, there was no reply.

"The connection is broken," she told the clerk.

He shrugged. "It's the Atlantic, I told you. Do you want to try again?"

She looked at her watch. Already hours. No, she would return the following day.

"Next," he barked.

She went home to the harpsichord. She would no longer have to think about classes, as she was never ever going to return to the university.

Tante Aletheia was waiting, her expression grim.

"I have some more bad news," she said.

Lili gasped. "From New York?"

"Not New York. It's Frau Dierck. She won't be coming back."

"You mean she's dead too? Was she sent to a concentration camp like Dr. Morsch?"

Tante Aletheia shook her head.

"No, but it's bad. They've put her into an asylum."

Tante Aletheia recounted what Frau Dierck's aunt had told her. Frau Dierck had been having reunion coffee with family members when the news arrived that her husband had died of pneumonia at Buchenwald. This alone was distressing to contemplate. But, among the few personal effects that were sent to her was his shirt, the fabric blood-encrusted and ripped, shredded threads sticking up along the edges of the tears. For quite a while Frau Dierck simply sat, clutching the shirt. Then her fingers found something caught in the threads. Out came a tooth; a dog's tooth. Needless to say, this shed a different light on how he had died, and the stress of this new image was enough to send Frau Dierck into her worst spell yet. Her screams of grief, outrage, and accusations were enough for her to be pushed into a closet and the door closed. They could hear her throwing herself at the walls and door, wailing. The doctor who was summoned was not of the same school of thought as Dr. Morsch.

Lili flinched. Dr. Morsch would never help Frau Dierck, or anyone, ever again.

She must be taken away immediately, the doctor stated, precluding any argument. Investigations were to be undertaken to explore the possibility that she was subject to mental disorders of a more serious kind, the inherited kind that could affect her children too. He would arrange the place. These days it was not so easy. What with cost cutting and closures, many asylums were quite overcrowded. Perhaps the doctor noticed the looks of alarm; he reassured them that she would be well taken care of. If the asylum at Wiesloch, which was well on its way to being a National Socialist model concern, had no space, then the one at Eichberg or Hadamar would do just as well.

Frau Dierck, by then heavily sedated, was placed into a wagon with dark windows and taken away.

"Has anyone been to visit her?" Poor Frau Dierck.

Tante Aletheia shook her head.

"Her aunt is afraid to be associated with her. She is a kind enough woman in good times. But these times are not good, and now they are getting worse."

♫♪♫

The December days were advancing. Tante Aletheia, Bettina, Volker, and Lili sat upstairs, sharing a bottle of Dr. Morsch's favorite Schnaps. Lili remembered the day he had poured her the first glass, and how comforting he had been. Now he was gone. What sort of a death had he had in the concentration camp? She watched Bettina, who looked miserable.

Bettina's voice shook as she told them of her decision. It made her sick with guilt that she was going to do what she had too long refused her father. She was leaving Germany.

She gazed at Volker as if she were memorizing him.

"If only I had listened to Papa," she told them. "But I thought I could never leave. Everything about me is German. I know nothing else. I don't feel different from any of you—just different from those people who are doing this." She bowed her head. "I was wrong to make him stay because of me. If I had listened to him, he wouldn't be dead."

Lili swallowed.

"I want her to go to Argentina or America or Australia," said Volker. "Anywhere that's far away from here. But she wants to go to France so that I can come visit." He shook his head. "As much as I want to be with you, Bettina, I don't think that's a good idea. France is too close."

Tante Aletheia agreed. "Of course you would always be welcome to stay in the Friedberg house, but Volker is right. Go far away, my dear. That is certainly what your Papa would want for you. Volker will find a way of getting to you."

Bettina began to weep then, and although Lili wanted to wrap her arms around Dr. Morsch's daughter, she could barely allow herself to place a polluted palm upon Bettina's hand.

At last Bettina wiped her eyes, drew a long breath, and told them that she had already received papers for Argentina. Once the necessary documents from here were in order, she could leave.

Volker had grown pale. Tante Aletheia poured them all more Schnaps.

Character as Limp as a Wet Wash Cloth

The next morning, Lili placed yet another call at the Post Office; once again, winter storms across the Atlantic left the connection crackling and then dead. A cablegram would work, but it would be impossible to express everything with clarity. She would have to wait.

On the way home, she stopped before a shop window. There, right in the front, near the glass, stood a *Lebkuchenhaus*, thick sugar snow upon the roof. It reminded her of happier, innocent times. Paul would enjoy it; he was still innocent. Yes, she would send it to him. As she left with the package, she realized that here was the solution to getting the incriminating letter, still sitting in the desk drawer, to Papa and Mama.

Once back at Kornmarkt, Lili mixed together an egg white with sugar to form a sticky paste, and took it upstairs. With the letter opener she pried apart the roof and walls of the gingerbread house. She would hide the letter under the roof and then glue everything back together with the sugary egg white. She began stuffing the folded pages inside what would have been the attic of the Lebkuchenhaus. But, if she wanted to live on truly able to look Papa and Mama in the eye, she would have to tell them everything that she had done. Far away in Argentina as she would be, Bettina need never know, but Lili owed Papa the whole truth. When she had finished writing the additional pages, she added them to the rest. By now the egg white and sugar had already dried, so it was necessary to add some water to revive the mixture. The edges of the walls of the gingerbread house were then lined with the sticky mess and the roof pressed down until all was set. She tapped it and pulled at it but it stayed firm. There. It looked just as before. She would post it in the morning. Nobody would know that it carried such powerful, and dangerous, thoughts.

And unless Paul broke it into pieces, no one would ever know. Yet this was not a problem. All she had to do was send another letter, telling them to look inside the house. She would mail that message a day later. She bit hard into her lip, welcoming the pain. Despite her unending shame and remorse, at least one part of her life would soon be resolved with honesty.

♫♪♫

Bettina's leave-taking was short. She nestled inside Tante Aletheia's embrace then kissed her cheeks, tracing them with tears. She threw her arms around Lili, telling her that she would never forget her bravery and decency; that the world should have more people like Lili and then there would be peace. Lili's unvoiced confession and impossible atonement made her tremble so that Bettina hugged her tighter. Tante

Aletheia and Lili stood in the foyer while Volker picked up the one lonely suitcase, and then Bettina was gone.

At dinner the Poppes sniffed a few times and declared that the air seemed fresher than it had in quite a while.

"I have been wanting to ask you again," Lili said later as she and Tante Aletheia sat upstairs. "Why do you let the Poppes stay on?"

Tante Aletheiaa stroked Fragonard's belly where he lay upside down on her lap. "They are awful," she said, "but they are useful, although they themselves are not aware of just how. That is the only reason I let them continue on here."

Useful? How could the Poppes be useful to her? If anything, they were a danger to have around because they were always watching, commenting, and judging people on their committment. Again, Lili was struck by her sudden and continuing retreat from that same committment. After so many years of faith in the Führer and everything connected with the Third Reich, she now found herself turning on it.

This abrupt turn-around worried her: it could mean that the former fervor was still deep within her and could resurface at any moment. On the other hand, it could also mean that she had never truly believed it, and had gone along with it because it was so exciting. And then what did that say about her character? Limp as a wet washcloth. But no, ever since Kristallnacht, and her sickening role in it, she had begun to see and question. Surely that had to count for something.

"What is going to happen when the Poppe's baby arrives? Will they stay on?"

"That does present some problems," Tante Aletheia admitted. "As with so many things, we shall have to cross that bridge when we come to it. Step-by-step is the best way to proceed. In the meantime, it seems that at least for a while we will be spared Frau Poppe's presence at breakfast, now that she has morning sickness."

Herr Tischborn too seemed relieved by Frau Poppe's absence these days, especially when morning sickness struck her at dinner.

Occasionally he related boring anecdotes dealing with the selling of wine, but the man was so gentle that it was hard to find fault with him. Even Herr Poppe reacted to his wife's absence by recounting moments of his earliest days as a civil servant, in which he always came out the hero of the latest crisis in paperwork. Dr. Hempel was as good-natured as ever; as long as he had his music, he seemed at peace.

With no more classes or studies to consider, Lili was back at the harpsichord. Each day brought with it an increasing depth. Something almost mystical was happening to her playing. Her fingers were again flexible as ever, yet her playing had gained an undertone of something indefinable.

One afternoon, she had just finished with a particularly complex segment of a Couperin when Dr. Hempel knocked on her door. He stood before her, rubbing his bearded chin between thumb and index finger in the same way that Dr. Morsch had, as did Papa with his invisible beard.

"As long as has been my pleasure to know you, you have shown a remarkable technical ability on the harpsichord," he said. You are indeed a gifted performer." He paused. "But I must tell you something.

"For many years I had hoped that in my teaching I would come across a student who would display a true virtuoso's understanding of music." He shrugged his shoulders. "Alas, it has not been. Those students for whom I entertained some hopes have long ago disappeared into the crowds, and I am left with only that one insufferable pupil who has made me come to dread Thursdays at five o'clock." He adjusted his spectacles before continuing. "Nevertheless. Although you have never been a student of mine, I have found my hope fulfilled in you. Your playing just now was beyond words. I truly have no doubt that you will be the inspiring harpsichordist of your generation, Fräulein Lili."

For the first time since the horrors that she had taken part in that day in November, Lili felt a tiny shiver of hope. Perhaps, someday, there would be a way for her to inspire something good.

Jokes of the Third Reich

Christmas had come and gone, Lili making a very quick trip to Alt Eichendorf. She suspected that it had been the last time she would be seeing either of her grandparents and the parting filled her with longing for what had been. Hugging Großmama Maximiliana and Großpapa Hugo, she felt the beloved substance of them, still warm, with the familiar contours and hollows of the years. She had held them close for Mama too.

On the train back, two middle-aged men told jokes to each other. One stuck with her and she planned to tell it to Tante Aletheia.

"What's the difference between Chamberlain and Adolf? One takes a weekend in the country, and the other takes a country in a weekend." It was funny in an ugly way.

The sky was somber when she arrived at Kornmarkt. In one sense it had been foolish to come back to Heidelberg when just five days from now she would have to return to Berlin for the concert. But despite what had happened in Marktplatz, Heidelberg was home now. And home was a place you loved even if it was not perfect.

She wiped her feet and took off her coat, remembering her return from Alt Eichendorf last year. So much had happened since then. She had grown up.

"Tante Aletheia?" she called. Silence. "Frau Brinkmann?" Lili carried her bag up, dropped it off, and went to Tante Aletheia's room.

The door was ajar, the lights on. She could see Tante Aletheia immobile in an armchair. Lili knocked once and entered.

"Tante Aletheia?" she said, voice soft.

It was as if the old woman had been drained of blood right there in the seat. She seemed to be looking up, and her eyes, though palest green, had no light in them.

"What is it?" Lili gasped, going onto her knees at Tante Aletheia's side. "Are you unwell?"

Tante Aletheia swallowed, shook her head. Some color returned as she gazed at Lili.

"Oh, my dear," she said. "I have no choice but to tell you. I am so very very sorry."

"What is it? What's the matter?" Lili cried out, blood rushing to her head.

"It is your father, Lili," Tante Aletheia said, her voice weary. "Christmas Eve, my dear girl. Heart attack. He is dead."

The One Matter in Which Papa was Wrong

Lili did not weep for her father. She did not deserve the release, brief as it might be, that tears could bring.

Cablegrams went back and forth. Lili should stay in Germany for now because Mama and Paul would go there in the New Year. The shock was devastating. Paul and she were holding up as best they could. It was a mercy that Papa had gone quickly. The roof was safe. Christmas Eve was a blur. Be strong. Perform in the concert. For Papa.

Lili rubbed the cablegrams between her fingers. The reason for the existence of these small rectangular sheets was because her Papa was dead. Staring down, she moved her fingers back and forth against the tan paper, trying to grasp the terrifying reality.

Tante Aletheia and Dr. Hempel suggested she cancel her performance.

She wavered. It would be so easy to just stay in her room and never come out again, just wait for Mama and Paul to get here. Without Papa. Without Papa! No. How could he be gone from their lives? How was it possible?

And then she was back at the millstone of guilt and shame and grief.

"I have to do the concert," she told them, her voice flat.

Tante Aletheia went along to the station, sitting with her in the compartment until it was time for non-travelers to get off the train. As the wagons began to move, Lili stood at the window, watching Tante Aletheia where she waited on the platform, wrapped in a dark green cloak. A living link to Papa she was. When she could no longer be seen, Lili sat down, staring at the passing landscape for the rest of the journey.

She had made her own arrangements and went straight to her room in the Adlon. A rented harpsichord was already waiting for her. She didn't need to go out at all until rehearsal time.

On New Year's Eve, she lay in bed and heard the midnight explosions in the dark. The drapes were drawn so there were no colors tracing patterns upon the windowpanes. It was her birthday and her widowed mother was on the other side of the Atlantic. Her brother was five years old. And fatherless. As was Bettina Morsch.

Now it was January 1, 1939, and mandatory for all Jews in the Reich to carry identification. How would the authorities know who was Jewish? She tried to imagine Bettina being stopped and ordered to show her identification card. What would happen if she had forgotten it at home? But Bettina was safe now. Even alone in South America without her loving, caring father who had always wanted only to protect her. For Jews, even those who didn't look at all like the stereotypes, anywhere was now better than here.

In the afternoon, Lili entered the recently remodeled Deutsches Opernhaus that was under Dr. Goebbels' directives; the Staatsoper Unter den Linden was Göring's domain. Perhaps the Führer laughed about his commanders competing with each other. Perhaps he was silent about that too. He still hadn't said a word about what had happened in November. It was obvious that he didn't care. It was even likely that it had all been instigated under his directive, calculated; without moral conscience. He was not what she had for so long thought he was. Her mouth tightened as she went straight to the rooms backstage, found an empty one and sat down in a corner.

She was ready to perform; indeed, every movement of hers this evening would be a performance.

As for playing, that would be a Bach Prelude and Fugue in A Minor, and she now was sickened by the way it ended on a major note.

Her gaze was on the wood floor. If only she had listened to Papa. If only she had realized long ago how right he was. Had been. None of this would have happened. Together in New York, they could have waited out the National Socialists. All governments eventually changed—the Kaiser had given way to Weimar, Weimar to them. If only she had understood what Papa had said about the Führer, no, *Hitler*. She grimaced as she changed his name. That he was an entertainer performing a hypnotic trick on the people of Germany and that he was transforming them; performing magic to make their sense of right and wrong disappear. Perhaps he was turning them into those jellylike creatures she had seen along the shore. Perhaps the German people were like the bewitched monsters or poisoned villagers slumbering under dark clouds in fairy tales. But who was going to wake them up, and how? And now that she was awake, what was she going to do about it?

Oh Papa.

How she had wronged him.

A true messiah would never have let his people grow to be so callous.

Hitler was a fraud. But it was too late. His image was all-powerful. The myth of the messiah had become the man. Hitler was larger than life.

Oh Papa. Had he found her letter and died of shock? Or, perhaps even worse, had he died not knowing how she had changed?

Either way, his death, too, was due to her willful blindness.

All those years that she had wasted, so desperately wanting to have a contributing role in the great staged national tragedy directed by Hitler the puppet master. How she had wished herself here, longing to be back in her homeland when her true home had always been her family. She had destroyed it and now it was broken, gone forever; her father gone. Bettina's father gone. Just like the true fatherland.

What other falsities was Hitler fabricating? She sank her teeth down, tasting blood. She stared at the wall.

What was going to become of Mama and Paul when they came here? Mama would surely occupy herself with care of Großmama Maximiliana and Großpapa Hugo, finding some solace in Alt Eichendorf, but what about Paul? It had seemed so tragic that in America he would miss being a Pimpf and a member of of the Hitler Jugend. Now, being here would be a waste of his childhood. Whether he felt impelled to join in, or if he would be forced to, his American birth disregarded in light of his lineage, he would have sparse time to pursue anything other than his allegiance and activities geared to making him a cog in the machine of the Reich. And, like Papa had said, what if there were indeed going to be a war?

Oh Papa, Paul. Oh, what had she done? She buried her face in her hands.

The door opened.

She looked up.

"Leo," she whispered.

He must have seen something in her eyes, for he gathered her into his arms.

He was silent while she spoke. Everything rushed out in a great jumble as she apologized, for her departure, her silence, her omissions and lies. She told him that the doctor was dead, her father was dead, and that all of it was her fault. She told him about that day and that night and what she had done to so many innocents. It no longer mattered that he would know the full ugliness of her being. If he praised her then it was all she deserved, to have loved the wrong man, and Papa would be right again. And if he hated her for it, she deserved his abhorrence.

When at last she was finished, Leo still said nothing. His hands were upon her arm and waist, and Lili could feel the heat of them but they were motionless.

"How torn and wretched you have been, Lili, in what you have wrought. But I know you now. I know that you will find the right way. *We* must find it." His touch trailed upon her cheek. "What a terrible time we inhabit, my love."

Leo. In this, in this one thing, Papa had been wrong.

Later, his voice low and warm against her hair, he said that her father would always be with her, just as the fatherland they had once known lived on in their hearts.

The door burst open.

"Fräulein von Rittersburg zu Mertz-Tärnekow!" said a harried looking man in a gray suit. "Heil Hitler. Thank goodness I've found you. We have a dreadful situation and it seems that you are the one to step in."

Lili slid off Leo's lap and stood up.

"What do you mean?"

The man glanced at Leo's uniform and back at her. His speech was rapid.

"For some reason Frau Stadelmann has had to cancel her appearance this evening. The *Brandenburg Concertos* without a harpsichord—unthinkable. Professor Dr. Hempel of Heidelberg has suggested that you stand in for her."

Through pulsing waves of time and space she heard Leo's voice.

"Brilliant idea. Of course Fräulein von Rittersburg zu Mertz-Tärnekow can take over for Frau Stadelmann. After all, she's been playing the Concertos since childhood.

Lili's eyes widened as she looked over at Leo who spoke with such confidence. But as she stared at him, she knew the truth of his words. The *Brandenburg Concertos* had always been the comfort food of her practicing. And she had performed them in Mannheim only another lifetime ago.

"Yes," she said. "I'll do it."

What Lili Did Not Yet Know

It was because of Lili's solo that Leo, having only that afternoon arrived from duties in Dresden, had seen her name on the program and gone searching for her backstage. It was because of Dr. Hempel's trust in her abilities that she was going to play not only a Bach Prelude and Fugue in A Minor, but take Li Stadelmann's place in the *Brandenburg Concertos*. There were some hurried but reassuring discussions with the conductor, Furtwängler, who told her not to worry but just to feel what they were creating and then the music would soar, and then some bars played with the first violin. Soon enough, the concertgoers began to enter the hall, with palpable excitement, for that evening the Führer himself was in attendance.

When it came time for her to walk onto the stage for her solo, and the vast sea of the audience disappeared into the dimness of the Deutsches Opernhaus, Lili knew for whom she would be translating Bach's music. As she seated herself, she remembered how, long ago, on a late December evening in a certain building in Berlin, in a double salon with velvet drapes at the windows and potted palms in the corners, the man with the mustache had told her it would be her life's duty to perform for the fatherland. And now, as she played on this first evening of January 1939, all the love and sorrow and pain flowed from her through the keys and into the great hall, and none seated there knew that Lili von Rittersburg zu Mertz-Tärnekow was playing for no one but two dead fathers.

After intermission came the Concertos. Lili was attuned to the maestro, his baton a wand turning all the musicians into magicians. She could feel the subtle tone color and texture of each separate instrument and she was the harpsichord, transcending, creating a dimension outside herself, pure and true. By the time they arrived at her first solo she was running free through the waking dream. Bach was the spirit, she the medium. It was power and life and more. Burning with the essence of the great composer, the others joined and together they rose, self-aware; yet already she had heard and understood and knew. Like the music, exquisite pain, terrible joy. Her own path through the labyrinth of living would go on and on, until the very end; only she, alone, making its meaning along the way.

♫ ♪ ♫

She did not yet know that later, after the audience would have risen to their feet to applaud her long and loud, a young girl, blonde and blue-eyed and eager as once she herself had been, would come on the stage and present her with a bouquet of yellow roses, the slight scent of decay wafting up through the anise notes of their fragrance. She did not yet know that Adolf Hitler, TIME's newest Man of the Year, would speak to all those there in the Deutsches Opernhaus, pronouncing Lili von Rittersburg zu Mertz-Tärnekow a great German musician, a cultural treasure, and that his words would mean less than nothing to her.

She did not yet know just how remorse would fuel her in the years to come, but, some months later, having asked herself what one single individual could do, she would find one answer, minute as it was. She would tell no one, not Leo, not Tante Aletheia. She knew how to be silent. Yet, in countless towns and cities throughout the Reich, Lili would leave little white cards begging people to wake up and ask themselves if this, their only life, was all it could, or should, be.

Perhaps the message was so vague that even the Gestapo didn't understand it. After all, despite a couple close calls when someone saw her leave a card and she pretended that she had found it herself and was in a hurry to get rid of it rather than carry it on her to the police, she was never arrested. It would have been easy enough to eventually discover the source of the cards by making the connection with the locations and schedule of her performances. Years later, Rudolf Ditzen a.k.a. Hans Fallada would write a novel based on true events about a Gestapo inspector who was able to connect the dots in a similar scenario, postcards with more traitorous messages of civil disobedience, and the 'guilty' couple was sentenced to death.

As she played that Fugue in A Minor that evening in Berlin, Lili did not yet know, but already sensed, that she and Leo would share a love in which the music they made together spoke more clearly than any words. Everything they knew, about life, and each other, could be expressed through their playing; in it they would share that which cannot be said.

Through their playing they would give voice to despair as they lived the ironies and the inadequacies, the infamy that was in Germany growing with each passing day; the stain that was blotting out most of what had been decent. For some time, they would sound an underlying chord of hope until the last lingering note would fade into utter silence.

But first she would come to discover that, like the viola da gamba she had once longed to be, the knowing touch of Leo's hands would make her sound at the core. His beloved at last, she would know the heat of his blood pulsing within her, forging the peace of a homecoming, and in each other they would find a homeland, at times forgetting what was happening in the world around them. But that was only when they were together.

For most of her life, my Tante Lili would be alone.

She did not yet know that my father would get the measles and thus on April 1, 1939, my grandmother would have to cancel their cabin for the voyage to Hamburg.

She did not yet know that Hildegard would marry Gustav and that a nosy neighbor would inform the Blockleiter and Hildegard would be taken away and sterilized although she was already pregnant, and Gustav sent first to the countryside and later to the Russian front, and that they would never again see each other. And that years later Hildegard would open a shelter for abandoned dogs on the outskirts of Frankfurt, saying, as did Sartre's relative Albert Schweitzer, not considering the exception of Adolf Hitler and his dogs, that we can judge the heart of a man by his treatment of animals.

She did not yet know that Frau Poppe would decide that there was something odd about the man and rummage about in his room to look for proof that he was homosexual and thus overdue for a long stay in jail or a concentration camp where a pink triangle on his prisoner's shirt would afford him extra attention from guards intent on torturing out of him and the other homosexuals love for their fellow man, but, while looking in a drawer, she would discover one tiny overseen memento from his mother and then, excited by the unexpected result of her suspicions, contact the Gestapo, and, while Tante Aletheia and Lili were out one day, he would be taken away because it had been confirmed that despite his muted echoing of Herr Poppe's views and despite his great understanding of German wines and his enjoyment of smoked ham and his sorrowful need to keep a secret because his papers were false, Herr Tischborn was in fact Jewish. And that eventually he would die, first in Dachau. That two years later he would die again, buried by boulders in Mauthausen, and this time his body would die with him.

She did not yet know that because the Battle of the Atlantic, as it would later be called, had begun the week before, when Britain and France declared war on Germany, Mama would worry that their ship might be in dangerous waters and so she and Paul would not board the ocean liner on September 10, 1939, and my father would enter first grade in New York.

She did not yet know that Bettina would make it to Argentina and while waiting for the freedom of the day when Volker could join her in a world that despite grief and fear and horror still held possibilities, she would learn how to ride on the pampas, soft wind blowing through her long honey-colored hair, and one day there would be a snake and her horse would rear and she would fall, just missing with her torso the sharp edge of a rock, but that her head would strike a different stone and, unknowing, uncaring, the reptile would continue its path through the grass and even if her father had been at her side there would have been nothing that he could have done, for the serpent had set it all in motion.

She did not yet know that eventually Tante Aletheia and she would leave Heidelberg and, despite Alsace now German again and much of the rest of France occupied by the initially courteous German Wehrmacht and SS, move to the house in Friedberg where, when she wasn't practicing her French harpsichord or off performing around the Reich, leaving her pathetic little white cards, Lili would go outside to breathe in the forest air and stare at the stars that returned each night, trusting the blackness. She did not yet know that Tante Aletheia and some villagers of Friedberg would have already helped find ways out of the country for eleven Germans from Heidelberg who, if not for them, would, beginning September 19, 1941, have had to wear the yellow star, nor that she would come to know well two local members of the Resistance, courageous and moral, a hefty handlebar-mustachioed behemoth with the heart of a teddy bear and his buxom copper-haired fiancée aptly named Angèle whom decades later I would meet in their rundown house surrounded by garden gnomes.

She did not yet know that as she rode the tracks and roads of the Reich from concert to concert, she would look out the panes fogged in patches by her breath and see endless forests and hills opening up on vast valleys of fields and meadows and pastures, on villages whose houses were inhabited by people who had chosen a leader her father had seen through. She did not yet know how often she would stare at the passing buildings with their red and white and black banners hanging from the windows and wonder about the true colors of the hearts and minds of those who lived behind their sheltering walls.

She did not yet know that Leo and she would share one dazzling weekend in Paris in which Leo would take off his uniform to don civilian wear and, avoiding any more elegant places where SS officers might choose to gather, they would pretend that they could be but two lovers linked in the city of light. That their kisses would be deep and taste like almonds as they held each other in the shadowed lanes of the Marais. That they would dance to an accordion under swinging lanterns on a tiny square in the back streets of Montmartre. That early in the morning they would eat steaming onion soup while rats ran over their feet in an alley in Les Halles. That they would fall onto the lumpy mattress in their 17th arrondissement room and want to stay there forever. Later, when Leo was advancing into the Baltic lands and a lifetime of shame, and, even later, she would look back and remember those two magical days and still her heartbeat would echo an extra note.

As she played that particular Fugue in A Minor in the Deutsches Opernhaus that night in Berlin, my aunt did not yet know that Benno the geneticist SS member of the Ahnenerbe would one day come back into her life and that even though he would already know that the Aryan Himalayan connection had been but a mythic fabrication by Himmler and the like-minded, he would seek to make good on his visions of germ plasms and clinical experiments and arrange that after Latvia and Lithuania, Leo would be stationed near Friedberg so that he and she might know times of togetherness in the house in the forest and she might fall pregnant with the perfect offspring but that Leo would already be less than whole for what he had been a part of up in the north and that there would never be a child. And she did not yet know that

Benno would eventually disappear but that one day decades later she would see his name in an American scientific journal and she would wince, and wonder at the ways of the world.

She did not yet know that it would be her own hand that would spoon Tante Aletheia the final handful of crushed tablets mixed with warm water to dull her cruel suffering as she battled a fast consuming cancer out there in the depths of the Friedberg forest one autumn and that Lili would mourn her loss with a heart tight as a fist but without remorse. She did not yet know that she would inherit both the property and, for the briefest of time, a grieving white cat. She did not yet know that she would stay there and take into the house for some weeks a child whose parents had already been taken away, never to see their child again, and that she would make good use of her great-aunt's lessons in mushroom picking when a billeted SS officer would discover the four-year old and she would choose to take his life rather than let him take away the boy. And she did not yet know that Leo would know this and feel his shame even more.

She did not yet know, as she sat there pressing keys to pluck chords on the instrument that she still believed she would play throughout her life, even if during the last year of the war there would be no more concerts, that she would find herself hiking into the thickly wooded hills above the town of Schirmeck on the other side of the lazy Bruche. That she would go there trying to find out where Volker was because she heard that he had been caught with a bag of something printed and, instead of being shot like the others, had been sent to labor at the quarry in Natzwiller-Struthof, once a holiday destination, and she would think that if she dressed in a dirndl and wore her hair in braids pinned in a crown and flirted with the guards, they would answer her questions and let her see Volker. She did not yet know that she would be very wrong about that, but that when leaving the barb-wired perimeter of the camp after a stern scolding and going into the forest in a different direction than the one she had first taken, she would come across a solitary house with sealed windows.

Decades later, I would stand before that very same house and learn that it was a gas chamber built not for mass murder but for the murder of too many individual lives to count. And two kilometers away, in the painfully sweet verdant sweeping sylvan vistas of the Vosges in what is left of the only camp set on what was once, again, German-claimed land, I would stare at the photographs of some of those who lived, suffered, and died on that hill. I would stand in the medical experiments room, the clinically gray space with the cold and terrifying tiled tables that slant inwards with thin troughs set like stick branches of a leafless tree so that warm fluids could disappear into their depths. I would stand before what was real: long and deep and dark; the oven in the crematorium. Outside in the hilltop air I would see a platform and gallows and rows and rows of white memorial marks that are still not enough in number, for there is not enough space to remember each of the over 20,000 men, women, and children who died at that small camp above the forests.

Choking with shock and horror and shame, I would tremble at the beauty of nature and the hideous baseness of humankind. And even today as I think back to that one wretched afternoon I spent at Natzweiler-Struthof and to each of the countless accounts of the Third Reich and the Holocaust and the war that I have read over the many years, I know that I can never ever truly imagine the realities of the millions and millions and millions of the innocent and courageous who suffered so long and horrifically and irreparably because of one man and his followers.

Back in Berlin that evening in January 1939, my aunt did not yet know that the firm at which Ursula had found such intriguing work with numbers and columns and classifiers and cards with punch holes would be crucial in tabulating a wealth of statistics including pseudo-scientific racial data leading the Nazi murderers directly to the doors of hundreds of thousands of those with Jewish roots. Nor did she yet know, although Ursula had told her part of it that day on the Philosophenweg, that this firm Dehomag would have its own dark roots ineradicably intertwined with that entity, made monumental by the purchase of the card-reading machine invented in 1884 by a German-American named Hollerith, whose corporate motto would be "The Solutions Company" which she would later recognize as IBM, and that this company for whom only the money mattered would reveal hundreds of thousands more of the Jewish of other nationalities with the misfortune of having been counted by its well-selling machines along the black-booted path of the conquerors. She did not yet know that this fact—as well as another further bitter disillusionment by that which she would for some time imagine to be, but only when it was already too late to let her father know, nearly the only land in the world that seemed to believe in and honor and fight for the sanctity of human life—would keep her from ever returning to American soil. And that after the war she would only once more step upon German earth.

As she moved through the inner labyrinth of that Fugue in A Minor she did not yet know that Beate, the dark-haired girl from the BDM campfire up on the Schauinsland in the Black Forest, would leap at the chance to train in Ravensbrück from where she would go on to flaunt her harshness and heightened expertise in cruelty to torment hundreds of women, especially the ones who still retained a faint shadow of their former beauty, in Neuengamme and Flossenburg and wherever else she could, and when those times were at last ended she would spend decades as a *Putzfrau* scrubbing warehouse floors and telling anyone who cared to listen, that her years in the BDM were the best in her life.

My aunt did not yet know that through the imprudent talk by SS officers over beer in Friedberg in 1943 she would learn that, under the direction of Benno's old associates from the Ahnenerbe, and a colleague from his Tibet trip, 87 prisoners from Auschwitz were to be gassed in the A-frame gas chamber house at Natzweiler-Struthof, anatomical casts made of their bodies before being de-fleshed, and their skeletons taken to the Anatomy Institute at the University in Straßburg as displays in a collection underlining racial differences.

My aunt did not yet know the role she would play in the efforts to save some of those prisoners from this fate.

She did not yet know that there would be seven headless cadavers and seven heads and her wretched job would be to sew them together most likely so that when those prisoners would be transported, en route some clever and daring and brave members of the local Resistance would substitute the bodies for them. From where did the seven guillotined cadavers come? And who were those seven people to be rescued, and who had the agonizing task of deciding which seven to be saved?

My aunt did not yet know the feeling of such a labor but she who had despised sewing would come to know that she was strong enough to do it, stitch by stitch. And she did not yet know that none of the efforts to save the seven would be of any use, for all 87 would be delivered to Natzweiler-Struthof, one throwing himself at a fence to die at his own chosen time, and that despite all the ways she would find in which to try to atone for her role in the deaths of Dr. Morsch and Bettina and her own family and all the misery she had caused through this, she would never do so.

As my aunt soared through the Fugue in A Minor and thought of her parents and her brother and of the home and life she had once known and would never have again, she did not yet know that eventually my grandmother would despair of ever seeing her daughter and, leaving behind Paul, her son and my father, in the care of Lotte and Oskar, would find a way to cross the war-torn Atlantic and arrive in Hamburg on the exceptionally dry and warm Saturday evening of July 23, 1943 and that due to a cancelled train south, she would be in

Hauptbahnhof in time to experience Operation Gomorrah during the same early hours of Sunday that the 10-year old who would become the daughter-in-law whom she would never meet, my mother, would be in a cellar as one random bull's eye *Volltreffer* of the 2,300 tons of bombs dropped between 0100 and 0200 blasted through, ripping away the building and engulfing the street in flames howling and hissing and helping to create the 1,500 foot tornado of fire that raged through the city but leaving her and some others their scorched lives and a ceramic horse and a piano book which my mother would days later find in the rubble and which I still have, and that this first one night of nine more full days and nights to come lit up by firestorms and burning bodies shrieking and bubbling and silent would leave already more than 15,000 dead, including my ethereal grandmother Wilhelmine.

As her fingers pressed each of the black and white keys that would cause the quills to pluck the strings that played the myriad notes that formed the being that was that particular Fugue in A Minor, my aunt did not yet know that learning of the death of her mother would make her wail and weep at last, for she would understand that this death too had been caused by her own misguided allegiance and now that her mother was gone forever, barren tears would fall for the little brother who was left on the other side of the Atlantic.

My aunt did not yet know that with the death of her mother (and her two aunts along with their husbands who although they would all have been perhaps but temporarily spared that particular Friday night had they stayed at their homes along the Außenalster, had just been to visit an injured employee at the seamen's hospital near the port and stopped for a beer at a quaint sailor's Gaststätte), her brother's life would alter completely. She did not yet know that my grandfather's firm on Park Avenue would be taken over by someone or some body and disappear from sight, leaving Lotte and Oskar with not much more than my 10-year old father and two hastily chosen paintings from my grandmother's Berlin collection (one that would be sold to pay for my father's education and the other now in my possession) and their own savings, and that because of this they would take my father and move north to Westchester and then Bronxville where Lotte would find work as a housekeeper and Oskar as a driver and the three of them would live together in modest circumstances and without another word of German spoken until my father was a young man and went out into the world. She did not yet know that my father would come to look at Lotte and Oskar, simple, hard working, loving, as his true parents.

As my aunt played the harpsichord that night in a way that made Adolf Hitler sit up and take notice, she did not yet know that as the Allies advanced and she hoped for a German defeat, she would wonder what had happened to Leo. She did not yet know that even before the taking into custody of so many of those who had been part of the SS, Leo, seeking requital for that which he had done—and for what he had not done—would turn himself in to the American forces upon their arrival in Alsace. She did not yet know that she would wait for him for many months after the end of the war until, setting out to search for him, she would at last find him in one of the American administered barbed wire camps just out of reach of the tantalizing freshness of the Rhine, one of the mainly shelterless, mainly waterless camps that went from POW label to being classified as DEF, Disarmed Enemy Forces, and thus out of the bounds of the Geneva Convention. There, among the tens of thousands of men and some women and children, many on under a thousand calories a day and left without medical treatment for the diseases like dysentery, pneumonia, typhoid, tetanus, and septicemia that ran through them in the earth holes where they slept and squatted and starved, as partial vengeance for what had been done by the Germans to the millions of the Jewish, the Allied soldiers, and the countless innocents of a dozen lands; there, where, shutting out the press, access was denied to the International Committee of the Red Cross, and, as had been done by the Germans in the camps liberated some months before, too many of those in charge systematically refused to aid the survival of human beings and encouraged their liquidation through exposure and labor and slow starvation; there it was, on a day when the cold rain had paused, and not far from where a 70-year old man was staring out at the endless sea of gray sludge and its near naked creatures and a blank-eyed child was chewing on some short blades of grass and a one-legged former soldier was pulling his hips through the wet earth like a plow made of bones; there it was that Leo, succumbing to a shame that had no more sound, as well as to the ravages of dysentery and lung infection, curling up in his shit and slime-soaked mud hole, perhaps seeing before him once again the death pits in the Nordic woods, feeling once again the awful press of his finger against the trigger—once, twice, thrice, endless times—, shuddered once more with the unfathomable horror of it all and was still. There it was that he would be found, leaving behind a scrap of brown paper with her name and the Friedberg address on it, a scrap of paper which one day she would discover in an envelope in the postbox next to the blue spruce by the lopsided gate, mailed to her by a kind stranger who had found it wrapped around a rock and thrown over the barbed wire by someone inside who still trusted in something, and the stained paper would have on it too some notes scrawled in a melody that would haunt her always, for she could hear what could not be put into words. There it was, through the arbitrary bizarreness of reality, that she would arrive just in time to see Leo's body pushed out of the gate of the camp in a wheelbarrow and that she would look into the glazed faces of those who pulled him off by his long stick legs and then grasped him by the bones of his ankles and the arms whose hands and once beautiful fingers had known how to make sing the strings of the viola da gamba and the deepest chords of her heart and who then threw what was left of him onto a truck with a heap of others, and that she would have one last glimpse of his hair falling back from his face and the angles of his cheek bones and his eyes below the stained forehead she would have wanted to have kissed one last time if not for the horror of his image, and there it was that she would begin to understand not only the German nation's full weight of atrocities and guilt, but the silences deemed necessary to safeguard the future generations of Germany and the other lands in a changed world. She would never know, for even today the figures conflict according to sources, how many of those who died at those post-war camps would be stacked in layers and covered with quicklime and that their personal possessions would have been ordered stripped off them by other prisoners and put into bags as spoils of war or sold on the black market; that hundreds of thousands would be packed into trains, traveling empty-bellied for days, peering out through cracks in the wooden cars as they rumbled over the war-ravaged lands, then find themselves in other American or Soviet or French or British-run camps where many collapsed into death before they could set out to labor, imprisoned for weeks, months, years, decades. That in France there were others who survived only because they were passed food and kind words by French villagers and farmers who still believed in human decency and humane actions although some had themselves been prisoners in Germany. And although my aunt would perceive that vengeance and retribution are not the same, and justice is not always possible, she would consider the years she had already spent in the birthplace of the *Declaration of the Rights of Man* and would decide to return, alone, to France.

As the final measures of the Fugue in A Minor resounded in the expectant air of the Deutsches Opernhaus, my aunt did not yet know that once back in France she would never again be moved to play the harpsichord nor leave long that home deep in the Friedberg woods. She did not yet know that although nearly all was lost, there would come the possibility to play a part, minor as it was, in helping the European Court of Human Rights in Strasbourg, translating those documents that would, perhaps, bring realization one step closer to those who might care about humanity and how to safeguard and honor its sanctity in this world, however naively. She did not yet know that her enduring shame and guilt and remorse would keep her hidden from her brother until he was a grown man wondering about the sister whom he barely remembered; the American brother who would one day come to find her in the house in the forest, bringing along his German wife and his German-American daughter who, one afternoon in the future, would enter the attic and discover there a shrouded harpsichord; the niece who would then press one key, breaking a silence.

♪

ACKNOWLEDGEMENTS

Kristallnacht was a turning point in the hideous landscape of the Third Reich. It marked the beginning of the end for far too many people, in too many lands. For some other people, it marked the beginning of disillusionment with their leaders. But it was already too late to change these without outside help.

There are some acknowledgments to be made here, and the first is to thank Heidelberg, a city for which I feel great affection. I have taken creative liberties in this novel; an incident like that of Dr. Morsch in Marktplatz did not take place there.

There are also some people to whom I would like to express my thanks although I don't know their names: helpful archivists at both the city and university archives in Heidelberg. The understanding official who allowed me to wander backstage at the Kunsthalle. The dark-eyed musician whose performance gave life to Leo, the schoolgirl whose smooth forehead let me see Lili.

And of course Marcia Kelly-Gerritz and B.L. Sauder for their Khao Yai critiques during the earliest versions of *Fatherland*. Others whom I wholeheartedly thank include Catherine Texier, Alison McKelvey Clayson, Anette Pollner, James Clayson, Edward Steinberg, Somtow Sucharitkul, Norman Sherry, Karl Alfred Wolken.

It is my closest family whom I wai with recognition and gratitude: the long gone ones whose histories I have absorbed over the decades, and my husband Arvind, daughter Katya, son Niki, and daughter-in-law Sheila. Your understanding, support, and quiet faith in me have been my eaux de vie. To all of you, my love, immer und ewig.